Word
of Honor

NEWPOINTE 911 BOOKS 3 & 4

Trial
by Fire

Books by Terri Blackstock

Soul Restoration
Emerald Windows

Restoration Series
1 | *Last Light*
2 | *Night Light*

Cape Refuge Series
1 | *Cape Refuge*
2 | *Southern Storm*
3 | *River's Edge*
4 | *Breaker's Reef*

Newpointe 911
1 | *Private Justice*
2 | *Shadow of Doubt*
3 | *Word of Honor*
4 | *Trial by Fire*
5 | *Line of Duty*

Sun Coast Chronicles
1 | *Evidence of Mercy*
2 | *Justifiable Means*
3 | *Ulterior Motives*
4 | *Presumption of Guilt*

Second Chances
1 | *Never Again Good-bye*
2 | *When Dreams Cross*
3 | *Blind Trust*
4 | *Broken Wings*

With Beverly LaHaye
1 | *Seasons Under Heaven*
2 | *Showers in Season*
3 | *Times and Seasons*
4 | *Season of Blessing*

Novellas
Seaside

TERRI BLACKSTOCK

#1 bestselling suspense author

Word of Honor

NEWPOINTE 911 BOOKS 3 & 4

Trial by Fire

ZONDERVAN®

ZONDERVAN.com/
AUTHORTRACKER
follow your favorite authors

ZONDERVAN®

Word of Honor/Trial by Fire Compilation Lifeway
Copyright © 2007 by Terri Blackstock

Word of Honor
Copyright © 1999 by Terri Blackstock

Trial by Fire
Copyright © 2000 by Terri Blackstock

Requests for information should be addressed to:

Zondervan, *Grand Rapids, Michigan 49530*

ISBN-10: 0-310-61027-3
ISBN-13: 978-0-310-61027-4

Published in association with the literary agency of Alive Communications, Inc., 7680 Goddard Street, Suite 200, Colorado Springs, CO 80920.

Interior design by Jody DeNeef

Printed in the United States of America

08 09 10 11 12 13 14 • 22 21 20 19 18 17 16 15 14 13 12 11 10 9 8 7 6 5 4 3 2 1

Word of Honor

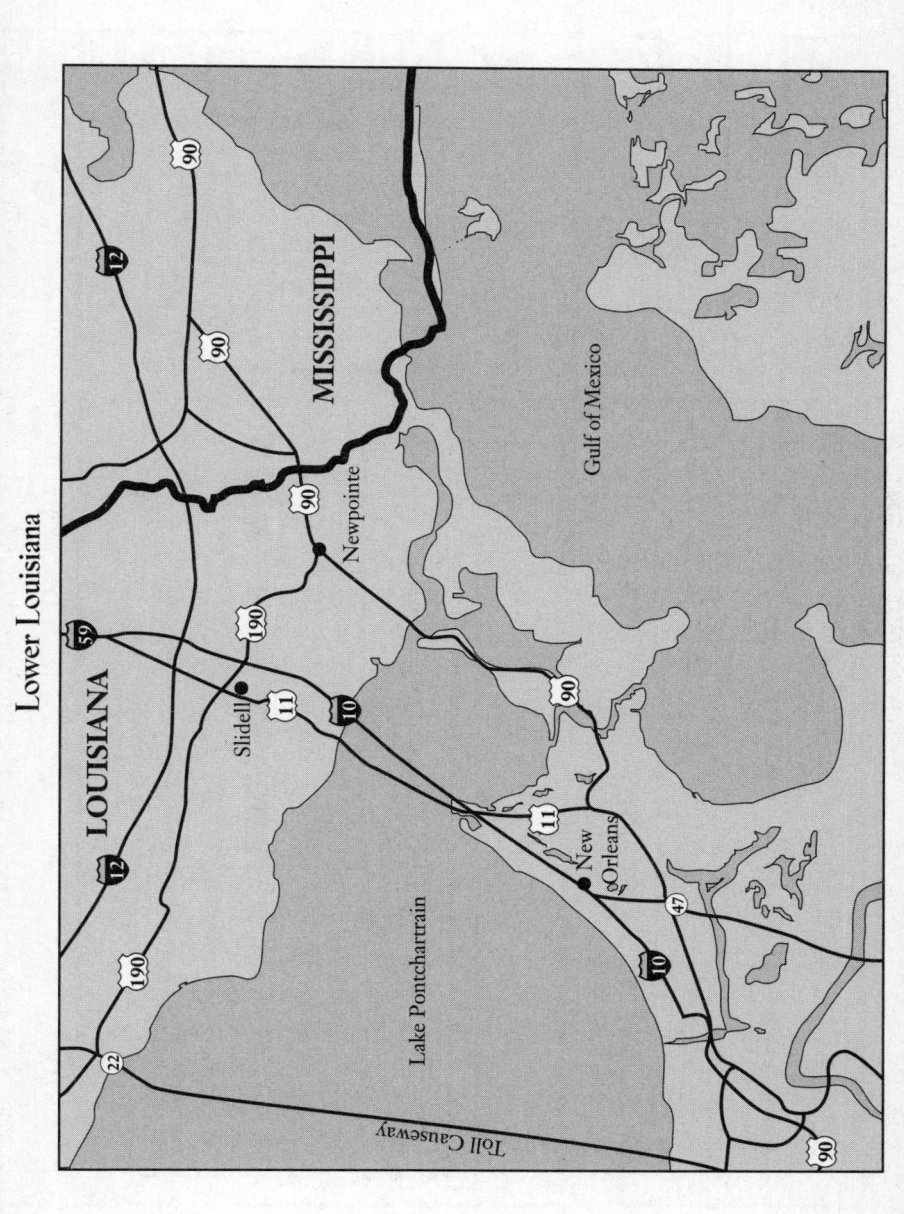

Lower Louisiana

Newpointe, Louisiana

Jill Clark

Shepherds

Larkins

Clearview Street

Brumings

Clearview Street

Broussards

Mill Street

Ingalls

Sid Ford

Ray Ford

Mill Street

E. Leake

W. Leake

Burgundy Drive

Delchamps

Walmart

Rue Main

Jefferson Avenue

Calvary Bible Church

Antoinette Boulevard

Bonaparte Apartments

Post Office

Drug Store

Bonaparte

LaSalle Boulevard

Jacquard Street

Bloons 'n Blossoms

Huey Long Boulevard

Aunt Aggie's

3rd Street

2nd Street

1st Street

Police Station

City Hall

Jill's office

Fire Station

Courthouse

Purchase Street

Gaston Boulevard

Elementary School

High School

Edwards Avenue

Long Street

2nd Street

2nd Street

Joe's Place

Dan Nichols

Bayou Lafayette

Newpointe Noncritical Care Hospital

90

190

Acknowledgments

I would like to express deep gratitude to Angela Hunt, Alton Gansky, Jack Cavanaugh, Athol Dickson, and Lisa Samson for brainstorming with me on this plot. I feel so privileged to have such wonderful authors offering me ideas. During a novelists' retreat in Grand Rapids, Michigan, we sat together over breakfast, talking about villains, car chases, and bombs. Before we knew it, I had a conclusion to this book. I couldn't wait to get home and write it.

I'd also like to thank Zondervan Publishing House for bringing their novelists together to encourage each other. It was one of the highlights of my year.

And once again, I'd like to thank Dave Lambert, Sue Brower, and Lori VandenBosch for their untiring efforts to keep my books coming. I am very pleased to be able to work with such quality people.

This book is lovingly dedicated to the Nazarene

Chapter One

The small, hot post office smelled of mold and dust and hummed with the sound of several air conditioning units placed in windows around the building. Cliff Bertrand, the Newpointe postmaster, held his hand in front of one of the vents, and realized it was blowing hot air. No wonder the building was so warm. He gave the side of it a bang with the heel of his hand, as if that would shock it into spitting out cold air. But he knew it wouldn't work.

Sue Ellen will be whining all day, he thought. He looked over his shoulder at Sue Ellen Hanover, his postal clerk, who stood at the counter fanning herself as she waited on a customer. With a fake fingernail, she punched out the amount of postage that Mary Hampton's packages would need.

"You wouldn't know it was July," she commented as she applied the sticky metered strips to the boxes. "You'd think it was Christmas, what with all these packages."

"Just some of Mama's stuff," Mary said. "She went to live with my brother over in Waco, so I'm shippin' her some of her things."

"You two couldn't get along?" Sue Ellen asked sweetly.

Mary looked offended.

Cliff knew it did little good to scold her, but he gave it a shot, anyway. "Sue Ellen, that was rude. Everybody knows her mama just went to help with her new grandbaby."

Sue Ellen shot him a look that said his intrusion wasn't appreciated. "Cliff, you really need to fix that air conditioner. It's hot as blazes in here." She fanned herself with a manila envelope and turned back to Mary. "Yep, them babies always do outshine the older grandkids. Where's your youngun, anyways?"

"Out there." Mary nodded through the glass doors at the child playing on the floor with a toy fire truck.

"Scrawny little thing," Sue Ellen said, taking Mary's check. "Can I see some ID, please?"

Cliff shook his head at the absurdity of the request, since Sue Ellen knew Mary well enough to wag her tongue all over town every time the single mother stepped outside her house. He heard Sue Ellen tapping her fake fingernails on the counter, as if she had a million better things to do than wait for Mary to dig her driver's license out of her purse.

Disgusted, he grabbed his keys and the refills for the stamp machine, and headed out to reload it. As he pushed through the door into the outer room, he saw Mary's sandy-haired five-year-old crawling along the wall, running his fire truck as fast as he could. He smiled, but the boy hardly noticed him.

Cliff jangled his keys and opened the machine.

Instantly, the boy was on his feet, peering into the machine as if glimpsing something sacred. "Hey, there," Cliff said.

"Hey." The boy watched, fascinated, as he stacked the packages of stamps in the appropriate places. "Can I do one?"

Cliff grinned and handed him a stack. "Put those right here."

Pete's eyes rounded, and he slid them carefully into their slot.

"Good job. What's your name, son?"

Pete looked up at him. "Peter Jacob Hampton."

Cliff held out his hand. "Nice to meet you, Peter Jacob Hampton. I'm Clifford Wayne Bertrand. How do you do?"

The little boy shook. "D'you do this everyday?"

"Every single one, except weekends," he said, closing the machine back. He looked down at the truck lying on the concrete floor. "Nice truck you got there."

"Thanks." Pete fell back to his knees and began making an engine noise as he ran along the wall.

Cliff chuckled and picked up his box. "See you later, Pete."

"Bye."

As Cliff pushed through the door in the back room, he glanced back and saw the child watching him with awe, as if wondering what treasures lay behind the mailboxes.

• • •

Pete watched the door close behind the man, and decided on the spot that he was going to be a mailman when he grew up. That, and a fireman. He went back to pushing his truck.

The door at the far end of the building opened, and Pete's attention shifted to the man coming in from outside. He was sweating hard and breathing fast, and carrying a box that looked like it held a big present. Pete stopped pushing the truck and sat up, trying to imagine what could be inside. The man stepped past him and set the box down against the wall, then started back to the door.

"That ain't where you put that, Mister," Pete said. "It goes over there." He pointed to the slots in the wall.

"That's right where I want it, kid." The man hesitated as he looked down at him. Pete noticed that the man was missing some fingers, and he bent some of his own to see how it felt. He started to ask him what had happened to them, but the man spoke first. "Hey, you know, that truck sure would fly on that half wall outside. Why don't you go out there and try it?" Not waiting for an answer, the man pushed back through the door he'd come in. Pete watched through the glass doors as the man climbed into the passenger seat of the blue pickup. The driver pulled away.

Quickly, Pete's attention moved from the blue pickup to the half wall he'd suggested outside the building. He glanced through the glass doors and saw his mother paying for their package. If he went outside, just this once, would he get in trouble?

Deciding that the wall's incline was worth the trouble it would cost him, he pushed through the door and hurried to the wall. His throat made a rumbling sound as he set his truck on the wall and gave it a shove.

He would never see it hit the bottom of the incline.

• • •

The explosion was so loud Jerry Ingalls heard it from half a mile away. "What in the—?" He slammed on his brakes. The blue pickup skidded across the street.

"What are you doing?" Frank shouted. "Drive, man! Drive!"

As Jerry tried to right his pickup, he looked back through the rear window. He could see the black smoke rising from where they'd been, filling the sky. "That's the post office!" he said.

"Up here," Frank said. "Take a right up here."

Sirens began to blare a few blocks away. Jerry turned in the direction he'd been told, his heart racing. "Do you know anything about what happened back there?"

"Yes," Frank said. He was dripping with sweat now, and the humid Louisiana air crept through the pickup in spite of the air conditioning. "But I can't tell you about it now. Just drive."

"Drive where?" Jerry demanded. "If you're involved in something, man—"

"I need your help!" Frank's bellowed statement left no room for argument. "Drive to the Delchamps parking lot. I have a car. Drop me off, then you head for Chalmette. There's a motel right on the outskirts of Chalmette. The only one in town. The Flagstaff, I think it is. Go there and rent me a room. Don't use my name or yours. Tie a hand towel over the knob so I can find you. I'll meet you there tonight and tell you everything."

Jerry's head was reeling from the orders. "Frank, if you had a car, why did you just have me drive you to the post office? What have you gotten me into?"

"A fight for your country!" Frank yelled back. "You're in, now. There's no turning back. You owe me, Jerry! And you owe your country."

"My country?" Jerry asked. "What are you talking about, man? The war's been over for twenty-five years!"

"I've been a POW, Jerry. For twenty-five years, and there were others there with me. They told you the war was over, but it came home with us. Communism is infiltrating our government, Jerry. The captain was part of it."

"The captain? What captain?"

"Bertrand, man! He works for the feds, and he's part of the whole thing."

"*Cliff Bertrand?* Frank, he's retired from the army. He's just a postal clerk, not some kind of spy."

"He's helping them to take over, Jerry. I don't expect you to understand. You weren't held all those years, like I was. But we have to stop it."

Jerry gaped at him. "Frank, you weren't a POW. You were in a VA hospital."

"That's what they want you to think, but there were others held there," he said. "You don't know what's going on. It's worse than the Viet Cong. They're going to take away everything, Jerry. They're trying to lull us into a false sense of security, and then we'll let them do anything they want. They already have our government."

Jerry's heart was racing. He pulled into the Delchamps parking lot and turned his pickup so he could see the black smoke still hovering above the post office. "Man, you didn't blow up that post office, did you?"

"You just don't understand," Frank said. "But I'll explain everything. I'll tell you at the motel. Be there. You owe me, Jerry."

With that, he launched out of the pickup and took off between the cars.

Jerry didn't wait to see which car was his. The sirens were getting louder, and the smoke billowed with urgent fury as he pulled out of the parking lot. Something told him he had just become a wanted man.

He reached behind him, got his hunting rifle from its rack, and set it on the seat next to him. He hoped he wouldn't need it, but he had a real bad feeling.

Frank was right. He did owe him. He could at least meet him and find out what was going on. Maybe he could talk him out of pulling any more sick stunts, make him go back to the hospital that had been his home for so long.

As he headed out of town, he looked back toward the post office. The black smoke of Frank's iniquities rose like a tragic prayer into the sky.

Chapter Two

The ambulance at Midtown Fire Station pulled out of the driveway first, just moments after the explosion six blocks away. The firefighters, who had just settled down to a lunch of shrimp gumbo, headed for their turnout pants.

Dan Nichols stepped into his rubber boots and pulled the pants up. As he snapped them shut, he grabbed his turnout coat and helmet. "Where's the fire?" he yelled as George Broussard, already decked out, jumped onto the pumper truck.

"Post office," George answered. "Explosion of some sort."

"Felt like next door!" Dan got into the truck. As the siren came on and Mark Branning pulled the truck out of the bay, Dan peered up through the windshield. The black smoke from the explosion just six blocks away had already made its way down Purchase Street and was billowing up into the sky, visible to everyone.

"Mail bomb?" Dan asked.

"Probably," Mark said.

As they rounded the corner and reached the block where the post office was, all three of the firemen on the truck went silent.

Dan had never seen anything like it. The roof and two of the walls were gone, and the walls left standing were consumed in flames at least twenty feet high. Fallen electrical wires sizzled and sparked. Dan dreaded the idea of digging through live wires and burning rubble to get to any bodies that might be under it all.

The ambulance was already there. Issie Mattreaux, the paramedic, climbed from the truck, joined by Bob Sigrest, an EMT.

Dan jumped out and waved to them. "Stay back!" he commanded. "Stay with the ambulance!"

They nodded, understanding. Since the ambulance squads weren't equipped to head into heavy smoke, it was up to him and the other firefighters, also trained as EMTs, to find any survivors.

Dan snapped down his face shield and pulled on his air pack. He pulled the gauntlets of his sleeves over his gloves to protect his skin, but he could already feel the skin-melting heat of the explosion, heavy on the July air. He wondered how any of them would make it through this. The breathing tank weighed thirty to forty pounds, a lot to carry when they were digging through bricks, steel, and glass. It had only about twenty minutes of air, not nearly enough for a job like this. They'd be swapping tanks left and right for the next few hours. He hoped the 911 dispatcher had radioed Slidell to send backup crews.

"Here! Help, here!"

Through the haze Dan spotted Penelope Houston, the owner of the drugstore across the street. Her face was smoke-stained, and she was coughing. Wildly, her arms gestured toward a body on the ground. *A child*, Dan realized, his heart jolting. He ran to the ambulance. "There's a child! Give me the megaduffel! He'll need oxygen."

Issie thrust the equipment at him, then handed Mark the spineboard and pediatric collar. Grabbing the gear, they took off into the smoke.

The child looked tiny on the scorched pavement, and he didn't seem to be breathing. He had been thrown in the explosion. Blood pooled on the ground from a wound on the back of his head, and his body was covered with glass and soot.

Wasting no time, they got the neck splint on him, slapped the oxygen mask on his face, and carefully moved him onto the board. Then they ran him back to the ambulance. "He's not breathing!" Dan yelled. "And he's got a bad head wound."

Even as he spoke, Issie began running a tube down the child's trachea to clear his airway. Dan fought the urge to watch to see if the soot-covered boy would live. Already, Mark was going back into the smoke to look for more survivors. Dan grabbed Penelope Houston. "Penelope, do you know of any other survivors?"

Penelope's face was streaked with smoke and tears as she babbled hysterically. "I heard the explosion, Dan." She coughed. Her voice was cracked and broken. "It shook the building and knocked my windows out. I . . . I come out and seen . . . all the smoke and flames . . . and this little boy was layin' here like he'd been throwed. I didn't see nobody else."

The town's other ambulance unit was just arriving, along with a convoy of other fire trucks and rescue units from neighboring towns. Dan waved for Steve Winder as he got out of the rig. "Steve, get her on some oxygen and out of this smoke!"

Steve tried to usher her back to his unit as Ray Ford, the fire chief, pulled to the curb between two of the trucks. He was dressed in full gear, face shield down, as he approached Dan. "Anybody inside?"

"Of course there was somebody inside!" Penelope shouted, turning back from Steve's ambulance. "Sue Ellen Hanover was there. And Cliff Bertrand. They're always there. They never leave, not even for lunch!" Again, she surrendered to a series of coughs.

"So we need to look for Sue Ellen and Cliff," Ray shouted. "How many cars in the parking lot?"

"Looks like a couple," Dan said.

Stan Shepherd, the town's only detective, came running up to the ambulances. "What in the sam hill—"

"Those cars could be Sue Ellen's and Cliff's," Ray cut in. "Who's the kid?"

Still coughing, Penelope turned around and shouted back, "That's Mary Hampton's boy. They were in the drugstore before they went to the post office."

Stan swung around. "Are you sure? Mary and Pete?"

"You know them?" Dan asked.

"Yeah," Stan said. "She goes to our church. Divorced. Some of the guys put a new roof on her house last year." He went to the ambulance and looked down at the boy as Issie struggled to stabilize him. "Pete's five years old. I've taken him to a couple of Saints games. Where's his mother?"

"He's all I've found so far," Dan said. He closed the doors of the ambulance to keep the smoke out, and ignored the stunned look on Stan's face. "Get out of the smoke, Stan. Keep everybody back."

As Stan ran to where they were setting up a barricade at the end of the street, Dan headed back into the heat to look for any survivors. But even as he did, he knew that there wouldn't be any. No one would have survived this blast. It was a miracle that the boy was still alive.

Chapter Three

Celia Shepherd had been shedding a lot of hormonal tears lately, and she suspected it would get worse as these last three weeks of her pregnancy passed. But the news of Mary Hampton's death, and the deaths of Sue Ellen Hanover and Cliff Bertrand, had sent her over the edge of her emotional precipice. She hadn't been able to stop the tears for Pete, the funny little boy in her Sunday school class. The thought that he had been orphaned in the space of a moment was too much to bear.

So she had gotten into her car and headed to Slidell, where he'd been transported. Pete's father had run off with his secretary two years earlier, and the boy had undergone quite a bit of emotional upheaval since then. No one knew where the father was, or how to reach him. And his grandmother, who had been living with them, had recently gone to live with her son.

The child was incredibly alone.

Celia's tears streamed down her face and she wiped them away as she drove. She set her hand gently on her pregnant belly and felt her own child kick within her. What a terrible thing it would be to leave your child behind. What a horrible nightmare for a little boy, to wake up from an accident and learn that the person he loved and needed most in the world was gone.

Trying to see through her tears to drive, she picked up her cell phone and dialed out her husband's number at the police department. "Stan Shepherd, please."

"Celia, Stan ain't in." She recognized the voice of LaTonya Mason, the rookie cop who did desk duty. "He's still at the post office. I'll leave him a note that you called."

"Just tell him I'm going to the Slidell Hospital."

LaTonya gasped. "The baby?"

"No, no. I want to go see about Pete Hampton—the little guy who was in the explosion. Just tell him he can get me on my cell phone."

She clicked the phone off, then dialed her Aunt Aggie and waited for the old Cajun woman to get to the phone. "*Hola?*"

"Aunt Aggie, it's me," she said. "Did you hear about the post office?"

"Hear 'bout it?" Aunt Aggie asked. "Near wet my pants when I heard that bang. And the smoke ... it's still arrywhere."

"Aunt Aggie, Mary Hampton was killed, and her little boy was injured ..."

"The little blonde, T-Celia?" The Cajun prefix was a shortened version of *petite*, her version of "little Celia." Aunt Aggie had called her that since she'd been a child.

Celia sniffed and wiped her tears. She could hardly see through them to drive. "Yes. The one in my Sunday school class. The one you said would be a heartbreaker someday."

"Celia, don't tell me—"

"It was him," she cut in. "His mother's dead, Aunt Aggie. And he's pretty badly injured. I just wanted to let you know I'm heading for Slidell to be with him."

"You okay, *sha?*" Aunt Aggie asked, using her drawled form of *chere*.

"I'm fine," she choked out. "I just can't believe they're all dead. Mary and Sue Ellen and Cliff."

"They got the crazy yet?"

"I don't know. I haven't been able to talk to Stan. Oh, pray, Aunt Aggie. Pray that they catch the person who orphaned that little boy."

Aunt Aggie paused for a moment. "You sure you don't want me comin' with ya?"

"I'm halfway there already."

"You take care of your baby, you hear? That little boy's gon' be all right."

"I'm fine," Celia said. "He doesn't have anyone, Aunt Aggie. I have to go help. At least until his grandmother gets back to town."

"You could try findin' that no-count daddy of his."

"He hasn't been heard from since he left them. I doubt seriously he'll turn up now."

"You might be surprised," Aunt Aggie said. "If he knew his wife was dead."

"I wouldn't have a clue where to start. Anyway, I'm almost there, and I'm fine, so don't worry about me. I just wanted to let you know."

"Okay, *sha*. You be careful, hear?"

Celia hung up the phone as she reached the outskirts of Slidell and checked her watch. The boy would have been here about half an hour by now. She wondered if anyone had notified his next of kin. She wondered if they even knew how.

She began to weep again, and not knowing what else to do, she picked up the cell phone and dialed out Nick Foster's number. He was the preacher at her church—a bivocational pastor who worked part-time as a firefighter. She had no idea if he was on duty right now. Even the off-duty firefighters were, no doubt, still working on the fire at the post office.

His voice mail picked up. "Your call is very important to me," he said, and she knew he meant it. "Please leave your name and number and I promise I'll call you back as soon as I can." She waited through the series of beeps that testified to the number of messages he had waiting already, then after the long beep added her own. "Nick, it's Celia. I just wanted to let you know that I'm headed to Slidell Hospital to be with little Pete Hampton. If you get a chance to come over there, would you do it, please? I'm kind of at a loss as to how to deal with things. I know it would help the relatives if you were there when they get there, and Mary's mother really likes you. Not to mention Pete." Her voice trailed off, and she cut off the phone and wiped her eyes again. What in the world was she going to say to that little boy? What in the world could she do for him?

She reached the hospital parking lot and parked near the emergency room. She hurried in to the receptionist booth in the ER.

"Maternity?" the receptionist asked through the glass.

"No," she said. "I'm looking for Pete Hampton. The little boy who was brought in from the explosion in Newpointe."

"Are you his mother?"

"No." She swallowed, and her lips trembled as she said, "His mother was killed in the blast."

The receptionist, who probably saw all kinds of tragedies on a daily basis, looked stricken. "I didn't know. That poor little boy. Are you a relative?"

"No, but he doesn't have anyone here, and he needs somebody. I'm his Sunday school teacher, that's all, but I love him, and no one else here even knows him." She broke into tears again.

The nurse peered up at her as if trying to decide whether to let her go back. Celia hoped she didn't recognize her. She'd had a colored past, and people who remembered her not-so-distant history often looked at her as if they'd spotted Al Capone.

"Just a minute, let me ask someone." She got up and headed through the swinging doors, and Celia began to pace in front of the window, back and forth, back and forth. This place brought back so many memories. So many close calls with death, so many friends in the midst of refining fires. All of Newpointe's crises seemed to culminate here.

She caught her reflection in the mirror, her blonde hair and wet blue eyes, her huge belly just weeks away from delivery. Again, she looked down and patted her stomach. "It's gonna be okay," she whispered to her baby. "We've just gotta go be with Pete."

In a moment, the nurse came back out. "The doctor said you can go back. It's through those doors, the third door on the left."

Celia searched the woman's face. "How is he? Is he gonna make it?"

"He's still unconscious," she said.

Celia headed through the emergency room doors and down the hall until she came to the room where Pete lay on the bed, surrounded by a team of doctors and nurses. A tube ran down his throat, his face was bruised, and his eyes were swollen shut. She threw her hand over her mouth to muffle her horror. "Is he . . . is he okay?"

The doctor left the bedside and met her at the door. "He has a skull fracture and a concussion," he said. "Both lungs have collapsed, so we've put him on a ventilator. Looks like he was thrown a good distance in the explosion. Fortunately, he was far enough away that he didn't sustain any burns. He's got a broken arm and multiple lacerations. He's unconscious right now, but he did wake up on the way to the hospital and spoke. Then he slipped back into a coma. We're running some tests to determine if there's any swelling in his brain. We're probably going to have to transport him to New Orleans, since they have a better equipped head trauma unit there, and a pulmonary specialist who has more advanced equipment. You're not one of his relatives?"

"No . . . I'm his Sunday school teacher. His mother . . ." She lowered her voice to a whisper, in case Pete could hear. ". . . was killed."

His face slackened. "The paramedics weren't sure when they brought him in. Do you have any way of getting in touch with his relatives?"

"I can try," she said. "I should have done it before now, but I wasn't thinking clearly."

"He may not wake up for a while. Right now, it would be a huge help if you could find his relatives. Where is his father?"

"No one knows," she said as a wave of anger surged through her. "But his grandmother . . . she lived with them until a couple of weeks ago, and then she went to stay with her son because his wife had a baby. It's so sad . . . because . . . she didn't know when she left that she'd never see her daughter again." She covered her eyes and sucked in a deep sigh. "Oh, what if she hasn't been notified yet? Shouldn't I wait until the coroner or somebody gets in touch with her?"

He touched her shoulder gently. "It's very important that we reach her right away. We need consent forms signed, decisions need to be made . . ."

"Yes, of course," she said. "Okay, I'll do what I can. Can I . . . just see him first?"

"Of course." He escorted her to the side of the bed, and she looked down at the tiny, limp body. He was a rascal in Sunday school, always asking the hard questions, delighting in everything they did. He had an imagination that never quit, and he soaked up stories of Joseph and David and Daniel like they were local heroes. She didn't remember ever seeing him quite this still. With all the tubes and wires they had attached to him, she hardly recognized him at all.

The fact that his mother wouldn't be here to nurse him back to health overwhelmed her. She lifted his little hand. It was limp in hers, but she could feel a light pulse beneath his wrist. "Hang in there, Pete," she whispered. "Hang in there. Don't let go." But even as she said the words, she wondered if, maybe, he *should* let go. Maybe staying in this life was going to be too tough. Orphaned, possibly brain damaged, even crippled. She just didn't know. Was this more than a little child could bear?

She leaned over and pressed a kiss on his little forehead, then stroked his cheek gently. "You're gonna be all right, Pete," she said. "You're gonna be fine. Can you hear me?"

No answer.

"Pete, this is Miss Celia. You just keep fighting, okay? I'll be here fighting right beside you."

There was no indication that he heard a word she said. She let go of his hand and looked up at the doctor. "I'll go try to make some phone calls," she said. "I know his grandmother is with his uncle. I'm just not sure what his uncle's name is. Maybe their neighbors know."

The doctor nodded. "As soon as we can stabilize him, we're going to be transporting him to New Orleans where they have better head trauma facilities and a team of neurosurgeons. If they have to do surgery, they'll need consent right away."

"I understand. I just don't know if I can make it through that phone call."

"Somebody's got to do it," the doctor said firmly. "It's better coming from a friend of the family."

She took strength from the doctor's calm, insistent gaze. Turning, she left the room to find a phone.

• • •

Four phone calls later, Celia had the name and number of Zack Lewis, Mary Hampton's brother in Waco. She was about to dial when Allie Branning pushed through the doors to the emergency room.

"Celia, is Pete all right?"

"No," Celia said, as Allie pulled her into a hug. "He's not. I'm trying to reach his relatives." She released Allie and wiped her tears. "Where's Justin?"

Allie was rarely seen without her eight-month-old baby. "I left him with a sitter. Mark's still working the fire at the post office."

"Well, I'm glad you came." Celia turned back to the phone. "Right now, I've got to do one of the hardest things I've ever done."

"You've done a lot of hard things," Allie said. "What could be so bad?"

"I've got to track down Mary Hampton's mother," she said. "And when I get her on the phone I have to tell her that her daughter has died, and that her grandchild is lying here, unconscious, with a crack in his skull." She pulled her tissue from her pocket and blew her nose, then picked up the phone and began to dial. Her eyes locked with Allie's as the phone began to ring. She almost hoped no one was there.

A man answered the phone. "Hello?"

"Uh . . . yes." She swallowed hard and cleared her throat. "My name is Celia Shepherd. I live in Newpointe, Louisiana. I'm looking for Thelma Lewis . . . or Zack Lewis. I'm a friend of Mary's."

"Yes," he said. "This is Zack, her brother."

She pinched her tear ducts. She could tell from his tone that he didn't know of his sister's death. For a moment, she hesitated, wondering if she should ask to speak to his mother or give the news to him directly. She wasn't sure what was the right thing to do.

"Is there something wrong?" he asked.

"Yes, I'm afraid there is." Her voice trembled as she spoke. "There was an explosion at the post office here."

"An explosion?"

"Mary . . . uh . . . she was there . . . inside . . ."

Silence settled like dust between them.

"I'm so sorry, but your sister was killed in the blast."

She heard the phone drop, heard him talking to someone else, heard a woman's wail. She covered her face and pressed it against the phone. Allie touched her back. Suddenly, the man picked the phone back up. "What about Pete?" he asked breathlessly.

"He's in the hospital," she said. "That's where I'm calling from. He was injured badly, but he's still alive. He's in critical condition at Slidell Hospital, but they plan to transport him to New Orleans to a head trauma unit as soon as he's stabilized."

"Head trauma?"

"Yes. He's got a fracture in his skull, and they don't know if there's any swelling in his brain or not. He's got a broken arm, and some cuts and bruises, and two collapsed lungs. Fortunately, no burns. They need his next of kin to sign consent forms for treatment . . ."

Zack was having trouble speaking. "We're gonna call the airport right now," he said. "If we can't get a plane tonight, we'll just drive. We'll be there as soon as we can. Meanwhile, maybe we could fax our consent. If someone from the hospital could call us on my cell phone—"

"That would be good," she said. She took down his cell phone number. "Pete's gonna need someone here in his corner. I'll stay until you come. When he wakes up, he's going to need to be told . . ."

She heard the man comforting his mother, who was still wailing. Then in a broken voice he asked, "You'll stay with him?"

"Yes. And here's my cell phone number, in case you need to get in touch. I'll keep it with me." She called it out to him. "I'm so sorry to give you this news."

He couldn't answer.

"I understand the shock. I'm kind of in shock myself. Please hurry."

She hung up the phone and fell into Allie's arms. The two women wept together for several moments, before Celia could muster the strength to go back to Pete's room.

Chapter Four

The firefighters at the Midtown Station were exhausted and emotionally spent as they returned from fighting the blaze. It had taken hours to make sure the fire was out, and a pall of death hung over them like the smoke that still hadn't cleared entirely. They had found partial remains of three unidentifiable bodies, and could only conclude that they were Sue Ellen Hanover, Cliff Bertrand, and Mary Hampton. Five firefighters, two from Newpointe and three from other towns nearby, had been treated for heat exhaustion, and six utility workers who'd come to help with the electrical lines had been treated for smoke inhalation.

The firefighters peeled out of their heavy coats and stepped out of their pants. Drenched with sweat, they grabbed jugs of ice water and went into the TV room to soak up the air conditioning before they showered. None of them had eaten lunch, but few of them had appetites. Some of them coughed and gagged on the smoke caught in their lungs. Though they tried to remain protected at all times, there were times when they didn't have access to their tanks, and they inevitably breathed what they shouldn't.

Dan and Nick couldn't get cool, so they headed for the cold showers. "Man, I thought my bunkers were gonna shrivel right off of me," Dan said.

Nick, the bivocational preacher who also served as the protective services' chaplain, had mistakenly taken off his hood and face shield once to cool off, and as a result, had soot streaks and blisters on his face from the smoke. "I thought my *skin* was gonna shrivel right off of me. Man, I'll never cool off."

As they cut through the kitchen, Nick noticed Issie Mattreaux standing at the back door of the fire station, her face and arms stained black from the smoke. She had a vacant, dull look in her eyes as she stared out the door. Tentatively, Nick approached her. "You okay, Issie?"

His question seemed to startle her out of her reverie. "Yeah ... uh, sure." A moment of contemplation followed, then, "No ..."

"Need to talk?"

She looked up at him for a moment, as though that concept surprised her. Then without a word, she pushed out the screen door and stepped onto the back lawn. Issie wasn't as hot as he— she'd been in a cool ambulance for some of the afternoon as she'd transported Pete Hampton and treated the firemen and electrical workers. Despite how badly he wanted to step under that cold spray of water in the shower, Nick followed her, wondering if he was supposed to. It was a sweltering July day in south Louisiana, and the humidity hung in the air like a curtain blocking any breeze. The smell of smoke still hung in the air. He imagined there was no place in the small town where it could be escaped.

He felt drained and dizzy, but he'd been praying for Issie, and didn't want to lose a chance to talk to her about her spiritual condition. He figured that if he passed out, she'd understand.

Issie went quietly to a bench near the bayou running behind them. It was a beautiful bayou, well-maintained and part of the pride of Newpointe. Ski boats pulled skiers behind them further down, where it was wider, but here, only an occasional fishing boat drifted by without an engine. Patricia Castor, the mayor, had outlawed boat engines in this part of the bayou, mainly because her city hall office was across the street and she wasn't big on noise pollution. They had all half expected her to outlaw sirens, as well, but she hadn't found a way to do that yet.

Nick watched Issie sink down on a bench under a tree dripping with Spanish moss. She had her black hair pulled back in a ponytail, as she always did at work, but wisps of it hung around her face in thoughtless disarray. He wondered if she knew her face was stained with smoke, or if she cared. He knew his was, but it was the least of his worries. He sat down next to her, his elbows on his knees. "Talk to me," he said.

She looked out over the water. "It's just ... the kid. I don't understand."

"Understand what?"

"What happened to him." Her voice was hoarse, raspy from the smoke, and she turned her big, dark eyes to Nick's and locked into them so tight that it felt like she was clinging to him. But Issie didn't cling, and they weren't even touching. "He came to for just a few minutes when we were en route."

"He did?" Nick asked. "Well, that's good news, isn't it?"

Her eyes ripped away and scanned the still water again. "He was crying for his mom."

"Did he know?"

"No, I couldn't tell him." She pulled her feet up onto the bench with her and set her chin on her knees. "That's the worst thing a child could ever hear."

Nick tried to put himself in the child's place. "I'm sure you're right." Again, silence ticked off the seconds. He saw tears well up in Issie's eyes, the first of her tears he'd ever seen. She wasn't the kind to cry at the slightest emotional tug, but they were each going to suffer the aftermath of this crisis in their own way. He saw how hard she tried to keep those tears from shattering and rolling down her face. Her throat moved as she swallowed hard.

"I was eight," she whispered.

He wasn't sure he'd heard her right. "You were what?"

"Eight," she said again, a little louder. "Eight years old. And there was this huge commotion downstairs, and my dad was cussing and yelling at somebody, and I got out of bed and started down the stairs ..." Her voice trailed off as the memories assaulted her, and he could see in her eyes that the memory was painful. He couldn't believe she was saying it. She'd never opened up to him, not ever. In fact, she went to great lengths to stay away from him. Something about his preacher status normally made her uncomfortable.

He didn't prod her on, didn't ask any questions that would make it easier for her to continue. Instead, he only waited, his eyes on those tears still balancing in the rims of her eyes, unwilling to let go.

"I went into the living room and asked Pop what was wrong, what he was so mad about, and he swung around and yelled out, 'Your mother's dead!'"

Nick's face changed, and he unfolded and sat up straight, gazing at her as the tear finally let go and made its slow path down her face.

"I'm sorry, Issie," he said. "I never knew."

She breathed a laugh that had no humor in it. "Well, why would you? She was in a car accident, driving back from my grandmother's, and no one found her until it was almost morning. My pop had gone on to bed, thinking she'd be home around eleven, but he'd slept through the night and never realized she hadn't made it in. And then they came and told him, and he was out of his mind with grief. Never got over it until the day he died three years ago." She stopped and looked at Nick with dull eyes. "Everybody's forgotten by now. It was a long time ago."

"But you haven't."

She shook her head sadly. After a moment, she brought her eyes back to his. "I know you're a preacher and everything,

Nick. You've got this whole thing figured out. But you know, I have a hard time understanding why mothers of little kids have to die."

"Everybody has a hard time understanding that," Nick said. "You know, you've got me all wrong. I don't have all the answers. I just know that I couldn't make it myself without—"

"Don't do it," Issie warned. "Don't preach to me, Nick. It'll just make me mad, unless you can answer my question and tell me how somebody could walk into a post office and leave a bomb, hoping to blow people to smithereens."

"The same way some guy could be a serial killer or poison somebody. It's not like it's the first terrible thing that's happened in Newpointe. I've heard these questions over and over, Issie. We live in a sinful world, and so there's unspeakable evil in it. You can't put the blame on God. He's—"

She shot him a look, cutting off his words. "Don't do it, Nick. Don't you preach to me."

"I'm not preaching," he said. "I'm trying to answer your question."

"You can't, and you know it." Another tear ran down her face, making a trail through the smoke smudges.

"No, I can't. Not the way you want, anyway. Issie, you're not the only paramedic or EMT who's ever come to me with that question. As the chaplain of all of the protective services, I hear from firefighters and cops and you guys all the time. It's an occupational hazard, to hit that wall of despair." He rubbed his dirty face. "It's gonna hit each of us hard, this one. It's tough finding people you know blown to bits and burnt beyond recognition."

She breathed in a deep sigh and then blew it out. "I gotta get a better line of work."

"Like what?"

"I don't know. I could go to nursing school and treat appendectomies and viruses. Give flu shots."

"You wouldn't be happy doing that."

She shot him a look. "Why would you say that?"

"Because you like living on the edge. That emergency feeling that keeps that adrenaline pumping. That life or death scenario."

"How do you know that?"

"Because I like it, too," he said.

"In the pulpit, or in the fire truck?"

He chuckled. "Both, actually."

She kept her gaze on him for a moment, her big eyes considering his words. He looked away. She caused way too many distracting thoughts, and she wasn't the kind of woman he'd been waiting for. She hung out at Joe's Place, the bar across the street, and got involved with married men and ex-cons, just for the thrill. Now, getting a peek into her childhood trauma, he thought he knew why.

Aunt Aggie, the eighty-one-year-old dynamo who cooked all of the fire department's meals, opened the door and shouted for both of them. "Come eat, T-Nick! Issie, you hungry? I got cold fruit and watermelon."

"I'm already off duty, Aunt Aggie," Issie said. "If you don't have enough, I'll just—"

"Have enough? You insultin' me, *sha?* I always got enough."

"I'll be there in a minute, Aunt Aggie," Nick called.

The old woman, dressed in a gold-glittery blouse and black wind-suit pants, looked as if she'd taken special care with her looks today. Her white hair looked freshly done, and she sported a smile that Nick knew was for their benefit. Aunt Aggie always liked to cheer them up when they'd fought a battle like the one today. "Ya'll need to get outa that heat and get some liquids down, not to mention food. I'm gon' have folks droppin' like flies around here, me."

They watched her go back inside, fussing and mumbling. "I wish I had answers for you," Nick told Issie softly. "All I know is that God is still in control. He was when you were a kid, and he still is."

"Why do you religious people always say that? That God's in control? It's like the catch-all answer."

"It's *exactly* the catch-all answer. In a world that doesn't always make sense, we can only trust in him."

"Trust him for what?" Issie demanded, growing angry now. "What can that little boy trust in him for? His mother trusted. She was one of your church members, wasn't she?"

"Yep. Sure was."

"Then how could this happen?"

"We may never know," Nick said. "But God will be faithful. I know that. Regardless of what happened . . . regardless of how tragic this was . . . God has a plan, and he will be faithful to carry it out."

"Well, excuse me for saying so, but if that's his plan for Mary Hampton . . . for Sue Ellen Hanover . . . for Cliff . . . for Pete . . . If it was his plan for me when I was eight years old . . . I don't know that I want God's plan in my life." She got up and headed back inside.

Nick sat motionless, realizing that he hadn't helped at all. Once again, he had failed. This woman for whom he had prayed so many times had finally come to him with a spiritual question. And he had not had answers that satisfied her.

The screen door opened and Aunt Aggie came out again. "You awright, Nick?" she asked him.

He looked up at her. "I guess. I just . . . Issie was asking me some questions about God. I didn't help her much."

"You prob'ly helped more than you know, *enfant.*"

"No, Aunt Aggie." He got up, took off his glasses, and cleaned them on his shirt. "Everything I say just goes in one ear and out the other. She just thinks I'm a big joke with silly ideas."

"Ain't that what I use ta think?" Aunt Aggie asked. "Used to say so, right to your face. I thought you was no better than a con artist, peddlin' your bill o' goods to that church full of folks. But look at me."

Nick couldn't help smiling. Aunt Aggie had been as close to a lost cause as he'd ever seen in his life. But a few months ago, she had shocked the town by showing up in church, and had almost caused collective coronary arrest when she'd gone down the aisle to tell him that she'd met Christ. "Tell me something, Aunt Aggie. Back then ... when you equated me with a con artist ... did anything I said ever sink in?"

"Arrything you said sunk in," she said. "I just didn't know it. One day, it all came cavin' in on me, all at once. You keep workin' on that Issie, *sha*. She'll come around."

Wearily, Nick followed Aunt Aggie back inside. The table was filling up with tired, quiet firemen.

Dan was out of the shower and stood in front of the mirror combing his hair, as if the right style might hide his receding hairline. Mark Branning was on the telephone, and when he got off, he turned to the rest of the guys.

"Do ya'll have any idea where Pete Hampton's father is?"

Ray Ford, the fire chief, was just coming in as Mark asked the question. Ray frowned and took his place at the head of the table. "I knew Pete's daddy, Larry, when he was still here. We went to school together. Even played ball on the same team. He worked as an insurance salesman over on Bonaparte Street. Up and disappeared one day with his secretary. Hasn't been heard from since."

"The kid needs somebody. Allie said his uncle and his grandmother are on their way, but if we could locate his father ..."

"I'll make some phone calls," Ray said, "soon as I get back to the office. Maybe we can come up with some leads and find him. But if I remember his daddy, I think little Pete might be better off with his grammaw."

Nick met Issie's eyes across the table. Those tears had sprung back into her eyes.

Chapter Five

Jill Clark didn't think she had the energy left to make it back across Lake Pontchartrain from Chalmette, where she'd spent ten hours taking depositions today. She didn't know how the injured Cajun roughneck had found her, but he had begged her to represent him in his lawsuit against the oil company responsible for the loss of his leg. Since most of the work required being away from Newpointe, she had tried to get everything done in one day.

But she hadn't finished, so she would have to be there early tomorrow morning. It was hardly worth it to drive the hour back to Newpointe. As she drove the outskirts of Chalmette, she looked for a motel where she could crash.

The song on the radio was grating on her nerves. She was reaching over to turn it off when a news bulletin cut in.

"Newpointe police are investigating an explosion that took place at the post office on Bonaparte Boulevard at 4:00 this afternoon ..."

She caught her breath and turned it up.

"The source of the explosion is under investigation. Three people are dead, and one survivor—a child—is in critical condition."

Jill raked a hand through her short brown hair and tried to think. Three people dead at the post office? Sue Ellen Hanover and Cliff Bertrand had to be two of them, she realized as her heart sank. An explosion? How could it have happened?

She was distracted as she pulled into the parking lot of the Flagstaff Motel, and sat there a moment, punching different stations on the radio, trying to get more news. But all she heard was crying-in-your-beer tunes, knee-slapping zydeco, heavy metal ...

Quickly, she got out and went to the office, checked in, then hurried to her room. She dropped her few things onto the bed and grabbed the telephone. By rote, she dialed the number of the fire department, tapping her foot as she waited for someone there to answer the phone.

"Midtown." It was Dan Nichols. She knew his voice immediately, and wondered if she had been wise to call. It had been eight months since their relationship had ended, yet every time they passed or saw each other, she still got that little pang in her heart.

"Dan?"

"Jill?" He recognized her voice, too, and she wondered why that warmed her.

"I'm sorry to bother you, Dan," she said. "It's just that I've been in Chalmette, and I just heard about the explosion."

"Yeah, it was bad. Sue Ellen Hanover is dead, and so is Cliff Bertrand. And Mary Hampton was killed."

"So the child ..."

"Mary's little boy. He's in a coma."

She sank onto the bed with her hand over her mouth. "Dan, what happened?"

"We're not sure yet. Looks like a bomb. A couple of witnesses saw a pickup truck there just before the blast. Apparently, they've identified a suspect."

"Any guess why he did it? Was it terrorism?"

"In Newpointe? Doubtful."

"Was he trying to get revenge for something? Has Cliff fired anybody lately?"

"I don't know, Jill. The cops are playing this one close to the vest. Looks like the FBI's getting involved, too, since it was a government building. We'll just have to see how it plays out."

That was it, she thought. That was as much as she was going to get. She took a deep breath as her head reeled with the information. She was about to thank him, when he spoke again, his baritone timber softening. "So how are you doing?"

She tried to line her thoughts back up. "Uh . . . fine. Just fine. And you?"

"I'm okay. It's been a long day. So you're in Chalmette, huh?"

"Yeah. I decided to stay in a motel since I have to be back at the courthouse at seven in the morning. I'm at the Flagstaff."

He was quiet for a moment. "Jill, it's good to talk to you. Real good."

She smiled and looked into the mirror above the bureau. Her tawny hair was tousled from a long day of raking tense hands through it, and her blue eyes looked tired and red. As she stared at her reflection, she was painfully aware that Dan's tastes ran blonder and more petite. Pageant material, Jill was not. "It's good to talk to you, too, Dan. You sound a little raspy."

"Yeah, there was a lot of smoke at the post office. We fought the fire for hours. It was the worst I've ever seen."

She sat back on the bed. "Who found the bodies?"

Again, seconds of silence ticked by.

"Dan? Was it you?"

"I made a few discoveries," he said.

She sighed. People thought Dan was self-centered and egocentric. He was, in some cases, but he also had a gentle, sensitive side that she cherished. "What did that cost you, Dan?"

"A lot." The words seemed to take a lot out of him.

"I'll bet. Wanna talk about it?"

"Maybe when you get back."

She tried not to let that statement give her hope. He was just feeling lonely and vulnerable. Death did that to you. It didn't mean anything.

A rap on the door made her jump, and she dropped the tele-phone. It clanged and she picked it back up, put the phone back to her ear. "Dan . . . hold on a second. Somebody's here."

She went to the door, looked out through the peephole, and saw blue lights flashing. Startled, she pulled back the curtain and peered out. The parking lot was full of police cars, with lights flashing in a broad array of blue and red. The knocking sounded again, and she realized they were not at her door, but at the room next to hers. When there was no answer, one of them shouted for the occupant to open it.

Shaken, she went back to the telephone. "Uh . . . Dan, this is really weird. The parking lot's full of cops, and they're bang-ing on the door next door—"

A gunshot ripped through her words as it tore through the adjoining door, and she screamed and hit the floor. The phone crashed to the ground. Another shot whizzed past her head, and she rolled out of the way. The door crashed open, and a man with a rifle burst in, his eyes panicked. He got one look at her and bolted toward her, knocking over a chair to get to her. He grabbed her up and thrust the nose of his rifle at her throat.

She heard the police breaking down the door to his room, yelling at fever pitch as they filled it. One mistake, and it would all be over, she thought. One overzealous police officer, one overactive twitch of this guy's finger on that trigger . . .

Two cops came to the door, their guns aimed at the man. "Drop the rifle!" one of them shouted.

"I'll kill her!" the man holding her yelled. "One more step and I'll kill her!"

She screamed again as he jabbed the barrel of the gun harder into her throat. He twisted her arm behind her to hold her still. She felt him shaking as he held her.

"Back up!" he bellowed. "Back up and close the door. Now!"

Slowly, the police backed away. "Just drop the gun and nobody'll get hurt."

"Shut the door! Now!" the man shouted. "I'm telling you, I'm gonna pull this trigger."

Jill's muffled scream frightened the cops back, and the door closed between them. Dragging her with him, the man kicked the door on their side shut. Jill screamed again.

Chapter Six

The sound of the gunshot shattered through Dan's brain with as much impact as if the bullet had traveled the phone line. He clutched the phone and shouted, "Jill! Jill!" She was no longer holding the phone, and he could hear screaming in the background, things crashing, people yelling.

Then the phone went dead.

"You okay?" Mark Branning had just come in from the truck bay, and stood there staring at Dan.

"No!" Dan slammed the phone down.

"What is it?"

"Jill! I've gotta run next door." He dashed out of the station and crossed the yard to the police station adjacent to the fire department, bolted up the steps, and pushed through the glass doors. Stan was heading out, and Dan almost ran into him.

"Stan, I was just talking to Jill at a motel in Chalmette, and something happened. There were police cars there, and I heard a gunshot, then we got cut off."

"The Flagstaff?" Stan asked, shooting him a look. "That's where I'm going."

"What's going on there?"

"We've got the suspect for the post office bombing cornered there," Stan said, trotting down the steps. "We had an APB on the pickup someone identified at the post office just before the bombing, and they spotted it at the Flagstaff. Apparently they've got the right guy if he's shooting back."

"He's not *just* shooting back!" Dan shouted, as if Stan had orchestrated the whole thing. "Stan, he's got Jill!"

"What?" Stan had reached his car and was unlocking it. "What do you mean?"

"I was talking to her and I heard a gunshot and *he came into her room!*"

"No way." He got into the car.

"I heard her screaming, Stan!" Dan opened Stan's passenger door and slid in. "I'm coming with you."

"No, you're not!" Stan said.

"He's taken Jill hostage!" Dan cried. "Call them and ask. You'll see."

Stan picked up his radio mike to check out the claim. In moments, he had someone from the St. Bernard Parish Sheriff's Department confirming that a hostage had been taken. "Okay, Dan. You're right. He has a hostage. But are you *sure* it's Jill?"

"*Yes!* Now, drive! I'm coming with you."

"All right." Stan turned on the flashing grill lights of his unmarked car and pulled out into the street.

Chapter Seven

The tortured dreams of napalm and Molotov cocktails, machine gun fire and mines, haunted Frank Harper, and in his sleep, he tried to cry out. But his screams were smothered by the sound of war, muted by the terror of death, or worse. He dreamed of comrades falling around him, of his captain's orders being bellowed over the fray. He dreamed of the pain that rent through him as a mine exploded, and the fingers tearing from his hands. He told himself it was a dream and tried to wake up, but the darkness was so profound, so dense, that he began to scream again, loud, agonized screams that went unheard and unheeded.

He tried to breathe, tried to remember where he was, tried to grope around for some sign. He was flat on his back, and he reached up and touched a wall above him, on each side of him, below him. A coffin, he thought, gulping in the air. He had been buried for his country.

Something crept across his leg, and he yelled again, then rolled onto his stomach and began to crawl away. The coffin wasn't closed on the ends. It was too long, and the farther he crawled, the more fresh air he felt. He crawled faster, faster.

It wasn't until he reached the end that he realized he wasn't in a coffin, but a culvert. He had hidden here.

He reached the end and pulled out, stretching to his full height, and looked up at the star-sprinkled sky.

It all came back to him, and he remembered stealing the Civic from the Delchamps parking lot after Jerry let him out, hearing the sirens as he hid under the bridge, hiding in the culvert to escape . . .

He looked around him in the darkness and wondered what he'd done with the detonation devices, the explosives, the wires . . . He was standing on the edge of Lake Pontchartrain, he realized. Maybe he'd thrown the explosives in.

But no . . . he'd needed them. He would not have gotten rid of them . . . not yet.

Had he left them in the culvert? He realized that he had, but couldn't—wouldn't—go back in to get them. What was he going to do now?

Jerry, he thought. He was supposed to meet Jerry . . . at some motel on the way to Chalmette. Would Jerry still be waiting? Had he slept too long?

He looked around, trying to orient himself. The bridge was too long, too far, to cross on foot. By now, they'd be looking for the stolen car. He'd have to find another one somewhere. He hoped that Jerry would wait.

Chapter Eight

The man let Jill go, and she reeled back into the wall, putting as much distance between herself and him as possible. He was breathing hard and beginning to sweat. The hum of the air conditioner gave a surreal feeling to the room, as if there wasn't a team of cops outside waiting to gun him down.

He pulled the chest of drawers in front of the adjoining door to make sure no one could come through, then satisfied, turned back to her. For the first time, he met her eyes, and she told herself not to shrink away.

There were certain things she'd learned in her years of dealing with clients who were both victims and criminals. Talk to them, she'd heard victims say. It was harder for them to kill people who seemed human to them. She'd also learned in dealing with criminals who occasionally wanted her to defend them that it didn't pay to let them know you were afraid. She lifted her chin and desperately tried to appear calm as she watched him get the phone off the floor and hang it up. But she knew her shallow, rapid breathing belied that calm.

Talk to him, she told herself. *Remind him you're a person.* "Why are they after you?" she managed to ask.

He turned to look at her with a surprised look on his face. Had he expected her not to speak? Or was it the question itself that stumped him? "I don't know," he said finally.

"You don't know?" she repeated. "Your motel room is surrounded by police, you've taken a hostage, and you don't know why?"

The phone began to ring, and he stared down at it as if it were some kind of live thing that threatened him. He made no move to answer it, and it kept ringing. Jill wondered if it was Dan calling back. She must have frightened him to death—the screaming and crashing. "Do you ... want me to answer it?" she asked.

He seemed to think it over for a minute, then shook his head. "No. Let it ring."

"But ... maybe it's them. The police, I mean. You could ... I don't know ... talk to them and ... straighten this out."

He rubbed his perspiring face with one hand as he clutched the rifle with the other. The expression on his face and his defensive body language gave Jill courage.

The phone kept ringing ... ringing ... ringing ...

"You must have some idea why they're out there. I mean, you're armed and holed up in here with me."

He aimed the rifle at her. "Get on the bed."

She eyed the bed where she had dropped her things. Dread overwhelmed her, and she struggled to find a weapon. The lamp, a ballpoint pen ...

He seemed to reconsider. "Wait."

The phone continued to ring ... ring ... ring ...

He ignored it and, still holding the gun to her, grabbed her briefcase and opened it. He pulled out the files, the documents, the day planner, the computer organizer, the pens. Satisfied, he put it all back, closed it, and put it on top of the chest of drawers blocking the adjoining door.

Surprised that he hadn't carelessly dumped it, she met his eyes. They were intelligent, not crazed, and she wasn't sure whether that comforted or disturbed her. Intelligence could be more deadly ... more calculated ...

The phone kept ringing ...

"Jerry!" The bullhorn voice buzzed over the hum of the air conditioner, startling them both. "Jerry, pick up the phone," the police voice said. "We need to talk to you, so we can bring a resolution to this. Just pick up the phone."

He walked closer to Jill, the barrel of the rifle against her temple, as if they could see him and infer that he was serious. She squeezed her eyes shut, bracing herself. "Go to the bed," he said again through his teeth. She moved toward the bed with the gun at her back. Why did he want her there? Was he going to hurt her? She got on the mattress and leaned back against the headboard, hugging her knees. As he got on the bed next to her, she squeezed her eyes shut. Her heart rampaged, making her dizzy. She had never been so afraid.

The phone kept ringing ...

Suddenly, he snatched it up. *"What?"*

She opened her eyes and saw the gun still aimed at her temple, but he wasn't looking at her. "Jerry, this is Mills Bryan, FBI." She could hear the telephone voice from where she sat. "You should know that you're making the situation worse for yourself. Keeping a hostage is going to hurt you more than anyone else. There are already three people dead. You don't want to add one more to that list."

Three people, she thought. He had killed three people.

"I didn't do it," he said. "You've got the wrong guy. I didn't have anything to do with that post office bombing."

She caught her breath as she realized that the man holding a rifle aimed at her head might very well be the terrorist that had killed three friends today.

"We can talk about that when you come out," the caller said. "Just let your hostage go and come to the door. Jerry, it would be so much better for you if you stop this now."

"How?" he shouted. "So you can gun me down and go on TV telling everybody that you caught the guy? *I didn't do it!*" He slammed down the phone and turned his raging eyes to her.

She balled herself tighter, and realized she was trembling. "Look ... you don't have to keep that gun on me," she said. "Just ... just put it down. I won't try to get away. I'll just sit here ..."

"Shut up!" he said. "I have to think." He kept the gun aimed at her, but thankfully got off the bed and began pacing back and forth, back and forth. She was able to breathe again. Occasionally, he looked at her, started to speak, then stopped. She didn't move.

Talk, she told herself. She had to keep talking. "I believe you didn't do it," she lied.

He stopped cold and turned around, that gun still aimed at her. He looked almost amused as he stared down at her. "You couldn't possibly."

"I do. I'm a good judge of character. You're not the kind of man who would kill anybody."

His scowl returned, and he shook his head hard. "You don't know what kind of man I am. You'll say anything to keep me from hurting you."

"No," she insisted. "I know because . . . the briefcase. You didn't throw it or dump it. You were almost . . . respectful. I believe you wouldn't hurt anyone. Even me." She prayed it would be a self-fulfilling prophecy.

He looked at her for a moment as if trying to decide whether to gun her down or befriend her. She had to keep talking. "Why do they think you did it, Jerry?"

He seemed to flinch at her use of his name, then tried to consider her question. His eyes went back and forth from the window to the bed as he turned that over in his mind. "My truck. It must be my truck. I was stupid. I should have known they'd be looking for it!"

Then he *did* do it, she told herself. They were looking for his truck, and they'd found it.

"There must have been witnesses," he went on as he paced. "I should have known. I should have said no."

"What do you mean?" she asked.

He seemed unable to go on as emotion overwhelmed him. He groped for the chair, pulled it out from the table, and sank down. "Debbie's gonna die."

She swallowed hard. "Who's Debbie?"

"My wife." He looked up at her, those probing eyes searching her face. "What's a matter? You don't think somebody like me could have a wife? I have kids, too. All these years, I've tried to protect them . . . and now this." His face twisted in pain, and tears shone in his eyes. As if to compensate, he aimed the gun at her again.

"Please . . ." she whispered. "Please put that away. If it went off . . . that would be four dead . . ."

"I didn't kill the other three. I didn't leave that bomb!"

"I know . . . I know you didn't. I just meant . . . four deaths that you'd be accused of."

"You don't know!" he flung back at her. "Don't pretend you know. For all you know I'm some kind of raving maniac whose elevator doesn't go all the way to the top. You don't know me."

"I know what you said."

"And why would you believe some guy who bursts into your motel room and holds a gun to your head? Huh?" His question was angry, insistent.

She knew he had her there. "I don't know. Instinct. I told you. The briefcase."

"Give me a break!" he shouted. "It's called *survival* instinct. Tell him what he wants to hear so he won't hurt you." He leaned back hard in the chair and leaned his head against the wall. "Look, I don't want to hurt you. I don't know who you are, don't care to know. All I do know is that I'm in a mess and I need time to think. You're buying me that time."

Somehow, she did believe him . . . but she didn't know if she should. "My name is Jill. Jill Clark." She hoped knowing her name would make it harder to pull that trigger.

He didn't answer for a long time, then leaned his elbows on his knees and gave her a tentative look. "Who were you talking to on the phone when I came in?"

She swallowed and tried to gauge whether his finger was right over the trigger. "A friend at the Newpointe Fire

Department. I had heard about the bombing on the radio, and I called to ask him what he knew about it."

"Small world, huh?"

"Yeah. It is something of a coincidence."

"And so . . . what did he say?" His eyes didn't look like those of a criminal. They were clear and green, and she imagined that he wasn't a bad-looking man when he wasn't drenched with sweat and waving a rifle. "Who were the three people killed?" he asked.

"Sue Ellen Hanover, the postal clerk, and Cliff Bertrand, the postmaster. And a customer . . . Mary Hampton. Her little boy, Pete, is in the hospital in critical condition."

His eyes widened with what looked like despair, and he turned his face away. "What have you done?" he whispered. She wondered if he was talking to himself. He brought his gaze back to her. "This . . . little boy. How old is he?"

"Five, I think."

"And his mama's dead?"

She nodded.

He took in a deep breath and wilted as his elbows hit his knees again. Slowly, he reached into his back pocket and pulled out his wallet. He took out a sheaf of pictures, tossed it on the bed. "That's my five-year-old."

Reluctantly, Jill picked up the pictures and studied the shot of the precious little boy in a baseball cap that was bigger than his head.

"You think a man with a kid that age would deliberately take a boy's mama from him?"

"No," she said. "Not deliberately."

"Not even accidentally," he said. He got up and grabbed the pictures back, turned the page, and showed her a little girl of about three. "This is my daughter. And my wife. I have a family. And a job. I'm a human, with feelings and a conscience. I don't kill people."

He waved the gun wildly as he spoke, and she held her breath, praying it wouldn't go off. His tears wet his face, and his nose was running, and he wiped it with the hand that held the gun. "I'll probably never see them again. My kids'll grow up thinking I'm a terrorist. My wife will wish she'd never met me." He batted at the tears on his face and breathed in a sob. "And I didn't do it!"

"Then tell them," Jill said, trying to keep her voice calm. "Go out there and tell them exactly what happened. Explain. If you didn't do it, you can prove it."

"No, I can't," he said. "Don't you think I've thought of this? I don't have an alibi. My truck was at the scene of the crime. They're gonna nail me to the wall. Only rich people are found innocent in this country. The rest of us poor Joes are automatically guilty. We don't have dream teams of attorneys spinning and posing for us."

"If you're innocent," she said, "then why *don't* you have an alibi? Why was your truck there?"

He just shook his head, got up, and began to pace again. When he refused to answer, she took a risk. "Jerry, I'm a lawyer. Not the five-hundred-dollars-an-hour kind, but I have a good reputation in Newpointe. They'll listen to me. You can turn yourself in, and I'll tell them you didn't hurt me. I'll help you prove that you weren't involved in the bombing. You have to try for your kids and your wife, Jerry. If you're not a criminal, don't become one just to avoid the fight."

He stopped pacing in front of the air conditioner unit and let it cool his back. "I didn't say I wasn't a criminal," he told her. "When they look at my rap sheet, they'll think I am one. But my record doesn't account for anything that's happened to me in the last ten years. They won't care who I am now. They'll only care about who I was then."

Her heart sank. So he did have a criminal record. Her hope that he was just a nice guy in a bad situation fled.

Keeping the gun trained on her, he came to the bed. She watched him—her breath held—wondering what he would do next.

Chapter Nine

Back in Newpointe, Jim Shoemaker, the police chief, hung up the phone and looked at the two federal agents in his office. "It's confirmed. The owner of the truck at the Flagstaff is a resident of Newpointe. He moved here six months ago when his wife's aunt died and left them her house. I knew the aunt. Good woman. Hard to believe she'd have a terrorist for a relative."

"What's his name?"

"Jerry Ingalls. Designs websites for a living, so he hasn't had occasion to get to know many of the townspeople yet. Kids aren't old enough for school, either, so the family kind of keeps to themselves."

"Are you sure it was him? The truck wasn't stolen, was it?"

"Nope. The men I sent over interviewed his wife. She said she hasn't seen her husband all afternoon. Apparently, he's the one in the truck."

"He's probably not working alone."

"Maybe not. But I have people going through his history, looking for affiliations and associations, groups he might have been involved with."

The door flew open, and Jim leaped to his feet. The agents swung around.

Patricia Castor, the mayor, bolted in. "Jim, I want to know what you know about that bomber. I can't have any more buildings go up in flames around Newpointe. Is he just targeting federal buildings, or government buildings in general? Should we evacuate?"

Jim frowned and looked at the two agents. "Uh . . . gentlemen . . . this is our mayor, Patricia Castor. Pat, these are FBI agents here working on the case."

"Then you tell me," she demanded, turning to them. "It's gotten so I'm scared to go to work tomorrow. Should we evacuate, or not?"

"Evacuate what?" one of the agents asked.

"The local government buildings. The social security office. The courthouse. City hall. This building right here! The homes around the downtown area."

"Pat, we can't evacuate all of Newpointe without cause."

"We have no reason to believe that other buildings are targeted, ma'am," one of the agents said. "We don't recommend random evacuations, but the minute we have reason to think evacuation necessary, we would let you know right away."

Pat wasn't satisfied. "I'm not so sure. You people blew the Kennedy investigation. I still haven't gotten over that."

Jim came around the desk, took Pat's arm, and gently turned her back to the door. "Pat, I promise, I'll keep in close touch with you about this. But right now, we have an emergency on our hands. We think we have the bomber holed up in a motel in Chalmette. We really need to get back to work on this."

"In Chalmette? Well, why on earth are you flapping your jaws in here, when you oughta be there?"

"There are dozens of law enforcement people there, Pat. Some of our own men. I'm working things from this end."

"Well, all right," she said, looking skeptically from Jim to the two agents. "As long as you catch him. You tell me the minute you do, Jim. I want to come over here and question him myself. I can't have people blowing up buildings in my town. What are we gonna do without our post office? Do you have any idea the position this puts me in, as the mayor? People will be looking to me for answers."

"I know," Jim said sarcastically. "Creates a lot of paperwork, doesn't it?"

"Now, don't you get smart with me, Jim Shoemaker! You know I care about the dead. I'm at practically every funeral in this town, whether they can vote or not." She stormed out of the office. Before Jim could close the door, she yelled, "You let me know the minute you get him, you understand?"

Jim closed the door and turned back to the agents. They probably thought they'd stumbled into an episode of the *Twilight Zone* in Mayberry. He hoped they wouldn't decide to disregard his department's help altogether.

Chapter Ten

In Slidell, Celia stood helplessly on the sidewalk of the Slidell Memorial Hospital as they loaded Pete into the ambulance to transport him to New Orleans. He still wasn't conscious, and some dreadful voice in the weariest part of her brain told her that he wasn't going to wake up. They had taken so long to stabilize him that she had almost believed they'd changed their minds about transferring him. When the ambulance had finally come, she had considered riding with him, but since she had her car here, she decided to follow behind them. She had tried to reach his uncle and grandmother to tell them where he would be taken, but hadn't been able to connect with their cell phone. Maybe they had gotten a flight out, she thought, and they were on the way.

"Celia." Allie stood next to her, looking distraught too. "Are you sure you don't want me to go with you?"

"No, no," Celia said. "You need to get back for the baby."

"But he'll be all right for just a little longer. I could follow behind you . . ."

"Really, it's okay. I'm just going to stay with him until his grandmother gets there."

"I don't want you to wear yourself out now," Allie said, patting Celia's belly.

She fanned herself with her hand. "If it just wasn't so hot . . . and it looks like rain."

They got the child into the ambulance, and Celia wiped her eyes again. "I hope he doesn't wake up in there and ask for his mother."

When they closed the doors, Allie hugged her. Wrenching herself away, Celia got into her car and followed the ambulance.

The ambulance made no attempt to move Pete there quickly, as she had expected. The siren wasn't on, and neither were the flashing lights, and she began to get nervous. Why were they wasting so much time? What if the child needed immediate attention?

Then she told herself to calm down, that they knew what they were doing. Maybe a smooth ride was more important than a fast ride. If they'd needed to hurry, they would.

She turned on the radio to divert her attention from her worries and fears, and flipped around until she came to the news. It was an update on the explosion, and she turned the volume up.

"The suspect is apparently cornered at the Flagstaff Motel in Chalmette, Bob. We are standing a good distance from the motel, since the suspect is armed. A few moments ago we heard gunshots, and it has just been confirmed that the gunman shot through the adjoining door in his room and took a hostage."

Celia brought her hand to her face. "Oh, Lord," she whispered, "don't let him kill anybody else." Quickly, she picked up her cell phone and began to dial Stan's number with her thumb. LaTonya Mason answered at his desk again.

"LaTonya, is Stan there?"

"No, he gone to Chalmette. They got the post office bomber there."

"I heard," she said. "So Stan's at the Flagstaff ... right in the middle of all that?"

"He's on his way."

"And the man is armed?"

"That's what I hear."

Celia swallowed back her protests. "All right. Just leave him a note that Pete Hampton's being transported to New Orleans. I'm going with him."

"All right."

She hung up the phone and realized that her heart was racing. Her husband was on his way to a motel where they had backed an armed, desperate man into a corner. There had already been gunfire. There was likely to be more.

Blinking back her tears, she stroked her swollen stomach as she drove and prayed silently that no one else would have to die.

Chapter Eleven

Outside, Stan Shepherd arrived on the scene with Dan Nichols. Dan leaped out before Stan could cut his engine off. Sid Ford—another Newpointe cop—was already there, and so were a dozen or so FBI and ATF agents, as well as the sheriff's department for St. Bernard's Parish.

"What are the feds doing in on this?" Dan asked Stan.

"Somebody blew up a federal post office. Everybody and his brother is going to be in on this."

Because of Stan's emergency lights, no one asked for either of their IDs. Dan pushed through the officers to Sid Ford, who had been the first Newpointe officer to arrive on the scene. "Sid, how's Jill?"

"We think she's okay," Sid said, distracted as he studied the blueprint someone had given him of the motel.

"Is that the blueprint of the motel? I can go in there," Dan said. "I could go through the attic ..."

Sid looked up, disgusted. "Dan, whatchu even *doin'* here? You ain't a police officer. Since when have the Newpointe firefighters responded to calls in Chalmette?"

"I came with Stan," he said. "I was talking to Jill on the phone when he took her hostage. Sid, you gotta let me go in."

Sid shook his head as if his friend had lost his mind. "I ain't even in charge here," he said. "We got all kinds of jurisdiction problems. The FBI's headin' this thing up. Local sheriff's department is already buttin' heads with 'em. Our best bet is to stay out of the way."

Dan wasn't satisfied. He scanned the federal agents until he saw one who seemed to be in charge. Dan pushed through the police and reached him. "Let me try to go in," he said, but as he did, Stan came up behind him, presumably to pull him away.

Preoccupied, the man gave him a sideways glance. "Who are you?"

"I'm Dan Nichols. I'm a firefighter from Newpointe, and if I just study the blueprint I can figure out—"

Stan stopped him with a firm grip on his arm. "I'm Detective Stan Shepherd from Newpointe," he cut in, reaching to shake the FBI agent's hand. "Excuse me a minute." He turned his back to the man and in a low voice said, "Dan, you need to get out of the way. You don't belong here, and you're just calling attention to yourself."

"But *somebody* needs to go in there."

"And what are you gonna do? Shoot him from one of the air conditioner vents? I'm telling you, get out of the way or I'll have to arrest you."

"You've got to be kidding," Dan said.

Stan's eyes pierced into him. "I'm not."

Dan stepped aside, and Stan engaged the FBI agent to see where they were on the case.

Sid was shaking his head as Dan came back to him. "Man, what is wrong with you?"

Dan's eyes flashed. "Jill is in there," he said through his teeth. "A homicidal maniac is holding her hostage! What's wrong with *you?*"

"Jill's tough," Sid said. "She can handle this." He touched Dan's arm, and Dan jerked away and turned to see which window Jill was behind. "Can you?"

"Say I'm overreacting," Dan said. "But I was just talking on the phone to someone I care a lot about, and heard some lunatic burst into her room shooting. It shook me up a little bit. Sue me." He raked his hands through his hair and took a step toward the motel. "Which room is it?"

"That one," Sid said. "One-fifteen. He came from 117 next door."

"There must be a crawl space in the attic, a window in the bathroom, *something!*"

"Where's Stan goin'?" Sid asked as Stan ran around the perimeter of squad cars. They watched as he went to the telephone van set up on the edge of the parking lot, tapping into the phone company's equipment on the corner of the property. Dan took off toward him, and Sid followed.

"The guy's making a phone call," one of the officers in the van was saying.

"Who's he talking to?" one of the FBI agents asked.

The agent monitoring the call shook his head and held up a hand to silence him. Dan wanted to jerk the earpiece away from him. He saw the tape recorder turning on the wall of the van. The cop monitoring the call turned up the volume, and Dan leaned in to hear.

"Honey . . ." The man's voice was overcome with emotion and wobbling.

"Jerry? Jerry, what are you doing? Where are you?" It was a woman's voice, and she was obviously upset. "Jerry, the police have been here. They're saying you blew up the post office. Just now, I heard on the radio that you were holding a hostage."

"I didn't do it, Debbie," Jerry said. "I'm telling you, you've got to believe me."

"Jerry, three people were killed!"

"Debbie, you believe me, don't you? I gotta know you believe me."

She began to sob. Jerry spoke again. "Debbie, honey, listen to me. Debbie, are you listening?"

"Yes," she choked out.

"Debbie, I want you to know that whatever happens, I love you. Please, no matter what people say I did, make sure the kids know that I'm not what they're saying."

"Jerry, you talk like you're gonna die!"

"It's a dangerous situation, Debbie. I'm surrounded by cops."

"Is it true you have a hostage?"

"Yes," he said. "I had no choice."

"Oh, Jerry, let her go!" she wailed. "*Please* let her go! This is getting worse and worse. How did it happen? What are you *doing?*"

"It's a long story," he said. "But I can't let her go. She's my only chance. I'm gonna ask them to get me a plane, and I'm gonna get out of here. Maybe by some chance ..."

"Jerry, are you out of your mind? You can't play games with these people! They have guns!"

"I have a gun, too," he shot back. "My deer rifle that was in the truck."

"What are you saying? That you'll *use* it?"

He was quiet for a moment. "Debbie, please, promise me, that whatever happens you'll tell the kids that I'm not—"

"That you're not what, Jerry?" she yelled. "That you're not a killer? What if you *do* kill somebody? What if you kill that hostage? What if there's a shoot-out when you try to go to the plane?" Her voice broke again, and in a high-pitched voice, she said, "Jerry, don't you know what you're doing to yourself?"

He was silent for a long time, and Dan could hear the despair in his voice when he spoke again. "Debbie, I'm as much of an innocent bystander as that little boy whose mama got killed. You know I don't have this in me."

"Then let the hostage go, Jerry. Let her go and walk out of that room, and we'll get you a good lawyer ... we'll do whatever we have to do. Just ... please don't make it any worse. Please ... I'm begging you."

He began to weep. After several moments, he said, "I love you. Just don't forget that."

The phone clicked.

"Call him back!" Stan said. "Maybe he'll be willing to come out now."

Someone dialed the number, and in the van, Dan heard the phone in room 115 begin to ring.

Chapter Twelve

The phone began to ring again, but Jerry made no attempt to answer it. Jill had been moved by the conversation she'd just heard. Though she hadn't been able to hear his wife's voice, she had seen her captor weeping. She knew by the pain on his face and the emotion in his voice that Jerry himself was in turmoil.

The phone's urgent ringing heightened the tension in the room, and she worried that it might send him over the edge. On the other hand, maybe he would decide to let her go and surrender. If she played her cards right, maybe she could push him toward that decision.

"Jerry, you could let me answer that phone," she said, just above a whisper. "I could tell them that you're coming out, that you haven't hurt me. I could tell them to put their guns down, that you didn't do it."

The phone kept ringing . . . ringing . . . ringing . . .

His face was wet with tears, but he began to laugh. "Oh, yeah. They'll believe that."

"Why wouldn't they?" she asked. "Some of those cops out there are probably from Newpointe. They know me really well. They know I'm a good judge of character and that I wouldn't say this if it wasn't true."

"They know you're under duress and you'd say anything to get out of here," he told her.

The ringing continued, shrill, relentless . . .

Her voice rose. "But if you're really innocent, they can substantiate your claims that you're not the one who planted that bomb."

"Oh, can they?" he asked. "How can they? Anyone who saw anything is probably dead."

"But if there were witnesses who saw your truck, then maybe they could confirm that you weren't there."

"But I *was* there. I just didn't know what he was doing!"

"What who was doing?"

He turned his back to her. The phone rang three times more as he stared at the wall, then quickly turned back around. "By now they've done a rap sheet on me and they know I served time for armed robbery. But it's been ten years since I got out, and I haven't had so much as a parking ticket since. And they'll find out I had post-traumatic stress disorder after Vietnam, and that I went for treatment. They'll call me crazy and say I've snapped. I know how this works."

"Well, excuse me for saying so," Jill ventured, "but you're not exactly acting sane right now."

Instead of getting angry, as she might have expected, he nodded his head in agreement. "You're absolutely right about that. But you see, I've never been in this position before. I don't quite know how to act." He wiped the sweat off of his temples and looked at the ringing phone. She hoped they wouldn't give up.

"What did your wife tell you to do?" she asked.

He looked up at the ceiling. "You can guess. She told me to let you go. That I was digging myself into a hole I couldn't get out of."

"Does she think you did it?"

His face twisted, and he swallowed hard. "She couldn't possibly. Not after being with me all these years. All she knows is she's hurting and scared right now." His face reddened, and as the anger seemed to rise up inside him like lava, he bared his teeth and kicked the bed table, knocking the phone off. Quickly, he hung it back up, as if the open line would give all his secrets away. Almost immediately, it began to ring again.

"Let me answer the phone, Jerry. Let me talk to them."

"No," he said. "I'm the only one who can talk to them. I've got to make some demands. I've got to have a plan." His hair was growing wet with perspiration, dripping down into his eyes, but still the air conditioner hummed and the telephone shrieked.

Finally, he bolted across the room and snatched up the phone. "I want an airplane," he said without prelude. "Get me a plane and a car that'll take me to the airport. If you don't meet my demands in two hours, I'll kill her, you got it? I have nothing else to lose."

He slammed the phone down, startling Jill. She stared up at him, letting the words sink in. Two hours, and he would kill her. She wasn't certain she believed him, but then, he was under extreme stress. There was no telling what he might do.

She decided she'd be quiet for a while, so that he could think his way out of this. Silently, she prayed for the men outside, that they would somehow know what to do.

Chapter Thirteen

Outside, it began to drizzle. The blue grill lights of Stan's unmarked car, and the unmarked cars of the FBI men, flashed along with those of the local police cars filling the parking lot. Dan's heart was flailing after hearing the man say he would kill Jill in an hour.

The Chalmette police and federal agents were arguing about whether to meet his demands to buy time, whether to try to go into the building, or whether to call him back and reason with him. Dan tried to stay back, out of the way, but the inaction was beginning to drive him mad.

"Why don't you jerks get busy and do something?" he shouted. "Time's ticking away. He may not even wait the full two hours!"

The head of the FBI contingency shot Stan an unappreciative look. "Somebody get him out of here."

Sid rolled his eyes and took Dan's arm. "Come on, buddy."

"They're just *sitting there*, like they have all the time in the world."

"No, they ain't just sittin' there. They're tryin' to make some rational decisions. Brother, you need to get back in the car, just to keep you from shootin' your mouth off where it ain't welcome. You need to stay out of the way, like we do when you fight fires."

He refused to get into the car, but leaned back on the hood. His head was beginning to ache, so he clutched it with both hands. "Are they gonna get the plane or what?"

"Maybe. Maybe not. It's their call, not yours."

"What about the wife?" Dan asked. "What if someone brought her here?"

Sid stared at him for a moment, processing the idea. "Now, that might be a good idea. The first one you've had all night. And if you stay here and don't start yappin' and yellin' again, I'll go throw that idea out to them. Can I trust you to do that?"

"Don't talk to me like some kind of idiot, Sid." Dan's face began to redden. "I've risked my life right alongside you, more times than I can count. Condescension isn't called for here."

"Neither is panic."

He banged his palm on the hood of the car. "I'm not panicked."

"Ain't you?"

"No! I just seem to be the only one concerned about Jill."

"You're the *most* concerned about Jill—I'll give you that. But you ain't the only one." Sid headed back to the others.

Dan stood on the fringes of the forces, feeling more helpless than he'd ever felt before. He saw some of the cops going into the motel's office, then heard that they were cutting off the circuit breaker that powered the air conditioner. It was eighty-five degrees out. Soon it would get so hot in there that Jerry Ingalls would be begging to come out. But so would Jill. He saw several of the cops clustering around the surveillance van again, and Stan seemed to be at the center. Slowly, he headed toward it, hoping he wouldn't be noticed. He saw that an FBI agent was calling Jerry again, letting it ring, ring, ring . . .

He started to suggest, loudly, that they not do anything else to increase the killer's tension, but just before he could get the first word out, the man inside picked up the phone and yelled, "*What?*"

Dan wiped the sweat from his face on the sleeve of his shirt and stepped closer, listening.

"Jerry, I think you know you're surrounded, and that the FBI is in on this, because blowing up a post office is a federal rap."

"I'm quite aware of that," Jerry snapped back.

"Then why don't you give yourself up, come on out, and spare your family any more pain?"

"I want you to listen to me," Jerry said, his voice quivering with rage. "I want you to get me that plane. I don't need a pilot. I can fly it, if you just have it waiting for me at the airport. I'm not bluffing, man. You've got two hours or she's dead."

"We're working on getting the plane, Jerry. But remember, she's an innocent bystander. You're not a cold-blooded killer."

Dan searched the agent's face, saw that he was feeling his way, trying to appeal to the human side of the man they'd heard in the phone call to his wife.

"You've got a lot more to lose than you think. Your family..."

"I've already lost my family," Jerry shouted. "You've taken them away from me. I'm gonna have to get on a plane and fly to who-knows-where, looking over my shoulder constantly, when I know I didn't do anything. So don't throw my family at me. Just do what I say." He slammed the phone down.

Dan shook his head.

"Okay," one of the agents told Sid. "Go ahead and get someone out to the wife's house and bring her here, fast. We'll bluff our way to the airport if we have to, but maybe the wife can buy us some time."

Stan and Sid got out of the van and headed for Stan's car. It began to drizzle, but that did nothing to help the sweltering temperatures. It only made it feel like a steam bath.

Dan stood close to Stan's car as he radioed the order back to Newpointe. When he'd finished, Stan looked up at Dan. "You okay?"

Dan could only shrug and look toward that motel room again.

"She's okay, you know," Stan said. "He hasn't hurt her yet."

"How do you know he hasn't? She's been in there over an hour and a half. We don't know what he's done to her."

"I just don't think he has."

Dan couldn't respond as he stared at the lighted window.

"You know, you and Jill haven't been an item for months. But you're acting like a husband negotiating for his wife. What gives?"

Dan breathed a sigh that spoke volumes. "I always knew she was okay. That I could pick up the phone and reach her if I wanted to."

"But you didn't want to."

Dan swallowed. It was too complicated to explain. He couldn't even sort out his feelings for his own sake.

"Now that she's being held hostage at gunpoint, you suddenly have feelings for her?"

"It's not sudden," Dan said. "Quit playing shrink and just get her out of there."

Chapter Fourteen

Inside the motel room, Jerry Ingalls went to the air conditioner and tried to make it come on, but it wouldn't. While he'd been on the phone it had gone off, and the room's temperature seemed to be rising dramatically as a result.

Jill heard rain drumming against the window, making the air even more humid than it had been. Jerry was drenched with sweat, and Jill was perspiring, too. So far, she'd stayed on the bed, her arms around her knees, protecting herself. Now she worried that the heat and his discomfort would add to his instability.

Slowly, she unfolded from her crouch and eyed the door to determine how long it might take her to rush to the door, turn the bolt, and push out into the night before he shot her. *Too long*, she thought. She'd never make it.

She peered into the darkened bathroom. No windows. And the ceiling in the small, stifling room was made of sheetrock. There was no way to push through to escape. Her eyes drifted back to the door. Maybe if she could just get closer to it, she would have an opportunity to run.

Cautiously, she got off of the bed and went to the air conditioner unit. "It must be broken."

He shook his head and slammed the cover down. "They did it. They want me to be as uncomfortable as I can be."

"How could they do that?" she asked. "They'd have to cut off all the electricity to do that, wouldn't they? The lights are still on."

"They could have tripped a breaker." He stood at a slit in the curtain, peered out, then turned back to her. He was still holding the rifle on her, but his finger wasn't poised over the trigger.

She crossed her arms nonchalantly and tried to get between him and the door. "Can I look out?"

"No," he said. "Get back over there."

His voice was tentative, almost timid, but he still waved that gun. She backed away, but didn't go all the way over to the bed.

"Did you mean that? What you said on the phone, about killing me in two hours?"

"Of course I meant it."

"But I thought you swore you weren't a killer."

"I'm not. But when you're surrounded by cops and falsely accused, you tend to do things you might not ordinarily do."

"And killing me will help you how?"

He gave her a disgusted look. "Just get back on the bed and shut up."

She sat on the edge of the bed but kept her eyes trained on him. He sat down, holding the rifle pointed at her, but his eyes seemed to move back and forth across the room, as his mind worked the problem over.

After several moments had passed, he turned back to the window. She thought of trying to rush him while his back was turned, but that finger was too close to the trigger. "It's sweaty," he said.

"What is?"

"The air." He turned back to her and looked at the floor. "It's what my little boy says. 'It's sweaty in here.' Like the air has the sweat floating around in it."

She forced a smile. "He sounds sweet."

His throat bobbed. "He is." His mouth twitched as emotion covered his face, and she knew he was wondering if he'd get to see his boy again. "You have kids?"

She shook her head, thinking that was probably a negative in his book. If she could say she was a mother, maybe he'd go easier on her. But somehow she felt he would know if she lied. She didn't think she looked much like a mother, or even a wife, for that matter. "I'm not married," she said.

"Engaged? Going steady?" It was the first hint of humor she'd encountered in him, but she didn't find it amusing. Neither did he. It was simply conversation designed to make the minutes tick by with fewer jolts.

"No." She began to realize it was a mistake to admit that to him. If she had no one who would mourn her murder, it would be easier for him to end her life. "But ... there's this firefighter I've kind of been involved with ..." It was a lie. She and Dan hadn't been involved in the last eight months, but she was still attached to him in some way. She thought about him more times during a day than she would ever admit to anyone. She wondered what he was thinking tonight after her bizarre phone call.

"That who you were talking to when I came in?"

She nodded. "Yes."

"Guess he's a basket case, if he heard all that."

Again, silence. He sat back in the chair at the window, and looked down at the floor, then at his watch, then at the phone.

She seized the opportunity to lean forward, ready to pounce toward the door as soon as she had the nerve. "Jerry, I could represent you, if you let me go. I could prove to them that you're innocent."

"But you don't believe that I am."

"Of course I do," she lied. "I could tell them that you haven't touched me ..." Her words faded out as quickly as she'd uttered them. She didn't want to give him any ideas. "I ... I could find the real killer."

"No, you couldn't. You'll never find him."

Jill frowned. "But with your help—"

Something she'd said was wrong, because his face hardened and he got up and turned back to the window again.

"Because all you have to do is tell them, and—"

"Shut up," he told her. "That's enough."

She checked her watch. Time was running too fast. "Jerry, please."

"I said shut up!" he yelled, swinging around. He looked at his watch, then peered out the curtain again. "What are they *doing?* They're just *sitting* there."

"They can't very well fly that plane into the parking lot," she said. "They're probably taking care of it by phone and radio."

He turned around and leaned his head back against the wall. "What if they think I won't really kill you? That it's a bluff? Maybe I need to shoot just to show them that I mean it." He began to pace across the floor, from the window to the bathroom, and back again. She sensed that he was getting more and more uneasy, more and more panicked, like a caged animal.

She eyed the door again, and watched him walk past her. He turned back around, like a sentry keeping guard, and passed her again. She sat up straighter, preparing to bolt. She had to get out of here, she thought. She had to at least try. She had to take the chance.

"One hour and twenty minutes," he said, grabbing a towel out of the bathroom and mopping his face. "They have one hour and twenty minutes."

"Jerry . . ." It came as a whisper, almost inaudible. In less than two hours he would pull the trigger. What did she have to lose by running now?

When he passed her to go back toward the bathroom, she took a deep breath and prayed a silent, pleading prayer. Then she pushed off from the bed and launched out for the door. He swung around with the rifle and yelled, "Don't!"

She turned the dead bolt and pulled the door open, but it caught on the chain.

Jerry crossed the room and slammed his gun against the door. It went off in his hand, shooting straight up into the ceiling.

She screamed and fell back, and he turned the gun on her. "Get back on that bed or I'll do it now!"

The phone began to ring, and still holding the gun to her, he sat down beside her and picked it up. He thrust it against her ear. "Tell them you're okay," he said.

She trembled as he pressed the phone to one side of her head, and the gun to her throat. "Hello?" she whispered.

"Jill, are you all right? We heard a gunshot . . ."

She glanced at Jerry and tried to find her voice. "I'm fine."

"Ask them about the plane," Jerry prompted.

"The plane . . ." she said, breathless. "Do you have the plane?"

"We're working on it. Jill, has he hurt you in any way? Are you—"

Jerry removed the phone and put it to his ear. "You've got an hour," he said, and hung it up.

Chapter Fifteen

On the east side of Newpointe, Debbie Ingalls saw the flashing lights of the police car through her window. She sat paralyzed in the dark of her living room as the walls went from blue-to-black, from blue-to-black. Had Jerry killed the hostage? Had they come to tell her he was dead?

"Mommy."

She jumped at the sound of her child's voice. Five-year-old Seth stood at the door with his hair all cowlicked and tousled, and those big freckles illuminated and darkened by the lights coming in the window. "Mommy, what's that light?"

"Come here, honey," she said, getting up and pulling her son to the back room with her. Her three-year-old daughter slept soundly there, and she crawled onto the bed next to her and held Seth with all her might.

"Why are you crying?" Seth asked in a whisper.

"Because . . . Daddy's in trouble."

"Why?"

"I don't know," she said, shaking her head. She pressed her forehead against her son's freckled face. She loved those freckles. She often told him they were angel kisses.

The doorbell rang, and she caught her breath and tried to calm herself.

"Who's that?" Seth asked.

"Um . . . Honey, I want you to stay here with Christy. Mommy has to go talk to . . . somebody."

She put the child down next to his sleeping sister and got off of the bed.

The doorbell sounded again.

Wiping her face with shaking hands, Debbie headed for the door. She touched the knob, pressed her forehead against the door, and gave in to another round of sobs. When the bell rang again, she forced herself to open it.

"Mrs. Ingalls?" the police officer asked, his hat dripping with rainwater. It wasn't the same officer who had been here earlier, to tell her that her husband was a terrorist.

She closed her eyes and nodded, pressing her hand against her mouth.

"Mrs. Ingalls, I'm Sergeant R.J. Albright, ma'am. I know you're aware that your husband is in some trouble. I also know he's been in touch with you . . ."

"Yes," she whispered.

"I was wonderin' if you would come with me to Chalmette and talk to him. We were thinkin' that if you could be there in person, maybe you could convince him to let his hostage go."

She opened her eyes wide and looked at him fully. "He's . . . he's not dead?"

"No. I'm sorry, did you think . . . ?"

"Yes." She collapsed against the door's casing, weeping.

The squad car's door slammed, and she saw a black woman storming up the sidewalk to her house, her silhouette stark against the flashing blue light. "You poor woman!" She reached the door and pulled Debbie into her arms. Debbie collapsed against her like a child running into the arms of its mother.

"Uh . . . ma'am, this is Susan Ford," the officer said awk-wardly, as if the embrace embarrassed him. "She's the fire chief's wife. Her brother-in-law, Sid, is a police officer on the scene in Chalmette."

Susan kept holding her. "He asked me to come see about watchin' your kids while you go deal with your hubby, darlin'."

"We're kind of in a hurry," the officer said.

"Give her a minute, R.J.!" Susan snapped, handing Debbie a handkerchief. "Can't you see she's upset?"

"He's given us a deadline," R.J. insisted. "We need to get you there as soon as possible."

Debbie straightened, and tried to steady her breathing. She took the proffered handkerchief from the woman, then quickly flicked on the light behind her. She looked the woman over. She was pretty and small, and her face was full of compassion. Debbie felt like she'd known her for years. "I'll go," she said. "The children are in the back bedroom. Seth is awake. He'll be scared when I leave. Tell them . . . tell them I'll be back soon."

"Don't you worry about a thing. Me and the babies, we'll have us a big time."

Debbie tried not to look back as she headed out to the squad car.

• • •

The rain was falling harder as they reached the Flagstaff Motel after a hair-raising, siren-blaring, light-flashing drive from Newpointe. Debbie looked around and saw the New Orleans television station vans broadcasting live with bright lights that lit up their field reporters. Over to the side stood a group of people that were, no doubt, motel guests who'd been evacuated after the gunfire.

Everywhere, she saw uniformed police officers and FBI agents. She began to cry again.

The sky flashed with lightning, and a thunderbolt crashed right behind it. R.J. ushered her out of the police car, and the crowd seemed to part for her. She kept her eyes on the one motel room that everyone's attention seemed to be focused on. "How much time left?" R.J. asked as they approached someone at a van. She recognized him to be Stan Shepherd. She had seen his picture in the papers.

"Thirty minutes," he said, turning around. "You Debbie Ingalls?"

"Yes," she said.

"Will you talk to him if we can get him on the phone?"

"Of course. I don't know if he'll listen . . ."

"He's demanded a plane, and he wants us to give him a car so he can drive to the airport. He says he'll fly it himself."

"Where does he intend to go?"

"We don't know that. But he's digging himself deep, Mrs. Ingalls. If you talk him out of all this, he'll be a lot better off."

She'd already figured that out for herself. "Where's the phone?"

Two agents filed out of the van to make room for her, and they gave her a seat next to the phone, where she could talk and still see out the windshield. She heard it start to ring, and realized that everyone was listening to the conversation. "Do you have to listen in?" she asked. "I . . . I feel a little nervous . . ."

"Just do the best you can," he said. "And yes, we do have to listen in."

She accepted that with resignation and put the phone to her ear. On the third ring, Jerry picked it up. "The clock is ticking," he said.

She winced at the words. "Jerry?"

He hesitated. *"Debbie?"*

"Jerry . . . I'm outside." She looked through the windshield to the motel room window. "They brought me here so I could talk to you."

"You're here?" he asked, and she saw the curtain in the room pull back slightly. She saw some of the rifles being lifted, and she grabbed the arm of the cop next to her. He signaled for them to hold their fire. "Where?"

"In the van," she said. "Over to the right of the parking lot. Jerry, this is crazy! You can't do this. You can't just get on a plane and fly out of here and never look back. We love you."

"I can't believe they're using you like this." His voice was deadly calm, quietly angry.

"I wanted to come," she said.

"Where are the kids? They're not out there watching all this, too, are they?"

"No, they're at home. The police sent a baby-sitter. But I'm here, Jerry. Don't make *me* watch it."

"Debbie, I'm doing what I have to do. I can't go back there. They'll stick me with terrorism and murder, and I haven't done anything wrong. They'll put me in Angola for the rest of my life."

The sky flashed again, cracking the line. "Jerry, we can prove your innocence if you come out now."

"Have they got the plane?"

She looked at the agent who seemed to be in charge, and he mouthed that they needed a little more time. "Jerry, they need a little more time. Besides, it's not flying weather. It's dangerous—"

She heard something crash. The police officers in the parking lot bent behind their cars and aimed their guns. She guessed there must be two dozen weapons aimed at that window in front of her husband.

"They think I'm bluffing," he said.

"Jerry, calm down. The plane is almost there. But you can't take a hostage and threaten to kill her, then hop on a plane and fly off in a thunderstorm and think you'll get away with it. Jerry, somehow we can prove you didn't do the post office bombing. So far, you haven't killed anyone. But if you hurt your hostage . . . if you add another victim . . . so help me, Jerry, I'll never know what to believe. I'll never know what to tell the children."

She heard him weeping into the phone, heard him sucking in a wet breath. "Debbie, I can't surrender. They won't listen."

"Yes, they will. Jerry, you have to try. I didn't marry a quitter. I didn't marry somebody who runs when things get hot. I married a fighter. An honest man. A *sane* man."

"Debbie, I want you to go home. They can't hold you here."

"I'm not going!" she shouted. "Jerry, don't make me watch you come out of that room with a hostage! Please!"

"Debbie, I said to go home."

"No!" she screamed. "Jerry, so help me, if you do this, I'll never forgive you. Don't you *dare* leave me. Don't you *dare* ruin your children's lives!"

He was silent for a moment, then finally, the phone clicked off and she was left with nothing but a dial tone.

"Aw . . . He's mad," the man behind her said, raking his hands nervously through his hair. "He's agitated. You gotta let me go in. Stan, tell them . . ."

Stan stared at the motel room, his eyes intent on it, as if he could see into it. "Maybe we do need to send somebody in at this point," he said. "But not you, Dan."

"Send somebody in?" Debbie asked. "And do what? Shoot him?"

"We have to protect Jill," Dan said. "He's unpredictable . . ."

"Shut up!" one of the agents ordered. "You're not a cop. You don't belong here!"

Dan backed away, shaking his head. He looked as nervous as she. "Is he . . . the hostage's husband?" Debbie asked Stan.

"No," Stan said. "Just . . . a good friend."

She looked back at the distraught man, then at the motel room, and knew that the man they called Dan was in love with the woman inside. It was written all over his face, even if no one else could see it. Suddenly, she had overwhelming sympathy for him, and for the woman inside. "Maybe I need to be the one to go in there," she said.

They all turned. "What do you mean?"

"I could knock on the door. Tell him it's me. Maybe he'd let me in. Maybe I could talk him into coming out."

"You're willing to do that?"

Dan approached the van again, his face growing hopeful. "Yes."

"But he's dangerous right now. He's armed."

"He's my husband," she said, lifting her chin. "He won't hurt me, no matter how desperate he is."

"Are you sure?"

She looked toward the motel room as if weighing the possibility, then finally, said, "Yes, I'm sure. Let me go in."

"I'm gonna warn him you're coming."

"All right." She got out of the van and waited in the rain with her arms crossed. Dan was watching her, and she knew he could see how hard she was trembling. Someone called the room, listened as it rang, but Jerry wasn't going to answer it. Finally, an agent brought the bullhorn to his mouth. "Jerry, your wife is coming to the door. Look out the window and you'll see her coming. Let her in."

Debbie started walking toward the door as the rain pounded on her and lightning bolted, and she saw the curtains being jerked back. Jerry motioned for her to go away, but she didn't stop until she was at the door. As long as she stood in front of his room, she knew they wouldn't shoot him through the window and risk killing her and the hostage.

She knocked and waited, but the door didn't open. "Jerry, let me in," she cried. "Open the door, Jerry." As she called through, her voice became more urgent, more emotional. "Jerry, please. Don't do this to me. Please, open the door. Look at me! I'm alone. Don't leave me out in this storm with all those guns pointed at me."

Several minutes passed, and finally, the door opened just a crack. Debbie pushed inside, and it closed again behind her.

Chapter Sixteen

Jill couldn't believe Jerry's wife had pushed her way in, and as their eyes met, the tiny woman seemed to be assessing her for injuries. She stood no more than five-feet-three, and had eyes that were too big for her face and wet hair that dripped into her eyes. She burst into tears again at the sight of Jerry's rifle. Jerry paid no regard to the fact that she was rain-soaked. He crushed her against him as she wept into his shirt, both hands clenched in fists against his chest. "Jerry . . . Jerry . . ."

Jill waited, breath held, praying that his wife would have the clout to get him to let her go.

Jerry turned Debbie's face up to his and gazed sadly down at her. "I need for you to go back out there."

"No, I won't go," she said. "Not until you let her go and turn yourself in."

"I can't do that."

"Jerry, how could you do this? You're going to make a widow out of me. I'll never see you again."

"No, I'm not. It'll all work out. When I get where I'm going, I'll find work and send you money, and you and the kids can join me."

"Jerry, they'll come after you, if they don't shoot you down before you ever get on that plane. You can't be naive enough to think you'll get away with this."

"I have no choice."

"Yes, you do!" She pushed him away from her. "You can be a man and fight this. You can walk out there and turn yourself in, and we can prove that you didn't blow up the post office! You won't be labeled a murderer." She grabbed his shoulders and stared up at him. "How did this happen, Jerry? Why do they think you were there?"

"Because I *was*," he said. "I was there right before the explosion. But I didn't know. I wasn't involved."

She wiped her face with both hands. "Jerry, the friend you were meeting. Was it him?"

Jerry turned away.

"*Who was it?*" she screamed. "Jerry, tell me!"

Jill waited, breath held.

"I can't," he said.

Debbie banged her fists on his chest. "Jerry, are you gonna die for this? If you do, you'll be the one considered a killer. They'll never even look past you."

It felt like an oven in the room, and Jill wiped her face on her sleeve. Jerry sank down into a chair, glistening with sweat, and shook his head wearily. "It's out of my hands."

"No! It *can't* be!" Debbie turned to Jill. "She'll tell them, won't you? You'll tell them that he hasn't touched you! It should carry some weight."

"How do you know he hasn't?" Jill asked.

Jerry's eyes whiplashed to Jill's.

Debbie's chin came up and her lips compressed. "I know my husband. He's a gentle, sweet man . . . a good husband and father . . . He'd never blow up a post office or kill innocent people or hurt anyone . . ."

The words seemed to chisel away at his constitution, and he wilted further with each one.

Jill sat straighter. "You're right. He hasn't hurt me. Yes . . . I'll tell them."

Debbie turned back to him and leaned down to him. "See? Jerry, this can still be all right."

"They'll put me in jail," he said. "Maybe Angola again. Are you sure you can stand to go through that?"

"Yes! At least I'll know where you are. At least there's hope."

"Hope," he repeated. "I don't know if there *is* any hope."

"Of course there is. There's always a chance, if you're here to fight. Jerry, I'll fight with you."

"I fought last time."

"I wasn't *there* last time. You were fighting alone."

Jerry seemed moved by that, and he stood back up and reached for her. She reached up to touch his face as their eyes met, and Jill held her breath, certain that he was about to acquiesce and let her go.

When he seemed to struggle with an answer, Jill decided to speak. "I told him I'm a lawyer, that I would represent him."

Debbie's eyes widened as they turned to her. "Really? See, Jerry? Look how much influence she would have, if she was the hostage you were charged with taking, and she wound up representing you! Jerry, don't you see how much help she could be?"

He looked at Jill, as if assessing her for honesty. She looked away.

"Jerry, I've never asked you for much," Debbie cried. "But I'm asking you now. If you love me . . . if you've ever loved me . . . if you love the children . . . I need you . . . we need you . . . to let her go and walk out there without that gun."

Jill began to pray silently as Jerry gazed down at his wife.

Chapter Seventeen

Outside, the lightning bolting angrily in the sky mirrored the energy coursing through Dan's soul. He could hardly breathe as he waited in the rain for something to happen. Moments passed, and he began pacing, never taking his eyes from the door. Overcome with emotion, he prayed silently for Jerry Ingalls, that he'd have a change of heart and mind and let Jill go, that Debbie would have enough influence over him, that Jill would remain unharmed . . .

Suddenly, the door opened, just a crack, then a little more, and Dan froze as a crack of thunder heralded the change. Officers all around the parking lot ducked behind the barricades of their cars and aimed their weapons. Headlights lit up the door, and they all waited. Then the storm grew silent for a moment.

Then Jill appeared, holding the rifle over her head.

"It's Jill!" Stan shouted. "Hold your fire!"

She broke into a run and headed toward them. Dan paid no regard to the guns aimed at her and took off between the cars to meet her. It wasn't until she was well past the headlights that she was able to see him, but she bolted into his arms and clung to him with all her might. Someone grabbed the rifle from her hands, and police officers surrounded her and pulled them out of harm's way.

"Where're the Ingalls?" Stan asked, keeping his eyes on the door.

"They're coming," Jill yelled. "They're unarmed. Don't shoot them."

They held their fire as the door opened again, and Jerry Ingalls came out with one arm around his wife and the other high in the air. Both of Debbie's arms were around him.

Slowly, they walked toward the police, one step at a time, as if they each expected to be gunned down at any second. When they were sure they weren't armed, the cops ran forward, pulled Debbie away, and threw Jerry down on the ground. Debbie began to scream that they were hurting him.

Suddenly, half of the reporters were shining their cameras on the scuffle, and the other half surrounded Jill.

"Miss Clark, are you all right?"

"Did he hurt you in any way?"

"What made him release you?"

She pulled away from Dan and stepped back as the rain drenched her. "No, he didn't hurt me. He let me go because his wife convinced him to."

"Why did he take you hostage?"

"Because he claims he's innocent of the post office bombing. He panicked when the police came."

She heard Debbie Ingalls sobbing hysterically, and looked back at her over her shoulder. "Wait! Stop!" Debbie screamed. "He has a lawyer! She's going to represent him! Jill Clark is my husband's lawyer!"

One of the agents pulled Jerry to his feet and began to drag him toward his car. Stan approached Jill. "That true, Jill?"

Dan let her go and stared down at her, and she was overcome with the sense that everyone here was looking at her, waiting for an answer. Even Jerry and his wife. A million conflicting emotions raged through her. "I ... I don't know what she's talking about," she said.

Debbie heard that and began to wail even more loudly, and Jerry looked at her with an anguished, betrayed expression. She put her back to them and looked up at Dan. "Will you drive me home?"

"I came with Stan," Dan said. "Besides, they'll want to take you back to the station. You'll have to give them a statement."

"I . . . I will," she said. "Just . . . drive my car. I just need some quiet. Just a few minutes."

"But they want to examine you, make sure you aren't hurt."

"I'm fine," she said. "Please, Dan. Get them to let me leave. I want to get out of here."

Dan secured permission to drive Jill alone in her car as two Newpointe squad cars escorted them back. She sat shivering in the air conditioning as her wet clothes clung to her skin.

Dan was quiet, and Jill got lost in her own thoughts. Why did she feel like a traitor? She had made a promise to Jerry and his wife, after all, but did a promise made under duress have to be kept?

She leaned her head back on the seat, breathing in the stream of cold air coming in from the air conditioner vents. "Jill, do you want the air conditioner off? You're shivering."

She shook her head. "No. It's been like a steam bath."

"But you're wet. You'll get sick."

She turned the vent away from her. "I'll be fine." She saw the concerned way he looked at her, and knew what must be going through his mind. "Really, Dan, he didn't touch me."

"Then why are you so quiet?"

She shook her head. "I was just thinking. He swears he's not guilty, wanted me to represent him."

"That would be a little crazy, if you ask me."

"Yeah, I think so, too. But I kind of had to make a promise to get out of there."

"Is that why he let you out?"

"One of the reasons." She thought back over the conversation with Debbie, her promise to help him, his final agreement to do as his wife had asked. "Maybe I should represent him, since I said I would. But what if he's guilty?"

"I guarantee you he wouldn't be holed up in a motel with a gun and a hostage if he wasn't. Any idea what his motive was?"

"I couldn't say. But he seemed concerned about the people who were killed, and Pete Hampton . . ."

"So he's a killer with a heart?"

Jill stared at the rain-splattered windshield. Steam rose up like a fog from the road in front of them. "Something like that."

"At least he didn't pull that trigger. When I heard that gun go off, I thought my heart was gonna explode through my chest."

She regarded his wet clothes and the pained expression on his face. It suddenly occurred to her that he wasn't supposed to have been there. This wasn't Newpointe, where firefighters were called to every emergency. "Dan, why were you there?"

He didn't answer for a moment, just drove into the night, across the long, lonely bridge over Lake Pontchartrain. "When I heard what happened on the telephone, there was no way I could just stay put. I had to find out what was going on."

"Yeah, I guess that was pretty scary," she said.

"Shook me up real bad."

"I guess anybody I had on the phone would have felt the same way."

"Maybe," he said.

Again, there was deafening silence between them, as Dan seemed to struggle with his words. "I was praying while I was out there," he said. "I was about to jump out of my skin. I just knew you were gonna get killed by that maniac. I just knew I was never gonna see you again."

She thought of asking him why that would have impacted him at all, since she rarely saw him now. But fatigue was coloring her perceptions and her thoughts, and it wasn't a good time to get into them.

"I made some bargains with God when I was waiting in the parking lot."

"Bargains?" she asked. "What kind of bargains?"

"Well, the most obvious kind, I guess." He seemed to be battling with the feelings he was trying to express.

"And what might those be?" she asked.

"I just started to realize that I'd missed you," he said, and glanced over at her. "And I told God that if you walked out of there alive, unharmed, I would quit second-guessing my feelings for you."

She gaped at him. "You have feelings for me?" It was asked almost sarcastically, and she hated herself for it.

He looked at her across the darkness. "Jill, you know I do."

"I thought you did," she said. "But they sort of fizzled out, didn't they?"

"Not for me." He looked at the road in front of him again. The windshield wipers stroked back and forth, back and forth across the window. "I told God that I'd quit trying to find ways out of our relationship. That I'd try to resume things with you."

The dread implied in that made her angry. "And what did God say to that?"

"He brought you out alive and unharmed."

She laughed bitterly. "So now you're obligated? Is that it?"

She could see that her levity bothered him. He shot her a puzzled look.

"Don't worry about it, Dan," she said, looking out her window again. "Don't you remember? A promise made under duress isn't binding."

"I mean for it to be binding," Dan said.

She shook her head and her smile faded. "Well, excuse me, but it takes two to tango, and I don't think I'm interested."

She knew his thoughts gravitated back to the way she had run into his arms and clung to him.

"It's been months," Jill said. "I had feelings for you before, but . . . well, I've had to move on with my life."

"You're not seeing anyone else," Dan said. "I'd know if you were."

She shook her head, unable to believe they were having this conversation. "It doesn't make any difference, Dan. I'm letting you off the hook. You don't have to resume things with me. I'm sure God won't hold you to it if I don't cooperate."

Again, Dan grew silent as they drove along, and Jill felt tears rushing to her eyes. She hadn't cried at all since she'd been held hostage. In the room fearing for her life, she'd been able to control her emotions. Now, suddenly, when her body was safe but her heart was threatened, the tears crept up on her, making it impossible for her to push them away. She began to cry, quiet tears at first, then deep, hard sobs that came straight from her heart and soul and seemed to have no place to go. After a moment, she felt Dan's hand on her shoulder.

She was too weak to resist as he pulled her head against him. His shirt was soaked—but it didn't bother her as she wept against his neck.

"Jill, you don't have to be a tough guy," he whispered as he drove. "I know it's upsetting being roughed up by some crazy guy who takes you hostage. No one expects your frame of mind to be level and unemotional right now."

She wanted to yell that she wasn't crying just because of Jerry Ingalls and being held hostage, that she was crying for Dan and for eight months of wasted days and nights.

But she couldn't say any of that. Slowly, she sat back up and wiped the tears from her face. "It's been a long day."

"It's about to get longer. When we get to the police station, they're gonna want to question you for hours."

"I can handle that," she said. "As long as it's dry and they have the air conditioner on. Maybe some dry clothes."

"If you'll give me your keys, I'll go to your house and get you some."

She shook her head. "Frankly, I'd rather stay in these than have you see the condition of my house right now. It's kind of a mess."

"Okay, then. I could call Allie and ask her to go. Or I could just run to my house and change, and get you something of mine to wear."

"Okay," she said.

"Which thing?"

She was too drained to make a decision. "I don't know. I'll decide before we get there."

"You know, you don't have to be embarrassed if your house is a little messy. You're a busy lady. I wouldn't think less of you."

She didn't answer. He reached across the seat to take her hand, laced his fingers through hers. She wondered why that mere touch meant so much ... why that hug moments earlier had melted her heart ... why his arms around her when she ran from the motel room had felt like heaven itself.

"So when were you the most afraid?" he asked.

She thought that over for a moment. "When I heard him set a deadline for killing me."

He swallowed and squeezed her hand. His eyes grew misty as he said, "Yeah, me too. Did you think he would?"

"He didn't seem to be the type," she said. "But I couldn't be sure. I don't know his mental condition, his ups and downs. I couldn't predict his behavior."

"Did he seem crazy?"

"Not really," she said. "He seemed like a very scared man who'd been accused of something he hadn't done. He just happened to be waving a gun in my face."

As they reached the outskirts of Newpointe, Dan glanced in the rearview mirror. "Some of the TV vans are following us," he said. "They'll want to interview you."

"I'm exhausted," she said quietly. "Telling the police all that happened is about all I can handle, and I still have to go back to Chalmette tomorrow and take more depositions for the case I'm working on."

"Jill, can't you take the day off in light of what's happened?"

"No, I can't. I have too much work."

He grew quiet. She knew her commitment to her work was one of the reasons things had cooled between them. Her heart sank further as any hope flew away like a carelessly blown dandelion puff. As they reached Jacquard Street, the main drag through town, Jill realized they were near the post office.

"Would you take a detour?" she asked. "Before we go to the police station, I want to see the post office."

"Sure, we can do that." He passed Purchase Street, where the fire and police stations were, cut through Second Street and LaSalle Boulevard, and reached Bonaparte. As they approached, they saw other cars parked along the curb, along with media vans. Lights from the reporters' spotlights illuminated the devastation, and Jill found herself unable to breathe.

"Pretty bad, huh?"

She felt the blood draining from her face. "They never had a chance. What was he trying to do? Blow up the whole block?"

"The windows were blown out across the street, but thankfully, there aren't many other properties around here. We had a tough time putting out the fire. It took hours. You think it was hot in that motel. I thought my coat was gonna melt right off of me. I've never seen anything like it."

She looked back at the devastated structure. People had placed flowers around the crime scene tape that kept them away from the building. Already, a pile had formed.

"Where . . . where was Pete found?"

He pointed to the corner of the parking lot. "Over there, where they've piled all those teddy bears."

The sight of the stuffed animals assaulted her heart, and she covered her face with both hands. "The man who was holding me . . . really did this?"

"That's what they think."

"But . . . it seems so impossible."

He stopped the car and let it idle for a moment. "Do you want to get out?" he asked.

"No. Let's just go to the station. If he did it, they need to book him. We don't need any delays."

"You want me to fight the media off of you?"

She looked out the back window and saw that they were still being followed. "That's okay. I'll just make a quick statement. Don't you have to get back to work?"

"I've probably been fired by now," he said, chuckling lightly. "I think Ray'll understand, though."

"I appreciate your coming, Dan."

"I appreciate you not getting yourself killed." He squeezed her hand again. This time, she squeezed back.

They reached Purchase Street and the Newpointe Police Department, and he pulled her car to the curb. "I'll walk you in."

Already the police cars were parking in front of and behind them, and she knew she would have no shortage of escorts. "It's okay, Dan. I can take it from here."

He leaned over and pulled her into a hug. She breathed in the scent of him—rain and soap and the slightest scent of smoke. The stubble on his jaw brushed her face, reminding her of other times . . . She hated to think how much she'd missed him over the past eight months . . . and how much she would miss him tonight, when she felt so shaken and alone.

"So what about the clothes?" he asked as their foreheads touched.

"I'll call Allie when I get inside," she said. "She probably needs to hear from me, anyway, if she's heard about this."

"All right." He touched her face and looked at her with adoring eyes that made her want to cry again. "You take care now. Call me if you need me, anytime night or day."

"I will, thanks." It seemed like such a cold, awkward response, but she couldn't manage more. He helped her out of the car, and Sid came to her side.

"You okay, hun?"

"I'm fine, Sid."

"We need you to come in and make a statement."

"I plan to."

As the reporters got out, microphones in hands and cameras on their heels, she was blocked from hurrying up the steps. She paused and watched Dan cut across the lawn before she began to answer their questions.

Chapter Eighteen

Frank Harper sat in the run-down motel in the seediest part of the French Quarter, watching his static-ridden television blare the news across the screen. Reruns of the tape of the post office just after the explosion replayed over and over on every station. He was so proud he could hardly contain it.

He watched as the reporter standing outside of the Flagstaff Motel in Chalmette described the surrender scene. Jerry had turned himself in. What a fool. It occurred to him that he might tell them what had happened, but then that old sense of peace fell over him. He knew Jerry wouldn't say a word. He knew he could count on him.

He had known it an hour earlier, when he'd stolen a car from a rest area as someone went in to use the facilities. As he'd listened to the play-by-play on the radio, he had known that Jerry would never talk.

Frank turned back to the papers on the table, picked up the ballpoint pen he'd found lying on the street, and returned to the most important work of his life. His manifesto. The reason for his blowing up the post office. There was no use committing an act that great without specifying his reason. To do less would mean cowardice, and he was not a coward.

He began writing as the news droned on about Jerry Ingalls's surrender, about his wife's part in the drama, about the woman he'd been holding hostage. Jill Clark was her name.

He looked up as they began to interview her. She looked shaken and sick, as if the day had taken its toll on her in more ways than one. Her brown hair was wet and beaded down into her face, and her nose was red as if she'd been crying.

"How many hours were you in there with him?" she was asked.

"Three or four. I'm not sure."

"Did he talk?"

"Yes."

"Did he say why he blew up the post office?"

"He claims he's innocent," she said, looking into the camera. "He says that someone else did it."

"Do you believe him?"

She didn't know quite how to answer that, and obvious seconds ticked by as she thought that one over.

"Did he say who did it?" someone else asked.

And suddenly Frank Harper's smugness fled, and he was certain beyond the shadow of a doubt that Jill Clark knew his name and had sent the authorities after him. Jerry Ingalls had given him away to save his own hide. The shock, the despair in that rose up inside him, and he knocked his manifesto off the desk.

He got up and raked both hands through his hair, suddenly paranoid, convinced they were surrounding his room even now. He went to the window and pulled back the curtain. Nobody was there.

He turned back to the television, and saw that woman, the hostage, still standing in front of the camera.

"Is it true that you're thinking of representing him?"

"It's true that he asked me to," she said. "Excuse me. I have to—"

"Miss Clark, are you going to represent him?"

"No comment," she said. She headed back into the police department.

She knew, Frank Harper told himself. If she was even considering representing the man who had taken her hostage, then he must have told her. That left him only one choice. He was going to have to kill her next, and he didn't have much time to waste.

Chapter Nineteen

Issie Mattreaux lay in her bed, staring at the ceiling, unable to sleep. Each time she dozed, she heard the explosion again, felt the world shaking, saw the flames and the smoke. Every time she closed her eyes, she saw five-year-old Pete Hampton, covered with cuts and blood, asking for his mother while he struggled to get a breath.

Somehow, she felt this was her fault. In some indirect, roundabout way, she had played a part in all that had happened.

She got up and went into her bathroom, turned on the light, and stared into the mirror. She looked younger with her dark hair down and tousled around her face. The little girl who had lost her mother at eight wasn't so far removed from the twenty-five-year-old she saw reflected there. But who was she? The flirtatious, sophisticated woman who played by her own rules, or the sad little girl who didn't have any rules at all?

She left her reflection and went into her living room, opened the drawer where she kept pictures in several Kodak envelopes, and began to flip through them. She saw picture after picture of herself with men. Most of them were men her mother would have warned her from. Some of them were married.

Like Larry Hampton.

She came to the picture she had kept of herself and him together. It had to be four years ago, when Pete was a baby. She had gotten to know him at Joe's Place, the bar that felt like home to her. She hadn't been that attracted to him at first, but then one day she had seen him with his wife. Mary was pretty and gentle, and a good mother, and she made him look good. Issie remembered the spirit of competition that had risen inside her at the thought that she might be able to turn Larry's head from his wife and baby.

Winning him would have been no big deal, if it had been just the two of them at Joe's Place. She had always been relatively successful with men. But the addition of his wife and child in the battle had raised the stakes. If she could win him from a pretty woman and a happy marriage, then she would be victorious, indeed.

So she had set about to win him.

She closed her eyes as she recalled that she was his first infidelity. He'd found it to be easy and harmless with her. They'd had their fling, and then she had moved on to someone else. But he liked the feeling of cheating, and he hadn't stopped with her. She hadn't been surprised when, a couple of years later, he had disappeared from town with his latest mistress.

What if she hadn't flirted with him at Joe's Place, lured him into unfaithfulness, started a pattern of cheating and lying? What if he had still been with his wife right here in Newpointe? Maybe she wouldn't have been at the post office that day. Maybe Pete Hampton wouldn't have experienced two losses in his young little life. Maybe Issie wouldn't have such guilt.

She knew her feelings weren't rational, that changing her behavior probably would not have stopped the bombing, but at the very least, Pete's father might have been here when he needed him most.

She wondered what Nick Foster would say about all this. All that forgiveness he preached . . . would he still believe in it with such guilt coursing through her? Or would he finally hit that wall of intolerance, and decide that she was one of those who had gone too far?

She couldn't stand her thoughts, so she headed back into her room and got dressed, pulled on her shoes, and grabbed her purse. She would go to Joe's Place and drown her troubles away. There were always people there to help her get her mind off her troubles. The men were especially happy to oblige.

Then she'd come home with her brain fuzzy and her body tired, and she'd fall into sleep without any problems at all. The alcohol could hold the nightmares at bay. And maybe it would cover the guilt, as well.

Chapter Twenty

Dan Nichols was met with a lukewarm reception when he returned to the station. Ray, the chief, was angry that Dan had run off without a word, but he had called Cale Larkins to replace him when he realized he wasn't coming back. Cale and some of the others were annoyed that Dan would create such hardship. But Mark Branning and Nick Foster were more concerned about Jill.

He filled them all in about what had happened, and before he knew it, the angry ones had forgotten their anger and were astounded at Jill's adventure.

When he'd finished describing the scene to them, he went out to the truck bay, which hadn't yet been closed for the night, and sat in a chair next to the pumper. From here, he could see Jill's car where he had parked it on the street. Media vans had pulled in around it, and some reporters still milled around in front of the station waiting for her to come out. He whispered a silent prayer for Jill, that she'd have the energy to get through the questioning from the federal agents tonight. She deserved to go home and relax, but he knew that wasn't going to happen for a while.

Mark came out of the TV room into the bay, and pulled a chair next to him. "Inquiring minds want to know," he said. "Are you and Jill about to be an item again?"

Dan had known the question was coming. He leaned his chair back on two legs and looked at his friend. "Inquiring minds. That wouldn't be Allie, would it?"

"Hey, my wife is her best friend. She's been rooting for the two of you to get back together."

"Yeah, when she hasn't cursed the day I was born."

"So she was a little ticked when you dumped Jill. She's defensive about her. But she's gotten over it. You know Allie loves you."

He drew in a deep breath to buy time, then dropped the chair down and leaned on his knees. "I don't know if we're starting up again or not, Mark. All I know is, when I heard that gun go off over the phone, and things crashing and Jill screaming . . . Well, nothing else mattered, you know? Every protective instinct in my body went into high gear."

"Now, that's how I've felt when Allie was in trouble. But I didn't really feel that way about Jill tonight, as good a friend as she is. I prayed for her, worried for her, rooted for her. But I wasn't rushing to the scene and thinking how I could take a bullet for her. But you did. See, that sounds like true love to me."

Dan grinned at his best friend's probing. "So are you trying to define it for Allie or yourself?"

"Both of us, I guess. It's kind of a hazard that comes with marriage. That feminine curiosity kind of eats into your brain cells, and male or not, next thing you know you're interested in people's love lives. Go figure."

"And this is a condition you recommend?"

"Sure, I recommend it. There's nothing like it. God knew what he was doing when he invented wives."

Dan looked at her car again, and slowly straightened. "I don't know where it's headed, Mark. It was a weird night. There's no telling what will come of it."

"But what do you want to come of it?" Mark asked. Dan shot him a look, and Mark laughed and held up innocent hands. "Hey, Allie's gonna ask."

"Tell Allie that I've been missing Jill. That tonight scared the hesitation out of me. That if it's at all in my power, I'm ready to have that fourth date."

"Fourth date? Man, you had way more dates with her than that when you were seeing her before."

"Yeah, but Allie'll know what I mean."

Mark thought about that for a minute, then began to laugh. "Oh, I get it. The guy with the three-date limit ... fourth date ... Allie'll love that."

"Tell Allie that it all depends on Jill."

"Uh-oh. The catch. I knew there had to be one."

"The catch is, does she want to be caught?"

"If I know Jill, she does. But she may not be willing to chase hard enough to catch you."

"Chase me? What do you mean by that?"

Mark chuckled. "Did you see your messages? You had three calls from women while you were gone tonight."

Dan waved that off as if it had no relevance. "They were just interested in the post office."

"Right, and they never call on other shifts." Mark's sarcasm caught Dan's attention.

"Okay, so they call. But that doesn't mean anything to me. I've never taken any of them on a fourth date. I wouldn't have rushed to Chalmette for them. I wouldn't have been begging the cops to let me go in and take on the gunman for any of them."

"So why did you?"

"Because it was Jill," he said, looking his friend fully in the eye. "She's different. She means ...." His voice broke, and he swallowed and looked off to the side. Finally, he met Mark's eyes again. "She means a lot to me."

Mark's amusement faded, and he nodded, as if he understood. "Like I said, buddy, sounds like true love to me."

Chapter Twenty-One

Hours passed as FBI agents questioned Jill about Jerry's behavior in the motel room, the things he had said to her, the threats he had made. When she'd told the story at least a dozen times, in as many different ways, they were finally finished with her.

When she and Stan were the only two left in the room, Jill leaned back in her chair and rubbed her eyes. Thankfully, Allie had brought her a change of clothes, and her hair had dried, but she felt bone-weary and wanted desperately to go home.

"So are you considering representing him?" Stan asked quietly.

"No," she said. "How can you ask that?"

"I know you," Stan said. "That, and the fact that he's still telling everybody that you're his lawyer. He's refusing to answer any questions until you're present."

She looked up at the ceiling and rolled her eyes. "I can't believe this. I told him that I'd represent him, just so he'd let me go. Surely he doesn't really think ..." Her voice trailed off and she shook her head. "Stan, there's got to be another lawyer in town who would represent him."

"There are only two, Jill. You know that. Frank Manning just passed the bar, and he's doing mostly contract work. Then there's Clive Martin. I guess he could represent him, but Ingalls wants you."

Jill was beginning to get angry, and she narrowed her eyes at Stan. "Don't you think it's a conflict of interest? I mean, how hard am I gonna fight for a guy who held a gun to my head and kept me hostage for hours?"

"That's what I tried to tell him," Stan said. "And no, I don't think you should. I was just asking."

She threw up her hands, got up, and went to the window. It was too dark to see anything on the outside, but raindrops still ran in rivulets down the glass. "I'd be afraid that if he didn't like the way things were going, he'd grab me around the neck and start making demands."

"I don't blame you," Stan said. "It would be hard."

"Hard?" she asked. "That's an understatement." Her eyes filled with tears and she motioned in the direction of the post office. "I got Dan to drive me by the post office on the way home. I can't believe the devastation. People are dead, Stan. This guy probably did it. I don't care what he says. I can't represent a person who might have done a thing like that."

"You don't have to."

She breathed in a deep breath and let it out in a huff, then slapped both hands on the table. "Then why are you badgering me about it?"

"Badgering you?" He breathed a laugh. "Why do you think I'm badgering you? I just asked you a question."

"You think I should keep my word, don't you? You think, since I told him I'd represent him, that I should do it." Her face was reddening.

"No, I don't, Jill." He leaned forward on the table. "Look, I think you need some rest."

"Don't condescend to me," she bit out. "Don't treat me like some distraught woman who's changed her mind! I have reasons. *Valid* reasons."

He was getting angry himself. "For what?"

"For not keeping my word!"

Stan looked as if he didn't know what to say to her. "Jill, you're putting words in my mouth. I'm not condescending, but I'm also not gonna sit here and let you chew me out for things I didn't say or think."

She wilted. "I'm sorry." She looked up at him across the table. "Okay? I'm really sorry. I'm just very tired."

"That's what I said."

"Yeah, that is what you said." She took a deep breath. "So can I go home now? I'm exhausted, and I have to get up early tomorrow. I have to go back to Chalmette to take some more depositions."

"I wish you'd stay in town in case we have more questions."

"What could you possibly have questions about? I've given you a play-by-play of every minute he had me in there. I have work to do, and I'm not gonna let some terrorist get in my way."

"All right, all right," Stan said. "I'll call your secretary if I need you. She'll be able to get in touch with you?"

"Of course. If Sheila can't find me, she hunts me down like an animal just for the sport of it."

He wasn't amused. He just stared at her with serious eyes. "Jill, at the risk of sounding 'condescending,' let me take off my cop hat for a minute and put on my friend hat. You know, you could stand to rest tomorrow. This is one of those days when no one would fault you—"

"Stan, I appreciate your concern, but I have to be there tomorrow." She was growing more and more exhausted, and her head was beginning to ache. "I'm going home now, okay?"

He nodded and got up. "We'll call if we have any more questions."

"Yeah," she said without much enthusiasm. "You do that."

"You sure you're all right?"

"Yep. Nothing a couple of Tylenol and a soak in a hot bath won't cure."

Chapter Twenty-Two

But neither the Tylenol nor the hot bath helped Jill to sleep that night. She kept having nightmares of a man bursting through her closet door with a rifle aimed at her face. A man leaving a box in her home, a box that exploded as soon as she discovered it. A man pulling her up from a deep sleep and attacking her.

She woke up for the fourth time, covered in sweat and trembling, and finally realized that she wasn't going to rest tonight. She sat up in her bed and looked wearily around at the shadows cast by clothes hanging over her chair and draped over her exercise bike. She'd been keeping so busy that she hadn't hung anything in her closet in days. Now each draped outfit looked like a crazed terrorist waiting to attack. She got up and turned on the lights as she went through the house, looking behind doors and in closets, making sure no one was lurking there, waiting to jump out and ambush her. Even as she did so, she realized the silliness of all this fear. She was not the type to be paranoid, yet something she had never expected to happen to her had happened today. It wasn't something she could get over easily.

Her den was somewhat neater than her bedroom, though old, unread newspapers lay rolled on the floor beside the couch, and unopened mail was stacked on the coffee table. She sat down on the couch, staring at the wall, trying to analyze her feelings. She was a mature adult, she told herself. A lawyer. She dealt with frightening people all the time. What was different about this?

It was that she had been out of control when Jerry Ingalls had shot his way into her room, she thought. She still felt out of control. Part of that, she realized, had to do with Dan, who seemed to be moving back into her life. She didn't understand his renewed interest, except that it had to do with his rescuing a damsel in distress—a role she hated playing. Why hadn't he called her in the last several months? There had been nights that no one knew about, nights she'd spent at home, watching movies alone and feeling as if she was drowning. He hadn't come to rescue her then.

She looked around at her messy home and realized she had lost control of it, as well. Nothing in her life was working very well. Now she wished the phone would ring, but she knew it would not. In the wee hours of morning, no one suspected that the big, bold attorney might need someone to hold her hand tonight. She coped. It was what she did.

The house creaked, and she grew more tense. Her eyes darted from corner to shadow. Her ears listened for a sound that broke the silence, a body that might burst through a door. But this was ridiculous. Jerry Ingalls was in jail, and no one was after her.

Oh, yeah. She was a big, bold attorney. Coping. But she couldn't stand to be here alone.

Finally realizing that she *wasn't* coping, that she was falling apart, she picked up the phone and dialed Allie Branning. She was her best friend, and she would understand more than most, even though Jill hadn't even revealed her deepest vulnerabilities to her. Anyone would understand her paranoias tonight. Allie would let her sleep on her couch.

It rang four times before Allie picked up. "Hello?"

"Allie, it's Jill."

"Jill, are you okay?"

Jill hesitated a moment as emotion blocked her throat. Finally, she forced herself to answer. "No, actually. I'm having a hard time. Do you think I could come over there and sleep on the couch?"

"Of course," Allie said. "Come on. I'm up feeding Justin anyway. I'll turn the porch light on for you."

Relieved, Jill hung up the phone, packed a quick overnight bag, and headed out to her garage. She got in the car and started the engine before opening the garage door. If someone was waiting there for her, she'd run over them, she thought.

Kicking herself for being so paranoid, she backed out, her eyes sweeping from side to side as the headlights lit up the front of the house. She closed the garage with her remote, backed out into the street, and headed for Allie's.

The porch light was on when she got there, and Allie opened the door before she even had a chance to knock. "Come on in." She was holding her eight-month-old baby in one arm, his little head on her shoulder, sound asleep, and she reached out to hug Jill with her other. "I'm so glad you're all right. I was so scared, I didn't know what to do." She took Jill's bag from her and led her into the den. "I was just about to put him down."

Jill waited as Allie put the baby back to bed. She loved being in Allie's little house. It smelled of flowers, probably because Allie and Mark owned a floral shop, and she brought fresh cut flowers home every day. She'd never been here when there weren't flowers and knickknacks and bric-a-brac and trinkets everywhere. But she had to admit that there were fewer now than there had been before they'd had a baby. In fact, the Blooms 'N Blossoms Florist was for sale, but they hadn't found a buyer yet.

When Allie came back in, she pulled her into another hug. "You look like you've been tied to the back of a truck and dragged for about a hundred miles."

"Not that bad," Jill said.

Allie laughed. "Well, maybe not. But you look awfully tired."

"As tired as you looked the first few months after you had Justin?"

"Worse," Allie said. "Come on. I've got your bed ready in the guest room."

"The guest room?" Jill grinned. "Allie, this is a two-bedroom house. I told you, I'm happy to sleep on the couch."

"No, there's an extra bed in Justin's room. I rolled his crib into our room so you could have the room to yourself."

"Oh, Allie, you didn't have to go to all that trouble."

"I'm happy to do it," she said. "Mark's on duty tonight. I didn't want you staying by yourself tonight, anyway. Jill, I'd be a wreck if what happened to you happened to me. No way I'd stay in my house alone."

"But I'm supposed to be this tough attorney, who doesn't crumble and copes with the best of them."

"You are the best of them. And forget all that coping stuff. You should have come straight here and not gone home at all. Did you get to eat?"

Jill realized she hadn't. "I ate before I checked into the motel."

"And you didn't lose it when . . . never mind. That was hours ago. Let me fix you something." She went into the kitchen, and Jill followed wearily behind her. As Allie moved around in the kitchen, fixing her a sandwich, Jill sank into a chair at the table.

"So Mark calls to tell me to turn on the television, that you've been taken hostage. And he says that Dan ran out of the fire station, just disappeared and left them shorthanded, and next thing they know, he's there at the Flagstaff. So are you two back together?"

"Hardly." Jill propped her chin on her hand and closed her eyes. "Actually, I don't know what to think."

"Jill, I've been telling you for months that Dan is still in love with you."

"He has a funny way of showing it."

"Exactly," Allie said. "He does have a funny way of showing it. When you were seeing each other, he was scared to death he was going to lose you."

"So he went ahead and threw me away?"

"Something like that." She handed her the plate and went back to the refrigerator. "It has a certain logic if you look at it from his point of view. I never said he was rational."

"Well, it's not like he's just been sitting around alone all this time. He has been seeing other people."

Allie poured her a glass of milk, then took it to the table. "Yeah, but he's back to his no-more-than-three-date rule. In fact, I don't think I've seen him with anybody twice."

"Well, that's just peachy," Jill said, taking the glass Allie handed her. "So many women, so little time." She bit into the sandwich.

"You're missing the point," Allie said, pulling out the chair across from her. "You're the only person I've ever known who could make him break his three-date rule. He never dated anyone over three times because he thought people would think of them as a couple. But he dated you dozens of times. *He* was the one thinking of you as a couple."

"He wasn't thinking of that when he decided to cool things down."

"I know," Allie said. "Right there in the hospital after I had Justin, he was mad at you for being so busy and leaving him out. I never thought that breakup would last."

"It's lasted eight months," she said. "Whoever said Dan couldn't keep his commitments?"

"Look, he could have stayed here today and monitored things from television. He didn't. He was right there."

Jill took another bite of her sandwich and stared into her glass of milk. "He cares about people. He would have been there if it had been you or Mark or any of his other friends."

"That may be true, but so would a lot of other people, and you didn't see them rushing to Chalmette. It was dangerous and we'd have been in the way. But that didn't stop Dan."

Jill realized she didn't have much appetite. She pushed her plate away.

"Mark said Dan drove you home," Allie said. "So did he talk about resuming things?"

"Not really. Well, sort of. In the context of a bargain he made with God."

"A bargain?"

"Yeah. Something like, 'God, if you get Jill out of there, I'll date her again.' Like the Lord has a dating service and Dan's sacrifice helped things along."

Allie wilted. "Jill, he didn't really say it like that, did he?"

Jill smiled. "Well, not exactly."

"I'm sorry. I didn't mean to sound so shallow. I just meant, wasn't anything mentioned about how he felt, why he was there, *anything?*"

"Well, he did mention that he was scared to death."

Allie's eyebrows shot up. "Scared to death. That's good."

"But he seemed ticked off that I was going to work tomorrow, that I have to go back to Chalmette. He tried to talk me out of it."

"And did he?"

"No, I *have* to be there. And once again, I'm too busy to do what he wants me to do, which is the reason we broke up in the first place. He was jealous of my time. Had a hard time believing I could be thinking about him when I was working hard."

"I don't really think that was all of it," Allie said. "I think he was mainly scared of losing you."

"Well, he did. He saw to it." Jill slid her chair back and took her plate to the sink. "And as soon as the emotional surge wears off and the danger has passed, he'll be back surfing his little black book and holding to his three-date rule."

"What if he calls me and asks about you?" Allie asked.

"Tell him I'm tall and have blondish-brown hair."

"I'm serious."

Jill sighed. "I don't know what to tell him, Allie. I don't have the energy to worry about Dan right now. And I don't feel like being in a relationship where I have to do double the work. Either someone wants me, or they don't." She rinsed out her glass and put it into the dishwasher. "Thanks for the food. I'm sorry I'm so cranky. I'm just tired and depressed . . . we drove by the post office on the way home. I saw all those teddy bears."

That deep compassion filled Allie's eyes again. "Yeah, I went to the hospital today to see Pete."

"How is he?"

"Not good. He's comatose, has a fractured skull, a broken arm, cuts all over him . . . Our biggest concern is that when he wakes up, somebody has to tell him his mother is dead."

"Who's with him now?"

"Celia."

"Good. That'll give him some comfort. And she has all those maternal hormones pumping through her. I'm glad she realized he needed her."

She nodded and assessed Jill's face. "You go on to bed. There's an alarm clock next to the bed, but you'll have to set it."

"I will," she said. "I'll probably be out of here before you get up in the morning."

"Wanna bet? Justin wakes up at the crack of dawn. Plus, I have a busy day at the florist tomorrow because of the deaths. I've got people working, but I feel like I need to be there. I'm taking Justin with me."

"I'm going to get up at five." Jill checked her watch. "That's only three hours. I'd better get to sleep." She squeezed her friend's hand. "Thanks for letting me come over. I was really having a hard time."

"Anytime. I'm always glad for company, especially when Mark's at the station."

Jill went into the baby's bedroom. It smelled of baby powder, a scent that brought back those feelings of being out of control again . . . defeated feelings that her life wasn't going the way she wanted it to. There were things lacking, things that would never be hers, things she could never count on.

But she did have good friends who loved her. Feeling more secure than she had in her own home, she got into the bed and pulled the covers up, wishing it was already morning.

Chapter Twenty-Three

As soon as Stan finished with Jerry Ingalls, he headed for the hospital in New Orleans, where Celia still kept vigil beside the bed of little Pete Hampton. Though he was in intensive care, they had allowed Celia to sit with him. A lot of exceptions had been made for the orphaned survivor of the post office bombing. She was exhausted, and her eyes were shaded with dark circles. When Stan walked in, she was lying on her side on the little vinyl sofa beside the boy's bed, and she seemed to be sleeping.

He stooped down in front of her and pressed a kiss on her cheek. She woke up slowly. "Stan . . ."

"Honey, are you okay?" he asked, stroking her cheek with his knuckles. "You need to go home and get in bed. You and the baby need rest."

"But I don't know what to do about Pete," she said, sitting up. "His family should be here soon. He needs somebody."

"Has he woken up yet?"

"Not at all." She burst into tears and reached out to pull Stan into a crushing hug. "I'm afraid he's gonna die, Stan. I've been praying for him all day, but I don't know whether to pray for him to live or die, because he's going to be in so much grief when he wakes up. He's just so young."

"Do you believe he's in God's hands?"

"Yes, I do," she wept. "It's just so hard to see him like this and know about Mary."

He could see that she had been battling these questions all night, and was exhausted with emotion, grief, and worry. Knowing that he couldn't offer her answers right now, he got up and sat down next to her, pulled her against him so that her head was leaning on his shoulder. All he could give her was comfort, and he felt she needed that the most. "Tell you what," he said, kissing her temple. "You go back to sleep, and I'll just sit here and hold you."

"Not yet," she said. "Tell me about the bomber. The guy at the Flagstaff."

Stan sighed. "His name is Jerry Ingalls. He and his family live in Newpointe, believe it or not. Nobody I've run into knows them, though. They moved here six months ago when Inez Pepper died. She was a relative of theirs and left them her house."

"Where does he work?"

"At home. Has some kind of business designing websites. I guess that's why we don't know them. New in town, working at home, kids not yet in school. I'll talk to their neighbors tomorrow."

"Why did he do it?" Celia asked.

He let out a heavy sigh. "I don't know. We can't get anything out of him."

She touched his stubbled jaw. "I'm glad you're okay. Jill, too."

"She's fine." He stroked her stomach gently. The baby wasn't moving. "Go to sleep now."

"Will you wake me up when his grandmother gets here?"

"Of course I will."

"And if he wakes up . . ."

"Nope. Not going to wake you up if he wakes up. I'm going to play a game of Go-fish with him and keep you in the dark."

She elbowed him hard. "You'd better—"

"Of course I'll wake you up. Go to sleep, now."

In seconds, he could feel her body relaxing into sleep, and he closed his eyes, as well.

• • •

It wasn't more than a couple of hours later that Pete Hampton's grandmother and uncle bustled into the room. Celia woke up instantly and sprang to her feet. They were tired, bedraggled, and their eyes were red as if they'd both been weeping much of the way.

Mrs. Lewis burst into tears as she saw her grandbaby lying there comatose with a tube running into his mouth. "What's that in his mouth?" she demanded.

"It's the ventilator. It's keeping him breathing."

"He's on life support?" the woman cried. "No, that can't be!" She leaned over the bed to gently touch his face, then kissed it, as tears fell onto it. "Pete, Pete! You wake up, you hear? You don't need this ole contraption. You can breathe on your own, can't you?"

The child didn't respond.

"Is he gonna wake up?" she asked. "We're not gonna lose him, too, are we?"

The uncle covered his mouth with his hands and bent over the bed. He began to sob, and Stan and Celia both felt as if they were intruders on a private moment. Finally, Stan touched the man's shoulder.

"I'm gonna take my wife home now. She's been here ever since Pete got here . . ."

The grandmother left the bed and hugged Celia. "Celia, thank you so much for taking care of him. I don't know what we would have done if we hadn't known you'd be here."

"I'll be back tomorrow," she said.

"You take care of your baby," the woman said. "He needs his mama." With that, she burst into tears again.

Chapter Twenty-Four

Frank Harper finished his manifesto and, while he still could, abandoned the sleazy New Orleans motel. He was certain that the police would surround the room at any moment, just like they had done with Jerry at the Flagstaff. They would pretend that he was the bad guy, make everyone think that they were trying to protect society. Then they would take him prisoner of war, and lock him up like they'd done for the past twenty-five years.

He headed for the bar across the street, its neon sign flashing in the night, and found a truck that wasn't locked. Like a gift, it had a rifle in the gun rack on the back window, and a box of cartridges lay on the passenger seat. He quickly hot-wired it, a skill he'd learned in his teenaged years, and headed back to Newpointe. He had to find Jill Clark. She knew too much. He couldn't let her ruin his plans, not when he'd finally gotten free and had the chance to save his country.

It was really very simple.

He would find her and kill her tonight.

In rapid-fire language, like some kind of holy tongue, he quoted the Bill of Rights as he drove, and tears came to his eyes as he thought of the sacrifices he'd made for his land. He wished the war would end. It had gone on for too long already, but the people were deceived, and didn't know. They thought they lived in peace. They didn't know of the battles being fought without their knowledge, the prisoners being held and tortured, the communist plans to get the people fat and lazy, then change their way of life into something that was intolerable.

He wouldn't let it happen.

He reached the outskirts of Newpointe and went into a convenience store to buy a map. As he paid, he asked the clerk where a local bar might be. The clerk told him about Joe's Place, a few blocks away.

The bars were part of their plan, he told himself. They were put there to lull the people into a false sense of happiness. He wouldn't be fooled. But he needed the bar tonight so that he could find Jill Clark. All it would take was a few loose tongues, a couple of drunk braggarts, and he'd have her address in no time.

He went in to the smoke-filled room and cringed at the sound of zydeco music pouring from the speakers. It was another communist weapon, he told himself. That, and heavy metal. And country music. And rap. He was certain they had all been carefully created by the regimes that wanted to pull the country down.

He looked across the bar and saw a heavy man, nodding in his beer. He took the stool next to him. The man looked up.

"How's it going?" he asked.

The man nodded. "Long day."

"Yeah?" He reached out a hand. "My name's Dirk Henderson."

"Sergeant R.J. Albright," the man slurred.

"Sergeant?" Frank asked. "You in the military?"

"Nope. Cop."

"Oh." Frank swiveled on his stool to face him. "So you people have had some kind of day, haven't you? What with the bombing and all."

"Yep."

"And didn't I hear something about a hostage situation?"

"Yep. The guy who blew up the post office took Jill Clark hostage."

The bartender brought his ginger ale, and Frank gulped it like it was scotch. "Isn't she a lawyer or something?"

"Yep."

"You know her?"

"She's a good friend of mine."

"Oh, yeah? Was she hurt?"

The bartender leaned across the bar. "Jill don't get hurt. She knows how to take care of herself."

"Somebody has to," R.J. said.

Frank lit up a cigarette and inhaled deeply. "Why? She married?"

"Nope. Lives all by her lonesome."

"Yeah," Frank said, tapping his cigarette on an ashtray. "Doesn't she live up on the north side of town?"

"Naw, man. She lives over on Clearview."

"Oh, that's right," he said, as if he knew. "Big blue house?"

The bartender chuckled. "Hardly. Littlest house on the block. You'd think she could afford more, with all the work she does." He wiped the counter as Frank finished his drink.

Frank smoked another cigarette, listening to more of the banter about the bombing and Jill Clark and Jerry Ingalls, holed up in the Newpointe Jail. He paid his tab and slipped out.

He checked his map and headed for Clearview Street. In just a few minutes, he thought, Jill Clark would be one less of his worries.

He found the street and drove slowly up it, trying to decide which was the smallest house. When he came to a little one-story house, he saw the name *Clark* on the mailbox. He couldn't believe his luck.

He parked a few houses down and loaded the rifle. It was 4 A.M. He could pick her lock and slip inside. She'd be dead by 4:15, and then he could get on with his work.

He left the truck and ran from tree to tree, the grunt on the alert, ready to do what was necessary for the sake of the war. He reached her backyard. Quickly, deftly, he picked the lock and slipped inside.

The only light on in the house was one glowing on the stove, but in the faint light it cast, he could see her bedroom off the hall. He made his way to the door and looked inside.

The bed was rumpled, empty. No one was home.

The clock on her bed table flashed 4:10. Where was she? Had she anticipated that he would come?

He tried to decide whether to wait for her here or go back out to the truck.

What if it was a trap? Any minute now police could surround him and cage him inside . . .

He decided to chance going back to the truck. He went back out, bracing himself for gunfire. None came, so he sprinted back to the truck. He decided to wait in case she came home. He couldn't forge ahead with his plans until he took care of her.

Chapter Twenty-Five

Jill didn't sleep until her alarm clock went off. She woke up with the first cries of the baby at 4:30, and decided to go ahead and get up. She had to prepare for Chalmette, anyway.

Allie was nursing Justin when Jill came out of the bedroom. "Jill, he woke you up! I'm so sorry. He's not usually up quite this early, but he's teething."

"Don't be sorry," Jill said. She leaned over the baby and grabbed his hand. "It's your house, isn't it, Justin? Besides, I wasn't sleeping that well."

"Well, have some coffee and sit down with me. I'll make you breakfast . . ."

"No way," Jill said. "You've done enough for me, Allie. I really need to get going, anyway. I brought clothes to wear in Chalmette, but I forgot to get the shoes I need. If you don't mind, I'm just gonna jump in the shower, then run home real quick and change shoes before I head for Chalmette."

"That's fine," Allie said. "The towels are in the hall closet."

Half an hour later, Jill headed for her house. The sun hadn't come up yet, and as her headlights lit up she shivered with the fear that had driven her to Allie's. She opened the door with her remote opener, and punched it closed again even before she was all the way in. Leaving the car running, she dashed into the dark house, cut through to her bedroom, and swapped shoes. Then, as if she expected someone to jump out of a closet, she went back to her car. She hoped the Chalmette courthouse would be open early. She had a lot to review before she got started today. And she wouldn't feel safe until she was around people again.

∙ ∙ ∙

Frank Harper couldn't believe his luck when he saw Jill coming home. Still parked up the street, he waited until she closed the garage behind her. Then he got out of the truck, and carrying the deer rifle, ran the few yards up the street until he was at her back door.

It was still dark outside, so he stood there, unseen, as she turned on her light and ran through the house. He waited for the light to go back out, or for her to settle in her bedroom before he picked the lock again, but in seconds, she was dashing back through the house and into the garage again.

Confused, he ran back around to the front of the house and saw her garage door opening. She backed out and headed south before he could even get her in the gun's sights.

Frustrated, he ran back to the stolen truck and followed her as closely as he could without being seen. He was surprised when she headed out of town, then got onto the bridge across Lake Pontchartrain. Where was she going?

The sun began to come up, and other early-morning commuters appeared on the road. He hadn't expected to follow her the hour's drive to Chalmette, but he supposed it was worth it if he accomplished what he'd set out to do. When she got to the courthouse, he found a parking place and watched as she went in. Was she going to court? Would she be there all day?

He decided that, no matter how long it took, he'd wait her out. But first, he'd make sure she didn't go anywhere. He got out of his car and went to hers. It was still early, and the parking lot was not full. The sun had now fully risen, but he didn't care. As long as he looked like he knew what he was doing, no one would notice him.

He went to her car and got down on the ground, slid underneath it. He made a few modifications, made more difficult because of his missing fingers. But he was used to accommodating. When he'd finished, he went back to his stolen truck. When she came out, at whatever time she did, her car would not start. He would then offer to help her, and he could quiet her before it was too late.

Time passed slowly, and finally, around midmorning, he began to doze. Parked safely in the courthouse parking lot, he slept for several hours. When he woke, he was startled to see that it was already late afternoon. But Jill's car was still there.

He hadn't lost her yet. There was still plenty of time to get her where he wanted her.

• • •

It was after 8 P.M. and almost dark before Jill came back out to her car. She was exhausted, but she and the attorneys for the defendant had finished taking depositions. She made her way back out to her car, tossed her briefcase onto the backseat, then shrugged out of her blazer and slid into the car. She tried to start it, but it wouldn't roll over. She tried again. Still nothing.

Frustrated, she dug through her purse for her cell phone, and called information for the local number of the auto club she belonged to. They weren't represented here, so she called the 800 number and asked how long it would take for them to come. They suggested that it was too late, that she should call a tow truck and try again tomorrow.

She was physically, mentally, and emotionally exhausted, unable to deal with this latest minicrisis. She sat there a moment, trying to decide what to do. Dan came to mind, as he had so many times that day, but she shoved the thought away. She didn't want him to think she was depending on him for anything, or that his actions last night had made her presume anything. But she couldn't call Allie, because she was so busy at the florist today. And Celia was probably still tied up with Pete Hampton. Sheila, her secretary, had probably already gone home for the day, and would make her life miserable if she asked her to come and get her.

Her mind drifted back to Dan again. He was the least encumbered of all her friends. Besides, she would feel safe with him. Reluctantly, she dialed his number.

"Hello?" He sounded out of breath.

"Dan, it's me. Jill. Is this a bad time?"

"No, not at all." He sounded glad to hear from her. "I've been running. I just came in. I tried calling you earlier. Are you home?"

"No. My car is broken down in Chalmette, and the auto club I belong to is turning out to be pretty worthless. I really hate to ask you this, Dan . . . but do you think you could possibly come and get me? I can have the car towed back to Newpointe, but I'm a little nervous about strangers right now, and I don't think I'd feel very comfortable riding with the tow-truck guy."

"Of course. I'm on my way."

"No hurry. If you need to shower and cool off—"

"No way. I'm coming now. Should be there within half an hour."

"Dan, it'll take longer."

"Not for me, it won't. I don't want you alone there."

When she hung up, she felt that warm feeling that she didn't want to feel. She was too tired to put up an emotional fight against her own feelings. Regardless of her better judgment, her heart looked forward to seeing Dan tonight. He was one of her biggest weaknesses. She wondered if she would ever overcome it.

She wished she didn't have to.

She laid her head back on the seat, locked her doors, and drifted off to sleep as she waited for Dan.

• • •

Frank Harper saw Jill sitting in her car, but only a few feet away from her, two deputies conversed as if they had absolutely nothing better to do.

He watched her carefully, knowing that he couldn't approach her to help her until she got out of the car and opened her hood—not unless the cops went away. But one of them leaned back against his squad car, settling in as he gave a play-by-play of last night's activities at the Flagstaff. She hadn't given any indication that her car wouldn't start. Why was she just sitting there?

What if she had called someone? What if she was waiting for someone to come?

It didn't matter, he thought, growing irritated. Whoever came to rescue her, their life would be at risk, too. He had to get rid of her, and anyone she may have told about him. He couldn't take the chance that anyone knew he was the one who'd left the bomb in the post office. Everyone who knew had to go. He didn't care if he had to take them each one at a time.

It would be well worth it to protect his privacy and enable him to get on with the serious work of defending his country.

Chapter Twenty-Six

When Dan reached the Chalmette courthouse parking lot, he saw two sheriff's deputies standing together, talking intently. He started to ask them where she was, but then he spotted her car. He pulled his Bronco close to it. She was there, her eyes closed and her head leaned against the window and the back of her seat, and her eyes were closed, as if . . .

His heart jolted. Then he realized how tired he had been today, and how tired she was last night . . . She had probably gotten up at the crack of dawn and worked here all day. She was only sleeping.

She had been through too much in the last twenty-four hours, and today Mark had told him that she'd spent the night at his house with Allie, because she was afraid. His heart kicked, giving him a personal indictment that he couldn't explain. Somehow, he felt responsible to protect her, even if she didn't want him to.

He pulled into the space next to her, then got out and knocked lightly on her window. She woke up with a start, then quickly opened the door. "Dan, hey."

He leaned in. "You okay?"

"Must have fallen asleep." She got out and tried to look alert and professional, but her business suit was crumpled and her hair was sticking out on one side. He fought the urge to smooth it back down.

"I've called a tow truck, but they haven't come yet," she said. "Then again, they may have, and I just didn't see them because I was sound asleep."

He slipped into the driver's seat and tried to start the car. The engine wouldn't turn over. "Have you been having problems before this?"

"No, not at all. The car's only a year old."

They heard the sound of the tow truck, and looked out toward the street. "There it is now." Dan waved it down, and the truck pulled into the almost empty parking lot.

When the tow truck had the car in tow and on its way back to Newpointe, Jill got into Dan's Bronco. "Dan, I really shouldn't have called you. I could have ridden in the tow truck."

Dan set his wrist on the wheel and looked over at her. "Jill, I would have been hurt if you'd called anybody but me."

"Thanks," she said. "I feel like I'm turning into a basket case. I couldn't even sleep at home last night. Truth is, I didn't sleep much, even at Mark and Allie's."

"I didn't sleep much myself," he said, "and I wasn't even the one held hostage last night. Why don't you just kick back and get comfortable?"

She relaxed back into the seat. As her eyes drifted closed again, Dan pulled the car out of the parking lot, and headed back to Newpointe.

She was asleep again by the time they reached the edge of the I–10 bridge over Lake Pontchartrain. Looking in his rearview mirror, Dan began to realize that the beat-up pickup with one headlight had been following them since they'd left Chalmette. He had noticed him first pulling out of the parking lot at the courthouse. Now he wondered if that person had been watching Jill.

Jill seemed to sense a difference in the way he was driving, and she woke up. "Something wrong?" she asked.

"No, nothing." He glanced in the rearview mirror again. "Everything's fine."

"Why do you look so worried?"

He looked over at her, then back to the rearview mirror. "Do you know who that is in the pickup behind us?"

She looked out the rear window. "Never seen that truck before. Why?"

"I think he's following us."

"Are you sure?"

"No. It just seems—"

"Why would anyone be following us? Jerry Ingalls is in jail."

"I don't know. Maybe it's a reporter, trying to get an exclusive."

"Oh, for heaven's sake. It's not like I'm tabloid fodder."

"If I speed up, maybe I'll lose him. That junk heap won't be able to keep up." But as he sped up, so did the truck behind them.

Suddenly, he realized that they weren't just being followed, they were being chased.

He touched his brakes to slow down, and the man almost hit him. "Uh-oh, I think I've made him mad now," Dan said, watching in the rearview mirror as the man pulled into the opposite lane and passed him. Dan sped up to be even with him, and tried to see the driver. It was too dark to see into the truck, but as they drove side by side, the driver turned his wheel and grazed Dan's Bronco.

Dan erupted. "What is he, crazy? He did that deliberately!"

"Slow down, Dan."

The car swerved and hit them again. "What's he doing?" Dan yelled.

"Trying to run us off the road," she said. "Stop! Stop the car!"

"I can't. What if he has a gun or something? He's insane!" He grabbed his cell phone and dialed 911. He didn't know to which dispatcher the call would go, but he hoped they would send the closest highway patrolman quickly. Before the emergency dispatcher had them on the phone, the truck rammed them again, this time crumpling Dan's door. The impact forced the front of the Bronco to slide to the right and scrape into the wall of the bridge. Jill screamed as metal sparked against concrete. Dan fought with the steering wheel and tried to move the Bronco away from the wall.

The truck picked up speed and made a hard right turn, crashing into Dan's fender and stopping them. They sat there for a moment … waiting. "I'm getting out," Jill said, panicked.

"No!" Dan stopped her as the truck backed up again. The maniac shifted into drive, and headed for his left fender again.

Frantic, Jill opened the passenger door as the Bronco was shoved against the wall again, and her arm twisted. She yelled.

Somehow, Dan managed to grab the cell phone again. The dispatcher answered, "911, may I help you? Hello? Is anyone there?" But he dropped the phone and Jill scrambled to pick it up.

"Help! Somebody's trying to kill us on the northbound side of the I–10 bridge over the lake! He's ramming our car, trying to make us go over. Do you have anybody in this area?"

"We'll send someone right away," the dispatcher said.

The truck bashed them again. "We're almost to the end of the bridge!" Dan shouted to the phone. There was nothing but wooden rail between them and the lake. Their front right tire hung precariously off the bridge, its weight threatening to pull them over.

"We have to get out," Dan whispered. Jill started to come up from the floor board, but suddenly, there was one more ram, and the car fell further over the side, its other front wheel suspended in air.

They heard a siren coming from behind them, and the truck took off as fast as it could go, leaving a trail of black smoke behind it.

Dan didn't have time to worry about him. He had to get Jill out of the Bronco. "Climb over the seat and get out the back," he shouted.

She was almost hysterical, so he grabbed her hands and made her look at him. "Jill, climb over the seat! We have to get out."

She nodded, then got on her feet and crawled over the seat. The left side of the car was bashed in, but there was just enough room to get through. Dan pushed the button to disengage the back door, but it was stuck.

"Dan, I can't open it!" she cried. "Hurry!"

He crawled back, his way made more difficult by his size and the injuries he was just beginning to feel. He felt the car rocking, felt its weight shifting, heard Jill screaming for him to hurry. The police cars screeched to a halt as the Bronco began to bob ...

Finally, with one last thrust, he got the door open.

Jill fell into his arms as they stumbled out of the Bronco, and clinging together, they watched as it rocked ...

Once ...

Twice ...

Then fell over the bridge into Lake Pontchartrain.

Chapter Twenty-Seven

Jill couldn't stop shaking. She sat in the rescue unit as they splinted her swelling wrist—which was, miraculously, the only injury she'd suffered—and watched the highway patrolmen who had converged on the scene, directing traffic across the bridge. An all-points bulletin had gone out on the man who had run them off the road. They had found the beat-up truck abandoned not far from the bridge, but the man had apparently fled into the woods on foot. When they traced the truck, they learned it had been reported stolen early that morning. Police were combing the woods on the other side of the bridge, but they weren't having any luck. Somehow, the man had gotten away.

Jill fought back the tears, knowing that if she gave into even one, she wouldn't be able to stop crying for days. She watched as Dan stood on the edge of the bridge, his arm in a sling. He was in pain, she could tell, and probably had a broken collarbone, but he had refused to let the rescue unit transport him to the hospital just yet. He had too much to tell the police about what had happened, and he was determined to see the man caught. The blue flashing lights of the police cars lit one side of his face as he gave as much information as he could to the police.

Jill tore her eyes from him. Had she brought this trouble on him? If so, he was going to rue the day he'd ever met her. Hostage situations, car accidents . . . What would happen next? She wasn't safe to be around.

Finally, when Dan was satisfied that he'd told the police everything he could, he allowed the rescue unit to transport them to Newpointe Hospital, where there was a noncritical care emergency room. They couldn't treat head traumas or gunshot wounds, but they could do X-rays and set broken bones.

As they rode, Dan pulled Jill close. "You okay?" he asked for the hundredth time tonight. "How's your wrist feel?"

"Okay," she said. "I feel sure I don't have any broken bones."

"Sprains hurt plenty."

"I'll take a sprain any day. I'm supposed to be dead. That guy was after me."

"How do you know it wasn't me he wanted dead? He wasn't real discriminating in the way he came after us."

"It had something to do with yesterday," she said without doubt. "Something to do with Jerry Ingalls."

"You don't think Ingalls is behind this, do you?"

She thought it over for a moment. "Why? Because I refused to represent him?"

"Maybe that's enough. Maybe it's revenge."

"Or intimidation to make me give in."

Dan wasn't convinced. "Don't look now, but that was no threat. I think you and I were both supposed to be dead on the bottom of Lake Pontchartrain by now. If he wanted to make you represent him, he's not helping his cause."

The thought sent chills down her spine. "It's so confusing. I was with Jerry Ingalls for several hours yesterday. I mean, I know he had a gun to my head, but I just don't think he's the kind of person who would have someone hunt me down to kill me."

"What about his wife? Do you think she would send someone after you?"

"No! She was as meek as a mouse. Besides, wouldn't they know that they would be the number-one suspects? What good would it do them to kill two more people?"

"What good would it do them to blow up a post office? We're not dealing with rational people here."

"I don't know. I just don't know."

They rode in silence for several moments, and finally Jill looked up at Dan. "I want to talk to him."

"To who? Jerry Ingalls?"

"Yes," she said. "I want to find out what's going on. And I want to talk to his wife."

"Why? They'll just lie. They aren't going to tell you."

"But I'll know," she said. "I'll be able to look into their eyes and tell if they're lying. I'm a pretty good judge of character. People lie to me all the time. I'll know, Dan. I'll be able to tell."

"But what point would it serve?"

"It might give me a clue as to who tried to kill us, and who it is that's still out there. He failed, Dan, so he may come back and try again. I want to find him before he finds us." She turned her anguished eyes up to his. "I'm so sorry to drag you into this, Dan. If I were you, I wouldn't get within ten feet of me."

He tightened his embrace and kissed her. "Do I look like I'm afraid to be near you?"

She steeled her heart against his kiss. "If you're smart, you are."

"Well, I've never been accused of being all that smart."

She knew that wasn't true, but he made his point. Still, she didn't expect him to hang around much longer.

Chapter Twenty-Eight

Frank Harper had swum several miles down Lake Pontchartrain by the time he took the chance to look back at the lights flashing on the bridge. Police were everywhere, and he could hear dogs barking and voices yelling.

Clutching the rifle, he went back underwater and swam farther, then came up at the edge of a campsite. He saw campers with their lights shining through windows, and the sounds of singing coming from a rec building at the back of the grounds.

Slowly, cautiously, he came up out of the water, thankful it was July. Dripping, he skirted the edge of the lake and zigzagged through pine trees and over downed logs, until he came to the parking lot.

He went from vehicle to vehicle, looking for one that wasn't locked. When he finally came upon an unlocked van, he slipped in through the side door.

The van was plush, comfortable, a good place to get some sleep. First, he had to get it out of here, though. If those cops and their dogs made it this far, the dogs would sniff him out for sure. No, he had to be far away.

He saw a duffel bag lying on the backseat, and hurried to open it. A man's T-shirt and some gym shorts and flip-flops were stuffed in there, along with a water bottle and a racquetball racket. Unable to believe this stroke of luck, he laughed out loud and began pulling off his wet clothes to don the dry ones.

Then he slipped between the front seats and bent down to hot-wire the car. It cranked to life, and he shifted into reverse. Without turning the lights on, he pulled out of the parking lot and headed for the road.

He knew they would probably have a roadblock west of the campground, so he turned east.

As he drove farther and farther from the scene, he wondered if he had succeeded in killing Jill Clark and her friend. He had seen the Bronco go over the bridge and had felt a moment of joy. He turned on the radio to see if there were any reports.

He flicked from a country song to a Cajun tune, to Christian music, to a rock sound, then finally came upon the news. He listened carefully through news of the Asian economy, the illness of the Russian president, Congress's latest bill to pass . . .

Finally, they got to the local news out of New Orleans, and he turned it up. *"Police are investigating a murder attempt that took place earlier this evening when an unidentified suspect ran two people off of the I–10 bridge over Lake Pontchartrain. The driver's Bronco went over the bridge, but, amazingly, the two escaped before going with it. The suspect, who was driving a stolen pickup, escaped on foot. Police are still looking for the unidentified man, and warn residents in that area to stay inside and keep their doors locked. The assailant is said to be armed. And in other news . . ."*

Frank Harper slammed his fist on the steering wheel and cursed. So they had gotten away. He would have to try it again, and this time he had no room for mistakes.

He turned the van around and headed north to Newpointe, hoping he could find them before the police found him.

Chapter Twenty-Nine

The Newpointe Hospital sent Jill and Dan home after confirming that no bones had been broken. Dan had one arm in
a sling and a bottle of painkillers clutched in his hand. He had a
dislocated shoulder and some torn ligaments, and the pain of
resetting it had been worse than if a bone had been broken.
They warned him against working for at least a week.

Mark and Allie picked them up and took them to rent a car.
Jill's had been towed to her mechanic in Newpointe, and she
hoped it would be repaired tomorrow. She was certain that the
man who had run them off the road had tampered with her car.
She wondered what he would have done if she hadn't called Dan
to help her.

Dan insisted on driving Jill home in the rental car, since they
had both been asked to stop by the Newpointe Police Department to make a statement about what had happened, in case it
was related to the post office bombing. As they went back into
the station, Jill couldn't believe she was back for the second time
in twenty-four hours.

"This is becoming a nightly event for you," Dan said.

"Tonight'll be different, though," Jill said. "I'm gonna talk to
Jerry Ingalls before I leave."

Dan stopped in his tracks. "Jill, it's been a long night. Don't
do that."

"I am," she said. "I have to look him in the eye. I have to see
if he had anything to do with this."

"It's after midnight. They probably won't even let you in."

"Watch," she said.

They found Sid and Stan sitting head to head at Stan's desk with a couple of the FBI agents from yesterday. They all stood up when Jill and Dan approached.

"Are ya'll all right?" Stan asked.

"We'll live," Dan said. "You wanted a statement?"

"Yeah, if you don't mind. We'll just move into the interrogation room . . ."

Jill hung back. "I'll give you a statement, Stan," she said. "But first I need to see my client."

"Your what?"

"My client. Jerry Ingalls. He doesn't have a lawyer yet, does he?"

Stan and Sid looked at each other. "Well, no, but . . . You're not really gonna represent him, are you, Jill?"

She took a deep breath. "Let's just say I need to talk to him before I can commit. But I need to talk to him now."

"But it's after midnight. He's asleep."

"I'll wake him up," she said. She waited, chin up, for one of them to make the decision to let her in. "Come on, Sid, Stan. I've had a rough couple of days. Give me this, will you?"

"Are you sure you ain't gon' walk in there and pull out a pistol?" Sid asked.

"Let LaTonya search me. I just want to talk to him."

"And then you'll represent him?" Sid asked.

"I told you, I won't commit until I talk to him."

Sid shot Stan and the agents a look. "Well, maybe if she does agree to represent him, he'll finally talk to us. I say we go ahead and let her wake him up."

"All right," Stan said, "but we're not letting you in his cell. You stand outside the bars and say what you have to say. Dan can start with his statement while you're doing that."

Jill nodded and shot Dan a victorious look, but he only shook his head. "Be careful, Jill. Real careful. Stay way back. Sid, don't let her get too close."

"I won't," Sid said. "All right, Counselor. Let's go."

Since Ingalls was the only one incarcerated right now, Sid opened the jail, turned on the light, and allowed her to go in. Sid came in with her and stayed seated in a folding chair at the end of the hallway. She walked across the concrete, her heels clicking irreverently in the night. She saw Jerry Ingalls sound asleep on his cot.

Anger exploded inside her. For all he knew, she could be dead now. She went to the bars. "Wake up, Jerry Ingalls," she shouted.

He stirred and squinted in the light. He saw her and slowly sat up. "What's going on?"

"I want to talk to you," she said. "Get up."

He rubbed his eyes. "What time is it?"

"After midnight. I would have come earlier, but I was too busy giving a statement to the police and getting patched up at the hospital. This may not come as a surprise to you, but somebody tried to kill me tonight. I want to know who it was."

He got up and walked toward her. "How am I supposed to know?"

"Because I have a feeling you had something to do with it."

His brain seemed to clear, and a slow frown darkened his face. "I have no idea what you're talking about."

"Tell me who's working with you," she demanded.

Jerry only stared at her for a moment, then looked down at his feet. "What did he do?" he asked finally.

The question surprised her. Was he admitting that he knew who had done it? "He ran us off the bridge over Lake Pontchartrain. We barely got out of the car before it went over the side. We're supposed to be dead right now. I want to know why."

Jerry slowly brought his eyes back to hers. "I have no idea."

That answer enraged her even more. "Did you have anything to do with this or not?"

He looked pale, suddenly, as he stepped closer to the bars. He grabbed them in his fists, and she took a step back. "Look, I know you must be shaken up," he said, "but you've got to believe me. I didn't have a thing to do with it."

Her eyes were beginning to fill with angry tears. "Are you threatening me into representing you?" she asked. "Is that what this is about?"

"No!" he said. "I gotta admit I was disappointed that you wouldn't, since you said you would. In my life, a person's word means something."

"So it *was* revenge?"

"No! How could I do that from in here? I'm not gonna kill you because you broke your word. How would that do me any good?"

"I don't know that it *has* to do you any good. Just like blowing up a post office didn't do you any good . . . killing three people and maiming a child."

"*I didn't do that!*" he yelled at her. "I told you, I was set up!"

"By whom?" she demanded just as loudly.

He shook his head and turned away. "Look, I didn't send anyone to kill you, I didn't blow up the post office . . . I need a lawyer, and if you're not going to represent me, then I need to find somebody else."

"I'm *not* going to represent you," she said through her teeth. "I don't represent killers. Especially when they've come after me twice."

"You're wrong," he said, more quietly. "Did I once hurt you yesterday? Did I so much as leave a scratch on you? I could have. We were in there for hours."

"So I'm supposed to give you a round of applause and pledge my life and my vocation to you because you didn't hurt me? Maybe you're a coward," she said. "Maybe you don't like to hurt people when they can look you in the eye. Maybe you prefer to do it differently, like running them off a bridge."

"*I am in jail!*" he yelled, throwing up his hands. "Does it look to you like I could run anybody off the road tonight?"

"Some people have connections," she said. "I don't know how you would have gotten in touch with them or why, or whether there's some allegiance in this that's making them help you out, but *somebody* is trying to kill me. I take that real personally."

He went back to his cot and sank down, looking between his knees down at the floor. "Look, I know you don't believe this," he said, not looking up at her, "but yesterday I was minding my own business, working at my job, not planning to hurt a single soul, and the next thing I knew I was being charged with terrorism and murder, and now you think I tried to kill you. I don't know how to convince you that I'm innocent, that I've been set up. Maybe I *can't* convince you."

Her face grew hot as her voice rose. "If someone set you up and you know who it is, why haven't you given them a name? That's the only thing that will get you out of here."

"There are reasons why I can't," he said.

"What kind of reasons?"

He looked up at her again. "Reasons that someone like you couldn't understand anything about. It has to do with keeping promises."

She wanted to scream. "I find it amazing that you can malign *my* character this way, when *you* are the one accused of heinous crimes. I haven't blown up any post offices. I haven't killed anybody."

"And neither have I." He got back up and faced her across the cell. "Look, it occurs to me that you seem to be caught up in this whether you like it or not. All I can tell you is to be careful."

"Then you *are* threatening me?"

He looked frustrated. "I told you to be careful, and you interpret that as a threat?"

She didn't know if she did or not. Suddenly, her head hurt, and she raised her hands to her temples. He saw the splint on her wrist.

"Did you break any bones?"

"No," she said. "It's a sprain."

"Any other injuries?"

She tried to filter out the kindness she heard in his voice. "The man who was with me dislocated his shoulder." She swallowed back the anger in her throat. "Look, I just came here to warn you to call off the dogs. So help me, if there's another attempt on my life, I'll make sure you pay for the rest of your life."

"And what if I'm the wrong guy to pay?"

"I don't think you are." With that, she clicked away from the cell.

"Don't go home," he said, stopping her.

She turned back to the cell. "What?"

"I said, don't go home. Whoever this is . . . he'll come back. He'll find you. I don't think he'll give up easily."

A foreboding chill went over her, and she stared at him for a long time.

"No, it's not a threat," he said, as if winded. "It's just good advice. You don't need to go home tonight. If I were you, I wouldn't go anywhere I usually go. Be careful."

Her anger seemed to dissipate like escaping air from a balloon. She walked out past Sid and back into the stairwell. Then, as Sid locked up, she stood at the bottom of the steps and took in a few deep breaths before she went back up to the police station.

She was exhausted and terribly afraid. She wondered if Mark and Allie really didn't mind if she slept in Justin's room again. They had insisted, but weren't *they* afraid to have her near them? She supposed they wouldn't have suggested it if they didn't want her there.

She only hoped the killer didn't somehow get wind of where she was. The last thing she wanted was to draw Mark and Allie into danger, too.

Chapter Thirty

Mark and Allie were both still up when Dan brought Jill to their house. When they saw saw the exhaustion on Jill's face, Allie quickly ushered her to the baby's room where she was going to sleep. Mark, worried about the pain and tension on Dan's face, stepped out on the front porch with him.

"You okay, buddy?" Mark asked.

"No, I'm not okay," Dan said. "I don't want to leave her alone."

"Man, she's not alone. I'm here with her."

"Yeah, but there's no telling what could happen. Somebody's out there, Mark. He got away. I'm scared for her." He turned around quickly as a thought came to his mind. "How would it be if I just slept on your couch?"

"Dan, you don't need to sleep on the couch. Not unless you're worried about him coming after you. I mean, you're welcome to stay here, but I don't think it's necessary."

"I don't know what I'm thinking," Dan said. "You'd be crazy to want both of us here, making you a sitting duck."

Mark frowned. "That's not it at all. That guy is probably still hiding out in the woods around Lake Pontchartrain somewhere. He doesn't know to look for her here, anyway. What about you? You think he knows who you are?"

"I don't know." His hand went up to his shoulder, and a pained look came across his face.

"Maybe you need to take a pain pill. Want to come in and get some water?"

He shook his head. "No. I don't want to be out of it if something else happens. Mark, are you sure you can protect her if—"

"Yes. Relax. I have it under control."

Dan began pacing in front of the porch steps. He looked as though he had more to say, but he seemed to catch himself. Taking a deep, weary breath, he said, "I guess I'll go and let ya'll get some sleep. I could use some myself." He started out to the rental car.

"Hey, Dan?"

Dan stopped midstride and turned around. "Don't worry, man."

Dan didn't answer as he got into the car.

Chapter Thirty-One

Dan had trouble sleeping because the pain was too great, and he didn't want to take a pain pill with a killer on the loose. The phone woke him at about 9 A.M. Startled, he jerked it up. It was someone from the highway department, telling him they had retrieved his Bronco from the bottom of Lake Pontchartrain. They wanted to know where to have it towed.

He got up and called his insurance company, and they promised to take a look at the car as soon as it got to Newpointe. He didn't have to hear from them to know it was totaled. As many times as the maniac had rammed it, it was totaled even before it had gone into the lake.

He showered, then decided to go to the fire station to tell Ray, the fire chief, about his dislocated shoulder. He supposed it was for the best that he couldn't work for a while. It would keep him available to look out for Jill until the killer was caught.

As he headed to the station, he racked his brain for answers about the killer. If Jerry Ingalls was locked up, who could have run them off the road? Curious, he pulled over to a pay phone and, in the phone book hanging at the booth, he located Jerry Ingalls's address. He didn't know why he needed to see the Ingallses' house, but he supposed it came from the same place as whatever had sent Jill down to Jerry's jail cell last night.

He changed his route and headed for Spencer Street on the north side of town. He counted out the addresses, then slowed down when he got to the Ingallses'. It was a little house, no bigger than where Mark and Allie lived. For a moment, he just sat there and stared up at the frame structure with wisteria vines growing up the porch post and full ferns hanging from hooks. It boggled his mind that a man who lived in a neat little house like this, with a tricycle on the side and a ball lying beside the front door, could actually be a killer. And it puzzled him even more that he might have others working with him. Maybe his wife was the one who had run them off the road last night. The wife who hung the ferns and swept the porch and planted the flowers. He had assumed the culprit was a man, but in the darkness he hadn't been sure.

Frustrated, he went to the station, tempted to take off his sling so he wouldn't call attention to his injury. He was known as the one in great shape, the one who never had a problem with his weight, the one who jogged five miles a day and bench-pressed more than anybody in the department. He didn't suppose he would be bench-pressing anything for a while.

He found Ray Ford in the office they had recently built on to the back of the Midtown Station. Dan broke the news that he wouldn't be able to come in for a while, and was barraged with questions from Ray about what had happened last night. Dan gave him a few sketchy answers, then headed into the kitchen.

Nick—his coworker and preacher—was sitting at the table with books and papers spread out in front of him. "Whatcha doing? Writing your sermon for Sunday?"

Nick looked up at him. "No, I'm getting ready to do two of the funerals tomorrow." He nodded toward the sling on Dan's arm. "I'm sure glad it won't be yours, man."

"You and me both." Dan pulled out a chair and sank down. "Pretty stupid, but I guess I forgot about the funerals. So much has been going on."

"Wanna talk about it?" Nick asked.

Dan shook his head. "Don't know what to say. Don't even know what to think."

"Well, we could start with why you've made yourself Jill's rescuer."

"I haven't rescued her," Dan argued. "Night before last, that man could have blown her away and I couldn't have stopped him. Last night she called because her car broke down, which wasn't a coincidence. The scumbag did something so it wouldn't run. If I hadn't shown up, he might have killed her right there."

"But you did show up. And then you got her out of the car before it went over the bridge. I'd call that a rescue."

Dan couldn't help feeling defensive. "So what should I have done? Let her go over?"

"No, of course not. But that kind of danger does kind of bond you, doesn't it?"

"Yeah, it does." Dan stared down at the wood grain on the table. "Nick, have you ever considered marrying a woman just so you could protect her?"

Nick started laughing, and Dan grinned. After a moment, both of their smiles faded. "I'm laughing, but it's not so funny. Truth is, I *can* understand the feeling."

"Really?" Dan asked. He stood up and went to the refrigerator, got out some orange juice. "'Cause see, I know that Jill's not safe. And I have this overwhelming, irrational feeling that I'm the only one who can protect her. But I can't move in with her and hover over her. I know it. So it's actually been crossing my mind that maybe I should marry her so I could be there." He got out a glass and began to pour. "Like she would even consider that in the first place. She's not even sure she wants to date me yet, much less marry me."

Nick's grin returned. "I don't think I have to tell you that's the wrong reason to get married, and I would not do the ceremony."

"But you said you understood it."

"I do," Nick said. "There's this woman that I think about . . ." His voice faded out, and Dan came back to the table.

"Yeah? You've got a thing for a woman?"

Nick shot him a look. "Being a preacher doesn't exempt you from normal feelings, Dan. I wouldn't call it 'a thing.' I just think about her sometimes."

Dan was riveted. "Go on."

Nick couldn't meet Dan's eyes as he spoke. "She's not a Christian, and she's a little reckless, and I keep feeling this heavy burden for her, like I'm the only one who can save her. Only she doesn't listen to me. But so often, I'm tempted to ask her out to dinner or something . . . but then I know that if I did I might get more involved with her, I wouldn't think clearly . . ." He looked up at Dan again. "The idea of rescuing someone is not a good basis for a relationship. Especially not a marriage."

Dan looked into his glass, as if the answers swirled there in the pulp. A wry grin stole across his face. "So you wouldn't marry us," Dan said, thinking out loud. "We could go to the justice of the peace. Who's got that job now? Jesse Pruitt?"

"Yeah, I think he's still holding it. Come on, Dan. You don't want to do that. You don't want to marry her on a technicality. You want to get married under God."

Dan chuckled, considering that as he took a drink. "Well, all right. So what if I thought it over and realized that I really wanted to marry her for the right reasons? Because I want to take care of her for the rest of her life."

"You're not ready," Nick said.

Dan's grin fled. "How do you know?"

"Because I've watched you and Jill for the last year. I've watched all the women you've taken out over the last few months, and all the ways you've avoided her. Just because she's in danger now is no reason to start shopping for rings. Marriage isn't going to protect her. Even if you're married, you can't be with her every minute."

"I know that," Dan said. "It's more than protection. For the past few months, I've been thinking about her a lot. Wishing I could call her. But there was part of me that just couldn't. I didn't want to start it up again, because I knew . . ."

Nick's eyes bored into his. "You knew what?"

"I knew that if I called her one time, if I went out with her, if I gave an inch, that I'd be in for the long haul."

"The long haul?" Nick asked. "Now, that's a healthy way to look at marriage. And if it took a crazy man with a gun to get you to make that move—"

"So it takes a lot to break through this tough skull of mine."

"What does it take to break through hers? You said she doesn't even know if she wants to date you."

Dan realized he had a point. "But she did call me when she was in trouble last night. There were a million people she could have called, right? But she called me."

"That's a good sign," Nick said. "But how many successful marriages claim close calls with death as the foundation? On the other hand, she's vulnerable right now. So are you. Maybe you should just see how it goes. Spend some more time with her. Some time that isn't filled with stress."

"If people would stop taking her hostage and running her off bridges, maybe we could do that." Dan shook his head. "I don't know why he wants her dead. I don't understand it. She never does anything but help people. She spends her whole life trying to keep people out of jail. Keeping them from being sued, keeping them from getting taken. Why did they come after her so brutally?"

"They came after you, too, pal."

"Only because I was with her," he said.

"That would make most guys avoid her like the plague," Nick said. "But not you."

Dan shook his head. "I stayed away too long already."

Chapter Thirty-Two

Jill had been so tired the night before that she had not set the alarm, and she slept right through the baby's crying and didn't wake up until nine. The moment she noted the time, she leaped out of bed, threw on her robe, and ran out of the room.

"Morning, Jill," Allie said, standing in the kitchen with the baby on her hip.

"I overslept!" Jill said, rushing for the telephone.

"That's okay," she said. "You're the boss."

"But I had appointments." She punched out her office number, then winced at the pain in her wrist.

"Jill Clark's office," her secretary said.

"Sheila, this is Jill."

"You're still alive?" Sheila asked.

Jill swallowed back the aggravation she often felt when talking to the woman. If she wasn't so competent, Jill would have replaced her years ago. The one time she'd fired her, she'd learned that there wasn't anyone else in town as capable, so she'd hired her back. "No, I'm not dead," she said. "Did you hear that I was?"

"No, if I'd heard that I probably would have taken the day off."

"Sorry I spoiled your fun." She raked her fingers through her hair. "Look, I overslept. I'll be in shortly."

"If you don't mind my saying so, I don't want to be within a mile of you today, and I don't think any of your clients do, either. They've got enough problems."

Jill frowned and opened her mouth to argue, then realized that Sheila was right. "All right, Sheila," she said. "Cancel my appointments. I guess I could use a day off."

"What a relief. I'll go home, too."

Jill closed her eyes. "You're right. Why don't you forward the calls to your house? I hadn't thought about it, but my office probably isn't the safest place to be right now."

"Sure thing."

"And don't tell anybody where I am."

"Where *are* you?"

Jill closed her eyes. "Never mind. Don't worry about it."

"What if somebody really wants to know?"

"Then I want you to *really* not tell them."

"And what if they come after me and torture the information out of me?"

"Then you'll be safe, because you won't know."

She heard Sheila pause long enough to light up a cigarette. The woman constantly denied that she ever smoked in the office, but every time she came in she was certain she smelled smoke.

"My doctor thinks I'm under too much stress as it is," Sheila said. "I don't need bombs going off around me and bullets flying . . ."

"Sheila, I said you could go home."

"Well, if you'd let me off the phone, I could go."

Jill slammed the phone down and bounced down on the couch. Allie was standing in the doorway watching her. "When are you going to fire her?" she asked. "She treats you with so little respect."

"Even smart alecks have to work somewhere," Jill said wearily. "Besides, she's a whiz in the office. I don't have to like her very much."

Allie put Justin on the floor near a play center, and Jill got down on the floor next to him. He grinned up at her as he chewed on a set of plastic keys. He handed them to her, and she arched her eyebrows. "Thank you, Justin!" She looked up at Jill as she stroked his soft hair. "He gets sweeter every day."

"You need to get you one," Allie said with a smile.

"Nope," Jill said. "I think I'm called to be single."

"Yeah, right."

"You don't think people can be called to the single life?"

"Oh, sure I do. Paul the apostle apparently was. Lots of people are. Just not you. And if you're not, then Dan just might be the guy."

"And if I can prove he's not, will you leave me alone about this?"

"Hey, you don't have a mother nagging you for grand-children," Allie said. "So I have to do it."

Jill's expression faded. She missed her mother, who had died while she was in college, and wished she could be here to talk to. Allie saw her expression and instantly regretted her words.

"Oh, Jill. I'm so sorry. I didn't mean to sound so flip about your mom."

"It's okay," she said, holding a mirror up for Justin. He saw his reflection and grabbed at it. "So my children will be your grand-children? Do I need to remind you that I'm older than you are?"

Allie laughed. "I'd always hoped we were going to have chil-dren grow up together. It's not too late, you know."

Jill shook her head. "You're hopeless."

"Actually, I'm full of hope. You're the one who's afraid to dream. Besides, there's nothing I love more than a good wedding."

Chapter Thirty-Three

Lately there was nothing Aunt Aggie loved more than a good funeral. She cut through the funeral home to the visitation room to get a look at Sue Ellen Hanover before they closed the coffin. But to her chagrin, it hadn't been opened. So she wandered into the room next door, where a ninety-eight-year-old woman lay. Aunt Aggie recognized her right away, and pretended she had come to pay her respects as the family greeted her. The funeral director came into the room, as he always did when Aunt Aggie was on the premises. It was as if he was a security guard hired to keep her in line.

"Who did her makeup, *sha?*" she asked him.

"Paula Bouchillon," he said.

"When I go, I want her," she told him. "Now don't you let them put no silly wig on me, nor poof my hair up like Dolly Parton. I want to look natural, me. And I want to wear my tiara from the beauty contest." Aunt Aggie had been Miss Louisiana in 1938, and she never let anyone forget it.

"Yes ma'am. I'll put it in your file." He had been taking notes like this on Aunt Aggie's funeral for the last several months, since she'd become obsessed with her own death.

"Now T-Celia gon' want to put me in my purple dress," she went on, "but I don't like that dress. I don't know yet what I want to wear, but I'll let you know before the time."

"Yes, ma'am."

Celia, who had been looking for her, spotted her and hurried into the room. "Aunt Aggie, we need to sit down."

Aunt Aggie followed dutifully as Celia led her into the chapel where the funerals were held. "Aunt Aggie, you've got to stop planning your funeral. You need to be concentrating on the grieving family, and Sue Ellen, instead of all this morbid talk."

People started filling in around them, but Aunt Aggie didn't speak to any of them. They were carrying the closed coffin into the room, and her eyes followed it. "This is the quietest I ever saw her," Aunt Aggie said. "Didn't know she had it in her, me."

Celia was mortified and looked around to see if anyone had heard. "Aunt Aggie, she's *dead*."

"Might be, might not be. Sue Ellen would do 'most anything to get attention." The man in front of them shot them a disgusted look over his shoulder, and Celia looked as if she might crawl under the pew. "*Aunt Aggie!*"

"I didn't know he could hear me," she said. "But you know it's true." She patted Celia's leg. "I don't want that kind o' coffin, me," she said. "It ain't worth it. I want the cheap kind, 'cause there's no use spendin' all that cash on the dead . . ."

"Aunt Aggie, please quit talking about your death!" Celia sat back and set her hand on her belly. "You know, I think I'll go to Mary's funeral alone. I just don't want to sit through it with you if you're going to do this."

"Why you so upset when I talk about dyin'?" Aunt Aggie demanded. "Ain't like I'm gonna be floatin' down the river Hades. If I die, I'm gon' shoot right straight up to heaven, so why you actin' like it's some awful thing, *sha?*"

Celia managed to smile. "You're right, Aunt Aggie." She had been trying to disciple her aunt since she'd come to know the Lord a few months earlier. But the old woman was still a babe in Christ. Her faith in the basics—that Jesus Christ had died for her and rose again so that she could go to heaven when she died—had not wavered. "I just don't want you to go yet."

"Well, I ain't got no intentions," she said, "so don't you worry yourself." Allie and Mark slipped into the pew next to

Celia, and Aunt Aggie wrenched her neck to see around Celia.
"Allie ..."

"Hey, Aunt Aggie," Allie said, as if the old woman had
greeted her. "How are you?"

"Don't mind that," Aunt Aggie said, waving her off. "Who
sent that spray over there?"

Allie looked at the spray of flowers Aunt Aggie was pointing
to. "Uh ... Grant Hargis."

"*Sha*, if they want to order mums for my funeral, you tell 'em
I hate 'em. You hear?"

Celia groaned.

"Aunt Aggie, you're gonna live to be a hundred and thirty
years old," Allie said. "Quit planning your funeral, for heaven's
sake."

"It's only because I'm allergic, me. Make me sneeze."

"You won't sneeze if you're lying in a coffin," Celia whispered.

"I might." Aunt Aggie leaned further around Celia, then got
up and moved between her and Allie. "And I want you to put the
flowers around the coffin so folks don't stand too close. Keep
folks from breathin' down on me with they rancid breath—"

"Aunt Aggie, people are going to hear you!" Allie said.

Offended, Aunt Aggie got up again. "Well, then, I'll go sit
with somebody who appreciates what I got to say." With that she
slid out of the pew and headed for the cluster of firefighters she
saw at the back of the room. Regally, she walked back to them,
and they all got to their feet and hugged her. She felt like the
most popular girl at the school dance.

She was just about to sit down when she saw Hank from the
newspaper coming in with a camera around his neck and a pad
and pencil in his hand. "Hank, you ain't botherin' folks for a
story, is you?" she asked.

Hank looked cornered. "Uh ... yes ma'am, Aunt Aggie. I
thought the funerals would be a good human interest story after
the bombing."

"Well, you take care that you don't upset these folks now, you hear? This is a serious occasion."

Several of the mourners shot her disgusted looks as she sat between two of her firemen.

Chapter Thirty-Four

Jill knew she should have gone to the funerals, but she just couldn't manage to pull herself together enough to do it. She was exhausted and still nervous about getting out in public, where she could be an open target for reporters and curiosity seekers, not to mention whoever had tried to kill them last night.

Allie and Mark had taken the baby and gone to the Blooms 'N Blossoms shop early to make all the sprays that would be sent to the funerals. They were also attending the funerals, but she had opted to stay at their house alone.

When her cell phone rang, she answered it quickly. "You got an urgent message," Sheila said, as if she was the boss and Jill had been negligent about her job.

"Who's it from?" Jill asked, doubting the real urgency of anything today.

"It was from a Debbie Ingalls." Jill caught her breath. "She sounded very nervous and insistent that she talk to you today."

"Debbie Ingalls?" Jill repeated.

"Ingalls . . . isn't that the name of the guy who's in jail for roughing you up?"

"He didn't rough me up. He just held me hostage for a few hours."

"So how did he run you off the bridge if he's still in jail?"

"Apparently, he didn't," Jill said. "We don't know if he's working alone or with someone else, which is why you're at home today, remember?"

"Oh, yeah. Anyway, this Debbie woman . . . is she his wife?"

"Yes."

"So what does she want with you?"

Jill figured it had something to do with Jerry's desire for her to represent him. "I won't know until I call her back. What's the number?"

Sheila barked out the number, then added, "I work in the middle of the hot seat and nobody wants to tell me anything. I'll just be an uninformed sitting duck. Don't worry about it."

"Sheila, if there's anything I need to tell you after I talk to her, I will. I won't make you a sitting duck."

Sheila muttered something that Jill was glad she couldn't hear and hung up. Jill took a deep breath, then dialed the number on her cell phone.

"Hello?" The voice sounded anxious, upset.

"Debbie, this is Jill Clark. I understand you tried to call me."

"Yes! Oh, thank you for calling back, Jill." It sounded as if Debbie burst into tears. "Jill, I need to talk to you. Please, it's very important."

"Why?"

"It's about Jerry, and all this mess. Please, Jill, can you come and see me? Can we talk somewhere? I could come to your office."

Every red flag in Jill's mind sprang up. "No. I'm not in the office today."

"Just tell me where. I'll come anywhere, as long as I can bring the children. I don't have anyone to keep them."

Jill frowned. Could a woman with two preschoolers really be dangerous? "Look, I'm a little nervous about meeting with any of you. Somebody tried to run me off the bridge into Lake Pontchartrain last night, and I'm not feeling exactly congenial right now."

"Someone tried to run you off the road? Jill, don't you see? That's proof that Jerry isn't involved."

Jill didn't answer.

"Jill, please . . . there are some things I could explain to you. Things that might help you understand. You seemed like a decent person when I saw you the other night, and you know that my husband didn't do anything to hurt you. You gave your word about something and you didn't keep it. That's okay, because I understand, but there are some things that you need to understand. Please. I'm begging you."

Jill closed her eyes as the guilt rose within her again, and those red flags fell to half-mast. If she refused to represent Jerry Ingalls, the least she could do was meet with this woman. She seemed like a harmless person. She was the one, after all, who had talked Jerry into letting her go. She supposed she owed her that much. "All right," she said finally. "I'll come to your house."

"You would do that?" Debbie exclaimed. "Oh, Jill, I would appreciate that so much. That way I could get the children down for a nap before you come, and we could talk."

"What time?"

"How about three? They should be sound asleep by then."

"All right. I'll be there." She hung up the phone and leaned her head back on the couch, her eyes closed. She couldn't believe she had agreed to do this. What in the world would Debbie have to tell her? There was nothing more that she wanted to know about Jerry Ingalls, and Debbie didn't have a prayer of convincing her to represent him. Besides that, she was worried what it might mean to go into his home. What if it was a trap of some kind?

She got up and paced across the floor, raking her fingers through her hair. She tried to think it through, then began to pray that God would give her direction. Would he stop her from going if it was a trap? Would he intervene somehow? She honestly didn't know, but by the time she finished praying, she felt an urgent need to keep this appointment with Debbie. Maybe that was God speaking to her. Maybe if it was the wrong thing to do, God would have let her know it. She just wasn't sure about her feelings anymore. Sometimes they made no sense, and sometimes they led her wrong.

The phone rang and she jumped. She tried to catch her breath as she picked it up. "Hello?"

"Jill, it's Dan."

She breathed out a sigh of relief. What had she expected? For the killer to call her to let her know he'd found her? Somehow, she'd have to get over this paranoia. "Hi, Dan."

"You sound a little out of breath," he said. "Anything wrong?"

"No," she said quickly. "The phone just startled me."

He was quiet for a moment. "I just wanted to let you know that they've set a time for Mary Hampton's funeral. Tomorrow at ten o'clock. I wondered if you wanted to go with me."

She closed her eyes and sank back onto the couch. "I don't know, Dan. I'll have to think about it. It's not that I don't want to go pay my respects . . ."

"I know," he said. "All the questions about the hostage thing and the bridge . . . I kind of dreaded that, too."

"And I don't know if I'm up to going out in public with this person still out there. I missed Sue Ellen's . . ."

"Me, too. What happened last night kind of has its lingering effects, doesn't it?"

She nodded, though she knew he couldn't hear.

"Have you eaten?"

"No. I was just about to go to the kitchen and see what Allie and Mark have in the fridge."

"Why don't I just bring you something over?" he asked. "It's lunchtime, and we both have to eat."

The thought of his company made her feel instantly better. "Okay," she said, "but I have an appointment at three, so I'll have to cut it short."

"An appointment?" he asked. "You're working today? I went by the office earlier and nobody was there."

"Yeah, well. I decided not to go in, and I sent Sheila home. Just in case." She was quiet for a moment, then finally said, "Debbie Ingalls wants to meet with me."

Disapproval screamed out of his silence.

"Dan . . . are you there?"

"Yeah, I'm here," he said. "You're not actually considering meeting with her, are you?"

"Actually, yes."

Silence again. "Look, I'll be over there in thirty minutes, and we can talk about it then." He had hung up before she had the chance to respond, and for a moment she sat there with the phone in her hand, staring at it angrily, almost rebelliously thinking that he had no right to talk to her about anything, that this had nothing to do with him.

She remembered the arguments they'd had when they'd been seeing each other before, when she had spent long hours working on a client's behalf. Dan had complained that she took too many risks and worked too many hours. Then he had just lost interest altogether.

"I'm not the kind of guy who really hooks up with one woman very long, Jill. You know that about me," he had told her. And then it had been over. Tragically, humiliatingly over.

Now he was back . . . temporarily, she assumed. Again, making her feel vulnerable and guilty for doing her job.

She was still turning the thoughts over in her mind when the doorbell rang. She looked outside and saw his rental car in Allie and Mark's driveway. As she opened the door, her anger melted away. He was too handsome for his own good, and the sling on his arm just gave him an endearing air of vulnerability. He was still the catch of the town, and she thought of all the women who would be sick to know he was bringing her lunch again.

Their eyes connected and her heart jolted. She hated the fact that he still had this effect on her.

"How ya doing?" he asked.

"Fine," she said. She stepped back from the door and allowed him in, and he set the bags on the table. "I got you sweet and sour chicken. I remembered you liked that."

"Yeah, it's my favorite."

Their eyes locked for a moment longer, and finally, he swallowed hard and looked at the floor. "Look . . . I had a long lonely night, and all these thoughts have gone through my mind about last night and how close we came . . ." His voice broke off and he looked up at her again. "A hug would be really nice right now."

A smile crept across her mouth as she stepped into his arms. He held her tightly, in a way she didn't think she'd ever been held before, almost as if she was cherished or . . . loved. Emotions both confusing and painful welled inside her, and she suddenly wanted to cry.

This, she told herself, was even more dangerous than walking into Debbie Ingalls's home.

Their eyes met again, and she tried not to let herself read the eloquence in his. She couldn't trust anything her heart translated for her. Quickly, she turned and went to Allie's cabinet and got out two glasses and some silverware. He stood there with his hands in his pockets, watching her with his head slightly tilted as she moved around the kitchen.

They sat down and he said grace, and then they began to eat in silence.

"So are we gonna talk about this?" Dan asked finally.

She looked up at him. "Talk about what?"

"About your going to Debbie Ingalls's house."

She looked back down at her food. "I don't really know why we would have to talk about it," she said. "It's just something I'm gonna do, that's all."

He seemed stung by the words, and she noticed a pink hue flushing over his face. "I'm not trying to get in your way," he said, "or to tell you what to do or anything like that. I'm just concerned. Last night somebody tried to kill you."

"You, too."

"Yeah, but it's you they were after. Your car was sabotaged. You're the one who was held hostage two nights ago."

She couldn't take her eyes off her food. He touched her hand to make her look at him again. When they met, his were probing, intense. "Jill, someone is still trying to kill you, and I don't want them to succeed. I really, really don't want that to happen."

She moved her hand away. "I don't want it to happen, either, Dan."

"Then why are you meeting with her?"

"Because I think she's a decent person," she said. "I met her the other night, and she's the one who talked Jerry into letting me go. She's a young, pretty mother who loves her husband."

"And what does she want with you?"

"Probably to try to talk me into representing him," she said, "which I'm not going to do under any circumstances, but I felt I at least owed it to her to give her a chance to have her say, since she is the one who got me out of that situation."

"Do you understand that you could be walking into a trap? If Jerry Ingalls does have people working for him . . . if he is the one behind that guy running us off the road last night, then Debbie Ingalls could be in on it, too. She's on her husband's side, Jill. Whatever their agenda is, she could be right there with him."

"They have two little kids," Jill said. "Why would she do that?"

"Why would anybody do anything?" he asked. "There are three people dead because he blew up the post office. There would be two more dead if he'd succeeded last night."

"I just have a gut feeling about this," she said. "I don't think Debbie is involved. She's just fighting for her husband and her life, and the lives of her children."

"But you can't always follow your gut feelings," Dan said. "Jill, look at me."

Grudgingly, she looked up at him. "Jill, you're an emotional person. I've known you long enough to know that your emotions do get tangled up with people. That's a good thing. It gives you compassion. But it also makes you exhaust yourself and spend yourself completely, and sometimes your emotions are wrong."

She felt the heat rising to her face, and her anger returned. "Tell me about it," she said.

"What's that supposed to mean?"

"It means that you're right. Sometimes my emotions are wrong. Like eight months ago when I started to fall for you."

He looked surprised that she would throw that at him. "What makes that wrong?"

"Well, it kind of became obvious when you told me that you're not the kind of guy who hooks up with one woman very long. It was pretty obvious then that my emotions were leading me wrong." She could see that her words had stung him, and she hated herself. What was wrong with her? Why would she lay her cards on the table like that?

"Jill, I know what you must have been thinking for the last several months. But there's a reason why I don't hook up with people very long."

"No kidding," she said. "Dan, I figured these things out about you a long time ago. You don't like to get attached. You don't want to love anyone."

Now it was his turn to look down. He had yet to touch his food, but he stirred it around on his plate as if he intended to.

"Jill," he said in a soft voice, "I didn't sleep much last night or the night before. This has been really hard for me. But it's been hard for the last eight months. I've thought about you every day, and I've wanted to pick up the phone . . ."

"But you never did," she said.

"It was a fight," he told her.

She hated the tears that sprang to her eyes. She looked down to hide them. "And you're so strong. You were able to win that battle."

He leaned forward and coaxed her cheek up with his finger. Slowly, their eyes met. She gave herself a desperate reminder that she didn't want to be in love with Dan Nichols. That was the last thing in the world she needed right now.

"Jill, my not calling you had nothing to do with strength. It's a weakness, I'll admit."

"A weakness for other women?"

"No, not for other women."

"Because I distinctly remember seeing you with . . . what . . . two, three dozen? Your never-a-fourth-date rule seems to be working very well for you. I didn't know there were that many single women in Newpointe." She couldn't believe the jealousy seeping out of her own tone.

Dan sat back in his chair, and Jill gazed across the table at him.

"Jill, the reason I wanted to stop seeing you was exactly this kind of thing right here."

"What? That I speak my own mind?" she asked. "That I say what I feel?"

"No," he said, leaning forward, his eyes intent on hers. "Not that at all. That's what I like about you. But what I don't like about you is your walking into danger, putting your life at risk. Maybe you're not used to knowing that other people care about you. Maybe it doesn't matter to you. But I didn't want to lose you."

"Dan, excuse me for not understanding the rationale of your breaking up because you didn't want to lose me."

"Okay, so it wasn't rational!" he admitted. "Nobody ever said it had to be. But I was scared and I didn't want to lose you. But the minute I knew you were in real danger, I couldn't control myself anymore. I had to get involved."

"Don't do me any favors," Jill said.

Dan's face was redder than she'd ever seen it, and he got up and headed for the door. For a moment she thought he was going to leave, and dread fell over her. It was just as she could have predicted.

But Dan didn't leave. Instead, he stopped and turned back to her. "Look, I'm trying to be honest, here. This isn't easy for me."

She sighed, knowing he was right. He was not usually that direct or open with his feelings. This must be hard for him. "Look, I know what's going to happen, here," she said in a softer voice. "I don't even blame you for it, Dan. It's just like Celia hanging around little Pete Hampton's bed. She feels a sense of responsibility to him because she's his Sunday school teacher. You feel a sense of responsibility to me because we once meant something to each other. And when you heard I was in danger, you came to my aid. It's a guy thing," she said. "You can't help yourself. Last night, I shouldn't have called you when my car broke down. I should have called someone else. I just thought of you—"

He looked down at her, and she could almost see the hope in his eyes that she would say she needed him. But she wouldn't let herself say that.

"And then when we were run off the road, you felt protective again. You saved my life, Dan. You're off the hook."

He shook his head slowly, then came back and bent over her. He put his hands on the armrests of her chair. His face was only inches from hers. "I don't want to be off the hook, Jill," he said. "That's what I'm trying to tell you."

She didn't know why his nearness made her heart ache so much. "Then what's all this about your not wanting to be involved with somebody who takes risks?"

"Not wanting to and not doing it are two different things," he said. "Besides, the irony hasn't escaped me. I'm the one who works as a firefighter, and you're not making ultimatums to me."

"It hasn't escaped me, either."

"So how come you keep getting into more trouble than I do?"

She grinned slowly. "Just lucky, I guess."

He didn't seem to find that funny. He gazed down at her with misty eyes. "I tried to forget about you. I tried to go out with other women. I tried to tell myself all the ways that you and I are incompatible."

"So did I," she whispered.

"But then when I heard you were in trouble, I almost couldn't stand it, and all these regrets came rushing through me. Regrets that I had been so stupid to give up the time I could have spent with you, and here you were about to be snatched away and I'd never have that chance again. It was a selfish thing, Jill. That's why I showed up there that night. Not as much to save you as to save myself."

Somehow, that admission changed everything.

"I know I'm not making a lot of sense," he said. "But bottom line is, I want to resume things with you. I care about you, Jill. I haven't been able to get you off my mind, and now I'm beginning to realize that it's stupid of me to deprive myself of you because I'm afraid I might lose you. It makes no sense. It's totally irrational, and I don't want to live like that anymore."

A tear stole through her lashes and crept down her cheek. She wiped it away. She couldn't believe he was admitting this. It was something she had dreamed of him saying at night when she had no control over her thoughts, but she hadn't believed he ever would.

"I want us to be a couple," he said. "I want to take you out more than three times. I want to break my record again." He grinned slightly, and she couldn't help meeting that grin through her tears. "But this kind of stuff just drives me crazy," he went on. "Knowing that you're walking into danger, possibly a trap, that you could be killed. That after I've finally said this to you, and you're right in my grasp . . ." He dropped down into the chair next to her. "What am I saying?" he asked. "You may not even *want* to resume things. This all may be totally moot."

Again, she wiped at her tears. "Don't jump to conclusions," she said.

"What's that mean?"

She smiled. "It means that I want to resume things, too. But I want to understand you. I want to understand what happened before."

He leaned back hard in his chair and looked at the ceiling, as if he could find the answers there, written out concisely, in a way they could both understand. "I don't want to be left behind," he said.

She frowned. "Left behind? What do you mean?"

He shook his head, got up, and turned his back to her. "When I was a kid, we had all that money."

She nodded. It was common knowledge that the Nicholses were one of the wealthiest families in town.

"My parents hired nannies," he said. "And they went off and traveled to Europe and to the Middle East and to Aspen. They were never home on Christmas," he said. "I was left behind. I told myself when I grew up, I would never be left behind again."

It all made sense as the words processed through her mind, and she softened. She got up and touched his back. He turned around and looked down at her. "Don't look at me like that. There's no reason for pity. My background made me who I am today, but it just made me want certain things and not want others."

"I can understand that."

"But I think I can get over it, if you'll just be patient with me."

She smiled.

"It's not gonna be easy," he admitted. "I'll be a basket case if you go to her house today. It's gonna be painful." He plopped back into the chair.

She sat across from him and scooted her chair close to his until their knees were touching. Their foreheads met, and she looked down and took his hand lying in the sling. There was so much she would love to say to him, about how she wished for him at night, and occasionally allowed herself to pray that he would have a change of heart. She had never expected that prayer to be answered.

Big tears dropped off on their hands, and finally, he looked up at her and wiped the wet spot under her eyes. Then he looked down at her lips and kissed her. It was as if the months of longing had built up in her soul, and she suddenly missed him with all her heart, and thought that if this was the last kiss between them, she would never be able to stand it.

When the kiss broke, he touched her face, and she met his eyes. "Dan, how would it be if you came with me to Debbie Ingalls's house?" she asked.

He dropped his hands and pulled back to look at her more clearly. "You wouldn't mind that?"

"No," she said. "I think it would make me feel safer."

His eyes lit up into a grin. "That would make me feel a lot better."

"Just this time," she said. "And I won't ask you to take me on your firefighting calls."

He chuckled, then pressed a kiss on her lips again. "Thank you," he whispered.

"Thank *you*," she countered softly.

And then he kissed her again.

Chapter Thirty-Five

It was midmorning when Frank Harper finally woke at the wildlife refuge just east of Newpointe. The captain's chair in the middle of the stolen van had made his back ache. He stretched and tried to think. He was hungry, but he had no money. He dug around through the glove compartment of the van, and into the overhead compartments, until he came up with a folded ten-dollar bill. He yelled jubilantly, thrilled that he could now buy enough food to get him through the day.

He would drive through a fast-food place and get some breakfast, and then he could think better to find Jill Clark. Brain food was what he needed. Brain food and a little more time.

He headed back toward Slidell, wondering if anyone from the campground had noticed the van was missing yet. If they had reported it, would they have already made the connection that he could have been the one who took it?

The thought filled him with urgency, and he realized that he needed to lose the van if he didn't want to be found. He needed another car, one that was nondescript, just like a million other cars on the road today.

He drove for another twenty minutes before he reached Slidell and navigated his way to the Piggly Wiggly. The parking lot was scattered with people: a young woman trying to keep three toddlers together as she unloaded her basket; an elderly woman tipping a bag boy; three teenagers loading an ice chest. No one seemed unduly interested in him.

He sat in the van for a moment, scanning the different choices of cars, and saw at least six Honda Civics. One of them had to be unlocked, he told himself, so he grabbed his almost dry clothes and shoes from the floor of the van, stuffed them into the duffel bag, pulled his rifle to his side, and left the van behind. It took only three tries for him to find a green Civic that wasn't locked, and in seconds, he had the engine running and was on his way.

He headed back to Newpointe. He would pay his respects to Jerry Ingalls's wife. Maybe she could tell him where Jill Clark would be, and who the man was in the Bronco with her. Maybe he could send Jerry Ingalls a strong warning through her—a warning to keep his mouth shut, or his wife would suffer.

He reached the edge of Newpointe and headed for the Ingallses' house.

Chapter Thirty-Six

The little house where Jerry Ingalls lived was immaculate, except for a tricycle on the porch and a ball lying in the yard. Jill could hardly believe that they were standing at the front door of the man who, quite possibly, had blown up the post office.

The house looked freshly painted, and a garden of impatiens lined the sidewalk. Dan stood next to her, his face looking tense and concerned as his eyes scanned the property as if he might find a hidden bomb there or a grenade launcher hiding behind a bush. "I don't know what I expected," she said. "But not this."

"I know," he said. "I drove by here earlier and felt the same way. I think I expected a dirt floor shack like the Unabomber had. Not flowers and toys."

Jill rapped hard on the door, trying to look more like an attorney than a victim.

Behind her, Dan touched her shoulder, and she felt the reassurance of his presence and the warmth of his need to be with her. The door opened and she came face to face with Debbie Ingalls again. The woman was smaller than she, with delicate features that suggested fragility. She probably weighed a hundred pounds and stood about five-foot-three. Her hair was black and pulled into a loose chignon at the back of her head, but the dark circles beneath her eyes and the lines around her mouth made it apparent that this ordeal had been taking its toll on her.

She gave Jill a shaky smile. "Thank you for coming," she said. "I worried that you might change your mind."

Her smile was endearing, but Jill tried to ignore it. She didn't want to like her. "This is Dan Nichols," she said. "He's a good friend. I hope you don't mind that he came with me."

"Not at all," Debbie said, reaching out to shake Dan's hand. "Come on in. The kids are asleep."

They walked cautiously into the house, and Jill was surprised at the amount of sunlight coming through the back windows. The house was decorated with live plants and craftsy items that she suspected Debbie had made herself. It reminded her of Allie's house, and again she was amazed that Jerry Ingalls lived here.

"Sit down," Debbie said, and Jill noted that her hands were shaking as she gestured toward the couch.

Nervous herself, Jill went to sit on the couch, but Dan remained standing for a moment. Jill knew he still wasn't sure this was aboveboard. All of this—Debbie's nervousness, the lovely little house—could have been a clever scheme to give them a false sense of security.

Debbie looked up at Dan's sling. "Broken arm?"

"Dislocated shoulder," he said.

"Ouch. I'm sorry."

"You should be."

Debbie stiffened. "What do you mean?"

"I told you, we were run off of the bridge last night," Jill said. "Somebody was trying to kill us."

Debbie's mouth came open in a look of defensive disgust. "You can't possibly think that Jerry had anything to do with this."

"Well," Jill said, "he obviously wasn't in the car. But you've got to admit, it's a coincidence."

"If he'd had his way," Dan added, "they would have been dragging the lake for us this morning."

"Jerry doesn't want that," Debbie said. "You've got to believe that. He wants you alive so you can keep your word to him!"

"My word?" Jill repeated.

"Yes. You told him if he would let you go the other night you would defend him. I was there. I talked him into it based on your promise."

"Give me a break! You would have said anything, too, to get him out of there. He had threatened to kill me."

"In our family, when you give your word, you keep it. Jerry feels real strong about that. We've come to expect it from people."

Jill was stung, but Dan breathed a sarcastic laugh. "Real honorable," he said. "But that's not really worth a hill of beans when you go around blowing up post offices."

Debbie's eyes flashed. "My husband did not blow up the post office."

"You weren't so sure of that the other night."

"Yes, I was. I've always been sure of that. Jerry doesn't have that in him." She got up, paced across the floor, turned back to them. "Look, I don't blame you for breaking your word. To you, Jerry's a criminal. But he's *my* husband. Jill, I know you don't have any reason to represent him, especially if you think he's guilty. But I wanted you to come here today so I could explain some things about his past, so you could understand who this man is and why I love him."

Jill looked at the floor. She didn't want to see the tears in Debbie's eyes. Dan sat down next to her. "I'm not sure there's anything you could tell me, Debbie. A killer is a killer, no matter what made him that way. I'm not of the school of thought that says it's society's fault and everybody's a victim."

"Neither am I," she said. "And Jerry isn't, either. That's not what I meant. He's not a killer, so I don't have to make excuses or explain that away." She started pacing frantically back and forth across the room. "I didn't know Jerry before he went to Vietnam, but everyone who did says he was the sweetest guy you'd ever want to meet. Everyone loved him. But when he came back from Vietnam, he was a different person. He'd been through some terrible things. And he had a hard time coping."

"Most Vietnam vets are productive citizens," Dan said. "Lots of them had harrowing experiences. You don't see them killing people."

"Please, just listen! That's not what I meant. What I'm trying to tell you is that he went through a series of jobs and had a really hard time staying focused. He finally got involved with the wrong people and started doing drugs and other things he shouldn't have done. He wound up being a part of a group that robbed a liquor store one night, and he was the one that got caught."

The admission caught Jill off guard. She had expected her to wax poetic about his virtues, not share his criminal record.

"He did mention he'd been in prison," Jill said, bringing her eyes back up to Debbie.

"That's right," Debbie said. "He's an ex-con. He served five years for armed robbery. But he considers it the biggest blessing of his life."

"Prison?" Dan asked. "You've got to be kidding!"

"No," she said. She came back to her chair and sank down, intent on making them understand. "There was a prison ministry that came in three times a week and they told him about Jesus." Her voice broke. "I don't know if you're believers, but Jerry is now. He became a Christian while he was in prison. And when he got out, that sweet spirit that he once had was back. He had been changed forever. I met him after that."

Jill's brows furrowed together. She had seen lots of prison conversions, but she had trouble trusting them.

Dan wasn't sold either. "And that was before he took up terrorism?"

Debbie didn't appreciate the comment. She ignored it and addressed Jill instead. "The first five years after he got out of prison he went to therapy. He'd had some terrible experiences in

Vietnam, was badly wounded, and he still had nightmares. But he started to get better. Eventually, he was helping the other people in his group. Leading them to Christ and discipling them."

Dan shot Jill a skeptical look, but she kept quiet. It didn't sound like a bill of goods. It sounded real.

"Jill, my husband is innocent. Someone else blew up that post office, and he doesn't even know why."

"So what happened?" Jill asked. "Why was his pickup on the scene? Why was he in the motel? Why did he shoot his way into my room?"

"I've asked myself those questions a dozen times," she said. "I wish I could explain all of that to you, but there are things that I don't know. Things he won't tell me."

"You better believe there's something he won't tell you," Dan said. "By the way, honey, I have this little hobby . . ."

"No, you don't understand," she said, cutting him off. "That morning, the day the post office bombing happened, Jerry got a phone call. He seemed a little shaken up by it. When he got off the phone, he told me he had to go to meet a friend from his unit in Vietnam. I didn't really like the idea, because now and then he still has nightmares, and I didn't want all those memories dragged up again. Stuff that he couldn't even talk about with me. But he insisted. He said this was a really close friend. Somebody that he cared a lot about, and hadn't seen in years. He wanted to make sure that he was all right, because the man sounded like he was in a little trouble."

"Who was the friend?"

"He wouldn't say. He just told me to trust him."

"He didn't say what kind of trouble the guy was in?" Dan asked.

"No, he sure didn't. I don't think he *knew* what kind of trouble."

"Didn't you wonder why he couldn't invite the man here? Let you meet him, if they were such great friends?"

"I asked that," Debbie said. "He told me the man was kind of rough around the edges, and might scare the kids. He said it was best if he met him alone. I didn't see him for the rest of the day. The next thing I know, the FBI are at my house asking about Jerry . . . I honestly didn't have a clue. Then I realized . . . they thought he did it. Then I saw the reports about the hostage situation, and Jill . . ."

"You're *sure* you don't know who this friend was?" Dan demanded again.

"I don't know," she said, " he wouldn't tell me his name. He still won't tell me. I don't know why he would cover for him after he committed such an awful crime and got Jerry thrown in jail. But I think he is covering for him. You've got to believe me!"

"It's hard to believe," Jill said, "you have to admit."

"Of course it is. I'm aware of that. *But my husband is not a killer!* He's a wonderful father and a wonderful husband. He's active in our church. He's active in prison ministry. He goes to Angola twice a month and does Bible studies there. I think something must have happened that day, something he couldn't control. He got backed into a corner and he didn't know what to do but to come out shooting. But he didn't shoot *anybody*, Jill. Nobody got hurt."

"Except three people are dead at the post office."

"I would bet my life on his innocence!" she yelled.

Silence fell like a curtain around them. Finally, Jill spoke again. "What do you want from me?"

Debbie covered her face and tried to calm herself. "I want you to talk to him again."

"I did talk to him. Late last night. Didn't he tell you?"

Debbie looked at her over her fingertips. "No. I haven't been able to talk to him today. Did he tell you anything?"

"Not really, but I told *him* a few things. I was sure he was involved in what had just happened to us."

"Think about it," Debbie said. "This guy, whoever he is. He's still out there. He's the one who wants you dead. I don't know why. I can't imagine, but you've got to consider that Jerry doesn't have anything at all to do with it."

"If he was innocent, why wouldn't he be the first to tell who really did it?" Dan asked. "He has you and the kids. Why would he sit in jail like that, and not say a word?"

"I don't know," Debbie said, "but that's how Jerry is! He takes his friendships very seriously. And all that happened in Vietnam was so serious that he hasn't even been able to share it with me! But it's like a big scar right through the middle of his heart. I think maybe he thought he could turn this person around or something. Somehow he got sucked into this, and he doesn't know how to get out of it."

"Mommy? Are you crying?"

Jill was startled as the little boy came out of the bedroom, rubbing his eyes. His brown hair was tousled, and he had wrinkle prints on his face.

Instantly, Debbie's expression changed from pleading to pleasant. "No honey, I'm fine. Come here." The five-year-old padded barefoot across the carpet. Debbie pulled him into her lap.

"Seth, I want you to meet Ms. Clark and Mr . . ."

"Nichols," Dan said.

"Nichols," Debbie repeated. "They're our friends."

"Hey," the child said.

Dan got up and shook the little boy's hand with a flourish of respect. "How you doing, buddy?"

"Fine, thank you."

Jill's heart melted. She wouldn't have expected a killer to have polite children.

"Did you have a good nap?" Debbie asked.

"Yes, ma'am." They heard a child crying from the other room, and she put the little boy down. "Just a minute. Let me go check on your sister." She looked up at Jill and Dan as she got to her feet. "My three-year-old. Excuse me."

She left the room and the little boy sat in her chair, staring across at Jill and Dan, like a grown-up at a meeting.

And Jill felt a sudden sense of dread that this child would soon face the stigma of having a father who was known as a terrorist.

Chapter Thirty-Seven

Frank Harper saw the rental car parked out in front of Jerry Ingalls's house, and decided now was not the time to go in. Instead, he parked in the driveway of an apparently vacant house a few doors down and watched for the visitors to come out.

He angled his rearview mirror so he could watch without wrenching his neck, but time rolled on and on. Whoever was there was staying an awfully long time. He wondered who it was, what she was telling them. Did she know about him? Was she telling them everything Jerry knew?

Someone knocked on the glass, and he jumped. An old woman stood at the window, smiling congenially and waving in at him.

Dread overcame him, but slowly, he rolled the window down.

"Hello," the woman said. "I'm Dora Higgins, next door. I couldn't help noticing you waiting over here. Are you waiting for your realtor to show you this house?"

He nodded. "Yes, ma'am."

"Well, I certainly will be glad to have a neighbor. It's a little creepy having it vacant, if you know what I mean. Would you like a piece of pie while you wait? I just took a fresh apple pie out of the oven. My grandchildren are coming this afternoon, and I like to have something sweet for them."

He shook his head. "Uh . . . no, ma'am. Thank you."

She looked disappointed. "Well, I reckon you can't go takin' apple pie from ever'body who offers you some. Not with the kind of things goes on around here. Guess you heard about our neighbor over there, Jerry Ingalls. Blew up the post office a couple days ago. Such a nice man, too, and those children ... oh my, they don't deserve what they've gotten. But I can assure you that the rest of us on this street are decent people. Are you interested in this house for rental property, or will you be living here?"

He glanced back in the rearview mirror. No one had come out of the Ingallses' house just yet. "Uh ... I haven't decided yet."

"Well, all it needs is a little yard work and a few repairs on the inside. The lady who lived here was one of my dearest friends. She lived here for years before she died. It fell into a little bit of disrepair at the end because she was ill and couldn't do much, but oh, in her day, she was able to keep this garden blooming all the time."

"Yes, ma'am."

"Are you sure you don't want some pie? It looks like your realtor is late. You could call them from my house."

He shook his head hard. "No, ma'am. I'll just wait a little longer."

"All right, then. So nice to meet you."

He watched her as she headed back to her home, and thought how her whole house probably smelled of baked apples. A memory assaulted him, a memory of his paternal grandmother when he was only four or five, pulling an apple pie out of the oven and letting him cut his own piece, as big as he wanted. She had died when he was six, and there hadn't been anyone in his life like her.

He missed her. For a moment, he eyed the vacant house, wondering what it would be like to have her as a neighbor. He fantasized about flowers in the garden, a pie cooling on the windowsill, a perfect lawn. Those were dreams that weren't available to him, he thought with contempt. They hadn't been since the communist threat peeled the blinders from his eyes. Instead, he'd had to give the best of himself for his country, and he was still giving. But it was for people like Dora Higgins that he fought. So she would have the freedom to bake apple pies for her grandchildren.

He glanced in the rearview mirror and hoped that he didn't have much longer to wait. He had too much to do, and he needed to get on with it.

Chapter Thirty-Eight

Do you know my daddy?" Seth Ingalls asked them as his mother went to get his sister.

Jill gave Dan a sad look. "We've met."

"Do you know when he's coming home?"

"No, I don't, honey. I'm sorry."

"Mommy cries at night," he said. "She misses Daddy."

"What about you?" Dan asked. "Don't you miss your daddy?"

Jill supposed the question was designed to expose Jerry's evil. Maybe Dan expected the child to scream out that he'd been abused by his father for years, and hoped he would never come back. Instead, the corners of his mouth began to droop and his eyes filled with tears. He began to rub them as he nodded his head. "He read to me at night."

Jill's own eyes filled, and she met Dan's eyes. He looked stricken, as if he knew he'd made the wrong call. She turned back to the child. "What would he read?" she asked.

"*Charlotte's Web*," he said. "Last time, *Winnie the Pooh*. My sister loves Tigger. He's her favorite. She cries, too."

"Have you been able to talk to your daddy?" Jill asked softly.

"I can't," he said. "He's on vacation." He rubbed his eyes again. "He shoulda took us."

Jill couldn't fight the tears welling up in her eyes. Dan squeezed her hand, as if to tell her that the child was no reflection of the father . . . that you could have a killer for a dad and still be a sweet kid.

Debbie came back into the room carrying the little girl. She was a tiny replica of her and looked too shy to speak to them. She buried her face in her mother's chest as the boy gave the chair back to his mother. "Sorry I took so long. Christy's a little shy, and she didn't want to come in here." She glanced at the boy, saw that he'd been crying, and shot Jill and Dan an accusing look. "Honey, what's wrong?"

"He was just telling us he misses his daddy," Jill said softly.

Debbie kept one arm around the sleepy little girl, and slid the other around him. She hugged him tightly, and when she looked at them again, her eyes were full of tears. So were Jill's.

"This is a hard time for our family," she whispered.

Jill got up. "We should go now." Dan stood up beside her.

"Jill, I'm begging you," Debbie said. "Won't you please reconsider? Somehow we'll pay you. We'll come up with the money. He just needs a good lawyer."

"It's not the money," Jill said. "Why me? Why not someone who's unbiased, objective?"

"Because you know he didn't hurt you. You were with him for several hours and you know what he's like."

"I don't know anything of the kind," Jill said. "I met him for a few hours in some strange circumstances—"

"That's right!" Debbie cut in. "You've got to realize what kind of stress he was under or he would've never—" She caught herself and looked self-consciously down at her children. "Otherwise, he would never have done anything like that." She brought her eyes back to Jill's. "Jill, I truly believe you're a woman we could trust. That you saw my husband's character. In your heart, you know . . ."

"You'd be a whole lot better off with someone else."

"Well, we don't *have* someone else," she said. "He wants you and I want you. There was something about you," she said.

"Something that made me think you were a woman of honor and integrity, even though you didn't keep your word."

Jill rubbed her temples. She was beginning to get a headache. "I can't promise to represent him, Debbie."

Debbie covered her mouth and sobbed. The little boy reached up and touched her face. "Mommy, don't cry," he whispered.

When he couldn't stop his mother's tears, he turned his angry little face to Jill and Dan. "My daddy is good," he said. "He wouldn't do anything bad."

"Honey, that's all right," Debbie said. "They know."

Jill bent down to the child. "It's sweet of you to defend your daddy that way." She breathed in a deep breath and let it out quickly. Dan squeezed the back of her neck. "I'm sorry, Debbie," she said finally, straightening again. "I believe that you believe in your husband. And I believe that you don't know what's going on. But I can't do it."

Debbie squeezed her eyes shut, then finally nodded her head. "All right," she said. "I guess there's nothing more I can say."

"No." Jill and Dan headed for the door before that little boy won her heart, before that little girl, so shy and sleepy, sitting in her mother's lap, began to affect her ... before Debbie Ingalls convinced her to change her mind.

"Thank you," Dan said as they drove home, "for deciding not to let her emotionally blackmail you."

"I hope I did the right thing."

"You did," he said. "Just because a guy has a cute kid and a sweet wife, doesn't mean he's not a killer."

"I know," she said. "But I've got to tell you, I wish he wasn't."

"Yeah, it would be nice to find out that he was innocent. But things don't always happen that way."

"I know they don't."

"Besides that," he said, "his wife could have been putting on an Oscar caliber act."

Her gaze drifted out the window. "I guess."

"You just never know."

But Jill felt that deep in her heart she did know. Debbie Ingalls hadn't been putting on an act.

• • •

Frank Harper watched as Jill Clark and her boyfriend came out of Jerry Ingalls's house, and suddenly overwhelming rage filled him. The sense of stark betrayal by Jerry's wife, a woman he didn't even know, was so fierce that he wanted to hurt her.

But he had no time right now. He would have to wait until later. Meanwhile, he had to follow the man and woman until he could finish what he'd started last night.

He wasn't going to sit still for betrayal. Vengeance had to be paid, or the war would never be won.

Chapter Thirty-Nine

Celia stayed with Pete Hampton while his grandmother and uncle made arrangements for his mother's funeral. Celia had been praying since the explosion that he would wake up with no lasting brain damage, but now she caught herself praying that he would not come around while his family was away from the hospital. Her greatest fear right now was that she would be forced into telling him that his mother was dead.

She couldn't think of a more horrible task.

But as the hours ticked by, he began to give indications that he was coming out of his coma. First, just an arm moved, then his head rolled, and he brought a hand up to scratch his face.

She stood frozen in front of him, trying to decide whether to try to reach his grandmother at the funeral home. Before she could make the decision, his eyes fluttered open.

Her heart jolted. "Pete? Can you hear me? Pete?"

His eyes closed again, and he was out. Celia went around the bed to call the nurse, but his eyes opened again. She stopped at the side of the bed and leaned over, waiting. "Pete? Can you hear me, honey?"

This time, his eyes focused on her. "Pete?" she said more loudly.

He opened his mouth to speak, but the tube in his throat prevented him.

"Don't talk, honey," Celia said. "There's something in your throat helping you breathe. Just nod if you know who I am."

He nodded. She breathed a laugh and stroked the side of his face. Her eyes filled with tears, and she realized that, if he knew—if he really knew—there might not be any brain damage.

"Then let's take a little test," she said softly. "I'll give you a name, and you nod if that's who I am. I'm Aunt Aggie Gaston."

He shook his head.

"I'm Miss Allie."

He shook his head again.

"I'm Miss Celia, from Sunday school."

He nodded.

"That's right!" she said. "You know me, don't you?" Maybe he would be all right, she thought. She reached for the buzzer, pressed it once, then a second time just to punctuate the urgency.

Pete tried to talk again, but the tube kept him from it.

"Shhh, honey, don't talk."

But he kept trying, and she could see from his lips moving what he wanted to say. "Mama."

She swallowed and stepped back. Her mind raced as she sought the right answer. She couldn't tell him, she thought. She needed help. *He* needed help. She pressed the buzzer again.

"Yes?" one of the nurses asked on the intercom.

"Pete's awake!" she said. "Please hurry."

Within seconds the two nurses were in the room standing over him checking his vital signs, asking him questions that he answered appropriately. Celia stood back as tears ran down her face in anticipation of the question she was going to have to answer. She prayed that his grandmother would return soon.

Her heart ached as she waited for the nurses to finish with him, and she tried to think of the best ways to tell him. Would it be better just blurted right out? Or should she pretend his mother just wasn't here, that she would be back later? No, she didn't believe in lying to children. But the truth was just too painful.

As the nurses worked on him, he became agitated and tried to pull the tube from his throat. His face looked panicked and scared as Celia came back to the bed, and he kept trying to speak. "Ma-ma . . ."

Celia bent over him. "Honey, she's. . . . not here." She wiped at the tears under her eyes. "Pete, does your head hurt? Are you in any pain?"

He fought to pull the tube out of his throat. The nurses got his hands away and strapped them down. Tears began to pour from his eyes, and his face reddened with his frustration.

A doctor rushed into the room and leaned over the bed and spoke to Pete, and began examining his eyes and asking him questions. Still crying, Pete answered with nods and shakes of his head, but that word kept forming on his mute lips. "Mama."

The doctor looked back over his shoulder and prompted Celia to answer him. She shook her head, indicating that she couldn't. A sob rose up in her throat, and she muffled her mouth to keep from frightening the child.

This is silly, she told herself. She was being a coward. The boy was confused, and she could clear that confusion up.

She tried to level her emotion and took a step toward the bed.

Just then, his grandmother came through the door, and Celia felt as if she'd been delivered. "He's awake, and he recognizes me. But I haven't told him yet . . ."

Pete's grandmother burst into tears and rushed to his bed. He struggled to free his arms.

"Oh darlin', we're so glad you're awake," she said. "We thought we'd lost you. How do you feel?"

Again, he mouthed the word and tried to free his hands to pull out the tube.

"Why is he strapped down?" she demanded.

"He was trying to take the tube out," Celia said. "They couldn't get him to stop."

"Oh, no, honey," his grandmother said. "You have to leave that in so you can breathe." She bent over the child and stroked his hair back from his eyes. He looked up at her, his big eyes focusing on her with every ounce of energy he had. "Honey, do you remember what happened at the post office?"

He shook his head.

"There was an explosion," she said. "That's why you're here. You were in it."

He looked as if he couldn't quite grasp that.

"And so was your mama."

Celia stepped up behind the grandmother and put her hand on her shoulder, encouraging her to go on.

"Honey, your mama's gone to heaven."

He looked at her for a moment, not quite grasping what she'd told him. And then his eyes changed to an expression of horror. His face began to redden, and he shook his head viciously.

"She got hurt real bad," his grandmother said. Her voice cracked as she tried to go on. "Honey, Mama died."

He sat up, shaking his head and fighting the straps that held his hands. One broke free from the Velcro that held them, and he pulled the tube out and began to yell in a hoarse voice, "You're lyin', Grandma! Why are you lyin' to me?"

He collapsed back on the bed, struggling to breathe, and the nurses and doctor rushed back to him and began trying to calm him down. He couldn't breathe, so he stopped fighting. They put the tube back down his throat, and when he was calm and breathing again, his grandmother took his limp little hand.

"Oh, honey. I'm so sorry I upset you. But I wouldn't lie about a thing like that."

He was too weak to fight, so he just closed his eyes as the tears squeezed out through his lashes.

They all stood there helplessly until he cried himself to sleep.

It was hours later, after Pete had fallen asleep and awakened again, that they had been able to convince him that it wasn't a cruel joke. His mother had been killed, and he had been left behind. Celia didn't have the heart to leave him, partly because his grandmother looked so torn and alone. Mary's brother Zack was busy taking care of the funeral arrangements and calling relatives, so he wasn't able to be there with her. So Celia hung around, trying to be whatever help she could be.

She was glad to see Stan arrive, but the tense look on his face told her he hadn't come to keep vigil with her. "I need to interview Pete," he said.

"No," she said. "Stan, this is not the time. He's not ready for this. He can't even talk while he's on the ventilator."

Mrs. Lewis got to her feet and moved closer to the bed, as if to protect Pete from him. He tried to smile at the distraught-looking grandmother. "Excuse me. I need to speak to my wife in the hall."

Celia followed him, ready to put up a fight to protect the little boy. "Stan, he just found out his mother is dead. He doesn't want to talk about the post office. He doesn't even remember any of it. I don't want him getting upset again."

"Honey, I know you're feeling real protective of him right now," Stan said. "It's a tragic situation, but I have to talk to him, because he's our only eyewitness to a terrorist act. Now, if I can get enough information from him, maybe we can head off the FBI agents who also want to interview him."

"But you've got the guy in jail."

"We have reason to think there's someone else who acted with him. Last night, Dan and Jill were almost killed on the I–10 bridge. I don't think it's a coincidence that that would happen the day after the bombing. Someone is still out there, and Pete might be able to identify him. Jill's life could be at stake, and Dan's, and who knows who else's?"

She sighed heavily. "All right, Stan, but so help me, you'd better be gentle with him. He's just a little boy."

Stan promised, so she led him back into the room. "Mrs. Lewis, I'm so sorry, but my husband needs to talk to Pete for a minute."

"Well, okay, but don't expect him to talk back." She took the boy's hand protectively.

Pete looked despondent when he looked up at Stan, nothing at all like the bright-eyed youngster he had delighted in. "How you doing there, Pete?"

The boy shrugged.

"Pete, I've got to ask you something about the explosion at the post office. You're the only one who can help us. Just nod or shake your head, okay? Do you remember being at the post office?"

Pete thought for a moment, then nodded his head. His mouth pulled down at the corners, and he covered his eyes with fists to hide his tears. His grandmother squeezed his hand.

"Did you see anyone you didn't know in there?" Stan asked. "Someone bringing a package or anything that wasn't where it was supposed to be?"

Pete nodded.

Stan stiffened. "Was it a man?"

Pete nodded.

"Did he mail anything?"

Pete shook his head.

"Did you see anything with him?"

Pete nodded and looked around. He pointed to the box of tissues on his table.

"Tissue?"

He shook his head and pointed to the box.

"He means box," Celia said.

Pete nodded that she was right.

"So the man came in and brought a box." Stan pulled Jerry Ingalls's mug shot from his coat pocket. "Pete, was it this man?"

Pete looked at the picture, then frowned and shook his head.

"No? Are you sure?"

Pete nodded and held up his hands. Two fingers on each hand were bent down. Stan frowned up at Celia. She didn't know how to interpret that.

Pete took the picture and pointed to Jerry Ingalls's fingers holding the sign with his number on it. Then he held one hand up with two fingers bent down again, and pointed at those with his other hand.

"Something about fingers?" Celia asked.

Pete nodded.

"He didn't have none?" the grandmother asked.

Pete shook his head.

"The man didn't have some of his fingers?" Stan asked.

Pete pointed at him, indicating that he'd gotten it right.

"So Jerry Ingalls didn't bring the bomb." He studied the picture. "Pete, is there anything else about the man? Were his eyes brown? Blue? Gray?"

Pete shrugged, but then he pointed to his face and made a full gesture.

"He had a beard?"

Pete nodded.

"What color beard? Blonde? Gray? Brown?"

Pete nodded at the color brown.

"Was his hair brown, too?"

Pete nodded and indicated that it was a little long.

Stan let that sink in for a moment. "Pete, I need to know if anyone was with him. Did you see anyone inside the post office with him?"

Pete shook his head, then pointed to the door.

"Outside?" Celia asked. "Someone was outside?"

He shook his head and held his hands like he was holding a steering wheel.

"In his truck?" Stan asked. "Someone was in the truck?"

Pete nodded.

The truck that Jerry Ingalls drove was blue, so he decided to give Pete another test. "Pete, was it a gray truck?"

Pete shook his head.

"Was it white?"

Again, he said no.

"Was it blue?"

Pete nodded.

"Which side of the truck did he get in on?" Stan asked. "Right? Or left?"

His grandmother looked up at Stan. "He doesn't know his left from his right," she said quietly. "Why don't you draw a picture?"

Stan grabbed the pad out of his pocket and sketched a truck. "Was the truck going this way, Pete?"

He shook his head.

"The other way?"

He said yes.

"And which side did the man get in on?"

The boy pointed to the passenger side.

"So, he wasn't driving. It was Jerry Ingalls's truck, but this mystery guy is the one who brought the package in."

"So, who was he?" Celia asked.

"I don't know," Stan said. "And Jerry Ingalls doesn't seem real inclined to tell us." He looked at the child again. "Pete, you've been a big help. We might be able to catch the guy who did this because of the information you just gave us."

The little boy closed his eyes again, and fresh tears squeezed out.

Stan leaned over the rail on his bed, and his face softened. "You must be pretty special, because God saved your life when you could have been killed. He must have something real important for you to do some day."

Big tears rolled down the boy's face, and he wiped them away.

Celia stepped up to the opposite side of the bed, and defensively touched his hand. The boys lips twisted. His grandmother leaned over and pulled him into a hug.

Stan shot his wife an apologetic look. He could see that the day had taken its toll on her. "Celia, I want you to go home and get some rest," he said quietly.

"I was about to. I'll just follow you home."

They said their good-byes, and walked together to the elevator. Celia was wiping her eyes as she got on.

"Honey, I'm worried about you. You don't need to be going through this with them."

"Just until tomorrow," she said. "I'm going to sit with him, while his grandmother and his uncle go to the funeral."

"This is way beyond the call of duty for a Sunday school teacher," he said.

"That's okay. He's worth it." She sighed and looked up at him. "So ... Did the missing fingers ring any bells for you?"

"Nope. But at least that's something to start with," he said. "At least we know that Jerry Ingalls isn't the one who delivered the package into the post office. Maybe he's telling the truth. That he gave somebody a ride to the post office and didn't know what he was delivering."

"Not on your life," Celia said, growing angry again. "Don't you let that man go, Stan. He killed people we know, friends of ours. Little Pete is an orphan because of him."

"Celia, you of all people should understand my concern about locking up an innocent man."

"He isn't innocent if he drove the car. He was involved, Stan."

"There's no question he was involved. The question is, whether he knew about the bomb. And why he won't tell us who he was driving that day."

"You think he didn't know him?" Celia asked. "Just picked him up somewhere and gave him a ride to deliver the bomb? How likely is that? And why wouldn't he give you a description?"

"Got me."

They got off the elevator and walked out into the parking lot. "So what's the next step?" Celia asked.

"With this new information about his fingers, maybe someone can identify him. Meanwhile, we keep questioning Jerry Ingalls. But he swears he won't talk until he has a lawyer. And he wants Jill Clark."

"She's not considering it, is she, Stan? She'd have to be out of her mind to represent the man who took her hostage."

"I don't know," he said. "Jill doesn't always think like the rest of us. There's really no telling what she might do."

They walked across the parking lot until they reached Celia's car. He opened the door for her, helped her in, then reached in and gave her a long, sweet kiss.

She smiled and leaned her head back on the seat. "Stan, can I ask you a big, big favor? One of the biggest I've ever asked?"

"Anything."

"Find Pete's dad. You can do it. Somebody needs to. Pete needs his dad back."

"I've already set the wheels in motion," he said. "I've got a few leads."

She reached up and kissed him again. "I knew I could count on you."

Chapter Forty

Frank Harper followed the car Jill Clark was in for several miles before he panicked. He saw her talking on her cell phone, and could have sworn that the man driving was watching him in his rearview mirror. Had they spotted him? Was she calling the police?

He was a lot of things, Frank thought, but he wasn't stupid. No, he wasn't going to be drawn into a trap. Quickly, he changed lanes, almost grazing the car next to him. Then without signaling, he took a right turn and got out of town as fast as he could.

• • •

In the rental car, Jill spoke to Pete Hampton's grandmother and learned that the boy was awake and had been moved out of ICU. He had been told about his mother and was despondent. Jill wanted to go see him.

"It's not wise right now," Dan said. "You'd be crazy to cross that bridge again tonight. Let me just take you back to Mark and Allie's."

She let out a deep sigh. "I guess you're right. Celia's been at the hospital most of the day. Anyway, he probably just needs quiet tonight." She stared out the window. "It's a terrible thing to lose your mother."

Dan glanced over at her. "It is, isn't it? I guess you would know."

She nodded. "Mom's been dead for almost ten years. But I still miss her so much sometimes. There are so many things I need to tell her. So many things I need help with."

"Ironic," Dan said. "You want yours and can't have her, and mine's alive somewhere and I haven't talked to her in ten years."

She studied his expression for a moment. "Do you miss her?"

He shrugged. "You can't miss something you never had. My mother wasn't like yours, Jill."

"How do you know? You never met my mother."

"She wasn't like most mothers."

"Are your parents still married?"

"Dad died eight years ago," he said. "A heart attack at Pebble Beach. Right on the golf course."

"I'm sorry."

"My mother cried her eyes out. And it occurred to me that she would have never cried that hard for me."

"I bet she would."

He shook his head. "Nope." He stopped at a red light but kept his eyes on the road in front of him. "I think I kind of hoped she would hang around Newpointe a little more after he died. You know, since it was just the two of us." He breathed a laugh. "She hasn't been back since."

"Do you hear from her?"

"No," he said. "But that's okay."

"Is it?"

"Yeah," he said. "I don't have any expectations anymore. That makes it okay."

She turned that over in her mind for a long moment, realizing how sad it was not to have any expectations of people you were supposed to love. People who were supposed to love you. She wanted him to have expectations of her, and she wanted to fulfill them.

But she wasn't sure he could fulfill any of hers.

• • •

Frank Harper stole another car. It was like laundering money, he thought. You just kept it moving so no one could ever trace it back to you. With the cars, he just kept swapping them back, and the thefts were blended into the car theft count without anyone ever tracing them to him. When they found them unharmed, they probably assumed some kid had stolen them for a joy ride and never even tried to find the thief.

When he had found an Accord, he tried, but failed, to locate Jill. As he drove around town trying to find her, he realized that he had probably been paranoid when he stopped following her earlier. Just because she'd been on the phone didn't mean she had spotted him. In fact, now that he thought back, they hadn't acted as if they'd seen him, except for the instant in which her friend had looked in the rearview mirror. Now that he ran it back through his mind, he was pretty sure that the man had been straightening his hair. He wouldn't have done that if he'd been panicked about someone following him.

No, he had just overreacted. And now he couldn't figure out where she was or what she was doing. He didn't know how he was going to get to her in time to kill her tonight, and he didn't have much time to waste.

He decided he wasn't going to waste any of it looking for her. Instead, he would get a message to Debbie Ingalls about how dangerous it was to talk to his enemies. It would be a loud, clear message.

Doing something—anything—made him feel better than doing nothing, so he drove out of town to Slidell and bought the supplies he would need for the message. Then he drove back to the Ingallses' house and sat out front, watching for the lights to go out.

When all had gone out, except for the one in the front bedroom, he began to get ready. Just a few more minutes, and Debbie Ingalls would know what it meant to betray him.

Chapter Forty-One

Inside the house, Debbie Ingalls sat in the front bedroom rocking her little girl to sleep. She was lonely, so desperately lonely that she didn't know how she was going to survive it. She wished that Jerry could call her from jail and reassure her that everything was going to be all right, but she had a strong feeling that it wouldn't.

She held Christy close and rocked. The baby was already asleep, but Debbie didn't have the heart to put her down. She needed the contact, the sweet comfort provided by her children. Seth was sound asleep already, and she didn't want to experience the silence of the house, nor the fears that kept barreling through her mind. If only she had been able to convince Jill to represent Jerry, there might be hope.

Leaning her head back on the rocker, she tried to pray, but the words just wouldn't come. Her heart was too heavy, and her hopes were too thin.

Then outside, she heard tires screeching as they rounded the corner. The glass at the window shattered as something flew into the room. She screamed and jumped up, knocking the rocker over and waking the child. Christy began to shriek.

Then Debbie saw it. Some kind of flaming device beginning to lap in flames across the carpet. She screamed louder and ran from the room, closing the door behind her.

"Seth!" she cried. "Get up, honey!"

She bolted into his room and jerked him out of bed.

"Hold Mommy's robe and follow me!"

Christy kept screaming, and Seth began to wail. She grabbed the cordless phone as they ran out into the night. Blocks away she could hear the car screeching around corners, fleeing from the neighborhood.

She took the children to the far side of the yard, then frantically dialed 911. "Someone just threw a bomb through my window," she cried. "My house is on fire. 203 Spencer. Hurry!"

The dispatcher told her they'd have someone there quickly, and she pulled her children to the side of the house, in the shadows, so that they wouldn't be open targets if the person came back. Sitting down on the edge of the yard, she began to weep as her children huddled closely against her.

Chapter Forty-Two

Dan heard the call on Mark's scanner as he and Jill were eating dinner with the Brannings, and he and Mark sprang out of their seats. "I'm going," Mark said.

"Me, too," Dan echoed.

"But your shoulder!" Jill cried. "Dan, you're on leave until it heals. They aren't going to let you fight a fire!"

"I just want to be there," he said. "I'll be back when it's over."

Jill and Allie stood at the door with their mouths open as Mark and Dan pulled out of the driveway. "You'd think it was a volunteer fire department and they couldn't do without them."

"Yep," Allie said. "Welcome to the world of firefighters."

"Next time, I'm going to insist they keep that scanner turned off."

"Get used to it. Mark has a scanner in both of our cars and in the house. He never wants to miss a call."

"But if he's not on duty ..."

"If he's not on duty, he'll overlook the cats in trees. But if there's ever a fire, he's outa here."

"Even with an injury?"

"They can keep him from being officially on duty," Allie said. "But these guys are never really off duty."

"And he's worried about *me* taking chances." She came back into the house and locked the dead bolt. "Now what? Do we save their dinner for later, or just throw it out?"

"Save it," Allie said. "Always save it. They'll come home starving to death, and Aunt Aggie doesn't make house calls."

Chapter Forty-Three

Dan didn't realize the call was to Debbie Ingalls's house until they rounded the corner and saw where the emergency vehicles were. The woman who had fought so hard today on her husband's behalf was sitting out on the grass in her robe, holding both of her children on her lap. The little girl was screaming, but the boy seemed enamored of the flashing lights and the sirens as the trucks and squad cars pulled onto the scene.

Dan crossed the yard to Debbie. "Are you okay?" he asked.

She looked at him like he was an accessory to the crimes that had been committed against her. "Yes, I'm fine."

"What happened?"

Her voice trembled. "I was rocking Christy, and some lunatic threw a bomb or something through the window."

"A bomb?" he asked. "Did it explode?"

"No. It just scared me to death . . . it was on fire and caught the carpet on fire, and before I knew it, it had climbed up the curtains . . ."

"Did you see what the car looked like?"

"No," she said. "I was busy getting the kids out." Her clipped tone suggested that she wasn't interested in his sympathy, not after their visit today. It occurred to him that her stress level had been even greater than his and Jill's, and tonight's events had only made things worse. Still, in the back of his mind, suspicions lurked.

Sid Ford and R.J. Albright, from the police department, cut across the yard to question Debbie, and Dan stepped aside. He looked at the house, where the current shift of firefighters worked. He wanted to help, as Mark was, but without the full use of his arm, his presence could actually hinder things.

Mark came out of the house, no longer hurrying.

Dan met him at the sidewalk. Lowering his voice, he asked, "How's it look?"

"Looks like the fire was confined to that one front room, and we've put it out. The rest of the house can be saved. The smoke damage is minimal."

"Did you notice the glass fragments where the window broke? Did they fall inside or outside the house?"

"I saw them inside," Mark said. "Why?"

"Just wondering if this was a trick."

"Why would it be a trick?"

"To get Jill's sympathy. Make us think she couldn't possibly be involved if someone's trying to kill her, too."

Mark looked over at the woman still sitting on the grass, clinging to her children. "I don't see her jeopardizing her kids that way."

Dan followed his gaze, then shook his head. "No, me either. But I had to consider it." He looked at Mark again. "So the glass fell inside, huh? Just like she said, something came into the room through the window."

"Looks that way. Could have been a lot worse."

"Guess so," Dan said. "Meanwhile, what do we do with her? She'd be nuts to stay here. If it's the same guy I had a run-in with last night, I don't think he's gonna give up that easy."

Ray Ford, the fire chief, was just coming out of the building. He wasn't required to fight fires, either, except when they were understaffed. But like Mark and Dan, he rarely missed an opportunity. "So this is that Ingalls guy's house?" he asked in a low voice.

"Yes," Dan said. "I was just here this afternoon with Jill. Ray, we probably need to help her make some arrangements tonight."

"No kiddin'," Ray said. "I'm a step ahead of you. I already called Susan."

Dan wondered what Ray's wife had to do with this. "What's she gonna do?"

"She gon' get Ben's room ready for 'em. I'm gon' take her to my house tonight."

"You sure you want her sleeping in your house?" he asked. "I mean, she is the wife of the guy who blew up the post office."

"Somebody's got to do it," Ray said. "Might as well be me. Besides, she don't look much like a killer."

"They never do."

Ray chuckled. "Spoken like a man who got run off a bridge last night."

"You better believe it. I don't trust anybody right now."

"Well," Ray said, "the way I figure it, if she's what she seems . . . an innocent victim . . . then Susan will nurse her back to normal. And if she's an accessory or even a killer herself, Susan'll have her baptized by the end of the week."

Dan couldn't help chuckling. He just hoped Susan understood what she was getting into.

Chapter Forty-Four

Dan's and Mark's food was still waiting when they returned back home, and Allie warmed it up for them while they filled them in about Debbie Ingalls's latest problems.

"It just shook them up a little. Ray Ford took them home to Susan, and they'll be staying there tonight."

Jill gaped at him. "Dan, who did this?"

"Obviously not her husband," he said. "I don't know why he'd do that to his own family . . . his own house."

"You think it was the guy who ran us off the bridge?"

"Probably," he said. "But she didn't see the car."

Jill was silent for a long moment as she stared down at the table. Dan took her hand. "You okay?"

She looked up at him. "Dan, what if he's telling the truth?"

"Who?"

"Jerry Ingalls. What if he's telling the truth about not being involved? About somebody else being the one to blow up the post office?"

"Even if he did, you don't have to get involved, Jill. It's not your job."

"But somebody has to. I want to know who did this, Dan. I want to get to the bottom of it before someone else winds up dead."

"You can do that without being his lawyer."

"Maybe not," she said. "I don't know. I'm so confused." She rubbed her face hard, then dropped both hands on the table. "I'm gonna go to the Fordses' house and talk to Debbie."

"Now?" Dan asked. "Jill, it's pretty late. They might be in bed."

"If there aren't any lights on, I won't knock. But I need to talk to her one more time."

"I don't like the idea of you out on the street at night."

"Me, either," Allie agreed.

Jill threw up her hands. "I'm a lawyer," she said with frustration. "I have to do what I have to do."

"All right," he said, holding up his palms in surrender. "Would you consider . . . Jill, could I come with you?"

Frustrated, she looked from Dan to Allie to Mark, then back to Dan. "All right," she said. "You can drop me off so I won't have to drive myself. But I'm not making this a habit."

He grinned and mouthed the word *yes*, then took his plate to the sink and rinsed it off. Quickly, he followed Jill out the door.

● ● ●

Susan Ford opened the door when Jill and Dan got there. *"Girl!"* She reached out to hug her and brought her right in. "Jill, what are you doin' out at a time like this? You shouldn't be out by yourself this late."

"I'm not," Jill said. "Dan is waiting in the car. Susan, I heard about the fire and I needed to see Debbie."

"She's right in the kitchen," she said. "I been trying to calm her down. We been praying together."

Jill's eyes locked into Susan's. She fought the urge to ask if Susan thought this could be an elaborate, expensive act. Was it all a play for sympathy? But she knew Susan never thought the worst of people. She would defend Debbie just because she felt sorry for her.

Jill walked into the kitchen, and Debbie looked up. "Jill! You and Susan know each other?"

"Honey, everybody in Newpointe knows each other."

"Except you," Jill said. "Nobody knows much at all about you."

"Oh, I don't know," Debbie said bitterly. "We seem to be the talk of the town right now."

Jill saw the tears come to Debbie's eyes, and she ducked her head, suddenly ashamed of her careless remark. Debbie looked shaken, and it didn't seem to be an act. The woman looked like she hung onto control by one fraying filament.

"Tell Jill what happened, Debbie," Susan said as she gestured for Jill to take a chair.

Debbie touched her forehead and swallowed hard. "I had put Seth to bed and I was rocking Christy, when all of a sudden something crashed through the window. The next thing I knew my house was on fire, and I had to get the kids out . . ." Her voice broke off. "If I'd been in bed, or if I'd put Christy down before Seth . . . He must have aimed for the only room with the light in it, but I always leave a lamp on in there, because she's afraid of the dark. If I hadn't been in there, the fire could have engulfed her before I even realized it. It *must* be the same guy who blew up the post office, but why is he after me now? My husband is taking the heat! I haven't done anything."

Jill pulled out a chair and sat down, her suspicions beginning to melt away. Would Jerry have had someone throw a bomb through his child's window? Not the man who'd shown her their pictures when he was holding her hostage, and worried what they would be told. Then again, whoever he was involved with could have acted without his approval. "Debbie, do you think Jerry knows who did this?"

"I don't even know if he's being told about it," she said. "Every now and then they let him call me, but I haven't heard from him today."

"That doesn't answer my question," Jill said. "Do you think he knows who did this?" She didn't know why she bothered to ask. She fully expected Debbie to cover for her husband at all cost.

Debbie dropped her face into her hands for a long moment, then looked up at Jill again. "Yes, I think he does."

Jill hadn't expected that answer. "Do you think he'll tell the police?"

"I don't know," Debbie said. "I don't know why he wouldn't tell after the post office was bombed. He has this loyalty thing sometimes. He means to do the right thing. I don't know."

Jill stared at her for a moment. "I'm gonna go talk to him tomorrow, okay, Debbie? I'll consider representing him."

"You will?" Debbie's mouth fell open, and she gaped at her. "Oh, I'm so happy to hear that."

Susan patted Jill's hand. "Good for you, honey."

"I didn't say I would. I said I'd consider it. I want to hear what he has to say about the guy who did all these things. I want to hear what he thinks about who started the fire in your house. I want to see his face when he says it."

Debbie's eyes were bright with tears. "You'll see, Jill. You'll see that he's not a killer. You'll see that he didn't have anything to do with this. And when he finds out about me and the kids—"

"When he finds out, if he still won't tell, Debbie, it isn't going to look very good."

"He has to," she said. "He just has to."

Chapter Forty-Five

As Dan drove Jill back to Allie and Mark's house, she kept looking behind them to see if anyone was following them. She realized that the killer could follow just as easily in daytime, but for some reason night seemed more threatening. Especially this night, when he had already been active in another part of town. She doubted he had called it a night and gone home to watch a movie.

But it didn't appear that anyone was following them. When they got to the Brannings', Dan walked her to the door and kissed her good night.

Allie was nursing the baby in her bedroom when Jill came in, so she told Mark good night and went on to Justin's room to get ready for bed.

When Allie put the baby down, she knocked and peeked into the room. Jill was sitting on the bed, staring at the air. "Everything okay?" she asked.

Jill shrugged. "As good as it can be with an insane killer on the loose. I thought they had him locked up, but now it looks like there's one still out there."

Allie sat down in the rocking chair. "I wish they'd catch him before Mary Hampton's funeral tomorrow. It would go a long way toward healing that family."

Jill felt sick. "Are they taking Pete?"

"No. He's still on the ventilator; he can't leave the hospital. Celia's staying with him while the grandmother and uncle go."

"Are you going?"

"Yeah, I plan to."

"I'm not going," Jill said, looking at her feet. "I just don't feel safe yet, out in public."

Allie's compassionate eyes rested on her. "Do you feel vulnerable to another attack?"

"A little," she said. "But I've got to get over it. I have a lot to do tomorrow, and I don't have time to slink around in hiding."

"I thought you were taking the rest of the week off."

"I'm going to the jail to talk to Jerry Ingalls. I may decide to represent him."

Allie just stared at her for a moment. "Did you tell Dan?"

"No. He won't like it. But I have to do it anyway."

"Why?"

"Because it might be the right thing. The man who held me hostage the other night ... he doesn't seem like the type to do these things ..."

"He sure had a gun to your head, Jill. They were real bullets."

"But he didn't pull the trigger. Not on me. He showed me pictures of his children. When his wife came in, he let her talk him out of it. I could tell he loved her."

"And because he loves his wife, you don't think he was even an accessory to the bombing?"

Jill considered that and realized it didn't make sense. "I'm just considering that he may not have been."

Allie came to the bed to hug her. "You've always had good instincts," she said. "All I know to do is pray for you."

"That's the best thing. And as for Dan ... well, I'll just have to deal with that as it comes. Our relationship is kind of fragile right now. I don't know. He may decide it's not worth it."

"Can you live with that?" Allie asked.

"I don't want to," Jill said. "But either we're compatible or we're not. We might as well find out now."

Chapter Forty-Six

The police station was abuzz with activity after the last strike by the killer, and Jill walked in and looked around. She didn't see Stan or Sid anywhere, so she headed for the front desk and asked to see Jerry Ingalls in an interrogation room where she could question him privately.

"Are you questionin' him as his attorney, Jill?" R.J. Albright asked her.

"I think so," she said.

"Didn't you do that the other night? Sid says you chewed Ingalls up one side and down the other, and still didn't commit to representing him."

"Well, maybe I'll commit today."

"Why?"

"Because he needs an attorney, and they're about to appoint one."

"Don't have to be you."

"Maybe it does," she said. "Which room can I have, R.J.?"

He pointed to the first room at the back of the station, and she headed back to wait for him. She went in and dropped her briefcase on the mahogany table, and went to the barred window to peer out. There wasn't much to see, even though they kept the back lawn lit up. There was an eight-foot wall that went around the jail's recreation area, obstructing the view from the police station to the bayou behind them. But she supposed the prisoners needed sunshine now and then, so she didn't blame them for the wall.

The door to the room opened, and Jill turned around. She crossed her arms as Jerry came in. He was unshaven and looked as if he hadn't slept in days. Wearily, he sat down and slumped at the table. "Did you come to ream me again?" he asked.

"No, not really." She waited for the door to close, then fought the chill running down her back. This was the man who had threatened to kill her just a few days ago.

"For somebody who refuses to represent me, you sure are showing up here a lot," he said.

She sat down and leaned forward on the table, meeting his eyes. "I'm still not sure I'll represent you, but I wanted to talk to you."

"About what?"

"About what happened to your wife and children last night."

He looked confused, and she studied his face earnestly for some sign of guile. There was none. "What do you mean, what happened to my wife and children?"

"No one's told you?" she asked.

He stiffened, and his eyes grew wide as his face reddened. "Is my family all right?"

"Yes, they're fine," she said. "But last night, while Debbie was rocking Christy in the front bedroom, someone threw something through the window and started the house on fire—"

He sprang up out of his chair, knocking it over, and backed against the wall with both hands to his head. "He didn't! Tell me he didn't!"

"*Who* didn't?" Jill demanded through stiff lips.

His hands fell limp to his sides, and he came back to the table and bent over it, breathing hard. "Just . . . did they catch him?"

"No," she said. "He got away. We don't know how he keeps escaping, but somehow he does. Jerry, if Debbie hadn't been in there with Christy at the time, if she'd been sitting a little closer to the window . . . they could be dead now. You've got to tell us who this is."

He began to pace across the room. A fine layer of perspiration glistened on his skin. "Where are they now?"

"They're staying with some friends of mine. Ray's the fire chief in town, and his wife Susan . . . she's the one who took care of the kids when Debbie came to the motel . . ."

His eyes shifted from side to side across the room, as if considering all his options. "I don't know what to do! My family—"

"Tell the truth," she said. "If you're not involved, Jerry, your only hope is to tell us who did this."

He slammed his hands on the table. "But he can't help it. It's not his fault."

"Why isn't it his fault, Jerry?"

He turned his face to the wall, banged a fist on it. Someone opened the door to see if Jill was in danger. She waved them away.

"I can't believe he would do that. We had a covenant. We're supposed to protect each other's families."

"A covenant? What do you mean by that?"

"I mean that we—" He stopped cold and turned back around, as if he'd said too much already. "Nothing. I didn't mean anything."

She couldn't believe he was going to clam up now. She got to her feet and came around the table. "Jerry, your children could be in danger. Your wife could be a target for him. He's still out there. He isn't giving up. He's tried to kill me, your wife, your kids, and he *did* kill three people and orphan and injure a little boy!"

"How is that boy?" he asked.

She hesitated a moment, surprised by his concern. "He woke up yesterday. He's grieving because they're burying his mother today."

Jerry looked away and rubbed his eyes roughly. "I don't believe this. This wasn't supposed to happen."

"Jerry, are you protecting this man out of some sense of honor?"

He shook his head, unable to answer.

"Because there's no honor in protecting a crazed killer. No honor at all."

"A covenant is a covenant," he bit out.

She frowned. "Jerry, look at me."

For a moment, he kept his back to her, then finally, he turned around and met her eyes.

"If you want me to represent you, you're going to have to be straight with me. You're going to have to tell me a whole lot more than this."

He rubbed his temples, then stepped toward the table and sank back into his chair. He looked as if the last drop of energy had just drained right out of him. "What do you know about covenants?" he asked.

She thought this was another challenge about her not keeping her word. "I know it's an agreement. I know about honor and all that—"

"No," he cut in. "I mean, what do you really know about the Jewish custom of cutting covenant?"

She twisted her face at the question. "Well, nothing, I guess."

"I didn't think so." He got up again and began pacing across the room, thinking hard as he spoke. "They used to take animals and cut them in half, longwise, and lay them opposite each other, and walk between the two pieces. It was how they sealed a covenant."

Jill remembered she had heard that before. "Yeah. Just like in Genesis when God told Abraham to cut the animals in half."

"Yes!" Jerry said, pointing to her, as if she—a simpleton—had just understood a complicated concept. "And God was the one who walked between the pieces of flesh, in the form of a smoking oven and a flaming torch. And that was the Abrahamic covenant."

Jill wondered how in the world this could possibly have anything to do with Jerry's case. She hoped he was going to tell her.

"At Jewish wedding ceremonies, the fathers would do the same things."

"What things?"

"They would cut the animals in half and lay them opposite each other, and the father of the bride and the father of the groom would walk between the pieces. In doing that, they were saying, 'I will give my life for this covenant. If my child fails to keep it, may the Lord do the same to me that I did to these animals.'"

"I still don't understand what this has to do with the post office—"

"Just listen," he said, sitting back down opposite her at the table, his eyes boring into hers. "When people made a covenant, they kept it, because it's witnessed by God. It's very serious."

"I understand that," she said. "Now, you tell me. Are you in a covenant with this person?"

He got up and turned his back to her again. Frustrated, Jill leaned on the table. "Jerry, if you are obstructing justice and enabling him to commit more crimes, maybe against your own family, God will not honor that."

"Just listen," he said. "Jonathan, Saul's son, entered into covenant with David. They swore to protect each other with their lives. Everything that was Jonathan's became David's, and everything that was David's became Jonathan's. They were identified with each other."

She shook her head. Maybe he was unstable, she thought. Maybe he needed to be hospitalized. She rubbed her forehead. "Jerry, you don't have to keep telling me these things."

"When Saul, Jonathan's father, set out to kill David, you didn't see Jonathan siding with Saul. He had a covenant with David, and that superceded his relationship with his father. He was sworn to protect David. That's what it means when you enter covenant with someone. You keep it. You take it seriously. You defend and protect them. You give them what's yours . . ."

"And is this what you did with this person?"

He closed his eyes and sat down again, and she could see the struggle on his face, as if he was fighting a memory. A terrible, painful memory.

"Jerry, if this is what binds you to this person, he didn't keep his end of the bargain. He betrayed you when he went after your family."

"The covenant stands, even if it's one-sided," he said. "God kept his covenant, even though the Israelites broke it over and over."

"You're not God!" She slid her hands down her face and looked at him over the fingertips. "Jerry, do you or do you not know who blew up the post office?"

He banged his fists on the table again. "I'm telling you, when you walk between the pieces, you're in covenant."

Now it was her turn to slam her hands on the table. "So you take the fall for some maniac and go to prison for the rest of your life for something you didn't do? What about your covenant with your wife?"

He closed his eyes as he struggled with that thought. "Yes. I do have to put that first. My wife and children . . . But what if this was a message to me? A warning not to talk? What if I give you his name and he goes after Debbie and the kids for revenge?"

"Jerry, he's a crazy, unpredictable, reckless killer. Your family will be much better off if we know who he is so we can find him and stop him."

"But he'll feel justified in his revenge if he thinks I broke covenant. He has a rationale for everything." His voice broke and emotion twisted his face. "We went between the pieces. I didn't walk. I was carried." He stopped and swallowed, trying to rein those emotions in.

Her eyes narrowed. "What do you mean 'carried'?"

"I was bleeding to death," he bit out. "I wasn't the only one. But he came back for me. I do owe him."

It was the first thing he'd said that made any sense to her. Had it happened in war? Had the killer saved Jerry's life? "Jerry, are you talking about Vietnam?"

He didn't answer, which was answer enough. He leaned on the table and stared into her face. "Some people can't be held accountable," he said. "Some people don't have the mental faculties, and sometimes . . . that's our fault. We have to protect them because we swore we would."

"Jerry, you're the one who sounds like you have mental problems. This sounds crazy. They're just gonna think you're insane, that you blew up the post office because you don't know right from wrong. I'll only represent you if you're innocent, Jerry. I'm not going to do the 'guilty by reason of insanity' defense. If you would just give me the name, tell me what really happened, the last time you saw him, why it was your pickup at the post office, why you were at the motel . . ."

He covered his face and shook his head harder with each question she posed to him.

"Jerry, your arraignment is the end of the week. They're going to appoint an attorney for you if I won't represent you."

"You could do it," he cried. "You said you would. That's why I let you go."

"And what would you have done if I hadn't? Killed me? What did you expect me to do?"

"Some people, when they give their word, they stand by it."

"When it's done under duress, I don't think it counts."

"Read about the Gibeonites," he said. "Read about the deceitful way they got Israel to enter into covenant with them.

Joshua kept it, anyway, even when they knew they'd been deceived, because Joshua knew how serious covenant was."

Jill didn't remember any of these stories. She vowed to herself that tonight she would start reading the Old Testament again. "I don't know anything about Gibeonites, Jerry. I don't know anything about Joshua's covenant with them. All I know is that I am not obligated to represent you, and if I don't feel that you're being straight with me, I'm not going to. So you have a choice. You can either tell me who did this, or you can get yourself another attorney."

When he didn't answer, she took her legal pad and pen and her laptop, which were spread out on the desk, and began to pack them back into her briefcase. She got up and started to the door, then turned back around midstride. "I only came here because your wife convinced me to. She's very persuasive. When I saw that there had been an attempt against your family, I hoped you weren't involved. I started to believe you, Jerry."

"You can believe me now, too."

"Still, I don't know the whole story. I can't represent you with only half of it. Meanwhile, whether I represent you or not, I can't go home. I have to look over my shoulder every minute, scared to death he's going to come out of nowhere. Even where your family is, Jerry, he could find them. This guy seems to be everywhere . . . and then nowhere . . . While you're in your cell waxing poetic about this glorious covenant of yours, he could be out there blowing up another post office. Or a football stadium with kids in it, or an airport!"

"It's not that hard to figure out!" Jerry shouted. "You can do it without my betraying him!"

She dropped her hand from the doorknob and stared at him, dumbfounded. "So you're telling me that if I figure out who he is, that's one thing, but you're not going to help me?"

"You can figure it out," he said.

"All right. Fine. I'll go tell your wife you said that. While she's sitting up, unable to sleep tonight for fear of some flaming,

flying thing crashing through her window, killing her baby ..."
She brought her trembling hand to her forehead and tried to
calm her voice. "Jerry, you should care more about your own
family and the innocent bystanders who have been drawn in and
may be killed because of this. Talk about honor ... Jerry, *you*
pulled *me* into this. I didn't ask for it. You *owe* it to *me* to tell me
who wants me dead before they finish the job."

He stared down at the floor, struggling with the tears in his
eyes. "He was in my unit. He saved my life. He won a Purple
Heart and a Congressional Medal of Honor."

"I don't care if he won a Nobel Prize!" she yelled.

"He had brain damage because he came back for me! It
doesn't take a genius to figure this out!"

Suddenly, she realized he was feeding her information. It
wasn't a name, but it was close.

He got up and went to the door, opened it. "I'm ready to go
back," he told the guard.

Jill stood frozen, watching him leave.

"Tell Debbie I love her," he choked out. And then he was
gone.

It took a few moments for Jill to get her thoughts back in
line. She grabbed her briefcase, stepped out into the noise of the
police department, and scanned the room for Stan.

Chapter Forty-Seven

Jill spotted Stan at the doorway of Chief Shoemaker's office, with several men she didn't recognize.

She cut through the desks, stepping around people, and made her way back to where Stan stood. He caught her eye, and she mouthed, "I need to talk to you." He nodded, then excused himself and headed to his desk. She met him there and plopped down in the chair across from him.

"I'm sorry if I interrupted something," she said.

"Don't worry about it. It's just the feds trying to make our lives miserable. If they'd get out of our way we might solve these crimes."

She looked back over her shoulder at the group of men still talking to the chief of police and Sid Ford. "Is this about Jerry Ingalls?"

"You got it. If he had to blow up something, I sure wish it hadn't been a federal building. It got the FBI involved, and there's a certain amount of head-bashing involved in working on a case with them."

Jill leaned forward, propping her elbows on his desk. Lowering her voice, she said, "That's why I'm here, Stan. I just talked to Jerry, and I think he gave me some vital information."

"Oh, yeah?"

"Yeah, but I'll give it to you as a trade. I'll give you what I know, but you have to repay the favor."

Stan didn't commit. "What did he tell you, Jill?"

Jill knew Stan well enough to know that he would help her whether he committed to or not. "He has some kind of covenant agreement with this person, and out of some sense of honor, he won't give a name. But I gathered that the guy is someone who served with him in Vietnam. He has a Purple Heart *and* a Congressional Medal of Honor, so it couldn't be too hard to narrow him down. He apparently was wounded saving Jerry's life. Brain damage. Jerry feels real conflicted about betraying him because of that."

Stan leaned back hard in his chair. "Anything else?"

"No, nothing. I still don't know how Jerry is involved, but at least you can get a name and maybe a picture, and catch this guy. The FBI could probably get that information in minutes. I want to know when they do."

"I can't promise you that, Jill. A lot is out of my control here."

"Stan, my life is in danger. I want to know this guy if I run into him. And Pete Hampton's life could be in danger, too."

A deep frown furrowed Stan's brow. "Jill, do you have good reason for thinking that?"

"It's just common sense, Stan. If he thinks that little boy is a witness, then he'll come after him, just like he came after me, and just like he came after Debbie Ingalls."

"I hope not."

"Find him, Stan. Lock him up."

Stan got up. "Wait here. I'll go get the agents on this. Maybe they'll prove competent, after all."

Jill waited, fidgeting all the while and watching the front door as Stan, Sid, and the FBI agents made phone calls and pounded on their computers. Every time someone walked into the station, she eyed them with suspicion, wondering if they were the right age to be a Vietnam vet. Anyone could walk in and hang around without being noticed. There were people everywhere: cops and perpetrators and people filing complaints.

After ten minutes, Stan came back to his desk. "We're still working on it, Jill, but we did just get a list of the men in Jerry's unit. A lot of them were killed in action." He handed her the printout. "That's all I have so far."

"I'll take it," she said.

As Stan crossed the room and returned to the FBI agents working near the chief's office, she took a pen from his desk and crossed off the names with the word *deceased* beside them, and saw that there were only five left. Jerry Ingalls, Jack Canady, Frank Harper, Michael Mills, Cliff Bertrand . . .

Her breath caught in her throat. Cliff Bertrand, the postmaster, had been in Jerry's unit? She got up and looked for Stan. He was standing beside an agent as he was talking on the phone and punching a computer keyboard. She almost tripped over a chair as she made her way to him.

"Stan, did you see this list?" she asked. "Cliff Bertrand—"

"Yeah, Jill, we saw it. There's gotta be a connection here. We're working on it right now."

"Do you think he targeted the post office because of this connection?"

"Could be."

Jill realized she wasn't going to get very far with Stan in front of the agents, so she went back to his desk. She crossed through Cliff's name, and Jerry Ingalls's name, and studied the three remaining names. Jack Canady, Frank Harper, Michael Mills . . .

She knew better than to use the police computer, so she got out her laptop and plugged in her modem, got on the Internet, and began searching the databases she had at her disposal, for information about which one of these men had won a Congressional Medal of Honor. When she wasn't able to find it, she tried keying in all three names and searching for a phone number. Jack Canady's name came up, and she saw that he lived in Vermont. She picked up the phone and dialed it. An operator's voice came on and said that the phone had been disconnected.

Not one to give up easily, she did a search on the next person on her list, but found nothing. She was typing in the third name when two hands fell on her shoulders.

She jumped and knocked over a glass of water. Grabbing a tissue to mop it up, she glanced back and saw that it was Dan.

"Jill, why are you here?" he demanded.

The question seemed unreasonable. "What?"

"Did you come here to talk to Jerry Ingalls again?"

"Yes," she said. "And he gave me some leads, Dan."

"Jill, he's dangerous. And it's dangerous for you to be here. Do you realize anybody can walk into this place?"

Though she'd already considered that, she acted as if she hadn't. "It's the police station, Dan. Where could I be safer?"

"Probably anywhere but here. These cops aren't worth the tin their little toy badges are made from if somebody starts shooting or leaves a bomb. You've got to get out of here, Jill. Have you forgotten how crazy this guy is?"

"What did you do, anyway? Just drive by to check on me?"

"No. We were coming back from a call and I happened to see your car out front."

"Dan, the FBI agents are this close to finding the guy's name, and probably a picture of him. I'm staying until I see it." She glanced at his arm. "What were you doing out on a call, anyway? You're not supposed to be working."

"I just heard it on the scanner, so I went. I didn't do anything much." Dan looked at his watch. "I have a doctor's appointment later today. I'm hoping to get my medical release so I can go back to work."

"Dan, you're not ready."

"Sure, I am. The shoulder's feeling fine. Now, if you insist on staying here," he said, setting his foot in a chair and leaning on his knee, "then I'll just have to stay here with you."

She struggled not to grin. "Fine. If you think you're a better guard than a couple dozen cops, you can guard me."

Dan pointed to the sergeant whose desk was beside the front door. Technically, no one should get in without going through him. But the paunch-laden officer was reading a magazine. "Look at that guy," he said. "Sitting down on the job, reading a magazine. You tell me how he's gonna protect you if that killer bolts in? What's he gonna do? Beat him with a copy of *TV Guide?*"

"He's got a gun."

"He's not gonna have time to use it, Jill. This guy is too good."

"Dan, I'm not leaving here until I know something, and that's that." She went back to her computer, torn between anger and the mildly pleasant feeling of having someone care about her.

"All right," he said. "Then I'll just sit right here with you." She didn't argue, but got back on the Internet. She found the number of the third guy on the list, and dialed it. A machine picked up.

She moaned as a man's voice told her he wasn't home but that he'd get back to her as soon as he could. She thought of leaving a message, but something told her not to. If this was the man who had blown up the post office, and run her off the road, and tried to blow up Debbie Ingalls's house, she sure didn't want him to know she was checking up on him.

She hung up the phone and moaned.

"Who are you calling?" Dan asked.

She looked up at him. "I'm trying to get in touch with some-one from Jerry Ingalls's unit in Vietnam. The killer won a Con-gressional Medal of Honor. I have three names, I just don't know how to find out which one it is. I thought if I talked to one of them ..."

"No way," Dan said. "You can't just call them up. What if word gets back to him that you're close?"

"It could," she said. "You're right." She studied the list again. "Dan, I found out that Cliff Bertrand was in their unit."

He frowned. "Cliff was in the army?"

"Yep. I don't think it was a coincidence that it was his post office that was targeted, do you?"

"No." He thought for a moment, then began to look at the screen over her shoulder. "There's gotta be an easy way to find out about a Congressional Medal of Honor."

She looked behind her at the group of agents and cops around the computers near the chief's office. "I'll bet Stan knows by now, and he's not telling me."

"Stan? I'll get it out of him."

Jill realized that he might have more clout with Stan, as a comember of Protective Services. He got up and headed toward the activity, but Jill couldn't stay back. She hurried to catch up with him.

"Stan, have you got the name of the killer yet?" he asked point-blank as he reached the police detective.

Stan shot them a look that said he couldn't talk in front of the agents. But thankfully, one of them turned around and addressed Jill. "So Ingalls told you the guy had brain damage? Did he say anything about any physical abnormalities?"

Jill shook her head. "No. What kind of abnormality?"

"Missing fingers," the agent said, turning back to his screen as a list scrolled across it.

"No, he didn't say anything about that."

"The kid did," the agent said. He sat straighter. "Here we go. Guys, we have a match."

"Which name?" Stan asked.

"Frank Harper." He typed in a few more things, then looked up at the other agents. "We've got to track down a picture of this guy and get it to the television stations immediately, along with an 800 number so people who've seen him can call."

Jill's heart threatened to pound right through her chest. She had known the killer was out there before, but somehow, knowing his name and his history made it all the more urgent.

"One problem," the agent said, typing frantically on the keyboard. "He's been in the psychiatric ward of a Veterans Administration Hospital in Jackson, Mississippi, for twenty-five years. If he's there, how could he have done the bombing?"

Stan jerked up a telephone and got the number of the VA hospital in Jackson.

"No wonder Jerry is so loyal to him," Jill said softly. "I guess you'd feel pretty loyal to a guy who saved your life and wound up in a mental hospital for the rest of his life."

Stan routed his call to the administrator and identified himself as a police officer in Newpointe, Louisiana. "I'm looking for information on a patient of yours. Frank Harper. Could you tell me if he's still a patient there?"

Stan listened, frowning. "What do you mean, technically? You're kidding. Disappeared how?"

Jill looked at Dan. They had their man.

"Then you do consider him violent. Do the police you reported this to have any information on where he's been? Can you tell me who I can get in touch with about that?" He bent over and began to write the name of a Jackson police officer. He stood back up. "Could you tell me the nature of his illness?"

He took a few more notes. "How did this happen?"

More notes.

"Could you tell me ... does he have all of his fingers?" He glanced at the agent who was looking up at him, listening, and shook his head that he didn't.

"I appreciate your help. Yes, please do. And I'll get in touch with the Jackson PD. Thank you." He hung up and looked down at the federal agents who were staring up at him, then at Dan and Jill. "He escaped a couple of weeks ago. Overcame an aid and got away. Apparently stole about a hundred dollars from a petty cash drawer in one of the offices. He's there because of a brain injury sustained in Vietnam after he saved some of his buddies. A mine went off. Somehow it blew some of his fingers, and he hasn't been right in the head since. He's normally heavily medicated with antipsychotics and antidepressants, but of course, he hasn't taken them since he broke out."

One of the agents grabbed up a phone and Stan's notes. "This the number of the PD in Jackson?"

"Yeah," Stan said. "They've managed to trace him to a few places, but haven't caught up with him yet."

"I got a picture!" one of the other agents said, turning his monitor so that they could see. "This one was of their unit in Vietnam, but it's really old. Here's one from the hospital a couple of years ago."

Jill went to the screen and stared down at it. She had never seen that face before. His hair was scraggly and long and peppered with gray, and his eyes looked drugged and vacant. He wore a beard which needed a trim. If he'd shaven or cut his hair, he could look totally different. But the fingers were unmistakable. He couldn't disguise those easily.

"You know this man?" the agent asked her.

"No," she said. "So this is the one who tried to kill me?"

The agent didn't answer. He was printing the photographs out and calling a television station.

Jill felt sick and rushed to the ladies' room. She threw up in the toilet bowl, then washed her mouth out at the sink. She looked in the mirror. She was white, and dark circles underscored her eyes. What had come over her? Just the sight of the killer had turned her stomach upside down.

Dan was waiting beside the door when she came out. "You okay?"

She nodded. "Yeah. It just … kind of caught me off guard." She looked up at him. "Dan, I'm going to represent Jerry Ingalls."

He looked pained. "Jill, you can't."

"Why not? Now that I know who did it …"

"Jerry Ingalls could still be involved. There could be a whole group of them."

"But I don't think he is. I think he's an innocent bystander who feels a debt to this man because of some covenant he made with him once. He needs a lawyer, Dan."

"But not you, Jill. It's not your job."

"Then whose is it?"

"I don't know," he said, his face reddening. "But you've gotta know that if you do this, you'll make this Harper guy even madder than he was before. This may be exactly what he was afraid of. The reason he wanted you dead. He'll come after you with everything he's got. He's mentally ill, Jill. I don't want you in his path."

Jill didn't especially want to be in his path, either. "Dan, I appreciate your feelings. Really, I do. But I can't help thinking that God put me in that motel room for a reason, and that he yoked me with the Ingalls family for a reason. Like it or not, he did."

"I can't believe God is telling you to do this."

"But you're not listening objectively."

His face softened, and he took her hands and pressed his forehead against hers. "You're right, kiddo. I'm not."

It was as close to an admission of love as he had given her, and warmth flowed through her. It was almost enough to make her back down. But not quite. "Will you trust me on this? Will you not go berzerko if I follow my gut on this?"

He closed his eyes. "All right, Jill. Go tell Stan that you're going to represent him. But I can't promise that I'll let you out of my sight until Frank Harper is caught."

"Come on, Dan. Your job is much more dangerous than mine, and I can't make you stay away, even with a torn shoulder. You walk into fires, into caving buildings, deal with explosions ..."

A slow grin crept over his face, conceding defeat. "Okay, you win. I'll try to quit hovering."

She shook her head and pressed a kiss on his lips. "Don't do that. I kind of like it."

Holding hands, they went to tell Stan.

Chapter Forty-Eight

Issie Mattreaux knocked on the door to Ray Ford's office, which was attached by a breezeway to the Midtown Fire Station. Ray yelled, "Come in," so she pushed through the door.

"What's up, Issie?" he asked, only glancing up for a moment before going back to his paperwork.

She sat down on the old couch facing his desk. Her uniform had a stain on the leg from an IV bag that had sprung a leak earlier, and brown streaks of iodine stained the front of her shirt. "I was . . . just wondering if you'd had the chance to find Pete Hampton's dad."

Ray set his pen down and leaned back hard in his chair. "I've made a few calls. Talked to his sister, who I remembered lived over in Baton Rouge. She was pretty shook up when she heard about Mary. I think if she knows where he is, she'll find him."

Issie looked down at her hands. "So you think he would return your call?"

"He might," Ray said. "I knew him okay when he lived here. He went to my church. I guess you could say we were friends. 'Course, he kind of kissed all his friends good-bye when he hauled off and left his wife. I don't know what in the world gets into some people."

Issie contemplated that for a moment. There had been a time when she had been among the "some people" he spoke of. The things that had thrilled her before seemed suddenly too heavy to carry.

"Maybe I'll try her again today," Ray said. "She's probably been thinkin' things over. She's a decent person, I think. Maybe she's come up with some ideas where he might be."

"Too bad you can't go over to the police station and get some of the feds to find him."

"Not a bad idea," he said. "Maybe I could get Stan to do it. Thing is, he's been so busy with the bombin' and findin' the dude who almost killed Dan and Jill, that he ain't had time to think."

"But he has a vested interest," Issie said. "Celia's at that hospital night and day. If he found the dad, maybe she could come back home and take care of herself."

"Good point," Ray said. "I'll call him."

She slapped her knees and got up. "Well, I just wanted to check. Poor kid's been on my mind a lot." Her lips trembled as she got those words out, and Ray regarded her with thoughtful eyes.

"Issie, do you need to talk to a counselor? That bombin' was pretty heavy, and you ain't the only one havin' some problems. I've had some others come in here real shook up, and they're bigger and tougher than you."

She shook her head. "No, I'm fine. Really."

"I hear you been spendin' a lot of time at Joe's Place."

She grinned. "I always spend a lot of time at Joe's Place."

"Yeah, but you ain't been puttin' 'em away like you been doin'."

Her grin faded. "Do people really have nothing better to do than to talk about what I do when I'm off duty?"

"There are people who care about you."

She laughed aloud, but there was no joy in it. "I don't need that kind of caring." She opened the door and started out, then turned back. "Let me know if you find Larry Hampton, will you?"

Ray had a puzzled, concerned expression on his face as he watched her leave.

Chapter Forty-Nine

Jerry Ingalls's eyes were more alive than she'd seen them since she had met him. He'd been told that Jill had agreed to represent him, and now he had hope as he sat with her in the interrogation room.

"Jerry, I want you to know that I've decided to represent you for one reason. I figured out who it is you're covering for."

He looked down at the wood grain on the table, obviously not surprised.

"It's Frank Harper," she said. She didn't know why it was necessary to say the name out loud. Maybe she just wanted to see the reaction on his face.

He got up, putting his back to her, but didn't say a word.

"I admire your loyalty to the man who saved your life, Jerry," she said. "He was a hero. But he's not a hero anymore. The Frank Harper who blew up the post office and ran me off the bridge and caught your house on fire is not the same man who saved your life in Vietnam."

"Tell me about it," he said, swinging around to face her. "He gave his life for me, and that *means* something to me."

"I know," she said. "It means something to me, too. I'm a Christian. I know about someone giving his life for me."

"No, you don't." He pulled the chair back out and plopped into it, looking smugly across the table at her. "You don't know about that. If you did, it would change every area of your life. Not a day would go by, not an hour, that you weren't thankful for what he did for you. You'd wear it like a robe. It would be all over your face. His light would shine out of you. But you don't."

She felt as if she'd been slapped. "How dare you? You don't know me. You don't know what I'm like."

"I know that you don't have much faith. You have enough honor to take me for a client, but it didn't bother you at all to break your promise to me at first."

She was getting angry. "Then why do you even want me for your lawyer?"

"Because I believe God threw us together for a reason."

If she hadn't uttered those same words to Dan less than an hour ago, his comment wouldn't have had much impact. Now it sounded like a sign. Was God speaking to her through Jerry? She honestly didn't know.

She threw her hands up. "Jerry, you make me feel really helpless. I don't even know where to start with you."

"Start by understanding what I understand."

"I can't make myself understand something that has no basis in logic!"

"How much time do you spend each day studying God's Word?" The question came like a spear through the air, impaling her right through the heart.

"I'm a busy woman, Jerry. I have people running me off of bridges and putting guns to my head ..."

"When life is normal," he said. "How much time? Fifteen minutes? Thirty?"

"Sometimes," she said.

"Sometimes what? Fifteen or thirty? And how much time do you spend in prayer?"

"I pray!" she said. It was getting hot in the room, and she got up and turned on the fan in the corner. "You know, Jerry, meeting with you just wears me out."

"Just think about it," he said. "A man gave his life for you, and you mostly ignore him."

"I do *not* ignore him! I'm in church three times a week . . ."

"So you think he died for you so you could walk in and out of his house three times a week?"

She knew her face was red. She snatched up her briefcase. "Look, just forget it. I thought I could represent you, but now I see that I can't—"

"Why? Because I say what I see? Because I pointed out that you can't possibly understand my loyalty to the man who saved my skin, since you obviously don't have much for the one who saved yours?"

"No! Because we need to be talking about the case, not about my spiritual life . . . which happens to be just fine, thank you very much!"

"Okay," he said, holding up his hands innocently. "I'm sorry. I'll leave you alone. Just . . . don't leave."

She sat down and looked at the table until she could calm her thoughts. Finally, she said, "We have to talk about your arraignment tomorrow."

"All right," he said. "Let's talk."

Jill only hoped she could get through their conversation without losing her temper.

• • •

When she'd finished with Jerry, Jill stopped by Stan's desk. He was just getting off the phone and looked up at her as he hung it up. "Everything go okay in there?" he asked. "You look a little ragged."

She felt more ragged than she'd ever felt, and she wasn't sure why. "Everything went fine. Did you find out anything about Frank Harper?"

"Yes. He checked in at a little hole-in-the-wall motel in the French Quarter the night of the bombing, but didn't stay all night. We also found out that he was here, at Joe's Place, early that morning. R.J. Albright talked to him, but couldn't remember anything specific they'd talked about."

She shivered. "I don't know why that bothers me. I mean, I figured he had been here. But to know he was that close."

Stan studied her for a moment. "Jill, are you sure you're all right?"

"Yeah. I'm fine. Just ... trying to process my meeting with Jerry. He's not an easy man to get along with."

Stan's phone rang, so he picked it up. "Stan Shepherd."

"I'll see you later," Jill whispered. "Call on my cell phone if you need me."

He nodded and waved.

She stepped out into the light and took in a breath of hot, humid air. She glanced next door at the fire station. Dan's rental car was there, and she knew he was back on duty, waiting for the opportunity to destroy his shoulder again, since it wasn't ready to be tested. She wondered how he had gotten the doctor to give him a medical release.

Irritated, she cut across the lawn.

Aunt Aggie was in the kitchen ordering everyone to the table. Jill stood in the doorway and looked at her watch. She hadn't even realized it was dinnertime yet.

The old woman was the first to spot her. "Jill, *sha*, bring yourself on in and have some eats with us. We got plenty!"

Dan heard Jill's name and appeared from another room. "Jill, how'd it go?"

"Fine," she said. "Uh ... I'm not hungry. I can't stay ..."

"Yes, she can, Aunt Aggie. She needs to eat. Jill, humor me on this one thing, okay?"

Jill grinned, then became aware of the eyes of all her firefighter friends on her. They were assessing her relationship with Dan, trying to decide if they were fully on again. She hoped they didn't ask her, because she wasn't sure herself.

"All right. Maybe I am a little hungry."

"You don't want to hurt an old woman's feelin's," Aunt Aggie said. "Now sit yourself down here and let me get you a plate. Preacher, you want to say the prayer?"

Jill still had trouble picturing Aunt Aggie as a Christian. The last few times she'd eaten here, Aunt Aggie had seemed resentful of Nick Foster's insistence on prayer before eating. It was strange to see her asking for it.

Jill bowed her head as Nick thanked God for Aunt Aggie and for her cooking, and for the food they were about to share. As he went on talking to God about protection on their calls, Jerry Ingalls's words came back to her. Had he been right about her spiritual life? Were there things she needed to examine? And if so, when would she find the time?

She decided at that moment that she needed to be alone with God tonight, and it couldn't happen at the Brannings' house.

She ate quietly, conversing neither with Dan nor with his coworkers. She sensed Dan's tension next to her, as if he knew something was wrong. Once when she looked up, she saw Nick Foster, her preacher, looking at her. She wondered if he was assessing her heart, as well.

After they had eaten, Dan walked Jill into the truck bay. "Are you sure you're all right?"

"Yeah, fine."

"You're sure quiet. Are you mad that I came back on duty? Because I got my medical release, you know. They said I could come back."

"I admit, I was a little aggravated when I saw that. You know your arm isn't ready, Dan."

He propped his good arm over her head and leaned against the wall. "It's fine. I'm still stronger than most of the guys here."

"At least you're modest."

He grinned and gazed down at her. "So tell me the truth. How did the meeting with Jerry Ingalls go?"

She crossed her arms, then realized how defensive that looked and let them drop to her sides. "I'm just smarting a little. Jerry challenged my biblical knowledge and my prayer life. It kind of stung."

"A known terrorist is questioning *your* beliefs?"

"Yeah. You believe that?"

"I told you he was crazy."

She pushed off from the wall and put some distance between them, as her arms crossed again. She looked down at the concrete floor. "The thing is, he isn't, really. The things he said, they made an awful lot of sense."

"Things like *what?*"

"Things like the attention I give to Christ. Things like how important he is in my life. Things like this concept of covenant that I don't know anything about, even though I've been a Christian for years."

"Jill, I don't think Jerry Ingalls's level of spirituality is something you should aspire to."

"I know," she said. "But as he was talking, I started feeling really defensive. See, I think God can speak to us through all kinds of people. Even people like Jerry. Before, when he was talking about all those Old Testament covenant stories, it rang true, Dan. This isn't about Jerry. It's about me, and my relationship with God."

He slid his hands into his pockets. "All right. I can't argue with that."

"I'm going to read all about covenant tonight," she said. "Everything I can find. I just want to know . . . to understand. If it's there, in the Bible—and I guess it is—then it must be important, don't you think?"

"Maybe. Or maybe Ingalls is one of those kooks who makes mountains out of molehills."

"I don't think this is a molehill, Dan."

"Okay," he said. "Whatever you say. We can look it over tomorrow after I get off. I'll bring my concordance."

She looked up at him, shaking her head. "I can't wait until tomorrow. I need to know tonight."

"Well, okay. I'll dig some tonight, too."

"Okay. I just . . . feel really fragmented lately . . . scattered . . . I could use a little grounding, and some serious quiet time with God."

"I guess we could all use some of that. You could probably stand some time without me, too. I've been hovering over you pretty good lately."

She didn't object as adamantly as she should have. "No, Dan. It's not that."

"Are you sure?" his tone was flat, as if he didn't believe her.

"Yes, of course."

The fire phone rang, and seconds later, the alarm went off, alerting all the firefighters that there was work to be done. She stepped back against the wall, out of the way, as Dan and the others ran to get geared up. When they had pulled out of the bay, she hurried back to her car, hoping she could continue this with Dan later.

Chapter Fifty

Jill called T.J. Porter, a cop who took jobs as a security whenever he could, and hired him to stand guard outside a hotel room so that she could be alone. Allie didn't like the idea.

"Jill, are you sure you're ready to stay in a hotel with that man out there looking for you?"

"Yes," Allie said. "I'll rent a room at the Biltmore in Slidell. I have some things to think about, and I need to be alone."

She hadn't considered how Allie might take that, until she saw her reaction. "I'm sorry if we're too noisy for you."

"No, no!" Jill said. "Nothing like that. It's just . . ." She dropped her bag on the floor and looked down at it. "Oh, I might as well tell you. Jerry Ingalls threw some stones at me today. Some spiritual stones."

"I don't understand."

"He challenged my Christianity."

"He what? The guy who held you hostage for hours is challenging *you?*" Allie moved the baby from one hip to the other. "Well, that just goes to show you that he doesn't have a clue. He doesn't know you at all."

Jill wasn't so sure. "Maybe he does. He had some good points. I want to be alone so I can do some studying. I don't read my Bible very much, Allie, and I don't take much time to pray . . . I just . . . need to reevaluate some things."

Allie began to look worried. "You're not questioning your salvation, are you?"

"No," Jill said. "Not that at all. But I am questioning my relationship with the man who died for me. I think I *need* to question it."

"Well, okay. Then you do need to be alone. But couldn't you just lock yourself in Justin's room? We'd be quiet."

"No, Allie. It's not you. I just need to be totally alone."

Allie sighed and shook her head. "All right. Call me in the morning, okay? Let me know you're all right."

"Okay." She leaned over and pressed a kiss on Justin's fat cheek. "I'll see you two later. If Dan calls, tell him to call me on my cell phone, okay? I'll just let him think I'm still here."

"Why won't you tell him where you really are?"

"Because then there would be this big argument over it, and I really want to concentrate on the Bible tonight."

"All right, I guess I can do that."

Jill smiled. "Thanks so much for being here for me. What would I have done without you?"

"It's not over yet, Jill. The invitation always stands. After you get this spiritual thing worked out, you're welcome to come back."

Chapter Fifty-One

Jill felt safe with the armed guard outside her hotel room door, but she wasn't sure if it was his presence that calmed her, or the distraction of Jerry Ingalls's accusations about her spiritual life. She hadn't had to go home for her Bible. It had been lying on the backseat of her car, exactly where she'd left it after church last Sunday. Dismally, she realized that was where she kept it most of the time.

She threw herself onto the bed and wondered where in the world to start reading. Should she start with the four Gospels, or the Epistles, or go back to the Old Testament? Then she remembered Jerry's mention of the Abrahamic covenant.

She looked in her concordance for the word *covenant* and found the first reference in Genesis. She turned to the story of Noah and began reading.

She was completely absorbed when the cell phone rang. It was Dan.

"Don't tell me," Jill said. "You've dislocated your shoulder again and you're on your way to the hospital."

"Nope. It's been a real slow night, and my arm is great. I've been doing a little reading . . ."

"Me, too," she said.

"I've also been talking to Nick. I think I've gotten a little insight on what Jerry might be thinking about this covenant stuff. Wanna hear it?"

"Yes, of course."

"All right. Well, see, there were these two guys who were best friends. I mean, really, really close friends. Closer than brothers. They wind up going to war together, and they sort of bond, you know?"

She frowned, assuming he was talking about Jerry and Frank Harper. "Yeah. I can understand that."

"So one day Friend One tells Friend Two that he wants them to have a covenant with each other, right? He wants to know that whatever happens, Friend Two will protect him. And he promises to do the same. He also wants to be sure that, if anything happens to him, his friend will protect his family, and take care of them. Again, he promises the same. Are you with me?"

"Yes," she said, sitting up on the edge of the bed. "I'm with you."

"So as a symbol of this covenant, they swap clothes."

"Clothes?" she asked. "Isn't that a little crazy?"

"Just stay with me. See, Friend One is a higher rank than Friend Two, so when he gives Friend Two his clothes, it's like he's giving him all the privileges and rights of that rank. When his subordinates see him, they think he's the other guy. But his enemies consider him a greater target than he was when he wore his own clothes. So with the privilege comes awesome responsibility."

"Wait," Jill said. "That's not allowed in the military. You can't just swap each other's uniforms."

"But they did," he said. "And what it symbolized to each of them was this: 'I'm in you, and you're in me.' They were so closely identified that they were literally willing to give their lives for each other. Over and over, the higher ranking friend protects his subordinate friend."

"Yeah, go on."

"Then one day, a great tragedy befalls Friend One's family, and he's killed along with his wife and children ..."

She got to her feet. "I thought you were talking about Jerry and Frank Harper. Dan, who *are* you talking about?"

She could tell he was grinning, and his tone was escalating, as if he couldn't wait to get the whole story out. "Just listen. Friend Two grieves deeply, and just about never gets over it. He gets promoted, big-time, and is very successful, but he still never gets over the death of his friend. Then one day, years later, he finds out that Friend One has a son that is still living. He's excited, right? Because he thought all the children had been killed.

"He finds out that this son was injured in the tragedy that came on his family, and it crippled him. But his nanny got him out of harm's way, and she's raised him ever since. Now he's an adult, living in poverty, still crippled."

Jill had stopped trying to figure out who these people were. Instead, she was captivated. She felt like a kid waiting for the next chapter of the storybook. "Uh huh."

"So Friend Two asks the son to come talk to him. The son is frightened. He's not sure if this man is a friend or an enemy, and let's face it, he's got a little touch of paranoia because of what happened to his family when he was a kid. But he agrees to come. And when he sees him, Friend Two tells him that he was in covenant with his father, and that he is sworn to protect him, too. So he invites him to move into his expensive home, and eat at his table, and live like one of his own sons. In one day, the son is transformed from being a poverty-stricken, crippled recluse to having all the riches that Friend Two can offer."

Jill smiled. "That's a beautiful story, Dan. Who are the people?"

He paused, just long enough to raise her anticipation. "They were Jonathan and David, from the Bible. And the son was Mephibosheth. Second Samuel chapter nine."

She closed her eyes, ashamed that she hadn't recognized it. "No wonder it sounds familiar. Jerry told me parts of the same story."

"Really? Well, I was telling Nick about all this covenant stuff, and he showed it to me. Whoever said the Bible isn't a great read?"

She turned to 1 Samuel in her Bible, and flipped through until she found the first passage about Jonathan and David. "It sure is. I can't believe I haven't been reading it."

"But there's more," Dan said. "The coolest part. Nick showed me in Galatians 3 where it says we're clothed with Christ, so when we accept Christ, we take his robe, so to speak. And we're identified with him. His family is our family. His enemies, Satan and all who fight with him, are our enemies. Jill, we just gloss right over Jesus saying this is the new covenant in his blood. But *we* are in covenant with Christ. Isn't that great?"

Tears filled her eyes. "Yes. That is great." She swallowed. "I was just reading about the Abrahamic covenant, where God passed between the pieces of flesh ..."

"Yes!" Dan was getting more excited. "Nick said that we do that when we enter into covenant with Christ. We symbolically pass between the pieces of Christ's flesh. He showed me in Hebrews 10:20, where it says we can enter the holy place through—and I quote—the veil, that is, Jesus' flesh. So you see? We do walk between the pieces. We are in covenant with Christ, in just that way. This is the coolest thing!"

She nodded, unable to speak. "I sure don't live like much of a covenant partner."

"Neither do I." He was silent for a moment. "Listen, I just wanted to share this with you, because it seemed important to you today."

"It is." She wiped her tears. "But all this doesn't explain why Jerry would still defend Frank Harper after he started killing people." She frowned and tried to remember what Jerry had said. "He told me something about the Gideonites or somebody, who deceived the Israelites. Oh, I should have taken notes."

"I'll ask Nick."

"Okay. Call me back on the cell phone if you find out."

"Will do. Say hi to Allie for me."

She felt a slight pang of guilt that he didn't know where she was, but she wasn't prepared to tell the truth and get into a long, distracting discussion. She wanted to bask in this new information she had about her savior. "I'll talk to you later, Dan. And thanks for the story. I needed that tonight."

She hung up and stared down at the pages of her Bible. There was so much she needed to know, so much she had never understood. How would she ever be able to absorb it all?

She had a good, repentant cry, then prayed a while before going back to the Bible. And as she read, a gentle peace fell over her, even as more questions about Jerry and Frank were raised.

Chapter Fifty-Two

Ray Ford's kitchen was alive with the sounds of laughing children playing on the floor in the corner. His sixteen-year-old daughter Vanessa sat cross-legged on the linoleum. He came into the room and smiled down at her. He hadn't seen her playing in years. She wouldn't have done so now, if her mother hadn't put her in charge of the Ingalls children while Susan and Debbie cleaned up the supper dishes, then relaxed with a cup of coffee. Vanessa still sat there with them, though she probably could have turned them back over to their mother at any time along the way. He enjoyed watching her delight in the children.

"Debbie got a contractor to come look at the repairs on the house today," Susan told him. "It's gonna take a lot longer to get it fixed than we thought."

"You stay as long as you need to," Ray said. "Don't you worry about us. We got plenty of room here."

Debbie smiled that humble smile that made him feel even more sympathy for her plight. "I don't know why you're being so kind to me, but I appreciate it."

The phone rang before Ray could answer, and he turned around and picked it up. "Yello?"

There was a long pause, then . . .

"Ray Ford? Is that you?"

Ray didn't recognize the voice. "Yeah, it's me. Who's this?"

"Larry. Larry Hampton."

Ray slowly straightened from his end-of-day slump and shot Susan a look. "I been tryin' to find you," he said into the phone.

Again, a long pause. "My sister told me."

"She said she didn't know where you were," Ray said.

"She didn't, exactly. But she knew how she could get in touch with me."

"Well, did she tell you why I called?"

Again, silence. When Larry spoke again, his voice was broken. "She said . . . that Mary . . ." He couldn't finish the words. He swallowed back the emotion in his voice, and cleared his throat. "How's Pete?"

"Well, he ain't doin' so good. He's in the hospital and still on a ventilator. He got some cracks on his skull, cuts and bruises all over his body, but that ain't the worst part. The hole in his heart is the part we're most worried about."

"How's he taking it? His mom's death . . ."

"How do you *think* he's takin' it?"

Larry was silent for a long moment. "I know what you must think of me, Ray. But trust me, there's nothing you can think about me that I haven't thought about myself."

Ray leaned back on the counter. "I ain't here to make judgments, man. I just want to reunite a family."

"Maybe it's too late for that."

"Well, sure it is with you and Mary. It's past too late. But you got a kid, you know. A kid who right now thinks he's a orphan."

Larry's voice was full of tears and regret. "I want to come back . . . get him . . . but his grandmother . . ."

"You think his grammaw gon' turn you away, when you the only parent he got left?"

"She should," Larry said. "The way I left town. I never planned on showing my face there again."

"Well, you need to change your plans," Ray said. "Comes a time in life when you need to worry about your own kid more than your reputation."

"That's easy for you to say," Larry told him. "I'm just not sure that Pete isn't better off with his grandma."

"Grammaws are nice," Ray said. "She'll do fine, if she's all he's got. After a couple years, he'll get over the pain, move on, grow up. That crack in his skull'll heal, his bones will get strong again, them cuts and bruises'll go back to normal, but that hole in his life, it ain't ever gon' go away. He needs his daddy."

"But what will I tell him?" Larry asked.

"Tell him you love him. Tell him you won't leave him again."

Larry's raspy voice came with much effort. "I don't trust myself to keep that promise."

Clutching the phone, Ray glanced at Susan and Debbie, then stepped into the laundry room, pulling the cord as tight as he could for privacy. "You know, all this regret is real movin' and all, but it don't mean nothin' if you don't come back and take care of your boy."

"I called, didn't I?"

"Yeah, you called. But that don't make you a man."

"What do you mean, it doesn't make me a man? I'm thirty-five years old."

"Only a coward would stay away when his boy needed him like this. I never took you for a coward, Larry, till you up and left your family. But it ain't too late to change things."

"Well, if I had been trying to be your champion, I guess I wouldn't have left."

"You ought to be your boy's champion. That's what fathers are s'posed to be." He knew he was making Larry mad, that it was quite possible that he'd get ticked off and hang up the phone, and Ray would never be able to get in touch with him again. But it needed saying. And he didn't have a lot of patience for tact these days. "Are you coming back, or ain't you?"

"I don't know," Larry said. "Just tell me where he is. What room?"

"He's in the Pendleton Memorial Hospital in New Orleans." Again, that choked emotion in his voice. "Has he been asking for me?"

"Are you kiddin' me?" Ray asked. "He don't know to ask for you. He don't know where you are. All he knows is you took off and left him one day. And it was just him and his mama, and now his mama took off and left him. Now it's just him and his grammaw."

"I can't take care of him. I can't raise him. Not by myself. My life is a mess right now, Ray. It's upside down."

"You don't think *his* life is upside down?" Ray asked. "All I'm askin' you to do is come back here and show that boy that he ain't a orphan. Let him know you didn't leave him without lookin' back. Let him know he's still got one parent alive on this earth who loves him."

Silence on the phone line was almost audible. Ray thought back over his history with Larry. They'd never been close friends, but they'd played Little League baseball on the worst team in the league. They'd both played in the band in high school. They'd been in the same vacation Bible school class year after year. They knew much of the same Scripture. "Man, I know the guilt is eatin' you up. I know you think it's too late to ever make things right with your boy. But you remember all the Scripture they taught us way back in Bible school? You remember that verse they taught us in fourth grade? Romans 5:8? They hammered it into us so we'd never forget it. It was practically tattooed on our foreheads."

"But God demonstrates his own love for us in this," Larry whispered. "While we were still sinners, Christ died for us." His voice broke off, and Ray heard him weeping.

"You remember the way home," Ray said. "Come on home, Larry. People need you here."

Finally, Ray heard a barely discernible click, followed by a dial tone. Larry had hung up.

Ray breathed a deep sigh and closed his eyes, wishing he hadn't been so hard on him. Maybe a little gentleness, instead of anger, could have lured him back. He went back into the kitchen to hang up the phone.

Susan was waiting. "Was that Larry Hampton?"

Ray stared down at the cord still swinging against the wall. "Yeah, that was him, all right."

"What did he say? Is he coming back to see Pete?"

He stared down at the floor between his feet. "Got me. I did my best."

"Pete Hampton," Debbie said. "Is that the little boy who was in the explosion?"

"That's right," Ray said, looking down at her. He started to add that it was the explosion her husband was probably a part of. The one they had spent hours fighting. The one that had killed three of their friends. But he knew it wasn't Debbie's fault. When they had taken her in, he and Susan had made a decision to minister to her and the kids without any condemnation. He wasn't going to start condemning now.

"His daddy left him a couple of years ago," Susan explained. "We've been tryin' to find him."

"How sad."

"Yeah, it's awful," Susan agreed.

"Susan, I don't know if he might call back," Ray said. "But if he does, and I ain't here, you get a number, if you can. I need to be able to call him back."

"He didn't give you one this time?"

Ray shook his head. "There's no tellin' how I might get in touch with him again. At least he's been told."

"So you don't think he'll come back?"

"It depends," Ray said, "on how much a coward he's come to be."

Chapter Fifty-Three

Dan couldn't sleep that night as thoughts of his conversations with Nick and Jill about covenant kept reeling through his mind. Finally, he quit trying to sleep, got up and dressed again, then went into the workout room and began to lift weights with his good arm. It was how he always worked out his frustrations and his anxieties; he tried some form of self-improvement. But he didn't understand why the subject of covenants, while it brought such joy, also brought such anxiety. Was there something in him that needed repentance?

Then his mind drifted back to Jill. Covenant. Wasn't that what people entered when they married? Was that why this subject inspired such anxiety? Was it the fear that someday he might enter into a covenant with Jill, or the fear that he wouldn't? Was it the fear that he wouldn't have the guts, or the fear that he couldn't keep the promise?

He saw a light come on in the kitchen. He put the weights back in their places, then stepped into the doorway to see who was there. He saw Nick sitting at the table with his Bible and papers spread out in front of him. He was, no doubt, working on his sermon for next Sunday.

Nick looked up and saw Dan standing in the doorway. "Couldn't sleep?" he asked.

"Nope," Dan said. "I've got a lot of things on my mind."

"The stuff we talked about?" Nick asked.

Dan nodded and took the seat across from Nick at the table.

"Did something I said bother you?" Nick asked. "Anything you didn't understand?"

"No, I understand it all," Dan said. "I passed it on to Jill. It's really pretty exciting stuff."

"Sure is," Nick said. "But most of us preachers don't talk about it much from the pulpit. I guess we feel like it's too much stuff to fit into a thirty-minute sermon."

"Maybe you need to go overtime."

"Right," Nick said. "They'd be nodding off all over the room. No, in this sound-bite culture, I can't hold them that long."

"Maybe you could do a series on it."

"That's what I was thinking," Nick said. "That's why I decided to get up and work. It was fresh on my mind. I'm working on a covenant series right now."

"Good," Dan said. "I think I need to hear that." He regarded Nick for a moment, wondering if he should tell him what was on his mind about covenants and Jill . . . and the fear he had of failing. But suddenly the door opened, and Issie Mattreaux, one of the paramedics who got off at eleven, came in and headed for the refrigerator.

She started when she saw them. "Oh, hey. I didn't think anybody was in here."

Nick seemed to sit straighter, and smiled up at her. "You just get off?"

Dan noticed something between them—a tension in the way they avoided each other's eyes and spoke in short phrases.

"Yeah. I just needed to get something out of the fridge."

Dan looked up at her. She was a beautiful woman with silky black hair, tanned skin, and the build of a teenager. She probably wore a little too much makeup, more than Dan's taste, but she certainly stood out in a crowd.

He watched Nick's eyes following her across the room.

"So what are you guys doing?" Issie asked as she pulled her drink out of the fridge.

"I'm working on a sermon," Nick said. "You should come hear it."

She grinned. "You know I don't do church." She took a drink, then headed back to the door. "Well, I guess I'll go home."

"You gotta be somewhere?" he asked.

She turned around. "No, I just thought I'd go get some sleep."

"Why don't you pull up a chair and talk for a while?"

Dan knew right away that something was up. It wasn't like Nick to waylay a beautiful woman unless he had an agenda. He suspected the agenda had more to do with his heart than his head. Issie Mattreaux was bad news.

Instead of sitting beside Nick, she sat next to Dan. "So, Dan, what's up with you? Anybody tried to run you off a bridge lately?"

Dan didn't find that amusing. "Been a couple of days."

"So what did you do about your car?"

"They totaled it. The insurance is giving me a check tomorrow. Guess I'll be shopping for a new one."

Nick kept looking from Dan to Issie, as if there was something he wanted to say, and suddenly Dan felt as if he was in the way. He slapped his hands down on the table and stood up slowly. "Well, guess I'll hit the sack."

Issie sprang to her feet, as if she didn't want to be left alone with Nick. "Me, too. I gotta go. See you both later."

She headed out as quickly as she'd come in, and Nick's eyes followed her to the door. "She's not going home," he said when the door had closed. "She's going to Joe's Place."

Dan sat back down. "Why do you say that?"

"Because that's what she does. That's where she goes every night when she gets off at eleven."

"How do you know?"

"I've seen her go there."

Dan stared at him, trying to evaluate why that would matter to him so. "She's a big girl. Makes her own choices."

"Yeah, I know," Nick said. "But I wish she wouldn't, because they hurt her."

Now, Dan's eyes narrowed, and he half-grinned at his preacher. "Nick, you're not interested in her, are you?"

Nick looked down at his Bible again, and stared at the words as if he was reading, but Dan knew better. The question was probably circling around in his mind, and he was framing it, trying to figure out how to answer . . . probably searching his soul for the truth, because he didn't know, himself. Finally, Nick looked up at him. "I can't be interested in her, Dan. But I do have a real burden for her. She's lost and unhappy, and she constantly gets herself into situations that get her into trouble. I worry about her."

"You know, it's not your job to be the caretaker of the whole world. That's God's job."

"I really do know that," Nick said. "But she's a special case."

"Why? Because she's good-looking?"

"No," Nick said. "Because she seems like such a sad person."

Dan made a face. "She doesn't seem that sad to me."

"That's because you don't know her that well."

He breathed a laugh. "And you do? You two could hardly look each other in the eye."

Nick looked at him as if he couldn't believe he'd said that. "That isn't true."

"It *is* true. If I didn't know better, I'd think you two had a crush on each other."

Nick laughed out loud, but it seemed a little overdone. "The last person in the world Issie would ever get involved with is a preacher. It's not just us Christians who don't want to be unequally yoked, you know. The unbelievers aren't real crazy about it, either. You're lucky, you know," Nick said. "You and Jill, you start off with a lot going for you. You care about the same things. You both want to be fruitful for God. You care about how he sees you. You'll both make Christ the center of your relationship. If you two got married, you'd start off way ahead of the game already."

"You act like we're engaged."

Nick stared into him. "Well, haven't you thought about it?"

Dan didn't want to answer that. It made him real uncomfortable. He shifted in his seat. "We're a long way from that."

"Oh. My mistake. I thought you two were getting along real well."

"Well, you don't marry someone just because you get along real well. At least you shouldn't. I mean, there has to be more to it, doesn't there? There has to be a lot of trust."

"You don't trust Jill?" Nick asked.

Dan rolled his eyes. "Oh, come on. Of course I do. But maybe not in that way. Not enough to know that she'll stay with me for the rest of my life."

"What about yourself? Do you trust *yourself* to stay with her for the rest of your life?"

Dan shook his head. "I don't know. I honestly don't."

"Are you thinking about it?" Nick asked.

Dan rubbed the stubble on his face. "Maybe. But this covenant stuff kind of got me thinking. It's pretty serious stuff . . . that two-becoming-one business. I don't think most Christians realize how serious it is."

"I'd say you're right."

"I mean, if they realized that marriage really is a covenant . . . and it's binding and can't be broken without ripping—"

The telephone rang suddenly and Dan jumped. He realized he was tense, perspiring. Did the subject get under his skin that much? Thankfully, he got up and answered the phone on the wall. "Midtown Station."

"Dan, is that you?" He recognized the voice of Lisa Manning, one of the women he'd taken out a time or two before Jill.

"Hey, Lisa. What's up?" He noticed that Nick looked accusingly up at him, as if Dan had solicited the call.

"I hate to call so late," she said. "But I figured you'd still be up. I have to go to this big dinner tomorrow night. One of those coat and tie functions, and I thought it was a shame to get all dressed up and not have a date."

He felt his muscles tightening. It was getting hotter in the room. He wondered if something was wrong with the air conditioning. He turned his back to Nick.

"So what do you say?" she asked. "You want to go as my date, or not?"

He breathed out a hard sigh. "I don't think I'd better, Lisa."

"You busy?" she asked.

He glanced back at Nick. The preacher wasn't hiding the fact that he was listening. "Yeah."

"Oh, I get it," she said. "It's Jill Clark, isn't it? Are you two on again?"

"You might say that."

"I heard you were with her when you had your accident the other night."

"Bad news travels fast."

"It's a small town. She's bringing you bad luck, you know."

Dan laughed. "I don't believe in luck." He glanced at Nick again, hoping that would please him.

"So you two are an item?"

"I don't know," he said. "I mean . . . I'm not sure. I just . . . don't think I can go tomorrow night."

The back door opened and Mark came in. Apparently, he'd been in the backyard of the station, talking on his cell phone, probably to Allie. Dan felt suddenly self-conscious. "Uh . . . thanks for the invitation, though."

"No problem," she said. "I'll just find somebody else."

"All right. Thanks for calling."

He hung up and turned back to Nick and Mark as they both stared at him. "Who is that?" Mark asked.

Dan started to tell them they needed a hobby, that his life didn't need to be their sole source of entertainment, but he knew that was a little defensive. "It was Lisa Manning."

"Lisa Manning?" Mark asked. "What did *she* want?"

"She asked Dan out," Nick said.

"Thanks a lot," Dan shot back.

"Are you going?"

"Of course not." He pulled his towel from around his neck. "You know, I appreciate your concern, but you're not Jill's caretaker just because she's staying at your house." He walked away.

Mark frowned. "Jill's not staying at our house. At least, not tonight."

Dan turned back around. "What do you mean? Where is she?"

"She's staying in a hotel. Didn't she tell you?"

"No!" he said, his face reddening. "I just talked to her a little while ago."

"What did you do? Call her cell phone?"

"Well, yeah, after Allie told me to. I assumed she was there and just didn't want to tie up your line or something."

"She wasn't there. She was in a hotel."

Dan slammed his hand into the wall. "What in the world would possess her to do that? She knows this guy's still after her."

"She hired a guard to sit outside her room. It's okay."

"No, it's not okay," he said. "She's in danger."

"She said she needed to do some research for the case. She needed to be alone so she could focus. Something about the Bible."

"Why didn't she tell me she wasn't at your house?"

"Calm down," Nick said, coming to his feet. "Maybe there's a logical explanation."

"There's no excuse for her lying to me."

"*Did* she lie to you?" Mark asked. "Did she ever say she was at our house?"

"No," Dan said. "But she knew I thought she was still there, and she didn't tell me. To me that was lying." His face was crimson, and he headed for the phone and jerked it up. He jabbed out Jill's number.

"Hello?"

"Why didn't you tell me you were in a hotel room?"

There was a long pause. "Dan, I just didn't want you to worry. I knew you'd overreact."

"Overreact?" he asked. "Because I care about you? Because I'm looking out for you? You said you like that, that you didn't want me to stop."

"Dan, I have a guard right outside the door. Nobody can get past him."

"Unless he blows him away! Jill, you're a sitting duck for this guy!"

"I'm a sitting duck no matter where I am. I needed to be alone tonight, Dan. I needed some time to read about covenant and figure out what's going on with Jerry and Frank Harper. I needed some time to pray. I knew you wouldn't understand."

"You knew I wouldn't understand?" Dan repeated, incredulous. "Just because I don't approve means I'm so dense that I can't understand?"

"That's not what I meant, and you know it."

"I can't believe you'd lie to me!"

"I didn't lie. I just didn't tell you where I was. It didn't come up."

"So, let me get this straight," Dan said. "Just because I didn't think to ask you if you'd moved in the last twenty-four hours . . . Excuse me if I misinterpreted our relationship to be close enough that you, at least, told me where you slept at night."

"Dan, you're blowing this way out of proportion. This really has nothing to do with you."

"Oh, well, thanks a lot. Guess that puts me in my place." He slammed the phone down and pressed his forehead against it.

"That didn't go well, did it?" Mark asked.

Dan shot him a piercing look.

"Man, I'm sorry I started all this. I wouldn't have said anything if I'd known—"

"That she lied to me?" he asked. "No problem. You know why? Because there are other fish in the sea." He picked up the phone and began to dial again. "Lisa Manning is one of them."

"Man, don't do it." But Dan kept dialing. "Dan, you're making a big mistake."

Dan swung around. "Don't tell me what I'm doing. She's putting her life in danger, and she doesn't care what I think about it. She lied to me to keep me from reacting, and I'm not even important enough for her to consult about this at all."

"She doesn't have to consult with you, Dan! You're not married."

"We're not going to be, either."

"Dan, you can't run every time she disappoints you."

"This is the last time she's gonna disappoint me," he said.

Lisa answered the phone, and he snapped, "Yeah, Lisa. Listen, about that invitation. I think I will take you up on it."

"Good. Pick me up at seven."

"You pick me up," he countered. "I may not have a car yet."

"All right," she said. "I'll see you then."

When he hung up the phone, he turned back to his two friends. "Don't say a word," he said. "Jill Clark doesn't care about me or my feelings, so I'm not going to care about hers."

He started to storm away, but Mark grabbed his arm. "What are you doing?"

"What do you mean, what am I doing? You heard me."

"Are you and Jill still an item, or not?"

"I don't know."

"Well, who would know?" Mark asked sarcastically.

"Apparently, you!" Dan said. "Why don't you tell me?"

"I think you are an item, but that self-destructive part of you that is scared to death of a committed relationship is looking for the slightest little excuse to call it off. You pump iron until you look like Arnold Schwarzenegger, jog five miles a day, comb your hair every time you pass a mirror . . . But you're your own worst enemy. You sabotage yourself the minute things start going right for you. It's like part of you doesn't *want* to be happy."

"I don't need you playing shrink on me, Mark."

"All right, then," Mark said, glancing at Nick. "Then let Nick tell you. Tell him, Nick. You're his pastor. He'll listen to you."

"Oh, brother . . ." Dan said.

Nick got up and set his foot on a chair. "Dan, you were just talking about not trusting yourself with that kind of commitment. From the looks of things, you were right."

"Great," Dan said. "So much for pastor confidentiality. You two are amazing." He started to leave the room, then turned back to them. "Get this straight. I'm not going out with Lisa Manning because I'm so weak that I can't help straying. I'm going to make a point."

"To Jill, or to yourself?" Mark asked.

"Maybe both of us," he said. "If our relationship is so superficial that she doesn't even tell me when she's walking into the line of fire, then it's too superficial for us to have an exclusive relationship."

Mark's voice dripped with sarcasm. "You'll show her."

Dan went back to the weight room and began to pump iron with a vengeance.

Chapter Fifty-Four

The van that Frank Harper had stolen after Dan's car went off the bridge was found in Slidell's Piggly Wiggly parking lot that night, after the Civic was reported missing. It belonged to one of the employees inside, and he was distraught, cursing and pacing, as the police took the report. There were no witnesses who had seen the thief.

When someone from the Slidell Police Department learned that the van had been stolen from a campsite near the I-10 bridge, he called Stan Shepherd to tell him that the thief was probably Frank Harper himself, and that it was highly likely that he was driving a green Civic.

Stan put an APB out, alerting all the cops on duty in several surrounding counties that the killer may be in a green Civic. And as he cruised the town in his unmarked car, trying to think like an insane terrorist, he racked his brain for where Frank Harper might be.

He went to every motel in town and showed Frank's picture, asked if anyone had seen him. No one had. He cruised the parking lots of Delchamps, the Newpointe Library, the Bonaparte Court Apartments, the Bijoux movie theatre, looking for the stolen green Civic, but found nothing.

Where was this guy? What was he up to? Who was he going to try to kill tonight?

Around ten o'clock, he called home to check on Celia. "Hey, babe. Were you in bed?"

"No," she said. "I'm cleaning out the closets."

"Cleaning the closets? Why?"

"It needed doing. I want the house to be clean when we bring the baby home."

"But we still have two weeks."

"Maybe, maybe not."

He frowned. He had heard that women had a burst of energy before they went into labor, that they often got into a cleaning spree that was almost obsessive compulsive. "You're not nesting, are you?"

"Probably," she said, "but don't worry about it. It doesn't mean anything."

"You know, they say that you're supposed to get as much rest as you can, even if you don't feel like it, because if you do go into labor, you'll wind up being too tired to deliver."

"And what?" she asked, amused. "I'll have to carry the baby the rest of my life? Stan, honey, this baby is coming whether I'm tired or not."

"You still need your rest. Our closets are clean enough."

"Okay. I'll go to bed. When are you coming home?"

Before he could answer, he got a call on the radio. "Hold on," he said, and turned it up. Slidell police had spotted the Civic at a parking lot when they'd been called about another car theft. "What kind of car was stolen this time?" he asked.

"A maroon Cavalier," the dispatcher told him. "Tag number's SEW 365."

Quickly, Stan put an APB out on the maroon Cavalier and alerted all available police that Frank Harper was driving it and that he could be armed and dangerous. He picked the phone back up. "Honey, it's gonna be a while before I can get home. You just call me if you need me. I'll keep the phone on. And go to bed, will you?"

"Okay," she said. "I promise."

He clicked off the phone and drove past Jill's house. Nothing there. Then he drove to Debbie Ingalls's place. She still wasn't home.

An uneasy sense of having no control plagued him as he drove. Something was going to happen tonight. He could feel it. He only hoped he could stop it before it was too late.

Chapter Fifty-Five

Jill hadn't slept at all that night. Despite her need for rest, Dan's words tumbled through her mind. By the time she'd checked out of the hotel the next morning, paid T.J. Porter, and headed for the jail, she looked as exhausted as she felt. She had dark circles under her eyes, but she had applied her makeup to hide it.

Still, Jerry noticed right away. "You look like you didn't get much sleep last night," he said. "Have you been crying?"

"No," she lied. "I was just up late reading about covenant."

His eyebrows shot up. "Really? You read about covenant? Everything about it?"

"Everything I could find," she said. She sat down wearily and looked up at him. "But there's something I don't understand. You said something about the Gideonites. I looked and looked and I didn't see anything about the Gideonites having to do with covenant."

"No," he said. "Not the Gideonites. The Gibeonites."

"Who are they?"

She could see that Jerry was a born teacher. He leaned forward, and his face came alive. "Just before Joshua led the Israelites into the Promised Land, God told them not to make a covenant with anybody, and to destroy all of the people in the cities of the Promised Land. So the Gibeonites, who lived in the Promised Land, decided to trick the Israelites into entering into covenant with them. They got old wineskins and old clothes and dried pieces of bread, and made it look like they had come from a long way away to make covenant with them. They knew if the Israelites knew they were from the Promised Land, they'd never make covenant with them. So they lied. Joshua didn't consult God, and he fell for it. The Israelites entered into covenant with them, and it was binding."

"But it was deceitful, " she said. "If they were tricked, they wouldn't have to keep the covenant, would they?"

"Oh, but they did," Jerry said. "If you read about it you'll see that's exactly what happened. When they found out the Gibeonites just lived around the corner, they realized they'd been had. But the covenant itself meant more than the deceit. They had to honor it. When the Gibeonites were attacked by the Amorites, they called on the Israelites, and they had to defend them. So that tells me that it doesn't matter if one per-son deceives you in covenant, or if they break it. Regardless, you're obligated for your side of the bargain. There's another example of that, with Jacob and Leah. He worked seven years so he could marry Rachel, but after the wedding he found out he'd been had. Was the covenant he'd made with Leah broken? Nope. He had to honor that covenant."

"Okay," Jill said, trying to understand. "So even though Frank Harper is a maniac and is going around targeting people at random, including your family, who is part of your covenant with him . . . you still have to keep your part of the covenant. Is that what you're saying?"

Now Jerry looked confused, and he slumped back in his chair. "No. That's not what I'm saying. My covenant with my wife is more important than that. But I've talked to her and she sounds like she's in good hands. And you know who blew up the post office, so I'm not keeping anything from you."

Jill rubbed her temples. They were beginning to ache. She was bone-tired, and her soul felt bruised. "All right, Jerry. Just a few more questions. I'm curious. You told me that you didn't become a Christian until after Vietnam, when you were in jail. So how did you have such a strong feeling about covenant before you even knew God?"

Jerry sat straight again. "See, Frank is a messianic Jew."

Jill frowned. "What do you mean? A Christian? Are you trying to tell me Frank Harper is a *Christian?*"

"That's right."

"No way!" She got to her feet and shook her head viciously. "Oh, no way! You've got some real distorted view of Christianity if you expect me to believe that a terrorist could be a Christian. A cold-blooded killer? The violent person who was chasing me on the causeway?"

"He's mentally ill, Jill. He's not himself."

"So . . . before this . . . this mine or whatever it was . . . he was a real Christian? A Jewish Christian?"

"Well, he was half Jewish. His mother was a Jew. He knew all about covenant. I did believe in God and I believed God punished people for breaking his laws. Frank taught me about the gravity of covenant, and about his covenant with Christ. He was very devout then. A great influence. He impacted so many people. I didn't accept Christ then, but he laid the groundwork in me. Later, when things changed for him, I couldn't forget that."

She didn't want to think that the same Christ who loved her also loved Frank Harper. She didn't want to think he had the same access to God that she had. "I'm sorry, but this is a little much."

"I don't know how God holds the mentally ill accountable," Jerry said. "All I know is that before he got blown up trying to save me, he loved Jesus. He hasn't been right since, but I think God must make allowance for that."

She felt sick again. She rubbed her eyes, unable to comprehend all of this. Since she couldn't grasp it, she decided to switch gears. She opened her briefcase. "Jerry, I'm going to do my best to represent you at the arraignment this morning, but they're not going to release you."

"I realize that," he said.

"Unless you intend to tell them about Frank Harper. Then maybe there's a chance they would be lenient . . ."

"I'm sure you've already told them," he said.

"But it would mean so much more coming from you. If you could just tell them the truth about how things worked, how you wound up at the post office, how you wound up at the Flagstaff."

"I can't do that," he said.

She slammed her hand on the table. "Why not? They need to know how Frank got you involved, Jerry. They need to know why your pickup was there, why you took a hostage, why he went after Cliff Bertrand."

"No, they don't. They only need his name, and they didn't get it from me. When he hears about it on the news, he won't hear that I spilled my guts. Maybe he'll realize I didn't tell them."

"Jerry, what difference does it make if you did? He knows his picture and name are all over the news."

"It makes a difference because he'll go after my family again if he thinks I broke covenant! He isn't sane, Jill. He isn't rational. I'm trying to protect my family!"

As frustrated as that left her, she knew she couldn't argue with his logic. She wasn't sure that he wasn't absolutely right. Unable to go on, she closed her briefcase, told him she would meet him in court, and left the room.

While she waited for court to convene, she went into the bathroom, pulled her phone out, and tried to call Dan. But there was no answer. She called Allie to see if Mark was off duty yet and if he knew where Dan was.

"No, he may be trying to get something worked out about replacing his car," Allie said.

Jill sighed. "We kind of got into a fight last night about my staying in the hotel. I just wanted to try to talk it out."

Allie was quiet for a moment. "Jill, there's something I need to tell you. I'm your best friend and I'm not going to let you find out about this from someone else."

She fought the urge to hang up. She didn't know how much more she could take. "Find out about what?"

"Jill, last night, Mark said that Dan was so mad at you that he kind of went off the deep end. Lisa Manning asked him to dinner tonight, and he said he'd go."

"He what?" She swallowed hard, trying not to let her emotions get the best of her before she went into court.

"I'm sorry. I don't know what's gotten into him, but the man has so much pride. And apparently, you wounded it when you didn't tell him where you were. So he's going out with Lisa. He's a jerk, Jill. That's all I can say. Just a big jerk."

Jill didn't know how to react. She felt tears pushing to her eyes, but she told herself she couldn't allow it. Not now. Not when she had to go into court and defend Jerry Ingalls.

"Well, I guess that speaks volumes," she managed to say.

"No, I don't think it does," Allie said. "Don't give up on him. I'm sure it's just an overreaction."

"You just called him a jerk. Which is it?"

"Well, he's a jerk that overreacts. Come on, Jill. I really like the two of you together. If you got married, we'd be best friends married to best friends. Don't let this ruin my dreams."

She knew Allie was teasing her, trying to make her laugh, but there didn't seem to be any mirth left in her. "You know, he can go out with anybody he wants. We don't have an understanding or anything. We're not engaged, for heaven's sake. We're not even going steady ... or whatever they're calling it now." Her voice wobbled as she spoke, and she tried to steady it.

"Jill, I know you're hurt."

She squeezed her eyes shut as tears pushed out. She wouldn't be taking this so hard, she told herself, if she had slept last night. And she would have slept last night if she hadn't taken her fight with Dan so hard.

For a moment, she didn't answer. "I thought we had something. How stupid." She pinched her tear ducts, trying to stop the tears. Taking a deep breath, she said, "Look, I've got to go to court."

"Are you okay, Jill?"

"I'm as okay as I've ever been. You know me. I always land on my feet. Knock me down, I bounce right back up."

"Like one of those Weebles? You wobble but you don't fall down?"

Allie was still trying to get a smile out of her, but she didn't think she had one in her. "Yeah, something like that." Her voice cracked with every word. "I'll talk to you later, Allie."

She hung up the phone and leaned over the sink to splash water on her face. She tore a paper towel out of its dispenser and blotted her face as she looked in the mirror. Why had she ever believed she could hold someone like Dan Nichols? He needed someone like Lisa Manning, someone beautiful, young ...

Forcing her thoughts back to Jerry Ingalls, she grabbed her briefcase up and left the bathroom, determined not to think about Dan Nichols again for the rest of the day.

Chapter Fifty-Six

Stan got up early the next morning and drove to Jackson, to the Veterans Administration Hospital where Frank Harper had been a patient for so many years. Some of the FBI agents who were working with him on the case were waiting for him there. They had already cleared it with the administrator to search Frank's room.

Stan didn't know what he had expected, but the men on the ward looked relatively normal. He and the other agents came in, and an orderly pointed them to the bed Frank Harper had used. Next to it was a locker, and they opened it and saw dozens of articles taped to the inside walls, articles about Waco and Oklahoma City, and the Unabomber, ads for survivalist gear and articles about conspiracies in the government. They found handwritten manuscripts, pages and pages of the same theme. Frank Harper thought he was a prisoner of war, and believed communism had infiltrated the government. The FBI agents took the contents of the locker for evidence. As they tagged and bagged it, they ran across an address book. Jerry Ingalls's name was written in red ink with several tally marks beside it.

"Wonder what the tally marks are?" one of the agents said.

The psychologist who had worked with Frank for years had led them to his bed, and he stood back, out of the way, as they worked. "Can I take a look?" he asked the agent.

The agent showed him the marks. "That's the number of times he visited him," he said. "He kept score of who came and talked a lot about how only one of the men he saved kept in touch anymore."

The agent counted the tally marks. "He came fifteen times. Over how long?"

"Years," the doctor said. "There's no telling how long. But he trusted this Ingalls guy because of that."

"Maybe that's why he went to Newpointe and got Ingalls involved," Stan said. "He was the only one he trusted."

"So now that Ingalls is locked up," Stan asked, "where else could he be?"

Chapter Fifty-Seven

Jerry had a tearful reunion with Debbie in court before he pled not guilty. The judge accepted the plea, but denied Jill's request to send him home pending trial. It was as Jill had expected, but she still felt like a failure as they led him out of the courtroom.

When Debbie had left, Jill went back across the street to the police station, and saw Stan driving up. He was beginning to look as tired as she.

"Stan, have you found Frank Harper yet?" she asked.

He shook his head and led her into the station. "We found his trail. We know he's been in New Orleans, and there's evidence that he's been in Newpointe and Slidell, but we haven't been able to find him yet. We think he's driving a maroon Cavalier, but he's changing cars every few hours, so there's no telling."

"You've got to find him," Jill said. "Stan, he's ruining my life. Please." Her voice broke off, and she covered her face, desperately trying to hide the emotion. "I can't go home, I can't go to my office . . ."

He looked at her with surprise, then took her arm and led her to his desk. Urging her to sit down, he asked, "Jill, are you all right?"

Jill realized she was losing her professionalism. She had never done this before. "Yes, I'm all right." She wiped at the tears falling, and shook her head. "I don't know what's wrong with me. I just—"

Stan handed her a box of Kleenex. "Jill, you've been under a lot of pressure. This would be stressful for anybody. You may even have a little touch of post-traumatic stress disorder."

"Give me a break," she said, jerking a Kleenex out of the box and wiping her nose. "I'm fine, I told you."

"You don't look fine."

"Are you speaking as a detective? Collecting clues?"

"No," he said. He got up from his desk and came around to take her arm. Gently, he pulled her to her feet. "I'm speaking as your friend. Come on, let's go to the interrogation room so we can have a little privacy, and you can tell me what's got you so upset."

She didn't object, just allowed him to usher her into the room. When he closed the door behind them, she sank miserably into a chair. Stan leaned on the edge of the table and looked down at her. "So what's going on, Jill? I've known you to have all sorts of run-ins with danger, but I don't think I've ever seen you like this. Is it Dan?"

She shook her head, but her face belied her denial. Finally, she realized that there was no use denying it. She was as transparent as glass, and she felt that everyone saw clearly what was in her heart—good and bad. "Last night I had this great prayer time, and I came to understand God on a deeper level than I ever have before. And today, everything's falling apart. This case is cutting into my relationship with Dan," she said. "It's ruining everything."

"What is?" he asked.

"The fact that somebody's trying to kill me. It kind of throws a wet blanket on my mood."

Stan smiled. "So you think Dan's going to quit seeing you because of your mood?"

"I'm not any fun!" she shouted. "I'm high maintenance. Too much trouble."

"Wait," Stan said, holding up a hand to make her back up. "Has Dan told you this? Because he doesn't seem like the party animal type to me, and he's not that shallow. In fact, the Dan I know has been more interested in you *since* Jerry Ingalls took you hostage. I haven't seen him backing off because it put you in a bad mood."

She got up and shook her head, as if he could never understand. "I'm constantly butting heads with him. It's like he thinks I'm suicidal, like I'm going to throw myself in front of a bus, just to get that adrenaline rush."

"Dan is not that unreasonable," Stan said. "Jill, have you and Dan had a fight? Have you broken up again?"

She laughed hard, though there was no humor in it. "It's worse than that. It's gone past fighting to indifference. He's got another date tonight."

Stan frowned. "I find that hard to believe."

"Well, believe it," Jill said. "He's going out with Lisa Manning."

Stan's face went slack. "Lisa Manning? She's not his type at all."

"*Au contraire*," she said. "He obviously likes her better than me." She covered her face, hating herself for exposing her feelings this way. "Oh, Stan, look at me. I've never acted with anything less than total professionalism with you, and here I am falling apart like some kind of lovesick teenager. It's so stupid! I hate myself for this."

"Jill, you're too hard on yourself. I'm not just a cop you butt heads with. I'm your friend. Your brother in Christ. And I do happen to be your deacon, so technically, it's very normal for you to come to me with your problems." He hesitated as she looked hopefully up at him, then he felt suddenly inadequate. "The thing is, I don't have a clue what to tell you."

She couldn't help laughing through her tears. Poor Stan. He'd never bargained for any of this. He'd just been in the wrong place at the wrong time.

"Have you tried talking to Dan?"

"He's not answering my calls," she said. "And last night he was really upset. I think he's finished with me."

"Then he's not worthy of you."

"Right."

Stan looked down at the floor, as if racking his brain for wisdom. "Well . . . he's not. If he takes off at the slightest little thing . . ."

The door flew open just then, startling them both, and Sid Ford stuck his head in. "Stan, Celia's on the phone. I think it's an emergency."

"Excuse me," Stan said and dashed back to his desk. Jill followed, wiping her face.

"Celia?" he asked. "Honey, are you all right? Really? Are you sure? No, no, I'll be right there. Can you wait? Do you need an ambulance?"

Jill forgot her own problems. Her heart began to pound. Celia was in labor.

Stan slammed down the phone and yelled out, "We're having a baby!" Then he grabbed his keys and ran out of the building without another word.

Jill began to laugh as she watched him. Then her laughter melted into more tears, as she realized that the whole world was rotating and moving and changing all the time. But it was all passing her by. Friends were marrying, having babies, buying homes, saving for college . . . And the only relationship she'd ever had with that kind of potential had just slipped through her fingers.

She thought of going to the hospital with them to get her mind off of Dan, but she knew it was no use. Celia would probably be in labor for hours, and she would just be in the way. No, she didn't belong there. She didn't really belong anywhere.

Feeling safer in the police station than anywhere else, she asked to borrow the phone at one of the empty desks. She called Sheila for her messages, then spent the next couple of hours returning calls, realizing that she was just marking time, waiting for the minutes to pass.

She wished with all her heart that she could go home, but she couldn't. Mark and Allie's was the closest to home she could go tonight. And as soon as she could pull herself together, that was exactly where she would go.

Chapter Fifty-Eight

A storm was moving in as Jill headed out to her car, and black clouds darkened the sky. Any minute, it would begin to rain. It would pound down on Dan and Lisa on their date, she thought, and if there was any justice, they would have forgotten their umbrellas. Lisa would get drenched and look like a wet cocker spaniel.

With her remote key, she clicked "unlock," and saw the light inside the car come on. She opened the back door and dropped her briefcase on the seat.

"Jill!"

She turned around and saw Nick standing in the truck bay at the fire station next door. She closed her door and headed across the lawn. "Hey, Nick. Don't you ever leave this place?"

Nick shrugged. "For some reason, we single guys are the ones they call when they want to trade shifts." He bent down and looked into her red, bloodshot eyes. "You've been crying."

"No, I haven't," she lied. "Why do you say that?"

"The Dan thing," he said. "I've been praying for you."

She rolled her eyes and looked away. "I guess everybody knows. He didn't even bother to tell me himself."

"I know. I'm sorry, Jill. But if it's any consolation, he's a miserable man right now."

She looked up at her preacher. "Yeah, that is some consolation. He deserves to be miserable."

Nick gave her a wry grin, but she couldn't seem to return it. "Don't give up on him."

"He gave up on me," she said.

"He's a complicated guy. Just hang in there. I still think you two are meant for each other."

"Whatever," she said. "Thanks for the encouragement, anyway."

"But you're not encouraged."

Tears came to her eyes again. "It's been a long few days." She choked back the emotion in her throat. "I'll see you later."

She crossed the lawn to her car. A mud-splattered pickup truck passed her as she got in, and she closed the door and started the car. The truck pulled to the side of the road as soon as she got behind him. He honked at her, and she wondered if she had done something to make him angry. Were her bright lights on? She checked and saw that she had not even turned her lights on. She passed him feeling uneasy. He pulled out behind her, tailgating her and honking and flashing his lights. A chill went through her.

Frank Harper had found her.

She slammed her foot on the accelerator and flew around the corner and into the left lane, almost hitting another car. The truck pulled up beside her, still honking and weaving, and she saw the man behind the wheel motioning to her to pull over. He didn't look like the pictures she'd seen of Frank—no beard, shorter hair—but he looked crazed, and that was enough for her. His eyes were wild and his teeth were bared, and his mouth moved in vicious dialogue as he tried to make her stop.

She made a quick left turn, and the truck cut across a busy lane of traffic and followed.

Trembling, she groped for her cell phone. She found it and pressed 911 with her thumb, then pressed *send*. The phone only beeped. She glanced down and saw the words "Low Battery" displayed on the small screen.

The truck bumped her, just like on the bridge, and she almost ran into the opposite lane of traffic. She crossed in front of him and got in the right lane, and again, he bumped her, trying to run her off the road.

She wove in and out of traffic, trying to decide what to do, but the truck stayed with her, weaving and honking and bumping her, trying to run her onto the shoulder. He didn't care who saw him, she thought. Cars were stopping and pulling off the road, and drivers were cursing and yelling as they flew by them. She skidded around a corner, and the truck came after her.

She had to find people out of their cars, she thought, people who could protect her. She had to drive into a well-lit area where lots of people were, and run for help. But her fear of stopping was too great.

The truck made its way up beside her, and the driver waved his hand at her, telling her furiously to pull over, as if the words would force her to comply.

She skidded around another corner, and was back on Jacquard, the main strip through town. But the traffic and visibility didn't stop him. He kept bumping her, urging her off the road, and she realized with a chill that he wasn't going to give up, and she couldn't lose him. She saw him reach under his seat, and he came up with a gun, waved it at her. She swallowed back a scream. Any minute now he would start shooting.

Not knowing what else to do, she skidded into the parking lot of a convenience store where several people stood outside at the gas pumps. She swerved to a stop, then threw the door open and ran for the door. The truck slid to a halt behind her, and the driver stumbled out.

Patricia Castor, the mayor, was inside paying for gas. She looked up as Jill bolted through the door.

"Help me!" Jill screamed. "He's after me! Please!"

The mayor pulled her into her arms, but her surprised eyes were locked on something outside the door.

"Call the police!" Jill screamed. "Hurry! That man—" She pointed out the doors, and saw the man from the truck. He wasn't running, and he wasn't coming in after her. Instead, with his gun in one hand, he opened her back car door and reached in, and jerked a man out of her backseat. It was Frank Harper.

Jill started screaming. He had been in her car. Frank Harper had been close enough to cut her throat, but that man . . . that truck driver . . . had stopped him. She couldn't stop screaming, and Pat Castor tried to calm her down. Outside, the men were struggling. Frank Harper knocked the gun out of his hand. He swung his right fist across the trucker's jaw, knocking him back, and took off running.

Jill bolted through the doors. "Catch him!" she screamed. "That's Frank Harper! Don't let him get away!"

A squad car pulled up with its siren on and lights flashing. Someone witnessing the traffic violations had probably called him, she thought, and R.J. Albright jumped out. "What's goin' on here?"

"R.J., go after him! Please, go after him. Frank Harper . . . He was . . . in my car . . . my backseat . . ."

R.J. ran back to his car and radioed for help.

The truck driver's lip was bleeding, and he stumbled toward Jill. "Lady, I was trying to tell you. I drove by you when you were getting in your car on Purchase Street, and your light came on and I saw him hunched in your backseat."

She covered her mouth, unable to stand the horror of such a chilling brush with death. "But I put my briefcase in the back-seat. I looked. He wasn't there!" She realized then that she had left the car unlocked as she had talked to Nick. He must have gotten in then. "I thought you were him! You had a gun!"

"I'm a deputy in Ouachita Parish, so I always have a weapon. Ma'am, when you didn't stop, I thought I might have to shoot him myself. I could see him risin' up in the back."

She began to sob, and Pat Castor bustled out. "R.J.," the mayor said, "you go after that man, hear? Don't you let him get away."

"I'm not, ma'am," the chubby officer said. "I've got folks chasin' him down as we speak."

But something about that didn't sound good to Jill. R.J. was too out of shape to chase down a perpetrator, and she feared that too much time had been wasted. Frank Harper was going to get away again.

Chapter Fifty-Nine

Celia's contractions were ten minutes apart, but when Stan got to the house, he had spent half an hour looking for a baby blanket Celia insisted on taking with her. When he'd finally found it, he had hurried her into the car.

Celia didn't seem to understand the urgency as keenly as he did, a fact that baffled him. Didn't she know that this baby was coming with or without that blanket? Didn't she understand that they'd never make it to New Orleans on time if they didn't get on the road *now?* "You know, it's crazy, us taking time to go all the way to New Orleans, when we can be in Slidell in ten or fifteen minutes. I'm calling the doctor and telling him we can't make it."

"Don't you dare!" Celia said. "We *can* make it. We agreed that the latest technology and that neonatal unit were at the New Orleans hospital, and we wanted to make sure we had everything we needed in case of a problem."

"There isn't going to *be* a problem! Everything's great with the baby, so why can't we just—?"

"Stan, my doctor is in New Orleans. And Pete's at the same hospital, so I can check on him. Now, calm down."

His hands trembled as he cranked the car and pulled out of the driveway. He ran over the garbage can, bashed it in, and dragged it several feet before it rolled out from under the car.

"Stan, are you all right? Do you want me to drive?"

He shot her a disgusted look. "You can't drive. You're in too much pain. No, I'm fine."

"Actually, I'm not having that much pain yet."

"Then why are you sweating?"

"Because you haven't turned the air conditioner on."

He caught his breath and cut it on, then aimed the vent at her. "Is that good?"

"Fine," she said. "Uh, Stan, you're running a red light!"

He slammed on the brakes, almost sending her through the windshield. "I'm sorry, honey!"

"Stan, you may be a little too nervous to drive. Why don't you just let me?"

"I'll calm down," he said, panting. "I'll do better."

He turned on the radio, a classical station from New Orleans, hoping the music would calm him down. "They say Mozart makes babies more intelligent. I heard that in some states they give every mother a Mozart tape to take home from the hospital with her."

"Is that Mozart?" she asked.

He shrugged. "I have no idea. But it sounds good, doesn't it?"

She smiled. "Yes. It does." She reached across and took his hand.

They heard a siren pulling out of Purchase Street, and Stan quickly turned off the radio and cut on his scanner. He focused immediately on what was going on. Frank Harper had been seen at a convenience store on the corner of Jacquard and Clearview, but he got away. They were combing the woods, trying to catch him.

"They're gonna get him!" he shouted, then shot her an apologetic look. "I'm sorry, sweetheart. I didn't mean to yell."

She was still sweating, and leaning her head back on the seat. "You need to go there, don't you?"

"Go where? Don't be silly. We're going to the hospital."

"But this guy ... you need to catch him. You know, you could turn around and go back to Aunt Aggie's, and she could take me.

It's probably going to be hours before I actually have the baby. By then you could lock this guy up and get to the hospital in time."

He hesitated a moment, giving that some serious thought. What he wouldn't give to be there when they caught Frank Harper. What if they weren't thorough and he got away? What if they didn't catch him?

Then he realized that worse than that would be missing the birth of his baby. No, he thought. He wouldn't turn back now. "There's nothing in the world that would make me turn back now. Not even the chance to wrap up this case."

"Are you sure? I really would understand."

He turned off the scanner and touched her stomach. He felt it slowly tightening as she entered a contraction. His baby would be here before the day was out. Suddenly, his heart soared joyfully, and he couldn't wait to hold it in his arms.

"I've never been more sure of anything," he said.

Chapter Sixty

The moment Lisa came to pick him up, Dan realized what a mistake he was making. The dark clouds in the sky gave him a foreboding sense of doom, as if this date was a mistake he would soon regret. He wasn't in the mood, didn't even like the idea of riding in the car with her, much less going to a dinner as her date. He didn't want to act charming or funny; he didn't want to laugh at her jokes, or tell her she looked nice.

They got to the dinner and were seated at a table of ten people. Then he realized what an idiot he was. His very presence here was a nail in the coffin of his relationship with Jill. What had he been thinking? Conversations abounded around him, and every now and then Lisa would look back at him and ask, "Are you all right?"

"Yeah," he'd say, irritated. "I'm fine." He was getting tired of her asking, but he supposed he didn't blame her. She wasn't being forced to go out with him, after all. If he hadn't accepted, she would have found someone else, and she would have had a better time.

He tried to concentrate on his food, but wound up just stirring it around on his plate, wondering where Jill was staying tonight, hoping she wasn't alone somewhere, hoping that she wasn't in danger. And then he realized that she *was* in danger, that Frank Harper could walk right into that hotel, shoot down the guard, bust through her door, and take her life before she even had a chance to react. His stomach tightened and his eyes misted over at the thought of that. Then how would he feel?

Vindicated, because he'd been right? Validated, because she'd deserved it?

She didn't deserve it. Nobody deserved it. He didn't deserve it, either. Yet he was doing this to himself. Instead, he could have been spending this evening with her, keeping her out of harm's way. Instead, he was sitting here with another woman, realizing what a cowardly jerk he was. He made himself sick.

He looked over at Lisa. "Uh . . . I need to make a phone call. I'll be right back."

She nodded as if she couldn't care less. He didn't blame her. As a date, he was sadly lacking tonight. But he couldn't help himself. He got up, went to the foyer, and found a pay phone. He deposited the coins and quickly dialed Jill's cell phone.

A recording came on. "The cellular customer you are trying to reach is not available at this time."

He slammed the phone down. She was trying to avoid him. He was sure Allie or Mark had told her about the date by now. Did he blame her for avoiding him? No, he didn't, he thought. But if she was avoiding him, why had she tried all day to call him? Maybe *his* avoidance of *her* had made her so angry that she'd given up on him entirely. What had he expected?

He dug some more coins out of his pocket, deposited them into the phone, then quickly dialed Mark and Allie's number.

"Hello?" It was Allie.

"Allie, is Jill there?"

Allie hesitated. "I thought you were having dinner with Lisa Manning."

"Allie, please let me talk to Jill."

"I didn't say she was here."

He didn't like the taunting tone in her voice. "Is she, or isn't she?"

"What do you care?" Allie asked.

"I *care*," he said. "That's why I'm calling. Please. Is she there or not?"

"You know, if you ever wanted a relationship with her, this is not the way to do it, Dan."

He tried to calm himself, and hit his forehead into the phone. "Look, I realize that. But I need to talk to her, okay? She made me really mad last night, but I've been worried about her, and I'm tired of worrying about her when I don't have to. If she would just be more careful and quit doing such stupid things!"

"*She* does such stupid things?" Allie asked. "What about when you went on calls before the doctor cleared you? You're one to talk, Dan."

"Okay, so I do it, too. But it doesn't make it easier when it's the person you're having a relationship with."

"Yeah, tell Jill about it!" Allie said. "But you didn't see her going out with another man just because she couldn't manipulate you into doing everything she wanted."

"Look, I'm not used to the constant struggle. She made me mad and I reacted."

"Well, grow up!" Allie shouted. "It's time you learned how to have a real relationship, and you don't do it by going out with some other woman every time you get mad at the person you care about."

He was sorry he'd called. "Look, if you see Jill, will you please tell her I called, and I'll call back later."

Before she could answer, he slammed the phone down.

Dan went back to the table and took a seat beside his date. She shot him an annoyed look. "Everything okay?"

"Uh ... no," he said, keeping his voice low so he wouldn't embarrass her. "It's not okay, as a matter of fact. I never should have come out with you tonight."

She grunted. "You sure know how to make a girl feel great."

"I'm sorry, but this has nothing to do with you. None of it. But I do have to go."

"Go? You're gonna leave me here?"

"You have your own car," he said. "I'll take a cab. You know a thousand people here. You're not alone."

"Well, sure, but it's a little embarrassing."

"I know," he said. "I'm sorry, but this was really stupid. The whole thing was stupid. I shouldn't have come here with you. I don't know what I was thinking ..."

"All right, then," she snapped. "Go then. I'm sorry I called. You can bet I'll never do it again."

"That's good," he said. "I think that's the best thing."

She looked at him like he was crazy.

"Look, I'm out of here, okay? Thanks for inviting me. And ... I'm really sorry." With that, he was out the door.

Chapter Sixty-One

Frank Harper heard the sirens and knew they were after him. He ran through the woods as fast as he could, determined to do what he did best: survive. But then he heard dogs barking and voices from several different directions. He pulled his shirt off, then flung it into the trees, hoping to slow them down as the dogs came upon it. Then he took off in another direction. But he saw flashlights coming toward him.

Somehow, he had to throw the dogs off. He ran, crouched, then leaped to a high branch and scurried up a tree. He crawled out on one of the strongest branches, then dropped his feet and hung there, swinging. The branch protruded over the bayou, and Spanish moss draped it on either side of him. He swung harder, making sure he had enough momentum to launch directly into the water without touching the ground. The dogs would smell him on the tree, but they wouldn't be able to tell where he'd come out.

He swung and let go, and fell into the warm, muddy water of the bayou. He came up on the opposite bank and ran, crouched down, from bush to bush and tree to tree.

The barking got closer, and he leaped to another branch and pulled himself up. His legs and arms were as strong as a cat's, and he knew that even the dogs couldn't keep up with him.

But then he saw a dozen flashlight beams crossing through the woods, too close to him. They came from all sides, and there were dogs on this side of the bayou, too. He was surrounded, and they were growing closer. His head hit a catalpa nest, and he brushed it off.

He swung again, trying to hit the water again and make a run for it, but the splash sent the dogs into a frenzy, and all of the flashlight beams shone on him. He let out a blood-curdling, torture-chamber yell, then tried to run through the water as its mud bottom pulled and sucked at his feet.

"It's him!" someone cried. "We got him!"

Someone grabbed him and fought him to his knees, the nasty seaweed and skin-sucking mud pulling at him harder. He was handcuffed and jerked to his feet, and someone read him his rights as they dragged him out of the water. All the while, he kept his eyes closed and his face down to his chest, refusing to engage with the enemy. He had been through this before. He knew how to hold his secrets.

Chapter Sixty-Two

Dan called a taxi, and Jacob Baxter, a fireman who moon-lighted with his cab, picked him up. They were halfway down Jacquard when he saw the traffic bottlenecked up ahead. He leaned forward on the seat. "What's going on up there, Jake? You know?"

Jacob rolled down his window and leaned out to get a better look. There were police lights flashing up ahead, and one cop was directing traffic toward a detour. "Don't look like a wreck. Looks like they're all at that convenience store."

"You got a scanner in here?"

"Yeah, but I don't use it with customers in here."

Dan shot him a look. "Turn the thing on, will you?"

Jacob reached under the dash and turned the scanner on, and immediately they heard the police activity. *"Subject has escaped on foot in the wooded area east of Jacquard, south of Le Fleur Boulevard."*

"He got away again? What's the matter with you people?"

"R.J. was first on the scene and claims he didn't go after him because he had to see about Jill Clark."

Dan's hands hit the dashboard. *"Jill?"* He looked at Jacob. "Something's going on with Jill! Let me out here. I'll run the rest of the way."

"But you didn't pay me!"

He reached into his pocket, got his wallet, and threw it at Jacob. "Take what I owe you." Then he took off, running between cars, zigzagging in and out of bottlenecked traffic, trying to get closer to the convenience store that seemed to be at the center of the crisis.

"You forgot your wallet!" Jacob yelled out the window. "Dan!"

But Dan ignored him, reached the yellow line at the center of the road, and began to run as fast as he could.

He reached the block that was roped off and jumped the crime scene tape. An ambulance was on the scene, its lights flashing, and he saw Sid Ford standing at the back of it as they loaded someone in.

His heart threatened to leap out of his chest as he tore around the ambulance. "Jill! Where's Jill?"

He saw that the person on the gurney was a big, burly man with a bloody nose, and he turned to Sid and grabbed him. *"Where is she, man? Where's Jill?"*

"I'm here, Dan."

He swung around and saw Jill coming around the ambulance. She was in one piece, unharmed, and he grabbed her and crushed her against him. He felt her weeping as she wrapped her arms around his neck, and he held her so tight that he lifted her feet from the ground. "Are you all right? I thought you were hurt, or worse. I didn't know . . ."

"I'm fine," she said. "He came after me, Dan. He was in my car, and I was driving and didn't know it. . . . He was going to kill me . . . But that man, that truck driver, he saved my life . . ."

Dan couldn't let her go. He closed his eyes and kept holding her, his hands stroking her hair and his face pressed against her neck. "Jill, I love you. I thought I'd lost you. I'm so sorry . . . so sorry . . . can you ever forgive me. . . . ?"

"Yes," she whispered.

It was the most beautiful word he'd ever heard. He loosened his embrace and looked at her, wiped the tears on her face. He didn't even realize he had tears of his own until she reached up and wiped his. "Jill, that Lisa thing was just childish revenge . . . I was mad at you about the hotel . . ."

"You were right about the hotel . . . He could have gotten me there if he'd wanted to . . . It was foolish . . ."

"But the date was just a stupid whim, and the minute I was with her I knew how miserable I was going to be, and I left her sitting there in the restaurant . . . like a real jerk . . . but all I could think about was getting back to you and making things right. I didn't know you were almost killed . . ."

She touched his lips with her fingertips. "Shhh. It's okay. I'm just so glad you're here. I thought I was going to fall apart." She breathed in a sob. "You feel so good."

He tightened his embrace of her again, and made the decision that he was never going to let her go.

Chapter Sixty-Three

Jerry Ingalls was lying on his bunk when the main door opened, and he heard them bringing someone in. He sat up and looked between his bars. The moment he saw Frank Harper, he sprang to his feet. "Frank?"

As they passed his cell, Frank held his arms over his head, as if protecting himself.

"Frank! It's me, Jerry!"

Frank slowly dropped his arms and peered at his friend over them. "Jerry?"

"Yes, it's me!"

They both stared at each other, surprised, as the police officer unlocked another cell and let Frank in, then locked it behind him.

"Frank, are you all right?" Jerry asked through the bars.

"No!" Frank yelled, his voice echoing off of the cement block walls. "They hunted me down like an animal, then beat me and brought me here."

In the dim light, Jerry tried to see evidence that Frank had been beaten, but saw none. His scraggly hair was wet, evidence that he'd had the usual shower they insisted on before processing new inmates. He doubted there had been any beating, unless Frank had put up a fight.

"I almost had her," Frank yelled. "I almost got her. I was gonna follow her to wherever she was going, but then the Lord gave her into my hands. She left the car unlocked and went to talk to somebody, and I just left the car I was in and slipped into her backseat, as bold as you please. She didn't see me when she got in. I could have just put my hands around her throat, but the car was running out of control. I was gonna wait till she stopped."

Jerry frowned. "Who are you talking about?"

"You know who," Frank said. "Your lawyer lady. The one you've told so much. The one who's part of the whole government scheme . . ."

Jerry shook his head. "Frank, I didn't tell her anything. Anything she knows she's found out on her own. And she's not part of some conspiracy."

"We had a covenant. You were supposed to keep your end."

"I did keep my end," Jerry said, grabbing the bars between their cells. "But you didn't keep yours. Especially when you targeted my wife and children."

"Only because she's in on it with your lawyer!" Frank shook his head frantically. "I can't sit still for people betraying our freedoms. *Somebody's got to do something.* I thought I could count on you, but I learned. I've known all along, since Nam, that someday you would betray me."

"Frank, it's been twenty-five years. I haven't yet betrayed you. I kept the covenant all these years, just like you taught me."

"But you told them. You told them that night, when you held her hostage, you told her everything. I knew you had, because they were after me, and they wouldn't have known about me if you hadn't told them."

"I didn't tell them, Frank. You've got to believe me. That's why I'm sitting in jail. They think I did it." He tried to calm his voice. "Frank, why did you set me up that way? Why would you get me to drive you to the post office, and not tell me you were gonna blow the stinking thing up?"

"Because I didn't want you to stop me," he said. "I had to do it. And once you were involved, I knew you would help. You were committed because you owed me, and you owed your country."

"Why did it have to be done?" Jerry demanded. "Why that post office?"

"Because of the captain. He betrayed me, too. After I was decorated, he handed me over to the enemy. He knew."

"Frank, Cliff Bertrand put you in the hospital. You needed to be there. The man was retired from the service. He was just working, earning a living. He didn't do anything to you."

"He was in on it. I had to get him out of the way." Frank got up and came close to the bars, grabbed them and leaned close to Jerry. "I had to get him out of the way so that I could get on with the important work. We have to make our mark, Jerry. We have to get out of here and finish the job. We have to hit other federal buildings, like that guy did before in Oklahoma. We have to take them out, before it's too late. The Viet Cong are part of this. They're on our soil now, infiltrating the government. You think the war is over, but it's not. It came home with us."

"You blew up a post office and killed three people. Wounded a little boy. He's an orphan now, Frank. His mother died. He's five years old, grieving with a fractured skull and who even knows what other injuries."

Frank's face seemed to change. "I tried to save him. I told him to go outside. Where is he now?"

"He's in the Pendleton Hospital in New Orleans, scared to death and no doubt in serious pain. One minute everything is fine, the next minute he's in the hospital and his whole life has changed. How can you think you're the good guy in that, Frank?"

"Every war has casualties. You ought to know that."

Jerry moaned. "Frank, you ran two people off of a bridge, and almost blew my wife and children up ... Those people didn't have anything to do with communism, Frank! Do you realize what you're doing? This is not you. You're not thinking clearly. You're not making sense."

"I'm making more sense than you with your cute little house and your freshly cut lawn, and that little wife . . ."

Jerry shook his head. "Frank, maybe you need to go back to the hospital."

"I ain't going back to the hospital," he said. "I'm a free man. They can't hold me there forever. Bunch of fascists. I got away, and I'm never going back."

"You got away? You told me you were released. Frank, did you escape from there? Is that what happened?"

"Yes," he said. "I don't have to be a patsy for this communist country. I'm not going to be theirs anymore."

"Frank, we live in a republic. We're not communist."

"Yeah, but if they win the war it'll be communist. First it was Cambodia, now . . ."

"We're not in Vietnam, Frank, we're in Louisiana, and there aren't any communists around. This is not war!"

"It *is* war!" Frank shouted, kicking the bar. "Everything is war."

Jerry backed away from the bars and sank helplessly down on his bunk. It was no use. Frank was too far gone. Jerry knew Frank had been mentally disabled since the mine had exploded, but he'd never realized the severity of it until now. "Frank, you need help. Medication. You need that hospital."

"There's nothing wrong with me that another bomb won't fix!"

Jerry felt nauseous, and his heart ached with a deep, abiding sadness that his friend had come to this. "Frank," he said quietly, "you must be tired. Why don't you get some rest?"

"I can't sleep here," Frank said. "What if we get ambushed? What if they're out there?"

"They're not," Jerry said, "but just in case they are, I'll stand guard while you sleep."

"You will?" Frank asked suspiciously. "You won't let me down now, will you?"

"Of course not."

"We have a covenant, you know. I *carried* you between the pieces. There were dead bodies everywhere, blown to bits, and I came back for you when you were bleeding to death. I carried you through, with bullets flying and mines exploding. You have to protect me. What's yours is mine."

"I haven't forgotten," Jerry said sadly.

Frank went to his bunk and lay down on the top of the covers, without taking off his shoes. "I know I made you mad, what I did to your house and all. But I never intended to hurt anybody. It was just a little fire bomb. I knew she'd have plenty of time to get the kids out. It was just a warning."

Jerry looked up at him over his fingertips. "A warning about what?"

"Not to talk to anybody else. I wanted her to realize she couldn't do that."

"But we swore to protect each other's families, Frank. We had a deal."

"And that's what I did. I protected her."

"*How?*"

"I stopped her before she went too far."

"That's not the agreement, Frank. That's not what you promised. I trusted you with them."

"I didn't hurt them, I swear. They're not hurt, are they?"

"No, but they're scared to death, and my house is damaged ..."

"But they're not hurt, are they?"

Jerry sighed heavily. "No, they're not hurt."

"See there?" He got comfortable on the bed. "Now you keep watch. I'll just get a few winks, and then I'll guard."

"Okay," Jerry said.

It wasn't long before Frank Harper was sound asleep, and Jerry could hear him snoring rhythmically.

Jerry muffled his mouth and began to weep. This man had saved his life so sacrificially, so heroically, when he was minutes from death. Frank Harper had run into a firefight with no regard for his own life, had thrown Jerry over his shoulder and had rushed him to the medics as bullets shot past him. He had gotten him safely to the gurney that would take him to the helicopter.

Then, as Frank had backed up and let the copter take off, the wind had knocked him back. He had caught himself with his hands. . . . directly on a mine. Jerry had never been able to forget the sight of that explosion that had almost killed his friend. He had lost several fingers and shattered his skull, and his brain had never recovered. How could he stop repaying? His friend was sick, and he didn't need to be in a jail cell or out on the street. He needed to be safe . . . medicated . . .

He knelt down beside his bunk and began to pray that Frank would get help before the justice system sealed his fate.

Chapter Sixty-Four

Jill wanted to kiss Sid Ford when he told her Frank Harper had been caught. Now she felt comfortable going back to her home, taking a shower, eating from her own kitchen, and lying in her bed for the first time in days. It was heaven. She'd never realized how precious her own home was.

She checked on Celia once before going to sleep, and was told that the baby still had not come. She tried again in the morning, and learned that Celia was still in labor. She decided to head for the hospital, anyway, with the hopes of visiting Pete if Celia hadn't delivered yet.

She drove to New Orleans, thankful that she didn't have to look over her shoulder for Frank Harper anymore. She was back in Dan's good graces, and he'd already asked her to hold tonight open for him. Things were looking up. Funny how much things could change in twenty-four hours. Yesterday she had been a basket case melting into tears at the slightest thought of Dan. Today she was floating.

She stopped along the way and bought Pete a gift. When she got to the hospital, she was told that Celia had just been taken to delivery. The baby should be born in mere moments. Unable to contain her excitement, she went to the waiting room and saw that Mark and Allie were waiting there. Aunt Aggie, she was told, had been with Celia and Stan all night. "How long have you been here?" she asked.

"An hour or so. Poor thing. It's been a long night for her."

She sat down. "Does Stan know about Frank Harper?"

"Yep. But he's a little distracted."

Allie went with her to Pete Hampton's room, and they found his grandmother sitting beside his bed, and the child lying under the ventilator mask. She walked in and smiled at the little boy. "Hi, Pete. How're you doing?"

He lifted his hand in a weak wave.

"Miss Celia's up here having her baby. Did you know that?"

He nodded.

"She came by when they first checked into the hospital," his grandmother said.

Jill leaned on the rail of his bed and smiled at his grandmother. "How are you holding up, Mrs. Lewis?"

She could see the remnants of grief on the old woman's face. "I'm doing fine. A good night's sleep would do me a lot of good ..."

"It's been a long week," Jill agreed.

Allie went to the other side of the bed and stroked the boy's hair. "So how's he doing? Are they going to take him off the ventilator soon?"

"Not for a while," his grandmother said, and the lines of worry grew more pronounced on her face. "He's not breathing right on his own yet. There's no telling how long he'll need it." Tears burst into the old woman's eyes, and she turned her back to the boy so he couldn't see.

He didn't have to see. He carried his own pain. He looked off in the distance, his eyes vacant, troubled ...

"I just wondered if you knew that the man who did ... this ... is in jail?" Jill asked.

The child looked up at her, suddenly interested. He held up his hands and pointed to his fingers.

"Yes, he was missing some fingers, just like you told Stan."

He nodded.

She knew the vacant look in his eyes reflected the thoughts that crept through his mind, thoughts of his dead mother and the explosion that had put him here. She reached into her bag and pulled out a gift she had bought him on the way here. It was a Game Boy with a Mario Brothers game inside.

His eyes widened.

She wished she could see a smile break through all the tragedy on his face. "Do you have one?"

He shook his head.

She handed it to him, and he turned it on. His eyes brightened instantly. He showed it to his grandmother with great interest.

"Well, I'll be," the old woman said. "Jill, you shouldn't have."

Jill looked down at little Pete, and saw that, at last, he was smiling through that mask. It was such a little thing, she thought. She wished there was something more she could do.

•   •   •

Celia still hadn't had the baby when Jill returned to Newpointe. She went to the office, revelling in her new freedom from Frank Harper.

Sheila was already there. "Sheila! I didn't expect you to be here."

"I thought I'd come back and catch up on some things, since your friend is locked up," she said, picking up a stack of files and heading for the file cabinet.

"He's not my friend," Jill assured her.

"Well, at least we don't have to worry about him throwing bombs through the window or trying to set the place on fire." She began to file the folders. "You know, you really have the jinx syndrome."

"What, pray tell, does that mean?"

"You're bad news. A danger to be around. A person could lose their life."

"You're perfectly safe with me now," Jill said.

"Hey, I'm just saying . . . a lot of bad stuff happens to you."

"Not anymore."

"So what's the deal with you and Dan Nichols? I heard the two of you were practically shopping for rings, and then I saw him out with Lisa Manning last night."

Jill wondered if there was anything in Newpointe that escaped Sheila's attention. "It's a long story."

"So you two are off again?"

Jill smiled. "No, actually. We're on again."

"And you don't care about his other women?"

Jill was not about to get into this with her. "Sheila, I'll be in my office if you need me."

"Because you can't just let him walk all over you, you know. You gotta lay the law down with these guys, or they'll think they can treat you any way they want. I've been through this, you know."

"So have I," Jill said. "I can handle it. But thanks." She went into the office, closed the door, and began to try to catch up on all the work she'd fallen behind on since the explosion.

Chapter Sixty-Five

At one o'clock, Sid Ford took Frank and Jerry out to the walled-in recreation area behind the police station where they could get some fresh air and sunshine. It was department policy ever since Patricia Castor, the mayor, was threatened with a lawsuit claiming the jails were unfit. She had immediately funded thousands of dollars to clean up the jails and build the recreation area. She had also wanted to outfit the cells with television sets and VCRs, but the city council had voted her down. They had also voted down the Nautilus machines she had proposed. It wouldn't do to turn the prisoners into puffed up, buffed up muscle men, they said.

So instead of weights, they had this yard, where they could soak up sunshine and feel the wind on their faces. It wasn't freedom by any means, but it was better than the cell. Jerry sat on the bench in the shade and watched as Frank paced like a nervous, caged animal from one corner of the wall to the other. Sid Ford was sitting in a folding chair by the door, reading the newspaper.

As Frank passed Jerry, he whispered, "I'm getting out of here."

"You're what?" Jerry asked.

Frank glanced back at Sid. He was absorbed in a newspaper article. "Getting out of here. They can't hold me."

"How do you figure that?"

"I'm gonna go over the wall. That's how I escaped from the POW camp in Jackson."

Jerry got to his feet. "Frank, don't try it. He's got a gun and he'll shoot you before you can get one foot over."

"No, he won't. I'll be gone before he knows it."

Frank glanced at Sid and saw that he was still engrossed. They weren't even in his view. "Frank, you're not going to get away with this," he said. "What are you gonna do? Go after Jill Clark again?"

"Yes, and anybody else who stands in my way. And that kid . . . I'm gonna take care of him."

Jerry shot him a look. "What do you mean?"

"I mean, I'm gonna make things right for him."

Jerry didn't know how much more he could take. "Frank, you're not gonna get out of here. You're only gonna make things worse for yourself."

"Watch me," Frank said.

Jerry knew he was going to give it a try, and probably get gunned down trying to climb over that wall. He had to talk him out of trying. "So you want to get out so you can see the boy? How are you planning to make things right?"

"Maybe he just doesn't need to hang on anymore," Frank said. "Maybe if he could be with his mama . . ."

As Jerry realized what he was saying, he covered his face. "Frank, you're a hero. Don't you remember in Vietnam, when you saved my life? Why would you want to go from being a hero to a killer?"

"Sometimes being a killer *is* being a hero," Frank said. His eyes were getting wild as he mentally measured the height of the wall. "I don't have a choice, anyway. I have a war to fight. That little boy can just make a peaceful exit, slip right on into heaven with his mama. Then I can finish the battle."

"What battle?"

"I'm gonna take out that hospital. Think of the statement. Think of all the attention it would call to what's really goin' on in our government."

"That is not a government building, Frank."

"That's what they want you to think. But they're all government buildings. They hold dozens and dozens of POWs in there, and they have their headquarters there and manipulate the multitudes in the name of good. When they find the kid dead, everybody will be there investigatin'. The FBI will fill the place up lookin' for me, and that detective and some of these Newpointe cops...I could get them all with one explosion."

He had little doubt that Frank could pull it off, if he could just get out of jail. But that seemed remote, and he was thankful to the point of tears. It occurred to him for a moment that he needed to get Sid's attention somehow, just in case Frank did manage to get over the wall. But then he told himself it was ridiculous. Frank would never make it. The very suggestion could get Frank into more trouble than he was already in, and Jerry wasn't about to bring that on him.

The sun was about to go down, and Jerry kept expecting Sid to take them back in, but he was apparently enjoying the cool of the day too much, and was letting them stay longer than usual. If it became dusk, he thought, and the sky began to darken, there was a possibility Frank would try. He couldn't let that happen. Somehow, he was going to have to stop him.

Chapter Sixty-Six

Dan called Jill at the office that afternoon. "I got my new wheels."

She grinned. "Really? What kind?"

"Another Bronco. The insurance almost covered all of it."

"Good for you."

"So . . . what are you doing tonight?"

She sat back in her chair. "I really wanted to go to the hospital. Celia should have that baby any time."

He was quiet for a moment, as if he wasn't sure if that was an invitation. "Mind if I come along?"

She grinned. "I was hoping you'd take your new Bronco."

A few seconds passed as a million thoughts seemed to file through both of their minds. "Jill, I know I've said this already, but . . . about Lisa last night . . . I'm still so sorry."

She looked down at her hands and wondered at the way her heart hammered and her nerves raged when she talked to him. "Dan, I was hurt. Really, really hurt. But you came back, like my hero riding in on a white horse, just when I needed you. I forgive you, and I don't want to think about it again."

He seemed too moved to speak. "You know, I could look the world over, and I'd never find anybody like you."

She smiled. "That could be a good thing."

Again, silence lay like a breathing thing between them. "I don't know how to explain how I feel," he whispered. "This . . . attachment to you . . . it almost hurts."

A tear rolled down her cheek, and she wiped it away. "You don't have to explain it," she said. "I know just the feeling."

"What I said last night, when I found you. That I love you . . . Jill, I've never told another woman that before."

Her heart melted in gratitude, and she closed her eyes as more tears made their way out. Then fear crept in to crowd out the warmth in her heart, and she wondered if he regretted it now.

As if he read her thoughts, he went on. "I meant it, Jill. I meant it last night, and I mean it now, and I even meant it eight months ago when we stood in front of that nursery at the hospital and parted company. I didn't say it then. I couldn't. But I knew it every day that passed without you, and every phone call I wouldn't let myself make, and every time I drove past your house just to see if you were home, but wouldn't let myself stop . . ."

"You did that, too?" she asked.

"Jill, I love you."

She sucked in a deep, ragged, wet breath at the words. "I love you, too."

She could almost hear the smile on his face. "Good," he whispered. "That's good." He drew in a deep breath. "I'll be over there in a few minutes, okay?"

"Okay."

When Jill hung up the phone, she sat there for a moment, basking in the afterglow of the truth of his love. She pulled her knees up to her chest and dropped her forehead against them, and began to pray. She thanked God for Dan, and for the conversation they'd just had, for bringing them together . . .

She had a lot to talk to God about. There was so much grace to acknowledge. So much generosity. So much love.

Chapter Sixty-Seven

Still outside in the police yard, Frank began to eye one corner of the wall where some jasmine grew over it. He seemed to think he could get a running start and hurl himself over. Jerry knew he couldn't. No one could jump that high, and if he tried to climb, Sid would be on him in a second. But just as he was rationalizing his silence, one of the younger cops came bolting out. "Sid, Stan wants to talk to you. He thinks Celia will deliver in the next hour or so!"

Sid jumped to his feet. "Finally. I thought Stan was gon' tear up Pendleton Hospital waitin' for that baby! Man, ole Stan's gon' be a daddy. Which phone?"

"My desk," the rookie said.

Sid rushed inside to take the call, and the rookie picked up the paper and started to read.

"Now's my chance," Frank whispered.

Jerry looked at the uniformed cop with the weapon on his hip. "Frank, don't do it. They'll kill you before you get off the ground."

Frank seemed to enjoy that challenge. "I told you, watch me."

Jerry could feel the heat in his face. He didn't want to see his friend die. "Frank, I'm begging you. Please . . . just wait . . ."

"I can't wait. I have to go now."

"Frank . . ."

"But don't worry. I'll see you again, Jerry."

Jerry fought the tears burning in his eyes. He knew his friend was crazy . . . had been for years. But he also knew that this man, this once heroic man, had given him a second chance to get his life right and fall in love and marry and have a family. Without him, none of that would have ever belonged to Jerry. Yet Frank had never known those things.

He grabbed his friend's arm and glanced at the rookie cop, wishing he could get his attention, make him call them back in. But the guy wasn't looking.

"Frank, things are gonna be all right, man. In this life or the next . . . You and me, we're brothers. We take care of each other, man. And I'm trying to take care of you."

"I'm taking care of myself," he said. "It's for you. For the whole country. My contribution." He stood stiffly, gave Jerry a salute, then took off running from one corner to another. He scaled the wall in the corner, one foot on each wall, pulling by the vines until he was over the top.

Jerry stood, stunned, waiting for the cop to start shooting, waiting for Frank to fall back down, for his problems to end . . . But Frank was stronger than he thought. He had the stealth of a cat, and he was going over.

The rookie heard Frank's shoes on the bricks and looked up as he reached the top of the wall. "Freeze!" he yelled, trying to get his gun out of his holster. But it was too late. Frank Harper was long gone.

Sid ran back out, and Jerry was pulled back in as sirens blared and police dispersed. It was just a matter of time before they would catch him, he thought. Just a matter of time before they gunned him down. Just a matter of time before Frank was released from the real prison that had held him all these years.

Chapter Sixty-Eight

Frank managed to cross the bayou and hot-wire a car before the dogs found his trail. He got out of town before they set up any roadblocks, and headed east to Hammond. He found a little Cajun Mom and Pop store on the outskirts of town and went in pretending to look for a gas treatment for his car. As they went to get it out of the back, he stole a pair of scissors and a pack of razors. He took one look at the gas treatment and told them he didn't like that brand.

He got out of there before they could get suspicious, then drove to a filthy gas station a mile away, locked himself in the bathroom, and cut his hair and shaved.

It had been years since he'd shaved, and he cut himself in several places, both on his jaws and his head. But by the time he was finished, his hair was piled in the trash can beside the sink, and his head and face were as smooth as marble.

He felt ten pounds lighter as he went back out to the car he'd stolen. The car next to him, at the gas pump, had a purse sitting on the seat. He looked around, and saw the driver inside paying for her gas. Without missing a beat, he opened her passenger door, grabbed the purse, threw it into his car, and drove off.

As he drove, he laughed at the treasure he had found. She had at least six credit cards, all in her husband's name, and about thirty dollars in cash. He was a different person, he thought. He had a different look, and a different identity. He could do anything he wanted. Nothing could stop him now.

Chapter Sixty-Nine

The rookie who had allowed Frank to escape threw Jerry Ingalls back into the cell and slammed it shut. "You've got to listen to me!" Jerry shouted. "He's headed for New Orleans! For the hospital where that boy is."

"Why should I believe you?" the cop demanded, kicking the bars. "You helped him escape! You been coverin' for him all this time. I'll probably lose my job over this. I've been here one month, and then you come along and—"

"I didn't help him! I didn't think in a million years he could get over that wall! You've got to listen to me. That's where he's going!"

"No, that ain't where he's goin'!" the kid yelled. "You heard us say that's where Stan was. You're just tryin' to throw us off!"

"He has some distorted idea that he could help the kid by killing him! A put-him-out-of-his-misery kind of thing. Please, listen to me. He said that when they find the boy dead, the FBI will come, and when they do, he's going to blow the place up."

"I'm not stupid!" the rookie shouted. "You're working with him. Everybody knows it. You covered for him the whole time we were looking for him. Why would you fink on him now?"

"Because . . . I see that I can't help him as long as he's out there. He needs help. He's sick. Please, you've got to stop him! Let me talk to the chief."

"Right. I'm really gonna call more attention to the fact that a prisoner got away while I was watching! Like I'm not in enough trouble already!"

Jerry didn't know how to get through to him. "Then call my lawyer. Call Jill Clark. I have a right to talk to my lawyer!"

But even as he spoke, the rookie left him alone, and he knew that he was going to cover his own tracks to save his job. They wouldn't catch Frank and wouldn't figure out where he was until it was too late.

"Hey!" he yelled, his voice reverberating over the room. "Somebody listen to me!"

But they were all too busy chasing the escaped prisoner.

Chapter Seventy

I t was midafternoon when Frank got to the Pendleton Memorial Hospital in New Orleans. He didn't park at the front of the hospital; that was too dangerous. Instead, he parked in a crowded parking lot at the back and walked around until he found an unlocked entrance.

He knew better than to go to the lobby and ask the volunteers there for the Hampton kid's room, so instead, he went to a pay phone and dialed the hospital's number. He asked for the room number, and without a hitch, they gave it to him. "Would you like me to connect you?" the lady asked.

"No, thanks," he said. "I'll connect myself."

He hung up, and chuckling to himself, went to the stairwell and ran up to the third floor. No one paid him a bit of attention as he counted down the room numbers, then came to the child's open door.

His grandmother was in there, sound asleep in a rocking chair in the corner of the room. Pete lay limp on his back, a ventilator mask over his face, and its tube running down his throat. Frank's stomach lurched. The child was in bad shape. His head was bruised and misshapen where it had hit the pavement in the explosion, and he had tubes and cords running like webbing around him.

Frank suddenly wished he had grabbed the kid up when he'd seen him in the post office, and taken him with him. He even would have gotten the mother out if he could have done it over.

But it wasn't too late.

No, he couldn't bring the kid's mother back, and he couldn't heal the child. But there was a way to set things right. He could end his suffering. Stop the ache in that broken heart. He traced the tube from the oxygen mask back to the ventilator, then found the power cord and unplugged it. He heard the oxygen output ceasing.

He glanced across the bed to the grandmother. She was snoring lightly. In the corner, a television was turned down low, and he saw his picture flash across the screen. It alarmed him, but then he realized that he didn't look like that anymore. He looked into the mirror and didn't recognize himself. He grinned.

The little boy's eyes opened, and he coughed. He looked up at Frank, squinting as if trying to determine who he was. And then the boy saw his fingers.

He tried to gasp for breath, but the air wouldn't come. His face was beginning to drain of whatever color it had left.

Frank hurried out of the room so he wouldn't have to watch. If the grandmother could just stay asleep, maybe Pete would slip away. It would be so merciful ... so kind. It would set things right once and for all. In just a few minutes, the kid would be with his mother.

He went back out into the hall, feeling more useful than he'd felt since he blew up the post office. He saw three security guards at the nurse's station, so he went the other way and slipped out into the stairwell.

He waited there for a moment, trying to think. The building smelled of antiseptic and brought back memories of his twenty-five years in captivity. The scent of iodine and blood filled his senses, along with the smell of cigarette smoke and body odor. His head began to hurt, and he sat down on the top step and clutched it.

He shouldn't have come here. But he had to help the kid.

And he had to do something about the government. And that detective. His wife was here somewhere having a baby. Where were they?

He went up to the fourth floor, looked out into the hall. It looked like the third floor, so he went up one more. He pushed into the hall and saw the nursery window a few yards away. And then he saw her. Jill Clark, standing there with the man he had almost killed with her.

He couldn't believe his luck.

They were all right here, right under his nose. Shortly, they would discover that Pete wasn't breathing, and they'd call the FBI and more police, and they'd all be here, like corralled sheep waiting for the end.

He ducked back into the stairwell and hurried down. When he got to the first floor, he bolted out, but his paranoia kept him from going through the lobby.

Were they looking for him? Did they know he was here?

He slipped into the cafeteria and headed back to the kitchen, as if he knew where he was going. The people in the kitchen were too busy to notice him as he cut through. There was a delivery door at the back left corner of the room where two guys were unloading some boxes of bread from a truck. He slipped behind a steel refrigerator, and waited until they began rolling the boxes further into the kitchen. When it was safe, he jumped on the truck and got behind a stack of boxes.

After a moment, the guys came back out and closed the doors of the truck. In moments, he felt the truck moving.

He laughed lightly to himself. He had escaped again. They were never going to catch him. As the truck pulled out of the hospital parking lot, he got up and peered out the small back windows. He saw a police car and convinced himself they were really the FBI, looking for him.

Perfect, he thought. The more the merrier. With everyone here, he could fulfill the rest of his mission. He could do away with all of them. He didn't have to worry about Pete Hampton anymore. By the time Frank got back, Pete would be gone.

He could get the feds, the detective who was having a baby, the communist doctors who ran the place, Jill Clark and her boyfriend, all of the ones who were responsible for the communism bleeding the country of its freedoms. All he would need was this truck, a few barrels of fertilizer, some diesel fuel, and a few other critical items. When he was finished, they'd give him another Medal of Honor.

All he had to do was wait until the drivers parked it for the day. Then he could take the truck and gather the ingredients he needed. Before dark, he'd have the whole place going up in flames.

Chapter Seventy-One

Ome, two, three, *breathe!* One, two, three, *breathe!*" Stan wiped his forehead on the sleeve of his shirt. Celia squeezed his hand with all her might as she tried to follow his instructions.

He could see from the contraction monitor that her contractions were getting intense, and he couldn't imagine that this would go on much longer. When he saw the line peak out on the monitor and then begin to descend, he grabbed the wet towel next to her and began to dab at her face. "You okay, baby?"

She was relaxing now, letting go of his hand. "Yeah," she said, breathless. "That was a bad one."

"Sure you don't want an epidural?"

She closed her eyes. "I don't know. Maybe."

"It's not a contest, you know. You don't have to do this natural stuff."

"How much longer do you think it will be?"

"Not much longer."

She took in a deep, cleansing breath. "I don't want to slow things down. I can do it."

"The contractions are two minutes apart," he said gently.

He heard something crash out in the hall, then a man's voice rising. Over it all, he heard, "You let me through them doors or you gon' be all over that floor, you!"

He knew Aunt Aggie's voice. Celia met his eyes. "You might as well go in and rescue her," she said. "She's gonna get in here one way or another."

"Are you sure you're up to it?" Stan asked.

Celia nodded. "I love Aunt Aggie. Just let her come in and see that I'm okay, and then we'll get her out of here when the next contraction starts."

Stan hurried to the door and leaned out into the hall. "Aunt Aggie, what are you doing?"

"Tellin' me I need to stay in the waitin' room!" she spouted. "Don't nobody belong in there if I don't!"

Stan took her hand and pulled her into the room. "You can't stay very long, Aunt Aggie. Celia's having a real hard time."

"They call the doctor?" she demanded. "They told him she's havin' trouble?"

"Not trouble-trouble," Celia said, wiping the sweat from her forehead. "It's normal. I'm just getting to the end."

"The baby ready?" Aunt Aggie cut in. "Where's the doctor at? Why ain't he in here with you?"

"He'll be here shortly," Celia said. "They're checking on me regularly."

"Checking on you?" Aunt Aggie shouted. "If you wanted me and Stan to deliver that baby, we coulda did it at home, you. Don't need to pay no doctor for dancin' in here when he feels like it, and *checkin'* on you!"

Stan saw the line on the monitor beginning to rise, indicating another contraction, and Celia reached for his hand. "Aunt Aggie, you need to go now," he said gently. "Celia's having another contraction."

"I'll call the doctor!" the old woman said, heading for the door.

"No, you don't need to call the doctor. It's not time yet."

"Look at her!" Aunt Aggie said. "She's in agony! *Sha*, you gon' be all right?"

Celia was clenching her teeth and breathing hard.

"Come on, baby, let's count," Stan said. "One, two, three, *breathe!* One, two, three . . ."

"She don't need you countin' at her, you!" Aunt Aggie shouted.

Stan stopped counting and decided to do whatever it took to get Aunt Aggie out. "Go get the doctor, Aunt Aggie. Tell him the contractions are a minute and a half apart."

Without another word, Aunt Aggie rushed from the room, on a mission to bring a doctor back with her.

Chapter Seventy-Two

Jill and Dan got to the maternity floor just as Aunt Aggie came running out of the room. "Doctor! Doctor!"

Dan grabbed her arm. "Aunt Aggie, is everything okay?"

"She in there having that baby and ain't no doctor for miles!"

Dan shot Jill a disbelieving look. "Aunt Aggie, this is a hospital. I'm sure there are doctors around."

"Ain't none where she needs 'em." She shook loose of Dan's grasp and started up the hall. "I ain't got time for you. I gotta go find me a doctor."

Dan let her go. Just as she headed up the hall, a nurse came from the other direction. "Uh, nurse," Dan said. "I think they may need you in that room there."

She nodded. "I was going to check on her."

Dan stepped back, tense, as Jill came up and stood next to him. They waited, hoping that nothing had gone wrong. Then the nurse came back out.

"Everything okay?" he asked.

"Just fine," she said. "She's progressing nicely. Won't be long now."

"Nicely?" Jill asked. "But Aunt Aggie sounded like the baby was ready to come."

"She's still got a little way to go," the nurse said. "She's not exactly having fun in there, but things are going well."

"You don't think you need to call a doctor?"

The nurse looked up the hall in the direction Aunt Aggie had gone. "The doctor's on his way. He'll be here any minute."

"Well, I hope you know that if he isn't, he's gonna have Aunt Aggie to contend with."

The nurse chuckled and headed back to her station.

Jill relaxed, realizing that Celia was okay. She walked over to the big glass window with all the babies behind it. Dan came up behind her, slipped his arms around her, and nuzzled her neck. "Does this bring back any memories to you?" she asked.

He lifted his face. "Yeah, this is where you dumped me."

She turned around, shocked. "*I* dumped *you?* You've got to be kidding. You're the one who gave me that song and dance about how you weren't the kind of guy who hooks up with one woman very long."

He grinned. "You sure didn't put up a fight."

She turned back to the nursery. "Hey, when you're ready to leave, take off. You won't see me begging."

As he pulled her back against him, she felt him laughing quietly. She turned around again and looked up at him. "Are you laughing at me?"

He caught her lips unexpectedly and kissed her, right there in front of the glass and all those babies and the nurses that were attending them. Her heart's rhythm went out of control, and she was glad she was in a hospital.

When he broke the kiss, she stepped back and looked up at him. She didn't know what to say. He smiled at the nurses behind the window, gave them a cursory wave, then pulled Jill to an exit door at the end of the hall. "Where are you taking me?" she asked.

He settled into the corner of the landing and pulled her against him again. "Somewhere where we won't be stared at while I kiss you." Again, he caught her lips, and this time, she settled into the kiss, sliding her hands up around his neck, into his hair. Her heart was beating so fast that she feared it would explode, and she could feel his raging pulse as she touched his neck. They'd been together many times, had even kissed, but something about the declarations of love and the life being born just a few feet away made everything seem a little more urgent.

They broke the kiss, and Dan's breath was ragged as he touched her face. His lips hovered over hers as he whispered, "You know we're going to have to get married, don't you?"

Jill looked up at him, startled, but he kissed her eyelids, one at a time. "Married?" she whispered. "Is that some kind of proposal?"

He brushed his face gently against hers, his own eyes closed as he found her mouth again. When he could speak, he said, "Paul said in the Bible it was better to marry than to burn with passion. The way I figure it, I'd rather be married *and* burn with passion."

Something about that statement made her stomach flutter, and she swallowed and looked up at him, wondering if he was joking, if this was a flippant statement about their getting too close too fast. But as he met her eyes and looked down at her, framing her face with both hands, she realized that he was serious. His eyes began to mist with tears, reflecting her own as she gazed up at him. "I'm serious, Jill," he whispered. "Marry me. I don't think I can stand it if you don't."

It took her a moment to find her voice. "But what if the passion fades?" she whispered, tears welling in her eyes. "What if we settle in and get comfortable with each other, and the passion doesn't seem to burn as bright?"

He only smiled. "I want to settle in with you, Jill. I want to get comfortable. I want to have babies with you and go to PTA meetings and eat popcorn while we watch movies at night, and sit next to you every time we go to church."

One tear rolled out of her eye and traveled down her face.

"I want to lose my hair and have you pretend it's still there."

Another tear escaped, and she laughed as she wiped it away.

"I want to look over at you in bed when I'm ninety years old, and still be amazed that you'd hang out with a toothless guy like me. I want to make a covenant with you, Jill. I want to love and protect you and cherish you until the day I die."

There was no use wiping the tears away. They were coming too quickly now. He smeared them with his thumb. "Will you, Jill?" he asked. "Will you be my companion and my partner and my helpmeet for the rest of our lives? Will you marry me?"

"Yes," she whispered, and rose up to slide her arms around him again. "Yes!"

As he crushed her against him, she wept with all her heart.

Chapter Seventy-Three

Jerry paced the cell back and forth, back and forth, like a wild lion suddenly held captive in the zoo. Occasionally, he went to the bars and banged and yelled, but still no one came. His hands were bruised from banging on the bars, and his voice hoarse from yelling.

He couldn't believe this was happening. Frank would be at Pendleton Hospital and have a bomb assembled and planted before Jerry could get anyone to listen to him.

He took off his shoe and began beating the heel of it against the bars, praying that someone up there would have the intelligence to come back and question him about what had happened. If they would just listen . . .

But still no one came.

Maybe they had caught him, he thought. Maybe he hadn't gotten far, and he was upstairs right now, being processed before being brought back down. Maybe the doors would open any minute, and Frank would be locked up again.

Or maybe Pendleton Memorial Hospital was going to be Frank's next project.

He started banging again, unable to give up. Eventually, someone had to come for him.

Chapter Seventy-Four

Outside, Larry Hampton pulled his early midlife crisis Camaro into a parking space and sat looking up at the huge, intimidating hospital. He was likely to see people he knew inside, people who knew he had abandoned his family for his secretary. What they didn't know was that the relationship had ended months ago, and he was now seeing a waitress who worked in the French Quarter. He'd been through three jobs, and now, looking back, he realized how funny it was that he had left his family so he could feel young and free again, but today he'd never felt older in his life.

He turned his car off, got out, and headed up to the hospital. His little boy was lying upstairs somewhere on life support. The fact that he'd even had to think about coming made him hate himself even more. He didn't deserve to be the boy's father. Yet ironically, except for his grandmother and a couple of uncles, he was all Pete had left.

He went to the information desk, asked for Pete Hampton's room, and was directed to the third floor. He went to the elevator and waited, then thought better of it. He didn't want to run into anyone he knew, so he decided to take the stairwell. The door echoed as it closed behind him, and he took the steps two by two.

He reached the third floor and stepped into the corridor. He looked up and down the hall for the right door number, and saw that Pete was just across from the nurse's station.

He slowed his step as he reached the door, dreading the moment of confrontation with his former mother-in-law. He hoped his visit didn't bring Pete any more pain.

The door was partially opened, and he pushed it slightly and peeked inside. Thelma, his former mother-in-law, was sitting up in a rocking chair, sound asleep. *Good*, he thought. That would give him a chance to look at his son, maybe give him a hello hug before she started throwing accusations at him.

He stepped tentatively inside, and saw the small form of his son lying on the bed beneath a tangle of wires and tubes. He wore a mask, and a tube ran through it into his mouth and down his throat. *The ventilator*, he thought. It was what was keeping his son alive, yet it looked so invasive, so painful, so alien . . .

He stepped closer to the bed and saw how pale and white the child's face was. He leaned over and pressed a kiss on his cheek as a tear rolled out of his eye. And then he heard the whistling, desperate sound of breaths not quite grasped.

The ventilator wasn't doing its job. Startled, Larry grabbed his little boy up from the bed and yelled, "Pete!"

The child's eyes opened, frantically, desperately, as he gasped for breath.

Thelma woke then, and sprang out of the chair at the sight of his father holding him. "Larry!"

"He's not breathing!" he yelled. "Quick, do something! Call the doctor! *Something!*"

In seconds, she had the nurses running in. One of them began breathing through the tube to give him air, as the others tried to determine why the ventilator had stopped. When they found the unplugged cord, they all moved into a new degree of frenzy.

It took several moments for them to get him breathing again, moments during which Larry stayed back against the wall, watching in horror as he realized that someone had unplugged the life support from his child. Suddenly, a fierce protectiveness rose up inside him, and any trepidation he'd had before about being back in his son's life vanished. He wasn't going to let anyone hurt him again.

When he saw his son breathing again with the tube running down his throat, he crumpled over and began to cry. There was no one there to comfort him. Instead, Thelma and the nurses shot him an occasional accusatory look. But it wasn't until the police officer came in and announced that Larry was under arrest that he realized they thought he had unplugged the ventilator.

He shook his head as they clamped the cuffs on his wrists. "I didn't do it. I came in here and he was gasping for breath."

Pete opened his eyes and reached a hand out, beckoning his dad closer to the bed. Tears rolled down his face as he tried to sit up, but he was too weak.

"Pete, I'll be back, son," he said. "I'm your daddy, and don't you forget you have one. I'll be back."

But Pete couldn't talk as they escorted Larry from the room.

Chapter Seventy-Five

As soon as Dan and Jill heard about what had happened to Pete, they came up to the room to see if there was anything they could do for his grandmother. They found her huddled over the bed, trying to make Pete stop crying, but he was distraught, and kept pointing to the door his dad had gone through, motioning for him to come back.

Jill felt sorry for the tired, ragged-looking old woman who hadn't bargained for any of this. "Thelma, I heard about Larry. Is there anything I can do?"

The woman looked up at her with tears in her eyes. "We were just so shocked to see him here, and now Pete can't get over it, but Larry's under arrest and I can't get him back."

The boy tried to pull his tubes loose, and the grandmother fought to hold his hands. Dan went to the edge of the bed, grabbed the boy's wrists, and held them firmly to his sides. "Take it easy, buddy. It's gonna be all right. You need that tube so you can breathe."

The boy was crying too hard to listen.

Thelma covered her face with her hands, and Jill pulled her into a hug.

The boy shook his head and Dan let one hand go. Pete pointed to the door again.

"What's he telling us? Something about his dad?"

Pete nodded his head. He pointed to the wall where the plug was, then held up his hand and bent some fingers. His grandmother saw that and pulled back from Jill.

"The fingers," she said. "Whenever he does that, he's talking about the man who planted the bomb. He saw him, and he said he didn't have some of his fingers."

Jill looked down at him. "Honey, that man is in jail. They caught him yesterday. He's locked up."

Pete shook his head and pointed to his hair. He moved his fingers like scissors on his hair, but Jill didn't understand. Again, he held up his hand and bent some of his fingers down.

A chill ran down Jill's spine, and she looked back up at Dan. He, too, seemed to seriously consider what Pete might be saying. Pete was getting more and more agitated, pointing to the door with tears rolling down his face. He wanted his daddy.

Suddenly, Jill felt overcome with the need to go and get Larry, but the police would never listen to her. Maybe they would listen to Stan, but he was still with Celia, waiting for his baby to come.

"I don't know what to do for him!" Thelma cried. "He's so upset. I wish Larry had never come back! And I'm so confused ... Part of me thinks he couldn't have unplugged the ventilator, but if he didn't, who did?"

Pete had stopped trying to pull out his tube, so Dan let his hands go and began stroking his forehead, trying to calm him down. The boy continued to cry.

"Do you really think Larry could have done that?" Dan asked.

"I never thought of that man as a killer," Thelma said. "But I don't know anything about what he's turned into in the last couple of years."

Jill shook her head. "No, I knew him when he was in town. Unless he's just gone off the deep end or something, I can't see him coming in here for that. Besides, if he wanted to ..." She couldn't say the words "kill him" in front of Pete, so she rephrased it. "If he wanted to unplug it, why would he try to ..." She glanced at Pete, and saw that he was looking up at her, hanging on every word. "To fix things, at the last minute?"

"Maybe when I woke up he got caught and had to cover his tracks," Thelma said. "But he was already holding Pete. I'm not sure, but I think I woke up *because* he yelled." She shook her head. "Or maybe he wanted to look like the hero, coming in on a white horse to rescue his child."

Jill thought that over for a moment. Maybe it was possible, but even as she considered it, Pete started shaking his head again, pointing to the door, kicking his feet with weak energy as tears rolled down his face. He wasn't going to rest until his father came back.

A doctor who had seen the activity of his heart monitor rushed into the room. "Pete, what's the matter, son? You've got to calm down."

"He wants his daddy," Thelma said.

Pete stopped kicking and nodded, as if at last he had been understood.

"All right," the doctor said. "I'll see if I can catch him before they take him out of the building."

His grandmother stiffened, as if she didn't know if that was a good idea or not. Pete suddenly grew still at the prospect.

"He doesn't think his father did it," Dan whispered.

Jill leaned over the bed. "Pete, do you know who unplugged your breathing machine?"

Pete nodded.

"Was it your daddy?"

He shook his head no.

"Who was it then?"

He held up his hand and bent some of the fingers again. Jill straightened, frustrated. "That's impossible. Frank Harper is in jail."

Dan frowned. "You don't think . . ."

"Let's go make a phone call," she said. "Pete, we'll be right back, okay? The doctor's going to get your daddy. You just rest for a minute, okay?"

Pete was growing tired and weak, and he nodded as they left the room.

Chapter Seventy-Six

It didn't take long for Jill to find out that Frank Harper had escaped from jail, and that they were looking for him in Newpointe at this very moment. Panicked, she ran up to the floor where Stan and Celia were having their baby. She began to pace frantically in front of the door, waiting for Stan to come out.

"Are you okay?" Dan asked her.

"Yes," she said, "but if Frank Harper has escaped from jail, and little Pete thinks that he saw him unplugging the ventilator, then that means he's here in this hospital!"

Dan was beginning to sweat. "You know, Jill, I'd really like to get you out of here. Let's just leave, okay?"

"But what about Pete? What about Stan and Celia? I mean, what is he up to? Why would he want to kill Pete?"

"Because he's a witness to the post office bombing," Dan said.

"Maybe," she said, still pacing. "We have to warn Stan. He could come after him. We have to tell the police . . ."

A nurse came through the door, and Jill almost attacked her. "Has the baby come yet?"

"Just about," she said. "It's crowning. Shouldn't be too much longer."

Jill wiped the perspiration forming on her forehead, and Dan took her hand and headed for the stairwell.

Chapter Seventy-Seven

It's a girl!" The baby's cry went up and filled the room, and Celia laughed with relief as she looked down at her beautiful daughter.

They put the baby into Stan's arms, and he began to mist up as he bent down to show his wife.

"She's beautiful," she said. "Oh, Stan, isn't she beautiful?"

"Just like her mama," Stan managed to say. He couldn't believe how blessed he was.

• • •

Jill and Dan found the police huddled just outside the hospital. Larry sat in a squad car as one officer questioned him.

"Excuse me. Sir, excuse me . . ." Jill pushed her way through the officers and reached the cop who was talking to Larry. "I just found out that Frank Harper escaped from Newpointe Jail this afternoon. I was just with Pete Hampton upstairs, and he's indicating that Harper is the one who unplugged the ventilator. I think Frank Harper is here, somewhere, in the building."

"Frank Harper?" Larry asked. "Isn't he one of the guys who blew up the post office?"

"Yes!" The cop seemed to be ignoring her. "Are you listening to me?" she asked him.

"Ma'am, they're looking for Frank Harper in Newpointe. He escaped on foot, and he couldn't have made it here."

"He could have if he stole a car, and that's one of the things he does well. I'm telling you, he's here. Pete saw him."

"I thought the boy couldn't talk."

"He can't. He motioned. Frank Harper is missing some fingers. Pete keeps holding up his hand like this." She showed him, and the man rolled his eyes.

"He wants his daddy. Now, why would he want his daddy if he was the one who tried to kill him?"

"Maybe he doesn't *know* he tried to kill him!" the cop shouted.

Larry was shaking his head. "They won't listen. They're convinced I came here to kill my son."

"People have done a lot of crazy things to keep from paying child support," the cop said.

"I don't *pay* child support!" the man shouted. "Never have. I've been hiding from my family for the last two years. Why would I come out of hiding now and make myself known to my son, just so I could kill him?"

Jill couldn't take anymore. She turned back to Dan. "Let's go back and find Stan. He'll listen."

"But the baby . . ."

"Stan needs to know that Frank Harper is in there!"

Dan nodded, took her hand, and pulled her back through the cluster of police.

They reached the fourth floor again, and were told that the baby had come. They asked the nurse to go tell Stan they needed to speak to him, that it was urgent. As they waited, they paced in front of the door, waiting for Stan to come out so they could tell him what had happened with Frank Harper. It seemed to take forever, but finally, he came through the door, grinning from ear to ear.

"It's a girl!"

"Yeah, we know. They told us."

Stan's grin faded. "What's the matter? You wanted a boy?"

Jill shook her head, unamused. "Stan, Frank Harper's escaped."

"He's *what?*"

"He's escaped. And I have reason to believe he's somewhere in this hospital, Stan."

"No way."

"Somebody unplugged Pete's ventilator and almost killed him. His father found him gasping for breath, and they've arrested him thinking he's the one who did it."

"No way," Stan repeated. "Larry Hampton may be a jerk of a father, but he's not gonna kill his little boy."

"Then you need to talk to them," Jill said, "and get him back up because Pete wants his daddy now that he knows he's here. But not only that, Stan. I'm scared to death of what Frank Harper is up to. The police downstairs won't listen to me. They're convinced that he couldn't be in New Orleans, but I know and you know that he could have stolen a car before they even got the dogs out. He's here. Little Pete kept holding up his hand with his fingers bent down . . ."

"He did?" Stan asked. "That would indicate Frank Harper, but how could he have gotten in without being recognized? His picture's been all over the news."

Dan put his arm around Jill's shoulders. "Stan, I'm thinking Harper may have cut his hair. Pete did a scissor-like motion on his hair, and kept holding up the hand with lost fingers."

Stan looked back at the door where his wife and child lay. "I don't like this," he said. He pulled the cell phone out of his pocket and called his office.

"LaTonya, it's me, Stan. What's going on with Frank Harper?"

He listened for a moment, then shot a look to Jill. "Let me talk to him." As he waited, he put his hand over the phone. "Some rookie who's been on the force for four weeks was guarding him when he escaped. She's going to get him so I can talk to him." Stan straightened again and looked down at the floor. "Yeah, I just wanted to know what Jerry Ingalls said about Frank's escape . . . What do you mean, what do I mean? You interviewed him, didn't you? Did you ask him what Frank told him before he escaped? . . . I don't care *how* busy you've been. I don't care if every cop in town is out looking for Harper. I want you down there talking to Jerry Ingalls. Call me back immediately! I want to hear from you as soon as you have any information."

By the time the rookie got back to him, Stan was pacing outside the door to Celia's room with the cell phone to his ear. Jill and Dan were huddled against the wall, waiting. "What did he say?" Stan asked the young cop.

"Well, he claims that Frank Harper is headed there. Where you are."

"*What for?*" Stan shouted.

"Something about wanting to put the kid out of his misery. Ingalls said he was feeling guilty about the kid's mother. And he said something else, Stan, but I don't know . . ."

"I didn't ask you to know or not know!" Stan said. "What did he say?"

"Ingalls said Harper talked about planting a bomb there."

"Oh . . . no . . ." Stan started to run even as he kept the phone to his ear, and Jill and Dan began to follow him into the stairwell, down the stairs, onto the first floor . . . He ran through the doors and found the cluster of cops still talking to Larry Hampton. Jill and Dan had trouble keeping up with him, but they managed to as Stan bolted through the cops and yelled, "Frank Harper is in the building! We've got to evacuate."

One cop turned around. "The guy who blew up the post office?"

"He's here," Stan said, out of breath. "We've got to get everybody out. Now. He told his cell mate that he was going to kill Pete Hampton, and that he might blow up the whole hospital." He pointed to Larry. "You've got the wrong guy."

The cop filling out the arrest report looked up.

"I told you what happened," Larry said. "He tried to kill my boy. Now, will you let me get back to him and make sure he's okay?"

"He didn't do anything wrong," Stan said. "He saved the boy. He'd be dead if his dad hadn't walked in."

Larry's eyes filled with tears. "I'm glad I came. I almost didn't." He turned back to the cops. "Can I go? Please, I have to get my son out of here."

When the cop hesitated, Stan stepped in. "You don't have time to take him in. You have to help me evacuate this building. It's gonna take all of us. We need to notify the FBI and alert the bomb division. We've got to find out if there's a bomb in this building, and we've got to find Harper, and we've got to get my wife and daughter out of here immediately."

"How much time do we have?" the cop asked.

"I have no idea. We'll just have to go on faith."

• • •

Unaware of what was going on in the hospital around her, Celia waited for them to bring her the baby after cleaning her up. Aunt Aggie was in her room with her, finally relaxed after the tension of the day.

"Where'd that Stan go?" Aunt Aggie asked. "He oughta be here with his wife."

Celia didn't know where Stan was, but she knew that if he wasn't here, there was a good reason. So she tried to be patient. "He'll be here, Aunt Aggie. Maybe he got a call or something. Or maybe he decided to contact relatives."

"I called ever'body who needs to know already."

"Did you call the Fords, Aunt Aggie?"

The old woman thought a moment. "Ever'body but the Fords."

Celia chuckled and picked up the phone. She dialed Susan's number in Newpointe.

Susan answered, and Celia could hear the children talking in the background.

"Hello?"

"Susan, it's me, Celia."

"Celia, honey! Where you callin' from?"

"I'm in the hospital! I had the baby."

A cry went out over the phone line. "Celia had her baby! Celia had her baby! Girl or boy?" she asked, coming back to the phone.

"It was a girl," Celia said. "She's beautiful. We're gonna name her Agatha Nicole."

"You're namin' her after Aunt Aggie! Oh, honey, I'm on my way."

Celia laughed. "No, you don't have to come. It's a long way."

"Forty minutes aren't anything," Susan said. "I'll be there. You just try and keep me away."

• • •

Susan hung up the phone and turned around to Debbie Ingalls. She looked tense and preoccupied, as she had since Ray had called to let them know that Frank Harper had escaped. "You haven't been out of this house in a couple of days. Why don't you pack up the kids and come with me to the South Shore to see Celia's baby?"

Debbie shook her head. "That's okay. We can stay here."

"Honey, as jumpy as you been, and with Frank Harper on the loose again? I don't think I'm gon' leave you by yourself. Now, you just get your stuff together and come with me. If they won't let the kids up, you can wait in the lobby, but at least you'll feel safe."

Debbie considered that for a moment, then looked back at her children. "I guess it wouldn't hurt. It would be a nice diversion."

"We'll get ice cream on the way," Susan said.

"They'll ruin your car."

Susan waved her off as if she didn't care. "We'll bring towels," she said. "There's nothin' they can do that a good washin' won't fix."

Chapter Seventy-Eight

Frank Harper was filthy from mixing fertilizer and diesel fuel with the other ingredients he needed to build his bomb. He had stolen a rifle from out of a pickup truck and pawned it to get the cash to buy the bomb materials from various hardware stores. He loaded the barrels onto the bread truck he had "borrowed" after the business had closed for the day. It had been so easy he couldn't believe it. And he had the detonator put together, and the timer ready to be set.

He headed back to the hospital. As he reached it, he saw the activity of the police cars and people being evacuated from the building. He realized they must have already found Pete and figured out he was here. Did that mean the boy had survived being unplugged from the ventilator? He hoped not. He wanted the boy to die peacefully, not in an explosion like his mother. But he supposed that dead was dead no matter how it happened.

The fact that he might have been found out didn't faze him as he crossed the parking lot in the bread truck. They were looking for someone going out, not coming in. He had the perfect cover.

He pulled the truck to the side of the building where he knew the kitchen was and pulled into the delivery drive. He climbed into the back of the truck and set the timer for fifteen minutes. Then grinning, he got out and left it there.

If he ran, he'd have plenty of time to get far enough away that the explosion wouldn't reach him, but he'd still be able to watch it. He looked around with pride as he saw the task force with their FBI T-shirts. A bomb squad had pulled up to the front door with the bomb robot, and they were taking it in as patients filed out of every exit.

They wouldn't get them all out, he thought. It was impossible. But he supposed that even those in the parking lot would be blown up. The statement would be loud and clear. And the people who heard would understand, and perhaps their eyes would be opened.

He took off from the side of the building and headed through the cars, trying not to run so he wouldn't call attention to himself. But he had to get out of here quickly.

Then he saw the car pulling into the parking space in front of him, and the black woman getting out. Two little white children climbed out of the backseat, and then he saw a woman he recognized. It was Debbie Ingalls. He couldn't miss her with that skinny face and those big eyes. Jerry had shown her picture to him every time he had come to visit him over the last few years.

Suddenly, he began to remember Jerry's words back at the jail, about how the covenant reached out to his family, how Frank had already violated it once. He had promised Jerry that he hadn't meant to hurt Debbie and the kids, that the fire bomb had just been a warning. Jerry trusted him.

Now he didn't know what to do. The women passed him without recognition, and were heading to a side entrance. Apparently, they hadn't seen the activity of the police at the entrance doors. He watched as the two women and children headed toward the hospital, and he wanted to yell out that they couldn't go in there, that they were evacuating because there was a bomb, that they needed to get as far away from there as possible.

But if he did that, the communist pigs he was trying to defeat would descend on him. He looked down at his watch. There were only twelve minutes left. He looked back at Jerry's family, and saw the two little kids holding hands and skipping beside their mother.

Jerry's kids.

He couldn't do it. He couldn't break his covenant with Jerry. It meant too much. It was too binding. They had sealed it by walking through the flesh. He had carried Jerry out on his back, between the dead and bleeding bodies, had gotten Jerry to the helicopter … And then there had been that explosion, that surprising blast that seemed to come from nowhere, and then darkness …

Jerry had been there when he'd come to, weeks later. They had hugged and wept together, and Jerry had promised to fulfill the covenant just as David had done for Jonathan. Frank had promised, too.

"Frank, things are gonna be all right, man. In this life or the next … You and me, we're brothers. We take care of each other, man. And I'm trying to take care of you."

Jerry had uttered those words just hours ago. They were covenant words. And they weren't one-way. That covenant that was so strong between Jonathan and David, between Abraham and God, between Christ and his church … that covenant that he had taught Jerry to honor … He remembered the import of it, and he knew that he couldn't keep the covenant if he let that bomb go off with Debbie Ingalls in the hospital.

Without another thought, he took off running back to the truck. He had to go the long way because new police cars were filling in nearby. He went around the hospital, dripping with sweat, and came up behind the cars with the flashing lights. He reached the truck and got back into it, and looked down at the timer. There were ten minutes left.

He tried to think how to stop it, how to break the connection, how to make the clock stop ticking … but he didn't have time to figure it out. Instead, he bent down and hot-wired the car again, started the engine, and backed out.

Chapter Seventy-Nine

Larry Hampton ran back into his son's room. Pete saw him and reached out to him. He went to the bed, unabashedly, and threw his arms around his little boy and began to weep over him. "Pete, I'm so sorry, I'm so sorry, I'm so sorry . . ."

The child clung to him with his weak little arms, and tears rolled down his temples. Larry wiped them away and looked up at Pete's grandmother standing at the side of the bed. "Hello, Thelma."

"Hey, Larry," she said.

"I'm so sorry," he told her, choking back the tears. "About Mary. And about . . . everything."

She nodded and smiled at the joy on the little boy's face as he held his daddy. "I know," she whispered. "The main thing is that you're back, and Pete needs you so much right now."

He wept at the sweetness of that forgiveness, and realized that grace wasn't just a word they threw out in church. It really existed. And now it had meaning for him.

A frazzled nurse rushed in. "We're evacuating the hospital," she said. "I've got them bringing a gurney in here for Pete, and we've got to keep his ventilator attached." As she spoke, she began disconnecting the cords that weren't vital. Her hands were shaking.

"We don't have to wait for the gurney," Larry said, picking Pete up. "I'll carry him, and his grandmother can carry the ventilator and the IV, can't you, Thelma?"

Thelma looked worried. "Well, yes. But what's going on?"

"It's a bomb threat," the nurse managed to get out. "Probably nothing, but we have to be safe." She disconnected the last of the cords and unhooked the IV bag. "Hold it up above him. And take the stairs. Hurry, please! Head for one of the ambulances so you can plug him back in. If he goes into respiratory distress, give him mouth-to-mouth."

They obeyed quickly.

•   •   •

Stan was trying to help Celia down the stairs with one arm and holding his baby in the other, when he heard Aunt Aggie shouting over the people in the lobby. "You don't let me go back up there and get my great-great-niece, you gon' wish you never been born, you."

Celia was pale and breathing hard, and Stan scanned the room for a free wheelchair as he yelled to Aunt Aggie. "I got them down, Aunt Aggie. Celia needs a wheelchair."

Aunt Aggie looked tremendously relieved, but much older than she had just hours before. She grabbed a wheelchair out of a nurse's hands and helped Celia into it. Stan handed Celia the baby and pushed the wheelchair out the doors as Aunt Aggie ran along beside them. He saw the people clustered around the outside of the building, but they weren't far enough away to avoid a blast. "Out there, Aunt Aggie," he yelled. "All the way across the parking lot."

He was running with the wheelchair, weaving between parked cars, trying desperately to get to the other side of the parking lot as orderlies ran by with patients on gurneys and IV poles rolling beside them. He saw Dan and Jill already on the other side, each pushing a wheelchair of a patient who couldn't help himself.

Cops tried to direct the flow of people, but they were ineffective as panicked loved ones fought to get patients out of harm's way. Stan knew he needed to help, but he wasn't going to turn back until he knew for sure that his wife and baby were safe.

And then he heard a scream and turned around. He saw the bread truck driving through the people, forcing them to leap and dive out of his way. The driver had a shaved head, but as the truck passed, Stan saw those eyes that he had seen in the pictures of Frank Harper . . .

"Aunt Aggie, stay here with Celia!" he cried, and he started to run after the truck. He heard feet running behind him, and Dan caught up to him.

"That's him!" Dan cried. "That's Frank Harper!"

The truck bobbed and wove through the cars and the people, not slowing at all but picking up speed as it got closer to the parking lot exit. But there were two police cars blocking the way. Stan ran as fast as his legs could carry him, knowing that his child's life and his wife's life and the lives of all the people in the parking lot and still making their way out of the hospital depended on it. He saw the truck slow down as it reached the blockade, but then it picked up speed in one last burst, and crashed the front fenders of the two squad cars, breaking through and skidding out of sight.

Stan pulled out his badge and flashed it at one of the stunned police officers. "I need your car!" he said, breathless.

The cop didn't say a word as Stan jumped into it. Dan got in on the other side, but Stan didn't have time to make him get out. He jerked the car in reverse, and his tires squealed as he turned it around and began chasing the truck. It was a mile up ahead of them, sliding around corners and grazing cars as it drove. It headed toward the highway, then opened up, burning rubber as Frank Harper stood on the accelerator to reach the truck's maximum speed.

"You can catch him!" Dan yelled. "That truck won't go that fast!"

They were gaining on him, narrowing the distance between themselves and the truck. "He's done something!" Dan yelled.

"There's a bomb back there, all right. He's trying to get away as fast as he can. He knows it's about to go off!"

Stan prayed silently that Celia and the baby and Aunt Aggie and Jill were far enough away from the building, but his heart told him they weren't. He had the sudden urge to grab the automatic rifle from behind his head and start shooting until Frank Harper was down.

Suddenly, three police cars came out of a side street and flew out in front of him. "Look out!" Dan cried.

Stan slammed on brakes and slid sideways, out of control, trying to avoid hitting them. He spun and hit a telephone pole head on. Air bags blew out, knocking them back against their seats.

Stan punched the side of his door, furious that the New Orleans police had almost killed them. He would report them, he thought. He would make sure he had all of their badges.

"You all right?" he asked Dan.

Dan opened his door and saw the truck pull onto the highway. "They've caught up to him!" he yelled.

Stan leaned out his open window and saw that the truck was surrounded by the cars, with one on either side and one behind. The highway cleared of cars as drivers pulled off to the side.

But the truck just kept on going. Frank Harper wasn't going to be stopped.

Chapter Eighty

Frank Harper ignored the cops chasing him down the highway. He glanced back at the timer, and saw that there were only fifteen seconds left. If he hurried, he could get far enough away that the hospital wouldn't be harmed ... far enough so that Debbie Ingalls wouldn't have a scratch, and Jerry wouldn't think of him as a covenant-breaker ...

Ten ... nine ... eight ...

He realized that it was too late for him to get out of the truck, too late for him to stop and run far enough that he could escape the explosion. He realized it was a sacrifice he would have to make. A sacrifice worthy of the covenant it represented.

Three ... two ... one ...

Bright, hot darkness closed over him, knocking him out, out, out into some other dimension ... and Frank was hit with a clarity he hadn't seen in years.

And then there was the light, beckoning for him.

Chapter Eighty-One

They heard the bomb from the parking lot and every station inside the hospital and the stairwell and the elevator shafts. Jill felt as if the earth had shaken as people threw themselves on the ground to escape the blast. Debbie Ingalls was running through the parking lot when she heard the explosion, and she threw herself over her children. Celia screamed and threw herself over their new baby. Larry threw himself over Pete on the ambulance's gurney. Aunt Aggie marched out into the parking lot, raising her fist at the fireball that had threatened to destroy her family, and yelling at it as if it was some part of Frank Harper rising into the sky.

Panicked, Jill made her way to Celia. "Where ... where is Dan? Where did he go?"

"He went with Stan," Celia cried. "They were following that truck."

Jill couldn't even voice her fears. "Celia, they were ... where the explosion ..."

Celia looked in the direction of the black smoke filling the sky. "No," she said. "No, they weren't. They couldn't be."

"They were!" Jill cried. "I saw them get in a squad car. They chased the truck out of here."

"No!" Celia cried. "No, they couldn't have. They didn't go that way, Jill!"

"Yes, they did!" she screamed. "They did!" She scrambled to her feet and started running in the direction she had seen them go, not knowing how far they were or how close she could get or what she would do when she got there. All she knew was that she had to get to Dan. She had to find him and know . . .

And then she saw a police car turn onto the road leading to the hospital, heading toward her, and she began to run faster, faster . . .

"Jill!" Dan jumped out of the backseat of the car and bolted toward her. Jill almost collapsed as he swept her into his arms and held her in a crushing embrace.

"Keep driving!" Stan told the officer who had picked them up. "My wife is over there!"

As the car drove past, Jill cried, "I thought you were in the explosion! I thought you were . . ."

"I'm not," he said. "I'm here. We're both here. We're still here." He was crying, too, and holding her with all his might. "I thought he was trying to get away from the explosion, but he was taking it with him. The police that were chasing him . . . they went up in the blast."

"Why?" Jill asked. "Why would he do that? Why would he drive away?"

"Only one reason I can think of," he said. "Because God is still in control."

Chapter Eighty-Two

The wedding took place at Calvary Bible Church, and two-thirds of Newpointe turned out for the occasion. Mark and Allie had seen to it that the church was filled with every kind of flower in bloom. It was a celebration, not just of a marriage between two beloved people in Newpointe, but of life itself, for so many of the attendees had come so close to death.

Jerry Ingalls was still in jail awaiting trial for holding Jill hostage, but Jill hoped that the judge would be lenient in sentencing him. Yes, he would serve time for his stunt at the Flagstaff, but she hoped her representation of him and her own testimony at the sentencing would cause the judge to make it a light sentence.

She had spent time with Jerry in his cell after the explosion and Frank's death and had seen the grief that had overcome him at the news. When he learned that his own wife and children had been at the hospital, and that she had passed Frank without recognizing him in the parking lot, he told Jill that he knew why Frank had driven the bomb away. It was that unending covenant between them, that promise to protect even their families.

But even in his grief, he seemed glad that his friend was no longer tormented by the illness that had plagued him for years. Jerry had latched on, instead, to the faith that Frank Harper had before his brain had been damaged, to the fruit he had borne, to the witness he had been. Jerry clung to the hope that Frank was at peace, living in the promise of the covenant that had held him like a dearly loved child ... even when he had been unable to hold it.

As Jill and Dan exchanged vows, they remembered the gravity of the covenant into which they were entering. When they exchanged rings, Nick told their friends and loved ones that it was like the ancient ritual of exchanging robes, symbolizing the merging of their identities and all their possessions. When they exchanged vows, he told how serious and holy and binding the covenant was under God, and how they were bound to love and protect each other, care for each other's families, and fight each other's enemies. When they kissed, he told how their union made the two become one. When he announced "Mr. and Mrs. Dan Nichols," he explained that Jill's taking of Dan's name was another way of identifying herself with him, just as we all take the name of Christ when we enter into covenant with him. When they cut the cake at the reception, Nick explained how the exchanging of the pieces of cake, each fed to the other, was the same as the old covenant custom of eating something that represented the covenant partner, just as communion represented our eating of Christ's body and drinking of his blood, to remind us of the new covenant. Then Nick led the guests, and the bride and groom, in partaking of that communion ... the ultimate covenant meal.

And he declared the Lord to be at the center of Jill's and Dan's marriage.

•　•　•

As the tears of understanding gave way to joy, and the reception grew more festive around the bride and groom, Nick saw Issie Mattreaux slipping from the room. Quickly, he cut through the crowd and caught her in the hall. "Issie?"

She turned around, and he saw that she was crying.

"Are you all right?"

She nodded. "Yeah. Sure. I was just ... moved. That was the most beautiful wedding I've ever seen. All that stuff about the covenant. I've never heard any of that before."

"I'm glad you like it. It was all Dan's and Jill's idea. I've never really thought of tying it all together in a wedding ceremony like that." He took a few steps closer to her and saw that the tears were still rolling down her face. "Are you sure that's all?"

"Yeah," she said. "I just ... get a little teary-eyed at weddings." She breathed a laugh. "You know how it is. It's always somebody else's wedding ..."

He chuckled. "I have that feeling myself sometimes, believe it or not."

She shot him a doubtful look. "You? I thought you were all philosophical about your bachelorhood."

"Not always," he said. "Sometimes I think I'd like to have a companion. A helpmeet."

"Where do you get these words?" she asked on a laugh. "I'm still trying to figure out all that covenant stuff. No new concepts just yet, huh?"

His smile faded into a pensive frown. "Are you really trying to figure it all out, Issie?" he asked. "Because if you are, maybe we could go have a cup of coffee and talk about it."

She looked at him as if she didn't trust him. "You aren't planning to get me cornered and beat me up with a sermon, are you?"

"No, not at all," he said. "I just want you to understand it. Besides, my work is done here. It wouldn't hurt me to commiserate with another member of the 'always the bridesmaid' club. Who knows? We might just cheer each other up."

Issie shot him a grin, and he counted it a personal victory that she wasn't crying anymore. "Okay," she said. "Let's go."

And as they walked out into the night, Nick prayed silently for a way to show her the Light that would chase all the shadows out of her life.

Afterword

I love to read, which is probably why I love to write. But lately, I've been increasingly concerned that some readers spend hours a day reading novels, and little or no time reading God's Word. Yes, I want to build my readership, and I want readers to like what they read. I have a message in my books and want that message to get into as many hands as possible. I am also sometimes forced to measure my success by the number of people who buy my books. If no one buys them, the bookstores will stop carrying them. This process makes it easy for me to get my focus off of my true purpose.

But if the only spiritual education you get is through one of my novels, then I have failed. My sole purpose for writing what I write is to point you to Jesus Christ. It isn't enough for me to point and have you give God a cursory nod. If you aren't drawn to his Word through reading mine, then I have no business writing these books. And you have no business reading them.

I don't mean to sound harsh, but the Lord has been working on me about what I'm doing and why. So often, we Christians soak up messages and ideas, and sometimes we even come under conviction, and wince a time or two. But then we forget and move on to the next stimulus.

Yes, I try to pass along the hard lessons God has taught me, and I try to convey truth as the Lord has revealed it. But if you read my work and accept anything I say as sound doctrine, without comparing it to the true Word of God, then you are an excellent candidate for false teaching. I am only a sister traveling the same road as you, learning lessons just like you learn them, grappling with the same growing pains, the same fires, the same trials. I have only one source for truth, and that does not lie in anyone's novel, or anyone's devotional book, or anyone's sermon, no matter how clever or eloquently written. It lies only in Scripture, which is "living and active and sharper than any two-edged sword."

I do believe that God sometimes speaks to my readers through my books, that he sometimes uses me to impart messages to you. But the Holy Spirit can only do that if I'm getting out of his way, emptying myself and offering myself as a vessel to be used by him. I can tell you, that's no easy task for me. As I agonize over the words and the plot and the characters, it's easy to lose sight of the truth God wants me to pass along.

So don't trust my words—trust God's. Study the book he has given us so that you can't be swayed by any false teaching. Know his Word inside and out, so that no one can deceive you. Then, and only then, read a novel, or a devotional, or a doctrinal text, and see if you agree with the human author who's walking the same road as you, that human author for whose sins Christ hung on a cross and died. And when you and I are sitting side by side at the wedding feast of the Lamb, you'll see that I got there the same way you did: through believing the Word of God and acting on it. "But what does it say? 'The word is near you; it is in your mouth and in your heart,' that is, the word of faith we are proclaiming: That if you confess with your mouth, 'Jesus is Lord,' and believe in your heart that God raised him from the dead, you will be saved" (Romans 10:8–9).

God bless all of you!

Terri Blackstock

Trial
by Fire

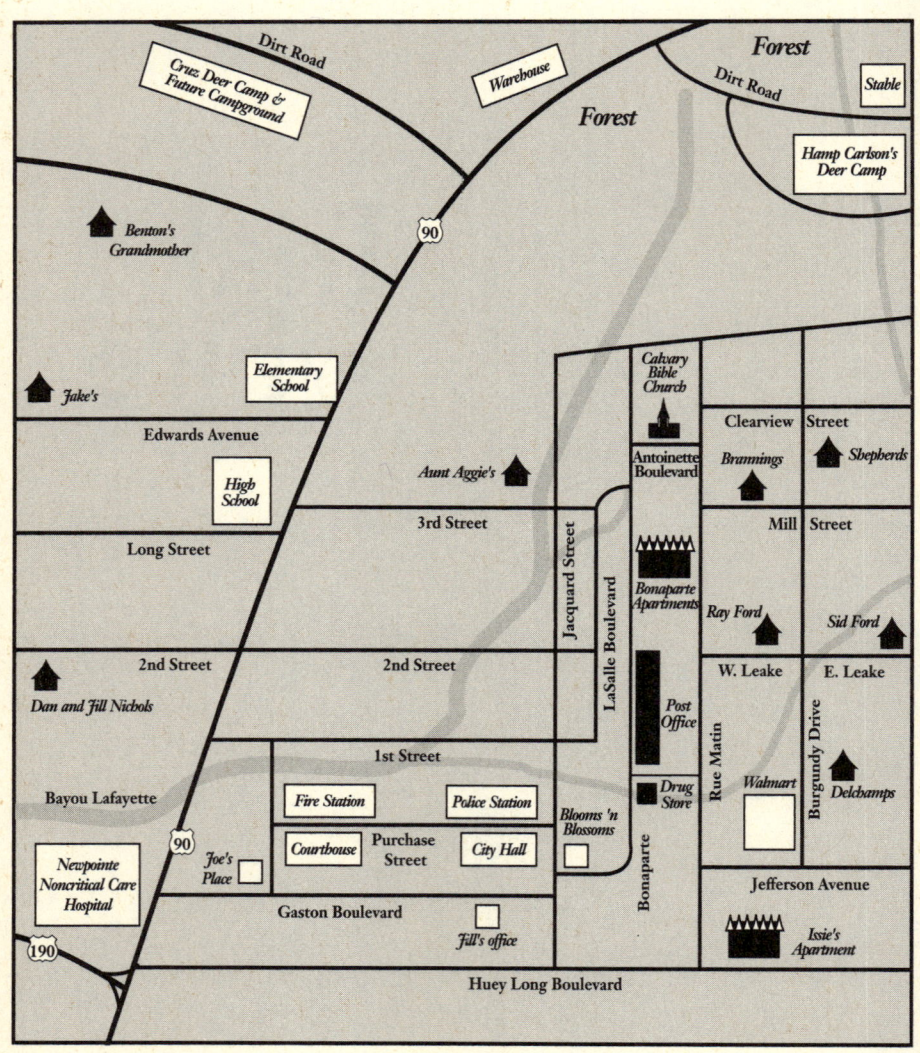

Chapter One

The fire alarm blaring at four A.M. jerked Nick Foster from a sound sleep. He swam through his groggy stupor and sat up, slipping his feet into the turnout pants and boots scrunched together next to his bunk. Mark Branning and Dan Nichols stumbled into their own gear and raced out of the room.

Adrenaline snapped Nick to attention, and his heart rate, which had gone from sleep to sprint in a matter of seconds, brought him fully awake. He grabbed the radio mike. "Midtown to Simone," he said to the dispatcher who sat in an upstairs room at the police station next door. "It's Nick."

"Nick, the church is on fire. Sounds bad."

"What church?"

"Your church, man! Calvary Bible Church."

Nick froze as the words filtered through his consciousness, then settled hard in the pit of his stomach. He forced himself to think clearly and grabbed his helmet from its hook. Pulling it on, he bolted out to the truck bay.

"Where to?" Mark yelled from the driver's seat of the pumper.

"The church." Nick grabbed his turnout coat and helmet and leaped onto the truck. "My church is on fire!"

Mark didn't comment that it was his church too, and Dan's as well. He turned on the siren, chasing away any remnants of sleep that might have dulled their senses, and drove into the warm October night as fast as reason would allow. A faint yellow glow lit up the night sky in the distance, and Nick could see the smoke billowing through the air as the fire truck approached Calvary Bible Church.

"Faster!" Nick shouted, but he knew Mark was driving as fast as he could. Maybe it was just in the rec hall, he thought. Maybe they could save the sanctuary.

But as they reached the street, he saw that the building was fully engulfed. Every wall was in flames, and the roof was a stage on which the fire did its wicked dance. The truck stopped and Nick leaped out, pulled on his tanks, and snapped on his mask. As he unwound the hose from the truck, he broke into warrior mode.

He heard the other fire truck from across town coming up Jacquard Boulevard, and behind their truck, the rescue unit screeched to a halt. The hose opened, blasting the way in front of him. As he entered the building and saw how thoroughly the fire had taken hold, he forced himself to think like a firefighter and not a preacher.

The fire had already consumed the west side of the building where all the children's Sunday school classes were held just yesterday, and the north side where they had fellowship and ate dinner together on Wednesday nights. He sprayed his way into the sanctuary, searching for the origin of the flames. The sanctuary was engulfed as well, and the air billowed with black smoke. It was tangible evil, blinding him to the source of the fire. But he would not give up. He was David facing down Goliath. His hose was like a few small stones, but if he aimed it well, he could knock Goliath to the ground. God would help him.

The gates of hell would not prevail against this church!

• • •

Stan Shepherd—Newpointe's only police detective—arrived on the scene just as the firemen began fighting the flames. As if he were watching his own home being consumed, he sat paralyzed behind the wheel. How had this happened?

Not so long ago, he and Celia had made the decision to lower their lifestyle so they could donate money for the building now going up in flames. All that money wasted ... all those hours of work sanding and scraping and painting ...

Stan tried to shake off his shock and got out of the car. A crowd of people was gathering in the street.

"Back up," he told them. "All the way across the street." Slowly, they did as he said.

"Stan, are they gonna save the building?" Mildred Buford asked.

He didn't want to pronounce the building dead, but it didn't look good. "I don't know, Mildred. Now get back."

"But I had some fish and a hamster in my Sunday school room. The kids'll never get over it if they can't save 'em! If I could just run in and get 'em —"

"You can't go in there. Now, come on, Mildred. I need you to get across the street."

"But could you tell the firefighters to look for them?"

"No! They're trying to put the fire out, Mildred. They don't have time to look for your pets."

He could tell that she was offended, but he couldn't worry about that now. As several more police cars came to the scene, he yelled for the uniformed officers to block off the street so that no other cars or curiosity-seekers would be able to come this way. Then he headed into the crowd reassembling on the opposite side of the street. "Did anybody see what started the fire?" he yelled. "Who made the call?"

"I did," Zeb Fox said. He was the old man who lived next door to the parsonage—Nick's home—across the street from the church. Zeb worked the night shift, seven to three, at the Mason Dean steel factory. "I seen smoke comin' up out the roof when I got home," he said, "then it started comin' out from under the doors and I knowed I'd better call somebody. I was just fixin' to call the po-lice when I seen the flames comin' from 'round the back."

"But did you see anybody nearby?" Stan asked. "Was there anybody in the church or any cars around?"

"I seen somebody," Thelma Fox piped in. She was Zeb's wife, and kept up with everything that happened in the community. She had mounted a rearview mirror at the perfect angle on her sink window, so that she wouldn't miss a thing while she was washing dishes. "I was fixin' breakfast for Zeb, and I seen a car full of young'uns over there just before the fire started. Three or four of them, and when I seen 'em in the parking lot, I knew they was up to no good."

"Did you get their tag number?" Stan asked.

"Why, no, I didn't think to do that," she said.

"Well, what about the kids? Did you recognize any of them?"

"No, but I believe it was a red car."

"What kind of car?"

"All I know is red."

"I seen those kids too," Cliff Breaux said. "I was rollin' my newspapers when they screeched around the corner and like ta hit me."

"Could you see them well enough to identify them?"

"No, it was too dark. But like Thelma said, they was young folks." He tapped his pockets for a pack of cigarettes and shook one out. He pulled it out of the pack with his lips. "Oh, I almost forgot. There was some bumper stickers on the car. One o' them Nazi symbols."

"A swastika?"

"Yeah, that's it. And they had a KKK sticker too."

Stan gathered the rest of the information the bystanders had to give him, then hurried back to his unmarked car and radioed the dispatcher.

"Simone," he said, "put an APB out on a red car full of kids, with a swastika sticker and a KKK sign on the bumper. Possible suspects in the church burning."

He looked out through the windshield and saw that George Broussard and Cale Larkins, as well as several other off-duty firefighters, had arrived on the scene to help. Most of them kept turnout gear in their trunks in case they were called from home.

For the first time, he wished he was a firefighter so he could go in there with them and take on this raging enemy.

Chapter Two

Ray Ford, the fire chief of Newpointe, had heard the call on his scanner as he got ready for work that morning. He hurried out the door without telling Susan goodbye, and sped to the scene.

He got out of his car and reached for his boots and gear, gaping in horror at the building that meant so much to him. But like the others, he shoved his emotions down. There was no time for grief or shock now. He had a job to do.

He saw Mark and Dan emerging from the building, and bolted toward them.

"What happened?"

"Looks like arson," Mark said. "I don't know how else it could have gone up so fast. The place wasn't locked, so anybody could have walked in."

They heard yelling from inside. Ray recognized Nick's voice, but he couldn't make out what he was saying. He headed for the door, when something cracked overhead. "Get 'em out!" Ray yelled. "The roof's cavin'!"

• • •

Inside, flaming roof beams fell, missing Nick by inches. He jumped back, almost tripping on something under his feet. He bent down and tried to see through the smoke. It was a body, lying facedown. He had stepped on a hand.

"Over here!" he yelled. "I've got a victim!"

He saw the fluorescent stripes of two turnout coats as firemen headed toward him, but he couldn't make out their faces through their masks. "Unconscious, unresponsive!" he yelled.

"Is he alive?"

He bent to check, but another beam fell, cracking around them and spreading across the carpet.

He turned the victim over to lift him, but froze when he saw his face. "Aw, no . . ."

Another beam dropped, just missing the four of them. "We gotta get outta here!" George Broussard said.

Nick slung the victim over his shoulder as George and Cale headed out. A beam cracked overhead, and the front half of the flaming roof caved in. Nick screamed as beams and sheet rock knocked him to his back, the victim on top of him. Pain shot through his chest and legs, and he fought to throw off the beams that lay across them both. The tanks under his back must have been damaged, and his mask had been knocked askew, so he could no longer get the air that they had provided. He managed to move one of the beams from his chest, but one on his shins was flaming, burning through his fireproof clothes, melting his skin . . .

He tried to kick it free, but his legs were trapped.

More of the roof caved and bounced on the floor behind him. He'd have to get out of here on his own. No one could come in after him. Smoke seeped under his mask and filtered through his lungs.

With one adrenaline-filled, panic-driven kick, he got the flaming beam off his legs, and wincing at the pain, tried to get up with the victim. But he couldn't do it. Collapsing in a fit of coughing, he fell back.

• • •

When Ray saw George and Cale emerge without Nick, then saw the roof cave in, he broke into a run, Mark was right behind him.

They heard muffled screaming, and behind them, Dan came in with the hose, spraying a path through the flames, George and Cale followed on their heels. "Where's Nick?" Dan shouted.

"He was right behind us when the roof caved!" Cale shouted.

"He found somebody hurt," George said. "I couldn't see 'im in all the smoke."

Ray yelled, "Broussard, Larkins, go out and surround and drown. The fewer of us in here, the better." George and Cale hesitated, obviously reluctant to leave Nick again.

"Nick!" Mark yelled.

"Over here!" they heard, then coughing, and they fought their way to where Nick lay.

Cale threw off his mask and shrugged out of his tanks, handed the gear to George, then ran out, holding his breath until he was in fresh air.

Ray saw from the soot around Nick's nose that he was breathing smoke instead of oxygen, and it was clear from the scald marks on his torn turnout legs and boots that he had been burned. Mark got on his knees, and working fast, threw off Nick's dysfunctional mask and replaced it with Cale's. "Help me get him!"

They got Nick to his feet and threw him over Mark's shoulder, knowing he could be doing terrible injury to his spine if there was a break, but there was no time to hesitate. They would all be dead if more of the roof fell.

But Nick yelled something incoherent, then pointed frantically toward the pile of flaming beams. Dan soaked it down, temporarily extinguishing the flames, until they could see the victim lying under them.

Ray and George attacked the beams. Ray managed to lift the victim, but the smoke was so thick that he couldn't see his face. "Outta here!" Ray cried. "Everybody! *Now!*"

As they burst out into clear air, Ray checked the victim for a pulse. He couldn't find one.

He put him down to try again, and only then saw his soot-covered face.

It was Ben, Ray's only son.

The sound that shrieked out of Ray's mouth seemed unnatural and foreign. Life seemed to screech into slow motion as Ray took his son from George and carried him further from the flames and the smoke and the yelling firefighters and the tumbling, fiery roof, to the paramedics waiting just out of the perimeter of the smoke. It was as if his spirit stood back in shock and looked on, helpless to save his child's life. But his body continued to do as it would do for anyone they had found in a fire, and his mind ran through practical facts about Ben's condition. He was burned badly on his legs and back, worse on his hands. His legs looked broken where the beams had crushed him. The smoke alone would have been enough to kill him, and Ray knew he had probably been inhaling it from the beginning. The paramedic pushed him out of the way and fell to Ben's side, urgently searching for a pulse.

And then he saw the worst injury of all, the one that made all the others seem like nothing at all ...

"Noooo!" he shouted. "His head!" he wailed. "A bullet hole. *Somebody put a bullet into my boy!*"

Not able to accept the verdict Issie Mattreaux was about to declare, Ray threw off his mask and fought his way back to his son. His face dripped with sweat as he pressed a finger against his neck, waiting for some hope, any hope at all. "*Please, God,*" he whispered, "*please ...*"

When he felt nothing, he shook his son, then gritted his teeth. "You listen to me, Ben Ford. You better not be goin' nowhere! *You listen to me!*"

Issie tore open Ben's shirt. "We need to defibrillate, stat!" she yelled, and opened the megaduffel to hand Steve an oxygen cylinder. "Ray, do compressions while I get the defibrillator!" she ordered, and Ray began compressing his son's chest, desperately trying to force his heart to beat. As Ray worked, Steve put an oral airway down Ben's throat, then pressed the mask against Ben's face and began administering pure oxygen.

Issie pulled the two pads out and peeled off the backing. She attached one at his ribs and another under his collarbone. She looked at the small screen of the monitor and yelled, "Stop!"

Ray rested a moment, streams of sweat and tears dripping into his eyes. He heard the whine of the machine charging, then the automated voice, "Press to shock."

"Clear!" Issie yelled. Steve and Ray got back, and she pressed the button. A 200-joule jolt shook through Ben, and Ray held his breath, praying for a pulse. But there was none.

The machine whined again, recharging, and they repeated the process. "Come on, Ben!" he shouted through his teeth, his eyes as hot as the flames swallowing the building. Issie pressed the button to shock him again. "Fight! Don't leave me, son!" But, again, there was no pulse. Someone behind him pulled Ray away as Steve and Issie made last-ditch attempts to revive him. Ray was shaking and could hardly stand on his legs. He felt as if his knees would buckle and he would collapse like a marionette. He thought he might throw up.

"Nooooooo!" The word ripped out of his heart with the same violence as if he'd torn off a part of his body.

Chapter Three

Nick threw his hands over his face, elbows in the air, as Ray's anguished cry told him all he needed to know about Ben's condition. Ray's firstborn child and only son was dead.

He wailed out his own lament, oblivious to Karen and Bob, the paramedics who worked quickly to swap Cale's tank for their own oxygen mask. He sat up, clutching the mask, straining to see the boy.

He saw Ray fall onto his son's body and lift him up, as if by holding him he could bring him back to life. Issie's smoke-stained face twisted with momentary despair. Then, wiping her tears, as if rolling up her sleeves, she abandoned the body and ran over to Nick.

"Is he all right?" she asked Karen, as if Nick couldn't speak for himself.

"Smoke inhalation," Karen said. "Airway doesn't seem patent. Nasal hairs are singed. Carbonaceous residue in the nose and mouth. He needs immediate transport. Also several pretty bad abrasions . . . Second-degree burns on the legs . . ."

"Let us take him," Issie said. "Nick's a friend of mine. You take care of Ben."

Nick couldn't take his eyes from Ben, limp in his father's arms. "He's dead, isn't he?" Nick managed to croak out.

She seemed to ignore him as they lifted his gurney into the ambulance. "There was nothing we could do," she said in a dull monotone, as if he hadn't already seen the tears streaking through the smoke stains on her face. "He was probably dead before the fire."

"What do you mean?"

"There's a bullet hole through his head."

"Bullet hole?" Nick tried to sit up again. He hadn't seen a bullet hole, not with all the smoke and soot and rubble covering Ben. He wanted to ask where it was, but he couldn't make his voice function, and as Issie hung the bag and began to examine his legs, pain shot through him, clearing his mind of anything but that.

Steve Winder jumped into the unit. "Ready to go?"

"Yeah," she said. "Radio in, Steve. I need permission to intubate before the airway closes."

"Intubate?" Nick choked. "No, I don't—"

"Nick, let me be the medic, okay?" Issie said. "I have to do it to keep it open, or it'll be so edematous that I can't get a tube in. But I'll do the nasotracheal."

He heard Steve talking to the receiving physician, and the doctor giving them the go-ahead. He tried to hold himself still as Issie threaded the painful tube into his nose and down his trachea. "I know it hurts," she said as she worked rapidly. "But I have to use as big a tube as I can get in, just to keep the way open. That's good. Don't try to talk."

But Nick had so many questions. If Ben had a bullet hole through his head, who had shot him? Had Ben started the fire, or had the killer?

He arched at the pain as she checked his burns again.

"Second degree, partial thickness, Steve. Eight percent. He feels it, all right."

As Steve radioed that into the receiving physician, Nick tried to remove his mind from the pain. She opened his clothes carefully, trying not to peel any cloth from the burns. "Nick, where else are you in pain? I only see burns on your legs."

He pointed to his right side. She began to palpate him. "Feels like broken ribs," she yelled to Steve. "Possible internal injuries."

But Nick's mind wandered from his own injuries to the fire chief and deacon in his church, who had just encountered one of the worst tragedies of his life.

Chapter Four

Susan Ford ran two stop signs and a red light, then screeched around a corner. The smoke billowing above the trees on Antoinette Boulevard was her target. She didn't know who had called to tell her that her son had been found in the fire. She couldn't remember if the caller was a man or a woman, or whether it had been someone she knew. All she remembered were the words, hitting her like a cruel blast of evil.

She heard a siren and saw an ambulance heading the opposite direction, and her mother's heart almost made her turn around and follow. But something told her that wasn't Ben.

Maybe it was the voice on the phone, the finality of the tone, the very words they had chosen . . . *It's too late, isn't it, Lord? Don't let it be too late.*

Her brown hands trembled as she punched on the scanner that Ray kept in the car. She tried to tune to the police frequency for information, but all she got was static.

She ran another red light, then peeled around a corner. The church came into view and she saw the flames that had devoured it, saw the firefighters still spraying it, saw the emergency vehicles parked in haphazard fashion wherever they had found a place on the street.

Paying no regard to the yellow tape blocking off the road, she drove right through it and came to a halt in front of the pumper truck.

She threw the door open and bolted out of the car. Another ambulance was parked at the curb, but there was no light flashing and no siren blaring. The paramedics were not hurrying.

She looked around for someone who could help her, then screamed, "Ray!"

Mark surrendered the hose to another firefighter, then jogged to be at her side. She didn't like the look on his face. "Susan . . ."

"Where's Ray?" she demanded, unable to ask where her son was. She didn't want to know yet, didn't want to hear the words. Somewhere in the pit of her stomach, she already knew.

"He's in the ambulance," he said, "with Ben."

Something about the way he said that gave her hope. She turned and ran to the ambulance, tried to get the door open. When she couldn't, she just banged on it, screaming, "Ray! Ray, let me in!"

The door came open, and she looked up and saw her husband slumped inside.

And next to him she saw a body with a sheet over it.

Her head was suddenly cloudy, her vision blurred, and she collapsed onto the asphalt. Ray leaped out of the rescue unit and gathered her back up.

"My baby." Her words, couched in pain and brokenness, were barely audible.

"He's gone," Ray said. "Shhh. He's gone." His voice was hoarse, high pitched, and she could feel the pain coursing through him as he held her.

"What was he *doin'* here?" she asked through her teeth.

"Nobody knows."

Not satisfied with that answer, Susan pulled out of Ray's arms, straightened with determination, and climbed into the rescue unit. She went to the body, grabbed the sheet and pulled it back, saw his face and his charred arms, the hair singed on his scalp . . .

Then she saw the hole through his forehead. Another anguished scream ripped out of her. "He was shot! Ray, he was shot!"

Ray nodded, but couldn't manage to speak a word.

"Who shot him?" she screamed. "Who shot my baby?"

He tried to guide her away from the body. She wailed in rage and despair, as if her very cries could bring him back from the dead.

· · ·

Outside the ambulance, Mark and the other firefighters began to realize the hopelessness of the situation. Already, most of the building had been consumed, and it was obvious that nothing was going to be salvageable. The roof had continued to cave in, little by little, and now some of the walls were beginning to crumble. Whoever was responsible for this had done a thorough job.

Mark ran to the truck to switch air tanks. Dan was already there doing the same.

"It's gone, man," he said. "The church is history."

Mark shook his head and stared back at it. "I can't believe it. In the blink of an eye it's totally gone."

He didn't have the heart to fight the fire anymore, but still he put his mask back on and plunged back into the smoke. He had a job to do whether it looked possible or not, but he knew as soon as the fire was put out, the real work would begin.

Chapter Five

Issie couldn't get Nick off her mind as she finished her shift that afternoon. In an uncharacteristically busy day, she had transported another fireman for smoke inhalation, then Miller Henderson over on Spencer Circle had gone into cardiac arrest. Apparently, he had been the carpenter who'd made the pews and pulpit for the church, and had keeled over at the thought that his work had all been destroyed. She'd revived him before she had gotten him into the ambulance, and the last word was that he was stable. Then there'd been a wreck over on the highway, and a teenaged boy escaped with his life.

It had been one of those days. But it was precisely because of the busyness of the afternoon that Issie found herself too tense to rest now. She was filled with nervous energy, and her thoughts kept gravitating back to the preacher. Nick had been diagnosed with smoke inhalation, bruised ribs, and second-degree burns that would keep him in the hospital overnight. The receiving physician had dealt with his airway first. Because both sides of his lungs sounded good, he was able to rule out a collapsed lung and determined that he was ventilating and oxygenating properly. He rushed him into the X-ray room and saw that there was no significant damage to the lungs. He had decided to take the tube out and administer oxygen through a mask. The medics had done the right thing, he told them in a rare compliment passed from doctor to paramedic. The chances of his airway closing en route had been high.

Because the doctor seemed reasonable, she had bucked pro-
tocol and stayed with Nick while he debrided the top, blistery
layer of his burned skin. She'd made sure they gave him pain
medication before they started the excruciating scrub-down
with the antibacterial solution. He'd clung to her hand, his grip
almost crushing her fingers, and yelled without inhibition as
they ministered to his wounds. She had stayed, talking him
through it like a Lamaze coach, until they applied the Silvadene,
an antibiotic ointment which gave some relief. She had left him
as they were dressing the wounds, knowing that someone back
in Newpointe might need her again.

All the way back, she and Steve had been quiet. They'd kept
the usually loud radio station off, and had both been lost in their
thoughts. She couldn't get Ray and Ben out of her mind. Daily,
they witnessed tragedy, sometimes were active players in it. It
rarely made sense, and this made the least sense of all. Tragedy
and death were no respecters of persons. They happened to
good and bad people alike. Living the "good life" was no protection against life's blows, she thought, so what was the point
in walking the straight lines?

She wasn't hungry enough to eat when she got off duty, and
it was too early to go to Joe's Place, the bar where so many of the
protective services employees hung out, so she decided to go
back to the hospital in Slidell to see how Nick was doing. She
donned a pair of blue jeans and a pink blouse. Her uniform was
so colorless and bland that she tried to wear bright things as
often as possible when she wasn't on duty.

As she took her hair out of its binding and shook it out, she
wondered why she was making such a fuss. It wasn't like she
was trying to impress Nick Foster, of all people. He was as different from her as the east was from the west. That was a quote
from the Bible, she thought with a smirk, though she had no
idea of the context. She doubted it had anything to do with
personalities.

She touched up her makeup and applied lipstick to match her blouse, then stood back and took a look. She was still a pretty woman. She knew that because men's heads turned wherever she went. Only recently had she realized that was not necessarily a good thing.

The men who turned *her* head were nothing but trouble. For years that hadn't bothered her. The more trouble the better, as far as she was concerned. If they were married or ex-cons or escaped cons, or drinkers or druggies, or daredevils, or irreverently charming or roguish, they were her type.

But it was only lately that she realized the domino effect her own behavior had on other lives. She didn't live in a vacuum, and nothing she did affected her life only. There were wives and children, jobs at stake, even her own physical well-being . . . and she had found lately that she was known by the company she kept.

She wondered why it was that once you got on the wrong track it was so hard to get off. You just kept going, hoping somewhere the road would turn. But it never did.

She tugged herself away from the mirror, telling herself that she didn't need to stroll down this dark lane where she started hating herself and counting regrets.

She hurried out of her apartment as if fleeing from the thoughts pressing down on her, and dashed out to her car. She turned the radio on as loud as she could stand it. All the way to Slidell, she listened to blaring rock music, as if the volume could chase any random thought from her mind. The music kept her from thinking too hard about herself and her regrets. It always worked. If she just drove fast and kept busy, stopped thinking, hummed along to the music, she would eventually forget those thoughts that haunted her, and get back to living her life, without indictment, guilt, or apprehension. By the time she got to Joe's Place tonight, she'd have a clear mind and be able to start all over again, drinking what she liked, meeting whom she wanted, going home with whomever caught her eye.

The other paramedics would arrive there with various degrees of fatigue, ready to swap stories about their medical adventures that day ... whose lives they'd saved, whose they'd lost, disgusting things they had dealt with, funny things patients had said ... And then there were always the stories about the hospital personnel—young doctors who didn't even know how to properly intubate a patient, grumpy nurses who treated the medics like inferiors. Tonight she would tell of the doctor who'd admitted Nick, and how he'd treated her like someone who knew what she was doing. He was rare enough to make a good story.

They were her family, even more than her own family had ever been. Her mother had died two years earlier, but she hadn't grieved, for the woman had left her to fend for herself long before it was civil to do so. She had worked at a bar in Slidell until the day she died, chain-smoked, and never rebleached her hair until the black roots were two inches long. Issie had been ashamed of her.

When she'd needed a woman's ear, Issie had turned instead to Karen Insminger, the thirty-year-old medic they considered something of a matriarch in a young profession. She had a lot more miles on her than her age would suggest, and had managed to keep from burning out like so many other paramedics did. She thrived on the thrill of saving lives, of leaping giant obstacles, of doing what others could not do. She had seen things that normal humans should never see, had patched up gore and prolonged both life and death. She always had a story to tell.

When Issie couldn't talk to her father, an alcoholic who had abandoned her and moved to Las Vegas to strike it rich when she was eight years old, she talked to Steve Winder, her wiser, married, slightly older partner who shot straight with her. He dispensed advice to her, welcome or unwelcome, like he dispensed IV bags and epinephrine, and didn't mind telling her if she was stupid when, in fact, she was. He had never shown a romantic interest in her, which was why they worked well together. Instead, he seemed slightly amused and a little disgusted at her life, though his didn't seem that appealing to her, either. Since he left his wife at home with the kids while he hung out at Joe's Place almost every night, she figured his credibility was slightly impaired. Yes, he was like her father in many ways, except that Steve did occasionally show interest in Issie's life.

And then there was Bob Sigrest, the jokester of the group, who turned every horrible, ugly call into a stand-up routine, and had them laughing over their beer when they could just as easily have been crying. He was the great stress-reliever, the one who helped them keep things in perspective. He was the one who forced them to stop dwelling on death and gore, and kept them functioning. The two of them had shared a couple of trysts over the last couple of years, when night bled into morning and the alcohol had properly dulled their good sense. It usually took weeks for their friendship to recover, but eventually, it always had. The times following those "mistakes," as she called them, were some of the loneliest she had ever spent. There was nothing worse than having to avoid someone's eyes because you'd done things in the dark that you would never have done in the light. If the lights could just stay perpetually off, if she never had to look in the mirror in daylight, her life might be easier to live.

But regardless of their past, she still enjoyed being around Bob, and Frenchy, and Twila (built like a linebacker and able to restrain the most combative patients, though her name made her sound like a petite blonde), and all the medics who showed up at Joe's Place every night. Sometimes a couple of firemen or cops would join them, and they'd try to outdo each other, implying that the other occupation was for wimps and old ladies, and that only theirs was the noble profession of heroes and champions.

They were a family, all right, not always a happy one, but they served their purpose much better than her real family did. Issie didn't waste her time trying to explain that relationship, or her need to spend each evening at the bar, to people who judged her. No one but another medic could really understand. She supposed firefighters and cops had the same relationship, that they, too, suffered stress unequaled in regular jobs.

She didn't know how Nick Foster managed to get through an ordinary night without a stiff drink and comrades who'd seen what he'd seen that day. Mark and Dan, she could understand. Being married, they had companions waiting at home, though she couldn't imagine how Allie had any understanding at all of Mark's job, when she did nothing more dangerous than pricking her finger on a rose thorn at the florist. Jill, Dan's wife, was a lawyer, so she wasn't exactly sheltered from the things they encountered. But it still wasn't the same. That was why, for a while, Mark had come to Joe's Place at night to sit around the table and swap stories and insults. As the alcohol filled their bloodstreams, the talk inevitably grew more serious, until Issie and Mark would be left there alone, in deep conversation about his marriage and her singleness.

But Allie had straightened him out somehow, and now he avoided both Joe's Place and Issie, as though either of them had the power to cast a spell on him that would lead him right back to destruction.

Or maybe it was Nick casting the spells. The preacher did seem to have a strong influence on those who attended his church. Like the pied piper, he had a charisma that she didn't understand, charisma that led people to do as he said. She wondered if it had anything to do with his blue eyes under those glasses he always hid behind, or his teddy bear look that made women want to hug him. He seemed harmless enough, yet he sure kept his people marching straight.

She got to the hospital in Slidell, got his room number from information, and headed up. His door was wide open, and she stepped over the threshold. Nick lay in bed with an oxygen mask over his face. He was attached to an IV replacing critical fluids in his body, and he lay staring out the window overlooking the parking lot. She rapped lightly on the door.

He turned, and she saw the shadows under his eyes. He wasn't wearing his glasses, and it was clear from the strained look on his face that he was in a lot of pain. He pulled the mask down. "Issie," he said, but his voice was damaged. He wouldn't be singing tenor for a while.

She grinned and came inside. "I've been upset all day that they undid my hard work and took the tube out, so I came by to put it back in."

He smiled weakly and held out a hand to stop her. "Don't come near me with any tubes."

She laughed and came to the bed. "You're not mad, are you?"

He shook his head. "I owe you a big one. You looked out for me. Thanks."

She shrugged off the gratitude. "I sure wouldn't recognize that voice over the phone. I'm surprised you're not worse off. Smoke inhalation can be deadly. Your nasal hairs were singed, you know. That's a bad sign."

"It was only seconds between my tanks failing and the guys bringing me oxygen. Seemed like a long time, but I still had my mask on and had that little pocket of air. I wasn't inhaling any more than I had to."

His voice just about cut out. Issie saw the ice chips on his table and offered him some. He lifted his mask and let her feed him.

"Thanks," he whispered when his throat was wet again. "I don't even know why they're keeping me here overnight. I'm fine. I have too much to do to be stuck here."

Issie dropped her purse on a chair and set her hands on her hips. "Don't kid me, Nick. Smoke inhalation, second-degree burns, bruised ribs. They have to keep you on this IV at least overnight, and get you set up on the dressing care program. In the morning, they'll probably get you to physical therapy for a whirlpool cleansing of the burn. And you know, you could still have internal bleeding. They have to watch you and make sure your stomach doesn't start swelling up and that you keep breathing normally. Not to scare you or anything."

"Thanks," he whispered. "You give me great peace."

"Hey, medics don't do peace. We give great pre-hospital care, but peace is where we draw the line." He smiled, and she turned her attention to the bandages on his legs. "So how are these feeling?"

"Ever been fried in a cauldron of hot oil?" he asked.

"Not that I recall."

"Well, it's something like that."

"Ouch," she said. "That's gotta hurt. So are you using the painkillers?"

"Morphine." He held up the pump. "I just click here if I need a dose. I'm trying to use it as little as possible. Don't want to get hooked."

"Use it if you need it, Nick. You won't get hooked."

"My point is, I can hurt just as easily at home as here. Except for the fact that they haven't finished torturing my legs yet, and the infernal internal bleeding ..."

She grinned again. "At least your sense of humor is holding up better than your voice. So why are you in such a hurry to go home?"

"I have to take care of things with the church," he said. "It's gone, you know. The whole building ... gone."

She knew, for she had gone back by the site several times during the day. There was nothing left of the building. They would have to clear the land and start completely over.

"You'll rebuild," she said.

He shook his head. "Don't know if I've got it in me."

Issie pulled a chair close to the bed and sat down, trying to look relaxed. But she didn't feel relaxed. "Come on, Nick. Where's your faith?"

He grinned then. "*My* faith?" he asked. "Coming from you ..."

"Yeah, kind of a left-field question, huh?" she asked. "I just thought I'd throw you off guard a little."

He smiled again, and this time the smile made it to his eyes. He looked at her for a minute, and she realized that he was seeing her, not as a colleague who'd just shown up at the hospital, but as a pretty woman sitting in his room.

Something about that satisfied her. Yes, she still had it. She could turn men's heads, even if they were preachers. "But really," she said finally. "There's not much you can do for the church tonight."

"I have people to see," he told her. "I need to talk to my church members, maybe call a meeting."

"Where would you meet?" she asked.

"That's another thing," he said. "I've got to find a place to hold services. And there's a funeral coming up." His voice cracked, and he put his hand over his face. "Susan and Ray ... have to ... bury their child. Got to figure out where to hold the service. Got to talk to them, got to apologize."

"Apologize?" Issie asked. "For what, Nick? You didn't do anything wrong."

He turned his head and looked out the window again. "I left the church unlocked. I thought we should have an open-door policy, twenty-four hours a day. I didn't know somebody would die—"

Issie reached out to touch his shoulder, but stopped her hand before it made contact. "Nick, there's more to this story than we know," she said softly. "There was nothing you could have done."

"I don't know that for sure," he said. "If I'd listened to the deacons and locked the church, maybe it would have never been burned. Maybe Ben would be alive. Maybe none of this—"

"Stop it," she said.

He turned around and looked in her eyes. She hadn't seen him without his glasses very often, if ever, and she hadn't realized his eyes were quite that blue. They glistened with moisture from the pain he had endured today. She could still smell the smoke in his hair.

"You can't do this to yourself," she said. "You and I, we rescue people all the time. For every life we've lost, there's a hundred that we've saved. Some things just happen, Nick. We can't control them."

"Have you talked to Ray and Susan?" he asked.

She shrugged. "Susan and I aren't very close, and I figured Ray didn't want anybody around. Word is he's taking it really hard."

"'Course he is," Nick said. He closed his eyes. "Ben had just been home from LSU for the summer. A friend of his, who was spending the summer on a special job in London, had offered him his apartment while he was gone. Ben had gotten a job and was doing construction work for the summer. Even though he'd eaten almost every night at home, he'd seemed to enjoy having his own place. He was happy. Right on the cusp of so many things."

His voice broke, and he cleared his throat, reached for the ice chips again.

Issie sat there for a moment, silence hovering between them. He was, after all, the kindest man she knew, and it didn't seem right for kind, gentle men to suffer so much guilt. Before she realized what she was doing, she touched his shoulder.

He didn't seem to notice. "I failed the church," he said. "It was under my care."

His guilt made her angry. "Nick, look at me."

He met her eyes. His were red, tired.

"You didn't fail that church. In fact, you're probably the only one who's going to hold it together."

"I don't know if I can," he said. "Now that we don't have a building, the church could just disperse and go to other congregations where their preacher isn't so distracted with fires and shootings and domestic quarrels."

"Oh, so now you're beating yourself up because you're bivocational? Like that's your fault? You're right, Nick," she said with sarcasm. "If you'd been demanding a full-time salary, none of this would have happened."

"I might have been in the church when it happened," he said. "I might have been there when Ben needed somebody."

"Even if you were full-time, you wouldn't have been there all night. It's not your fault. I want you to say that after me. 'It's not my fault.'"

Nick couldn't say it. He just turned back to the window.

A knock sounded on the door, and Issie turned to see Stan Shepherd leaning in. He nodded at her, then moved closer to the bed. Nick took a deep breath and wiped his eyes. He grabbed his glasses from the night table and shoved them back on. "Hey, Stan," he said in a rasp. "How's it going, man?"

Clearly, Stan couldn't make light of such a horrible day. "Been better," he said. "I hear you've been better too."

"Me? I'm fine," Nick said. "I oughta be home." He studied Stan's face for a moment. "Have you talked to Ray and Susan?"

"Briefly."

"How are they taking it?"

"Just as you'd expect." Stan took a chair across the room and sat down with his elbows on his knees. "Nick, I've got to crack this case before anything else happens."

Nick started to sit up, then remembered his bruised ribs and dropped back. "Something else?"

Stan stood up and paced across the floor, his head down, then stopped and turned back to Nick and Issie. "If you want to know the truth, my gut feeling is that this was some sort of hate crime, racially motivated."

Nick's mouth fell open. "No way."

"Think about it," Stan said. "Our congregation is mixed. We have blacks, whites, Creoles, Indians, Chinese, Hispanics. We never discouraged anybody from walking through our doors. We're right at the beginning of this investigation, but I got to tell you, Nick. It's all pointing to that."

"But who?" Nick asked.

Issie shook her head. "Does Newpointe really have people like that? People who are hateful enough to destroy the building people worship in because their skin is a different color?"

"The KKK group in Newpointe has been quiet for several years. But you can bet I'm gonna be all over them to get as much information as I can."

Nick looked thoughtfully at Stan for a moment. "It could very well be what you think," Nick said. "But a thought keeps nagging me, and I can't let it go."

"What thought?"

"Remember that kid who was coming to our youth group, stirring things up? Him and his sister?"

"Yeah. Cruz and Jennifer Somebody."

"Well, just a few weeks ago, when I broke up his party at that gay ball at Mardi Gras, he threatened to get even."

Stan got to his feet and began to pace as he rubbed his chin. "I had forgotten all about that."

"What?" Issie asked. "Who is this kid?"

"Well, it's kind of a long story," Nick said. "See, back around the first of the year, he and his twin sister started coming to church. Everybody called this kid Cruz. They were eighteen, pretty popular, instantly likeable. Seemed like good kids. Claimed to be Christians. They seemed real interested in our doctrine, but they started challenging the Sunday school teachers. The teachers got frustrated and asked me to talk to them. So I did. I went out to their house, hoping to answer some of their questions so they wouldn't have to keep interrupting their teachers. But as soon as I got them alone, I started to realize they weren't quite the upstanding, likeable kids I thought. They had an authority problem and didn't think I had a thing in the world to teach them. Their mother was just as much of a smart aleck as they were. Said they knew the Bible inside out and didn't need the likes of me snooping around trying to change their thinking. I left there kind of baffled.

"But I started noticing that the kids were following this boy around like he was their leader or something. I mean, the pied piper kind of thing. They started missing youth group functions because they were with him. It was almost like this ingenious recruitment effort, you know? Like he was only there to win our kids over one by one."

"Win them over for what?" Issie asked.

"Well, that's what I wasn't sure of. When I tried to get to the bottom of it, I got vague answers about how he was mobilizing them to win Newpointe for Christ. Sounded fine, except it didn't ring true. The kids I had tried to get through to weren't the spiritually conscientious types. And then I heard through the grapevine that he had rounded up a group of them to go protest during Mardi Gras, outside one of the gay balls. I got worried and decided that I'd show up and see what this was about. And lo and behold, there they were. Most of my youth group were following this kid around in circles like puppies on leashes, and they were holding some of the most contemptible signs I've ever seen."

"What did they say?" Issie asked.

Stan slid his hands into his pockets. "They were vicious, hateful signs that claimed God hated homosexuals."

"That's right," Nick said. "And I lost my temper."

Issie was confused. "Why? I thought you Christians believed that."

"Well, you thought wrong. God doesn't hate anybody. He may hate their sin, but he hates mine too. So I got out of my car and stormed to their picket line and started grabbing those hateful signs out of the hands of my kids. I was so mad that I smashed them against a brick wall and broke them. Then I told that Cruz fellow that God didn't hate anyone, and I wouldn't allow him to fill the minds of my youth with lies and hate." Nick stopped and went for the ice chips again, coaxing his voice into finishing. "I told him he wasn't welcome back in my church if all he wanted was to lure my kids into this kind of activity. I loaded all those kids into my van, and it was a real tight fit. He cursed at me and yelled threats as I got them in. Before we drove off, he yelled to me that it wasn't over. He told me he'd get even, that my 'heretical' church and I would be sorry for what I'd done."

"Maybe I'd better see what I can find out about this kid," Stan said.

"I'm not saying he did it. He was mad, not crazy. I can't see anyone burning down a church and murdering somebody just to get back at me."

"Stranger things have happened," Stan said.

"Yeah," Issie agreed. "It sure wouldn't hurt to look into it."

Chapter Six

When Issie returned to Newpointe it was still too early to head over to Joe's Place, so she went home. The phone was ringing when she came in, and she snatched it up. "Hello?"

"Issie, it's Mike." Her brother sounded irritated. "Do you know where Jake is?"

Issie hadn't seen her sixteen-year-old nephew in a couple of days. "No. Why would I know?"

"Well, we thought maybe he had dropped by your place."

She knew where he probably was, but wasn't about to tell them. She and Jake had a special bond. He was just like she had been at his age, and she knew that his occasional tastes of the wilder side of life were harmless. She had even aided and abetted them on occasion. "I haven't seen him," she said.

"Well, if he does happen to drop by your place, give us a call, will you?"

"If I see him, I'll call." She hung up the phone, knowing she had no intention of doing any such thing.

She thought about it for a moment and realized that her brother did have a right to know where his son was. She supposed that was a father's prerogative, though she couldn't rely on her own experience, since her father had never cared about anything she had done.

She checked the clock and saw that it was only eight. Where would Jake be at this hour? He could be at one of his friends' houses, but usually they didn't go there until after the parents were all in bed.

No, if she had to guess where he was, she would start with the old vacant house over off the highway. The grandmother of one of his friends had died, and his parents had kept the house until they could get the place cleaned up enough to sell it. That was where he and his friends liked to hang out when they wanted their privacy. She knew because Jake had taken her there a time or two. The kids felt independent sitting out in the back-yard or in the stale rooms, smoking cigarettes, cursing and neck-ing where nobody could stop them. He'd recently gotten into a band and told her they used the house for practice.

She went back to her car and drove to the wooded outskirts of town to the vacant house, and as she pulled into the drive-way, she realized that she'd been right. Jake's ten-year-old Escort sat in the garage, and some of his other friends' cars were on the street.

Since the front of the house looked dark, she walked around to the back. There was a bonfire back there and three guys stood near it, but inside she could see a light.

"Hey, guys," she called down to the bonfire, "is Jake here?"

The kids all turned, but none of them answered. One of them stepped out of the crowd.

She tried to see his face, but he was silhouetted against the bonfire. "Who are you?" he called.

"I'm Jake Mattreaux's aunt," she said. "I'm looking for him. Is he here?"

He came closer, looking her over. As the dim light from the house caught his face, she realized she had never met him before. He looked like a lifeguard and wore a tank top and a pair of camouflage pants. He came too close, squinting down at her with blue eyes that might have mesmerized her if she'd met him in a bar. "How long have you been here?" he asked.

"I just got here," she said, puzzled by the suspicious ques-tion. "Do you know where he is, or do I need to go in?"

He didn't answer, just kept looking down at her, as if wondering if she was friend or foe. "This could be very serious," he said, and a chill went through her at his tone.

"What could?" She was beginning to feel like she had stumbled into a national security meeting.

"She's awright, Cruz." Instantly, she recognized the name. This was the guy Nick had told Stan about. And her defender's voice was familiar. She looked behind Cruz to see Peter Benton, Jake's best friend and the one whose family owned the house. He was draped in shadows, as the kid behind him was. Only Cruz had come close enough to separate from the light of the fire.

Around this Cruz person was an aura of respect, a held-breath kind of anticipation, that seemed to keep Benton and the other kid a few steps behind him.

She stuck out her hand. "I'm Issie Mattreaux. And you are …?"

He glanced down at that outstretched hand but didn't take it. "Benton, go in and get Mattreaux out here."

She watched as Jake's friend retreated into the house. She looked up at the lifeguard/leader and tried to keep things light. "So what's the bonfire for?" she asked. "Roasting marshmallows?"

He grinned then, and she saw a perfect row of bleach-white teeth. "Didn't you hear us singing 'Kum Ba Yah'?"

She breathed a laugh, and tried to sound unconcerned. "Really, what's it for?"

"Call it a pep rally," he said.

"Oh?" She glanced at the fire, wondering if anyone was watching it. She hoped no sparks flew into the nearby trees. They hadn't had enough rain lately.

The screen door opened, and Jake bolted down the back porch steps. A tall girl with long blond hair sashayed out beside him.

"Issie!" Jake came toward her. "What are you doing here?"

"Looking for you."

The girl stepped up next to Cruz with an authority that set her apart from the rest. Issie noted that she stood as tall as he and had the same compelling eyes. She wore a cross around her neck, but her neckline scooped too low, and her shirt was at least two sizes too small.

Issie realized Jake would be mortified if she acted like an older aunt who had come to tell him his mommy was looking for him, so she tried another tact. "I didn't have anything to do so I wanted to hear your band practice. But I didn't know about the pep rally." She grinned and shoved her nephew playfully. "Since when have you had school spirit?"

He looked a little confused, but one look by Cruz seemed to set matters straight. "Yeah, well. We didn't practice tonight, so—"

"Bummer." She shrugged. "Oh, well. Guess I'll find something else to do then. See you guys later. Oh, Jake, you might want to give your folks a call. They're looking for you." She gave a flippant wave, then ambled back to her car.

She drove away without a look back, but she had no intentions of leaving. Something about the way that Cruz guy had looked at her, and the way Benton and the other kid had stayed silently behind him, and the look of anger and fear in Jake's eyes, all added up to something being wrong.

That was no pep rally.

She made a U-turn and headed back to the Benton property, but this time stopped before she got to the house. There were no houses for a mile or so on either side of the vacant house, so she doubted she would be seen as she slipped quietly out of her car. She cut through the pine trees and wild azalea bushes, stepping over fallen branches and tangled vines. She wished she could use a flashlight. She looked out at the bonfire and saw Benton and the kid she didn't know standing on the north side of it. Cruz, Jake, and the girl had apparently gone into the house.

She steadied herself on tree trunks and tried to push through the brush as she headed toward the fire. She had to see what they were burning. Kids didn't start bonfires, then stay inside. No, the two who were guarding it were watching something burn. What it was, she couldn't see.

As the ground cleared into overgrown grass that needed to be mowed, then dirt farther toward the back of the property, she stayed in the perimeter of the trees and made her way closer to the fire. She heard the popping, crackling sounds she had heard this morning at Nick's church. She hoped these kids didn't start a forest fire.

Afraid to get closer, she tried to see what they were doing, when something in the flames caught her eye. She strained to see it, but wasn't close enough.

Slowly, she inched closer ... closer ...

It looked like rolled up carpet, and a big dark spot stained it. She hunched over and ventured out of the trees, moving closer, until she was satisfied that it was, indeed, carpet. The stain was the color of blood.

What had Jake gotten involved in?

She retreated before they spotted her and went back the way she had come, but curiosity drew her to the house. She went to one of the back windows and peered inside. She saw a dozen kids sitting on a concrete slab.

The carpet had been pulled up.

In front of them, one hip resting on a wooden stool, sat Cruz, talking as if he was the teacher and they were his pupils. His tanned face was lit up in a smile, and his expression was warm, animated, nothing like the closed expression he'd worn when he stood face-to-face with her just moments ago.

Jake sat among those on the floor, next to the tall blond, leaning into her as if the mere brush of her shoulder warranted lies and secrets.

He had it bad for her, Issie realized. At best, the girl looked merely tolerant of Jake.

Issie stood at the window for a moment, trying to sort through the barrage of images and impressions. The bonfire, the bloody carpet, the way Cruz had blocked her from coming closer, the charismatic way he spoke to the group . . .

What was going on?

"Hey!"

The voice behind her spun her around, and she saw one of the kids from the fire running toward her. "What are you doing? Hey!"

She took off running back along the trees, back out to the street. She heard the screen door slam, heard voices yelling, heard them getting closer. She made it to her car and jumped in, quickly jabbed the key into the ignition, and screeched away before they had crossed the street.

She was over a mile away before she caught her breath and realized she might have been in danger.

She needed a drink.

Still shaking from the scare, she headed to Joe's Place.

The parking lot was full, as always, and as she walked in, the haze of smoke assaulted her. The bar didn't have the appeal that it usually held for her. The faces here were the same every night, and tonight the Cajun music grated on her nerves. Fiddles and accordions were not calming enough after a day like she'd had. She looked around for the other medics who usually showed up here around nine, but none were here yet. She went to the bar, took a stool, and looked up at Joe, the bartender.

"Where y'at?"

"Awright," she said, returning the Cajun greeting as if it was second nature. She ordered her drink, then spun around slowly on the stool and scanned the customers. Already she'd caught the eye of several of the men across the room. There was no one here who particularly thrilled her.

R.J. Albright, one of the cops of Newpointe, sat at the end of the bar in his usual place.

"You heard anything about Nick?" he asked.

She nodded. "Saw him a little while ago."

"How's he doing?"

"Worse than he'll admit," she said.

Joe brought her the drink and she took a sip. Someone tapped on her shoulder, and she looked up to see one of the new electrical workers who'd come to town recently. She'd met him on a call when he'd been shocked on a job, and she had stabilized him and had rushed him to the hospital. It was amazing the number of people she met each day, and most of them never forgot her even though their faces became blurry in her memory. This guy looked better standing up than he had on a gurney, and she decided that the night had promise after all.

Chapter Seven

It was after eleven before the visitors all left the Fords' house, with their empty casserole dishes and emptier platitudes about the death in their family. A few relatives remained, and Susan had spent hours trying to figure out where she would put them for the night. Usually, she let guests stay in Ben's room, but tonight she wanted to keep that room closed off until she could go in there alone. She didn't want the evidence of his life to be disturbed. She wanted it left untouched, just as it had been the last time he'd stayed at home.

Vanessa, her brokenhearted teenage daughter, needed her room. The girl was distraught and exhausted, and Susan wanted her to have a good night's sleep in her own bed. Susan would have given up her own bed, since she doubted there was much sleep in her future, but she knew that Ray needed rest.

So she made pallets on the living room floor for her sister and her husband, her nieces, and Ray's parents. Sid, Ray's brother, had graciously taken some of the other relatives into his home.

But now that the house was winding down and people were getting quiet for the night, she found that there was no place she could go to be alone. She had some things to say to God, and she meant to say them alone. She didn't want anyone standing over her telling her that there was a purpose in all this, that God would comfort her, that Ben was ready to be with God. She didn't *want* him with God, and she didn't want God's comfort.

She wanted Ben, her firstborn, whom God had given her, never warning he would snatch him away.

She waited until the clattering in the kitchen stopped as her sister found creative places in the refrigerator to store the food, waited until she heard no more sniffing from Vanessa's room or the living room, waited until the silence from Ray's side of the bed finally settled into a light snore. Then she went to Ben's room, quietly slipped in, and closed and locked the door behind her.

The lamp was shining. She wondered who had been in here to turn it on. She looked around at the baseball memorabilia on the wall, the trophies he had won growing up, the framed certificates and ribbons. His childhood was trapped, frozen in this room, but he had moved on. He had become a man and moved into an apartment, had excelled in school, had forged dreams and plans that would have made her proud.

The pain wrapped around her, sharp tentacles of grief that cut into her flesh, straight to her heart, and threatened to immobilize her. Rage spiraled up inside her, like the grief from her heart making a pilgrimage to her head. Someone had to pay. Someone had to suffer. Someone had to explain to her why her son, her only son, had been chosen.

She muffled the grief moaning out of her mouth and squinted her eyes as her hands folded into fists. She looked up at the ceiling as if God was there, and thought of taking the lamp and flinging it at the Sheetrock, lashing out at the God who would allow such a thing.

"How could you, God!" she whispered. "How could you take my baby?" She sat on the bed and pulled her feet up, hugged her knees to her chest, and rocked back and forth, back and forth, as if recoiling from the touch of the Lord who could comfort her.

Explain it to me, God! I don't understand this. I need to understand.

She had known people who'd lost children before, had even visited them in their home the day of the tragedy, had taken food and mumbled things that sounded wise at the time. Some of those had been sick; others had died in car accidents.

But none had been shot, or left in a fire to die. None had so much mystery surrounding their last hours.

What had gone through Ben's mind before he died? Was he tortured? Tormented? Had he suffered?

"I can't do this, Lord!" she cried. "I can't. Let others do it, who are stronger." She thought of the pain she had endured after being shot in the chest a couple of years earlier, left to die in a fire much like the one that had taken Ben. Ray had found her in time and saved her, and the Lord had allowed her to have a second chance at life. "Did you save me for this?" she asked. "So's I could grieve my son?"

So many today had told her she would get through this, that they would help her and love her, that God would give her what she needed. "No," she said now. "I *need* my son back! That's all that would help me. I don't want to live ... I didn't survive so I could learn to get along without him." She shook her fist at the ceiling. "Do you hear me, God? I cannot do this! Just take me too. Take me on outta here. Take me home, 'cause I don't want to stay."

But she knew he wouldn't. For some reason, he had given her life back, and he had taken Ben instead. Not an even trade, she thought. She would never have agreed to it. But God hadn't asked her.

She didn't know if she could forgive him for that.

She pulled the pillow from under Ben's bedspread and buried her face in it as her anguish wailed out of her. She wanted to break things, kick things, scream and rant and rave ... even hurt herself. But then the family would come, and they wouldn't leave her alone again. The cycle of being surrounded would continue, and she wouldn't have time to think . . .

So she didn't throw anything, didn't break anything, didn't scream or hurt herself. She just lay on Ben's bed, moaning and sobbing into his pillow as her mother's grief dragged her through the worst night of her life.

Chapter Eight

Though Issie was sometimes gullible and reckless, she wasn't naive. She had been around the block a few times and knew when things weren't right, and lately, she'd made a point of raising her standards. It had taken her a little over an hour to figure out that the man hitting on her was married. There were subtle signs, like a white stripe on the ring finger of his left hand. She didn't know why men didn't realize that it was obvious when they took their wedding rings off.

While this wouldn't have bothered her in days past, she found that it irritated her now. She didn't like being treated like a fool. Twice during the conversation he'd gotten a call on his cell phone, and he had kept it short and sweet. She felt like grabbing the phone and saying hello to his wife, telling her to come get him before he made a victim out of some girl who wasn't as smart as she was.

When she'd finally been able to shake the guy, she'd decided that she needed to go home. Maybe Joe's wasn't the place for her tonight. Anyway, it wasn't doing the trick. Her spirits were just as low now, and her nerves just as shot as they had been when she'd left the Benton property.

She paid her tab, said her goodbyes, and headed out to her car.

The night air was cool, and a breeze whispered through the Mimosa tree next to Joe's Place. A couple of college-age kids were standing at a truck on the perimeter of the parking lot.

The wind picked up their laughter and carried it to Issie, making her almost jealous that others found smiles after a day like today.

She got into the car and jammed her key into the ignition, turned it, and shifted the car into drive. A loud rap song beat out its morbid message, and she changed the station as she stepped on the accelerator. The song changed to a softer, more harmonic song by a popular boy band. But the car stalled.

She gave it more gas, and the wheels began to turn slightly, but they fought the movement. Frowning, she shifted back into park and got out, leaving her door open, and looked at her tires.

All four were flat.

Anger roiled inside her. She punched the button to open her trunk and pulled out her flashlight. She shone the light on one of the tires and went closer, looking for the source of the problem. Had she run over something big enough to deflate all four tires?

Then she saw the slash, and realized that someone had taken a knife to the tire. She went from wheel to wheel, shining the light, and saw that they had all been slashed.

Who would have done such a thing? Had she been chosen randomly, or was it a deliberate act?

The autumn breeze whipped through her hair, fluffing it into her face, and she pushed it back and looked around, first to the right, then the left, hoping whoever had done this was still in the area. She had visions of catching and restraining them, and somehow getting them across the street to the police station. There she'd have them locked up and the key thrown away until they bought her four new tires and gave her an apology.

But there was no one in sight.

The college kids still laughed and horsed around, oblivious to the rage coursing through her. She stormed over to them. "Did any of you see someone around my car?" she demanded.

"No," one of them said. "Why?"

"Because all four of my tires are slashed. You didn't see anybody?"

"Ma'am, we just got here," one of them said. "There hasn't been anybody in the parking lot since we got out of the truck."

She muttered something under her breath and stomped back to her car. Not knowing what else to do with her rage, she kicked at the tire. This was all she needed after a long day.

She looked across the street and saw the lights of the fire department and some of the firemen milling around in the truck bay, and next door the police department with its squad cars parked out front. At least there was someone over there who could take her home.

She headed across the street to the fire department, went inside the truck bay, and saw Dan Nichols lifting weights. "Issie," he said, setting down a barbell. "What are you doing here?"

"I was at Joe's Place," she said, "and somebody slashed my tires. I need a ride home. Can you take me?"

Dan hesitated. "Why don't you ask somebody else?" he said. "No offense, Issie, but I'm a newlywed and I don't want to start rumors."

That made her even madder. "Oh, no, of course you wouldn't want to be seen with a piranha like me."

She bolted into the fire station, slamming the door behind her. She saw Mark Branning sitting in front of the television watching a ball game. George Broussard was sprawled out in the recliner across the small room. "Mark, I was just over at Joe's Place and my tires were slashed. Can you take me home?"

Mark just looked at her for a moment, and she could see that he was trying to come up with an excuse.

"Oh, come on, Mark," she said. "It's not like I'm going to attack you in the car. Give me a break."

Mark shrugged. "Allie and I are doing real well, Issie. I don't want to rock the boat."

"Would Allie want me to walk home at night?" she asked. "Come on, I'm a lady in distress. You're a public servant."

Mark grinned. "Nice try, Issie, but I'm gonna pass. Get George."

She looked at George. "George, surely you can do it."

The big Cajun was a young widower, left alone with a little boy. He looked up at her as if it pleased him to be asked. He dropped his feet and got up. "I'll brought you home," he said, and looked down at Mark. "I got the scanner in the car. Won't be long, no way." He bowed with a flourish and said, "After you."

Issie started out without saying goodbye to Mark or Dan.

When they were on their way home, George grinned over at Issie. "Sorry 'bout them attitudes back there."

She shrugged and looked out the window. "I guess I deserve it. But Mark doesn't have to be scared of me. We never did anything wrong. And I have no idea why Dan Nichols would have to worry about Jill. The whole time he was a bachelor he and I never went out once. We weren't each other's type."

"What type you like, Issie?" George asked.

She sighed and shook her head. "I have a broad range of types, George. I'm not that specific."

"Maybe ya ought to be, pretty girl like you," George said.

Was he hitting on her? She glanced at his double chin and his Santa Claus paunch. He was the last one she'd be attracted to. She looked out the window, quiet until they reached her apartments. "Thanks, George," she said. "I really appreciate it."

"So how ya gon' get to work tomorrow?" he asked.

"I don't know. I'll call Steve or somebody. Guess I'll have to get AAA out to change my tires. My insurance doesn't cover tires, so it's going to cost a small fortune, which I don't have at the moment." She groaned and dug through her bag for her keys. "I've got to get a better-paying job."

"You can do like me," he said, "save lives one day, sell smoke alarms the next."

"Yeah, I'll have to consider that," she said without much enthusiasm. "Thanks again."

She got out of the car and trotted up the steps to the apartment on the second floor. She put her key in but found that the doorknob turned too easily. Normally it took a little effort unless it was unlocked.

She turned the doorknob and pushed inside, quickly flipped on the light, and looked down at the knob again. Had it just been her imagination, or had the door really been unlocked? That wasn't like her. She never left it without locking it. Maybe the stress of the day had distracted her into forgetting.

She locked it now, then dropped her purse on an end table and headed for her bedroom. She kicked off her shoes toward the closet as she rounded the corner.

Then she saw it. Written in red spray paint across her wall were the words, "Ignorance is bliss."

She gasped and stepped back, and quickly ran for the gun that she kept hidden in her closet. Her hands trembled and her heart raced as she tried to load it, then she went around the apartment from room to room, looking in closets and behind doors and under things. Someone had been in her apartment, and they had left her a message. What did it mean, ignorance is bliss? What kind of ignorance? Ignorance from what?

She had no idea what it meant, but as shivers coursed through her, she realized that it had something to do with the four slashed tires.

She got to the bathroom, turned on the light, pulled back the shower curtain. There was no one there. She was sweating now, and she stumbled out of the bathroom, still holding the gun, and grabbed the telephone next to her bed.

She picked it up and started to dial 911 when she noticed a small lump under her comforter. Aiming the gun at it as if it was a live thing that would jump out and grab her, she pealed her comforter slowly back. She screamed as she saw the dead cat, brutally slain.

The sight backed her against the wall, and she stayed there, pushing against it as if it would let her slip through. She saw a note attached with a rubber band around the cat's torso. Still holding the phone and the gun, she forced herself back to the bedside, pulled the note out from under the rubber band, and unfolded it.

"Tell the police about anything you've seen and you're as dead as this cat."

There was no signature. No need of one. The message was clear. Issie didn't know what things she knew or what they were referring to, but the fact that she had picked up the phone to dial 911 reminded her that someone was looking in on her thoughts, figuring out her moves just before she made them.

She slammed the phone down. It was those kids with Jake, she thought. He and his friends were worried that she was going to tell something.

Did it have anything to do with the carpet that she'd seen them burning in the bonfire? Was this about the church burning? Had they killed Ben?

She was shaking so hard she could hardly grab the phone again, but she picked it up and dialed her brother's number. He answered quickly. "Hello?"

"Mike, it's me," she said, her voice wobbling. "Some weird stuff is happening around here and—can I come and bunk at your house tonight?"

"What's wrong?" he asked.

"I've just got to get out of here. Somebody slashed all four of my tires, so I don't have a car. I'll need you to come get me."

"Slashed your tires?" he asked. "Who would do that?"

"The same person who'd put a dead cat in my bed and leave me threatening messages!" she shouted.

"Issie, what have you gotten yourself into?"

The question would have enraged her if she hadn't been so exhausted. She rolled her eyes and shook her head. She didn't have the heart to tell him that it very likely had something to do with his own son. "I don't know," she said. "That's the bizarre thing."

"Have you called the police?"

"No. They left a note telling me not to, and frankly, I don't think I want to mess with them right now. Will you come get me or not?"

"I was asleep, Issie. I'm not even dressed."

"What don't you understand?" she bellowed. "Someone has been in my apartment. You're my brother! I don't have anybody else to call!"

"All right, all right," he said. "I'll be right over."

"Can you put Lois on the phone until you get here? I'm a little spooked."

"Let me see if I can wake her up." She knew he expected her to tell him not to bother, but she was too frightened to be selfless right now. After several moments, Lois came to the phone. "Issie, what's going on?" her sister-in-law asked irritably.

Blinking back her tears of frustration and indignation, Issie told Lois what had happened while she waited for her brother.

Chapter Nine

When they got back to her brother's house, Issie spent two hours convincing Mike that they were not to call the police. She didn't want to provoke whoever was after her, she said. She needed a few more clues before she went to them.

But the truth was that she didn't want to implicate Jake.

When Mike and Lois finally went back to bed, Issie stayed up waiting for Jake to come home. She didn't know what had gotten into her brother, raising a teenage boy without a curfew. He should know better. If not from his own teenage days, then from hers. She had been a wild one, staying out sometimes all night, watching the sun come up with her dates, then sleeping all day. It wasn't a very productive life, she knew. It hadn't been until she started showing her own self-imposed discipline that she'd even been able to get through her paramedic training. Now she saw Jake following in her footsteps, and the thought worried her.

He rolled in about 4:30. When she saw his car drive up, she went to his bedroom and sat on his bed. She wanted to surprise him.

It worked. He came in and flicked his light on, saw her on the bed, and sucked in a breath.

"Issie, what are you doing here? You scared me to death!"

"I couldn't stay home tonight," she said through her teeth. "My tires were slashed at Joe's Place, and then when I went home, someone had been in my apartment."

She could see the guilt on his face, but he straightened and tried to look innocent. "Oh, really? Did you call the police?"

"No," she said. "You can tell whoever it is that I didn't call them. But I won't be manipulated by a criminal. I want to know what you know right now."

Jake threw up his hands as if he couldn't believe the accusation. "Issie, how would I know anything about this?"

"Because in my mind it's no coincidence that after I came to your playground and saw what you were up to, my tires get slashed and a dead cat turns up in my bed!"

"Dead cat?" he asked. "Gross!"

She nodded. "Yeah, it's gross, all right. Thank goodness for your father. He came over and got it out of my apartment, but I'm afraid the mattress is ruined. So now I'm stuck for four new tires and a new mattress if I want to sleep in any kind of peace, not to mention the fact that I don't know how they got into my apartment. But I was thinking that maybe someone who had a key let them in."

"I don't have a key to your apartment, Issie."

"No, but your dad does, and it's hanging in the kitchen on a hook. It doesn't take a genius to know which key it is."

He swallowed and turned around, putting his back to her.

"And incidently, I've already checked. It's not there right now."

He turned back to her. "What did you tell Dad?" he asked.

Her laughter was dry and brittle. "I didn't tell him that I found you in the vandalized house of some old lady who died. So you don't have to worry just yet. He doesn't know anything."

"That's good," he said, "because there's nothing to know."

The obvious lie made her livid, and she got up, crossed the room, and put her face inches from his.

"I know I'm not a whole lot older than you, and I know that I don't have any authority where you're concerned, but so help me, Jake, if that was more than cat blood on the carpet I saw in that fire, you'd better cut yourself loose right now before you wind up in prison. The police need to know about that bonfire and that carpet."

Jake's eyes hardened. "I wouldn't do that if I were you, Issie."

"There you go, threatening me again. What'll it be this time? A dead snake in my bed? A *live* one?"

"I'm not threatening you," he said. "I'm warning you. I don't have a lot of control over some people. I can't be held responsible for what they might do."

"Then you are threatening me," she said. "I thought so." Her eyes began to fill with stinging tears, but she blinked them back, refusing to let them fall. "I'm warning *you* of something," she said. "You get out of this group or this gang or whatever it is that you're calling it. You get out of it, you remove yourself from those friends, and you save yourself while it's not too late, because, so help me, those kids are going to go down if I have to take them down myself."

With that, she went back to the guest room, closed the door, and locked it. For the first time in her life, she didn't trust her nephew. She didn't even know who he was.

Chapter Ten

The fact that Nick was single rarely bothered him, though he had expected to marry by now. Most of the time he was so busy that he didn't have time to think about his loneliness, but on days like today when he was getting out of the hospital with no one to take him home and care for him, he inevitably wondered why God had not answered his prayers for a helpmeet.

Though he had only been here one night, it would have been nice to have a wife come from home and bring his toothbrush and his shaving kit, a change of clothes. Last night he had been barraged with visitors, but no one had thought to bring him the necessities that a wife might have thought of.

Now as he signed the papers and prepared to leave, he thought how nice it would have been if his wife had been there to fill out the paperwork for him, to fuss over him and make sure the nurses gave the proper instructions for caring for his burns and his broken ribs. It would have been nice to have someone look at him with concern in her eyes, and maybe even pamper him a little when he got home.

He didn't like to admit it, but it had been nice having Issie stay with him through the worst of the treatment yesterday. She had held his hand, talked him through the agony, pleaded with the doctor on his behalf. He wasn't used to that, but he had appreciated it.

A knock sounded on the door. He looked up and saw Jill and Dan Nichols standing in the doorway.

"Hey, guys," he said, his voice still raspy from the smoke inhalation. "Thanks for coming."

"We were glad to do it," Dan said. "Somebody's got to get you home, man."

Jill came in and hugged him. "How are you feeling, Nick?"

"Sore," he said. "I'm not liking these burns too much, but it could have been a lot worse. Voice is shot, but that's no big loss. Some people will love having me shut up for a while."

She looked around the room. "Where's your suitcase?"

He chuckled. "What suitcase? They brought me here in an ambulance."

"But no one brought you any clothes?"

He stood up carefully, showing her the T-shirt and gym shorts he'd been wearing when he was brought in. It was what he'd slept in at the station, and he had pulled his turnouts over them. "If I'd had a change of clothes, do you think I'd be wearing this?"

Jill tried to muffle her laughter.

"It's you," Dan said. "I really like the look."

"Hey, buddy, you were wearing the same thing when we got called to the fire. But you got to change." Nick grinned and went back to signing the papers. "I'm expecting the fashion police to arrest me in the parking lot."

"Hey, why didn't you get one of us to go by your house and get you some clothes?"

"Last night I didn't think of it. It never occurred to me until this morning that I didn't have anything to wear. I'll be fine. If you can just get me home without anybody seeing me, then I can change clothes and go visit Ray and Susan."

"Visit Ray and Susan?" Dan asked. "Nick, you need to be in bed. You don't need to be out visiting people."

"I'm not visiting 'people,'" Nick said. "They lost their son. I'm their preacher. I have to go see them."

Dan shot Jill a look that said they weren't going to be able to change his mind.

"Well, use your own judgment," Jill said quietly. "I hear they're taking it real hard."

"Of course they are." Nick's voice caught, and he shoved the papers away. "I never thought I'd be burying one of their children."

He got up and drew in a deep breath. It caught in his bruised side, and he winced. And putting weight on his legs made his burns hurt worse. "Let me just go find the nurse and get these forms turned in and we can go," he said.

He walked carefully as he stepped out of the room. But it wasn't his wounds that were keeping him down now, he thought. It was the heaviness of his heart over a destroyed church, a broken family, and a sense of failure that had enshrouded Nick since the fire yesterday.

Chapter Eleven

Stan and Celia were waiting at Nick's house when Jill and Dan got him home, and he was grateful to see that Celia had vacuumed and dusted and put away the few scattered things that he had left out. Already, at least a dozen casseroles lined his countertops. Someone had loaned him a freezer, and had delivered it to his carport this morning. Celia was trying to figure out what dishes could be frozen and which could not.

They'd moved his furniture around slightly so that he could rest more easily in the recliner and still reach reading materials and coffee on the table next to him. He hadn't thought of arranging the furniture quite that way before, but the woman's touch certainly added something. He gave Celia a hug and thanked her.

"Now sit down," she said. "Let me get you something to eat. You must be starved. I know how that hospital food can be."

"No, I can't. I've got to go visit Ray and Susan."

Celia's silence spoke volumes. She had been trained well, being married to the one detective in town. She knew better than to lecture him about taking it easy or being careful. Stan never listened.

"I'll go with you," Stan said.

Nick frowned. "It's not necessary, Stan. I can do it myself."

"No, you can't," Stan said. "I've been kind of putting it off. I need to talk to them about the case anyway. I think maybe we can answer some of their questions."

"Okay," he said, "but let's not wait much longer. I feel like I should have been there yesterday when they were going through the worst part of it. I just need to change clothes."

Celia grinned. "You sure you want to? Your gym shorts make a nice statement."

Nick looked down at his bandaged legs and the shorts he'd slept in at the station. "Yeah. It says, 'I'm an idiot.'" He shot her a grin and limped back to the bedroom.

He sifted through his drawers, looking for a pair of khaki shorts. Were they dirty? It was October, but it was still shorts weather most of the time in south Louisiana. He'd worn them just a couple of days ago. He began to feel overcome with weariness, and he sat down on the bed and tried to think. Had he washed them? If so, had he folded them, or did he need to go look in the dryer to see if they were still there? He dreaded the walk back in there. The scorched skin on his legs was covered tightly with bandages, but every flex of the muscles seemed to stretch the skin and cause undue agony. Just standing was an ordeal.

He forced himself to get up and look in the next drawer. He found them there, carefully folded, then sat back down to put them on.

Is this how it's going to be? he asked the Lord. *Is every movement going to wear me out?* He was going to have to do these things for himself, because soon he would be alone.

He could do this, he told himself. Carefully, he stepped out of his gym shorts and stepped into the khakis. The seam hit his bandage on the way up, and he winced. But he got them up, then sat there a moment, trying to catch his breath. His lungs felt as if they'd trapped half the heat of yesterday's fire in them, and his throat and trachea felt parched. He needed something to drink but didn't want to take the time.

His mother would come to take care of him if he asked her. But that wouldn't work, because she might bring his dad. The last thing he needed was his military father rummaging through his things and lecturing him on the need to do something with his life. No, he didn't need his father calculating what rank he should be, had he joined the military, or what income bracket he would be in. He didn't want him reminding him what kind of house and family he should have at age thirty-two.

No, he wasn't up to that now. He could handle this himself. In just a minute ... he would catch his breath ... and the pain would cease, and he could go visit Ray and Susan.

He slipped on a pair of flip-flops, and as he did, he thanked God that the burns hadn't been over his joints. At least he still had mobility in his feet and knees. It could have been so much worse.

He trudged back into the living room. Stan was ready to go, and he leaned over and gave Celia a kiss. "Pray for us," he said.

Celia nodded. "I will. You know I will. I've been praying for Ray and Susan all night. You too, Nick."

"Thanks," he said. "I needed it." He didn't know why he got choked up as he walked out to the car.

Chapter Twelve

Nick had hoped he and Stan would be able to visit with Susan and Ray alone, but he was surprised to see that the house was full of people when he got there.

Susan's parents were in the kitchen organizing the food that people from the church had already brought over. He figured they had doubled the recipes, and he had the counterparts at his house. Vanessa, Ben's sister, sat in the living room with her eyes swollen, talking on the phone in quiet tones. Several cousins and aunts and uncles milled around the small house. Susan was nowhere to be found, but they discovered Ray in the backyard hammering nails into a trellis he had been building during his time off.

Grief was a funny thing, Nick thought. Some people kept busy, some withdrew, some chattered. Some curled up in bed and cried, while others ate. He never knew what he would find.

After the introductions, Nick stepped into the living room to speak to Vanessa. He gave her a hug and she burst into tears. He told her how sorry he was. She nodded, suddenly unable to speak even with the phone next to her face.

"Where's your mother?" he whispered.

She shrugged. "I don't know. Probably in the bedroom. Mama's not feelin' well."

That didn't surprise him. He looked around and found Stan at the back door, saw that he was about to go out and talk to Ray. Nick crossed the room and followed him.

When they stepped out into the yard, they saw that Ray was hammering with more strength than was necessary. He didn't look up as they came out, just kept hammering as if his life depended on finishing this trellis and making it stand.

Next to the trellis, Susan had already planted jasmine, and Nick supposed that within a year the fast-growing vine would be covering the whole structure. Life went on.

They crossed the yard and finally caught Ray's eye. Nick put his hand on his shoulder, but Ray just kept hammering. "Thought you was in the hospital," Ray said.

"Just got out."

"You s'posed to be out and about?"

Nick shrugged. "I figured this was important enough."

"You didn't have to come." Ray stood back, surveying the trellis. "I was lookin' for a weak spot that needed a nail."

Stan looked down at his feet and saw some of the nails that Ray had already dropped. He bent down and picked a couple up, rolled them around in his hand.

"Do you think we could talk to you and Susan?" Nick asked. "Is there someplace we could go?"

Ray dropped the hammer to his side and looked down at it. "I don't know if Susan wants to talk. She's in the bedroom feelin' sick." He gave Stan a thoughtful look. "Is it about the investigation?"

"Yeah, it is. I wanted you to know where we are on this."

"Okay," he said. "I can go get her. I know she'll want to hear that." Ray dropped the hammer onto the fence next to the trellis, dusted off his hands, and started back into the house. "Let me just give Susan some warnin'," he said, "and then we can go talk to her in the bedroom. It's the only private place in the house right now."

"We'll just wait out here," Stan said.

Ray went into the house, and Stan sank down onto a patio chair.

Nick sat down next to Stan and looked out across the yard, thinking how miserable it felt to come here like this, to minister to a couple who had lost a child with no explanation, no warning. It was the part of his job he liked the least.

They sat in silence until the back door opened and Ray stuck his head out. "Come on in," he said. "Susan's waitin' in the bedroom."

Nick got up, trying not to wince when his legs protested, but he headed in and Stan followed him. They cut through the crowd of people meandering through the house and made their way back to the master bedroom. It wasn't a big room, just large enough for a full-sized bed and dresser, but one of the uncles had brought some chairs in so they could all sit together and talk.

Susan was already sitting in one of them, looking out the window.

"Hey, Susan," Nick said softly. He bent over to give her a hug, but she didn't respond at all. He squeezed her shoulders and backed away. Stan didn't even try.

Ray took the seat next to her and held her hand, and Stan and Nick sat on the bed across from them. Nick had never seen Susan like this. Her eyes were dull, and her face was as lifeless as Ben's had been.

"What you got to tell us, Stan?" Ray asked.

Stan leaned forward, his elbows on his knees. "Ray, Susan, we think this killing was racially motivated. Witnesses saw several people in a car leaving the scene, and the car had a swastika and a KKK sticker on the bumper."

Susan's face twisted as those words sank in. "My son was murdered because he was *black?*" She pressed the heels of her hands against her eyes and shook her head. "God help me! God help me!" she whispered.

"I think it's possible," Stan said. "The church burning could have just been a way of disposing of the body, or it could have been racial. We are a mixed congregation. If the KKK was involved, I'd say it was some kind of statement against us."

Ray's lips stretched tight across his teeth. "What statement could they have to make with my son?"

"I don't know," Stan said quietly. "They've been pretty quiet for a number of years. Sidney Clairmont, the grand wizard, is in his seventies. Probably doesn't have the venom he used to. Recruitment's way down. On the other hand, this could have been his way of letting us know that their activities are starting up again."

Ray got up and started walking around the room. Susan's dismal eyes followed him. "All these years," he said, "I've raised my children not to think of theirselves as bein' a different color. I told them that you could be anything you wanted to, that God had plans for everybody, no matter the race. Here I am, fire chief of Newpointe, and my son was a year away from havin' his marketin' degree at LSU. He was gon' be somebody. And you're tellin' me that because of the color of my skin, somebody come along and shot my son, burned down my church, all for some kind of sick statement he wanted to make?"

"I don't know for sure," Stan said. "But it's a lead."

Ray's face turned marble hard as he met his wife's eyes. "I'm gon' go out there and find 'em, Susan. I'm gon' find who did this and I'm gon' kill 'em with my bare hands."

Nick drew in a deep breath. "Ray, I know you feel that way now, but you can't go off half-cocked and try to do something about this. You have to let the police handle it."

Stan shifted in his seat. "Ray, we're not going to let this go. I have a personal interest in it. I don't take it lightly when friends of mine are murdered. Calvary was my church too. I'm going to find who killed Ben, and we're going to put him behind bars and he's going to stand trial and suffer for what he's done. You've got to let us do it."

Ray sank back down into the chair. Susan touched the back of his head. "He's right, Ray. I don't want to lose both the men in my life. Let Stan do it."

Ray began to weep, and Nick found himself staring at a spot on the carpet, making a valiant effort not to break down himself. When Ray had pulled himself together, Nick tried what he had come for.

"Ray and Susan, I need to talk to you about the funeral, if that's okay."

Ray drew in a deep breath and wiped his face roughly. "We didn't know if you'd be up to it," he said, "so we asked Susan's Uncle Thomas to do it."

"Oh, a relative?" Nick was not sure whether to be relieved or offended. Truth was, he really *wasn't* up to it, but he could have mustered the strength for them. He told himself this decision wasn't rejection of him. He didn't have time for wounded pride. "Well, that's understandable. I can see why you'd want him."

"I gotta tell you, Nick," Susan choked out. "We're mad at God. Real mad."

"I understand," he said. "That's normal. I think God understands that too."

"I want answers," Susan said through her teeth. "I want to know why—with all the violent, hateful, malicious people in this world—why did he take Ben?"

Nick met her eyes. He had always loved Susan. She had been a dynamo in the church, was always the encourager and the one to bring food when someone needed it, the one to baby-sit kids or take in a family who was down on their luck. She was always willing to give. Now she needed for someone to give back. He wished he had the answers for her. "God allowed this to happen for a reason," he said. "We may never know why, Susan."

"Don't matter *why*," she said. "There was no *reason* good enough to get my baby shot through the head and left in a ragin' fire to die. None! You hear me, Nick? And God and I won't be on speakin' terms till he convinces me otherwise."

She looked out the window again as tears rolled down her face. Nick dropped his eyes. Her child was gone and she couldn't hear reason. There was no rationale, only questions that couldn't be answered.

Chapter Thirteen

Nick was silent all the way home, but Stan kept lecturing to him about the fact that Susan and Ray had been through trauma, and that their reaction was only temporary. But Nick would rather have them blame him than God.

When they got to Nick's trailer, he saw the arson inspector from Slidell across the street sifting through the rubble. Several of the firefighters were on fire watch, to make sure that nothing ignited into flames again. Several members of his congregation were sitting in a circle on the lawn, holding hands and praying. The sight didn't evoke the usual paternal pride he felt when he saw his flock acting without him.

"What are they praying for?" he asked in a dull voice.

Stan shook his head. "There are a lot of things to pray for right now, Nick. Everybody feels real vulnerable. Our hearts are tender. Maybe this is just where God needs us to be."

Nick went in and watched from behind the screen door as Stan drove away. The trailer smelled like a celebration, with the different scents of lovingly cooked dishes. Ordinarily, he would have let the scents draw him and comfort him, but he had no appetite. And looking at those prayer warriors across the street, praying right out in the open, where anyone who drove by would see . . . that should stir the spirit in him. Were they praying for the people who had done this to their church? Were they praying for Ben's killers? He hoped they were praying for Susan and Ray, or for him.

But somehow he felt those prayers were falling on deaf ears.

"How does it glorify you, Lord," he whispered, "to see our church in a heap of ashes? How does that work to the good of those who love you?"

He closed and locked the door before anyone could cross the street to speak to him. He had nothing to say to them, nothing to give. Nothing at all.

He sat down and tried to get comfortable. He realized that since the church was no more, maybe he was no longer a preacher. He didn't have a funeral to preach, didn't have a pulpit, and his library of books which he kept in his office in the church had been burned away.

Every hope and dream had been consumed. And if Nick was no longer a preacher, then who was he? Maybe being a firefighter was enough. But the truth was that he had even been a failure at that. The irony overwhelmed him, that here he was a preacher and a firefighter, and his own church had been destroyed by fire.

The doorbell rang, and he closed his eyes tight and decided not to answer it. He couldn't see anyone right now. He couldn't talk.

His stomach told him it was lunchtime, so he ate a dinner roll. He was too tired to get up and serve a plate from one of the dishes in the kitchen. Sometimes a person needed to just lie there and stare at the ceiling. There seemed to be no alternative.

He tried to nap for a while, but sleep wouldn't come. When the phone rang, he let the machine get it.

The call from Stan telling him the elders of his church had called a meeting to discuss what needed to be done hit him like a dull thud between his eyes. He wasn't ready to meet with the elders, not until he'd managed to drag himself out of this melancholy.

But he didn't know if he'd be able to do that. Despair had never weighed so heavily on his heart. There was nothing left. Someone might as well admit it.

For some time he had been insecure about his calling. Every time he failed a church member by saying the wrong thing, saying too much, not saying enough, he wondered if he should be a preacher at all. Every time he lost a member, every time he saw one backslide, every time he couldn't address their needs, he realized how much better a full-time preacher might do. Maybe being bivocational was his downfall, but he couldn't afford to live on what they paid him at the church. Maybe someone else could.

He went to his computer in the tiny living room and turned it on. He sat staring at the screen, wondering what he would say if he composed a letter of resignation and gave it to the elders tonight.

But his resignation seemed almost moot at this point. What was there to resign *from*, after all? Still, he felt he needed to make the gesture just for the purpose of offering closure to the congregation who depended on him. They would all be free to scatter in their own directions. Some could go to the Baptist church that worshiped on Jacquard. Others would decide to try the Presbyterian church over on Second Avenue. Methodists worshiped on Rue Matin, and then there was, of course, the Catholic church on the west side of Newpointe. Nick supposed that he would find a place to worship, where it wouldn't be so uncomfortable being a sheep instead of a shepherd.

He typed a letter that was straightforward and to the point, then punched the key to print it out. He watched as it scrolled through the printer. In a few seconds it was a done deal. The elders would have to accept the demise of the church, put the land up for sale, and move on with their lives. Somehow, he would get over the Lord's removing his calling. He had to fight the bitterness welling up inside, and this debilitating sense of failure. He had to get rid of the pride that was making him bitter.

Somehow, he had to swallow it all and find a way to look up to the Lord with his hands open and say, "What next, Lord? You tell me. I'm yours." He was a jar of clay, and some jars of clay were meant to be used for noble purposes. Others were not. Maybe he was one of those instruments of mediocrity, one of those common vessels with no significant purpose. Maybe he'd just been kidding himself, thinking that the Lord had marked him for special service.

Fighting back the tears in his eyes, he bathed himself as best he could without getting his bandaged legs wet, and tried to wash the pain and regrets away.

• • •

Nick was a few minutes late for the meeting, which was being held in the kitchen at the fire station. He went in and saw that most of the church leaders were there. Mark and Dan, still on duty, Stan Shepherd, Frank Dupree from the hospital lab, Jesse Pruitt, retired schoolteacher, Vern Hargis and Sid Ford, cops, and Andre Bouchillon, who owned most of the apartments in town, were all at the table, waiting. Aunt Aggie, as comfortable in the fire station's kitchen as any of the firefighters there, was cutting pieces of cheesecake and pouring coffee. They were already engaged in discussion when he arrived, but the room got amazingly quiet the moment he limped in.

He stood in the doorway, looking from one man to the other, wishing he didn't feel so vulnerable and broken. He felt like telling them there was no point in going on with this. They didn't have to pretend anymore. It was over. They could just pronounce the church dead and move on.

"T-Nick, you get off 'em feet and prop them legs up, you!" Aunt Aggie cried, pulling him toward two chairs. She had fashioned an ottoman out of one of them. "I tried tellin' 'em you didn't need to be out runnin' around with burned up lungs and fried legs. Want some cheesecake, *sha*?" The Cajun forms of *petite* and *chere* rolled right past him.

"No, thanks." He was too tired and out of breath to refute any one of Aunt Aggie's claims about him, so he just lowered to the chair and propped his legs up.

"So how are you feeling, buddy?" Jesse Pruitt asked him gently.

"Fine," he said. "Really, I'm fine. I'll be good as new in a few days." Each man reached across the table to shake his hand, and as he greeted them, he realized that one of the deacons was missing. Ray Ford. Of course. A man preparing to bury his son didn't come to church meetings. Especially if he blamed his son's death on God.

His heart twisted with as much pain as his bandaged shins. When the greetings were done, the men sat back, giving the floor to him, as if he would open the meeting and lead them in some enlightened discussion about the state of the church, making them all feel better.

He could hear some of the firemen—probably Slater Finch, Marty Bledsoe, and Jacob Baxter—working out in the truck bay. Today was truck cleanup day. They would have their work cut out for them, after yesterday. Tomorrow they would do yard work when they weren't on a call. The next day was housecleaning day, when they scrubbed toilets and mopped floors. Despite all the menial chores that kept them busy, fire fighting was an important job, nothing to sneeze at, nothing to make him feel deprived. At least he'd been properly trained for that. It was preaching he wasn't adequately educated for. Taking seminary classes at night wasn't the kind of training that made one a great pastor.

He shifted in his chair, wondering if the fatigue brought on by his damaged throat and lungs, the stress from yesterday, the burns and bruises, might be making him feel extraordinarily defeated. Maybe he needed to sleep on it, pray on it, and wait a little while before handing them that letter.

But he didn't have the energy to wait. The sooner this door was closed, the better. He didn't have what it took to see them through the life-support efforts when the church was nothing but a corpse.

He cleared his throat. When they kept waiting, he knew he should open with a prayer. But he was too tired. He needed to economize his words, save his voice. "I want to thank whoever called this meeting," he said finally. "As you might imagine, I've been a little shaken up and haven't really been thinking too clearly. But we do have some decisions to make."

He pulled the letter out of his pocket, his hands shaking. He looked down at it, ran his fingers over it. After a long pause, he put it on the table in front of him. "I guess this can be the first decision we take care of."

The deacons stared at it as if they didn't know which one of them should read it first.

"What is it, Nick?" Sid asked.

Nick drew in a deep, raspy breath and pulled it back. "Well, I guess I'd better read it out loud," he said. "It's my letter of res-ignation."

There was a collective gasp around the room, and Mark slapped his hands on the table. "Nick, you've got to be kidding."

"No," he said. "I have to do it. God took my church away from me. I have to accept that."

"God didn't take your church away," Dan said, in a tone that suggested Nick was delirious. "Some maniac did. He didn't *fire* you, for heaven's sake. *We* didn't fire you. We still have a congregation, Nick. We need a pastor."

Nick fought the tears in his eyes, but they were stronger than he was. "Maybe I've led us wrong," he said. "Maybe I haven't been everything I need to be."

Stan sat at the end of the table, watching him with tired, serious eyes. "This is about Ray and Susan, isn't it, Nick?"

Nick met his eyes. "No, Stan, it's nothing to do with that."

"Of course it is," Stan said. He looked around at the others. "Nick and I visited Ray and Susan today. They said some things about being mad at God. Nick's taking that as a personal failure."

"Look, my brother's hurtin'," Sid cut in gently. "The whole family is."

Nick pinched the bridge of his nose.

"The point is," Stan said, "you can't base your decision on emotion after a tragedy."

"I'm basing my decision on a lot of things," Nick said, sliding his hands down his face. "I've failed the church. I've failed it miserably. When a kid is found murdered in your sanctuary and it's burned down before your eyes, you have to ask what God is trying to tell you."

"He's not trying to tell you anything," Dan said. "Nick, you've taught us a million times in a million different ways that sometimes God brings suffering to purify us. We've prayed for revival. Well, maybe this is it. Maybe this is really an answered prayer."

"An answered prayer?" Nick asked. "How in the *world* do you figure that?"

"Maybe people will get closer to the Lord through this. Maybe he can use it."

Stan leaned forward on the table, his arms crossed in front of him. "Nick, I think I can speak for all of us when I say that we won't accept your resignation. You need to pray about this. You don't need to do it the day after you've been through such serious trauma, both physical and mental. You need to give it some time. I guarantee you, when you're feeling better and stronger, when you've had time to rest and heal, when you see what God is going to do with the church from here on out, you're going to change your mind."

"No, I'm not, Stan. I'm not going to change it."

"Fine," Dan told him. "Then if you still feel this way in a month or so, you can always quit then."

Nick sighed heavily, then began to cough. When he stopped, he felt soul-weary and too tired to fight them. "I'll think about waiting," he said. "I'm not promising anything."

"Fine," Sid said. "Now then, we need to talk about where we gon' meet till we get that church rebuilt."

"I was thinking," Dan said, "of asking the mayor if we could use the courtroom. It's probably big enough, and it's empty on Sundays."

"Good idea," Stan said. "You get her to agree to it, and we can start calling people to let them know. If she doesn't agree, we can try the high school auditorium. Third choice might be the Ritz Theater. We might have to sweep up popcorn and drink cups before the service, but it's better than nothing."

"I'll find us a place," Dan assured them. "Leave it to me."

"Well, that's one problem solved," Sid said.

"Now we need to get the insurance adjuster out," Jesse Pruitt said. "Nick, you give me the information on the company, and I'll place the claim."

Nick hadn't even thought of that. Maybe they were right. Maybe he was too sick to make rational decisions. "Okay, Jesse," he said. "I appreciate that. I'm sure I've got a number or something at home, even though the policy itself probably burned in the fire."

Mark touched Nick's shoulder. "See, Nick? It's all gonna be okay. We're gonna take care of what we can, and God will take care of the rest. And I just have a feeling about Sunday."

"What kind of feeling?" Nick asked.

"A feeling that the Holy Spirit is going to do some mighty things," Dan said, as if he had the same feeling. "You wait, Nick. This is not the end of our church. It may just be a fresh beginning."

Chapter Fourteen

Because there was always the chance that a smoldering ember might blow into a flame again, Mark, Dan, and George took the evening fire watch the day after the fire. They hacked at parts of the wall still standing, making sure that every spark had died. There would be someone here around the clock for the next couple of days.

When members began showing up to see the charred structure, they kept them back. So the members congregated at one end of the property, far enough away from the debris not to get hurt, but close enough that they were still on the property.

Someone brought a guitar and they began to sing praise songs together, and slowly the crowd grew. From the way they sang and praised God, one would think that he had swooped down and struck them with a glorious gift instead of a devastating fire.

Mark didn't want Allie to miss it. He went back to the truck, got his cell phone out, and dialed his home number.

"Hello?"

"Hey, hon. How's it goin'?"

Her sigh told him she hadn't gotten over the shock of the tragedy. "Okay, I guess. I just got back from Susan and Ray's. It was bad, Mark."

"I know something that might make you feel better. They're holding a bona fide church service right on the church grounds. Singing and praising God, just like Nick taught us."

"You're kidding."

"No. It's really amazing. Jacob Baxter has his guitar, and people who drive by to see the damage keep stopping and getting out. I think it's a great testimonial to the community. Don't you want to come?"

"Do you think it's too cool out for Justin?" she asked, referring to their toddler.

"I think it's fine. He'll probably sleep through it."

"Then we'll be right there."

He clicked off the phone and leaned back against the truck, watching the spirit of his church declare that it had lived on, even if the building was gone. He wondered if he should go knock on Nick's door and give him the chance to join in. Then he thought better of it. If he wasn't aware of it already, it probably meant he was so wiped out that he needed his rest.

Allie arrived with little Justin, and the child slept on her shoulder as she sang and swayed in worship. Staying near the debris, Mark began to sing with them, and soon Dan and George joined in. Like the others, they began to feel a sense of hope rather than a sense of mourning. It was just as Nick had taught them to react to trials. "Consider it joy," he'd said time and time again. "Thank God when he refines you like silver."

Soon the praise songs turned to prayers, and the members prayed one by one, lifting up the Fords and their family and friends, lifting up Nick for healing both inside and out, lifting up the church body, which had challenges ahead, lifting up the community that still had so much to learn.

People began to weep as they prayed, and one by one, some dropped to the ground, with no concern for the dirt on their knees. Eventually, others fell to their faces, wailing out their combination of confession and repentance, mourning and thanksgiving, prayers of intercession and prayers of hope for the future.

As night fell over the group, the singing began again, interspersed with more prayer. The group grew, as if word had traveled that a prayer meeting was going on, and no one wanted to miss it. It was loud and heartfelt, passionate and private, purging and purifying, a tent revival without a tent or an evangelist.

Something was happening in the church, something Mark had never seen before. The Holy Spirit was here, his power brighter than the fire that had swallowed the building. They could set fire to the church and destroy the building, but their lampstand still stood.

• • •

It was about nine o'clock when a 1986 model Ford van drove by too slowly, its rattling engine disrupting the church, and its loud rap music blaring at eardrum-shattering level. The dirty white van slowed as it passed the worshipers, then it screeched off, running a stop sign. Sid Ford, who had joined the group halfway through, left the circle and went to his squad car, parked on the side of the road. It took him a couple of blocks to catch up to the van with the half-deaf occupants. He knew he had no grounds to arrest them, but at least he could shake them up a little, make them stop disturbing the peace while driving through town.

He turned on his lights and gave them a block to pull over. Holding his flashlight, he got out, walked toward the van, and saw a swastika sticker in the bottom corner of the rear window. An alarm clanged in his head. Hadn't a witness claimed she'd seen several kids leaving the church before anyone noticed the fire? But she'd seen a red car, with two stickers on the bumper, not on the window. Still . . . had these four had something to do with murdering his nephew?

The radio volume lowered as he continued to the driver's door, staying back as he'd been trained. He shone the light into the window.

"We didn't do nothin'," the driver said.

In the flashlight beam, Sid saw three white guys and a girl. They all looked relatively clean-cut. The driver was blond and more tanned than normal for this time of year. He had the look of one of those action-movie stars who hit celebrity overnight.

"Can I see your driver's license, please?" he asked through his teeth.

The driver pulled his billfold out and thrust his license at him. "What did you pull me over for?" He sounded weary and fed up.

"For going sixty in a thirty-mile zone, runnin' a stop sign, and disturbin' the peace."

"Disturbin' the peace?" the driver asked. "You've got to be kidding me. And I wasn't speeding."

"I say you was. And since I'm the cop, it's my word that counts. See, they listen to me down at headquarters, not to a vanload of punks with hate signs stuck on their windows. Besides, I got a couple dozen witnesses back there. Stay right here."

The driver opened his door and started to get out.

"I *told* you to stay there," Sid said.

The kid continued to get out of the van. "I don't take orders from people like you."

Sid laughed bitterly, thinking how much he would enjoy putting this kid in his place. Yeah, these white supremacists were superior, all right, with their smart mouths and stupid rebellion against authority. Real intellectual.

It occurred to him that he could show this little coward who he'd take orders from, but he decided to savor the moment. He needed backup, just to make sure he didn't lose them. Since they very well could be the killers and arsonists, he wanted to keep them here as long as he could. He put his hand on his weapon. "You got a choice. You can either get back in your van until I say you can get out, or you can stand here, provin' your superiority with a pair of handcuffs on your wrists, or you can come sit in the back of my squad car with those handcuffs on, since that's probably where you gon' wind up, anyway."

After trying to stare him down, the kid slowly got back into his car, as if it was his idea and had nothing to do with Sid's suggestion. Sid grinned and leaned down into the window. "There now. You are an intellect, ain't you? A veritable genius. Now you just stay there while I go back to my car for a minute, because if you so much as start your engine, you won't have to worry about gettin' arrested. I'll take care of you myself, before you even have time to turn that steerin' wheel. Now why don't you give me your driver's license?"

He left them sitting there and went back to his car. Keeping his eyes on them, he radioed in. "Three-three-two to Midtown. I just pulled over four punks for speedin' and disturbin' the peace, but I have reason to believe they could be suspects in Ben's murder and the church burnin'. Witnesses saw a swastika sticker on the getaway car, and this one has one. Need backup and a search warrant, fast as I can get it. And run this name through, see whatcha got."

After a moment, the dispatcher radioed back. "Sid, that Jason Cruz is the one Stan's been looking for. He said to tell you he's the one threatened Nick Foster."

"Score!" Sid sat still for a moment, feeling no joy that his nephew's murderer might be in that car in front of him.

"We have a search warrant on the way. Judge DeLacy was still at the courthouse. Vern Hargis is bringing it."

In moments, they had all four kids out of the van being frisked, while Sid and the others searched it for any clues that they had played a part in the burning or the murder. They found stacks of white supremacy and Aryan nation propaganda, but no gas cans or guns, no blood on the seats or in the carpet, no drugs or alcohol, nothing that would make it appropriate to impound the van and throw them in jail.

Nothing, except for the hunch that Nick Foster had had about Jason Cruz getting even. They had been looking for him, wanting to bring him in for questioning, but hadn't caught up with him until now. Sid Foster wasn't about to let him go.

"Okay, now, here's how it's gon' be," he said, trying to temper his voice so he wouldn't sound like a vengeful uncle. "Jason, here—"

"Cruz," the kid cut in. "They call me Cruz."

"Okay, *Cruz*. Cruz here's gon' come to the station with me. We got a few things to talk about, like where he was in the wee hours of yesterday mornin', what he knows about Ben Ford's death and the church burnin' . . ."

"Wait a minute," Cruz said. "I ain't goin' nowhere."

"Well, now, you can come peaceably, or I can handcuff you and drag you in. I prefer the latter, but we'll let it be your choice."

Cruz swallowed and looked back at his sister. "Jen, go back and tell everybody that we're being persecuted. That they ran us down on the road without probable cause and are taking me in without an arrest warrant. Tell Granddaddy to call his lawyer."

The girl flung her hair back over her shoulder and took a bold step toward Sid. She was almost as tall as he, and as skinny as a runway model. He could see that she didn't have much fear in her. "You ain't got anything on him."

"We have witnesses," Sid said. "Witnesses who saw some punks comin' out of that church just before they noticed the fire. Witnesses who saw a swastika and KKK emblem on the bumper. And the curiosity that had you drivin' by the church grounds tonight, what with the sticker on your van and your smart mouth, make you prime suspects, as far as I'm concerned. Maybe you'd like to come in with your brother and answer a few questions too." He pulled out his pad as if to write. "No problem to add Cruzette to our little party tonight."

"I go by Jennifer," she bit out.

"You can see how I'd be confused. That's J-e-n-n—"

"No," Cruz cut in. "Jen, you go back and tell them. Tell Granddaddy. I can take care of this until he gets there."

Jennifer didn't like it, but she nodded to the others and went to get in on the driver's side. Before she got in, she gave him a worried look over the door. "Cruz?"

"It's okay," he said, almost gently. "Don't worry. Just do what I said."

As Sid escorted Cruz to the backseat of his squad car, he watched that van drive away. He wished he could lock up the whole bunch. Eventually, he vowed that he would, if they had anything at all to do with Ben's murder. As soon as he took care of Cruz, he'd get a rap sheet on each of them, assign someone to tail them, find out who else they hung out with, what they did in their spare time, where they worked, what their agendas were. If they were involved in the killing of his nephew, Sid Ford was going to make sure they paid.

Chapter Fifteen

Because the Cain and Addison Funeral Home expected record numbers of mourners for Ben's visitation, they convinced Susan and Ray to have a four-hour visitation. That would help with traffic in the parking lot and through the building, they were told. It was simply a matter of convenience.

There had been some debate as to whether to open the casket, but the undertaker had promised that he could cover the bullet hole. There had been no significant burns to Ben's face, so Susan saw no reason to deprive his friends of the closure the viewing would bring them.

By the third hour, Susan and Ray were still on their feet, hugging tearful friends who'd lined up to pay their respects. Susan wasn't making sense anymore, and Ray wished he could call a halt to the rest of it and take her away where she could sit down and take her shoes off and let go.

But as many words of comfort were offered to them, Ray found that Susan was trying to offer just as many in return. She clung to each mourner, as if she knew their hearts were broken with hers. She told them each what precious friends they'd been to her son, even if she'd never seen them before in her life. She made them each feel that their presence here had made all the difference in her level of grief. He didn't know how she did it. He knew she had not slept last night. He had heard her sobbing in Ben's room, and had gotten up to see about her. The door had been locked, so he'd respected her need to be alone. He had gone out to the backyard then and wept his heart out under the stars. He wasn't sure anymore if God heard.

Someone whispered something to her, something Ray hadn't heard, and Susan burst into tears again and clung to that person as if he were Ben's best friend. She wept openly, without any stoic acceptance, without that glow that some were able to have in the face of tragedy, declaring God to be sovereign and all-knowing, and trusting in him. Instead, he knew that trust would be a long time in coming. She would have to work that out with God on her own . . . just as he would.

Lord, I can take the pain, he thought. *But help her with hers. She's so fragile. She can't take it, Lord.*

He watched, broken and weary, as they came one by one. And each time someone approached the casket, he saw Susan stiffening slightly, looking that way, as if desperately wanting to tell them not to touch him, that she didn't even want them looking at him long. He knew how she felt. He felt it too. It was all he could do last night not to come to the funeral home and insist on sleeping on the floor next to his son.

The fact that Ben was in heaven, and not lying in that casket, provided little comfort. He had searched his heart for all the Scripture he had ever learned about heaven and death, but it failed him now. He needed someone to quote it to him, remind him what it said. But he didn't want to hear it from Nick, because part of him blamed the preacher.

He blamed him and Mark and Dan, and all the guys who'd fought the fire that morning. He blamed Stan and the police force for letting lunatics run the roads and kidnap innocent victims and murder them. He blamed the paramedics who couldn't bring him back to life, and he blamed the coroner who must have seen Ben as just another job, even though it hadn't been obvious.

And if he were honest, he had to admit that he blamed everyone in line here, for not being aware enough of the evil in their community to call it what it was and purge it from their town. If someone, anyone, had seen them take Ben ... if one person had made a phone call ... turned someone in ... Ben might be alive.

He knew it wasn't rational, but he didn't care. And now he blamed the funeral home for a visitation that stretched beyond human endurance, and for the mourners who dared to smile in the halls and talk about things other than death and Ben.

And most of all, he blamed himself, for not being there when his son needed him, for not coming to his aid, for not protecting him as he had always tried to do. The big fire chief of Newpointe, the big rescuer, who couldn't even save his own son.

The irony almost buried him.

But still the people came, and whispered, and wept, and Susan kept clinging and crying and chattering empty phrases over and over ...

Ray just wanted it all to end.

Chapter Sixteen

Jennifer bolted into the house, all fury and rage, and slammed the door with an authority that silenced the dozen kids there. "They arrested him. Took him to jail without probable cause."

"Who?" Jake asked.

"Cruz, that's who!" she shouted like he was a fool. "Took him in handcuffs like a criminal, when he didn't do nothing wrong. We were just driving through town minding our own business . . ."

Jake decided it wouldn't be a good time to point out that Cruz *had* done something wrong. There was that little matter of murder, but everyone seemed to have forgotten it.

"I got my granddaddy to call his lawyer in Slidell, but the idiot is out of town and won't be back until morning. So Cruz has to sit there all night, in a jail cell, and he ain't done nothing wrong!" She waved her arm at the group as a thought came to her. "You know what this is about. It's about who we are. The grandchildren of the grand wizard of the KKK. But you know what? This is a free country, and you don't get to arrest somebody just because they're related to somebody you don't like."

"Did they say anything about the fire and the shooting?" Benton dared to ask.

Jake was proud of his friend's courage. He wished he'd managed to get that question out.

"Oh, yeah, that came up," Jennifer said. Her cheeks looked as if they'd been slapped hard, and she paced back and forth, back and forth, in front of them, like a caged tiger trying to find an escape. "We've got to intervene, that's all there is to it. We have to do something to divert suspicion."

"We should pray for him." The guy who came up with that was what Jake would have called a fanatic. Roy Decareaux had dropped out of high school in the ninth grade and worked at the Burger King for minimum wage. His dream had been to be an evangelist, until Cruz gave him a greater purpose.

"Okay," Jennifer said, almost as if humoring him. "Let's pray."

"On our knees," Roy said.

"Right. On our knees," Jennifer said, then flashed her eyes to the others. "Get down, everybody. Now!"

Jake looked around, feeling awkward, and realized that everyone else did too. Some of them stood on their knees, with hands clasped in front of them like toddlers beside their beds. Others sat back on their heels, balancing themselves with a hand on the floor on either side of them. Only Jennifer failed to kneel, but she stood at the front of the room with her hands raised high, and began to yell her prayers, as if God was hard of hearing.

Jake wondered if a real God would like to be talked to like that. Would he really want some raving girl, pretty as she was, spouting out confusing things like "confound the enemy" and "curse those who persecute us"? Or was that just what God wanted from them? Did you have to know his language to approach him? What if some ordinary Joe like him ever wanted to pray, and didn't know those phrases? Would God still hear? Would he hear now?

Jake looked up at Jennifer from his crouch on the floor, and saw the tears streaming down her face. His heart softened, and he realized her prayers were genuine. It broke his heart. He didn't like seeing her cry. He fought the urge to get up and put his arms around her and let her cry on his shoulder. It probably wasn't a good idea.

So he kept pretending to pray, wondering if there really was a God up there who was listening to their pleas to hide the murder they'd committed, and helping them get away with burning one of his churches. Was it true that God really favored white people? Wasn't Jesus from the Middle East? Wouldn't his skin have been dark?

But Jennifer seemed to think God was listening. Who was Jake to question it? After all, he knew nothing of God. She'd been raised from birth to believe. She knew tons of Scripture by heart, and Cruz, the most spiritual person he had ever known, had memorized the entire New Testament. If anyone knew God, he supposed they did.

He thought about the first time he'd seen Jennifer Cruz, a couple of years ago when he was fourteen and she was sixteen. She and Cruz had been at the ballpark after a game one night, when kids congregated on the dark field to smoke cigarettes and drink wine coolers. They had walked onto the field like some kind of rock star and super model, and had gotten everybody's attention. Especially Jake's.

He'd had a crush on Jennifer ever since, and unless he was mistaken, the feeling was mutual.

After all, she'd recommended him as drummer for their band, hadn't she?

Plus, Cruz was the most likeable guy he'd ever met, and had accepted Jake right into his group. What a relief to be taken for who you were after being labeled an outcast in high school, since he wasn't a jock or a junior politician. Jake felt like he was part of something important. The Twelve Disciples, Cruz called them, leaving himself and Jennifer out of the count. Jake and Benton had nothing but respect and admiration for all of the "brothers and sisters" of the group, from the illustrious "inner circle," consisting of Cruz, Jennifer, Redmon, and Graham, to Grayson and LaSalle who constantly lobbied to be among the favored few. And he respected the couples—Decareaux and his girlfriend Blair, Butch and Meg, and Drew and Kaye. They were all unified in purpose, and accepted without question.

When Jake and Benton had told Cruz about Benton's dead grandmother's house, they had suddenly become heroes. They needed a place to gather until they could start converting Cruz's grandfather's old deer camp into a compound in which they could all live. Cruz told them that God had sent them, because he knew they needed a place to hold their meetings and their band practices. Since this house was vacant and Benton's family had no plans to sell it for a while, it was perfect.

Suddenly, life got interesting. Though Jake still drifted home for a couple hours of sleep each night, he had bought his way into Cruz's following by donating anything he owned that they could sell. It seemed to be for a good cause. Cruz and Jennifer had goals, and he was part of them. He didn't think he'd ever had a goal before.

But now he wondered if it was getting out of hand.

Jennifer finished praying, then wiped her face and took the stool that her brother usually occupied. "It came to me during prayer," she said. "God revealed to me that we have to do something to divert attention from Cruz. If they think he was involved in the church burning and the killing, and that the others of us were . . . me and Redmon and Graham . . . then we have to give ourselves an airtight alibi tonight, and do it all again."

"Do what again?" Jake asked.

"Another church burning, and another black killing."

The crowd of kids roared out its disapproval, but she raised her hands and quieted them. "Just listen. This is a holy war. *Rahowa*. Say it with me."

All twelve followers muttered the word that had become a chant, symbolizing the racial holy war that Cruz said they were engaged in.

"Again!" she cried.

"Rahowa!"

"Like you mean it!"

"Rahowa!"

"We've had one taken captive," she went on. "If we're really what we say we are, then we can't stop now. We have to prove that Cruz ain't the one responsible for the killing. Something has to happen while he's in police custody, and while we're busy somewhere else. We have to throw them off. I need volunteers to do this for us. For Cruz . . . for me." She waited, and no one came forward.

An alarm blared in Jake's chest. She was asking him to be involved this time, to kidnap some kid and beat him to death or shoot him, to throw him into a fire and let him burn to death. She was asking him to get his own hands dirty, not to just stand back on the perimeter while somebody else did the dirty work.

He began to sweat as the silence in the room lingered. What if she chose him, as Cruz had chosen the ones who'd helped him with Ben Ford?

"Cruz ain't made disciples of cowards, has he?" she asked. "No, he's chosen only the best. The loyal ones. And when he comes into his kingdom, those of you he's counted on will reign with him."

Jake hadn't been with the group long enough to understand all of the things they believed about Cruz. This "coming into his kingdom" stuff still baffled him, but he knew there was something different about this genius who could memorize the Bible and build a compound and plan the security to protect it. He wasn't an ordinary man. Whether he was some kind of higher being, Jake wasn't sure, but he supposed he had more belief in Cruz than he had in God. He just wasn't ready to gamble his life on him.

When his best friend, Pete Benton, got to his feet, Jake froze.

"I'll do it," Benton said with a half-grin. Jake knew he didn't fully understand what he was volunteering for. His bulb had always been a tad dim. Jake thought he just had bad genes, since his father was an unemployed construction worker who only got a job when he ran out of drinking money. His mother supported them fixing hair twelve hours a day.

Jennifer's face blossomed into that charismatic Cruz smile, and she gave Benton a my-hero look and slid her arms around his neck. As she raised up to press a kiss on his lips, Jake felt a stab of jealousy that almost made him volunteer. But even the thought of Jennifer's attention wasn't enough to make him volunteer for murder.

But it was enough for Roy Decareaux, who was next to volunteer. Jennifer laughed with delight, as if he'd just asked her to the prom. Then Jack LaSalle, rumored to have a coveted relationship with Jennifer already, offered himself.

Jake was flooded with relief.

Jennifer turned all three around to face the group. "I always knew these three were chosen, that one day I'd need them, and that I could count on them. Now, here's the plan. The band plays at the Viper Pit tonight. I'll talk to Butch and set it up. We're all there, making a lot of noise. Meanwhile, our three heroes find another victim, take care of him, start another church fire, then rush back to the Pit, where we'll swear you've been all along."

She pulled her hair back from her face, and let it slip back down. "Of course, the cops will come looking for us first thing, but we'll have all been there. They won't have no choice but to start looking for some other group. With Cruz in jail and us at the Pit, how could we have done what they say? And then they got no choice but to move on and look for somebody else."

Everyone cheered, and Jake wondered if these poor idiots could really pull off such a thing. Chances were, they'd wind up in jail. Would they talk then? Name names? How would she keep them from it?

As the band members began loading up their equipment to take to the Viper Pit, Jake tried to shake the swirling doubts in his head at what they were all getting into. Another kid was going to die, and what was it all about? To purify the culture, by getting rid of those who were ethnically inferior?

Things were getting hazy, and now it didn't seem about any cause at all. The first death had been about getting even with some preacher guy who'd insulted Cruz. This second one was about diverting the police.

It was hard to get behind a cause that wasn't really a cause.

As they dispersed and headed for their cars to the Viper Pit, he moved slowly, thinking of speaking up, questioning what they were about to do. Jennifer approached him near his car. "Hey, Jake," she said in that sweet way that made him feel favored above all the others.

"Yeah?"

"I was thinking about your aunt. How safe do you think Cruz is with her out there?"

"I don't know what you mean."

"I mean, she was snooping around here last night. She saw things. Her apartment was hit. What if she goes to the police and tells them about the carpet in the bonfire? What if she identifies my brother?"

"Identifies him as what? She doesn't know anything."

"She could cause trouble, is all I'm saying."

"But she won't. If she did, she'd get me in trouble, and Issie won't do that."

"But she's mad about her apartment—the cat and everything. Maybe she's scared and won't feel safe till she exposes us."

He wanted to ask her why they didn't think of that before they'd terrorized her, but he managed to keep his mouth shut. "You don't have to worry about Issie. I talked to her last night, okay? She's cool. She doesn't want me to get tied up as a murder suspect, so she won't say anything."

"I was just thinking that . . . maybe we need to make sure."

Anger tingled in his face. "So what are you suggesting? Kill her too?"

"Jake!" She smiled and took his hands, pulled him close, and clasped his hands behind her back. He hadn't been this close to her before, and he smelled the strawberry scent of her hair. His heart was on overload, hammering out a maddening beat. He hoped the others saw this. "Of course I don't mean kill her. What kind of person do you think I am?"

He thought of saying that she was the kind of person who would order a murder just to throw people off of her brother, but the words seemed broken, incomplete in his mind. He couldn't think clearly when she was this close.

"I'm saying that maybe she needs to be watched. Maybe she needs to be a little more afraid than she is."

"She's plenty scared. She slept at my house last night because she was afraid to stay home."

"Excellent," Jennifer said. "Really, that's excellent. Then you talked to her?"

"I told her to stay out of it."

"Do you think she will?"

"Like I told you, Issie's kept my secrets before. The last thing she wants is to see me thrown in jail. Really, Jennifer, you can trust me and my family."

"I thought I could," she said, gazing down into his eyes. He saw adoration there, infatuation so deep that it almost mirrored his. She liked him too, he thought. It wasn't just his imagination. He wasn't one of those geeks that she was manipulating into committing crimes. This wasn't like that.

She leaned down and kissed him so suddenly that it startled him, and then he gave into it and gave back. Just when he thought his heart would leap out of his chest, she stopped. She released him and stepped back, looked down at the ground, swept her hair behind her ear. "I didn't mean to do that," she said, looking embarrassed.

His throat was suddenly dry, and he rasped out, "No, don't apologize. It was . . . it was good." He laughed then at his own poor choice of words. "Excellent."

"Yeah, it was excellent, wasn't it?" she asked. She leaned into him and whispered, "Just like I thought." Then, as if she couldn't bear to face him after saying that, she turned and headed back to the van.

Jake stood there watching her, his heart beginning to hurt. It wasn't just his imagination. She *had* singled him out.

How had he gotten so lucky?

Forgetting the doubts that had swirled through his mind earlier about the cause not really being a cause, he finished loading his drums.

Chapter Seventeen

So you're the grandson of Sidney Clairmont, the grand wizard of the KKK?" Stan asked Jason Cruz as he sat across from him in the interrogation room.

"That's right," Cruz said, thrusting his chin up as if they were talking about a former U.S. president.

"So what was his part in this murder and in my church burning?"

"My granddaddy had no part in this. He's an old man. The KKK ain't hardly even active in this town anymore. You're the cop. You ought to know that."

"Looks like we might have a new generation of hate mongers."

"Hate mongers?" He leaned up on the table, getting closer to Stan. "Hey, man, you're white. And if that was your church, then you're Christian. Don't you want your country back? Don't you want to take care of your own?"

"Some of my own are black," Stan said.

"Right." Cruz leaned back in his chair and leveled those hypnotic eyes on him. "Come on, be straight. Don't you ever imagine what our country would be like if every culture under the sun wasn't here?"

"I'm sure the Indians used to think that, when we whites were moving into their land."

"But they're inferior too. God gave the land to the people with the brains, man. The ones who could make it fly. And we have, except that the gays and blacks and Latinos and Jews and Muslims and who knows who else are in here corrupting everything and turning it into hell."

"Actually, it's people like your group turning it into hell," Stan said. "If it weren't for people killing each other and destroying each other's property, it might not be a bad place to live."

"But *they're* killing each other and destroying property."

"So you feel justified in killing them?"

Cruz sighed, as if Stan was too dense to understand. "I told you, I didn't kill nobody. That's not what we're about."

"Then what *are* you about?"

"We're about being left alone to worship and work and live together. We're about protecting ourselves from Big Brother."

Stan was getting weary, and he looked down at the boy's file. He had little on him, but much on his grandfather and mother, and even on his father who'd become an informant just before he vanished from town. He'd had many suspicions, himself, about what had happened to the man, after the first black mayor of Newpointe was murdered. Terrence Cruz had become an informant, but without any evidence of a body, they'd had to let the matter go.

He tried to find an approach somewhere in the file, but finally he shut it and slid it away from him. "I'm just gonna be honest with you, Cruz. I've known about your family for years. When your father vanished a few years ago, I spent a long time looking for him. I had my suspicions that something had happened to him."

Cruz seemed unduly interested in a spot on the table. "My father is dead."

"Who killed him?"

"God, according to my mother."

Stan narrowed his eyes. "God killed your father?"

"My daddy was eat up with sin," Cruz said, bringing his eyes back to Stan's. "He was an immoral traitor, and God rained destruction down on him."

Stan sat back in his chair, staring at the boy. "I think I know why your mother might call him a traitor. But why do you call him immoral? I thought you people thought everything you did was moral."

Cruz's jaw began to pop. "What has my daddy got to do with that church burning?"

"I'm just saying that one day he talked to the police about the murder of our first black mayor, and the next day he vanished."

"That was years ago."

"Sticks in my memory," Stan said, shaking his head. "I don't like having unsolved crimes."

"It's not unsolved," Cruz said. "I told you, he's dead."

"And God did it."

"That's right."

"But God hasn't struck your grandfather for burning people's houses down, terrorizing them into leaving town, killing the mayor . . ."

"My granddaddy was never convicted of nothin'."

"No, but some of his cronies were. If I remember, some of the informants who told us what happened mentioned that you and your sister were involved in some of the crimes the KKK committed. You must have been little then. What? Eight? Nine?"

"They weren't crimes," Cruz said. "They were battles. Little battles in a big war."

"Then you admit that you've been involved with the KKK since you were a kid."

Cruz breathed a laugh. "You know I have been. I was practically raised in their headquarters. I stuffed envelopes, answered phones, went to meetings."

"And you were with your father and grandfather when crosses were burned in people's yards . . ."

"I never did nothing wrong. The Klansmen are soldiers in a war, and war is not criminal. It's necessary."

"So was it war last night when you killed that kid? Or was it just getting even with Nick Foster for what he did to your picket line at the gay Mardi Gras ball?"

Cruz slammed his hand on the table. "Is that what that sleazebag told you?"

"He said you were angry. That you'd threatened him. Is that true?"

"Threatened him? I hardly even knew he was there!"

"He said he broke your signs and took home the youth from his church."

"I still had plenty of supporters, and we made new signs, okay? Nick Foster isn't going to stop me. And there is a thing in this country called freedom of speech. Picketing was perfectly legal. It's my duty as a Christian to point out to those people that they're bringing God's wrath upon themselves."

"But to tell them God hates them? I'd be interested in seeing where in the Bible it says that. Wanna show me?"

"I don't wanna show you nothing," the kid said. "You're as much the enemy as Nick Foster is, embracing those people and pretending to worship with them, like God can even hear you when you're such an abomination."

"Then you do consider Nick Foster your enemy?"

"I didn't say that."

"Where were you yesterday morning between the hours of four and six A.M.?" he asked suddenly.

Cruz seemed thrown by the sudden shift. "I was sleeping."

Stan began to write on his legal pad. "Where?"

"At home, of course."

"Was your sister there?"

"Yes."

"Then why did your mother say she hadn't seen you in a couple of days?"

"Because she hadn't. She was asleep when I got home, and gone when I got up."

"But she *said* you hadn't been *home* in a couple of days." Stan made a point of turning the pages in his legal pad, looking for his notes he'd taken when he'd gone looking for Cruz earlier. "She said, and I quote, 'Them kids never tell me nothing. They stay out all night and sleep all day, and sometimes don't come home at all.'"

"So you jump to the conclusion that I must be a murderer?"

"Actually, the conclusion I've drawn is that you must be a liar. You just told me you were home."

"Well, my mother misses a lot of things. She never has seen half the things going on in our house."

"I thought she home-schooled. Aren't most home-schooling moms real attentive?"

"We're both eighteen. We don't need home-schooling no more. But when we were young, a lot went on that she didn't see. Truth ain't one of her passions."

Stan looked down at the legal pad again, and he began to wonder what kind of childhood these kids must have had, with every adult in their lives engaged in criminal activity against anyone they saw as different. How many murders had they witnessed? How many lives had they terrorized? How could any child come up with a healthy view of society when they'd been taught nothing but hate?

And when they slapped the label of Christianity on that hate, it got even more confusing.

No wonder so many Americans thought Christians were hateful zealots with murderous agendas and evil hearts.

He looked across the table at the kid who had probably grown up too fast. What were the secrets he harbored about his father's immorality and his mother's blindness to it? What immorality had he borne as a child?

If murder wasn't considered immorality, he could only imagine what was.

The door opened, and Chief Jim Shoemaker leaned in. "Stan, can I see you a minute?"

"Sure." He got up and stepped outside, closing the door behind him. "What is it?"

"There's been another church burning," he said. Stan caught his breath. "Bayou Missionary Baptist Church. And there was a victim in this one too. My understanding is that this one isn't dead yet."

"Then maybe he can tell us who did it." He spun around and looked through the glass. The kid was sitting there with his face in his hands. Stan was pleased he had gotten to him. "Pick up his friends," he said. "And his sister. They had to have something to do with it."

"We have cars en route. Sid located them at a bar called the Viper Pit. We've had problems with them before for serving to minors. It's the teenage hot spot."

"I gotta get over to that church," Stan told him. He nodded toward Cruz. "Can we keep him here a little longer?"

"Yeah, I'll get somebody else to question him for a while, just to mark time until you've worked the scene. It's over on Briarson and Catalpa Street. I'll meet you over there."

Stan took off without a look back, hoping another kid wouldn't have to die.

Chapter Eighteen

Jennifer's three chosen ones were a wreck by the time they got back to the Viper Pit, after doing what she had ordered. They came in, soaked with sweat and trembling, and instantly split up to get lost in the crowd. Jake tried not to miss a drumbeat as he looked for his best friend. Benton looked like he'd been in a fight. He had blood on his shirt and scratch marks on his face. His eyes were wild as they darted east to west. He came to the edge of the stage and looked up at Jennifer as she banged on the keyboard. She nodded to him that she would come down, and quickly announced that they were taking a break.

Jake followed her off the stage and watched her usher Benton into a back room.

Benton was hysterical by the time she had the door closed. "We found some kid out ridin' his bike and LaSalle runned him down and he put up a fight when we tried to get him in the car and we started the fire and left him there unconscious . . ."

"Hush!" Jennifer said, jerking his shirt over his head. "Get this shirt off immediately."

He looked down, noticing the blood for the first time, and obediently pulled the shirt over his head. She rolled it up in a ball. "Let me look at the rest of you. You look like you were caught in a stampede. You didn't leave any witnesses, did you?"

"No, of course not!" Benton was trembling, like he was about to snap. He started to cry. "He put up a fight and started hollering and begging and I thought about my little brother and him pleading for his life and I couldn't really remember why we were doing this and what it meant except that it was something about throwing the cops off . . ."

"Stop it!" Jennifer ordered, taking him by the bare shoulders. "Now stop it!"

"You don't know my name, do you?" Benton demanded. "Tell me my name."

For the first time since he'd known her, Jennifer was at a loss for words. She looked at Jake for help.

"Benton," he said, and Jennifer's smile returned.

"Benton, you know I know who you are. I wouldn't have chose you if I didn't know and trust you."

"We did this for you and we don't even know why and now the police are gonna come and they're gonna question us and figure out that we did this . . ."

"No, they won't," she said. "It's gonna be fine." She pulled him against her, and he dropped his forehead on her shoulder and began to sob. Jake stood back, wishing he could just take his friend and get out of here. But they had to be here when the police came. "Come on, it's okay," she said, stroking his hair maternally. "You're heroes. All three of you. People will be talking about what you did years from now. You'll be legends. They'll write songs about you. Now, you go out and get a beer," she said. "You need to calm your nerves. Tell Butch at the bar I said to give you all you want on me. Don't worry about him asking for your I.D. He never gives us a hard time. He's one of us, remember."

Benton pulled back and studied her face. He tried to calm his breathing. "Okay. I just . . . need to know that this is gonna pay off, you know? That you ain't just gonna forget."

Jennifer's face softened, and she turned back to Jake. "Jake, leave me alone with him for a while, okay? I just need a few minutes."

Jake's stomach took a dive, and he got sick at the thought that she was doing to Benton what she had done to Jake just hours ago. She was using his crush on her to manipulate him, and she was good at it. He found himself seething with jealousy. He didn't want to leave them alone.

But as he headed back into the crowd, with the stereo music playing until they could get back to the stage, he noticed a buzz around the door. He pushed through and saw that police were swarming in.

Quickly, he dashed back to the room. "Cops are here," he said.

Benton looked as if he might as well be dead. "They know," he said. "They already know and they're coming after me and I don't want to go to jail . . ."

She slapped him and made him look at her. "Stop whining! You've been here the whole time with us. Nobody's left. You have fifty witnesses out there who'll swear to it. We all have alibis. If they ask you about the cuts and scrapes, you tell 'em you were fighting with LaSalle and . . . who was the other one?"

His face twisted in deeper dread. "Decareaux! Man, you don't even *know* us."

"You were fighting with *them*, okay? They have scratches and scrapes too." She went to a shelf and grabbed a folded black Viper Pit T-shirt, set aside for bar employees. "Here. Put this on. Now go out there and get lost in the middle of that crowd, and so help me, act like a soldier instead of a whiny little girl."

He stumbled out. Jennifer got back on the stage and signaled for the other band members to join her as the police made their way through the crowd.

Chapter Nineteen

Nick Foster was lying in bed, staring at the ceiling and listening to the scanner, when the call came through that the Bayou Missionary Baptist Church was on fire. The pastor was a friend of his, and he knew he had probably been called and would be heading to the fire with as much dread and despair as Nick had just days ago.

He got up and decided he had to go and provide whatever support he could. He got dressed as fast as his injuries would allow and headed toward the blaze.

• • •

The boy who'd been found in the fire was still alive, but just barely.

"I will not lose this one," Issie said through her teeth. She had worked for eight hours already—the three to eleven shift— but when the call came at eleven o'clock, she and Steve had answered it. "He's alive. We've got to stabilize him."

Steve Winder was busy intubating him since his airway had obviously closed.

"Issie, who is he?" Nick asked.

She cast a glance up at Nick. "I don't know. He's burned so badly he's practically unrecognizable. No identification, no nothing. But he's young, thirteen or fourteen. Pulse rate's dropping, guys!"

"He's gone," Steve yelled. "No pulse. Come on, get the defibrillator." They attached the probes to his chest, and as they pulled back to allow the shock to jolt him, Issie prayed to a God that she didn't know that this kid would not slip through their fingers like the last one had. He had a mother and father, as Ben had. He might have brothers and sisters, friends, relatives.

The heart didn't respond. She got down on her knees and began to pump furiously on his chest.

"Clear!" Steve shouted, and she pulled back and waited as he sent the jolt again.

Nothing.

"No!" she shouted. "We can't let him die!" She kept pumping.

"Clear!" Steve shouted again, and she stopped and pulled back. The jolt shook his body again, and she held her breath as she waited one second, two seconds . . .

"Beat, you stupid thing!" she screamed to his heart. "Don't you give up!" She began compressions again, pumping as if her own heart was connected to his.

"He's gone, Issie," Steve said. He stopped pumping air into his tube and wilted in defeat.

"No!" she shouted. "We can't stop! Don't stop, Steve." She kept pushing on his chest, trying to force the heart to beat. Had Jake had anything to do with this? Had that smart aleck Cruz thrown this kid into the fire?

Nick bent down and touched her shoulders. "Issie . . ."

"No!" she screamed. "I won't let 'em do it!"

"Let who do it?" Nick asked her.

She didn't answer, but the tears rolled down her face and she pumped his chest with fierce urgency, pleading with him to come back to life. "Pray, Nick," she cried. "Do what you do!"

He was silent behind her, and she wondered if he had closed his eyes, if he was sending up those prayers to God. Prayer was all that could help the boy now, but she wasn't sure that bringing him back was going to do him any good, not with the flesh dissolving on his body in horrible third-degree burns, and months, even years—possibly a lifetime—of excruciating treatments, not to mention the disfigurement that would come upon him if he lived.

She finally gave up and fell back, sobbing. Where was Jake? Was there another carpet rolled up in a bonfire with this boy's bloodstains on it?

She felt hands on her shoulders. She fell back, and strong arms came around her, embraced her, held her.

"It's okay." She recognized Nick's deep whisper against her ear. "It's okay. You did the best you could."

"He's dead," she sobbed. "Another kid is dead just because he's black."

"You don't know that," Nick said.

"I *do* know it!" she bit out. "How could they do this? How could they be so cruel? This kid has a mother, just like Susan." She slapped the tears on her face and got to her feet, pulling out of the security of Nick's arms. She didn't want to feel that security. She didn't want to feel any comfort right now. She just wanted to hang on to that anger and soak in it and wallow in it. She wanted to find her nephew and grab him by the throat and shake him until he told her who was responsible for this and why he was a part of it. But she couldn't leave the scene yet, not until the fire was out and all the firemen were safe. Someone might get hurt like Nick had the other day. Any number of things could go wrong. She had to wait this out.

Meanwhile, she prayed once again to the God she did not know, that the efforts of the kids who had done this thing would be thwarted until she had the chance to stop them herself.

Chapter Twenty

Due to lack of evidence, the police were forced to let Cruz go after they'd worked the fire and interviewed his followers at the Viper Pit. Cruz was able to reach Jennifer at the Viper Pit, and she told him she was sending someone to get him. She herself couldn't leave, she said, because there had been some new developments, and one of them needed to be there.

He trusted her, and told her he'd meet her back at the Benton house.

Sye Redmon—one of the members of Cruz's inner circle—came to get him. He seemed nervous, and Cruz wondered what was going on.

They were quiet until they got to the car. "Tell me everything," he said.

He got behind the wheel, even though it was Redmon's car. Graham got in on the passenger side and tossed him the keys. "There was another fire," Redmon said as they pulled away from the police station. Cruz glanced into the truck bay of the fire department and saw that it was empty. "Another church."

Cruz frowned. "Copycat?"

"No," Redmon said. "It was a ploy Jennifer came up with to prove you weren't involved. We were all making a big ruckus at the Viper Pit, so we've got alibis. It ought to throw them off."

"Like they don't know we could lie for our own?"

"Man, they interviewed us. They talked to dozens of the kids at the Pit, and didn't come up with anything."

Cruz was quiet for a moment as he drove. "Who did it?" he asked finally.

"Benton, LaSalle, and Decareaux."

"Why them?"

"Volunteered. Plus, they're expendable. If they have to take the fall, it's no great loss."

"We don't hardly even know them. What if they talk?"

"And get theirselves thrown in jail?" Redmon asked. "I don't think that'll happen. Besides, Jen has things under control. She has them eating out of her hand." Redmon chuckled. "She's good at this."

The comment sent a tide of anger rising up inside him, but Cruz held it back.

By the time they got to the Benton house, everyone seemed to be there. Cruz got out, slammed the car door, and headed into the house. The stragglers, still out at their cars, cheered for Cruz and high-fived him, as if he was MVP of the toughest game of the season. "Everybody inside," he said, bolting up the porch steps and into the house.

Jake was just inside. "Cruz!"

Cruz shot him a look. "Where's my sister?"

Jake hesitated to answer.

"*Where is she?*"

"She's in the back with Benton."

"Benton?" he spat out.

"Yeah," one of the others piped in. "He's freaking out and threatening to stop letting us use the house. She's trying to calm him down."

Jake looked as if he realized how dangerous Benton's instability could be. "Benton's all right. He's just worried about his parents finding out, that's all."

Cruz shoved past him and went into the kitchen, reached up over the cabinet, and pulled down a switchblade he'd hidden there. He engaged the switch, making the blade fly out.

"Cruz, what are you—?"

Cruz's head was beginning to ache, and his stomach burned, just like it had when they were kids and he'd heard Jen crying when her father was in her room . . .

He stormed back through the house, his angry step shaking the walls. He found the closed door and flung it open.

He saw them standing with their arms around each other, Jen with her back against the wall and Benton with his fingers all tangled in her hair.

Rage like that he'd experienced as a child crashed through him, blinding him to anything but that picture of his father using his sister . . .

He flew across the room, switchblade flying, but Benton reacted just in time. The blade missed.

"Cruz!" Jennifer screamed. "Stop it!"

He spun around and headed for Benton again and slashed the knife through the air, slicing into his leg. Benton screamed in pain.

Then Jennifer was on his back, crying and screaming that this wasn't their father, that Benton wasn't hurting her, that Cruz was confused . . .

Slowly, his rage deflated, and he tried to catch his breath. She whispered childhood memories into his ear. "It's okay, Cruz. It's okay. You've always been my rescuer. It's okay."

He swallowed and turned around and pulled her into a fierce, fraternal embrace. "I'm sorry, Jen," he whispered, sweating and breathing hard. "I'm so sorry. Did I hurt you?"

"No." She was out of breath too. "But I think Benton is in trouble."

He turned back to the kid he'd cut and saw him writhing on the floor as the puddle of blood beneath him grew bigger. "Get a towel," Cruz ordered Jake, who stood at the door, dumbly gaping in.

Jake ran out, then came back with a towel and fell down next to his friend.

"We have to stop the bleeding," Cruz said, taking charge again. "Put pressure on it."

"Cruz, he needs a doctor," Jake said. "We need to call somebody or get him to the hospital."

"He's okay," Cruz said. "He'll be okay as soon as the bleeding stops."

"But you can bleed to death in five minutes!" Jake said. "Cruz, we have to do something."

"I told you, he's all right!"

"I'll call my aunt," he said. "She's a paramedic. She could help Benton, and I swear she'll stay quiet. She cares about me and wouldn't want to get me in trouble."

"She's already been snooping around here," Cruz said. "We can't trust her." He got down beside Benton and held the wound. "It's all right, buddy. You're gon' be all right."

Jake was getting frantic. "He's my friend, man! He needs help!"

"He's my friend too," Cruz said more calmly now. "All right. I care enough about this man to risk calling your aunt. But only because he's indispensable. He's a courageous foot soldier, and when this is over, I'm goin' ta make him one of my lieutenants."

In spite of his pain, Benton looked at Cruz with pride in his eyes.

Jake ran out to find a cell phone so he could call Issie.

Chapter Twenty-One

Issie felt defiant enough to return to her apartment that night when she finally turned her shift over to Frenchy and Bob. Earlier today, the manager had painted the wall that was written on, but had tacked an extra hundred bucks onto her rent to cover it. She had dragged the bloody mattress to the street. She didn't know when she'd be able to buy a new one. The four new tires on her car had cleaned out her meager savings. With her gun within reach, she took a shower and washed off the residue of the smoke that soiled her face and uniform. She watched the water swirl down the drain and wished that her anger and fears would go with it.

She got dressed, dried her hair, then sat looking into the mirror. How would she get through to her nephew? Jake thought she was no different than he, and if she was honest, she had to admit she wasn't. At his age she had been following an equally dangerous crowd, except her friends had been threats to their own bodies, not those of others. She'd spent all her nights making and getting into trouble, but no one had ever suggested burning down a church or murdering a kid because of the color of his skin.

But what if they had? she wondered. Would she have followed along blindly like Jake was doing now? Would she have been needy enough to do whatever she was told in the interest of belonging? She hoped not, but she wasn't sure, and she knew Jake wasn't sure, either.

Even now, she teetered on the edge of risk in most of her relationships. Even her job was a risk, a constant jolt of adrenaline. She liked to live dangerously, and she was easily bored. Jake was just like her.

She decided to try talking sense into him again and picked up the phone to call her brother's house. His wife, Lois, answered.

"Hello?"

"Lois, it's Issie. I'm sorry to call at midnight, but it's important. Where's Jake?"

She sighed. "He's out, as usual. You know that boy never stays home."

Her heart sank. "Any idea where he is?" she asked.

"Your guess is as good as mine," Lois said. "He doesn't tell us anything."

"Okay. Maybe I can find him."

"What's this about?" Lois asked.

Issie thought of telling her what Jake seemed to be involved in, but something told her it was too soon. She needed to give Jake a chance. She needed to talk to him first.

"Nothing," she said. "I just had a message to give him."

"There isn't anything wrong, is there?"

Issie hesitated again. "Not that I know of." She sat there a moment longer, then finally asked, "Lois, what do you know about the kids he's hanging out with?"

"Not much," her sister-in-law said. "It's not like he brings them home for dinner."

That made her angry. Her own mother had never demanded to meet her friends. She had never held her accountable. "Then why do you let him hang around with them? I mean, what if they're dangerous or something? What if they're leading him down the wrong path?"

Lois chuckled as if the questions were incompatible with Issie Mattreaux. "I've never heard you talk about the wrong path before. You told me once the only path was the one you paved."

Issie knew that was true. She wished she could eat those words now. "Well, I used to think that, but I'm starting to wonder."

"Is there something Jake's doing that I need to know about?" Lois asked.

Again, Issie thought that one over. "I don't know, Lois. I just don't like his friends much. They look like trouble to me."

"More trouble than the ones you used to go out with?"

"Yeah, even more trouble than that," Issie said. "Maybe you need to get more involved in his life."

"Get more involved? How? He's hardly ever home, and he doesn't want to talk about anything when he is."

"You're his mother. Maybe you need to make him."

Lois was offended. "Issie, just a few years ago *you* were the one staying out all night and getting into trouble. Mike complained about you all the time. Your mother *never* knew where you were."

"Mama never cared."

"Well, maybe that was true," Lois said. "But Jake knows I do. And now you're telling me that I need to demand that he make me a part of his life?"

"I don't mean like that," she said. "I just mean, don't take things for granted. Don't assume anything."

"Anything like what? Jake's a good kid, Issie."

"Maybe that's exactly what you don't need to assume."

She heard Lois breathe her surprise, and realized she might have gone too far.

"Issie, if you have something to tell me about Jake, then go ahead and tell me."

Issie closed her eyes. She knew her sister-in-law was right. She needed to either spit it out or shut up. "I'm sorry. I'm just worried about him."

"Well, if you want to let me in on what you're worried about, I'll worry with you. I am his mother."

"It's nothing, really. Just a feeling."

"A feeling about his friends?"

"Yeah."

"Which ones?"

She shook her head. "I don't know for sure, Lois. That guy Cruz kind of gives me the creeps."

"Cruz? Is that his first name or last name?"

"I don't know. Last, I think."

Her sister-in-law was quiet, and Issie imagined the wheels turning in her head as she tried to figure out what she could do as a mother. She knew that her brother and his wife were both good parents. They had just abdicated their power.

"Believe it or not," Lois said, "I love him. Just because we're not real close right now doesn't mean I don't care about him. I'm just trying to give him a little more space as he gets older."

"Maybe space is the wrong thing to give him," Issie said. "Maybe you need to ride him . . . just stay on his back."

"And if anybody had told your mother to do that just a few years ago," Lois said, "you would have packed your bags and disappeared, never to be heard from again."

"Maybe," Issie said.

"I have certain parameters I have to work in as a mother," Lois said. "I have to give him his space and let him go and hope that maybe by doing that, I'll be able to hold on to him a little longer."

Issie was suddenly glad that she wasn't a mother herself. As she hung up the phone she told herself that she wasn't thrilled about being an aunt right now, either.

She went to the window and peered out on the parking lot, looking for a sign of anyone who shouldn't be there. She had found the key to her apartment hanging back on the hook in her brother's kitchen this morning, and she had taken it in case Jake tried to get into her apartment again. Still, she felt uneasy.

Though she was exhausted, she was afraid to sleep, so she lay down on her couch with the gun on her coffee table and turned on some mindless infomercial about skin care. Slowly, she drifted off to sleep.

She didn't know how long she had been asleep when the phone shrilled, waking her. She grabbed the gun and sat up. Her stomach tightened as she went to the caller ID and looked to see who it was. It looked like a cell phone number. Slowly, she answered, "Hello?"

"Issie?" It was her nephew's voice.

"Jake, it's you! Did you have anything to do with—"

"An emergency," he cut in. "Issie, we need your help."

"We?" she asked. "Who's we?"

"Me and some of my buddies," he said. "Look, we're in a lot of trouble. Benton got hurt, and we can't take him to the hospital. I need you to come over and see what you can do for him."

"I'm a paramedic, not a doctor," she said. "Jake, what's going on? How did Benton get hurt?"

"He cut himself," he said. "Can't you come look at it, try to stop the bleeding?"

"He's still bleeding?" she asked.

"Yeah, and it's bad."

"Where are you?" she asked.

"We're at the house. You know, Benton's grandmother's house?"

Issie closed her eyes. "Jake, I don't want any part of this. I've already told you."

"He cut himself, Issie. That's all. It's not illegal to cut yourself."

"I don't trust your friends," she said. "How do I know that if I come over there I'm not walking into a trap?"

"Because *I'm* here," Jake said. "I wouldn't let anything happen to you. Issie, I wouldn't have called you if you weren't the only one who could help us. Come on. The guy's bleeding."

She recognized the panic in Jake's voice. He wasn't faking, and the last thing she needed on her conscience was another death. "All right," she said. "Where is the wound?"

"On his thigh," he said.

"Well, then you need to wrap it and apply pressure to it. Have you done that?"

"Yeah, we wrapped a towel around it, pretty tight."

"That should help the bleeding to slow down until I get there. Jake, how did he get the cut?"

"It's a long story," he said. "I'll tell you when you get here."

She knew it was a story that she was better off not hearing, but quickly she got dressed, grabbed some dental floss and scissors, a bottle of alcohol, and a few other makeshift supplies from around the apartment. She threw them into a bag and lit out as fast as she could to her car, still clutching her gun, just in case anyone lurked around waiting to jump out and ambush her.

Chapter Twenty-Two

J ake was waiting nervously for her in the front yard at the vacant house, smoking a cigarette. She pulled her car into the driveway and quickly got out. He dropped the cigarette and stubbed it out with his toe.

"Thought you quit smoking," she said.

"I did," Jake said. "Cruz doesn't like it. But I'm a little stressed right now. This way, Issie."

He led her into the house to a back bedroom, and she saw the boy lying on the floor in a back bedroom. The tall blond girl sat against the wall with a worried look on her face. Cruz stood at the center of the room like a traffic cop. "Before you touch him," he said, "I need to warn you that you can't breathe a word about this to anyone. It was an accident. He was drunk and playing around with a knife . . ."

Issie fell to her knees beside Benton and tried to uncoil the boy. "Let me see, Benton. I can't help you until you give me your leg."

Cruz was getting impatient. "One word, and the next injury won't be an accident. Are you hearing me?"

Issie had coaxed Benton out of his coil and saw that the towel pressed against his cut was soaked. "Benton, I'm gonna move this towel. I need to see how bad the cut is."

"I'm talking to you!" Cruz yelled.

Issie shot a fiery look up at him and yelled back, "Do you want me to help him or not?"

Jennifer grabbed Cruz before he could react. In a soft voice, she said, "Come on, Cruz. Let's go to another room, and we can fill each other in about tonight."

He didn't want to leave, but he finally let her coax him out. Jake stayed behind.

"What is his problem?" Issie peeled the towel off the wound, and Benton groaned and tightened up, starting the bleeding again. She winced as she saw the depth of the cut.

"This is not a cut, Jake," she said through her teeth. "This is a stab wound." She looked up at him. "Isn't it?"

"No," he said. "He was just playing around with his knife, that's all. He got drunk and was playing around."

"You're trying to tell me that the guy was drunk enough to give himself a cut three inches long and at least an inch deep?"

"Yeah," he said weakly.

She shook her head. "I can't do anything with this. He's going to need lots of stitches. He needs to be in a hospital."

"Issie, he can't go. That's all there is to it. We need you to help him."

She got on her knees and tried to see if he was lucid. He was half-conscious. "Benton, can you hear me? I need to get you to the hospital."

He shook his head. "No, can't go," he slurred.

She groaned and looked up at Jake. "What is it with you people? I'll do what I can, but I'm going to need your help."

Jake nodded and got on his knees.

"You're going to have to hold him down. I'm going to have to clean the wound first, and it's gonna hurt. If he was drunk, maybe he won't feel it."

"Hope he drank enough," he said.

"Me too. Now, hold him down."

As Jake tried to keep him from writhing and recoiling, Issie began to do the best she could to take care of the wound.

• • •

Later, when she had sterilized it and stitched it up, Cruz came back in.

"We need to get him to a hospital," she said.

"But that isn't an option," Cruz bit out, dismissing the subject by leaving the room.

Issie started to object, but she caught Jake's eye, warning her not to pick a fight with him. Benton had passed out long ago, whether from blood loss or alcohol, she wasn't sure.

"Jake, you've got to figure a way to get him treatment," she said. "He lost a lot of blood. He needs fluids. Antibiotics."

"I can't," he said. "Cruz knows what he's doing."

Issie didn't doubt that for a moment. "What is their draw, Jake? What do they have that you want?"

"Nothing," he said.

"You're risking prison to hang out with them. I want to know why. Is it that girl?"

He glanced toward the door. "It's a lot of things. I'm somebody with them. Not just a freak who gets in the way. And they've given me something to believe in. Something important to *do*. We're all gonna help build the compound where we're all gonna live. And Cruz, he's special. There's something *different* about him. He's on a higher level than we are. Like, if there's a God, maybe Cruz has an in with him."

Issie couldn't believe what she was hearing. "So he's setting himself up as some kind of Messiah figure?"

"Yeah, kind of," Jake said. "Only it's not his fault. He was chosen, just like we are."

Issie brought her hand to her forehead, trying to puzzle this out. "Jake, have you quit school?"

"Well, not officially, but I haven't been there in a couple of weeks. Mom and Dad don't know. Since they're both at work during the day, the school hasn't been able to fink on me yet."

"Jake, you're sixteen! What are you gonna do without a high school diploma?"

"I won't need one," he said. "We're all gonna live together in the compound when it's built. We'll take care of ourselves and mind our own business."

"Where is this compound?" she asked.

He shook his head. "I can't tell you that."

She wanted to throttle him.

"They're good for me, Issie."

"Jake, another kid was killed in another church fire tonight. Did you have anything to do with that?"

He looked down at the crude stitches on his sleeping friend's leg. "Issie, I don't know what you're talking about. My band played at the Viper Pit tonight, until just a while ago. Since then I've been right here with Benton, trying to figure out what to do about his leg."

"Well, there's a lot of secrecy around here, Jake, and a lot not being explained. Where was Cruz?"

"At the police station, being questioned about the other church burning. So see? He couldn't have done it. The rest of us were all at the Pit. None of us could have done it. And the cops can verify it. They were there, giving us all a hard time." He met her eyes and seemed to read her doubt. "Why won't you believe me?"

"Because there are too many secrets. Scary secrets. The kind that get people like you killed."

Jake got quiet.

Her eyes stung as she stared at him. "You know, you remind me a lot of myself when I was sixteen."

"You're not that much older now."

"I'm eight years older than you," she said. "I know you think that's not very much, but there's something I've learned in the last few years that you apparently haven't caught on to yet."

"What?"

"I've learned that the kids I hung around with when I was your age, the ones who got into trouble and came up with mystery wounds and committed petty crimes ... they're all either dead or in prison right now."

"Yeah, right," he said.

"I'm not kidding, Jake. I have three friends from high school who are dead. One died of an overdose and one in a drunk driving accident. He was the drunk. Another was shot in the French Quarter on the south shore."

"Your point?" Jake asked her.

"My point," she said, "is that two other friends wound up in prison. These were the people I counted as my closest friends, the ones I depended on for everything, sometimes even my life. This Cruz guy is not going to get you anywhere, Jake, nowhere but maybe dead or in prison, and I don't want to see you in either place."

He pulled out a cigarette and lit it. His eyes narrowed as he inhaled. "You know, you're right," he said on the exhale. "You are a lot older than me. You're already starting to sound like my parents."

"Your parents don't want you dead or in prison either," she said. "These friends of yours don't care. If your parents had any idea what I've seen the last couple of days, this house you've vandalized, the bloody stain on that carpet I saw you burning the other night, the stab wound tonight ..."

"Come on, Issie," Jake said. "You need to just keep your nose out of it. We appreciate what you did tonight, but these things are still none of your business."

"Hey, Ray Ford is a friend of mine. If you had anything to do with his son's murder—"

"Of course I didn't," Jake cut in. "You really think that about me?"

"Don't act so hurt," she said. "You know I hardly even know who you are anymore. You used to be this sweet kid I loved to be around, and now you're turning into ... I don't even know what."

Jake looked hurt. "You were never so high and mighty when it was you that wanted to party."

His words were like a slap in the face. "I don't do dangerous things, Jake. I don't step over the line."

"What line?" he asked. "You don't have any lines!"

"I make better choices," she said. "You don't see me breaking and entering, committing arson, murdering innocent people."

"Give me a break," he said. "You live just as dangerously as I do, Issie."

"How do you figure that?" she demanded.

"Everybody knows you like dating ex-cons and married men, and spending every spare night at Joe's Place. You live on the edge, just like me. You just found a way to make a living at it."

"How dare you?" she flung back. "Don't you *ever* talk to me that way again!"

"Why not?" he asked. "You talk to *me* that way all the time."

"I'm trying to save your life, you little fool," she said. "I'm trying to keep you from going the wrong way."

"Well, when you figure out what the right way is, why don't you come tell me," he said, "'cause I don't see your path bein' all that different. At least these people have a purpose and a plan that lasts longer than one night. At least they stand for something!"

"You want to stand for hate and lies and death?" she asked. "Does that make you feel important?"

He made a face as if he couldn't believe she was cornering him this way. "I haven't done anything! Just because a church burns down doesn't mean I know something about it."

"Well, you knew something about the first one."

Again, he looked shocked. "What makes you say that?"

"The carpet I saw with the blood on it. The conversation we had when I brought it up."

He looked at the doorway, as if worried that someone was listening. "Issie, I'm going to tell you this one more time. You need to keep your mouth shut and get out of here now."

"Or what?" she asked. "Are you threatening me, Jake? Because I'm your flesh and blood, and those people in there aren't. You can pretend ignorance, but you need to know that tonight I tried my best to save that kid's life. We defibrillated him three times. I pumped his heart for twenty minutes. His skin was bubbled up like melted rubber. Even if he had lived, he probably never would have walked again, or moved, or had any of his organs function properly. If you're involved, I want you to know that his death was probably horrible, and you'll pay for it some day. And if you're not involved, then I want you to look around and figure out which one of your friends might have done this, because you might be next."

She had her nephew's attention now. He was staring at her, his face serious. She knew that he really was in over his head. "Who was the kid?" he asked.

"Some kid named Frankie Sardis who lived over on Twenty-third Street. He was thirteen years old. Seventh grade. What kind of coward goes around killing boys too small to even defend themselves?"

Again Jake kept staring at her. "We were all at the Viper Pit," he whispered, as if that was the story he was sticking to.

"Look, I don't know what any of you are involved in," Issie said, "but as a member of Newpointe's protective services I'm obligated to tell what I know."

"You don't *know* anything," Jake said.

"I do know some things," she said, her voice low. "I know what I've seen, and I'm going to tell it. I know that after I saw that bloody carpet, I had someone break into my apartment last night and put a dead cat on my bed. I know that I've had my wall written on and my tires slashed. I know that your friend was stabbed tonight."

"So what are you going to do?" Jake asked.

"I'm going to go to the police," she said, "and I'm telling you this, Jake, because I don't think it's too late for you to get out of here. I suggest you surgically remove yourself from this group of friends and make sure that you never become a part of this cancer again. Maybe if you go with me to the police, tell them what you know, this will have a better ending than it looks like it's going to have now."

He swallowed hard. "Issie, don't do it."

"I have to do it," she said. "It would be stupid of me to just sit here and keep my mouth shut, knowing that tomorrow another church might burn down and another kid might be found dead. And I'll be called to the scene and I'll have to try to save his life. Have you ever tried to do that, Jake? Have you ever tried to keep somebody alive who's slipping away, knowing that somebody in your family might have had something to do with killing them?"

"I had *nothing* to do with that," Jake bit out. "You have to believe me. I wouldn't do that."

"It's a sickening feeling," she said. "It makes you vomit. It makes your head ache, and it fills you with so much guilt that you don't know what to do."

"You don't have any reason to feel guilty," he said.

"Tell me about it. But you do. And you and I are related and I love you and I don't want to see you follow the path that these guys are following."

"Issie, I'm telling you. Don't go to the police. It's not a smart thing to do."

"Well, since you have such bad judgment about what's smart and what's not, I think I'll follow my own."

She left the room with Jake following behind, and they cut through ten disciples in the living room. Cruz seemed to be giving a lecture to the rest who were there. He had relaxed now and was sitting on his stool, and the group was laughing at something he'd said—oblivious to Benton on the floor in the back room. They got quiet as she came in. "If he doesn't take that kid to the hospital, then don't any of you believe that he cares about you," she said. "You could be next, hurt however Benton was and left to suffer."

Cruz got to his feet, his stance suggesting that she had crossed the line.

Issie bolted out of the house, and Jake followed her. "Issie! *Issie!*" She got into her car and slammed the door hard. She turned the key and flipped on her lights. Her nephew stood in the circle of headlights, and she could see the confusion and fear on his face. She wished there was some way she could talk him into coming with her, but she knew it wasn't going to happen. Something about that brother and sister was pulling him back toward the group.

She started backing out slowly, hoping he would run after her and get in the car with her, go and tell the police everything he knew, but he just stood there. Tears came to her eyes as she put the car in drive and set out down the road.

Chapter Twenty-Three

Cruz came out of the house and watched her car pull out of the driveway. "What was that all about?" he demanded.

"She just got upset," Jake said.

Jennifer came out with some of the others behind her. "Where is she going?"

Jake felt sick. He didn't know if he should tell them what she'd threatened to do. If he did, they would chase her down, and there was no telling what they might do. But if he didn't, they would all go down. "She's just upset because of the fire tonight. She tried to save the kid, but he died. She's a little suspicious."

"Did you tell her about my being in police custody when it happened? Did you tell her you and all the rest were at the Viper Pit?"

"Yeah, I told her."

"So what did she say? Where is she going?"

"I don't know."

Cruz stood there for a moment, just staring at him, then suddenly, he launched forward and grabbed Jake by the throat. *"Where is she going?"* he bit out.

Jake grabbed Cruz's wrist and tried to disengage it. "I don't know."

"She's going to the police, isn't she?"

"No!" he lied. "No!"

That grip on his throat tightened, and Jennifer stepped forward. "Cruz, stop it. Let him go!"

Cruz didn't. His thumb and forefinger cut into the skin of his neck, and Jake thought he would pass out.

"Let him go, Cruz!" she shouted. "Cruz, do it! Let him go!"

Finally, Cruz loosened his grip, and Jake fell on the gravel driveway. "I'm going after her," Cruz said.

Jennifer headed for their car. "I'm coming with you."

Jake watched from the ground as they got into their car and screeched out after Issie.

Chapter Twenty-Four

Issie hadn't gone five miles when she saw the headlights behind her. The car was moving up too close, right on her bumper, and she did what she always did to make it back off. She tapped her brakes and slowed, hoping the car would either pass her or slow down, but it stayed locked on her bumper. Someone was pursuing her, she realized.

Fear rushed through her and she slammed her foot down on the accelerator and jolted forward, but the car was right with her, not allowing her to get away. She made the next turn onto a street just as desolate as the one she'd been on, and looked for a public place where she could pull over and cry for help.

She reached for her cell phone, tried to dial the number for the police station, but it fell out of her hand and onto the floor. She bent down to grope for it, but couldn't feel it. She looked in the rearview mirror and saw that the car was coming up beside her. It was a red Camry, but she couldn't see who was inside.

A gunshot exploded the window next to her head, whistled past her ear, and shattered her windshield. She swerved and felt her wheels leave the road and sink into the dirt. Her car tilted, and the wheels skidded into the grass. Her headlights flashed a sequence of bushes and branches, tall grass and wildflower. Then a telephone pole loomed in front of her. She screamed and tried to avoid it, but her hands seemed frozen on the steering wheel, and her foot on the brake pedal made no difference in the skid. Metal crashed and glass shattered as she hit and fell forward, jamming her knee into something and crushing her sternum into the wheel. Her seat belt cut a diagonal line across her from shoulder to hip.

She sat there, dazed for a moment as her mind slowly cleared. She saw the car make a U-turn and start back for her. She reached clumsily into her glove compartment, felt for her gun. Her fingers closed over the metal.

• • •

Cruz made a U-turn and stood on the accelerator. "The gun," he shouted. "Give me the gun!"

Jennifer thrust it at him.

He slowed as he reached Issie's smoking car and rolled down his window. He aimed his pistol and fired. The bullet went through her shattered window and burst through the passenger side.

He slid into a U-turn again, and thrust the gun at Jennifer. "She's on your side. Don't miss."

He slowed, allowing Jennifer the chance to aim.

But before she pulled the trigger, a bullet whistled past his head. He cursed. "She's got a gun!"

Another bullet shot through their back windows, and he punched the accelerator again.

"Get out of here!" Jennifer cried.

"No, we have to go back. We can't leave her alive!"

"But she's shooting at us!"

"Not for long! Give me the gun!"

She handed it to him and ducked as they skidded past the wrecked car again. Issie fired before Cruz could aim the gun.

Jennifer jerked, and blood hit the dashboard. Cruz almost ran off the road. "Jen!" he yelled. "Jen!"

Another bullet whizzed past, and Cruz dropped the gun and reached for his sister.

She looked up at him, her forehead covered with blood. "Get out of here, Cruz! Please don't go back!"

He didn't need any more incentive than that to make him speed away from the scene.

Chapter Twenty-Five

Issie clutched the gun in a tight-knuckled fist, trembling as she waited for the car to come back. Her heart pummeled out a deadly rhythm.

She only had two bullets left, and she knew they had no intention of leaving her there alive. Keeping her eyes on the road, she groped for her cell phone on the floor and finally found it.

Then quickly, she stumbled out of the car, slamming the door behind her. Pain shot through her chest, and her knee threatened not to support her.

She limped down the grassy embankment and into the trees skirting the road.

She prayed that the phone would pick up a signal. Quickly she dialed 911.

Simone, the dispatcher, came on. "Nine-one-one. May I help you?"

"Simone, this is Issie," she said, breathless. "I'm on Meadow Road out in that wooded area. Car's wrecked. They've been shooting at me ..."

"Who has?"

"Cruz somebody. Send police, Simone. They'll come back." She knew she wasn't making sense. "Please hurry!"

"Issie, are you hurt? Do you need an ambulance?"

"No. Just ... please ... It was a red Camry and they're still in the area."

"We'll get somebody right out," Simone said. "What's your cell phone number?"

Issie spouted it off, then clicked the phone off and dropped down behind a tree. There was no sound of a car coming and she wondered if they were just waiting, trying to make her sweat, giving her a chance to get good and scared before they came back around again. She kept the pistol up, waiting to use it.

She had never felt more tragically alone. There wasn't anyone in the world she could lean on, except perhaps her brother, and Jake's part in this confused things. Overcome with despair, she began to cry. She pulled her good knee up to her chest and dropped her face on it. There was no loneliness like that of sitting in a black night by yourself, knowing that any minute wheels could screech and bullets could fly. And there wasn't really anyone who cared.

Her car sat just yards away, still smoking from the accident that wasn't an accident. She might die before the police came. With only two bullets left, she might not be able to defend herself. The need for human contact overwhelmed her, and her mind drifted back to the fire earlier tonight, when she'd wrestled with the dead boy to make him live, and Nick Foster had held her and whispered in her ear. *It's okay. It's okay. It's okay.*

She dialed information, got Nick Foster's phone number. It was one-thirty in the morning, and she knew she would wake him.

He answered on the third ring. "Hello?" It came out too loud, as if he'd been startled awake.

"Nick, this is Issie."

"Issie." He sounded surprised.

"I'm so scared!"

"What is it?"

"Nick, somebody just tried to kill me," she said in a wobbling, high-pitched voice, "and they ran me off the road and I hit a telephone pole. I'm sitting on Meadow Road waiting for the police to get here, but I'm afraid they're going to come back and—"

"Issie, where on Meadow Road are you?"

She heard a siren in the distance. "About halfway down the wooded block."

"I'll be right there," he said. "Will I be able to see your car from the street?"

"Yes," she said, "but I'm not in it. I got out and I'm sitting off the road. Hiding in the trees. I only have two bullets left, and I know they're coming back."

"I'll be there in five minutes," he said.

She clicked the phone off and wondered what was taking the police so long. She wondered if anyone was chasing down the car, and if her nephew had been in it. She wished she could jog back to the Benton house and see who was still there. She wondered if she had shot anyone.

For the second time that day, she found herself praying.

• • •

Cruz took the back roads on the outskirts of Newpointe and cut down a dirt road near his grandfather's deer camp. When he knew he was hidden, he stopped the car and groped for his flashlight.

"Jen, let me see."

"I'm okay." Blood rolled down her face and into her eyes. She smeared it away.

"That's it. I'm taking you to the hospital!" He put the car in reverse and tried to turn around.

"No, wait. I don't think I was shot. I think it's glass."

He stopped the car again and shone the flashlight more carefully on her face. "It is. It's not a bullet, Jen. It's glass from the window." He shoved his fingers through her hair to hold the back of her head still, and picked a fragment out of her forehead. "Man, the blood . . ." He pulled his shirt off, wadded it up, and pressed it against her wound. "You still may need to go. I'll take you, Jen, if you need a doctor."

"No," she said. "We've got to hide. She'll send the police after us. Just drive. I'll be fine."

He drove down the dirt road, then over the old swinging bridge near the place where he and Jen grew up. He threaded down the road until it came out near his grandfather's house.

"We'll go home," he said. "Mama can patch you up and make you good as new."

"I'm gonna scar up like a freak," she said.

"At least you're alive. That could just as well have been a bullet as glass. I never shoulda let you come with me."

"We're in this together, Cruz. I hate being left out. You know I do." She pulled down the visor mirror and shone the flashlight on her forehead. "The bleeding's stopped. Maybe the cut's not so bad. Maybe I won't have a Frankenstein scar. Should we tell Mama about the killin's and all?"

"Maybe," he said. "Only don't tell her it was revenge against that preacher. Let her think we were takin' up the cause."

"Ethnic cleansing, we'll tell her," Jen said. "She'll be proud of us. Mama always did get into the fight. It made her feel all patriotic."

"I'm not through with that preacher yet. Won't be through till he's as dead as them other two. And Jake's aunt with him."

"We've got to do somethin' about the car, Cruz. She'll describe it. And the shot-out window won't help matters any."

"I'll drop you home, then I'll take care of the car. Remember that old stable on the edge of Grandpa's land? I'll hide it there till we can get the window fixed and change the color."

Jen actually smiled, filling him with relief. "I knew you'd have a plan, Cruz. You always take care of everything."

Chapter Twenty-Six

Issie didn't emerge from her hiding place until two squad cars had stopped and R.J. Albright and Anthony Martin had stepped into the circle of light created by the street lamp. Then, on shaky legs, she'd limped back up to her car.

She had finished filling them in about her chase and the gunfire, when Nick screeched up to the curb. She didn't know why the sight of him drew her to tears again.

He was still limping and moving carefully, and those bandages on his legs reminded her how serious his own injuries had been. She felt guilty for getting him out tonight.

"Issie, are you all right?"

"Yes," she said. "Nick, I may have shot somebody ... I'm not sure ... but they were shooting at me ..."

His arms came around her and pulled her against him, and she pressed her wet face against his chest. His hand cupped and stroked the back of her head. "Anybody looking for the car?" he asked over her head.

"We put an APB out, but no one's found it yet," Anthony said.

"They will," Nick assured against her ear. "They'll find them."

"I want to get out of here," she said. "Please, can Nick take me to the police station? I want to talk to Stan. I have ... information ..." The words filled her with terror, as if a spray of bullets would come from nowhere to shut her up. "Before I lose my nerve, I have to stop them. That's why they were trying to stop me."

"You can give *us* that information," R.J. said. "Right here, right now."

"No. Not right out in the open. Please. I want to talk to Stan. It's about the church fires and the killings. I know who did it, R.J. Stan will want to talk to me."

"We'll have to wait for backup," Anthony said. "There's some strange things happenin' in this town, and if you don't mind my sayin' so, I don't want to be caught in the middle of 'em."

"Both of you stay, and I'll take her in," Nick said.

R.J. shrugged. "Reckon that'd be okay, since you're practically one of us. I'll notify Stan you're comin' so he can meet you there."

Nick released her, and she felt that cloak of security jerked away. He ushered her to his car, helped her buckle in, then went to his side.

"Nick, I appreciate you coming," she said. "I don't even know why I called you. Of all people, you're injured yourself and don't need to be rescuing damsels in distress."

"I like rescuing damsels," he said. "I'm glad you called."

She looked out the window, her eyes searching the streets for a red Camry that might come from nowhere and start shooting again.

"Issie, what's going on? What do you know?"

"I know who did the church burnings and committed the two murders. I think it was my nephew's friends."

"You've got to be kidding."

"No. It's exactly who you thought. That Cruz kid and his sister. Last night, right after your church burned down, I went to this house where they hang out, and I found them burning a carpet with bloodstains in a bonfire."

Nick gaped at her. "Why didn't you say anything then?"

"I didn't want to implicate Jake. But then my tires were slashed, and I tried to convince myself there wasn't a connection. I got home and there was a dead cat in my bed, and somebody had been in my apartment and written on my wall. And tonight Jake called and had me stitch up a kid who'd been stabbed."

"Stabbed?"

"Yes, and I warned Jake I had to go to the police, so next thing I know I'm being chased and shot at and run off the road."

"Issie, you really think he could have been involved?"

"I know his friends were," she said. "He's with them all the time. I can't see how it could have happened without his knowledge. My brother's going to have a heart attack when he finds out. My sister-in-law's heart will break. She just doesn't deserve it."

"But you can't cover for him if he's guilty."

He reached the police station and pulled up to the front curb. "No, I can't," she said. "But, Nick, when I tell what I know, my life is going to be worth about as much as Ben's was to them. They won't stop until I'm dead."

He stared at her across the darkness. "You're a brave woman, Issie."

"I'm not brave," she said. "I've just run out of choices."

He sat there for a moment, his eyes locked into hers, as if his mind worked on the puzzle of Issie though some of the pieces were missing. After a moment, he opened his door. "Well, let's do it."

He came around and opened her door, then put his arm around her shoulders as he walked her up. She wondered why he made her feel so protected. Was it his size, or just his character? She decided it was his character, since she knew so many strong, tall men who gave her more to be insecure about. She remembered earlier today when he had pulled her back against his broken ribs and held her as she'd wept over losing the boy. It was a feeling so different from that of men's lustful arms around her, hands groping instead of stroking, grabbing instead of calming.

He opened the door for her and they stepped inside. The lights in the squad room made her feel safer, and she looked around and saw the buzz of activity. She didn't see Stan, but she knew that R.J. had called him at home and asked him to meet her there. At least she was marginally safe here. Surely those kids weren't stupid enough to come firing into a police station, no matter how desperate they were. Again, she wondered what kind of damage her bullets had done. What if she had killed one of them? What if Jake had been in the car?

Her knee hurt and her chest ached. She would probably have a bruise in the shape of her steering wheel, and no doubt her neck would ache tomorrow. But at least she was alive.

She looked up at Nick and realized he was probably in much more pain than she was. It was selfish of her to keep him here. "I appreciate you getting me here, Nick. You can probably go on home now. I know you're not feeling very well."

"No. I'm staying," he said. "You called me, and you're stuck with me."

"But you really don't have to. I can take it from here. I mean, if I'm safe anywhere, it's in the middle of a police station."

"I just want to stay here," he said, ending the discussion. "If it's all right with you, I'll just stay."

She nodded, thankful that he didn't want to leave. Truth was, she was petrified, and even sitting here, she worried that her killer might return. Nick's calming presence was what kept her from cowering through the station. She wondered if this was what it felt like to have a father—someone who counted it his responsibility to walk ahead of her through the land mines. No, she thought. These feelings toward Nick had little to do with father hunger, but there were things about him that fed that, anyway. Until now, she'd spent her life trying to rewrite the ending to her father-story, with men just like him—detached, lustful, selfish, unavailable. Her heart had expected every love to fulfill itself better than her father's love had. But it always came out the same.

Now she wondered if her heart had been as clueless as her mind.

Don't look at it too hard or it'll go away, she told herself. *Good feelings never stay.* So she thought, instead, about the land mines dotting her personal landscape as she bolted across it.

Chapter Twenty-Seven

It was almost four A.M. when Stan and Sid went to make arrests. Issie stayed behind at the conference table in the interrogation room, staring down at her hands splayed out in front of her. Directly across from her, Nick watched the emotions pass across her face.

"You okay?"

She cleared her throat. "No."

He set one of his hands on top of hers and tried to get her to look up at him. "What is it?"

"I . . . I'm wondering if I should warn my brother . . . you know . . . that Jake might be arrested."

"I don't think you should," Nick said. "He might tell Jake, and Jake might tip off the others . . ."

"You're right," she cut in, trying to blink back tears. "I know you are. It's just . . . he's only sixteen, you know . . . He's been brought in before . . . disturbing the peace, drunk and disorderly conduct . . . I bailed him out. I don't think I can bail him out this time."

"Issie, they would have killed you tonight. He's *with* them."

"But . . . what if he's just gotten in over his head? That slime-ball apparently stabbed his friend. What if he's afraid he'll be next?"

"It doesn't matter why he's doing it, Issie. If he's involved— or even if he knew about it—he's accountable. He has to pay."

"But you're supposed to be all about forgiveness, aren't you?" she asked, looking up at him. "Loving the sinner but hating the sin."

He had to look deep inside himself to find the answer she needed. It was in there somewhere, way down, covered over by anger toward the people who had killed Ben Ford. "You're talking about two different things, Issie. God's forgiveness, and the world's consequences."

Tears filled her eyes, and she stared down at her hands again. "What do you mean?"

He swallowed. "Paul the apostle killed Christians. He told himself he did it in the name of God. But it didn't matter why he did it. He killed people. He murdered them. Later, when he realized how wrong he'd been, when he repented, when God forgave him . . . those Christians were still dead."

"But . . . I thought Paul was one of the good guys."

"He was. He was one of the greatest Christians who ever lived. He wrote most of the New Testament. He was responsible for spreading the gospel throughout the world. But those Christians he killed . . . he could never undo it. God forgave him completely. He even forgot. But their families were still missing loved ones. They couldn't forget."

"Then what good is forgiveness? How does it help anybody?"

"It takes away the guilt."

"But if they still have to pay . . ."

"The world still makes you pay for your crimes," he said. "God doesn't."

"Even when you die?" she asked. "He doesn't punish people who've been involved in murder? They get off scot-free?"

"In heaven, God still requires payment for your sins . . . all of them, great and small. That payment is death. But he provided someone to make that payment. Someone to take your execution, just as surely as if he'd walked onto death row, unlocked the door, and taken your place. But no one can sit through your execution unless you let them. He doesn't force you to take the pardon."

He could see from her eyes that she was turning it all over in her mind. He wondered if she was processing it for Jake, or for herself.

"What if you don't deserve a pardon?" she asked.

"That goes without saying," he said. "Nobody deserves it. But the offer still stands."

The door opened, and LaTonya Mason stepped in. "Sorry, folks. I need to use this room."

Issie nodded and got to her feet. "We're leaving."

Nick wanted to turn around and beg LaTonya for ten more minutes. Issie was close. So close. But still so far from embracing the truth.

She came around the table and took Nick's arm. She was still shaking. "Come on. Let's go."

He followed her out into the noisy squad room, with telephones ringing and printers buzzing. Perpetrators and complainants cursed and yelled.

He watched that hard look flood back over her face, as if the reality of a fallen world had wakened her from a deep sleep. "Thanks for staying with me, Nick." She looked down at his bandaged legs. "I know you can't be comfortable. I forgot all about your injuries, I was so wrapped up in my own problems."

"Well, go easy on yourself," he said. "They're pretty tough problems."

She sighed and shook her head helplessly. "I don't know where I'm going to go," she said. "I can't stay at home, and my brother's is kind of out of the question. Maybe I need to get a hotel."

"No, you'd be too nervous in a hotel by yourself. You wouldn't sleep a wink. Look, there are a number of places you could stay. I could call several different families in my church. Usually I call Ray and Susan first, but under the circumstances I don't think they're up to taking any guests tonight."

"No, I hate feeling like an intruder. I don't want to stay in someone's house, especially if I don't know them that well."

He drew in a deep breath and tried to think. "I have an extra bedroom, but it wouldn't be appropriate for you to stay there with me."

She gave him a smirk. "Can't you just see it now? The tongues would be wagging for years. Issie Mattreaux and the preacher. Wouldn't that be a hoot?"

He didn't find it amusing. In fact, the thought had already occurred to him too many times. *Issie Mattreaux and the preacher.* No, she couldn't stay at his place. He frowned as an idea came to him. "You know, there is somebody who would probably be glad to put you up, and you know her really well."

"Who?" she asked.

"Aunt Aggie. She's got plenty of room, and she likes you."

"Yeah, I could stay with her. Do you think she'd take me?"

"Let me call her and we'll see."

As he took one of the spare desks with a telephone, he propped his legs up, wishing he'd brought his painkillers. But the pain was worth it to walk Issie through this process. She needed someone, and the fact that she'd chosen him filled him with an inexplicable pride.

Nick let the phone ring several times, for it always took Aunt Aggie a little longer to get all the way down the stairs to the one phone she kept in her foyer. He didn't know why no one had ever been able to talk her into putting a phone upstairs, but the old woman had her ways, and no one was about to change them now.

She finally picked up the phone. *"Hola."*

"Aunt Aggie, it's Nick. I know I woke you up. I'm sorry to call so late ... or, so early."

"Hey, Nick," she said. "How them burns are?"

"They're okay, Aunt Aggie. Did you hear about the latest church burning?"

"Yep," she said, "and I hope you see that it ain't just your church burnin' down. It got nothin' to do with you so you can quit that down-in-the-mouth stuff and jus' get on back to preachin'."

"I plan to, Aunt Aggie," he said, "but we've got a problem. I need your help. Issie Mattreaux just named some people that she thinks might have something to do with the murders and the church burnings, and we think she's in a little trouble. She was shot at on the way to the police station, and she's afraid to go home. The police are making arrests right now, but if they don't round everybody up . . ." He hesitated, trying to get to the point. "Aunt Aggie, she needs a place to stay, and I wondered if you'd take her in."

"That girl can stay with me anytime," she said. "Only I ain't too crazy 'bout havin' bullet bait in my house."

"Bullet bait?" he asked.

"Yeah. If people out shootin' at her, I don't want her here, me."

"But, Aunt Aggie, she doesn't have any place else to go."

"Well, she can brought herself here, all right," Aunt Aggie said, "but I ain't got a man to protect us. I'll take her if you come too."

He frowned. "Me? I have a house, Aunt Aggie."

She didn't seem to find any relevance in that. "I'll put you downstairs in the guest room. Anybody comes in this house, they go by you first."

He sat back, thinking it through. Aunt Aggie had never been the frightened type, so her fears now didn't ring true. "Aunt Aggie, is this a trick? Are you just trying to get me in your house so you can hover over me?"

"You want me to take that girl in, or not?"

He grinned and met Issie's eyes. "Aunt Aggie, you're a sneaky little thing, aren't you?"

"You call it sneaky, I call it smart, me. If I got bullet bait in my house, then I gon' have a man to protect me. And if I have to cook and do for you to return the favor, then you'll jes' have to let me, you."

"All right, Aunt Aggie. You win."

"I'll take good care o' you, *sha*," she said with delight. "You ain't been pampered in a long time, you, so y'all come on over, we'll pass a good time."

He hung up the phone and sat there a moment, wondering how he'd been snookered into that.

Issie approached him. "What did she say?"

"She said you're very welcome to come." He looked up at her, wishing she wasn't quite so pretty ... wishing he wasn't quite so happy about staying in Aunt Aggie's house with her. "There's just one little catch," he said.

"A catch? What catch?"

"She wants me to come too."

"What do you mean? To spend the night?"

"Yeah," he said. "She said that she doesn't feel very safe without a man there and she'd like for me to come."

"Well, if you don't mind my saying so, she's probably right. I'm not the safest person to be putting up right now. But that doesn't mean that you have to take a bullet for me."

"I'm not going to take a bullet," he said. "Nobody's even going to know where you are. I'll just take you by your apartment and we'll go in and get your stuff, get whatever you need for tonight, and then we'll go by my house and I'll get my stuff. I'll just forward my calls to Aunt Aggie's. Oh, and I've got to try and change these bandages. I put it off all day, dreading it, but I guess I can't put it off any longer."

She looked down at his legs. "I'll be happy to do it."

He couldn't stand the thought. He wanted her to think of him as strong, invincible. Not wounded and disgusting. "No, that's okay. It's not very pleasant."

"Hey, I do unpleasant things all the time. I can do a lot better job than you can, Nick. When we get to Aunt Aggie's I'll change your bandages and apply the medication, and make sure everything looks all right."

The thought of doing it himself was almost more repulsive than the thought of getting her to, but he couldn't decide between the worse of two evils as they drove to her apartment to get her things.

Chapter Twenty-Eight

Cruz and Jennifer's mother let a string of curses fly when she saw Jennifer's face. At that, their grandfather had wakened and shuffled into the kitchen, his big paunch protruding like that of a pregnant woman.

"What are you two tied up in?" Sidney Clairmont demanded.

"It's them church burnings, ain't it?" Hattie Cruz spouted as she doused Jennifer's forehead with hydrogen peroxide. "Reminded me of the old days."

"Except for the bodies!" Clairmont boomed. "Whatsa matter with you two? You don't kill somebody first thing! You leave a warning, then you burn a cross. You make sure they know the KKK acted, but they can't narrow down who done it."

"We ain't like you, Granddaddy," Cruz said. "We ain't the KKK. We have different ways."

"Use the ways that work, fool!" he bellowed. "That way you don't get shot at and chased and put in jail before you have a chance to make a difference."

"They know how to do it," Hattie said. "Daddy, they was raised with this. They been follerin' you since they was knee-high to a grasshopper."

Cruz went to the refrigerator and got a beer out. "I hear the police been snooping around here."

His mother made a derisive noise. "Come wanting to talk to you, but I ain't seen you in days."

"We found a house we could use till we get the compound done," Cruz said. "When it's done, I want you two to come live there with us. We're gon' have massive security to keep the Feds out, and you can help us recruit older soldiers who have money. We need a cash flow, and the younger ones ain't got much."

"I ain't movin' nowhere," Sidney said. "I'm fine right here."

"But they'll come after you to get to us. I can't promise your protection if you ain't with us. When we get moved in, we'll have a supply of food for a year, an arsenal of weapons, and won't nobody be able to touch us. Just think about it. Think of all we can accomplish with the resources our recruits bring with 'em."

Hattie put a big Band-Aid on Jennifer's forehead and winked at her son. "I'll work on him," she said. "Time it's ready, we'll be set to go. Now ya'll ain't going back to the group tonight, are you? You gotta hide. They'll be back lookin' for you again."

"We'll need to hide the car for sure," Jennifer said. "They'll be lookin' for it. We put it out in the shed near Granddaddy's deer camp. You think it'll be all right?"

"Yeah," Sidney grunted. "And you two better stay at the camp. It's empty right now. They won't look there."

Cruz liked the idea. "Thanks, Granddaddy. I knew you could help."

By the time they got their things and set up at the deer camp, they were ready for a few hours of sleep.

Chapter Twenty-Nine

Aunt Aggie's house was one of the biggest and oldest in New-pointe, and was situated on one of the last undisturbed stretches of land in the center of town. The center point of her acreage dipped down into a valley that flooded when it rained, but her house sat half on a hill overlooking her well-tended garden in front, and half on pilings in back that protected her from rising waters. The driveway swung down and around to the back of the house, and she parked her huge, fifteen-year-old Cadillac underneath. Nick parked next to her car in the garage, and he and Issie carried their things up the steps and into her massive kitchen that smelled of cayenne pepper.

"Come right in, you," she said. "Issie, you look wore out, *sha*."

The old woman was wearing a hot pink satin robe and fresh red lipstick on her thin, wrinkled lips. "T-Nick, you takin' care of her?"

"Yes, ma'am, Aunt Aggie."

"We sure appreciate you taking us in, Aunt Aggie," Issie said. "I don't know where I would have gone if you hadn't. I've never been so scared in my life."

"Jes' let 'em try gettin' you here," Aunt Aggie warned. "Nick'll show 'em, won't you, *sha*?"

"They won't come here," he said. "My guess is they're hiding from the cops as we speak."

"So d'yeat?" she asked, going to a pot on the stove and taking off the lid. The smell of jambalaya wafted across the room.

He wondered if she just kept a pot on 24/7, or if she had thrown this together at the last minute.

"I'm not really hungry," Issie said, and Nick shot her a sharp look. She cleared her throat. "But it smells so good . . . I'll have some, anyway."

"Gettin' too skinny, *sha*. You ain't one o' them anorexics heavin' in the toilets, is you?"

"No, ma'am, Aunt Aggie. I wouldn't do that."

She spooned out the jambalaya and handed Issie a bowl, then started dipping Nick's. "I ever tell you I was Miss Louisiana in 1938? We needed curves then, not the bones and angles like today. Ma Dugas, he liked ma shape. Never did have nothing for them skeleton types. But I does try to keep ma figure. Ain't no excuse for letting yourself go. Who trying to kill you, Issie?"

Nick grinned at the sudden shift in thoughts as he took his bowl and sat down.

"I think it's the same people who killed Ben Ford," Issie said.

"Like t'get my hands on 'em," Aunt Aggie said. "Yellow-livered murderers."

She ranted and raved for a while longer before she began to wane. Finally, she retired to her bedroom, and Nick found that he felt awkward being here alone with Issie. He wondered what his church members would think if they learned he was spending the night in this house with Aunt Aggie and Issie Mattreaux. Was it really much better than putting Issie up in his own home? But he couldn't worry about that now. Issie's life was in danger until the police rounded up all those who were responsible for the church burnings and the murders.

He carried Issie's things up to her room, then came back down and found her standing in the dark, peering out the window. "They don't know you're here, Issie. It's gonna be okay." He came up beside her and closed the blinds, then turned a Tiffany lamp on. The darkness fled.

Issie took Nick's hand, making his heart jolt. "Okay, let's have a look at those burns," she said.

He shook his head. "It's okay, really. Now that I think about it, I can do it. It's really not that hard."

"Then why have you been putting it off all day?" she asked. "You know, you really should have done it this morning."

"They're feeling fine. I just—"

"You *have* to change the bandages," she said. She pulled him toward a chair and got too close, setting a hand on his shoulder and giving a little shove. She was such a flirt, and she was so good at it. He sat down.

"Come on." Her voice was gentle as she lifted his feet onto an overstuffed ottoman. "Let's put your feet up on this and I'll see what I can do. Where's your stuff?"

He nodded toward the guest room. "It's in there on the bed. In the little black bag."

"I'll get it." She took off toward the bedroom, and he closed his eyes and leaned his head back and prayed a silent prayer that he would keep this in perspective. He wasn't used to being alone with women or having one address his needs. Oh, occasionally someone would bring him a meal or come clean up his house when he was particularly busy, but usually it was one of the married members of his church. He had a few single women who had targeted him for husband material, but they weren't women in whom he was interested. And Aunt Aggie's ministrations didn't count.

Issie Mattreaux was someone he had spent too much time thinking about. He wondered if she was aware of just how attracted he was to her . . .

. . . And just how much he didn't want to be.

She came back, her black hair shimmering in the lamplight, and he wondered if she took any special care of it or if it came easy to her. He didn't think he knew any other women whose hair looked quite that silky. It was midnight-colored satin, and he told himself that it probably didn't feel as soft as it looked. In fact, it was probably coarse to the touch, and probably smelled like sauerkraut or old gym shoes . . .

Yeah, right.

She brought the bandages and the Silvadene cream that he was to put on the burns. He tried not to wince as she peeled the bandages off. Instead, he chuckled, amused that he would be concerned about impressing her with his toughness.

"What's so funny?" she asked as she worked.

"It's not funny," he said. "I was just thinking how big and strong I'm supposed to be—since I'm ostensibly protecting you and all—and here you are, making me coil up like a toddler about to get a shot."

She grinned. "Am I being rough with you?"

"No, it's okay." He chuckled again. He watched her work on his legs and she did it quickly, competently, and he realized that she was very good at what she did. The pain was making him sweat, and he tried to get his mind to shift gears.

"What would you have been if you hadn't been a paramedic?" he asked her.

"Oh, I don't know. I'd probably be in jail."

He hadn't expected that, and he laughed. "Jail? Come on."

She grinned. "I'm half serious," she said. "I really only decided to be a paramedic for the money. It looked pretty good, and there's a lot of time off. A lot of time on too, though."

"Give me a break. You love what you do."

"Sometimes," she said as her grin faded again. "But days like today . . . I think I'd opt for jail."

He wished her eyes were easier to forget. "Tell me you didn't have any feelings of wanting to help people, wanting to rescue them."

"I think I kind of liked the idea of the adrenaline pumping through my veins. You know what I mean?"

He nodded. "Yeah, I know. But I saw you today. You weren't trying to save that kid's life for the money or the adrenaline rush. You really cared about him."

She seemed to concentrate harder on the burns.

He winced. "And besides that, the money isn't that great," he said. "You could have been a nurse or a doctor and made a lot more money."

"Yeah, can't you just see me as a doctor?" she asked. "I couldn't care for patients long-term. I don't do anything long-term. I'm not like you, Nick."

"What do you mean, you're not like me?"

She kept her eyes on his burns. "I'm not the commitment type."

"And I am? You haven't ever seen me commit to a woman, have you?"

"Well, you've committed to a lot of other things. Your church, the people you're friends with. People rely on you. I, on the other hand, am not one that anyone relies on."

"Hey, if I was in a fix and needed rescuing, you'd be the one I'd call."

She gave a weak smile. "Thanks, Nick. I appreciate that, and obviously the feeling is mutual since that's exactly what I did tonight."

His face sobered, and suddenly he felt very vulnerable. It wasn't a bad feeling. "Why *did* you call me, Issie?" he asked quietly. "Me, of all people?"

She sat back then and looked a little embarrassed. "I don't know. I really don't."

She wouldn't meet his eyes. She just kept looking at his legs as she worked, and he forgot the pain and watched the pink color climb in her cheeks. He'd never seen her blush before. She wasn't the type. He wondered if it had anything to do with today when he had pulled her back against him and held her. It had been instinctive, something he probably shouldn't have done. He was a preacher, after all, and had to maintain a certain amount of decorum. But she had been so distraught . . .

He couldn't forget how small she had felt in his arms.

She finished bandaging his legs, then stood up. "Almost good as new," she said.

"I appreciate that. You just don't know how much." He carefully lowered his feet to the floor, then set his hands on his knees.

He was nervous, he realized, and that was so silly. He was almost always nervous around Issie. He didn't know why. Sometimes it felt as if she was playing with him. Other times he felt a fierce, overwhelming sense of protection toward her. He didn't know why he would think that God might appoint him protector over her. Surely, there were plenty of other men who wouldn't mind guarding her, men who were more her type.

She got up and sat facing him on the ottoman, her knees just inches from his. She had something on her mind, he sensed, something she didn't want to say from across the room. He expected coy flirtation, but instead, her face was serious as she looked into his eyes.

"Nick, can I ask you something?"

"Sure," he said. "What?"

She looked down at her hands, and he saw that she was fidgeting. Her voice was quiet, as though she didn't want Aunt Aggie to somehow overhear. "Sometimes . . . I look at my life . . . and it's not exactly the way I thought it would be. And I see my family . . ." She swallowed. "My father's an alcoholic . . . not that I would know it firsthand, since he's never been around. Before my mother died, she worked in a bar in Slidell and had very little interest in anything I did. She had . . . weird priorities, you know? Always did. And then I see my brother and Lois standing back at arm's length while Jake gets involved in such a mess. I start to wonder . . . what things might have been like if we were different."

He knew that she was leading up to an important question, one for which he needed an answer, and he silently prayed that God would give him the wisdom to answer it in the right way. It was tempting, sometimes, to tell someone what they wanted to hear, just to make them feel better. But Issie's life might depend on the truth. Her eternal life, anyway.

"Different how?" he prompted.

"Different, you know. Religious maybe. I mean, sometimes I look around at the people who go to church, people like you and Mark and Allie . . . Dan and Jill . . . Susan and Ray . . . and I think how together they all seem to have things. Sometimes I just look at them and think it's harder for them, you know? Like when Mark and Allie were having problems. Other people might have just gone for divorce, moved on, taken the easy way . . . but it was harder for them because they had this standard to live by. In some ways I felt sorry for them because of that. Angry even. But that's another story."

Nick couldn't meet her eyes on that one. He knew that she had been in love with Mark and wanted to see that marriage break up. The fact that it didn't happen had probably surprised her.

"But then I look at them now and I see how happy they are, and they've got the baby. They're a real family. And Dan and Jill. You know all that time when Dan was single, I used to watch the women line up for him. And frankly, I would have gone out with him in a second if he'd asked. He just never did, and I think I know why."

Nick met her eyes again.

"I wasn't his type," she said. "I was a little too loose and free. And, of course, most men like that, but Dan was of a different ilk."

Nick grinned. "You can say that again."

"But he was," Issie said. "He had that standard, that different set of rules he lived by."

"They're not rules," Nick said. "Really, Issie, they're not."

"Well, the Ten Commandments are rules."

"Issie, the only reason Christians live by a different standard is because they trust that God wants what's best. God gave those commandments for their good, not so they couldn't have any fun. He knows how sin hurts people. It really does, Issie. Look at what's happening to Jake. Look at the murders. Look at the church burnings."

She nodded. "Look at my life."

She was coming around, he thought as his heart rate sped up, like it always did when someone started to see and understand the truth. He wondered if Jesus had gotten that racing heartbeat when someone finally got it. He took her hands, as if to hold her there and keep her from backing away. "The cycle doesn't have to go on," he said. "You could stop it right now."

She was quiet for a long time, staring at a button on his shirt. "I don't know, Nick. I'm not the type to start living by rules. And besides that, I can't imagine a God who would care a thing about me. Some stupid medic who drinks and parties too hard . . . who has a past like I have."

"He does care, Issie. You have to believe that."

"Well, I wish I could believe it. I really do. It serves the people who believe it. Kind of a placebo effect, maybe. If they think it, then it makes things better for them. Maybe it's all psychological anyway. Maybe I just need to get my mind thinking right."

"Mark and Allie's marriage wasn't healed because of any psychology," Nick said. "It was because God worked on their hearts and changed them. Trust me, Issie. If there was a woman alive who could have lured Mark from Allie, it would have been you."

Her eyes rounded in surprise, and he realized the spiritual talk had given him solid footing and made him forget his awkwardness.

"Funny coming from you," she said.

They were too close, and he never should have taken her hands. He needed to get up, put some distance between them. But he couldn't seem to do it. He kept his eyes boldly locked with hers. "I have the same impulses you have, Issie."

Her eyes were the softest brown, almost hazel, and he felt he could see through them right into her heart. The air between them was charged with electricity, and he feared he would feel the shocking pop, telling him that the voltage was too high.

"I never would have figured," she said. Now he heard the expected flirtation in her tone.

"Yes, you would," he whispered.

It was clear by the grin in her eyes that she relished the power she had over him. "So you're telling me that even preachers have temptations?"

"They absolutely do," he whispered. He swallowed hard, trying to get his bearings. "But the Bible tells us there's no temptation too great that God won't give us the means of escape. And I've found that to be true every single time."

The pleasure seemed to fade from her eyes, and he sensed her disappointment. "Haven't you ever wondered what it would be like if you didn't escape it?" she asked. "Just once? If you gave in to something that you wanted to do?"

He wanted to say yes, that he was struggling with that now, that it would have been so easy to let her have that power over him as she sat knee to knee, holding his hands, grinning into his eyes. It would have been so easy to just lose himself in that moment, to taste of Issie Mattreaux and learn what he was missing.

But then there would be tomorrow, and the emptiness would set in, and when it did ... where could he run for comfort? How could he turn to the Savior he had betrayed? She would never understand.

"I *want* to please God," he said. "That's my first priority."

She sighed, as if disappointed. "I don't even know why I like you," she told him. "There are a million other people I could have called tonight. I could have called Joe's Place and just asked for somebody and ten people would have come to the phone wanting to help me. Ten medics, like me, sitting there unwinding together. We have a bond, you know. We're close. I could have called them."

Nick smiled. "But you didn't call them," he said. "You called me. Isn't that interesting?"

"So what are you saying? That that's a God thing?"

"I think maybe."

She lifted her chin high and leaned closer. Her eyes sparkled. "Maybe it was a chemistry thing," she said defiantly. "Maybe I called you because I'm attracted to you, God-only-knows-why."

He felt the blood rushing to his face and pulled his hands away. Had she just admitted she was attracted to him? Issie Mattreaux, to the preacher? He didn't know where to go with that.

"Maybe God's telling us that you and I are supposed to be an item," she went on, chiding him. "How would you feel about that, Nick, with all your rules?"

His mouth suddenly felt dry. "I don't know, Issie. I don't think that's what happened."

"Of course it's not," she said, "because a pious person like you could never get involved with a wretch like me, is that right?"

She was too close to him now, looking up into his face, daring him to back away. He smelled the scent of her hair. It was nothing like sauerkraut or gym shoes. Strawberries, maybe. He liked strawberries.

She turned her face up to his, her lips too close to his. "I'm not good enough for you, am I, Nick?"

He looked down at her, feeling her breath against his own lips, and wondered what it would be like to kiss her just once. He wanted to feel that sprinting of his heart and that sweet relief and urgent desire warring inside him. He wanted to tell her that he thought about her more than any other woman he knew, that her image was constantly on his mind.

But escape lingered there in the back of his mind. He could take a step backward, break this spell she seemed to have over him. He could close off the vision he had of holding her and kissing her, and focus back on the Christ who would not have orchestrated their coming together for the purposes of becoming a couple, not when they were so unequally yoked. Christ would want someone for him who could share his passion for the kingdom. Christ would have chosen someone who shared his passion for the Lord. A woman who had the same goals and purpose that he had, someone who understood the grace of the Cross, someone whose heart was broken over it.

Issie was not that woman.

He took that step back. "I'm going to bed, Issie."

"Did I scare you, Nick?" she asked, almost angrily.

"No," he said. "Let's just say I'm taking that escape." And before she could dare him further, he went into the guest room and closed the door.

Chapter Thirty

Jake woke to the sound of moaning. He opened his eyes and squinted at the light pouring in through the window. He had come home after Cruz had run out after Issie last night, and had brought Benton with him. The rest of the kids in the house had scattered, for fear that the latest killing, and Cruz's actions if and when he caught Issie, might bring police. Jake's parents were in bed when he got home, and now, at nine A.M., he hoped they were both at work.

He had called Issie's house at least twice an hour all night long, and she had never answered. His stomach burned. What had Cruz done to her?

There had been no news. His parents hadn't gotten a phone call in the middle of the night, and Issie hadn't shown up here in desperate flight.

So what did that mean? Had they gotten to her, shut her up? Or had she gotten to the police first?

He sat up in his bed and admitted to himself that his association with Cruz and his group wasn't working out to his advantage. Playing drums for their band was definitely a perk, and the idea of living in a commune without school or parents, growing their own food, and following a charismatic spiritual leader like Cruz had been cool enough . . . but he hadn't counted on murder and seeing his friends and family abused.

He heard the moan again, and squinted up to see Benton writhing on the twin bed across from him, his leg exposed where Issie had cut open his jeans last night. The dental floss stitches she'd made were crude and looked like something out of a Frankenstein movie. He wondered if the muscle beneath would heal without deeper sutures, or if Benton would have a limp for the rest of his life.

He got up and went to Benton, reached out to shake him, and felt that his skin was burning. "Benton?" he said. "Wake up, buddy. You're burning up with fever."

Benton's eyes barely slit open. "I'm f-f-f-reeezing."

"Chills," he said, grabbing a blanket to put over him. "Man, we need to get you to a hospital. You may need surgery or something."

"Cruz said no."

"I don't care what Cruz said," Jake threw back. "He's not the one with the gash up his leg."

"Don't even know what I d-d-did."

"Something about Jennifer. He sees red when anybody touches her. Goes ballistic, man. Like a total personality change. Jekyll and Hyde."

"She didn't do nothin' wrong, Jake. You're just mad 'cause she was with me instead of you."

"We need to get you to the doctor, and while we're there, we need to have our heads examined for hanging out with people like Cruz and Jennifer in the first place."

"You better sh-sh-shut up," Benton said. "He might kill you if he hears you talking like that."

"He's not even here. We're at my house." He bent over and touched the swollen place around Benton's stitches. "Come on, man. We've got to get you to a hospital before Cruz comes looking for us."

"B-b-but what'll we tell 'em?"

"We'll think of something on the way there. Now, come on."

Benton tried to sit up but was too weak. Jake bent down and helped him. "Man, you lost a lot of blood last night. No wonder you're weak. Wouldn't hurt to get you some food too, and something cold to drink. You're hot as fire. Here, lean on me and try to get to your feet."

He managed to get Benton up on one leg, and they limped out the door. With each step on his hurt leg, Benton moaned and winced. Jake looked down at his leg and saw that the stitches were pulling as the wound swelled, and the cut was beginning to bleed again.

"Here, just stop. Don't put any more weight on it, man. Just stand here against the house, and I'll back the car around. Can you do that, man?"

Benton seemed to be dizzy, but he managed to nod.

Jake ran to get the car, drove up in the yard, turned around, and put it in reverse. He backed up to just a foot or two from Benton, then got out and helped him into the passenger seat.

As Jake got back into his car, he realized that if Benton hadn't been so scared of Cruz, he would have gotten him to the hospital before now. At least he could have taken him home, where his parents could care for him . . . if they felt like it. But Benton's dad sometimes got a little crazy himself, and Jake wouldn't put it past him to beat Benton for coming home wounded, as if he'd miraculously heal if his dad gave him enough other injuries to concentrate on.

"What are we gonna tell 'em?" Benton slurred as he leaned his head back against the seat. "We can't squeal on Cruz."

"I know, I've been thinking about that," Jake said. "Let's tell them that we were out last night, and we got really drunk at the Viper Pit, and you fell on a broken bottle and it cut your leg."

Benton thought that over for a moment. "Does a glass cut look like a knife wound?"

Jake wasn't sure. "You got a better idea?"

"No."

"Okay, then."

"What about the stitches? Do we tell them about Issie?"

"No, man. We can't get her in trouble. We tell them that I did the stitches. That we got paranoid about coming in 'cause we were so drunk ..."

"Yeah, okay." Benton closed his eyes, thinking it over.

Jake tried to measure for flaws in the story, and decided it was okay.

Benton began to laugh. He threw his wrist over his eyes and shook his head. Jake glanced over at him, grinning. "What's so funny?"

"They'll probably lock us up to protect us from ourselves," he said. "Man, we're gonna look stupid."

"I don't care how stupid we look," Jake said. "Just so they take care of you."

Silence filled the car as they both ran the scenario through their minds. "It makes me sick ... Cruz doing me like that," Benton said. "I didn't do nothin' to him. I trusted him, looked up to him. Look what I did for him!"

"He turned on us, man. He's not the person he wants us to think. Cruz's dangerous. He doesn't tell us anything, but he expects us to jump in with both feet, no questions asked. Well, I don't work that way."

"We've both been workin' that way lately," Benton said. "I worked that way last night. That kid we killed ... He reminded me of my kid brother ..." He got quiet for a moment, his eyes closed and his head leaned back on the neck rest. "Man, you think I might go to prison?"

"Of course not," Jake said. But as he navigated his way to the Slidell hospital, he realized that prison was a secondary problem. First they had to keep Benton from losing his leg.

Chapter Thirty-One

Dan and Jill Nichols sat in the waiting room in Mayor Patricia Castor's office. They knew she wasn't busy. They had heard her through the wall talking on the phone to her daughter about what to get her grandchild for Christmas, but she always liked to keep people waiting for meetings, just so they would know who was in control. The only time she was prompt was during election years. Then she made a career out of being courteous and polite.

This was not an election year.

Jill checked her watch and gave a disgruntled sigh. "You know, I've got a lot of work to do. I probably ought to just let you handle this and get on back to the office."

"No, wait." Dan slapped down the bodybuilding magazine he'd been scanning and got up. "I've had enough. I'm going in."

The mayor's secretary looked alarmed. "You can't do that, Dan."

"Watch me." He went to the mayor's door and threw it open. "Pat, I'm sick of waiting. Now if you can get off the phone and quit talking about Christmas presents and grandkids, maybe we can get down to some of the town's business."

Pat Castor looked up at him, disgusted. "Where is my secretary? Why didn't she keep you—"

"I'm here, Mayor," the woman said, scurrying to the doorway. "I'm so sorry. I tried to keep him from comin' in, but—"

"Come on, Pat," Dan said, motioning for Jill to follow him as he bolted in. "It's not her fault. I sat there patiently listening to you talk about Beanie Babies and Play Stations until I was sick of it. Jill needs to get back to the office, so can we please get on with this?"

The mayor looked indignant, but she made her apologies to her daughter and got off the phone. "What do you want, Dan?"

It occurred to him that they hadn't gotten off to a very good start. This didn't bode well for the favor he had come to ask her. "I want to talk to you about our church."

She shifted in her seat and crossed her arms. As far as anyone could tell, Pat Castor didn't go to church, though she claimed affiliation with the Methodists on every campaign flier she had printed up. If she attended a Methodist church, they could only assume it was one out of town, since no one at Newpointe's Methodist church had ever seen her there. "Yes, that church burnin' was such a tragedy," she said. "And poor Ray. I've been meanin' to get a card out to him, expressin' my condolences."

Dan started to say that a card should make up for everything, but Jill anticipated the sarcasm and pinched his leg. "Pat, we appreciate your time," she said, though Pat hadn't given it willingly. "We're really upset about our church and the fact that it's completely devastated and there's no place for us to worship."

"It was a tough break," Pat said, "and I'm trying to get to the bottom of it. I won't have people in my town going around burning down institutions. Next thing you know, they'll be burning down the courthouse and the police station and my office, so's you're not safe anywhere. I'm thinking about getting a bodyguard. You just never know what you might run into."

Jill nodded sympathetically. Again, Dan bit his tongue to keep from expressing amazement that she'd managed to twist the conversation back to herself.

"Mayor, we wanted to ask you a favor," Jill said. "We want to ask if you would allow us to use the courtroom to have our services on Sunday."

The mayor just stared at her for a moment, then laid her head back and let out a laugh.

Now it was Jill's turn to be angry. "Would you please tell me why this is so funny?" she demanded.

"Because I can't believe you'd ask me that. You, a lawyer and everything. You know I can't let you have church services in the courtroom. Whatever happened to separation of church and state?"

Dan pinched Jill's knee, figuring that either of them had grounds for going across the desk and throttling the woman. "The separation of church and state," Jill said in her best legal voice, "had to do with preventing our states from telling us how, when, and where we had to worship. It had nothing to do with congregations using municipal buildings paid for with taxpayers' money to hold their services. In fact, they did it all the time in the early days of our country. Our founding fathers even worshiped in them."

"Well, if I let you," Pat said, "I'd have to let the Muslims and the Hindus and the Buddhists."

Dan shot her an are-you-crazy look. "First of all, there aren't any of those in Newpointe to my knowledge, and if there were, they'd have their own places to worship. Ours, on the other hand, was burned to the ground the day before yesterday. Every one of us is a taxpayer. We're asking to use this facility for a public assembly. We have the right to worship."

"But you don't have the right to worship in my courthouse," the mayor said. "Sorry, folks. I just can't let you do it."

Dan gave further consideration to lunging across the desk. "Pat, what is your problem? You've let us have meetings here for everything from planning the policeman's ball to organizing a fund-raiser for the public schools. You've even let Aunt Aggie cart food in here when people were meeting. It's one of the few rooms big enough for our whole congregation to fill."

"There've got to be others," she said. "Try the hotel. It probably has a conference room."

"A conference room is not big enough, Pat. We have two hundred members. Besides, we don't have a lot of money, and the hotels want us to pay for those rooms."

"So the city is supposed to give you a handout?"

"Not a handout," Jill said. "A place to meet. That's all."

Dan stood straighter as an idea came to him. "Pat, do you realize how many of your voters go to our church?"

That got her attention. Her eyebrows came up as she considered that fact. "Since I won by a landslide, I guess you're right. My constituency is everywhere."

"But if word gets out that you wouldn't let us meet here, how do you think they'll vote next time?"

"It'll blow over by then." She preened, patting the back of her short hair. "They have short memories. Anyway, they'll probably understand because they all know about the separation of church and state."

Jill stood up and went into attorney mode. "You mean, they're all *deceived* about the separation of church and state. As you are. You know, it really chaps me that our own elected officials don't know the Constitution any better than that."

"Well," the mayor huffed. "Insult me all you want, if that's the way your church operates . . ." She got to her feet, dismissing them. "I appreciate you stoppin' by," she said. "Wish I could help. I hope I can still count on your vote in the next election."

"My vote?" Jill asked. "I was actually thinking of running against you."

Her face hardened instantly. "Run against me? You?"

"Why not?" Dan asked. "She's younger and smarter and has more character. Better looking too. I think she could win it hands down."

They both knew they were bluffing, but Pat's reaction was amusing. Her face was turning red, and her lips were compressed as she looked at them. "Well, you just do that," she said in her saccharine drawl. "May the best woman win."

Dan and Jill left, still fuming, and headed to the school superintendent's office to see if they could use the high school auditorium. When they saw the man's reaction, Dan wondered if Pat Castor had already warned the superintendent.

He told them that he had enough trouble getting federal aid without turning the school into a church. One move like that and he'd be on a street corner trying to raise funds to pay teachers.

Then they tried the theater in town, but the owner told them that the first scheduled movies on Sunday were for eleven o'clock. If he allowed them to have church there, he wouldn't be able to start the movies on time.

Feeling defeated, they left there and went to the fire station to tell Mark and some of the others that they had struck out. Aunt Aggie was there serving lunch to the men.

The old Cajun woman was almost ninety years old, yet she still insisted on cooking for her boys every day. The habit had started decades ago when her own husband had been a firefighter and she'd been known as the best cook in town. Aggie, rich from her investments, had pitied her husband for having to eat their cooking, and had started bringing meals from home for him. When there was enough of an uproar from men asking to share what she'd brought her husband, she had started bringing her groceries to the station and cooking it all up there. She had been doing it ever since. It was one of the joys of her life, and theirs too. They'd had to start a strenuous workout program for the firefighters, to offset the extra calories they took in while on duty. Today they were having Cajun popcorn, which was really fried crawfish claws, and homemade seasoned French fries for lunch.

As Dan and Jill walked in, Aunt Aggie motioned for them to hurry. "Did ya eat yet, *sha*?"

"Not yet, Aunt Aggie," Jill said.

"Then sit yourself down. Hurry up. I gotta get this on the table while it's still hot, me."

"That's okay, Aunt Aggie," Dan said. "I'm off duty. We're not eating."

"I don't care if you off duty. You here, ain't you?" She pulled out a chair and ordered them to sit down. They both took their seats obediently as the firemen filed in.

"Well, what you two doin' here on your day off, Dan?"

Dan shrugged. "I was just coming by to tell Mark that I didn't have any luck with finding a place to worship. Pat Castor won't let us use the courthouse, and Dennis Fournier won't let us use the high school. The theater manager refused too. I can't think of any other places, but I thought maybe somebody here could."

"How 'bout my house?" Aunt Aggie asked. Mark was just coming to the table, and he looked up at her.

"Your house, Aunt Aggie? Your house is big, but it's not big enough for two hundred worshipers."

"I meant outside," she said. "We can get folding chairs and sit out in the yard. I got plenty of land and plenty of shade, *sha*, and it ain't too cold yet."

Jill and Dan looked at each other. "You know, that's an idea. We hadn't thought of meeting outside."

Aunt Aggie was a new Christian and was still a little green about the things of Christ, but she knew how to solve a problem. "I'll cook and we can have food and—"

"No, Aunt Aggie," Jill cut in. "You don't have to cook. If we use your property, that'll be enough. We'll be so grateful."

Mark's eyes were widening as he looked at Dan. "I think that's the answer. We can have services Sunday morning, can't we, Aunt Aggie?"

"*Mais oui*, you bet we can. I'll get Bradford over to the rental place to brought us the chairs. You boys can help set 'em up. We'll have us a church 'fore we even know it, right there under God. He'll be smilin' down at us."

Mark was getting excited. "And the neighbors around will hear us singing and praising the Lord. It might turn out to be a good witness. Maybe our numbers will even grow."

"I like it," Jill said. "I like it a lot. Aunt Aggie, are you sure?"

"I'm sure, *sha*," she said, "and I'll be insulted if you don't do it, me. I ain't never had much to give that church 'cept money, and that don't mean nothing now that the building's flat on the ground. If I can help keep the church goin', then that's what I'll do, me."

Chapter Thirty-Two

Sunlight shone through Nick's window as he lay in his own bed, staring at the ceiling. Issie had gone to work today, so he had gone home to catch up on some things. He hadn't slept well in Aunt Aggie's guest room, so he tried to rest now. He'd had several visitors today, all with food, but hadn't had an appetite. He had finally felt so exhausted that he'd put a note on the front door that he was sleeping, and had gone to bed. The soreness had settled in, but the pain was not as great as the depression cloaking itself over his soul. Issie's lure last night, along with the state of his church, had driven his spirits to ground level.

He heard tires on his gravel driveway and pulled up enough to look out the window. Dan Nichols was getting out of the car. He hadn't seen the note yet. Nick dropped back down on the bed. Should he go to the door? he wondered. Dan, after all, was more than part of his flock. He was one of his closest friends.

He got up and limped to the front door and opened it just as Dan started to turn to leave. "I'm up," he said wearily. "Come on in, Dan."

Dan came in and closed the door behind him as Nick went to his recliner and slowly lowered himself into it. "You don't look so good," he said. "You need to be in bed."

Nick almost laughed, but he didn't find it very funny.

Dan sat down on the couch across from Nick. "You looked pretty rough at the station yesterday, but you look worse now. Are you all right?"

"I'm okay," Nick said.

Dan cocked his head. "Come on, Nick. You can be straight with me. You look like you're in pain."

"I'm fine," he said, irritated. "My side is kind of sore, and the burns aren't feeling so great. Throat hurts. But my real problem is that I stayed at Aunt Aggie's last night and didn't sleep well." He chose not to mention that Issie had been there too.

"So Aunt Aggie's been taking care of you?"

"Some," he said.

"Good," he said.

"So what brings you by?"

"I thought you could use some good news."

"Good news," Nick said, as if that was a concept he hadn't thought of in a while. "Yeah, hit me with some good news."

"We have a place for you to preach on Sunday."

He moaned. "Dan, I'm not up to preaching."

"Then we'll get a guest preacher, or one of us'll do it. We were a church before we had that building, Nick. We're still a church. Remember, we used to have worship right here in this trailer when there were only ten or twelve of us that came."

Nick looked around and remembered all the places they had found to cram chairs. It had worked for a while until they'd been able to put up a makeshift structure on the church property, then raised enough money to build the permanent one. It was all wasted, he supposed.

"So where do you plan on having this service?" Nick asked.

"In Aunt Aggie's yard. We're renting chairs from Buzz Brady, and we'll sit out there and worship in the breeze under the sun, and people up and down the streets are going to hear us and want to join in."

Nick breathed a laugh. "Sounds a little optimistic."

"It's called faith, Nick. You remember that."

Nick received the barb as it was intended, and swallowed hard.

"You sure you don't want to preach?" Dan asked. "I know you're hoarse and your throat hurts, but I can't help thinking that getting back in the saddle will do you more good than harm."

Nick thought it over for a moment. He was jealous of his pulpit, and never liked to have anyone take his place. Maybe he'd feel differently by then. "I don't know," he said. "Maybe I could come up with something."

Dan leaned forward and put his elbows on his knees. "Look, Nick, I know you're depressed. I know you're upset and feeling defeated, but we need you, man. You're our leader, and we need for you to lead us. A lot of the congregation doesn't know what to do. They're all distraught. But sometimes this kind of thing makes us stronger, you know? You're the one who taught us that."

Nick let the words sink in. Maybe Dan was right. Maybe God had allowed this tragedy for a reason. They'd been praying for a revival, but he had not expected God to bring it with a fire and a murder. He hadn't expected it to come with so much pain.

He blinked back the mist in his eyes. "Dan, I want to do the right thing. I want to do what God wants me to do. I'm just not sure that preaching is it anymore."

"Why was your call last week so much different than it is this week?"

"Maybe it's not," Nick said. "Maybe I was never called in the first place. Maybe I was just kidding myself."

"How do you grow a congregation from a dozen people to two hundred and not really be called? Nick, I can't believe you're questioning this when it's so clear in my mind."

Nick's eyes softened as he fixed his gaze on Dan.

"Nick, I don't even think you realize what an opportunity we've been given. Something really special might happen because of this fire. And even the murder. You know what they say about the Christian's blood being seed. At the funeral, I just know that Ray and Susan are going to want the gospel presented in some way. They're not going to let Ben die without his death bearing some kind of fruit."

"I wouldn't know," he said. "I don't even know the guy who's preaching it. I don't know what he believes. And the last I heard from Susan, she's not on speaking terms with God."

Dan sighed. "She's upset and lashing out, but she'll come through it. Are you going to the funeral?"

"Probably. It'll be weird not preaching it. There's so much I'd like to say about Ben. He was a good kid." He rubbed his face roughly. "Aw, Dan, I think God's talking to me. Telling me it's time to pass the baton. But I just keep thinking about all the people I never reached. There are still so many I've been praying for. Issie Mattreaux, and some of the other paramedics. Some of the guys at the station. My father . . . He never even heard me preach . . . It's so hard to believe that the ministry is over, just like that."

"It's not over," Dan said. "Nick, you've got to believe that. It's not. God still has a purpose and a plan for you, and for our whole congregation. And our church burning down is not going to take that away."

But somehow the fire . . . and Issie Mattreaux . . . had blurred Nick's vision. Nothing was clear anymore.

Chapter Thirty-Three

Jake hadn't expected to be at the hospital so long. The emergency team started Benton on an IV of antibiotics and cleaned and stitched up his leg. It had taken hours for the bag to empty so that they would release him.

Benton had crutches by the time they left, but was so weak that he could hardly walk on them. As he got into the car, he held up a hand for Jake to high-five. "We did it, man. Pulled the wool over their eyes."

Jake wasn't so sure. They had asked a lot of questions and caught them lying about their names. When they'd finally demanded identification before they would treat them, they'd realized they were both minors. They had called Benton's dad, and the man had taken his time getting there. He'd been steeped in hang-over pain, and refusing to believe their story, had cussed Benton out for tangling with anyone who had a knife. When he hadn't been needed anymore, he had taken off, leaving Benton to ride home with Jake.

If Jake knew Benton's old man, he was probably planning to stop off at the nearest bar.

Jake was worn out by the time they got back in the car. "That's it," he said, starting the car. "I'm sick of Cruz. Look what he did to you, man."

"I'm okay," Benton said. "He didn't mean nothin'. We were all drunk."

"Well, he could have killed you. I'm going back to get my drums, that's all. I'm quitting."

"Man, you can't quit. It's my grandmother's house they're practically living in! I'm stuck. You're the one got me into this. I don't want to hang with them if you're not."

"Then throw them out."

"Oh, right," Benton said. "I'll just hobble up on my crutches and threaten them. They'll be runnin' scared, all right. Are you crazy? Besides, what I did to that kid last night makes me part of them whether I like it or not."

Jake knew he was right. "He's not gonna be happy that we went to the hospital. But at least maybe he'll be afraid to do anything to us. The thought that anyone knows anything might stop him. We can say that we didn't tell them anything, but that we're afraid they're on to us now, that they need to find another place to meet just to be safe. Then, after they move all their stuff out, we can just phase out."

"It won't be that easy, man. What if they use me for a scapegoat and tell the cops what I did?"

Jake knew he had a point. He tried to turn it all over in his mind as he drove. "All right, then. Let's just face this head on. We'll go back to the house and tell Cruz we went to the hospital. We won't say anything about them being onto us, because you're right, they'll get even. We'll just hang on for as long as we can until we make sure he doesn't trash the house. And I need to find out about Issie. I'm worried about her, man. I tried calling her all night."

"She's dead," Benton said. "No way Cruz let her get away."

Jake slammed his hand on the steering wheel. "Don't say that! She *can't* be dead. She can take care of herself. She's tough, man. We would have heard if he got her."

"Then why wasn't she home all night?"

Jake shook his head. "I don't know."

"If they didn't kill her already, they will."

"Shut up, okay?" Jake said. "Just shut up!" He rounded the curve leading to Benton's grandmother's street, and caught his breath. Police cars lined both sides of the street.

"They're onto us," he said. "They found the house." Still far enough away that he might not draw attention, he made a U-turn and headed back the other way. "Man, I can't believe this. They're going through the house. Maybe they arrested Cruz and the others."

Benton started to sweat. "You think they know about me? What I helped do to that kid?"

"I don't know. But your old man probably woulda said something, if they'd been looking for you. Don't you think?"

"We can't be sure." He twisted in his seat and tried to see if anyone was following them. "I can't go home," he said. "I can't let them arrest me, Jake. They'll try me as an adult, and I'll never make it in prison. Man, I can't go down for *murder*. What was I thinking? Why did I let her talk me into that? I killed a guy to impress Jennifer, and now I'm going to prison . . ."

Benton was getting on Jake's nerves. "Where can we go? We can't just drive around all day."

"The compound," Benton said. "If they weren't arrested, that's where they'll be."

He thought of Cruz's grandfather's deer camp, which they were converting into a secure compound where they could all live. It was far from ready. The water had been cut off, and there was no air conditioning or electricity. He couldn't imagine them staying there. But he didn't have any other ideas.

"I can still get out of town," Benton said. "I can just run."

"With what? You don't have any money. You're sixteen. What will you live on?"

"I can do odd jobs on the road."

"Get real, man. You're gonna take off by yourself, with that leg?"

Benton wiped his face, then slammed his hand on the dashboard. "You think Cruz can keep us safe? Hidden? You think we can trust him?"

"*No*, we can't trust him. Are you crazy? He cut you with a switchblade, Benton!"

"But he was just overreacting. Most of the time he's a great guy. And if all that stuff Jennifer says about him is true, about coming into his kingdom . . ."

"Give me a break! I'm trying to find him for one reason, and that's to find out where Issie is, and what's going on with the cops. He is not some messiah, and I'm not going to follow him!"

"But he's the only one who can save us," Benton was rambling. "He's the only one who knows and understands the cause and has our best interests at heart and . . ."

Jake was beginning to sweat, too, even though his air conditioner blew out as hard as it would. He wished Benton would shut up. He turned down the dirt road leading to the deer camp, and navigated his way through the trees and over a shaky bridge, until he came to the rotting old structure that Cruz was going to turn into Fort Knox.

He saw two pickup trucks backed up to the door. Cruz, Jennifer, Redmon, and Graham were carrying chairs and mattresses out to the truck beds.

"There he is, that jerk!" Jake slammed the car into park.

"What are you gonna do?" Benton asked. "You're not gonna get out waving your fists and cussing them out, are you? Because you ain't speaking for me."

"Fine," Jake said. "Then speak for yourself." He got out of the car and slammed the door. Cruz and Graham dropped the mattress into the truck bed and turned to look at him. "Where's my aunt?" he demanded. "What did you do to her?"

Jennifer came around the truck. "You mean, what did *she* do to us?" she asked. "She shot at us, Jake. She's crazy. She almost killed me." She pulled her hair back and showed the bandage on her forehead.

"Then she's alive?" he asked.

"Of course she's alive," Cruz said, in a maddeningly calm voice. "What did you think I'd do? Kill her?" He smiled that charismatic smile he had that disarmed people so quickly, but he didn't disarm Jake.

Jake wasn't sure he believed him. "Yeah, actually," he said. "Call me crazy, but when you chased out after her waving your shotgun, I couldn't help thinking that."

"Well, I didn't, okay? But she turned the cops onto us and they're looking for us. So now we have to set up a hiding place. We've got a place. They'll never look for us there, but we needed the mattresses and chairs that are in this place."

"They're swarming all over Benton's grandmother's house," Jake said.

"I know," Cruz said. "They've been hounding our mother, but we hid out last night in an old hiding place my granddaddy and his Klansmen used to use."

Benton got out of the car and balanced on one leg. Afraid he was going to step on his bad leg and burst the stitches, Jake angrily opened the door of his car and jerked the crutches out of the backseat. He thrust them at Benton, daring Cruz to ask about them.

Benton looked at them as if Jake had somehow betrayed him.

"Where'd you get those?" Cruz asked.

Benton gave Jake a sick, frightened look.

Jake was ready. "Man, this morning Benton woke me up moaning, and he was practically delirious. He had a fever so high I thought he was gonna croak on us. Leg was swollen up like a tree trunk."

Cruz looked suspiciously at Benton's leg. "So what did you do?"

"Took him to the hospital in Slidell. Don't worry, we didn't tell them how it happened. We made up a story."

"They bought it?" Cruz asked.

"Yeah, man," Benton said, wobbling weakly. "Not like it's a gunshot wound or nothin'."

Cruz's face softened, and he looked down at Benton's leg. "Man, I am so sorry. I owe you big time. You're a hero, man, for what you did last night. Now that Jenn has explained your part in things, I can't believe what I did to you."

Benton shot Jake a surprised look, then brought his blood-shot eyes back to Cruz. "Man, it's no big deal."

"No big deal?" Jake spouted. "Benton, this guy *stabbed* you!"

Benton looked torn in two. "He didn't mean it, Jake. I'm gonna be okay."

Cruz's jaw popped as he brought his dull glare up to Jake. "I'm sensing a lack of commitment from you, Mattreaux. You ain't thinking about turning on us like your aunt, are you? Because you should know that they're looking for you, too. They're trying to round all of us up today. You're as guilty as any of us."

"Hey, I didn't kill anybody."

"But you were part of the group that did. Now, we have a new hiding place if you want to stick with us. We have a new plan for getting ourselves out of all this, and you, too. If you decide to stay with us, no hard feelings."

"And if I don't?"

Jennifer came closer, her eyes as hard as Cruz's. "Don't bolt, Jake. It wouldn't be wise."

"Is that a threat?"

"You could say that," she said. "Yeah, that's just what it is."

"So why do you want me with you?" he asked, knowing that they didn't care if he lived or died, as long as he didn't talk.

"Maybe we want to keep an eye on our potential turncoats," Cruz said. "Or maybe we think you've got the kind of backbone we need. Maybe we're ready to bring you in."

"Bring me in where?"

"To the inner circle. No more secrets from either of you guys."

Jake thought of that inner circle—Cruz, Jennifer, Graham, and Redmon. They were the very ones who had committed the first murder. Now that Benton had killed, too, were they going to honor him with this? "Benton killed an innocent black kid last night to please Jennifer," he said. "He's already *in* your pathetic 'inner circle.'"

"Everybody has to pay their dues," Cruz said.

"So what are the dues?" Jake asked. "How many bodies?"

Jake's tone made Cruz angrier. "Either you're committed to our cause, Mattreaux, or you're not. Make up your mind."

Jake squinted. "So what *is* the cause again? I forget, since the first one was about getting that preacher, and the second one was about throwing the cops off."

Cruz's lips grew taut over his teeth. "I don't like your tone, man."

Jennifer sashayed closer to Jake in that way she had, and slid her arm around his shoulders. "It's a holy war, Jake. Superiority of our race. God's fight. *Rahowa*."

Jake stepped out of her reach. "It's not 'superior' to kill a thirteen-year-old kid who didn't do anything wrong. And what kind of statement did Ben Ford's death make? I mean, if you want it to change something, what did it change? Are you expecting the blacks to line up in a convoy and leave town? All that guy did wrong was go get something to eat late at night. You waylaid him in the parking lot, beat him to a pulp, put a bullet through his brain, and left him to burn in his own church. For what? Man, you *know* you just wanted to get at that preacher."

Cruz was getting angrier now, and he came over to Jake and put his face intimidatingly close to his. Jake's cheeks mottled with heat, but he didn't step back. "You know what your problem is, Mattreaux? You're not a visionary. You're a follower. Leave the planning to me, and you just do as I say. I'm the one who sees the whole picture. I'm the one with the plan."

"Okay, fine," Jake said through his teeth, finally backing away. When adequate distance was between them, he asked, "So . . . just explain to me how Ben Ford's death helped the cause."

"There's one fewer mud person walking around. The world is automatically a better place."

Jake wanted to throw up. But why, he wasn't sure. He wasn't a brotherly love kind of guy, and it wasn't his style to champion a principle. Was he truly concerned about Ben Ford, or about the lies being told to keep them all committed? Or was it fear of prison, or bitterness about what they had done to Benton? Maybe it was all of it together. "I guess I'm just wondering why you picked Ben Ford, and not some drug addict or pimp or loser who beats his wife and kids? Why Ben Ford, who was educated, worked, minded his own business?"

"Because he was there," Cruz said. "And he was black. Those were the only two reasons I needed."

"So how many more are you going to kill?"

"However many I need to."

They all grew quiet, and Jake realized all eyes were on him. They were assessing him to see if he was worthy to be called one of them. He told himself he was not. "Well . . . I didn't come into this group to commit capital murder and wind up on death row. I came to play drums. That's all."

"The band is just the cover, man," Cruz said. "It's the advertisement for our cause. The means of recruitment. But it's not who we are. There's a lot more to us than that." He pulled out his knife, switched it open, and ran his finger along the dirty blade. "This is serious business, and we don't take it lightly. Life or death. You get to choose. You can be for us, Mattreaux, or you can be against us. Life or death."

Jake just stared at him for a moment.

Cruz slapped the flat of the blade against his palm. "Choose, Mattreaux."

Jake looked up at Benton and saw the fear in his eyes. Jake swallowed but didn't answer.

"I'm with you, man," Benton said quietly. "And Jake is, too. He's just emotional because of his aunt and all."

Cruz didn't take his eyes from Jake. Jake knew he was in too deep to get out now.

"Are you with us or not?" Cruz asked again.

He sighed and looked at the loaded truck bed. Maybe if he just went along, it would all be over soon. Maybe he could figure out a way to thwart their next plan and make sure that they left Issie alone. They weren't likely to let him walk away.

"I guess I'm with you," he said, and the words made his stomach burn.

"Fine. Then help us get the rest of the mattresses out of here."

Jake swallowed and ambled back into the house. He saw the filthy mattresses lying on the floor and lifted one. As he loaded it into the truck, he wondered if he was kidding himself about stopping them, or if there was really a chance that he'd escape *both* death and prison.

Chapter Thirty-Four

The funeral service for Ben Ford was held in the Methodist church on Gaston Boulevard.

Nick limped into the building, nodding to those around him who acknowledged him. Pushing through the quiet crowd in the foyer, he offered a nod to his church members milling in the foyer and headed around to the side of the building where he knew the family would be. He found them in the fellowship hall sitting quietly with family and close friends.

He saw Ray and Susan in a corner with Vanessa, who leaned dismally against the wall. Susan's eyes were puffy and red, and it was clear that she had been crying most of the night. He wondered if she had slept at all since Ben's body had been discovered. Vanessa, too, looked as subdued as he'd ever seen her. The teenage girl had on too much makeup, as if it would cover the sorrow and sleeplessness on her face.

Ray just looked angry. He stood there with his hands in his pockets, a taut look on his deeply lined face. Slowly, Nick approached them.

Susan got up and greeted him with a hug. He held her tight, wishing he had words to snuff out her pain. When he'd let her go, he reached for Ray's hand. "You okay, Ray?"

Ray nodded without speaking.

What now? Nick wondered. "Lot of people out there," he said. "Ben was loved."

"Why did he do it?" Susan asked, her eyes boring into Nick's as if to nail him with the question. "Why did God take him?"

He searched his mind for wisdom, but found none. "We may never know this side of heaven."

Susan scrunched up both fists and looked at the ceiling. "I'm so mad!" she said. "It ain't fair!"

She put her hand over her mouth and headed for the bathroom in the corner of the room. Nick turned to Ray. "You're not blaming God too, are you, Ray?"

Ray shrugged. "I blame the hateful no-good slugs who did this, Nick. And like I told you and Stan, if I get the chance, I'll kill 'em myself."

Ray's words knocked the wind out of Nick, and he didn't know how to respond. He searched his store of Scripture verses and experience but found nothing to help. What was wrong with him?

A group of relatives came between them, and Nick went to the sanctuary and took a seat in the back of the room.

Several quiet moments passed, during which he struggled with the tears threatening to pull him under. He hoped no one would sit next to him, that he would be left alone. If he was forced to say anything to anyone, he would lose it for sure. His heart felt battered and bruised, as if it had been damaged along with his ribs and shins.

He saw someone pause at the end of his pew, and he looked over. Issie Mattreaux stood there, wearing a black skirt just above the knees, black stockings, and a black sweater that was a tad too tight. He started to look away, but she slipped into the pew and came to sit next to him.

"Hey, Nick," she whispered. "Do you care if I sit with you?"

He swallowed and shook his head.

She kept looking at him, and he knew she was taking in the tears in his eyes and the emotional struggle on his face. "Hey, are you okay?"

He nodded.

"You just look . . . a little shaken up."

"I'm fine."

She kept looking at him, and he fixed his eyes on the coffin at the front of the room, covered with flowers that Allie had probably made at the Busy Bee Florist. That was what he'd failed to do, he thought. He hadn't sent flowers. There should be a spray at the front with his name on it. He should have expressed his love that way.

But then he realized that it wouldn't have changed anything. What was wrong with him? Did he think a few flowers on a stand would assuage a mother's grief?

"How are your burns?" Issie whispered.

He shrugged. "Fine."

"You're still mad at me, aren't you?"

"Mad? I wasn't mad, Issie."

She looked down at her hands. "I'm sorry for acting that way last night."

He ran back over the frustrating thoughts that had kept him awake all night. "It's okay," he said. "I don't hold grudges."

He glanced at her and wished she didn't look so nice. It was hard to remember why he had rejected her last night, when her hair shimmered in that way it had, and she was by far the best-looking woman in the room. No, he had no business being a preacher.

The organ started to play, and latecomers hurried to take their seats. He watched as the family processed in, Ray and Susan and Vanessa clutching each other for support. The unemotional funeral director pointed the family to where he wanted them to sit. Nick watched the tears, the hugs, and the leaning and comforting and grieving. His own eyes filled with tears again, and he closed them to hold it in. But he wasn't successful.

Issie put her hand in his, and he found himself closing his fingers around hers. It was some comfort, even while it made him feel guilty. He needed the contact. He needed someone to be there for him, someone who wasn't someone else's wife treating him like a brother. He needed to feel, for this one moment, as if he had someone of his own.

He opened his eyes and looked over at Issie. She had tears on her face, as well. He marveled at how soft she looked with tears in her eyes, so unlike the tough paramedic who wrestled grown men when it was required. She wiped her face with her free hand and breathed in a broken sob.

Like him, she was probably second-guessing her actions when they'd found Ben too. She was probably remembering Ray's anguished cries as he realized his son was dead. She was probably thinking about the second kid she hadn't been able to save.

The desire to comfort her eclipsed his own private pain. He let go of her hand and put his arm around her, pulled her against him. She buried her face against his shoulder, and he held her tight as he felt her shaking with grief. The fact that she didn't pull away, didn't seem repulsed by his comfort, melted him even more.

There was something strangely soothing about holding Issie. Her hair smelled of some perfume he'd never known before, and he knew it would haunt him at night when he tried to forget. It was soft against his face, silky, and he stroked it with his fingertips. He couldn't stand to see her cry.

The service began as Susan's uncle took the pulpit, and Nick slowly let Issie go. She pulled back, took in a deep, cleansing breath, and wiped her face with both hands. He knew better than to touch her again.

They listened as the man spoke of Ben's love for Christ, and the things he would have wanted them to know about salvation and heaven, and where Ben was today. Nick found himself praying that Issie would hear. And as he did, he questioned his motives again. Was he praying it for himself, because of the fierce attraction he felt toward her? Did he think a conversion on her part would make it possible for him to think seriously about her? Or did he honestly care about her soul?

Both, he admitted to himself. He wanted both.

The funeral went on as some of Ben's friends from high school and LSU stood up to give eulogies, and others sang. He watched Ray and Susan sobbing at the front, and wondered why people thought funerals provided comfort. In this case, he thought Susan wasn't going to make it through. It was just too hard. Some things required too much.

• • •

Issie rode with Nick to the little cemetery where Susan's parents lay.

When the service was over, and the family had gone to the black limousines, he and Issie headed back to his car.

They didn't speak until they were in the parking lot. "Tough day," Issie said finally.

He squinted into the breeze. "Yeah. Not my favorite way to spend it."

She turned and looked up at him. "Would you mind giving me a ride to Aunt Aggie's? I don't have a car . . ."

"Of course," he said. "How did you get to the church?"

"Steve Winder dropped me off. I could get somebody else to give me a lift if you'd rather not be alone with me."

He smiled softly and opened the car door for her. "Get in," he said. He closed her door and limped around to the driver's side. When he had started the car, he shot her a grin. "I'm not afraid of you, Issie," he said.

"Good," she whispered.

As he drove out of the parking lot, he realized that it was himself he feared the most, whenever he was close to Issie.

Chapter Thirty-Five

Issie's insurance company pronounced her car totaled. Steve Winder loaned her the pickup truck he drove for hunting, complete with rust and caked mud and bondo where he'd tried to make some body repairs years ago. She was just glad to have transportation.

Knowing that Cruz was still at large, she decided she had to talk to Mike and Lois. She'd heard from some of the cops she knew that they had questioned her brother and sister-in-law about Jake's whereabouts, so she knew they were anticipating his arrest and were probably sick with anxiety.

But when she showed up at their door, they treated her as the enemy. "How could you do this?" Lois demanded. "How could you turn our son in when he didn't do anything? Make him out to be a murderer? You know Jake wouldn't kill any-body!"

"I didn't know what he had done," Issie said. "All I knew is that there are two kids dead and two churches burned to the ground. Jake's friends were involved, and they tried to kill me last night. My smashed-up car with bullet holes in it is in Sam Slater's salvage yard to prove it."

"But you could have told us first. You could have come to us."

"I had no choice but to go straight to the police to save my life. And believe it or not, I was hoping to save Jake's too."

"See, that's just it, Issie." Her brother stormed at her like he had when she was a kid and he wanted her out of his way. "If Jake was involved, nobody would have been shooting at you. He loves you. You're his favorite relative. He would never have done anything like that."

"I didn't think so either," Issie said, "but you don't know how much a kid can be influenced by his peers. I don't know what he's capable of."

"Not murder!" her brother shouted.

"How do you know? You don't even know his friends. You don't know that he hasn't been to school in over two weeks and doesn't intend to go back. You don't even know about the compound they're planning to build and the fact that Jake intends to live there with these people."

"You're lying," Mike shouted. "If those things were true, you would have told us sooner."

"I've been too busy dodging bullets!"

"Why should we believe you?"

"I don't *care* if you believe me. The plain simple truth is that if Jake knows something, and I *know* he does, he needs to tell the police. If he's involved, then he needs to be punished, and you don't need to stand in the way."

"That's just fine for you to say," her brother said through clenched teeth. "It's real easy for somebody who's not a parent to say, 'Just let him suffer the consequences. Let him go to prison. Let him go down for a murder he didn't commit. He'll learn his lesson.' But he's not your son!"

"Look," she said, clutching her aching head. "The last thing I want is for Jake to go to prison. That's why I didn't say anything when I first started suspecting his friends. But last night he called me to patch up Benton after he'd been stabbed. Does this sound safe to you? Do you want to shelter your son so he can be trapped under the influence of someone who's reckless with a knife?"

"You should have come to us then!" Mike said. "We had a right to know!"

"Well, which is it, Mike? Was I supposed to keep my mouth shut, or blow the whistle? You can't have it both ways!"

"You could have told us without telling the police," Lois said.

"Right. And then his pals would have come after you instead of me, when you tried to intervene. It's not that simple! So don't yell at me for going to the police, the only ones who can really stop this madness. Yell at me for waiting too long to do it. Has it occurred to you that he could be dead?"

"No!" Lois shouted on a sob. "Mike, tell her—"

The blood seemed to drain from Mike's face as he stood over her. "If he's dead, it's your fault. Look what you've done, Issie."

"Me?"

"Yeah, you. If they're as dangerous as you say, they may have taken your snooping around out on Jake."

"I told you, they called *me!* And I begged Jake to leave with me, but he wouldn't." They weren't listening to her. She wasn't even sure they could hear her through their pain and confusion. There was no use trying to bring them around. "Look, I came here because we have to find Jake. Whether he's in trouble or just hiding . . . or something worse . . . we've got to find him."

"Tell us about it!" her brother shouted.

"He was home last night," Lois said. "His bed was slept in. We didn't see him, but he was here. That's a good sign, isn't it?"

"Maybe," Issie said.

"It is," Lois insisted. "He's a smart kid. He'll be okay." She ran into her husband's arms, and he clung to her.

Issie would have given anything to be a part of that comfort they exchanged. But her brother had never been affectionate with her. She was part of their family, yet she was as alone as she had ever been. "I'm gonna keep looking," she said. "I haven't given up on him."

"If anything happens to him," Lois said, "we'll never forgive you."

"I know," Issie said. And knowing there was nothing more to say, Issie hurried out to her car.

Issie worked the three to eleven shift that day. Aunt Aggie had given her a key to her house, knowing she was working late. She wondered if Aunt Aggie would make Nick stay there again tonight. Would he lock himself away from her again, even after he'd held her at the funeral? She couldn't stand the thought of his avoiding her as he had last night.

So she headed to Joe's Place, knowing that some of the medics would have congregated there by now, and that she would be welcome among them.

She walked into the haze of smoke and noise, and vaguely wished she could get them to turn off the flat, nasal Zydeco music blaring on the speakers, and instead play something soft and slow, more compatible with her mood. She found her medic friends at their usual table in the corner. Karen Insminger was there, looking tired and pensive, and Bob Sigrest looked as if he'd already had too many as he dissolved into loud laughter at something Issie couldn't see. Frenchy and Twila were trying to quiet him.

"What's so funny?" Issie asked as she took a chair from the next table and turned it around.

"He's drunk, that's what's so funny," Twila said. "Maybe you can shut him up. He's making a scene."

"I was just telling them about the fat woman I treated today for low blood sugar, who had all these rolls on her hips."

"Rolls of fat?" Issie asked.

"No. *Dinner* rolls." He burst into laughter again, and dropping his head on the table, almost toppled it.

Issie didn't feel much like laughing, so she gave him a slight grin and rolled her eyes. She looked at the others, who had apparently already heard the story.

"What's wrong with you?" Bob asked. "Don't you get it?"

"I get it," she said.

"Then why aren't you laughing?" he demanded. "Come on, she had dinner rolls in her pockets. *Dinner rolls.*"

"Yeah, Bob. I said I got it."

"Well, you don't have to get an attitude."

"I don't have an attitude," she said. "I'm just not feeling like giggling myself silly, okay?"

Frenchy frowned at her. "You okay?"

She thought of telling them about her talk with Mike and Lois, and her fears about Jake, but decided against it. "Yeah, I'm fine. I just need a drink."

"Well, you're gonna have to go to the bar to get it. We haven't seen a bar maid in over an hour. I think Bob hassled her so bad she quit."

Bob spat out laughter again, and they all joined in.

Issie got up and headed for the bar. She slipped onto a stool, and looked around at the faces of those who were here. The usual clientele filled the place, sitting in their favorite places like their names were carved on the chairs.

She ordered her usual, then looked around, wondering how wise it was for her to be out alone at night. If Cruz and his gang were watching her, waiting for another opportunity to kill her, this was probably the first place they would look. Hadn't her tires been slashed here?

Down the bar, in his usual place on the end, sat R.J. Albright, still wearing his police uniform. He always came here when he got off duty. She wondered if she should consider him protection. Maybe she should just go on to Aunt Aggie's now.

But she didn't want Nick to think she was anxious to see him. No, she thought. She had to stay here until she'd had a couple of drinks to chase her depression.

She could get R.J. to escort her out when she decided to leave, and ask him to follow her to Aunt Aggie's. If he balked, she could offer to pay him something. Men usually didn't mind protecting damsels if there was something in it for them.

The thought that she would have to go to such lengths for protection broadsided her, and when Joe brought her her drink, she downed it quickly.

Haunted by the thought that her brother had turned on her, she took inventory of the men in her life and found that there were none. Her mind drifted back to childhood, when her appendix had ruptured and her mother had barely gotten her to the hospital in time. She had been there for over a week, but her mother had not been able to stay with her at night because she'd had to work her shift at the bar. Her father had been called about her sudden illness, but he hadn't shown up to see if she was all right.

He had sent her a card with a kitten on it and some Hallmark verse about getting well. She still kept that card in her top dresser drawer. She wasn't sure why.

"Another one, Joe," she said as he passed, and he refilled her drink.

She looked down at it, struggling to hold back tears that she had no intention of crying. She had dealt with the absence of her father, she told herself. She was beyond the lonely little girl who pretended that her daddy was away on important business of national security, pining away for his little girl and carrying her picture close to his heart.

The fantasy reminded her of Brenda Hamilton, a close friend of Issie's in the fourth grade. Brenda had almost drowned in Lake Pontchartrain as she and Issie played in a forbidden part of the lake, but it wasn't the trauma of her near-death that ached anew now. It was the desperation of Brenda's father as he'd tried to rescue her. He had fished her out of the water and done mouth-to-mouth resuscitation, breathing his own life into her to keep her alive until the paramedics had come.

She had gone to the hospital with them and waited in the hall as Brenda's father paced back and forth, back and forth, weeping for his little girl one minute and working as her advocate with unconcerned nurses the next. She remembered him chewing out a doctor who seemed to have given up on her. And then he had gotten on the pay phone and called every drowning expert in the country until he'd found one with a treatment that gave him hope.

Issie had sat in a cold metal chair and watched as Brenda's white knight fought her battles for her. Issie had never had a white knight, and from the depths of her soul, she had longed for one.

She threw back the alcohol now, and swiveled her stool to look for any white knights who might be looking for a damsel in distress. But it was just the same old faces. Bob had had enough, and Karen waved as she walked him out. One by one, she bade Twila and Frenchy goodbye, too.

She turned back to the bar and told herself that she was on her own. No white knights in her future, and certainly none in her past. The men she chose were only mirror images of the father who'd sent her a card without even a note when she'd been suffering in the hospital. They were not the knights, and she had to wield her own swords to protect herself from the pain they brought with them.

Her mind drifted to Brenda again. She had eventually come out of her coma, had gotten up and gone home. She had never quite been the same, but her father doted on her as if she was his special gift.

Issie had been so jealous of that love as a child, and had even wished that Brenda's dad would look up one day and notice Issie sitting there, and love her like his own, and offer himself as her advocate and her protector. But when her appendix ruptured, he had not come, either.

Joe refilled her drink again, and again, and again, as she replayed the tapes in her mind. One of these days she would find some shining knight who would swagger into Joe's Place and sweep her off her feet. He would be a man who came when she was hurt. A man who fought for her when she was threatened. A man who wept over the thought of losing her.

A picture of Nick Foster flashed through her mind, and she banished it quickly, telling herself that he wasn't the one who could rewrite her ending. She was more attracted to the ones who were unavailable, the ones who couldn't commit, the ones who were hard to get.

The ones like her own father.

Why was that? she asked herself. Did she really think the ending would ever change?

She finished off her fifth drink, and as Joe filled it again, she began to get tired . . . so very tired. She was tired of being alone, tired of fighting her own battles, tired of the reputation and the expectations and the disappointments.

She was tired of knowing that the white knight would never come.

"Fill me up, Joe," she slurred, banging her glass too hard in front of her. "I've been empty too long."

Joe filled her glass, but she remained empty.

Chapter Thirty-Six

When Issie passed out cold at the bar, with her head down between her arms, Joe was surprised. "What she doin'?" he asked R.J. Albright. "She ain't never done this before, passed out cold right here at the bar."

"Did she drink more than usual?"

"Maybe," he said, "but Issie can hold her liquor, *sha*."

R.J., who spent as much time at Joe's Place as Issie did, got up and waddled around the bar, tapped Issie on the shoulder. "Issie, wake up. Come on, darlin', wake up."

She didn't budge.

"So who I'm gon' call?" Joe asked.

R.J. shrugged. In a conspiratorial cop voice, he said, "Well, don't say I told you, but when she wrecked last night, she called Nick Foster."

"The *preacher*?"

"Yeah, and he come as fast as we did. Stayed with her the whole time."

"Awright, I'll try Nick." Joe picked up the phone and called information for the preacher's number. He got the number and it rang, then clicked as it forwarded the call.

He waited through eight rings before the old woman answered. "*Hola?*"

He pressed a finger to one ear. "Who's this?"

"Aggie Gaston," she said. "Who d'you want, *sha*?"

"Aunt Aggie, ya got Nick Foster there?"

"Who's this?" she demanded.

"Joe, over to Joe's Place. He there, or ain't he? It's an emergency."

"Yeah, he's here, awright. Just you wait." He heard her put the phone down and shuffle off.

• • •

Nick Foster was sound asleep when Aunt Aggie woke him up knocking on his door. He groped in the darkness and only found a lamp, then felt his way to the switch and turned it on. It was one A.M.

He must have been in a dead sleep. His sleeplessness of the night before was catching up with him. "Yeah, Aunt Aggie," he said, getting to the door. "What is it?"

"Phone for you," the old woman said, clutching the collar of her robe to her throat. "Joe over to Joe's Place."

Issie, he thought. Something had happened. He hurried out and grabbed up the phone. "Hello?"

"Nick, it's Joe. I got Issie here passed out on my bar, *sha*. I need somebody to come get her."

"Passed out?" Nick asked. "What do you mean, passed out?"

"I mean she's out cold."

"Well, that doesn't sound like her," Nick said. "Does it? Does she usually pass out like that? How much did she drink?"

"She been puttin' it away tonight too fast for me to keep up."

Nick looked at Aunt Aggie and waved that everything was all right. The old woman padded back up the stairs. "Well, okay, I'll be right there," he said.

He hung up and stood there for a moment trying to get his thoughts in order. He looked up and saw Aunt Aggie staring down at him over the banister. "Issie in trouble?" she asked.

He nodded. "Sounds like it. I have to go get her, but she'll be all right."

As he got dressed, he wondered why Joe would have called him. How had he known that he was staying here with Issie? If he knew, Cruz might know too.

He drove as fast as he could drive without breaking the law, and was in the parking lot of Joe's Place just moments after the phone call had come. He felt ridiculous walking through the door of the notorious bar that his church had picketed when it had gotten its license years ago. He knew that every person in the room would feel either self-conscious or amused that the preacher was there. He didn't even want to look around and see how many of his church members were in here boozing it up.

Awkwardly, he stepped inside and saw Issie there with her head flat down on the counter. Dreading the confrontation, he limped over to her and touched her hair. "Issie, wake up. Come on, Issie."

She didn't budge.

He shook her. "Has anybody tried to wake her up?" he asked Joe.

"R.J. tried," Joe said. "She didn't want to come around."

He pulled her hair back and felt her neck for a pulse. It was slow, but still beat against his fingertip.

He put her arm around his neck and tried to raise her up, but her legs were limp and her head hung heavily in front of her. He pulled Issie back from the bar and tried to lift her head. Her eyes half opened and she looked up at him, then tried to lay her head back down.

"Come on, Issie," Nick whispered. "People are staring."

He managed to get her to her feet and pulled her arm around his neck. Her legs didn't offer much support at all, but he managed to get her out to the car. He propped her up against the back door, then holding her there, fished in his pocket for his keys, unlocked the passenger door, and slid her in. She immediately wilted over onto his seat.

He lifted her shoulders up and got in. Her head fell against the door. He started the car.

"Issie, wake up," he said. "Come on. Wake up. I'm taking you home." But she was out cold.

He thought of bypassing Aunt Aggie's and taking her to her apartment, since he didn't want to start any gossip when the old woman saw her condition. But then he realized she wouldn't be safe there, and he couldn't stay there all night watching her. Deciding Aunt Aggie's was his best hope, he drove back to the old house.

When he got to Aunt Aggie's garage, he tried to rouse Issie again. When his efforts failed, he carried her up the steps. What had gotten into her?

He'd heard a lot of things about Issie, things about her promiscuity, things about her binge drinking, things about her reckless behavior, but he had never heard of her passing out in public before.

He got her to the front door and pulled her inside, flipped on the light and looked around, praying Aunt Aggie was sleeping soundly and wouldn't come down to check on Issie. He lifted her in his arms and carried her up the stairs to her bedroom and laid her on the bed. She curled up in a fetal position.

Worried, he bent down beside the bed and put his face close to hers. "Issie, can you hear me?" She didn't stir. "Issie, wake up."

She wasn't responding, so he took her pulse again, found that it was slow, weak. He went to the easy chair in the corner of the room and sat down, trying to think clearly. Should he take her to the hospital to get her checked, just in case?

After a few moments, he got up and went to the bed again. She had balled even tighter, and he realized she was cold. He looked in the closet and found a handmade quilt, then covered her with it.

What now? Should he go back down to the guest room, far away from where Issie slept, and trust that she would wake up in the morning with a horrible headache and little memory of what had happened tonight?

The thought of leaving her here like this seemed unacceptable to him, so he decided to lean back in the chair and try to relax. Maybe she would stir soon.

As he sat alone in the room, he looked around at the meager belongings she had brought here with her. Just some clothes, a bag of makeup, a toothbrush. Nothing that revealed anything about her.

That seemed to be the story of Issie's life. Nothing personal. That string of one-night stands she'd been known to have was nothing personal. Her nightly visits to Joe's Place were nothing personal. Even the passion she showed in her job was nothing personal. And the flirtations she showed him on rare occasions … Again, nothing personal.

He couldn't explain it, didn't know why it happened, but suddenly his heart ached for her, and he wanted very much for her to know something personal, something that could change her life, fill it up, give it purpose.

He decided to pray for her instead of sleeping or fleeing. One hour passed, then two as he laid this whole confusing mess on the altar of God.

Suddenly, she sat up and bolted off the bed, staggering toward the bathroom.

"Issie?" She disappeared, leaving the bathroom door open behind her. He stood there and waited, wondering if he would be needed …

Then he heard her retching into the toilet.

He went to the door, not knowing whether to offer her help or stand back and let her have this time alone.

"Issie, it's me. Are you all right?"

"Come in," she said weakly.

He looked behind the door and saw her sitting in the corner on the floor next to the toilet, her knees drawn up to her chest. Her face looked ashen, and dark circles underscored her eyes.

"I don't feel so good," she said.

He eased down the wall—careful not to hurt his legs—until he was on the floor across from her in the tiny bathroom.

"Joe called me," he said. "Do you remember my coming to get you?"

She shook her head, then winced as if the movement caused her great pain. "I'm so embarrassed," she whispered.

"Don't be. It's just me."

"Jus' you?" she slurred. "Jus' the preacher." She shook her head and slid her fingers up through the roots of her hair as if clutching her head together. "Head feels like it's gonna explode."

"I could get you some Tylenol."

"No, I'll jus' throw up again."

"That might be a good thing," he said. "You probably need to get it out of your system."

"No," she said, reaching out for him. "Help me up."

He reached for her hands. She was shaking as she took his. He tried to pull her to her feet, but her legs were too weak. Then she got that sick look on her face and dropped back to her knees. In seconds she was heaving over the toilet again.

He backed out of the room, trying to give her some privacy as she retched. He hadn't bargained for this. This was too intimate for him, something he hadn't expected. What would people say if they knew he was in the bathroom off of a bedroom in the middle of the night watching Issie heave into a toilet?

Then he chided himself for putting the approval of men before Issie. It made little difference what people thought. His church was burned to the ground. Soon they would have his resignation and his congregation would be scattered and it wouldn't matter what people thought of him anymore. It was what God thought that mattered, and God had put him here with this woman for some reason he couldn't fathom, and he had drawn him into this bathroom where she was sick. How could he walk away without helping her?

He had to stay, if for no other reason than to let her know she wasn't alone. It seemed critically important that he get that message through to her.

When she finished throwing up, he stroked her hair again. "Issie, do you want to go back to the bed?"

She nodded, and he helped her up. When she almost fell again, he steadied her and walked her into the bedroom. He helped her onto the bed, covered her with the quilt, then backed away.

"You gonna be okay?" he asked.

She didn't say a word, just closed her eyes as if she was sleeping again.

He tried to kneel beside the bed, but the pain in his shins stopped him. Instead, he bent down and touched her face with the back of his fingers. "I'm going downstairs," he said. "But you call if you need me. I'll be right here, okay?"

She nodded but didn't speak. Slowly, he left the room, but left her door open so he could hear her.

Chapter Thirty-Seven

Word about Issie's condition at Joe's Place spread like pollen, coating the conversations of everyone in Newpointe by noon the next day. And even greater news was the fact that Nick Foster had been the one who'd come to get her.

Issie had been the subject of gossip before and tried to ignore it the best she could. But as always, it did bother her. She hated herself for making such a spectacle of herself, and wondered what had made her do such a stupid thing. The fact that Cruz hadn't come along when she was vulnerable was sheer luck, she told herself. If she kept it up, she wouldn't be able to get Aunt Aggie or Nick to help her anymore.

Jake still hadn't been found, and Cruz and his buddies were still at large. Despite her hangover, she couldn't stay at home, not with somebody out to kill her and nothing to do about it. She might as well be working. Her seven-to-three shift came too early to endure with a hangover, but she managed to function. Steve was bad about swapping shifts to accommodate his softball games, his hunting, and his fishing. Some days he wanted to work late, others he wanted to work early. Issie tried to keep her schedule matched with his, because they were so used to working together.

Fortunately, today was a slow day. Forced to sit in their rescue unit at the Walmart parking lot—a central location in town from which they could reach most locations quickly—she and Steve usually passed the time listening to music and making up stories about the people walking by.

But today, Steve was more interested in Issie's story of the night before. "So what are you trying to do?" he asked. "Ruin the preacher?"

She shot him a look. "What do you mean?"

"I mean everybody in town knows that he practically spent the night with you last night."

"He did not spend the night with me," she said. "We were both guests in Aunt Aggie's home, on separate floors, for Pete's sake."

"And you just happened to be drunk, and you want me to think that you didn't throw yourself at him?"

"Throw myself?" She wanted to get out of the rescue unit and hitchhike home, but she knew she had to stay. "I can't believe you said that."

He leaned his head back on his seat and stared out the windshield. "Issie, I know you love living dangerously, but stay away from the preacher. A lot of people value him in this town. The last thing those people need after losing their church is to lose their preacher too. Or even their respect for him."

"They're not going to lose respect for their preacher," she said. "He's a nice guy. He was helping me."

"Find somebody else to help you, Issie."

Issie fought the anger boiling inside her. "You know, you really ought to mind your own business," she said. "This has nothing to do with you. It's not even your church. He's not your preacher so you don't have to defend his honor."

"All I'm saying is that I know how you work. Nick Foster is not who you need to be chasing."

"What makes you think I'm chasing him?" she asked.

"The rumor is that he's the one they called to come get you last night."

"Well, I didn't have anything to do with that decision."

"There's also a rumor says you called him yourself when you got shot at and had that wreck."

That was true and she couldn't deny it. "I felt like I might be dead by the time the night was over. You'd call a preacher too."

"I just hope you don't have anything up your sleeve. Remember Mark Branning?"

"Nobody's ever going to let me forget that! I don't have anything up my sleeve, Steve! Who did you want me to call? You? You were probably at home watching the *Brady Bunch* with your cute little wife and your darling little children. You probably would have checked the caller ID and seen that it was me and decided not to answer."

"I wouldn't do that," Steve said.

"Of course you would," she said. "Every time I've ever called you at home I've gotten the machine."

"I'm a busy guy."

"I called someone that I thought would be home and I thought would respond. And I was right. He did help me. He stayed with me the whole time and solved the problem of where I was going to stay. What's wrong with that?"

"What's wrong with it is that Nick Foster has enough problems without you in his life right now."

His scathing indictment crushed her. She tried not to cry. "So what am I, a piranha?" she asked.

"No offense," he said, "but a lot of people do think of you that way."

"Oh, give me a break," she said. "I thought you were my friend."

He stared at her, silence passing between them, then finally he said, "I am your friend, Issie. That's why I'm giving you good advice. I hope you'll take it."

"I don't need your advice about Nick."

A call came through on the radio, and they both came to attention. There was a wreck on Jacquard Boulevard and someone was claiming whiplash.

Steve started the unit and radioed that they were on their way. There wasn't more time to talk, and Issie decided to push her anger to the back of her mind. She didn't have a defense after all, and she knew that Steve was probably right.

Besides, there was nothing like working an accident to get her mind off of her own problems.

When they got to the scene of the accident, Issie was surprised to see Nick there. She hadn't expected to see him there with those bandages still on his legs. But there he was, dressed in complete uniform, helping Mark, Dan, and George assess the damage to the car.

The passengers were all standing on the sidewalk, and it was clear from her first glance that no one was injured. Still, she got out of the unit with Steve, found the woman who claimed her neck was sore, and began to evaluate her symptoms.

When she'd gotten the neck brace on her, she looked up and saw Nick watching her. She hadn't seen him this morning. He'd been gone when she'd gotten up, and now she had trouble looking him in the eye.

"How do you feel?" he asked.

She shrugged and stood up. "Oh, a little mortified. And my head feels like it's been run over fourteen times." She looked up at him, trying to change the subject. "What about you? I didn't think you'd get a medical release until your lungs and burns healed."

"I'm just on office duty," he said. "I came on the call in the capacity of chaplain. There are some things I can still do."

"Well, you be careful," she said.

"I will. But what about you? You're not planning a trip to Joe's Place tonight, are you?"

She blinked back the mist in her eyes and looked into the wind. "Nick, I don't even know what to say. I'm so sorry. And no, I'm not going back tonight. I'm ashamed to show my face."

He just stared down at her as if processing that thought, and she wondered what he was thinking. Dan called from the fire truck a few yards down the road, and Nick waved.

"Well, guess I'll see you a little later. You take care, okay?" He dipped his face to her ear, and whispered, "And next time call me *before* you get into trouble."

She looked up at him, and their eyes met and held for a moment, a moment that was full of unspoken words. Issie wondered if his thoughts were anything like hers. She was getting too attached to him, and that was dangerous. As Steve had said, the last thing Nick Foster needed in his life was Issie Mattreaux. Maybe she needed to do what he said and back off. Maybe the greatest act of gratitude she could offer him was to cut all ties with him before her heart was any more entangled.

Then she told herself that she was kidding herself if she thought Nick had given her a second thought. She wasn't his type, and she never would be. Nick was one of those rare white knights, but white knights never went for damsels like her.

• • •

As the firefighters drove back to the fire station, Mark, Dan, and George were quiet. Nick knew what they were thinking, but he didn't want to give them the chance to voice it.

Finally, as they pulled into the truck bay at midtown station, Dan looked back over his shoulder. "You're playing with fire, Nick."

Nick had seen it coming, so he didn't flinch. "Dan, there's nothing going on."

"I *saw* something going on," Mark said. "I saw the way she looked at you. Don't underestimate her power, Nick. She's trapped me with it before."

"Oh, man!" Nick said. "You trapped *yourself*. You got wrapped up in lust and started going to the bar with her and the next thing you knew, your marriage was on the rocks."

Mark looked at him as if he couldn't believe he had said those words. Nick had never been that bold with him. There had been many conversations between them about lust and temptation, but Nick had never looked Mark in the eye and told him he had been to blame.

Instantly, Nick regretted it. "I'm sorry, Mark. Look, I know you never had an affair with her. I know you rectified things before they got out of hand. But I'm just telling you that it's not all her fault. She's been a victim some too."

"I thought you didn't believe in victimhood," Dan said. "If I recall, you've said that people make victimhood an excuse for sin."

"I don't believe in overlooking sin so that we can justify anything we ever choose to do," Nick said. "But I've prayed a lot about her. I've wanted to reach her. I've never been able to. And lately she's been through a lot. For some reason, I'm the one that keeps getting called to help her. Now, you tell me. As a preacher, as a Christian, as a human being, what would you do if someone called you and told you they were in trouble?"

"If it was Issie Mattreaux," Dan said, "I think I'd pass."

"Well, I can't pass," Nick said. "I've thought about what people would say and what they would think. And then I've realized that I have to care more about her soul than my reputation. And if people want to think the worst about me, then they might as well go ahead. It's not like I have a lot to lose."

"Of course you have a lot to lose," Dan said. "You're still our preacher. We didn't fire you."

"No, but someone fired the church," he said. "It's not there anymore, guys. Wake up."

"There's still a church," Mark said. "There are still people who want to worship. They want you to lead them in that.

You're our shepherd, Nick. Don't let her lead you off in another direction. You aren't immune just because you're a man of God."

Nick didn't say anything. He just got out of the truck and slammed the door as he went into the station.

Chapter Thirty-Eight

No one expected to see Ray drive up that afternoon and go into his office without saying a word to anyone. They hadn't expected him back for at least another week.

Nick stood at the edge of the truck bay, looking out at the trailer parked between the fire department and police station, and wondered if he should go talk to Ray. Dan came up behind him and set his hand on Nick's shoulder. "He needs to talk, man."

Nick nodded. "I'm not sure he needs to talk to me. I never can think what to say when I'm around him. It's like all my experience goes out the window, all the Scripture, all the wisdom God's ever given me, and I just stand there, speechless and angry that Ben is dead."

"Man, I do even worse than that," Dan said. "You're his preacher, his chaplain, and his friend."

"I'm also the one who found Ben's body."

"He knows you tried to save him."

Nick nodded, hoping that was true. He slid his hands into his pockets and walked slowly across the freshly cut lawn to the door of Ray's office. He knocked, but there was no answer, so Nick turned the knob and pushed the door open.

Ray sat in the dark at his desk. "I didn't say come in."

Nick came in anyway. "I just wanted to tell you it's good to see you back."

Ray rubbed his face and nodded wearily. "What are you doing here?" he asked. "I ain't seen a medical release."

"Well, I'm not officially back," Nick said. "Just office duty. I figured with you out, I could take up some of the slack. I didn't have anything to do what with the church gone and all. Plus, I figured with the two murders, somebody in protective services might be needing a chaplain."

"Well, I better not catch you fightin' a fire. With those injuries you're liable to get in somebody's way and cost 'em their life. We've had enough death." He dropped his hands to the desk. "How are you feelin', anyway?"

"I'm okay. Getting better all the time."

"I've had burns like that before, Nick. You ain't kiddin' nobody. They don't heal up in four days."

"Well, I appreciate your concern." He looked down at his feet and sought to change the subject. "Have you heard about the church service we're having Sunday out on Aunt Aggie's lawn?"

Ray nodded. "Heard somethin' about it. I don't know if we'll be there."

Nick felt that personal stab of failure again. "Ray, don't turn your back on God. You need him now. Susan and Vanessa need him. Come back and let us help you heal."

"I don't *want* to heal." His voice broke, and he covered his face.

Nick didn't know whether to get up and go to him, or let him suffer alone. He cleared his throat. "I know," Nick told him. "That's a common feeling. You just want to grieve, you want to feel the pain, you want to hang on to it because it's kind of like hanging on to the person."

"Don't tell me what I feel," Ray said. "You don't know what I feel. I don't know *anybody* who knows how I feel."

Nick's mouth trembled as he tried to say the right thing. "You're right. I don't. There's no way I could."

"He had his whole life ahead of him, Nick!" Ray bellowed. "His whole life. He was gon' *be* somebody."

"Ray, he *is* somebody. In case there's ever been a moment's doubt in your mind about Ben's salvation, I mean ... I want you to know that I've prayed with him, talked with him myself. He cared about the Lord. I know he's in heaven."

Ray broke down again, and finally Nick got up and came around his desk. He leaned over his friend and put his arms around him. Ray fell into him and cried the tears of a broken man. "You can do this, Ray," Nick said. "We don't grieve as those who have no hope. This is not the end for you and Ben."

"Feels like the end," Ray said.

Nick just held his friend and let him grieve as he hadn't been able to do before.

Chapter Thirty-Nine

Nick was emotionally spent by the time he left Ray's office just after three, so he decided to go home. He got out of his car and looked across the street to the church that had been such a fixture in his life for so long now. It was odd to see the rubble piled on the property that had once been donated by someone who loved the Lord. He couldn't believe it was all wasted now.

He crossed the street and went to stand in the center of his scorched foundation, around the place where he estimated the pulpit had been. Had he taken his pulpit for granted? he wondered. He'd always thought it would be there, as if it had some hedge of protection around it and the Lord would never let harm come to it. He supposed it took losing it to realize how significant it was.

He sifted through the rubble and came to a pew that was still intact, though it was black from the fire. He sat down on it, testing it with his weight. It held him up, so he relaxed and looked around at the things that were scarred and soiled from the fire.

Some of the elders had met with the insurance agent, and he'd already been out to look at the damage. He hoped the church would get enough to rebuild. He hoped they had the energy to start again.

He covered his face with his hands as the despair of the last few days rose up inside him, and as he began to weep, he began to pray, asking God to show him what his purpose was in this, what it could possibly mean, and what he was to do with it.

A rattling, rusty old pickup truck pulled up to the curb, and he wiped his face quickly. It wasn't until the truck door closed that he saw that it was Issie.

She stood there in uniform, just off work, but she looked weak, pale, still ailing from the night before. He couldn't believe she had come here instead of going back to Aunt Aggie's to rest after a hard day on the job. She came to the scorched pew and sat down next to him. "Hey," she said softly.

"What are you doing here?" he asked.

She sighed. "I don't know. I saw you coming out of Ray's office awhile ago, and you looked kind of upset. I thought I'd come by and just see if you were okay."

He couldn't think of a response to that so he just sat there.

"What are *you* doing here?" she asked.

"I don't know," he said. "I thought I'd come over and just look at the place. Every time I look this direction I'm shocked. I can't believe the building's not still here, that my pulpit's not standing, that there aren't pews everywhere, that people can't come and go."

"But you know insurance will take care of it and you can rebuild."

"We can't rebuild Ben," he said. "We can't rebuild the sense of security and peace that we had in this building."

"You sure don't put much confidence in your congregation," she said. "I mean, it seems to me if this was such a great church, that a few problems like this wouldn't ruin everything."

She was right. He didn't have much confidence in the church. Most of the time he felt he was pushing an eighteen-wheeler uphill, heavy with the cargo they needed to bear fruit in God's kingdom, but they just never felt like turning the ignition on. Now he feared what energy they did have would die out completely, and he didn't know if he had the strength to keep pushing.

He didn't want to talk about it anymore, so he looked at her, assessed her face and her eyes. "How's the hangover?"

"Better," she said. "Thankfully, we didn't have any major trauma today."

"So have you had your fill of Joe's Place yet?"

She looked across the street at the trailer Nick lived in. "It's not Joe's fault. It's mine. Next time I won't drink so much."

He shook his head. "Issie, what's it going to take?"

"For what?" she asked.

"For you to wake up and realize that that's no kind of life."

"Hey, good people get hurt and killed too. Ben was at your church every time the doors opened and he's dead now. So living a high-and-mighty life doesn't guarantee safety."

"No, but the risk is higher when you pass out in bars and thumb your nose at the people trying to kill you."

"I didn't thumb my nose," she said. "What are you talking about?"

"You shouldn't have gone anywhere alone last night," he said. "You should have kept as low a profile as possible. Why would you go about your normal routine when Cruz is looking for you?"

"I don't know. I was depressed. My brother had all but thrown me out of his house because I turned Jake and his friends in. I guess I wasn't thinking clearly. I was upset and worried, and I needed a drink."

"You never *need* a drink."

"I *needed* to relax, get my mind off things." She looked frustrated as she groped for words. "You could never understand. You live some kind of unreal life, and I don't know how you do it, but I'm not like you. You've probably never had a vice in your life."

"Hey, I had plenty of vices before I became a Christian," he said. "I gave in plenty. I know what I'm missing, Issie. I'm missing a lot of heartache, a lot of turmoil, a lot of anxiety, a lot of remorse, a lot of self-indictment, a lot of guilt. I'm missing those feelings of waking up in the morning and running the night back through my mind, trying to figure out if I did or said anything that I was going to regret today."

"You?"

"Oh, yeah, me. The miracle is that God could take some-body like me and use me. I mean, he didn't just transform me into a new creature. He literally made me into something he could use."

"Well, that's you, Nick. You're a useful kind of person. He could never use me."

"Of course he could."

"Not with my past," she said. "You don't know all the stuff I've done."

She looked sadly off in the distance, and he reached for her chin and turned her face back to his. "Issie, look at me."

Those dark eyes came up to meet his.

"You have no idea how useful you could be. God has a plan for you. He's had a plan for you all along. You just wouldn't fol-low it. But if you started following it, you could do amazing things."

Her expression seemed soft, vulnerable, and for a moment he thought he might be getting through. Her eyes were stricken as they locked into his, and he thought he saw a fine mist paint-ing the inside edge of her lids, but then that hard look came back and she was skeptical again.

"When I think of God's plan for my life, I picture me in a black church suit with ugly pumps and my hair pulled back in a bun. I picture me going around with a fifty-pound Bible, wav-ing it in people's faces and quoting Scripture every time I open my mouth. It doesn't sound like much fun to me."

"Issie, you know a lot of Christians. Do they act like that? Do they look like shells that are going around repeating robotic phrases?"

"No," she said, "some of them don't. But some do. They talk about Christ and righteousness, and in the next breath they're declaring themselves superior to Jews and blacks and gays . . . and anybody who's not like them. Even Cruz and his group are Christians. They don't drink or smoke or do dope, but they kill people. And they think it's okay because they figure if they hate somebody, then God must hate them too."

"Issie, they're not us."

"They say they are."

"They're liars. They're using the banner of Christianity to camouflage their hate. They're defining who we are, Issie, but they're defining us wrong. Don't buy into their lies. Go to the Bible and see what God says. And look at the ones who follow that Bible, the ones who love and pray and cope and help people in need. The ones who think not only of themselves, but of others, no matter how different they are. The ones who hate sin but love sinners enough to rescue them, just as surely as you rescue people every day."

She looked down at her hands, turning his words over in her mind.

"Issie, Christians are not a bunch of clones without personalities. God doesn't want that. He needs all kinds."

She swallowed. "Well, I could be wrong. I have been before."

"Well, if you're wrong about this," Nick said, "then your eternity will be affected by it. I don't want that for you, Issie. I don't want you to miss this."

She breathed a laugh. "I don't particularly want that, either."

"Then come out of the cell."

Her smile faded. "What cell?"

"The one on death row. There's someone waiting to take your place. Your pardon is waiting. Until you take it, you're in bondage, Issie. You're trapped. You think you're free but you're not. You've just constructed your own prison."

"Oh, yeah?" She was starting to get angry. "And what exactly am I trapped by?"

"Sin," he said. "You hate it and you don't want it, but then every night you go back to Joe's Place and you drink and you pick up a man."

"Okay." She got up from the scorched pew and held up her hands to halt his direction. "I do *not* pick up men," she said. "But even if I did, it is not a sin to attract a man."

"No, but it's a sin to lust after them, make them lust after you, and take them home with you." He hated saying it. He didn't want her to turn on him, but if he let it end like this, he might never have another chance to be this honest with her.

"How dare you?" she asked. "Just because things aren't going great for me does not mean that I'm some kind of hell-bound sinner."

"You said there were things in your life that God wouldn't be able to accept," he said. "What do you call those?"

"Well, so what? Maybe they are sins. But you don't have to paint me to be some kind of harlot who prowls into the bar every night looking for her latest victim. I'm not like that. I go there to unwind, to talk to my friends."

"Oh, I know you're not like that," he said. "You're not a hunter. I think you're the hunted."

Her mouth fell open. "And who is hunting me?"

"Lots of people," he said. "They're all looking for a pretty girl with a big heart who just wants to be loved."

She rolled her eyes and shook her head and looked into the wind. It whipped her hair around her face, and she shoved it behind her ear. "I know what I'm doing, Nick. I'm in perfect control. I'm the driver in my life."

"You're contradicting yourself all over the place, Issie."

Again she shook her head with disbelief. "Okay, so I am, but you're confusing me."

"I'm confusing you because you're not making any sense."

"So the only sense to be made is that God has a plan for me and I'm supposed to follow it, and all his rules, and live like you live, constantly depriving myself of everything in the world that I want?"

"Well, see, that's the thing that's different," he said. "If you gave your life to Christ, you'd want different things."

"The other night you admitted that you don't," she said, lifting her chin defiantly. "You admitted that you're tempted just like I am."

"I'm tempted," he said, "but in my heart I want what God wants for me, and that's why I take that escape when he provides it."

"Well, maybe I don't *want* that escape," she said. "Maybe I *like* the so-called prison you say I'm in. Maybe I don't want to walk through the door that he's opening for me to get out. Maybe that's because I don't see it as a prison."

"No one ever does," Nick said. "That's what's so sad."

She groaned and combed her hands through the roots of her hair. "You make me crazy, you know that? You drive me right up the wall."

"Yeah, I've been known to do that."

She looked suddenly very weary, and he remembered her crouched like a little girl next to the toilet last night.

"I'm tired, Nick. I'm going to Aunt Aggie's. I just came by to check on you, see how you were doing. I guess you're getting back to normal, throwing your punches." She got up to leave.

"I'm not throwing punches, Issie. I'm trying to throw a life raft." Nick followed her, stepping over some of the rubble on the way to the pickup.

She reached the truck door but didn't get in right away. Instead she stood there and looked up at him.

He wondered if Mark was right, if she knew exactly the power she had over men. He didn't want her to have that power over him. Still, he stood there looking down at her, stricken with how his heart rate escalated when she looked up at him. Even when she wasn't at her best, there was something about her eyes that drew him in, something that had always made his heart jolt.

"I worry about you," he said. "Last night, I sat by your bed and prayed for hours."

He couldn't define the poignant expression that passed over her face. It was something between shock and sorrow, and for a moment, he thought she was going to cry. "No one's ever prayed for me before," she whispered.

"I have," he said. "I've been praying for you for years."

She looked down at the key in her hand, her eyes stricken. "My advocate," she whispered.

He frowned. "Your what?"

She swept her hair behind her ear. "Nothing. I was just thinking." Those tears filled her eyes now as she looked up at him. "Thank you for worrying about me."

He smiled. "You act like I'm doing it on purpose when, in fact, I just can't help myself. I guess it's this built-in protective mechanism that I get whenever I see a lady in trouble."

Her smile faded. "A damsel in distress, you mean?"

"It's not a sign of weakness, you know. Vulnerability and weakness are not the same things."

She tried to smile again, but quickly that smile faded and tears seemed to rim her eyes as she looked up at him. "You make me feel safe, Nick. I like to be around you. That's the real reason I came looking for you today."

A lump lodged in his throat, and he tried to swallow it back. "I'm glad," he said. "You deserve to feel safe."

She looked up at him again with those honest probing eyes, and as he regarded her, he wondered what it would be like if he reached out and slid his fingers along her neck, up her jawline, into the roots of her hair. He wondered what it would cost him if he leaned down just a few inches and grazed her lips gently with his.

It was almost as if she read his thoughts. "I wish I was different, Nick," she whispered.

"What would you do if you were different?"

"I'd probably pull out all the stops and chase the only white knight I know," she whispered.

He felt the blood coloring his face.

"Can you imagine Issie Mattreaux going after the preacher?" she asked, teasing.

He wondered if it was his imagination or if she was moving closer, testing him with her proximity. He didn't move back. Instead, he just looked into her eyes, glanced down at her lips. He was breathing harder than he meant to.

"Can you imagine the preacher falling for Issie Mattreaux?" he whispered.

She looked at his lips then, and he wet them, thinking how easy it would be just to dip down and touch hers.

"What would people say?" she asked.

"I don't know," he whispered.

They stood there like that, stricken and paralyzed as the cool breeze teased around them. Finally Nick opened her truck door. She took his cue with a disappointed look, got in, and started the engine.

"Feel free to call me if you get scared before I get over to Aunt Aggie's," he said. He leaned down, putting his face even with hers. His eyes were serious as he locked into her gaze. "No kidding, Issie. I have a few things to do at home, but you let me know if you need me."

"I will," she said, and that smile came back to soften her lips. "Thanks, Nick."

He closed the truck door, stepped back, and watched her drive away. He crossed the street and went into his trailer, turned on a lamp, and sat down in the chair that someone from his congregation had given him. He pulled his feet up and stared at the shadows on the wall.

What was it about Issie Mattreaux, he asked himself. Why was she on his mind so often, and why did she keep turning up in his life? He closed his eyes and confessed that to the Lord, told him he felt like Hosea falling for a prostitute. But in Hosea's case, God had ordained it. He knew better than that. God had not led him to Issie Mattreaux, because she was not a believer. He couldn't think of anything more miserable than being married to someone who didn't have the same values, the same goals in life, the same purpose, someone who didn't know where to turn in times of trouble, someone who didn't know the value of her life. Simply because of the blood of Christ, God would never put him with Issie. It just wasn't possible. These feelings he was having, they were lustful feelings. He wanted her because she was the unattainable, and because she was so darned pretty. He asked God to take this desire away from him, to make him stop thinking about her and stop caring. He asked him to make him think of her the way a preacher would think of a lost person, instead of the way a bachelor would think of one of the prettiest women in town.

Maybe he was playing with fire as Mark had said. Maybe *she* was. And then he told himself again that maybe he had misread his calling, that maybe he wasn't pure enough to be a preacher. If he was, wouldn't he be able to put her out of his mind and move on? If he was truly called to preach, why would he be having feelings like this for a woman like Issie?

Maybe God had brought him to the end of his preaching career for a reason. Maybe he was displeased with the thoughts skittering through Nick's mind. Maybe his weakness toward Issie was symptomatic of the weakness in his own faith. Maybe he had no business trying to uphold the faith of others when he had such a hard time fleeing temptations in his own heart. Maybe it was time to resubmit that letter of resignation.

Maybe this time he shouldn't take no for an answer.

Chapter Forty

Saturday morning, Nick woke before Issie did. Nervous about facing an expectant, wounded congregation the next day, he decided to leave Aunt Aggie's and go home to work on his sermon. Aunt Aggie wasn't anywhere to be found, so he assumed she was out walking. He left her and Issie a note, then drove up to his trailer and saw bulldozers on the church grounds. Junior Reynolds sat on one and Jesse Pruitt on another, clearing the rubble. Several dozen other people stood around the grounds in work clothes.

It was as if he was walking into a surprise party as he got out of his car and crossed the street, for the members of his church who had shown up to help began to cheer and holler.

"What's going on here?" he asked.

"We decided to go ahead and clear the land," Jesse yelled from the bulldozer. "That way we can get started rebuilding as soon as possible."

He hadn't had the chance to think of that himself. Instead, he'd been so blinded by the rubble that he couldn't see into the future at all. He looked around at all the faces and all the people in work clothes prepared to spend the day clearing the junk away from the church. There must have been forty or fifty people there. He felt the heaviness of his heart lifting as his mind flitted back to that letter of resignation he was planning to offer them. Maybe he would wait. There was no reason to put a damper on the work they would be doing. Instead, he rolled up his sleeves and began doing what he could to help.

• • •

Issie woke up a little later, thinking about Nick. She got up and showered quickly, then came out of her room to see if he was up. To her disappointment, he was already gone.

She kicked herself, wondering why she spent so much of her time thinking about the preacher. He wasn't the exciting, tough, alpha-male kind of guy that she usually fell for. Instead, he was sweet, sensitive, safe. So why did her heart pound out of control when she was around him? Why did her hands tremble and her mouth go dry? Why had she stood there at the truck yesterday, looking at his lips and waiting for him to kiss her? Why had she been so crushed when he had stepped away again?

The thought of her feelings for Nick began to make her hate herself. She could never be good enough for a man like him.

She went into the kitchen and found a note that Aunt Aggie had gone to take snacks to people working on the church grounds. She made a bowl of cereal and sat down, hating the thought of being alone today. She wished she hadn't made Nick feel like he had to avoid her. She wondered if that was a sign that he was attracted to her, or repulsed by her.

Still, as she finished breakfast, she began trying to think of reasons to see him today. The church grounds, she thought. Aunt Aggie said they were working on the church grounds. Maybe if she went to help . . .

She cleaned her dishes, then went to the truck and drove to Nick's street. But even as she drove, she realized that part of the reason she was thinking so much about Nick right now was that he was not interested in her. Had he been, she didn't even know if she would have given him the time of day. She felt a little bit like Mark Twain who would never join a club that would have him as a member.

For that, she hated herself.

She pulled onto his street and saw the bulldozer on the church grounds. Dozens of people sifted through rubble, and she wondered if she should keep driving to keep from stirring any further gossip about her and Nick.

But she had no place else to go, so she pulled Steve Winder's old pickup truck into Nick's gravel driveway and sat there idling for a moment.

She shouldn't have come here, she thought. She started to pull out of the driveway when she heard something bang on her truck. She looked out the window and saw Nick standing at the door. She rolled the window down. "Nick, I was going to volunteer to help, but I don't want to cause you any trouble."

"Cause me trouble? Why would you?" he asked.

"Just coming here. I mean, the rumors."

He shook his head. "They're all so busy over there, they don't care."

"What are they doing?" she asked.

"They're clearing the property," he said, "so we can start rebuilding."

She turned and looked out her rear window and saw that women and children and old men and young were all helping. "Looks like they could get it all done today with that kind of a turnout."

"That's what I was thinking," he said. "They planned all this without me. I didn't even ask them to come. I was going to try to find a way to do most of it myself, or scrounge up a committee. I thought I'd have to twist arms and beg and plead. But they turned the ignition themselves, and I didn't even have to give them a shove."

She thought she'd missed something. "Huh?"

"Never mind. I just mean that my job is to equip the saints to do the work of the church, but it always seems like it isn't really happening that way. Today it is. Come on and help, Issie.

They're all too busy to speculate about why you're here. All hands are welcome."

"Are you sure?"

"Of course, I'm sure," he said. "Come on." He opened her truck door and ushered her out. She followed him across the street, wondering if this was his way of getting her assimilated into the fellowship of the church. She wasn't sure, but whatever he was doing, it was working, because she really did want to be a part of this effort.

Chapter Forty-One

Allie had stiffened the moment she saw Issie drive up in Nick's driveway. She wondered if the rumors she'd heard about them were true. Had Nick been spending time with the woman who once tried to steal Allie's husband away?

"Oh, great," Mark said, coming up behind Allie and following her gaze. "Don't tell me she's coming to help."

They watched her get out of the car, and Allie turned back to tying up garbage bags. "Looks like it."

"Are you okay?" Mark asked. "We could leave if you're uncomfortable."

Allie tried to reassure him with her smile. She knew that Mark hadn't given Issie a thought in a long time now, and he had managed to rebuild her trust in him as they had built their family. But she wasn't sure she wanted to get chummy with Issie.

Celia touched her shoulder, and Jill approached her too. "Really, are you okay?" Jill asked. Celia had her blond ponytail pulled up and was covered with soot since she'd been sifting through the rubble for anything they could salvage.

"I'm fine," Allie said. "I forgave Issie a long time ago."

"Then why do you look so tense all of a sudden?" Jill asked her.

Allie turned back to gaze at Issie's truck. "Because I still get uncomfortable around her. I wish I could forget, but I just have problems with her."

Mark saw that Issie was coming into the crowd of workers, and Nick was treating her like one of them. "I'm gonna ask her to go home," he said.

Allie grabbed his arm. "You can't do that."

"But Allie, I don't want you to have to work beside her today and drag up all those memories. This is *our* church."

"No, it isn't," Allie said. "It's Christ's church. And if we can't welcome someone like Issie into our fellowship, even rejoice that she would come, then we're the ones who don't belong here. Not her."

His face softened and he studied his wife's face. "You're right. I know you are. I'm just trying to protect you from my own stupid past mistakes. Plus, I question her motives. I think she's after Nick."

Allie looked up at Mark again. Their eyes met, and she looked away. She had always secretly suspected that Nick had a thing for Issie. She wondered what the appeal was, and if he realized he was on dangerous ground.

Then she felt guilty again. If Jesus had shied away from the woman at the well, or the adulteress who was about to be stoned, just because of who they were . . . well, that would mean he'd have to shy away from Allie for her past sins, and Mark for his, and none of them would ever be forgiven. Suddenly one of her favorite Scripture verses struck her in the heart: "This is love: not that we loved God, but that he loved us and sent his Son as an atoning sacrifice for our sins. Dear friends, since God so loved us, we also ought to love one another."

There it was, she thought. She had to love because Christ loved her. It was very simple, really. Cut and dried. Black and white, with no gray areas. Issie had as much right to her love, as Allie had to Christ's. And it was Allie's job—no one else's—to make Issie feel that she could be accepted here on the holy land where God's house had been built.

Chapter Forty-Two

They gave Issie a job sorting through a pile of hymnbooks in a box, and salvaging the ones that could still be read, as well as the Bibles that had been in the pews. The fact that anything was salvageable was a small miracle, Nick said. Issie felt an awkward sense that she didn't belong when she saw Mark and Allie working alongside everyone else. She and Allie had had a difficult time speaking to each other ever since she had caused problems in their marriage.

As she sorted Bibles, she was peripherally aware that Allie and Mark were whispering to each other. Was Allie telling Mark to get her out of here? That's what *she* would have been doing. Was she threatening to go home if she had to lay eyes on Issie Mattreaux one more time?

Hours passed and everyone kept working. She worked quietly, not interacting much with anyone else, though occasionally someone spoke to her as if she did belong.

When they'd gotten the building leveled and cleared and everyone was backing away as the bulldozer made its last sweep through, Issie saw Allie heading her way. She stiffened instantly, bracing herself for whatever was coming. She wondered if Allie had waited for the noise of the bulldozer, so that no one would hear her chewing her out.

But when Allie reached her, Issie saw a smile instead of hostility. "I appreciate how hard you worked today, Issie."

Issie tried to return the smile. "No problem. I didn't have anything else to do."

"Some of us are about to go over to Aunt Aggie's and set up the chairs for tomorrow's service. Nick wanted me to ask you if you were interested in coming."

Issie looked up across the crowd and saw Nick on the other side of the bulldozer. He could have asked her himself, she knew, but there was something about sending Allie over that was supposed to speak to her heart. She looked up at the woman whose home she had almost wrecked.

"I don't know. Maybe I'll just go on home."

"Oh, no. We need your help. Besides, I wasn't going to say anything, but Aunt Aggie cooked a little extra for the firemen today and she said that we could eat when we got to her house."

Issie studied Allie's face and wondered if she was just a good actress, or if she really wanted Issie to come. "Why do you want me to go so bad?" she asked. "I would think you would want me as far away from your husband as I could get."

Allie's eyes saddened, and she looked away. "I have to admit, sometimes when I'm around you bad memories come back. But that's my problem, not yours. The truth is, we're all here cleaning up a church, and there's not a reason in the world that you shouldn't be there working right along beside me if you want to be. Believe it or not, Issie, I forgave you a long time ago."

Issie looked away. She hadn't asked for forgiveness, had never admitted wrong, but denying that she had been seemed like a waste of effort now. Her eyes filled with tears, and she looked down to hide them. "You have every reason to hate me," Issie admitted.

Allie smiled. "Christ has every reason to hate *me*. But he doesn't. So how could I hate you?"

When Allie went back to her husband in the crowd, Issie found herself unable to speak or think. The lump grew in her throat and she tried to swallow it back, but she knew she was going to burst into tears right here in front of everybody and cause another round of gossip if she didn't get out of here. Quickly, she crossed the street and headed toward the rusty pickup that was still parked at Nick's house.

She got in and sat there for a moment, covering the tears that were coming through her lashes. Suddenly there was a knock on the window. Nick stood there, looking in with concern. She rolled her window down.

"Issie, what's wrong?" he asked.

She wiped her eyes and tried to pull herself together.

"I saw you talking to Allie," he said. "Did she say something that upset you?"

"No, no. Not at all."

"What then?"

"She was very sweet," she said, bringing her misty eyes up to his. "And she has every right not to be. She's forgiven me for the way I intruded on her marriage. Thing is, I guess I'd be more comfortable with the hate, because I know how to deal with that."

Nick reached through the window and wiped a tear that was rolling down her cheek. She drew in a deep breath as if jolted by the contact. "I'm not a very nice person, you know," she said. "Even if I wanted to come to your church, be a part of this, I couldn't. I would never fit in."

Nick just kept smiling. "One of my favorite Bible passages is in 1 Corinthians 6," he said.

She gave him a smirk. "Haven't read it lately."

He grinned as if he knew she didn't even own a Bible.

"It says, 'Do you not know that the wicked will not inherit the kingdom of God? Do not be deceived: Neither the sexually immoral nor idolaters nor adulterers nor effeminate nor male prostitutes nor homosexual offenders nor thieves nor the greedy nor drunkards nor slanderers nor swindlers will inherit the kingdom of God.'"

More tears erupted in Issie's eyes. "Well, see there? That keeps me out on several counts."

"That's not my favorite part," Nick said, leaning in the window and getting too close to her face. "The next verse says, 'That is what some of you were. But you were washed, you were sanctified, you were justified in the name of the Lord Jesus Christ and by the Spirit of our God.'"

She looked up at him, her eyes intent on seeing the insights that seemed too natural to him.

"You think you don't belong in that group over there?" Nick asked. "Well, Issie, almost every one of them fits into those categories before they came to know Christ. Some of them just had heart problems. They weren't outward thieves and they weren't going around committing adultery, but they were doing it in their hearts. Others of them did these things openly. Just look at them, Issie. You've lived here long enough to know. You know who has changed and who hasn't. If people couldn't change, then Paul wouldn't have said, 'Such *were* some of you.' God doesn't keep those people out of heaven unless they decide to stay out. He can wash you and sanctify you and justify you in the name of the Lord Jesus Christ. And then you can be just as much a part of this congregation as anybody over there. We're just all a bunch of turned-around people."

"Turned around?" she asked.

"One hundred and eighty degrees. We changed our direction. We're striving toward Christ now instead of toward sin. That's the only difference between you and me."

She leaned her head back wearily on the headrest. "But I have a lot of baggage, Nick. A lot of people in this town have things to hold against me. And if I haven't hurt them, then they have preconceived notions about who I am and what I do."

"Those notions can be changed," he said. "I guess before this crisis with the church, I didn't have a lot of faith in my people. I guess I thought they wouldn't know what to do, how to act, unless I told them. Like they were all a bunch of sheep that would scatter if I wasn't there to keep them all together. But I'm learning differently. They've grown. They've matured.

They're wiser than I thought. And they're too wise to think that they're above you somehow. That life of sin is just behind every one of us. We're all sinners saved by grace."

"What does that mean?" she asked. "Saved by grace?"

He drew in a deep breath. "It means we don't deserve it. Not one of us here deserves to be in communion with Christ or to go to heaven. Not a single one of us. But for some reason that no one on this earth can fathom, God looked down on us and saved us from our emptiness. He filled us up, Issie. He can fill you up too."

Someone across the street called to Nick, and he waved. "Come on, Issie. We're headed over to Aunt Aggie's to set up for the service. Won't you come?"

She wiped her eyes with both hands. "You don't need me there, Nick. I'll find something else to do."

"I'd like for you to be there," he said. "Please come. I like your company."

The words spoke volumes and told Issie all she needed to know to persuade her into coming. If it was true that Nick liked her company, then maybe these feelings she'd been nursing toward him were not entirely absurd. Somehow it vindicated her. She drew in a deep breath and got out of the truck. "All right," she said, "I'll come." Then she followed Nick back across the street and into the crowd of church people, climbing into the back of Jesse Pruitt's truck, to be transported the few blocks to Aunt Aggie's.

It took a couple of hours to set the yard up in such a way that they could worship adequately the next morning, and as Issie found herself getting involved in the plans, she began to wish she could be in attendance. She had never come to Nick's church, had never heard him preach except at a funeral or two.

By the time the chairs were set up and the pulpit had been placed, and they had figured out where they would plug in the microphones, amplifiers, and speaker system, Issie found herself alone with Nick. Aunt Aggie had gone to the fire department to start supper, and the others had headed home. The dip in the land, so that the chairs were seated at the bottom of a bowl-shape in Aunt Aggie's acreage, allowed the hills around it to act as barricades against the breeze. Issie sat on one of the chairs like one of the congregants, trying to imagine whether she would feel out of place if she came. After a moment, Nick came and sat down beside her. "So what do you think?" he asked.

"I think I'm going to have to come hear you preach tomorrow," she said.

He grinned. "Are you kidding me?"

"Nope. I could hardly work this hard to get everything set up, and then not be here."

"Well, yeah, but you realize *I'm* supposed to be preaching, don't you? Really think you can handle that?"

She breathed a laugh. "It's not your preaching that's kept me away. Maybe it's the church building."

"So you have a paranoia about church buildings?"

She shook her head. "No, I have a paranoia about rules."

"I told you—" he began, but she cut in.

"I know you did. It's not about rules. It's about the heart. I think I saw some evidence of that today." She could see that that pleased him.

"So you're really coming tomorrow?"

"I'm really coming," she said.

"Then I guess I'd better go home and work on that sermon."

"You don't have it ready yet?" she asked.

"No, I guess I've been a little distracted."

She suddenly felt guilty. "I guess I'm the one that caused that. All the rescuing you've been doing."

"No," he said, "it's not that. I've just been a little depressed. I haven't felt like there was any point." He looked over at her with a grin. "But if you're going to be here, maybe there is."

"Glad to be of service," she said.

• • •

That afternoon when Nick went back to his trailer to work on his sermon, he got his Bible and his other study aids and piled them all on his kitchen table. He began to write the sermon that the Lord had laid on his heart today, while he'd been working with his flock to salvage the church. As he was writing, he pictured Issie sitting there soaking in every word, so he wrote the sermon directly to her and prayed while he wrote it that the Lord would penetrate her callused heart so that that empty look would vanish from her eyes, and instead he would see joy and peace like he'd only seen in believers.

The depression since the church fire, the murder of Ben, his own failure in rescuing the boy, his worries about what Cruz and his gang might do next, and his doubts about his own calling all vanished in light of the hope that he might lead one person to Christ tomorrow.

And that person might be Issie Mattreaux.

Chapter Forty-Three

The old furniture warehouse Cruz's grandfather provided for their new hiding place was musty and dirty, and had the peculiar smell of newborn rodents. It gave Jake the creeps, even though he realized it was the least of his troubles. He had noticed a difference in the way Cruz and Jennifer and the others treated him, for they weren't making plans or strategizing in front of him. They were taking all of their planning sessions into another room—LaSalle and Decareaux were now part of the inner circle—and he and Benton were left out, along with the others who hadn't earned that status.

That was fine with him, since he didn't want to be a part of any more of their crimes anyway, but Benton felt slighted. "Man, here I am hobbling on crutches, popping antibiotics and painkillers, and worried about being arrested for murder. I paid my dues, but they're still treating me like I'm not worthy of hearing their stupid plans."

"You're better off," Jake said. "Trust me. I'd leave if I could."

"Why can't you? Nobody's bound and gagged you."

"Not physically, but they sure don't let me out of their sight." He glanced toward the closed door to the small room that had once been an office. Cruz and his confidants were huddled in there for an "executive meeting." Grayson, Drew, and Herring sat near the door, as if guarding it from anyone coming in or going out. The girls—Blair, Meg, and Kaye—worked at a table in the corner, assembling pipe bombs that Cruz said were security measures to defend them. "I want to see what they're gonna do next," he said. "I want to hear if they're planning to use those pipe bombs on Issie."

"Issie *and* Nick Foster," Benton said. "A little while ago, when they were setting up the mattresses, I heard Cruz say they're an item now. Said Issie passed out in the bar the other night, and Nick came to get her. Nick's life already wasn't worth a dime to Cruz, and now the two of them together? Issie can really pick 'em."

Jake looked at Benton as if he was delirious. "Nick Foster, the preacher? You're outta your mind. Issie would never get hooked up with a preacher."

"Ask Cruz," Ben said, as if their leader's word was gospel. "And Cruz *hates* him, man. I'm surprised they didn't burn his trailer down when they hit his church. He lives right across the street from it."

"I think they made their point with the church . . . whatever that point was." He rubbed his face hard, as if to wipe off his confusion. "Man, I *have* to do something." Jake dropped his elbows to his knees. "I bet my parents probably think I'm dead."

"My folks probably *hope* I am," Benton said.

"No, they don't."

"You're right," Benton said. "They probably haven't given me enough thought to care one way or another." He sat down and propped his leg on another chair. "My kid brother's probably freakin' out, though. He worries a lot."

"Maybe you could get a message to him that you're all right. Maybe he could go tell my folks. Maybe warn Issie."

Benton looked toward the room where Cruz and Jennifer were. "No, I better not. If they found out, they might think I was turnin' on them."

Jake knew they already thought that about him. He was still uneasy about what they might do eventually. First chance he got, he was out of here, and the more he knew when he left, the better. Then maybe he could head off some of the damage they were planning to do.

Chapter Forty-Four

By the next morning Issie had almost talked herself out of going to the church service, even though she had given Nick her word that she would be there. She didn't know what to wear, for she owned very few dresses, but she went home long enough to sift through her various skirts and blouses, and finally came up with something that she felt was appropriate.

Then she worried about how to act. Did they kneel when they started the service? Maybe not out in the yard, she thought. Did they chant things she wouldn't know the words to? And what about singing? Should she just stand there and let everyone know she didn't know the first word—as if that would come as a surprise to anyone—or should she try to hum along and pretend she did? And what if they did something hokey like look at their neighbor and quote some Scripture she didn't know, hug, and say, "I love you"?

She wondered if she would be better off staying home. She found a million reasons to do so as she showered. She didn't feel well. Her muscles ached from her work yesterday. She had some reading to catch up on, friends to visit, a nephew to search for.

Yet tugging equally at her mind were the memories of Nick's excitement yesterday when she told him she would be there. It seemed to mean a lot to him, though she couldn't imagine why. The thought that he might like being around her as much as she enjoyed being with him seemed unfathomable to her. Still, she wanted to explore it a little more, and she remembered the feeling of belonging she had had yesterday working among the people of his church, and Allie's forgiveness and invitation to help set up for the service. She had worked hard. She wanted to see the fruit of her labor.

Finally deciding that she needed a friend to go with her, she picked up the phone and dialed Karen Insminger. It rang four times before the phone was answered.

"Hello." Karen sounded hoarse, and Issie knew she had pulled her out of a sound sleep.

"Karen, it's me, Issie."

"What do you want?" she asked, irritated. "I was sleeping."

"Then you shouldn't have answered the phone," Issie teased.

Karen didn't find that amusing. "This better be important, Issie."

Issie chuckled. "Well, I guess important is relative. I wanted to see if you would go to church with me."

"Church?" Karen started coughing as if the shock had been too much for her. "Excuse me. I thought you said 'church.'"

"I did, actually."

"I'm sorry," Karen said. "I must have really been out of it. I thought you said this was Issie."

"All right," Issie said. "So you don't want to go. All you have to do is say so."

"I don't want to go," Karen returned. "So, what's this all about anyway?"

"Well, it's the church that burned down the other day. Calvary Bible Church. I sort of helped them clear the land yesterday and everybody kept inviting me. And I've gotten to be pretty close friends with Nick Foster, the preacher."

"Issie, you're not after him, are you?"

Karen had heard the rumors, Issie thought. She wondered if all the medics sat around when she wasn't with them, speculating about her love life. "Don't you people have anything more exciting to think about?"

"I've just never known you to be interested in church, that's all. The only thing that could possibly get you there is a man."

"Thanks a lot."

"So, is that it?"

"No," Issie told her. "He's just a nice man. He's helped me. And also there's that community support kind of thing. The church burned down, but it didn't stop them from having services out on Aunt Aggie's lawn, and I just kind of feel like I ought to be there, just to show support."

"Oh, yeah, that's you," Karen said. "Little Miss Community."

Issie regretted calling. "I guess I've got my answer. Go back to sleep."

Karen had hung up even before she'd gotten the word "Bye" out, and Issie wondered why she had even bothered. Then, with her stomach in her throat, she headed out to her pickup to attend church for the first time in her life.

She was a few minutes late for the service, and as she pulled back up to Aunt Aggie's, she found a parking place in an empty lot beside her house. A couple of guys she knew from town waved her into a space.

She sat in her truck for a minute and rolled down her window, listening for any sounds that might clue her not to go to where the congregation was gathered. She heard the sound of a keyboard and a couple of guitars. Guitars in a church service? Then she realized that this was Nick's church. Nick probably had some of his personality tied up in it. Maybe it wasn't quite as stuffed shirt as she had imagined.

She eased out of the truck and looked down toward the congregation. So many people had come that they were setting up extra chairs. She hoped Nick was encouraged by that.

She saw that someone was standing up front and singing, a young girl, maybe eighteen or nineteen. Maybe now wasn't such a bad time to go in.

She closed her door quietly, then walked through the cars and made her way down to the yard near Aunt Aggie's house. When she saw that there was standing room only at the back behind the chairs, she decided she would just stay there. That way she could slink out if she felt the need to. But before she had a chance to get used to her position, three different men had stood up and waved for her to come sit in their place.

She started to shake her head, thank them very much and tell them no, that she would stay right where she was, when she met Nick's eyes from the front of the gathering. He smiled at her and waved for her to come up and sit down in an empty seat near the front.

She dipped her head, looking at the ground as she made her way up, wishing no one here knew who she was. She imagined she heard gasps as she walked up the grassy aisle, people shocked that Issie Mattreaux had come into the presence of the Lord. Lightning would probably strike the whole assembly. The sun would be darkened and Nick would be struck dumb. If there was a God, he sure didn't want the likes of Issie Mattreaux in his house, even if it wasn't a house anymore.

She took her seat and looked up to see that she was next to Dan and Jill Nichols. Jill patted Issie's arm. "Glad to see you here," she said. Issie just nodded.

When the girl stopped singing, Nick came to the front and grabbed one of the guitars. Issie's eyebrows came up as she watched him begin to play a chorus of "Amazing Grace." She didn't know where she had learned it, but somewhere in her past that song had become part of her consciousness. She couldn't make herself mouth the words, but as the others around her sang, she began to hum along.

The familiar sound of that tune was like a soothing balm to her soul. She couldn't imagine why she would respond so to it. She had never really concentrated on the words before, but now she listened, wondering why a song like this would be handed down from age to age, generation to generation, and why it would still be so popular.

She saw some of the people singing it with their eyes closed as if the song itself was a prayer that rose straight to heaven.

Chapter Forty-Five

Cruz and Jennifer had heard about the work done at the church site the day before, and all the people who had turned out for it. They'd heard about Nick Foster working right there along with the others, and the fact that the church burning had drawn the congregation together, instead of scattering them apart. And from the signs posted all over town, they'd learned about the church service on Aunt Aggie's lawn.

"Right up here, take a right," Jennifer said. "Where the cars are."

Driving the black van he'd borrowed from Decareaux, Cruz slowed down as he saw the cars parked on the side of the road. His eyes squinted as he came up beside the bowl-shaped lawn and saw the hundreds of people in folding chairs, worshiping in song.

He stopped the car and rolled his window down. The strains of "Amazing Grace" flew on the breeze. "You believe this?" he asked his sister. "There're more people here than they usually have on Sundays."

Jennifer pointed down to Nick, standing at the front of the crowd. "Look at Nick Foster. Standin' down there like they're worshipin' *him* or somethin'."

Cruz drove on, his face twisted as he tried to think it through. "So the church burnin' didn't phase 'em. They're stronger than ever. Nick Foster wasn't even affected."

"We have to do somethin' else," Jennifer said. "We can't let him win."

Cruz's hands tightened on the steering wheel as he drove faster. "Oh, we're gonna do somethin' else, all right," he said. "We'll show Nick Foster. And this time there won't be one black kid dead."

Jennifer's eyebrows lifted, and her eyes shone with the same light he'd seen in his mother's eyes when they were kids and his grandfather was preparing to go on one of his missions. "What are we gonna do?"

"We'll send people back over to mingle with them when they break up, and find out what they can about their next service. And then we're gonna be there to surprise them."

Chapter Forty-Six

When they had ended "Amazing Grace," Nick led them into a chorus of a faster song that Issie had never heard before, and those around her clapped their hands and sang along.

There was joy here, she realized, even though their building had just burned down and one of their families had lost a son. How could they find joy after that? She had expected a service of mourning, a service full of guilt, but instead, she felt the love of the people around her.

When it finally came time for Nick to give his sermon, he put the guitar on its stand and headed to the microphone at the front of the group. For the first time in her life, Issie Mattreaux heard the gospel of Jesus Christ presented in a way that couldn't be denied.

When he ended the service with a prayer of repentance and acceptance of Jesus Christ, she felt her spirit fighting her mind for control. She wasn't ready to pray with him, because she wasn't sure she believed it could all be that easy. But she listened to every word, contemplating what it meant. And just before Nick led them in the amen, Issie whispered a prayer to Christ. "I don't know if you're there, but if you are, you're going to have to prove it to me."

She knew it was probably blasphemous, probably something that didn't please God. She knew that people said he wasn't a God to be tested, but she wasn't sure he was God at all. How could she be sure he wasn't just some figment of these people's imaginations that they clung to because they were weak?

But as she looked up at the congregation which had already burst into song again, she realized that she was the one who was weak, and these people had a rare strength that she had scarcely seen in her life. Something inside her yearned to have that kind of strength.

She didn't know why tears came to her eyes at that very moment as people around her were singing and praising God, but she found them rolling down her cheeks, and she wiped them away as quickly as they came. She saw that Jill had noticed she was crying, and she looked as if she didn't know what to do for Issie.

Issie thought she had to get out of there, had to get in her truck and drive away where she could cry in peace, or wipe from her mind whatever it was that had started her crying in the first place. She reached down for her purse, but Jill touched her back.

"Don't leave," Jill whispered. "We're having lunch right out here after the service. I really wish you'd come."

Issie wanted to ask her why, but something made her really want to stay, so she let go of her purse and sat up straight. She told herself she would just have to fight the tears and get through this morning. Something told her it would be worth it.

• • •

As the church service broke up, Nick found Issie in the crowd. He tried to get to her so that he could invite her for lunch, but people kept coming up to him and giving him hugs, telling him it was going to be all right, that they didn't need a building to worship the Lord. The Holy Spirit's glory had not abandoned them.

He needed to hear those words, but he also needed to get close to Issie to make sure she stayed. She needed to be wrapped in the fellowship of these people. She needed to know what it was to be around those who trusted in Christ.

But the real reason he wanted to get close to her was to see if she had prayed the sinner's prayer with him. He had led the congregation in it just for her, but he'd had no indication that she had prayed it with him. It was suddenly very important that he find out if she had.

He cut through the group and found Issie standing with Jill and Dan. He was surprised that she hadn't made her way out yet. "Issie, I'm so glad you came," he said, in his best preacher voice. "I thought for a while you weren't going to."

She smiled up at him. Her eyes looked wet, red. He had seen her crying, and it had given him hope. "Sorry I was late."

"So, give me your best shot," he said. "How was it?"

"Not as bad as I thought," she said.

He looked wounded. "Is that all?"

She laughed softly. "You'd know what a compliment that was if you knew what I'd been expecting."

"Is it something about my personality that told you I was a terrible preacher?"

"No, not the preaching," she said. "I just hadn't been to a church service before. The only time I've even darkened the door of a church is when I went to a wedding or a funeral."

"Well, we'll have to keep you coming long enough to darken the door of ours when we get it built," he said. "So how about staying for lunch?"

Issie shrugged. "I was thinking about it, but I didn't bring a covered dish or anything."

"Don't worry about it. Aunt Aggie made enough for a dozen people. In our whole history of covered dishes, we've never had a shortage."

"All right," she said. "I guess I'll stay."

Issie forgot the tension with which she had approached church this morning, and as she ate lunch and fellowshiped with the people, most of whom she'd known all her life, she found that there was no judgment or condemnation among those who surrounded her. A few snubbed her, but overall, she didn't get the general impression that people were asking what a woman like Issie Mattreaux would be doing among them.

Finally, she realized there were so many people there that most had probably not noticed her. She sat on a lawn chair that Nick had brought for her to use, and tried to fight the feeling that she was special, that the preacher had singled her out to pay special attention to. But that was silly. It wasn't as if he was singling her out because she was an attractive woman. It had a lot more to do with her soul than she wanted to admit.

She scanned the crowd looking for people who might be whispering about her, when she saw two young faces milling in the crowd. She had seen them before. They had been there when she treated Benton's leg the other night. Her heart tripped into race mode, and she sprang up and started toward them. They must have seen her coming, for they put their backs to her and started to walk away. She broke into a trot, but they went faster, threading through cars and getting far away from the crowd. Finally, she caught up to them. "Hey, you!"

The boys turned around. "Yeah?" They were both wearing jeans and wrinkled T-shirts, and she knew they hadn't been in the service or she would have noticed.

"You were at the Benton house last night. You know my nephew. Where is he? Where's Jake Mattreaux?"

"I don't know any Jake Mattreaux," one of them said.

"You're lying," she told them. "I know you're lying. Where is he?"

They both stared at her, their faces suddenly serious. A chill went through her, and she realized she shouldn't have gotten so far from the crowd, not when their group had tried to kill her just days ago.

"I'm warning you," she said, stepping into her paramedic personality and approaching them as she would if she were in uniform. "I want you to listen to me. If anything happens to my nephew, so help me, I will spend the rest of my life searching for you and making you pay. Do you understand me?"

They didn't seem amused at her bravado, yet she knew they had not taken it seriously. But without another word, they both turned and walked away. Quickly, she searched the parked cars for the truck she'd been driving and ran to get into it. She could follow them. She could follow them and let them lead her to Jake.

She pulled the truck out of its place, then made the block and saw the two boys in a white Ford Escort. They were pulled over to the side of the road a couple of blocks from the church, and two other kids were getting in.

Where had they all been? Why had they been at the church? What were they up to?

She hung back, staying out of their sight, until they were on their way. Then she followed them, hoping they would lead her to Jake.

Chapter Forty-Seven

The arsenal of guns that Cruz and the group were bringing in clued Jake that they were planning something even worse than the church burnings. As he and Benton sat in a corner of the moldy warehouse while Cruz plotted in another room, he began to wonder if there was something he could do. "Somebody needs to turn these idiots in," Jake told Benton. "How many more people are gonna die?"

"At least two, if we try to turn them in," Benton said.

"Well, maybe we're both just cowards."

"Maybe we are."

He watched Benton devour a bologna sandwich as if he hadn't eaten in a week. "How's your leg, man?"

"Sore," Benton said. "Really sore. But I'm not feeling so weak anymore. Antibiotics . . . good stuff."

Jake tried to see through the glass door to the room where Cruz and the group sat. "All those cameras they had, and the Polaroids they brought back . . . what are they taking pictures of?"

"Who knows?"

He looked at his friend again. "Benton, you know we gotta do something, don't you? We can't let them kill any more people. Not if we ever plan to look ourselves in the mirror again."

Benton dropped the last bite of his sandwich, as if the words had stolen his appetite. "Hey, I can't look myself in the mirror now, after what I did."

"Then undo some of the damage by helping me figure out what they're up to, so we can stop them."

The door to the office room came open, and Cruz, Jennifer, and the others came out. Benton got to his feet. "I'll see what I can find out."

• • •

I ssie followed the car at as much distance as she could, trying not to be seen as they rounded curves and turned corners, heading into the warehouse district of Newpointe. They led her to one old warehouse set back from the street, with garbage filling a ditch out front, and about six cars and pickups in front of it.

Was this where Jake was?

She watched them all go in, then left her truck some distance down the street and got out to walk the rest of the way. She went to the window of the building and peered in and saw the pile of guns in the middle of the floor, and Jake's dangerous friends encircled around them. But she didn't see Jake.

He was in there somewhere, and something told her he was in trouble. Maybe he was in a back room, hurt. Maybe he needed her.

She went to another window and looked in, trying to determine if there was some way to get in and look for him. There was an open window on the side, and it opened into a dark room that was separate from the room where they seemed to congregate. She managed to lift herself into it, and dropped down into the room.

She looked around. There was a table, and it was covered with papers and snapshots. She went closer to study them. They were pictures of this morning's worship service, she realized, pictures of the congregation sitting in Aunt Aggie's yard. They looked as if they had been taken from the street down—into the bowl-shaped yard. Had there been more of them there, hidden on the hills surrounding Aunt Aggie's property, standing back in the trees where no one could see them?

She wondered why anyone would have taken pictures like this, then she realized that it had to have been the two boys she had spotted and followed. Was that why they had come?

She looked through the small window in the door, and saw them still huddled around a pile of firearms. They were planning something, and it involved Nick's church . . . and lots of guns.

She went back to the table and picked up one of the papers under the snapshots. It was a diagram of the grounds at Aunt Aggie's, the house and trees surrounding where they had placed the chairs, and on the hills surrounding the worship area, she saw stick figures with guns pointed threateningly at the crowd.

Her heart jolted. Quickly, she folded up the paper and stuck it into her purse. She had to get out of here. She had to take this to the police and warn them. She slipped back up to the windowsill, but as she did, her foot caught on a hubcap leaned against the wall, and it toppled and fell with a clatter.

She dove out the window and bolted toward her truck, praying that no one had heard. But behind her she heard someone yell, "It's that woman again!"

She saw Cruz explode out of the warehouse, and she ran with all her might to reach her truck.

Chapter Forty-Eight

Jake shot out behind Cruz, trying to stop him long enough for Issie to get away. But Cruz was gaining on her like a linebacker foiling the winning touchdown. He caught Issie and knocked her down.

"Let her go, Cruz!" Jake shouted. "Let her go!" He threw himself on top of Cruz, but three others descended on him and wrestled him off.

He tried to knock them loose, flailing his arms and kicking at them, but Cruz clamped his arms around Issie, and she kicked and bucked and tried to shake him free. "Jake, help me!"

Cruz wrestled her to a rusty blue Subaru. "Open the trunk!" he shouted, and Jennifer popped it open.

Jake fought to get away, but someone pulled him into a choke hold, immobilizing him. The harder he fought, the tighter the arm clamped against his throat. He drove his fingernails into the arm squeezing the life out of him, but couldn't break free.

He heard Issie scream, and Cruz lifted her and stuffed her into the trunk. She kicked and fought to get out, but Cruz hit her across the face, and it knocked her back into the depths of the trunk. Before she could fight her way back up, he had slammed the trunk shut.

Jake could hear her fighting inside, banging and screaming, but Cruz backed away, and turned, red-faced, to Jake. Jake kicked behind him, his heel tearing into the knee of the person holding him, and his captor cursed and let him go. Jake ducked out of his grasp.

He had to get help. He had to get out of here and somehow get to a phone. He started running, and heard feet behind him on the gravel. Cruz yelled, and he heard Benton telling Jake to run.

Jake headed for the woods and leaped over a log, tore through a cluster of bushes, and slid down a hill covered with dead leaves.

He heard a gunshot, and someone just behind him yelped and fell. He looked back and saw Decareaux in a heap at the top of the hill he'd slid down, and Benton standing with a shotgun in his hand. "Go, Jake! Keep running!"

Jake crossed a stream, then ran up the other bank, clambering to get out of sight. Another shot rang out, and he swung around and saw Benton standing hand to chest, a look of shock on his face. He stood there for a moment. His eyes met Jake's, and he mouthed the word, "Run." Then his friend dropped and slid limply down the hill. Jake turned and ran.

Somehow, Benton had thrown them off, and he heard them running in another part of the woods, footsteps and cursing and gunshots shooting without aim. He kept running in the opposite direction, pounding the dirt and the dead leaves and leaping over logs and branches.

When he thought he was far enough away, he hoisted himself into a tree and rested on a branch, waiting to make sure he was clear before he tried to help Issie.

•   •   •

The car began to move, and Issie lay trapped in the black compartment. She banged on the trunk door and screamed until her throat was raw. They drove for several minutes on the road, and then she felt them pulling off. She heard gravel beneath the tires and was jerked from side to side as Cruz drove the car into a place where she knew no one could find her. Would he kill her when he got her there? Was this how it would all end?

She screamed and banged against the trunk, using all the strength she had to make noise. Someone along the way might hear, maybe at a stoplight, and call the police. But all her efforts seemed futile.

Finally, she heard the engine cut off, heard the door close, heard other car doors slamming, then an engine driving away.

Silence. They were leaving her here, trapped in the trunk of a car in a place where no one would ever look.

Then she heard a car door again, voices, and the Subaru engine starting. She felt the car moving. She screamed and kicked again, to no avail.

They drove for twenty minutes or so, when finally she felt them crunching back through gravel, heard the scraping and scratching of trees. Then the car stopped, and she heard them getting out, heard another car behind them ... doors closing. The other car left.

The silence screamed out her hopelessness.

Meanwhile, Jake's friends were planning to ambush Nick Foster's church the next time they met together. People would be killed. Perhaps even Nick.

She wailed again and screamed, banging with her shoulder and elbow and trying to get out, but there was little hope.

●　●　●

Jake waited for over an hour before he dropped out of the tree. They weren't after him anymore, he felt sure, but panic still raged in his heart. What had they done with Issie? And was Benton dead?

He had to go back. He had to see if the blue Subaru was still there, or if Benton had been taken care of.

He tried to retrace his steps back through the woods, careful not to be heard. He had done a lot of hunting with his father and knew how to remember landmarks. He passed the log he'd almost tripped over earlier, the dead oak, the wasp's nest . . .

Then he came to the spring and ran along it, looking for the place where Benton had fallen. He went carefully, stopping and listening every few feet, waiting to see if it was a trick. But there were no sounds except those of the mockingbirds in the trees, the woodpeckers drilling out their holes, the crickets and frogs and wind.

Then he saw his friend still lying at the bottom of the embankment, as twisted and broken as when he'd first fallen. Jake's throat constricted as he raced toward him and fell at his side. "Benton!" he whispered. "Benton!"

There was no response, so he shook him hard. He saw the bullet hole through his back, and as terror rose up in his throat, he turned him over. The exit wound had taken most of Benton's chest.

"Benton, come on, man. Come on, get up!" He reached for his arm and tried to find a pulse, but there was none.

He sat there on his knees and tried to muffle the sob screaming out his throat. He had brought Benton into the group. He had led him into this trouble, and Benton had died trying to keep Jake from being caught.

"I'll kill them myself," he said through his teeth. "Don't worry, Benton, I won't let them get away with this." He left his friend on the dirt, then climbed up the embankment, intent on making someone pay. He slowed as he got to the top and looked carefully toward the warehouse. All of the cars were gone.

They had bugged out, just like a military unit whose security had been compromised. The blue Subaru was gone, and Issie was in trouble.

They were taking her away, locked in a trunk, and he didn't know where he could send anyone to help her. Still, he had to get help. He would have to forge ahead in the woods, hoping to come out somewhere on the other side, or find a hunter or someone else who could help him, and rescue Issie.

He got up and stumbled into the brush as fast as he could, knowing that death could catch up to him at any moment.

Chapter Forty-Nine

Nick was worried about Issie. He didn't know why she'd taken off the way she had, but an hour later, she still hadn't returned. He was getting nervous.

When Steve Winder, Issie's partner, called around three, he had even more reason to worry. Issie hadn't shown up for work.

"I was wondering if you'd seen her," Steve said. "I know you two have been together a lot lately."

He decided not to comment on that. "Well, no, I haven't seen her, not since our picnic this afternoon. She left in a big hurry. She hasn't come back."

"Well, she was supposed to be on duty at three," Steve said. "She didn't show up. It's not like her."

Nick frowned. "She didn't call or anything?"

"No," Steve said, "and I've been trying to call her apartment and nobody's home. I even called over at her brother's and he said he hasn't seen her."

"Has this ever happened before?" Nick asked.

"No way," Steve said. "I've been her partner for a couple of years now. She's never even been late."

Nick felt sick. Something had happened to her. "Look, I'll see if I can catch up with her. I'll get back to you."

"Thanks."

Nick hung up the phone and sat staring at the wall for a moment, trying to separate panic from concern. Where would she have gone so quickly? Who might she have seen? He grabbed his cell phone off the counter and rushed outside. He got into his car and set out to find her before it was too late.

• • •

Jake managed to keep running through the woods, desperate to get help. He was lost and it was getting dark and he didn't know how far he had to go to get out on the other side. All he knew was that he couldn't give up now. He had to get to someone who could help Issie before she wound up like Benton.

He reached the bayou and stood for a moment, panting and sweating and trying to figure out which way he needed to go to get out of the woods.

He took off running along the bank, hoping that he was right in determining that it would come out next to the place where the new post office sat. Then he could get to a phone and call the police. Maybe it wasn't too late to save Issie.

He'd never been so thankful in his life as when he heard cars up ahead and knew he was getting near civilization. He ran faster, harder, thickets and thornbushes tearing at his pants legs and his arms.

He crossed the street and went to the drugstore where a pay phone sat at the corner of the parking lot. He dug through his pants pockets, got out the money for the phone, then stood there a moment, trying to decide whom to call first.

He put the change in and started to dial his parents but realized that might be a mistake. They would want to come get him, but home was the first place Cruz would look for him, and he couldn't risk having them find him there.

No, he thought. He needed to call the police. They were the only ones who could help Issie. He didn't know the number so he dialed 911 and waited for the dispatcher to answer.

"Nine-one-one, may I help you?"

"Uh, yeah," he said. "Uh, I'm calling to report a crime." His voice was shaking and hoarse. He could hardly get it out.

"What crime?" the dispatcher asked.

"Uh, kidnapping, sort of. Issie Mattreaux. You may know her. The paramedic."

"Yeah, I know Issie," the dispatcher said.

"Well, she's sort of been kidnapped. A guy named Cruz has her. I saw him put her into the trunk of a car, and he drove away with her. I don't know where they are, but you might still catch them in the blue Subaru."

"Can I have your name please?" she asked.

His mind started reeling, and he thought she wouldn't send help until he gave her what she wanted. "Keith," he lied, "Keith Jones." That seemed to satisfy her, and she got off the subject.

"Keith, can you tell us where they were headed?"

"No," he said, "I have no idea."

"Was there some kind of fight, some kind of argument?"

"Sort of," he said. "She had kind of stumbled on some evidence and ratted on them. They want revenge."

"What kind of evidence?"

"About the church burnings and the murders. Also, a guy got shot over by the old Mayflower Furniture warehouse. He's in the woods, down an embankment. I'm pretty sure he's dead."

There was silence for a moment. He pictured her frantically trying to get a message to the cars she was dispatching. He started to realize that his call could be traced. At any moment now police cars could descend on him, and in moments he'd have handcuffs snapped on and be on his way to jail.

He hung up.

He started walking toward the edge of the woods, hoping to stay in the shadows enough that he could get away from this place in case they had traced the call. And as he walked along, he tried to rack his brain for a place to go. None of his friends could be trusted. He didn't want to put his own parents in jeopardy.

Nick Foster. The name came to him out of the blue, and he remembered hearing that Issie and Nick might be an item. He knew Nick would want to know that Cruz had it in for him, that the first fire and killing had to do with revenge against him.

Maybe Nick could help.

He knew that Nick lived across the street from the church that had burned down, so he headed that way, just a few blocks away, and hoped that Nick would be home.

It took him half an hour to reach Nick's trailer, and when he did, he realized there was no car there. He peered across the street to the place where the church had been and saw no sign of Nick. Where could he be?

Maybe he was at the fire station, he thought. What if he was there all night and Jake couldn't reach him without giving himself away? He stumbled onto the front porch, a weather-beaten structure that was in need of repair.

He walked up the rickety steps, wishing for the cover of darkness, though it was only five P.M. He sat down in a corner and leaned back against the rail. He didn't know how long it had been since he'd slept. Most of the people he'd been living with only fell asleep when daylight hit.

He closed his eyes and tried to relax, wishing that Nick would come home soon. If not, he supposed he'd have to sleep here all night, but he would have to leave before daylight. Maybe the police would take the information he gave them and find Issie by then, and then they could arrest Cruz and Jennifer and the rest of the gang before they did any more harm to churches or people, or Jake's own relatives or friends.

• • •

Nick searched everywhere he thought Issie could be but didn't find her, and as he drove, he felt the growing sense of panic that something had happened to her. She was in trouble. He knew better than to think she had just been irresponsible by not showing up for work. He had contacted everyone he knew who was a friend of Issie's, but no one knew her whereabouts.

Almost to the point of despair, he decided to head back home, get on his knees, and pray for Issie as hard as he could. It was the only thing he knew to do.

He drove back to the street where the church had burned and pulled into his gravel driveway. His headlights lit up the front of his porch, and he saw the shape of something he hadn't expected on his porch. Had someone left something, he wondered, or was that a person hunched in the corner waiting for him?

Issie, he thought suddenly. She was here, waiting for him to get home. He should have known. He stopped the car, lunged out, and raced up the steps.

"Issie?" But when he got to the front he was shocked to see that it wasn't Issie at all. Instead, a young man was hunched in the corner. Could this be Jake?

Startled out of sleep, the boy sat up straight. It took a second for him to orient himself, then as if he realized where and why he was here, he grabbed both of Nick's arms and pulled himself to his feet.

"Nick, Issie's in trouble!"

"Where is she?" he asked.

"I don't know," Jake said. "She was snooping around the warehouse where we were. I think she followed somebody there, and she went in. They must have heard her, because she ran out, and then Cruz went wild. He put her in his trunk and drove her off somewhere. I don't know where they went."

"In his trunk?" Panic almost stopped Nick's breath. Issie might not live through this. He pictured her somewhere locked in the trunk of a car. Was she dead or alive?

He unlocked his front doors and bolted inside, Jake on his heels. "We've got to call the police," he said.

"I already did," Jake told him. "I don't know if they believed me but I tried. I described the car, and I told them who was driving it. Maybe they can find her."

Nick dialed the number of the police department and asked for Stan's desk. Stan wasn't in, so he talked to Sid Ford.

"Sid, Nick Foster. Have you heard anything about Issie?"

"We've got an APB out on that same blue Subaru right now," Sid said, "but we ain't found nothin' yet."

"Come on, Sid!" Nick yelled. "This is a small town. How many places are there to look?"

"They coulda left town by now," Sid said. "They could be anywhere between here and the south shore. There's woods all around, man."

"Sid, he's got her in her trunk. He could kill her if he hasn't already!"

"I understand that," Sid said, "and we're doin' the best we can. We've got dogs out, and a helicopter, and everybody's looking for her. But we can't do more than that. Not unless you've got some more information that would help us."

"What do you need?" Nick asked. "You have the make and model of the car. You have the name of the person driving it."

"We're workin' on it," Sid said, "and when we find somethin' out, trust me, you'll be the first to know." Sid hung up, and Nick sat staring at the receiver in his hand. He slammed it down, almost breaking the telephone, then he turned on Jake.

"They're your friends," he said. "Now you tell me where they might have taken her!"

"I'm telling you, I don't know," Jake said. "I'm on your side, okay? She's my aunt. I've known her all my life. I don't want anything to happen to her. That's why I came here. I've been out of the loop on everything for the past couple of days, and then they killed my friend Benton. Shot him through the back, and he didn't deserve it. He killed a kid for them, all just to throw the cops off of Cruz. And look how they reward him!"

Nick felt sick. "Do you know where Benton is?" he asked. "Are you sure he's dead?"

"Absolutely dead," he said. "He's out by the warehouse, only everybody's gone."

Nick's mind raced. "Jake, it would be a good idea to take the police to him. Come on and get in the car."

"No!" Jake said. "They'll arrest me, man. Lock me up! Then who's gonna look for Issie?"

"I am," Nick said. "The cops are."

"But I *know* places," he said. "I *know* some of their hangouts. There's Cruz's deer camp . . . Besides, I already told them where he is near the warehouse. They'll find him there."

Nick tried to think, and he rubbed his temples with shaky hands. "So she was still conscious when he got her into the trunk?"

"Yes," Jake said. "She was conscious all right. Banging and kicking and screaming. It's a wonder he'd ever keep her in that trunk."

Nick hoped that was true. Maybe her rage and her emergency training and her strength would get her out of this. He was shaking, sweating, and his mind was having trouble following a logical train of thought. "Okay, Jake, we have to do something." He sank down on to the porch step next to Jake, still rubbing his face. He let his fingers slide slowly down his cheeks. "Jake, how do I know this isn't some kind of trick? I don't know you. I don't know what you've been up to. For all I know, you may have killed Ben Ford."

"No, I didn't," Jake said. "I knew they killed him, but I wasn't there. Man, I was stupid. I bought into everything. Cruz thinks he's God or something, and we all thought he was too. He had the Bible memorized, and he had this plan for us to build a secure compound and live together and grow our own food. It felt good to believe in something and have a goal."

"So you let them kill people and you sat by and didn't do anything about it?"

Jake looked down. "I know it's stupid. But I'm telling you the truth. By the time I got wise that he wasn't who he said he was, I knew they'd kill Benton and me both if either of us tried to get out. Plus Issie was getting involved where she shouldn't have, making a lot of people crazy, and I decided I'd better stay with them just to make sure they didn't get to her, 'cause you know they slashed her tires and they broke into her apartment and left a dead cat on her bed. *I* gave them the key and let them do it! I'm such a jerk!"

"Why didn't you call the police?" Nick asked.

"Because I was messed up," he said. "And I was scared. And to tell you the truth, I was worried that I would be the one going to jail. I didn't know what would happen."

"So your staying out of jail was more important than saving your aunt's life?" Nick asked. He could see the self-hatred on Jake's face.

"What can I say? I'm a coward. I admit it!"

Nick groaned and rubbed his eyes hard. He let out a heavy sigh. "At least you came now."

"Well, it's not going to do her a lot of good if she's already dead," Jake cried. He smeared his tears away. "How could I have trusted those guys? I knew they didn't care about anybody but themselves."

"It wasn't a matter of trust," Nick said. "It was a matter of you getting something out of it. You were having fun. You didn't have any restrictions on you. You had the freedom you thought you wanted. But just like all the freedoms we think we want, they wind up becoming a prison instead. You might have been trying to keep yourself out of jail, Jake, but you're in a cage as surely as if the police had put you there."

Jake didn't deny it. "I can't undo anything I've done," he said. "All I can do is try to find her, try to help *you* find her."

"Then think," Nick said. "You mentioned a deer camp. Can you take me there?"

Jake tried to calm down, and it was clear his mind was running through all the possibilities. "Yeah, I could find it easy."

Nick got to his feet and pulled his keys out of his pocket. "Okay, let's go."

They piled into the car, and pulled out of the driveway. "Which way?" Nick asked.

Jake pointed the direction he needed to turn.

"You know, this guy, Cruz," Jake said. "He's a lunatic. Really. He's insane. He stabbed Benton in the leg because he was kissing Jennifer or something. It was like he blacked out and went into some kind of rage. Didn't even make sense." He gestured to the next turn. "Up here, to the right."

Nick drove, the streetlights flashing then darkening his face as they passed.

"So what's your relationship with Issie anyway?" Jake asked. "I know she doesn't go to church, but you and her are the talk of the town. Even Cruz and them know you got her from the bar the other night."

Nick was quiet for a few moments. "We've gotten to be good friends lately."

"Well, if you don't mind my saying so," Jake said, "it doesn't seem like a match made in heaven to me."

"It's *not* a match made in heaven," Nick said. "We're just friends. I've been worried about her. She knew she could count on me, for several things," he said. "For coming out and looking for her, for rescuing her, for praying for her."

"Issie needs a lot more than prayer right now," Jake said. "Up here. Turn into this dirt road."

Nick turned onto the dirt road, feeling as if he might be driving into a trap, but he had to try. He put his headlights on bright and drove down the dirt road, weaving back and forth among the trees, till finally he came to an opening and saw an old, inactive oil rig in the middle of the property. There were no cars to be seen.

"Aw, man," Jake said. "We came here once with a keg of beer, so I thought they could have parked her here."

Nick slammed his hand on the steering wheel. "Then where are they?"

"I don't know," Jake said, "but there are a few more places that they've been known to go. I'll take you to each one of them. Just turn around and go back out the same way you came in."

Nick did that, but as he drove, he realized how hard this was going to be. Issie could be anywhere, and it might already be too late.

Chapter Fifty

Issie was bleeding. She had a cut across her cheek where Cruz had hit her, and a gash down her arm where she had wedged it between the trunk and the car, trying to keep him from closing it. As he'd wrestled her into the trunk, her calf had caught on a sharp metal corner, ripping open her pants and slashing her leg. She lay cramped in the darkness, folded in a fetal position.

The rough carpet beneath her was wet with her blood. She wasn't sure which was bleeding harder—her face, her arm, or her leg—but she couldn't maneuver enough to get to any of those places to apply pressure. She tried to turn or wiggle free so that she could move more easily, but she was wedged.

Pain shot through her leg, throbbed on her cheek, and the cut on her arm rubbed against the hard carpet as she tried to turn over. Her head ached, but worse than all that was the realization that if she didn't get out of this car and days passed, and Nick Foster's church met at Aunt Aggie's for the midweek service, they could all wind up dead, right down to the preacher himself. There was no one to warn them.

She wailed, then screamed for help again and banged on the metal roof. But no one came, and she feared no one would. Where had they taken her? They had driven for some time. They could be out of town, far away from Newpointe, way back in the woods where no one would ever find her.

She wondered if Jake had told them what had happened, if they were even looking for her, or if he had wimped out and decided to go back to his gang. Or had they killed him? She had heard several gunshots.

She managed to squeeze her arm free and began to reach above her head where she couldn't see, feeling around for the few items Cruz had left in his car. She found some greasy jumper cables and a tire gauge, but nothing else.

Was God trying to get her attention, or had he only turned away?

She closed her eyes and tried to take inventory of what had brought her here. She had to admit that her own influence over Jake might have led him to his association with these people. She hadn't shown him any reason not to get involved in evil.

Everyone was good, she had told him, because good was a relative term. She had told him that we defined our own good and evil. It was whatever you thought it was. But now she knew that wasn't true. There were clear lines between good and evil, lines that Nick understood, and all the people in his congregation did as well. It was only beginning to become clear to her.

What had brought her here? she asked again. Was it generations of a family who followed their own path? She wondered if her brother would even look for her, or if he'd simply drown his worries in a bottle of wine. That was how their family handled crisis.

But now it all seemed to have caught up with her, as if God was trying to get her attention. She wept harder and yelled out, "You've got it, God! You've got my attention now! What do you want me to see?"

She thought of Mark Branning and Allie, the forgiveness that Allie had shown her, yet the way that Mark avoided her as if she would bring plagues on him. She thought of how happy Dan and Jill were, and Stan and Celia, in spite of all the trials they'd faced.

She had never seen them go out and get drunk just because things went bad. She hadn't sat around the table with them at

Joe's Place reliving the cases they'd gone out on that day. They led quieter, cleaner lives, lives that she had considered boring until she'd found herself locked in the trunk of a car.

She had even considered Nick to be boring at one time, but something in her spirit had changed. Lately he had seemed like someone safe, a point of refuge in which she could hide. She didn't know why she had been so attracted to him lately, why she'd gravitated toward him in every situation, why he was the first person she thought of when she needed to call for help. But now *his* life was in danger, and she could do nothing about it.

She banged on the roof again, trying to get the trunk up, but it wouldn't budge. She was getting weak. If she didn't do something soon to stop the bleeding, the life might just bleed right out of her.

She groped down around her legs, and touched a towel that seemed stiff and greasy. She took the towel and bit until it tore. Then she ripped a strip and managed to bring her leg up as far as she could. Wiggling her way down, she was able to touch her calf. She inched the strip of cloth around it, tied it tightly to stop the blood.

"Please, God," she whispered, "don't let me die here. Get me out of here so I can tell them before they kill everybody."

She didn't care about herself anymore, or her past sins or her very soul. She didn't care what was going to happen to her in the future. All she knew was that Nick and his congregation were in trouble, and she could help them if she could just get free.

She tore off another strip and wrapped her arm, bandaged it as tightly as she was able in the small space she had. Then she wadded another piece of terry cloth and laid her face down on it. The pressure would stop the bleeding, she hoped, but it wouldn't stop the pain. And every time she moved she was liable to start it again.

She closed her eyes and tried to picture God watching over her from somewhere up in the sky too far away to reach her and unlock that trunk.

"I know you don't have anything for me, God," she said. "I'm not even worth your time. I'm probably so repulsive you can't even stand to look at me. But that's okay. You can turn your face from me . . . But those people at that church, they're your people. And Wednesday night when they gather for their service, Cruz is going to be waiting. And there's not going to be any place for them to run." She started to sob.

"Please, God. I don't want Nick to die. I don't want any of them to die. You've got to stop them or you've got to help me so I can. Do whatever you want with me. I don't care. I deserve every bit of it. But they don't."

She wasn't sure if the bleeding had stopped, and she almost didn't care. She felt the life drifting out of her as sleep pushed its way in. Finally, she drifted into a state of rest, weary from tears, fighting, and the loss of her own blood.

Chapter Fifty-One

Cruz drove the black van to the edge of Aggie Gaston's property. They had circled the block until her bedroom lights had gone off, and now they felt safe pulling up to the ridge circling her property. There were two of them—Redmon and Graham—besides himself and Jennifer, four guerillas brave enough to risk their lives to support the cause. They would make their mark. They would scatter that congregation and knock down their high-and-mighty preacher, and make a name for themselves even better than their grandfather's.

And if all his fame was postmortem, he supposed that was preferable to going to jail. He had always known he would lay down his life. He pictured himself walking through the pearly gates, rifle in hand, and seeing only the faces of Caucasians who cheered him like one of the heroes of his faith. God himself would greet him like a messianic prince and crown him with a jeweled crown, and take him to his new point of power, where he would rule the underclass with an iron scepter.

And Nick Foster would learn not to mess with him.

They got out and headed to their respective posts around the perimeter of Aunt Aggie's property. It was just a drill, a practice session to make sure everyone knew where they were supposed to be. They had to do it under cover of night to make sure no one saw them.

He chuckled lightly as he headed for the tree that he would stand behind on Wednesday evening before the sun set, and as this mixed congregation sat and prayed together, probably about rebuilding the church that had no business linking itself to God, they would rain hell and brimstone down upon them.

That is, if Jake didn't ruin everything for them. He thought of the kid again, somewhere out there waiting to make trouble. That was why he'd kept Issie alive. He hoped that one of the team he'd sent looking for him would find him, and Issie's life would be enough incentive to keep him from talking.

His only disappointment was that he hadn't been able to talk more members into following him in this mission. Jennifer was with him, because she had grown up as he had, and knew what it was like to experience the thrill of a mission well-planned and executed. But he'd had to be careful with the others. He'd kept his plans exclusive to his inner circle, and asked for volunteers who had the courage to finish this church off once and for all. Until they did, their plans for the compound would be on hold, and they would have to wait for critical new recruits with money who could finance their plans. Vengeance was the Lord's, he told them, and until he wreaked that vengeance, God's blessing would be withheld. He'd had a vision, he told them, and had received the clearest of orders.

So far, only Redmon and Graham had agreed to be a part of this. He knew they didn't quite understand why he was doing it—after all, Nick Foster had insulted and implicated him and Jennifer, not the others—but they had such a fascination with the other shootings across the country that he suspected they just wanted the notoriety. Both of them were detached from their families and outcasts among their peers, and had little to lose. Their commitment to him and their holy war was exemplary.

He saw that Jennifer, Harris, and Graham stood in their positions at the other corners of Aggie's property, with perfect shots down to the bottom of the bowl that was her land, where the chairs had been set up Sunday morning. He shone the flashlight on his face again and gave the signal for which they were all watching. He heard a series of pops produced by their mouths, as if they were kids pretending to shoot guns. But Wednesday night there would be no pretense. Wednesday night before the sun set, the bullet fire would be real.

Chapter Fifty-Two

Issie's throat was dry, and the gashes on her face, arm, and leg ached. Her muscles had gotten stiff, and she could hardly move. Her head throbbed with all the force with which she'd been slammed into the trunk.

Her eyes had adjusted to the dark, but she still couldn't make out everything in it. At least her bleeding had stopped and the carpet beneath her face had dried crisp.

She tried to squirm free so she could turn and see what was behind her in the trunk or what was at her feet, but it was too tight and she couldn't move. The air was getting stale, thin, and she was having trouble breathing. She was drenched with sweat.

It had been a cool October for Louisiana, but tonight it seemed sweltering. She wasn't going to make it. She would die of thirst if not hunger, or her wounds would get infected.

She reached up and tried to feel the junction between the trunk lid and its bottom, and felt the rubber strip that kept it sealed. If she could just peel back that rubber strip she'd be able to get some air. Maybe she would be able to see out in case anyone came. If she had warning, maybe she could scream and yell, or surprise Cruz with a counterattack.

She picked at it and pulled until part of it tore, and then she began to chip it away where the heat and age had made it flake. After a while she had a little slit where air was coming through. She saw that the car was in some kind of shed. It was still dark outside, and she wasn't able to see much of anything, but the cool air on her face was welcome.

She started to think of her mother, the woman who had died just two years ago. Issie had grieved even though their relationship was lacking.

Sara Mattreaux had once had a dream of being a singer, but according to her, she'd never had a break. She hadn't finished high school, for she'd quit early to follow a boy in a rock band that she thought was going to make her a star. Instead, she had wound up singing from band to band in the seventies, never lighting long enough to get a real job.

It was during that time that Issie's brother had been conceived. Sarah had never told the name of his father, and he had taken her maiden name. Issie wondered if she even knew who the father was. Years later she'd had Issie with an alcoholic who felt no familial responsibility at all.

She started to cry and wished she could call out for her, the mama who had so rarely been around to bandage her wounds and nurture her spirit. Her mother had always worked nights for tips. She and her brother had practically raised themselves. She wondered if her mother had died with regrets.

She wasn't bitter, she thought, trying to keep her mind occupied as she sought out the good memories she had of her mother. They had attended a Saints game together when Issie was thirteen, she recalled. She had thought it was something that her mother had chosen to do with her, but halfway through the game she'd realized that her mother was there because she'd met one of the Saints players who happened to be married at the time, and had gotten free tickets in exchange for her agreement to meet him after the game.

Fortunately, they had lost and the married football player hadn't been in the mood to spend time with the barmaid, who wasn't as pretty in the light of day as she'd been in the dim lights of the bar. Issie wondered what she would have done if the man had been interested. Would she have left Issie in the hall out-side the locker room or locked her in the car?

She searched her mind for other good memories. Christ-mases, Thanksgivings ... But she only remembered a lot of drunkenness, strange men in and out of the house, cursing and anger and blame. But she wasn't bitter, she thought. She had turned out all right. She didn't need a nurturing mother, any more than she needed a father.

She thought of Nick's sermon yesterday, of the way he'd referred to God as a loving father. That wasn't a concept that Issie had ever known. She couldn't quite grasp it. To her, the word *father* meant abandonment and neglect. It meant turning one's back, forgetting you ever existed. It meant pain and heartache and absence. No, she couldn't imagine any good com-ing from her thinking of God as a father.

She heard a car engine and wheels on the gravel, and peered through the slit trying to get a glimpse. It was impossible to see in the dark shed.

She waited until she heard the shed door open, then she began to bang and kick on the hood of the trunk, praying it wasn't Cruz.

"Help me!" she screamed. "Help me! Somebody, please come help me! I'm in the trunk."

She heard a key in the lock on the trunk, heard it turn, and the trunk sprang open.

Cruz stood over her as she raised up.

Double doors opened to the night, and a van idled there with its headlights shining in, blinding her.

"So you ain't dead yet?" Cruz asked.

She thought of trying to run for it but knew her legs wouldn't cooperate if she tried to leap from the trunk. She would wait until he had her out, until she was standing on her feet. He cocked his pistol and held it to her head.

"I've been tryin' to decide whether to finish you off or to wait till we find Jake. I'm thinkin' he might do everything we say if he knows your life is in my hands. Besides, Wednesday ain't that far off."

The significance of Wednesday shot through her brain with the velocity of a bullet. "You're planning to kill all those people, aren't you?" she managed to croak out.

He smiled. "Oh, that's right. You're Nick Foster's latest project, aren't you? I heard about him draggin' you outta the bar the other night. Like to drink, do you? Bet you're thirsty now."

"Please . . . ," she whispered.

"Sorry," he said, snapping his fingers. "I plumb forgot to bring you anything. So how's your sleeping quarters? Are you comfortable here?"

She took the opportunity to look around her in the trunk, now that there was light. She saw a two-liter bottle lying sideways in the wheel well where her feet had been. Next to it was an oily rag. There was nothing else there of consequence, but at least she knew that water might keep her alive until someone came. If he locked her back in, she would have to make sure that her head was near the bottle.

"Let me out, Cruz," she said. "Please. I won't tell anybody. I won't get in your way again. You don't want to kill me. I haven't done anything to you."

"We practiced tonight," he said. "We waited till Aggie Gaston was in bed, watched her turn her light off, then we went to the trees surroundin' where the church will be set up Wednesday night. And we practiced. Do you know what our signal is?" he asked.

Closing her eyes, she shook her head.

"Soon as I pull the trigger and kill the preacher, the others are gonna start firing."

She closed her eyes. "He hasn't done anything to you. Why him?"

"Because he thought he was better'n me, comin' to New Orleans and snatching away my army. Tellin' them that God loves everybody, that he died for the gays and the blacks and the

Jews and the Indians ... He's dangerous," he said, "full of lies and blasphemies, and I'm just makin' myself a vessel to be used of God for his own vengeance."

"You're insane," she whispered.

He grabbed her by the hair and ground his teeth. "I don't like it when people call me insane." He put his face up close to hers. She could smell his breath. She had the image of rotten meat hanging between his teeth.

"These gashes look pretty bad," he said, stroking his thumb along her torn cheek. "You're going to have a nasty scar there. That pretty face'll never be the same."

She slapped him away, but it only made him angry, and he grabbed her by the hair and pulled her up out of the trunk. Her chin hit the metal and she almost fell headfirst, but she managed to get her legs out and catch herself.

She took a deep breath and decided the moment she could get upright she was going to bolt. It was as if he was testing her, toying with her, wanting to see what she would do. She felt like a rat in a science experiment.

He pulled her straight, turned her around until she was face-to-face with him. She felt faint, felt the waves of dizziness and blackness washing over her as if she would drop right here on the concrete. If so, what would he do with her?

She couldn't faint. He could kill her. Or worse. No, she told herself. She would have to get away.

She tried to summon all her strength, as if by sheer will she could muster the energy to run ...

But he wasn't going to give her the chance.

He pushed her to the ground, then kicked her in the chin with his knee. She thought for a moment that he had broken her jaw and possibly knocked out some of her teeth. She fell back.

He pulled her back to her feet, turned her away from him, and pushed her as if giving her his blessings to run, but she was too dizzy, still reeling from the agony. She took a step and stumbled, caught herself with her hands, skinning the pads of her hands.

"Go ahead, Issie. Run," he said. "Let's see how far you can get."

She scrambled to her feet and tried to take a step, but he knocked her down again.

"Tag. You're it," he said. He pulled her back up by her hair, put one arm around her waist, and dragged her back to the trunk.

"Please don't put me back in there," she managed to cry, but he picked her up and slammed her down inside. Her head was at the wrong end. She wouldn't be able to reach the bottle, so she got up on her knees and tried to fight him before he could close the trunk. Though she knew she could never win, she managed to get her body situated where her head would be on the other side, and finally she gave up and sank back in.

The trunk slammed shut. She wept until she heard the doors to the building closing, and the car leaving again. He was gone, and she was still here.

It felt as if the wound on her leg had reopened, and she knew there were bloody places on her knees and hands. But at least she had water.

She reached for the two-liter bottle and saw that she could stand it upright in the small compartment. Why had Cruz had it here? she wondered. Was it in case his engine ran hot? Or was it even water?

She unscrewed the top and brought the lid to her mouth. A little of it spilled onto her face and down her neck and chest, and quickly she stood it upright again, making sure that no more was wasted. Yes, it was water, she thought. Real water. She screwed the top on. It might have to last her for days. She would have to be careful with it.

She let the water stay in her mouth, wetting all of her taste buds, and after a while she swallowed and felt the sweet sensation of it going down her throat. Then she lay there weak and in pain, and cried out, "Where are you, God? Can't you see that I'm locked away in this box and nobody's ever going to find me?"

She had a sense that God was listening, that he heard, that he saw her trapped in this little compartment that no one else could locate. What if there *was* a God, a Father watching over her, looking down on her, waiting for her to call on him? Nick was convinced that God loved even her, that Jesus' death on the cross had been as much for Issie Mattreaux as it had been for Nick Foster.

Issie had doubted that was true. Why would a pure and blameless God give his life for someone as miserable and dirty as she? But just as that thought came into her heart, another one followed.

"While we were still sinners, Christ died for us." Nick had read that in his sermon yesterday.

And on its heels came the words he'd said to her the other day about slanderers and swindlers and adulterers and idolaters . . . and the sexually immoral. She couldn't remember all the sins he had listed, nor the order in which they had come, but she did remember one thing: "That is what some of you were."

It hadn't sunk in when he'd said it before, even though he'd explained it like she was a little child. He'd wanted her to understand that that verse alone showed that even people with filthy sins in their lives could be cleaned up and changed.

Was it possible that that could happen to her too? She closed her eyes. She might never find out. She might never get out of this trunk alive and prove to God that she could be different.

But yesterday, Nick had said there was precedent for that too. There was a thief on a cross hanging next to a crucified Savior. "Today you will be with me in paradise," Jesus had said. He hadn't expected the thief to get down from that cross and go clean up his life. He had known there would be no chance of turning around. He just knew his heart.

Maybe God could know Issie's heart as well. Maybe that was why he had allowed her to be locked in a cramped trunk where no one could find her. Maybe it took that to get her to the point where her heart was ready to call out to him.

"Save me, Jesus," she cried. "You don't have to get me out of here. But whatever happens, I want to know that you're my Father, that you haven't left me, and that I can call on you. Even if I die here, that maybe today I'll see you in paradise."

A peace like she'd never felt before fell over her, and she filled up with an emotion so deep that it brought tears to her eyes, tears unlike the ones she'd been weeping since she'd been locked in here. Tears that seemed to come from the very bottom of her heart, cleansing tears that seemed to wash away the sins that had eaten at her for years, sins that had become a curse on her family for generations, habitual sins that had a hunger of their own.

Could it be that God could see her as a clean person now? Could it be that all the cycles of sin in her family could be broken in her through Christ?

The trunk didn't miraculously open the moment she prayed the prayer. Her wounds did not miraculously heal. She didn't hear a siren coming up the dirt road to her rescue.

Her situation was not different. But her heart was. And as she lay in the cramped dark trunk, she felt less fear than she had felt before. Her Father was watching over her, unwilling to abandon or forsake her.

She closed her eyes, and sweet sleep fell over her.

Chapter Fifty-Three

By ten o'clock Jake had run out of places to look for Issie, and Nick was growing frantic with the search. At one point he had called the police station to see if there were any updates, and Sid told him that she hadn't been located yet. Benton had been found where Jake told them he would be, however, and he was, indeed, dead.

Nick had broken the news to Jake, and watched him cover his face and begin to weep. Somehow, the kid had been holding out hope that his friend had made it.

He looked over at Jake as he drove. "Jake, I think you need to go home now."

"I told you, I can't. It's too dangerous. They're looking for me."

"You need to at least tell your parents where you are. When they hear about Benton, they'll think you're dead somewhere too."

Jake thought that over for a moment. "I want to. I really do. But I can't figure out how to do it without giving myself away."

"Well, how about if I call your parents and have them meet us somewhere? If anybody's watching your house, they won't know where your parents are going."

"What if they follow them?"

"I'll tell them to stay aware of it. They'll know. If they're looking, they'll know if someone's behind them."

Jake looked out the window for a moment, then turned back to Nick. "All right," he said, "but I hope this doesn't get anybody else killed."

Chapter Fifty-Four

Nick didn't tell Mike Mattreaux anything more than he had to. He asked them to meet him and said he needed to talk to them about Jake. Quickly, Jake's mother had grabbed the phone.

"Do you know where our son is?"

"Please, just meet me," Nick had said, "and be careful. Don't let anybody follow you. If you think they are, then turn around and go back home and call me on my cell phone."

Now he and Jake waited at the old abandoned gas station on the east side of town. As they waited, Jake leaned his head back against the seat. Nick could see how tired he was. He wondered how long it had been since the kid had had a good night's sleep.

"So what are you to Issie, really?" Jake asked him as they waited.

Nick was getting tired of this line of questioning. "A friend, I guess."

"No, you're more than a friend."

Nick met Jake's eyes and saw that he was searching. He hoped the kid didn't see more than Nick wanted to reveal.

"You two have something going, don't you?"

"No, we don't. We're cut from different cloth," Nick said.

"You can say that again."

Nick stroked his lip with a finger and gazed out the window. "Why are you so interested, anyway?"

"I just heard about you taking her home from the bar the other night. And everybody's saying that you two are getting to be an item."

"Oh, I wouldn't say that," Nick said. "I like Issie. There's something about her that's really special."

"Then you two do have something."

Nick didn't want to talk about it anymore. In fact, he didn't want to talk about anything. He just wanted to rack his brain for other places he should look for her, and get down on his knees and pray as hard as he could that God would hear his prayers . . . and hers if she was praying . . . and get her out of the mess she was in.

They saw headlights coming up the road, and Jake stiffened. The car turned in.

"My parents," Jake said.

Nick looked beyond them and saw that they were alone. "Nobody with them, nobody following."

"Good," Jake said. He got out of the car and stood beside the passenger door. The moment his parents saw him they slammed on brakes and lunged out of the car. Lois was already in tears.

"Jake, we've been looking all over for you! Where have you been? Are you hurt, son?"

Mike was more reserved as he came closer to his son. "Jake, you're not involved in anything criminal, are you?"

Jake evaded the question. "I got Issie in a lot of trouble, and right now we don't know where she is, but Cruz took her and, Dad, I think he's going to kill her. He'll kill me too, if he finds me."

Mike's face went pale. "Have you called the police?"

"Yes," Jake said, "they're looking for her. But they haven't found her yet, and it's been hours."

Mike turned his desperate face to Nick. "What have you got to do with all this?"

"Jake came to me," he said. "And I've been out looking for Issie."

"Have you been hiding him all this time? Keeping him from us?"

"No," Nick said. "He just came to me tonight."

He swung back to his son. "How did Issie get involved in this?"

"She's been involved all along, Dad," Jake said. "She snooped around where we were and saw things, and then she turned us in."

"They already tried to kill her once," Nick added. His voice cracked as he went on. "I'm worried about her, Mike. They're capable of anything."

Mike looked sick as he ushered his son into the car, and then he turned back to Nick and asked him what was being done. When he'd updated him, Mike drove off to hide his son.

Chapter Fifty-Five

Nick headed back to the police station, got an update on the search for Issie, and learned that she still had not been found. Every available police officer was looking for her, he was told, and off-duty cops were coming in to help with the search. They all took her disappearance personally, since they considered her one of their own.

But the all-out effort to find her had produced no results.

Frustrated and not knowing where else to look, he headed over to the fire station to ask for prayer. Mark and Dan were on duty, and George Broussard was filling in for Nick. Nick found all three of them in the kitchen, and he shuffled in. "Hey, guys."

They all looked up from what they were working on.

"Hey, Nick," Dan said. "I tried to call you awhile ago. I heard Issie was missing."

Nick came into the kitchen and plopped down at the table. Mark set his hand on his shoulder. "You okay, man?"

"No, I'm not okay," he said. "Her nephew said that his pals threw her into the trunk of a car and took off with her."

"You're kidding me," Mark said.

"No, she's in a lot of trouble if she's even still alive." Tears burst into his eyes, and his mouth shook as he tried to hold back his despair. "Look, I came by tonight to ask if you would pray for her."

"We have been," Mark said. "You can count on us."

"So what has Issie gotten herself into?" Dan asked. "Does this have to do with the killings and the church burnings?"

Nick nodded. "She knows who it is, and she gave Stan the names. It was exactly who I thought."

"That Cruz kid?" Dan asked.

"You got it. And so help me, if I could get my hands on that kid . . ." He rubbed his mouth to cover his emotion. "But see? That's what's wrong with me. I took the wrong approach with him from the beginning. If I'd treated him like a fertile lost soul instead of a false teacher, maybe he wouldn't be so dangerous. Maybe I could have gotten through to him. I had the chance, but I blew it."

"You were protecting our own youth," Dan said. "What could you do? He wasn't going to listen to you."

"He might have if I'd tried getting to know him instead of chewing him out. Now two people are dead, and Issie could be the third." He drew in a deep breath and brought his tired eyes up to Mark's. "I need your help, guys. I can't preach at the service Wednesday night. I'm too distracted, and I don't feel worthy of leading that congregation in anything. Would you two lead the service for me?"

Mark and Dan looked at each other. "We could give our testimonies or something, or kinda give a pep talk to the congregation," Mark said.

"Sure," Dan told him. "We can work it out." Dan pulled out a chair and sank down, looking intently at his pastor. "You're pretty shaken up, aren't you?"

Nick let out a deep sigh. "I can't stand the thought of her out there in trouble with a bunch of thugs . . . imagining what they could be doing to her, if she's even alive. And to think of her locked in a trunk . . ."

"Issie's strong," Mark said. "She's tough. I once saw her fight a delirious wrestler. She can handle herself."

"And I'm sure the police are doing everything they can," Dan threw in. "I heard they're treating this like they would if she were a cop. She's one of our own in protective services. They'll find her."

"They're not doing enough." Nick buried his face in his hands and shook his head hard.

Dan and Mark were quiet for a moment, then finally, Dan spoke. "Man, you really have a thing for her, don't you?"

Nick looked at him over his fingertips. For a moment he was quiet. Then finally, he whispered, "I know what you two think of her. Her reputation. Even the experiences you've had. But she's a special person. I've seen her brokenhearted over accidents she's had to work. I've seen her cry over pain that little kids have to suffer. I've seen her work until she was about to drop to try to revive somebody who'd flat-lined. Even now she's in trouble 'cause she was trying to save her nephew."

He looked up at both of them, pleading for them to understand. "I know she's not right for me. I know we're unequally yoked and all that. I know that it's pretty pathetic for a preacher to let a girl like Issie get under his skin, a girl who spends more time in the bars than she does in church. I know all that. But I didn't plan this. I know you think it's one of those damsel-in-distress kind of things, that I want to rescue her so I'm starting to think I have these feelings for her. Transference, or whatever . . ."

"It crossed my mind," Mark admitted.

"It's not that," he said. "Issie's gotten to me for the last couple of years. I don't know what it is about her. Just something. Maybe because she's so wrong for me. But I think I understand her better than most people do. She didn't have a good childhood, you know. She never knew her father very well, and her mother's value system was pretty messed up. She was never home. Issie and Mike practically raised themselves."

"It's not like you, Nick, to make excuses for sin."

"I'm not trying to make excuses," he said. "She's responsible for her behavior and for who she is and what people think of her. But I'm just saying that she's deeper than that. There's more to it. When God looks at her, he sees more." His voice broke off and his face twisted again, and he looked up at the ceiling. "God can see her right now. He knows where she is. Why won't he tell me?"

"You want us to pray with you, buddy?" Dan asked.

The tears spilled over Nick's cheeks, and he wiped them away quickly as if he couldn't let his friends see him this upset over a woman. "Yes, please pray with me," he said, and together they all bowed and began to pray.

Chapter Fifty-Six

As he finally drove home, Nick had another bout with his tears. He brushed them away angrily and asked God why he couldn't just tell him where she was, why he couldn't lead him right to the car and get her out of that trunk if she was still there.

He didn't understand why God would take a woman who was so close to turning to him, who had given Nick opportunities to share with her in a way that he'd never had before. Why would he let him get so close, only to snatch her away?

She couldn't be dead, he thought. She had to be alive. This couldn't be the end of her.

As he pulled into his driveway and his headlights lit up the front porch, he looked to see if there was any one slumped there, as Jake had been earlier. Maybe she was hiding, waiting for him to come home. But he saw nothing.

He turned off his headlights and sat in the car, staring at the dark house. What was he doing? he asked himself. Living in a parsonage, acting as a shepherd to the flock that was without a house? Was he tainted because he'd fallen in love with a woman who didn't know the Lord? Did that disqualify him for service to Christ?

"I want to do your will, Lord," he whispered. "I don't ask that she and I get together. All I ask is that you lead me to her, help me to find her. And if not me, somebody else. Lord, please help them to find her before she dies." He closed his eyes as tears squeezed out. "I'm giving it up, Lord," he said. "The calling. I know it wasn't real. I thought it was but I *can't* be called to do this. You're trying to tell me something, and I just don't know what it is. As soon as I find her, as soon as we know what's happened to her, I'll give up my church and you can bring in whoever you have called to that position. Someone who can lead them, protect them. Somebody strong, somebody who doesn't make so many mistakes."

He suddenly felt like a dismal failure because he hadn't led Issie to Christ. She might be giving up her spirit at this very moment. If so, he would never forgive himself, and he'd never get over it.

He got out of the car and went into the house, miserable and knowing he wouldn't sleep. He would call the police station every hour and check to see if they'd found her yet. He wouldn't rest until he saw her again.

Chapter Fifty-Seven

Issie woke up hungry. The hunger was a deep pain in the pit of her stomach, crying out to her loudly, demanding that she fill it. But there was nothing to eat. She didn't know if she would ever eat again.

"Is there food in heaven, Jesus?" she whispered, like a curious child who'd just been introduced to heaven as a new concept. Then she remembered hearing something about the marriage feast of the Lamb, how all the believers would be invited one day.

Would she be there, adorned like a bride at her own wedding? Would she be among all those in white? She couldn't picture herself in white. Scarlet, maybe. Yet the sense of cleanliness, of newness, washed over her as it had last night when she'd whispered her prayer to her Savior. She knew without a doubt that he had heard, and that he had accepted her, as she had accepted him.

"Me a bride," she whispered. "Imagine that." She hoped he would clean up her wounds, take the swelling away, heal the bruises. She didn't want to meet her Maker looking like this.

She reached for the bottle of water, unscrewed the top, and carefully took a sip. It went down her throat, filling her, nourishing her.

"Thank you, Lord," she whispered. She knew that she needed to ration it out, but she had a feeling she wasn't going to live long enough for it to matter. She was just so grateful that it had been there when she needed it. She had no doubt that God had prompted Cruz to put it there, probably weeks ago, then forget that he had.

Her head still ached and the gash on her leg had begun to swell. She suspected it was getting infected. She was thankful that it wasn't August, but even in the middle of October the heat sweltered in the building and turned the trunk into an oven.

Eventually the heat itself would kill her, if not the hunger. She hoped she could sleep until God saw fit to take her life.

But then she realized that something terrible was about to happen. The shooting was going to take place. When? What was today? Monday, Tuesday? She honestly wasn't sure. The hours had blended together, and the darkness had made it hard to mark the time.

Wednesday, Cruz and his thugs were going to show up at Aunt Aggie's and try to do away with the people of Nick Foster's church. Nick would be the first to go, and there was nothing she could do about it.

She began to weep again. "Lord, take me if you have to, but please don't take him. That church needs him. Oh, Lord, stop them somehow. Expose them. Let them all be locked up before the day even comes."

But God didn't always answer prayers the way she thought he should, which was why she was bent up like a rag doll stuffed into the trunk of a car. She didn't know how God would answer her this time. All she knew was that he would ... somehow ... in a way that fulfilled his will.

• • •

Nick spent the next two days looking for Issie again, and made the rounds to every place he could think of. He navigated his way to every fishing hole he'd ever heard about, both in and outside of Newpointe, and drove for hours and hours searching for any sign of her.

Finally, he called the elders of his church and asked them to come and pray with him for Issie tonight. He didn't know where she was or what he could do for her, but God did, and they needed to go to him.

Ten men showed up and sat in a circle in his living room, praying from deep in their hearts for the woman who wasn't even a part of them, because it was becoming increasingly obvious that Nick cared deeply for her.

He didn't even try to hide it anymore. His feelings were as obvious as the tears on his face.

Chapter Fifty-Eight

By Wednesday morning Nick knew the meaning of "praying without ceasing." He didn't remember if he had slept or not last night, for he'd spent so many hours praying for Issie. He was beginning to despair of ever seeing her again, and he felt sure she had never come to know the Lord. He considered it his own personal failure. He would never see it as anything less.

When Mark and Dan and some of the other elders of the church came to get him so that they could set up chairs on Aunt Aggie's lawn for that night's service, he didn't have the energy to go. But reluctantly, he allowed them to take him to the old woman's house. Aunt Aggie seemed as distraught as he at Issie's plight, and hadn't been able to cook for the firemen since Issie disappeared.

When all was done, he found himself alone with Dan. "How do you feel, Nick?" his friend asked. "If you can't preach tonight, somebody else can do it."

"No," Nick said. "I can't stand up in front of these people and tell them everything is going to be all right. All my preaching about suffering purifying the church ... I don't care if it purifies the church. I don't care if it purifies me. I just want Issie to be found, and I don't understand why she hasn't been."

Dan sat down across from him and stared out into the breeze. "I wish I knew what to say, buddy. Some way to help."

"If it was me who had to suffer," Nick said, "I'd do it gladly. And the church ... if God's trying to purify us ... okay, we prayed for revival. But Issie's not one of us. She doesn't even know where to turn." He got up and looked down at Dan. "What if she died not knowing the Lord? What if I had all those opportunities to tell her and I never made her understand?"

"Nick, you did tell her," Dan said. "You told her so many times you probably can't even count them. She wouldn't listen."

"She *couldn't* listen," Nick said. "She just didn't have the ears to hear."

"Who has to give her those ears?" Dan asked. "You?"

Nick shook his head. "No. I know only the Holy Spirit can do that."

"Then why are you beating yourself up, man?"

"You make it sound like it's simple," Nick said, "like all I need is a little assurance to soothe my conscience, then just wash my hands of her and forget she ever existed. But I can't forget! She might still be alive. And I don't know where she is!"

Dan looked down at his feet. "I've been praying for her day and night, Nick. I know you don't believe that. You think we have some kind of vendetta against Issie. But I've worked with her for years and I feel pretty close to her. I don't want to think anything happened to her. I'm still hoping for the best. Issie's tough. Don't forget that."

"Yeah, real tough," Nick said wryly. No one knew how vulnerable she really was. For some reason, she had only revealed that to him.

He looked at the men across the lawn from him, still setting up chairs. "Tonight after the service I'm going to give them my letter of resignation again, Dan. And this time I'm not going to take no for an answer."

"No, Nick!" Dan said. "You need time. You *can't* do that!"

"Watch me," Nick said.

Chapter Fifty-Nine

Issie didn't know how long she'd been here now, but if she was guessing right, it had been three days. She had seen daylight come and go, had tried to mark the dark hours, but the days were running together and her hope was running out.

Her body ached with the effort of lying still in this cramped position, her bruises and gashes were sore to the touch, and she was almost out of water despite her efforts to ration out her drinks. Her hands had been shaking so badly today that she had spilled half of what was left. She only had a little water left.

Her head throbbed and her joints felt as if they had been pulled apart. She was having chills and knew that she must have fever, for even in October it was still warm enough that she should have been sweltering in the trunk.

She tried to peek out where she had pulled the rubber back, but the building was dark and she couldn't tell whether it was late afternoon or evening. If it indeed was Wednesday, then this was the day that Cruz and his evil friends would be dispersing around Aunt Aggie's property, aiming their guns at the congregation of Nick's church. She wondered how many would die.

She closed her eyes and began to pray, knowing that she was probably never going to get out of this trunk in time to stop the madness. But God knew where they were. He knew what they were doing. Would he allow the shooting to proceed?

She thought of Nick's sermon Sunday about how suffering sometimes brought revival, how tragedy purified the church and made it more vibrant and alive. It had made no sense to her then. Now she wondered if it would work that way. Was God going to allow evil to have its day? Was he going to put these people through suffering that they'd never experienced before? Could they endure it?

She thought back on the shooting that had happened at a Fort Worth church not that long ago, and recalled the article she had read about how that church had become even more effective than they had been before, how it had bonded them more closely to each other and to the Lord, how it had brought them all to their knees and made them turn to prayer as a significant habit of their lives.

Had God used that evil for good? Had it rippled out from that church into the community, reaching people like herself and drawing them in? Could God make good of even this?

She tried to find peace in that hope but still couldn't stop thinking that if she could just make her way out of this place she would be able to go and stop them. She would be able to warn Nick before the first bullet fired.

There had to be other ways to suffer through, to purify a church, she thought. Surely the church burning was enough, and Ben's murder. But then she wasn't God and she didn't know what he knew.

She recalled the words she'd heard so many times but never really in context, not until she'd spent time with Nick. "Thy will be done." Could one really pray that even on the cusp of tragedy? she asked. Then quickly the answer came.

Yes, trust me.

"I do trust you," she said, "but please don't take Nick. Please don't take him. They need him."

She shivered with the chills coursing down her spine and wondered how long it would be before she would drift out of consciousness and into oblivion. She wondered if God would wait a while before taking her to heaven, or if he would come for her immediately.

It didn't matter much. Either way, the next time she opened her eyes she would see Jesus. The thought thrilled her. She couldn't believe it. She had never been that sure of anything before, yet some part of her longed to stay here, to explore what life could have been like if she had embraced it God's way. She'd love to try that again.

"Lord, I'll be the thief on the cross if you want me to," she said. "I'll be the one who never has the chance to come down and clean up his life. I'll be the one who will see you today in paradise. Or I can get down off this cross and walk back into Newpointe and let you change my life the way Nick says you can. I'll be a walking testimony, the bad girl turned good, the one who couldn't do it on her own but who finally figured out she didn't have to."

Either way was okay with her. God's hand was on her life now, and it was on her eternity. For the first time in her life she felt the peace of knowing that everything would be all right, however it turned out.

Chapter Sixty

The congregation started arriving for prayer meeting at five Wednesday afternoon. Aunt Aggie, still disturbed about Issie's disappearance, had not made her characteristic smorgasbord. But members brought covered dishes which they set up on rented tables.

They milled around the grounds as they ate and fellowshiped, none of them aware that their gathering made them prey for the hunters waiting to take them down.

• • •

From her state of half-consciousness, Issie Mattreaux thought she heard the sound of a car. She tried to peer out the little slit she had created by pulling the rubber away from the trunk, but all she saw was the daylight peeking through dirty boards in the building.

She told herself that she needed to cry out, needed to kick on the trunk and beat the top of it and scream so that someone would hear her. But she had so little energy left.

She kept her face on the carpet beneath her. She had to find the energy to cry out, she thought. She had to make some noise. She groaned, tried to make herself heard, but her throat was dry and it barely croaked out.

She hit the trunk with her fist, kicked against the metal. "Help!" she managed to get out. "Somebody help me!"

She heard a car door slam, then the doors to the small building were opened. Cruz, she thought. He was back, probably to speed her death.

Any minute now he would open the trunk and torture her a little more, dangle freedom in her face, then slam the door shut again.

She heard him doing something to the car, then heard the sound of water running. After a moment, the trunk opened. Blinded by the sudden burst of light through the open doors, Issie tried to raise up, but was too weak.

Just as she suspected, Cruz stood over her.

"Not dead yet, huh?" he asked. He saw the empty two-liter bottle lying next to her and pulled it out. "Where'd you get this?"

Her lips were cracked and parched. She just looked at him. The acrid smell of gasoline rose on the stagnant air. He leaned over the trunk and looked Issie in the face. "Have you ever thought of hell, Issie?" he asked.

Her mind raced for an escape. If she could grab him by the throat, pull him down, pull herself out of this trunk, maybe she could get away.

"'Cause in a few minutes," he said, "just a very few minutes, this car is gonna be on fire, and you're gon' be in the middle of hell. And then me and my friends, we're gon' go to where Nick Foster and his church are meetin', and we're gon' blow them all away. Most of them are already there, in place."

She reached up, tried to grab his collar, but he knocked her hand free.

Come on, Issie, she told herself. *Get up. You can do it.*

She reached up again, this time clawing his face. With as much adrenaline as she could summon, she threw herself up and tried to bolt out, but his fist came down across her face, reopening the gash on her cheek and knocking her back in.

The back of her head hit against the rim of the trunk, and she screamed out in pain. Before she knew it, he had her back in the trunk and darkness closed over her again.

The smell of gasoline fumes made her nauseous and she gagged, but there was nothing in her stomach to throw up. Had he doused the car with fuel? she wondered, panicked. Was he about to set her on fire? Was it almost over?

The words kept dancing through her mind as the pain in her head overtook her. *Today you will be with me in paradise.* The words gave her a strange comfort, and she let herself slip away.

Chapter Sixty-One

Cruz parked in the designated area where they had decided to leave their getaway cars. They had a plan to use pipe bombs to distract attention so they could get away, so he'd stuffed two into his pockets and pants legs, so he would be able to toss them when he was ready. As he got out of his car and headed through the woods that would come out at Aunt Aggie's property, he felt the thrill of knowing that soon his plans would pay off.

He got to the edge of the property and saw that Jennifer was already in place behind a cypress tree. He looked across the dip in Aggie's land for Harris and Graham on the other side.

They were ready.

From his position, he tried to see around the tree. He saw a plume of smoke drifting above the sky and knew that that was the old stable he had set on fire. The whole structure would go—from the wall he'd doused with gasoline, to the other old, brittle walls—and eventually the car would catch the flames. She was probably dead by now. Nothing was going to stop them now.

He checked his rifle, which one of his disciples had stolen from his father's gun cabinet. Satisfied that it was ready to go, he waited until the right moment.

Chapter Sixty-Two

The crowd milled toward their seats as Jesse Pruitt started playing his harmonica at the front of the assembly, leading them all in a chorus of "Blessed Be the Name of the Lord."

Nick's head throbbed with the ache of urgency as he walked to the back of the congregation and sat down. His people filled in around him, and as they did, he pulled his letter of resignation out of his pocket and quickly read over it again.

He hoped they wouldn't be too hurt by this. They'd had enough loss lately. But God was doing things in his life that he didn't understand. He didn't know how to work around them or through them. All he could do was follow what God wanted, and right now it looked as if he wanted him out of ministry.

As his congregation sang praise songs to the Savior, Nick's soul felt heavier than it had ever felt. He cried out in his heart to God, praying that he would lead him to Issie, that somehow she would be okay, that in spite of all the odds and all the fears and dreads that had coursed through him, that somehow God would bring her through this.

Are you still listening, Lord? The question came from an honest quadrant of his heart, pleading for an answer.

Then suddenly he opened his eyes and lifted them up to the heavens, and he saw a plume of smoke coming from somewhere miles away, over the trees. He got slowly to his feet.

He wondered if the fire department had been called. He tried to think where that smoke might be coming from, and realized there was nothing in that area but woods. Maybe someone had left a campfire, or a hunter was making his meal . . . Or maybe after the dry summer they'd had, a spark had caught into a giant conflagration. Or maybe . . . just maybe . . .

Someone was in trouble.

Issie! He knocked his chair over with a crash, leapt over it, and bolted toward Aunt Aggie's house. He pushed past her on the porch and headed inside.

"Where you goin', *sha*?" Aunt Aggie asked, following him inside. "T-Nick!"

"I saw smoke," he said. "There must be a fire back up in the woods."

He picked up the phone and dialed the number for the station. Junior Reynolds picked up the phone. "Midtown Station."

"Junior, there's a fire over on the northeast corner of Newpointe, back up in the woods, probably near Hamp Carlson's deer camp. Have you had any calls?"

"No," Junior said, "none at all. Does it look bad?"

"Not yet," he said, "but we gotta get over there before the whole forest catches. And I'm thinkin' that maybe it's where Issie is."

He hung up the phone and hurried back out to his car. He didn't even notice the attention he caught as he jumped in and skidded away.

In seconds, he heard the sirens coming behind him. If only he could find the smoke, maybe it would lead him to Issie.

Chapter Sixty-Three

Issie smelled the smoke as it began to seep in through the one hole she had to get oxygen, and with her hand she tried to cover it up. But the metal was hot, and she recoiled. She remembered the oily rag she had seen in the trunk and groped around in the cramped space until she found it. Quickly, she stuffed it into the hole. The smoke stopped seeping in. Despite her fever chills, she felt the heat being turned up around her. She closed her eyes and knew that it was almost over.

Soon her spirit would leave her body and it would float into heaven where she would be with Jesus in paradise . . . just as he had promised the thief on the cross. That was the option he had chosen for her, and it was all right. "Just please, Lord," she whispered weakly, "please protect Nick and his congregation. You must have angels that could take care of them. You must have ways."

She heard the fire crackling around the car. Soon the fuel tank would ignite.

She hoped it would be over quickly.

• • •

Cruz was a little thrown when he saw Nick running from the area, jumping into that car, and skidding away. And then he heard the sirens and that had shaken him as well, but the emergency vehicles had flown right past Aggie Gaston's house. They weren't coming here.

The possibility occurred to him that they might be going toward the fire. He cursed, realizing he should have ignited the car instead of just the structure hiding it. He had chosen that way to give her a slow, frightening death, in which she felt the heat rising by degrees, and had a long time to think before the car actually went up.

She was probably dead by now, anyway. She had probably died from smoke inhalation, and the fire had probably already claimed the car. If they were about to find her, it was probably too late.

He looked from Jennifer to Harris to Graham, and knew they were wondering when he would give the signal. But Nick Foster was gone. There was no use scattering the flock unless he could take the shepherd too. He wanted to wait just a few more minutes. Maybe Nick would be back.

He gave them the signal to wait, then he checked his watch and decided he'd give it ten more minutes. The service would go on for at least another hour. They had plenty of time.

Chapter Sixty-Four

The smoke was like a beacon as Nick got closer, and he felt as if the Holy Spirit was leading him just like the cloud over the Tabernacle when the Israelites were in the wilderness. It was telling him which way to turn, how far to go into the woods . . .

Behind him the fire truck forged through. The closer he got, the more certain he was that this was something to do with Issie, but he had a terrible feeling that they were getting there too late.

As the cloud of smoke thickened and made it impossible for them to see, he kept driving until he saw the blazing stable up ahead. Then he saw the flames and realized that it was the car inside that was engulfed. He jumped out—ignoring the pain in his legs—and headed for the flames.

Behind him the firemen leaped off the pumper truck and began unwinding the hose. He saw Junior Reynolds, Cale Larkins, and Ray Ford, the chief, working quickly. They ran the hose up to the building and began dousing the flames.

As they pushed the flames down with the water, Nick opened the door. A blue Subaru sat at the center of the building.

"*Issieeeee!*" He bolted in with the hose spraying alongside.

"I've got to open the trunk," he shouted. "Issie may be in there!"

They kept dousing the flames as Nick ran back to his car for a crowbar, then in just a few deft motions, was able to disengage the trunk lid. Coughing and gagging on the smoke, he threw it open. And then he saw Issie.

She lay limp inside the trunk, her lips dried and cracked, and her face bruised and cut. "Issie!" He lifted her out.

Just then he heard the sirens of the rescue unit and he rushed her toward it. He didn't even wait for the gurney. He just climbed with her in the back of the unit, and Steve Winder immediately began hooking her up to oxygen while Karen Insminger, the medic filling in for Issie, put a mask on Nick.

As soon as she could breathe, Issie's eyes came open. Nick came into her focus and she tried to rise up. "Issie, you're going to be all right. You're okay," he said. "Can you hear me?"

She tried to grab the mask off of her face, but he fought her to keep it on.

"Come on, Issie. You've got to breathe with the mask."

She shook her head and tried to say something, but the words wouldn't come out. "Please," she whispered. She pulled the mask off again. "How many did they kill?"

"How many did who kill?" Nick asked her.

"At your church," she said. "Wednesday night?"

"It's Wednesday night right now," he said. "What are you talking about?"

She managed to partially sit up. The urgency in her eyes was startling. "Nick, you've got to stop them."

"Stop who?"

"Cruz and all the thugs that burned your church down," she managed to say. "They have a plan … They're at Aunt Aggie's … they're going to kill everybody!"

Steve slowed his ministrations and shot a look up at Nick.

"Issie, just relax. Just calm down and rest a minute."

"No!" she cried. "You've got to stop them! Don't you see? That's why God led you to me. It wasn't to save me. It didn't *matter* if you saved me. You have to save the church."

"The church is gone," he said. "It burned down."

"Not the building!" she cried, grabbing his shoulders. "The people! Cruz is going to kill them. They have guns . . ."

Her words rang too true, and he stood there, frozen at the horror of it. "Please, Nick!" she said. "Please go!"

"Issie, are you sure?"

"Yes!" she cried. "Oh, Nick. Be careful!"

He got out of the rescue unit and saw Stan Shepherd getting out of his car. Nick ran to meet him.

"It's Issie, isn't it?" Stan asked. "Is she—"

"Yeah, she's alive," he interrupted. "But she says they're about to have a shooting spree over at Aunt Aggie's."

"The prayer meeting?" Stan asked.

"You got it," Nick said. "We better get over there."

Stan was already grabbing for his radio mike as Nick got into the car with him.

Chapter Sixty-Five

They had waited too long already, Cruz thought, and he was getting uncomfortable. Darkness was beginning to fall, and soon he wouldn't be able to see his targets well. Jennifer, Redmon, and Graham were getting impatient.

The person giving his testimony tonight droned on and on. Cruz knew the minute he quit, they would begin to pray. Once they did, he didn't know how much longer they would have. Soon they would break up and go home. He couldn't let it happen without doing what they had planned, even if Nick Foster wasn't here.

It was time. He nodded to Jennifer, who nodded to Redmon and then to Graham. They all raised their weapons and got their targets in their sites. Cruz got out a pipe bomb and held it under his arm.

He moved his finger to the trigger and fixed his gun on the one at the front, hoping that would be signal enough to get the others to shoot. His heart began to triple-beat as adrenaline rushed to his head. His finger closed over that trigger.

He heard a click at his ear.

He swung around and saw the barrel of a gun pointed at his head. That same black cop who had detained him the other night stood there with barely restrained rage in his eyes.

"You the one killed my nephew?" the cop asked. The barrel of the gun nudged against Cruz's face, and he almost dropped his weapon. Instead, he got his finger close to the trigger. If he could pull it, the others would shoot and it wouldn't matter that this man had a gun to his head.

"Might wanna drop that gun, scumbag," Sid said.

Cruz didn't even have to aim the gun. It didn't matter if he hit anything. All he had to do was make the noise, send the signal. He got his finger around the trigger and squeezed.

Bullet fire coughed across the property and he heard screams. And then the others went off and there was gunfire everywhere and people screaming and fleeing for their lives.

Sid grabbed Cruz's shirt, pulled him down, and wrestled the gun away from him. Before Cruz could defend himself, he was handcuffed behind his back.

* * *

Nick Foster was already running toward his congregation when he heard the first shot and screamed, *"Get down!"*

He threw the six-year-old Hampton twins to the grass and tried to cover them with his body.

He heard shrill, piercing screams around them as more bullets fired, and he prayed out loud, not even sure what he was saying. He saw Dan and Mark racing for their wives, Celia trying to cover her toddler, choir members scattering. He didn't know how many guns were aimed on the congregation, but it sounded like warfare.

And then a sharp pain shot through him, knocking him from the children. He lay there for a moment, trying to utter one last prayer, before all went black.

* * *

Cruz lay with his face in the dirt, waiting for the battle to be over. The count of fatalities would be worth whatever he had to pay for this. He had accomplished his mission.

His grandfather's lawyer would keep him out of jail, and he would win.

A bullet fired past him, startling him, and he realized someone was trying to knock off the cop to give him a chance to get away. Cruz got his knees beneath him and raised up, preparing to run for it.

People kept screaming as more bullets fired, and Sid turned to fire back.

And then a bullet jolted Cruz, and cut through his leg. He yelled and fell forward again, and realized that the bullet had ignited a pipe bomb.

He tried to stop the wick from burning, but locked in the cuffs, his hands couldn't reach. He let out a bloodcurdling yell. Sid turned and saw the sparkling wick on the side of Cruz's bloody leg, and dived away to take cover.

The explosion that followed sent further terror shattering through the crowd, as everyone saw Cruz dying by his own weapon.

Chapter Sixty-Six

One by one, Stan Shepherd and the other police officers captured the gunmen and disarmed them. In the wake of the gunfire, people were wailing and screaming and groaning.

Stan waited to make sure that there wasn't another guerilla hiding in the trees waiting until they least expected it. Finally satisfied that they were all accounted for, he headed down the hill.

He looked around at the bleeding people one by one. Eddie Neubig had a gunshot in his hand, and Andre Bouchillon looked as if he was clutching a bloody ear. Louis DeLacy, the town's judge, was sitting up, but he was clutching his knee. Stan could see that it had been shot.

He kept looking around, taking inventory of the wounds, but he saw no one bleeding to death, no one who looked lifeless on the ground, no one unconscious.

And then his eyes came to Nick. He was lying on his back and looked as if he'd been shot in the left side.

"Nick!" he screamed, and several of the men scrambled to their feet to help.

Paramedics rushed down the hill with a gurney and started triage. Stan surrendered Nick to them and tried to see who else was critical. Nick seemed to be the only serious casualty.

He heard sirens coming and saw that other rescue units from surrounding towns were arriving on the scene.

He heard a yell and saw Ray Ford at Nick Foster's side. "Save him!" Ray was yelling. "Get him outta here, *now!*" He ran along beside the gurney, and Stan followed. "Stay with us, man!" he yelled at Nick. "Come on, man! You gotta stay with us! We need you. This church needs you. We can't do without you, man!"

Stan saw Nick open his eyes.

"There you are," Ray said. "You're with me, ain't ya?"

Nick managed to speak. "I'm with you, Ray. I'm with you."

"You gon' be all right," Ray said. "You gon' bounce back. Me and Susan, we gon' be prayin' for you."

"Speaking terms?" Nick got out.

Ray was crying. "Yeah, man. We're back on speaking terms. God knows what he's doin'. You taught us that."

Nick managed to smile. "Appreciate that, man."

Stan watched as they loaded Nick into the rescue unit. Then he set about trying to help with the triage scene that had emerged around them.

Chapter Sixty-Seven

The waiting room outside the ICU at Slidell Memorial Hospital was full of people from Calvary Bible Church waiting to see if their pastor was going to live or die. Word was that he'd been shot in the left side near the kidney.

Allie and Mark, Stan and Celia, and Dan and Jill huddled together in a corner praying for their friend and spiritual leader, and for the doctors who would save his life if it was going to be saved. Other groups huddled in various parts of the waiting room. Some cried over the trauma that they had all endured; others chattered nonstop with a nervous energy that couldn't be assuaged.

When Ray and Susan came in, a hush fell over the room. They said their hellos to various people, then crossed the room and sat down with their closest friends.

"How is he?" Susan asked.

Allie looked up at her with red, swollen eyes. "It's touch and go, Susan. He may not make it."

"Well, he has to," she said. "He just has to." She burst into tears and Celia pulled her into her arms and held her. "What will our church do without him?"

No one had an answer for that.

Susan wiped her face and pulled back. "I had a dream," she whispered. "Last night, it was so vivid. I saw Ben."

Jill's face twisted in pain for the mother.

"He told me he was fine, just fine. That he was havin' a big time up in heaven. That he wouldn't come back for the world, not even if they let him. He tole me we would see each other soon . . . that it might seem long, but it really wasn't." She wiped her face and breathed in a sob. "And he tole me I needed to go back to the church, stop blamin' God. That death was the best thing ever happened to him." She broke down and began to weep, and Celia pulled her back into her arms.

They all clung together and wept, then prayed some more. Finally Celia got up. "I think I'm going to run and check on Issie," she said. "Somebody needs to tell her about Nick."

"Nobody told her yet?" Ray asked.

Mark shook his head. "Well, none of us. We've all been kind of preoccupied."

"You know, she's the one who saved the day," Ray said.

"How?" Allie asked.

"When we got her out of that trunk, the first thing she told us was that they were planning to ambush the church. If it wasn't for her, there's no tellin' how many would have been dead. Sid woulda never stopped Cruz, and those others woulda emptied their guns."

Silence fell over them as they realized how close they had come. Allie shivered. "Then we owe her a thank you," Allie said, "a big one. I'll go with you."

"I'm going too," Jill said.

Before they reached the door, Mark had joined them. "Wait for me," he said.

Dan was behind him, and Stan brought up the rear. Together they marched up the two flights of stairs to Issie's room. They found her lying in bed with cuts and bruises and an IV feeding nourishment into her body. Her brother and sister-in-law sat on the couch near the bed talking quietly.

Allie was the first to knock. Issie's eyes opened partially.

"Issie?" Allie asked, tentatively stepping inside. "Feel like company?"

Issie nodded. "Come on in, Allie."

They all came into the room, filling one side of it. Slowly they made their way around the bed until they surrounded her. She was pale as death and had dark circles under her eyes. Bruises and a gash colored one side of her face and both eyes. Her lips were cracked. Allie put her hand over her mouth.

"I saw the news," Issie whispered. "Said nobody was killed."

"Thanks to you," Allie said, beginning to cry again. "Oh, Issie, it was awful. We were running, but there was no place to go. If the police hadn't stopped them, there would have been fatalities." She stopped on a sob, unable to go on.

"We owe our lives to you," Jill said.

Celia took her hand. "Our children, people we loved." Her voice broke off, and she caught herself in tears. Swallowing hard, she said, "I really appreciate what you did, Issie."

"I didn't do anything," she said. "I just told the truth. I just wish I could have done it sooner."

"Are you okay?" Celia asked.

"Oh, yeah, I'm gonna be fine," Issie said. "Just sore and tired. I'm going to have to have a little plastic surgery to clean up the cut on my face, I'll be on antibiotics and fluids for a while, but I'm going to be okay."

She managed to open her swollen eyes and looked up at Jill and Dan. "Where's Nick? He was really worried about me when they pulled me out of the car, but he hasn't come by to see me."

Jill pushed the hair out of her eyes. "Issie, Nick was shot."

Issie sucked in a breath. "Oh, no. I knew it. I knew it."

"He's in surgery," Allie said, "but we don't know how bad he is."

"We'll let you know as soon as we get word," Mark threw in.

She began to sob, and her brother got up and came to the edge of the bed. He tried awkwardly to calm her with a pat on her hand, but she wouldn't be comforted. "Why Nick?" she wailed. "Why Nick, of all people?"

None of the others had an answer, so they just stood there, weeping along with her.

"I don't get it," she cried. "I didn't know it was going to be so hard. I thought after I gave my life to Christ that things would get easier, not worse."

Everyone just stared at her through their tears. "You gave your life to Christ?" Mark asked.

"Yes, in that trunk. And God kept me alive so I could tell them. But why didn't he spare Nick?"

"We don't know," Allie said, "but all we do know is that accepting Christ doesn't mean you're instantly immune to suffering. Look at all of us, Issie. We've all been through it."

Issie looked at Mark and Allie and thought about the killer that had gone after Allie two years ago. Mark had even been shot trying to defend her. She looked at Stan and Celia and recalled the poisoning that had almost killed Stan and how Celia had suffered in jail for weeks trying to prove her innocence in the crime.

And then there was Jill and Dan, and it had just been a few months ago that Jill had been held hostage by a man considered a terrorist, and had fought for her own life and Dan's while she tried to help justice be served.

No, she couldn't say that they had been immune to suffering. Even the very church that she had thought was so protected had taken its share of pain. Now it appeared that there was more suffering to be done.

"Then what good is it?" she cried. "What good is it to be one of God's children if you're not taken care of?"

"Oh, but you are taken care of." Allie leaned over the bed, putting her face close to Issie's. "Issie, you are. Because even if something happens to Nick, we know we'll see him again."

"It doesn't make it easier," she cried. "It makes it a lot harder."

"But we don't have to despair. God has his reasons, and they're bigger and broader reasons than we could even imagine."

If the words had come from anyone but Allie—the woman whose husband she had once tried to steal—they might have been intolerable. But she was aware that Allie knew the hard way.

"I know this is silly," Issie said, "but I was in love with him. I know it's ridiculous, somebody like me, falling in love with someone so unattainable. A preacher, of all things."

"Issie, I think Nick's had a thing for you for a long time," Allie said. "Maybe God does have a plan for you two. It's not over yet."

"We have to pray," Issie said. "It worked before, when I prayed that God would protect your congregation. And he did. He really did. Prayer works."

She struggled to sit up, and they raised the head of her bed. "Come on," she said, reaching for their hands. "Everybody, please. We've got to pray."

They all held hands and stood around the bed of the bad girl of Newpointe, who had been washed and restored and changed, and prayed with her that Nick would be all right.

Chapter Sixty-Eight

It was almost an hour later when they stopped praying, and Allie realized that Lois and Mike had had their eyes closed. They had been praying with them. They heard movement at the door and saw that Ray had come in sometime during the prayer. He had stopped in the doorway and waited for them to finish. "He's out of surgery," he said quietly. "It's a miracle."

Issie sat up straight in bed.

"The bullet missed his kidney," Ray went on. "It hit part of his intestine, but they took care of that. They've got him stabilized."

A cheer went up around the room, and Allie threw her arms around Issie. "I want to see him," she said. "Can I go see him?"

"Issie, you can hardly get out of bed," Lois told her. "Come on, lie back down."

"No!" she said, "I need to see Nick."

"He ain't awake yet," Ray said, "and when he does wake up they're gon' have him in ICU."

"I *have* to see him," Issie said. "Would you find out when the first visiting time will be? It's important, Ray."

Ray nodded. "I'll do it, Issie, and I'll come back and let you know."

As Ray left the room, the others laughed and cheered again. The Lord was with them, Issie thought. He had answered their prayers. Maybe there was hope after all.

Chapter Sixty-Nine

Nick wasn't sure he wasn't dreaming. He opened his eyes and tried to focus on the woman standing over him. *Issie*, he thought. But what was she doing here? She faded in and out of his consciousness, then came into clear focus.

"Nick," she was saying. "Nick, can you hear me?"

"Issie," he whispered.

She smiled and he saw the redness of her eyes, the bruising on her face, the gash, reminders of what she'd suffered at the hands of a madman.

"Nick, we thought we'd lost you!"

"I think they told me I was going to live," he whispered. "Unless I was dreaming."

"You better live," she said. "I have a lot to tell you."

He squeezed her hand and stroked the soft skin there. He couldn't believe she had been locked away in a trunk for three days. It was like being in the belly of a whale. He wondered if she felt anything like Jonah.

He blinked back the tears in his eyes. "You saved my church," he whispered. "You saved all those lives. You saved me."

Tears burst into her eyes again, and he saw the way her mouth trembled as she tried to hold back her emotions. "Not me," she whispered. "God."

A tear fell. "I'm glad you see that. I'm glad you understand. He was watching over us, wasn't he? My church was not a building, but I had forgotten that until I heard those bullets flying and people dropping to the ground. Those people are the church. Not a bunch of wood and bricks. The church is the people who inhabit it. It's the God who inhabits them. God didn't take my church away from me."

Emotion welled up in his throat, and he swallowed it back and closed his eyes. When he looked up at her again, she was crying too. Their eyes locked into each other's, and he felt an intense connection with her. He couldn't remember ever having that kind of connection before.

There was something about her, he thought, something that had always gotten to him, under his skin and into his heart. And it was still here, stronger than ever. Even when he had resolved never to be unequally yoked, when she bent over and hugged him, he couldn't help wrapping her in his arms, holding her close to him.

But they were unequally yoked. Then it occurred to him. She had agreed that God had saved the church. And if she understood that, then maybe ... He let her go and pulled her back enough to look into her face. It was only inches from his, and he could see the little golden flecks in her dark eyes, the pink rims, the redness of her nose.

"You said that God saved the church," he said. "You believe now."

Those tears came even faster down her face as she nodded her head.

"You've accepted Christ?" he whispered, astounded.

She only stared at him for a long moment, and in that moment he convinced himself that she was going to say no, that she hadn't gone quite that far. Maybe she had a cursory belief in God, understood that there was a supernatural power directing things around her. But a relationship with Christ was another thing.

"I have accepted him," she whispered, and his heart took wing. He tried to get up, but she made him lie back down. "That's not the amazing thing. The really amazing part is that he's accepted me."

Nick's mouth opened. He couldn't think of words that adequately expressed the joy soaring inside him. It was a miracle, an even greater miracle than God stopping the shooters from killing anyone in his church. God had saved Issie Mattreaux.

Overcome with the miracle of that grace, he framed her face with his hands and pulled her closer. Their lips met, and he kissed her hard and long with all the joy and sadness and grief and anxiety and desire that he had felt for her for so long. And he could feel in her kiss that she felt it too.

She didn't see him as a big brother, or a protector, or even the preacher who barraged her with customized sermons. No, she was kissing him like a man.

They heard someone in the doorway of the ICU, and a nurse's shrill voice cut across the moment. "Time for you to go, honey. Visitation is only fifteen minutes."

She nodded to the nurse, then turned back to Nick, her eyes swimming with tears.

"I love you, Nick Foster," she whispered.

He was so shocked he couldn't speak as she sat back down in her wheelchair and allowed the nurse to push her out. As she disappeared from his sight, he began to weep with relief and joy and hope like he'd never felt before.

Was God going to give him permission to pursue his relationship with Issie? The thought that that might happen overcame him as he closed his eyes and began to pray. And for the first time in a long while, he began to realize that God's plan for him might be even better than he expected.

Chapter Seventy

The courtroom was full of reporters from both national and local stations, all waiting to capture the arraignment of each of Cruz's followers. Thanks to Jake's testimony, the police had rounded up everyone involved in the murders and the church burnings.

Sidney Clairmont, Cruz and Jennifer's grandfather and the grand wizard of the KKK, hired his own lawyer from New Orleans to represent his surviving granddaughter. He marched into the courtroom with a suit that looked like it had fit ten years ago, and with a smug grin on his face that said this was a minor setback in their lives, but they would clear it up before long.

Jennifer sat in an orange jumpsuit with dirty hair and a gray cast to her skin. She had stopped eating since seeing her brother killed by the pipe bomb he had meant for the church. She was going to follow her martyred brother, she had declared, and didn't care whether she did it from jail or from home.

Judge DeLacy, who had been on the grounds of Aunt Aggie's when the shooting had occurred, and who had even had his kneecap shattered by a bullet, had excused himself from the case and had the hearing moved to Slidell so that another judge could handle it. Still, he sat in the courtroom, hoping the whole group got all they deserved.

When their case was called, Jennifer came before the judge.

"What do you plead?" the judge asked.

"I don't care," Jennifer said, her eyes fixed on the floor in front of her.

"You *have* to give me a plea," the judge said.

Her lawyer whispered something in her ear, and finally, she brought her dull eyes to his. "Not guilty by reason of insanity."

"Insanity," the judge repeated distastefully. He leaned up on the bench and glared down into their eyes. "Since you're so insane, you won't blame us for lockin' you up. Just to make sure you don't have a mental lapse again."

"Your honor," the attorney said, straightening his tie and shuffling papers as if this was a routine case. "She's just a kid."

"Not according to the law, she isn't."

"But we both know that she is," the attorney said. "She just lost her brother, and she hasn't been well. Their mother is a fine, upstanding Christian woman. Let her keep this young lady at home and get her through this bad time until the trial."

"We all know who her mother is," the judge said, "and who her grandfather is. Thank you, but I b'lieve I'll stick with my original order. She will be held in custody pending the trial, and I don't care if she eats or not."

Jennifer gave no response, but her grandfather got to his feet.

"Your honor," the lawyer said, "I'd like to have her mentally evaluated to see if she's even competent to stand trial."

"She's gon' stay in jail, Counselor."

"Judge, when you hear how this child was abused by her daddy for most of her life, you'll understand her instability. Jennifer here was sexually abused, and her brother was beaten repeatedly throughout his life. They were both exposed to repeated acts of violence throughout their childhoods, acts that seemed normal to them. I'd like a mental evaluation to prove—"

The judge banged the gavel again. "I'm sorry for their past history, Counselor. But thousands of people who were abused as kids live decent, law-abiding lives every day. They don't kill people. The victim defense won't work in my courtroom. I'm sick to death of hearing people come up with excuses for committing horrendous crimes. I don't care about excuses. I care about seeing that justice is done." He looked at his bailiff. "Next case."

Jennifer was compliant as the bailiff led her out.

Chapter Seventy-One

Six months later, the new sanctuary was filled to overflowing with people who had come to dedicate the building and listen to Nick preach the first sermon in it. Nick gave an invitation that day asking anyone there who wanted to walk the aisle and profess their belief in Jesus Christ to come to the altar.

Issie, whom he'd baptized in Bayou Lafayette as soon as he had recovered a few months ago, walked the aisle with her brother, Mike, his wife, Lois, and her nephew, Jake.

For the past several months she had been in a Bible study group that Nick had led in his home, and he'd found her to be an enthusiastic student of the Word of God. She soaked up the things he taught her with a hunger that surprised him, and gradually he saw the emptiness in her heart being filled with Bread of Life and Living Water. He saw her father-longing satisfied as she learned what it was to be embraced by the paternal arms of the One who loved her enough to die for her.

He had seen joy in her like he'd never seen before, and he'd seen purpose, for now she knew why she was here. As far as he knew, she hadn't been back to Joe's Place since the night he had rescued her from herself.

When the service was over, Nick took them to a room in the back and talked to Jake and Lois and Mike about their salvation. And then he deferred to Issie as she began to explain the simple concept of grace to her nephew, who had trouble believing he could be forgiven for some of the things he had been a part of. Awaiting trial for being an accessory to murder, he knew he would serve time in jail. How could God forgive him when the justice system could not?

Nick was proud of her, so proud that he could hardly stand it. And even as he listened to her teach those she loved about her own salvation, he found himself struggling to hold back the tears.

Later as she and her family left the church, he watched them walk out to the new parking lot and get into their car. He stood at the door, moved by what he had seen here today, the fruit she was bearing, the burden she had for telling those she loved about Christ.

He heard footsteps behind him and glanced over his shoulder to see Mark, Dan, and Stan come up behind him. Stan put his hands on Nick's shoulders and shook him roughly, affectionately.

"So what are you waiting for?" Mark asked.

Nick looked over at him, saw Mark leaning against the doorway's casing, his arms folded and a smug grin on his face.

"What do you mean, what am I waiting for?"

Dan grinned and nodded toward the car driving out of the parking lot. "It's pretty obvious that you and Issie are made for each other," Dan said.

Nick grinned then, understanding. "I've been waiting for a lot of things," he said. "I wanted to make sure I wasn't taking advantage of her in her vulnerability. A baby Christian, struggling to walk. I didn't want to get in the way of that, or interrupt it in any way. And I didn't want to wonder if she was trying to be something I wanted, or if I was trying to be something she wanted. I wanted to watch her for a while, make sure her salvation was real, and disciple her."

"She's bearing fruit," Mark said. "That looks like a good sign to me."

Dan shook his head. "She's not the same party girl that she used to be. She's really getting into this church thing. Her heart is different."

Nick nodded. "Yeah, her heart is different." But he hoped it wasn't too different, for he couldn't forget the words she'd whispered to him in ICU months ago.

I love you, Nick.

Since then, they'd dated frequently, but he had deliberately taken things slow. He didn't want to rush her, didn't want to get in the way of God's work in her life, didn't want to interrupt her healing.

But he didn't know how much longer he could wait.

He grinned as they all watched him watch her drive away. "I think she's getting better looking all the time too," he said.

They all roared as if their favorite team had just made the winning touchdown, and all of them patted him on the back and hugged him roughly.

They headed back into the church.

• • •

Mike took Lois and Jake to the restaurant they had chosen for lunch, so that they could hold a place in line while he took Issie home. She wasn't hungry, she said. She wanted to go home and be alone for a while.

She rode in the passenger seat of her brother's car, her gaze fixed on some invisible object outside the window.

"So is Nick coming over for lunch?" he asked.

"No," she said. "He didn't mention it."

"Then why don't you want to eat with us?"

She shrugged. "He said some things in his sermon today. I want to go home and look them up, and put them in context, and study them while they're fresh on my mind."

Mike grinned. "Man, you've changed."

"Not enough," she said. They rode in silence for a while, and finally, she looked over at him. "Mike, I've been thinking a lot about Dad lately."

"Dad?" he asked. "Why?"

"I don't know," she said. "The concept of God being my Father sort of keeps it coming to mind. That didn't sound like a good thing to me, you know? To me, fatherhood meant neglect, indifference, absence . . . I didn't get a warm, cuddly feeling when I thought of God as that."

"I can relate to that," he said.

"But lately, with Nick, I've felt that security and that love and that sense of being cherished . . . all the things that fathers are supposed to give to their children. All the things I missed with every single man I ever dated, because I never knew that I didn't just have to rewrite the last chapter in my relationship with our dad. I didn't know that I could rewrite the entire story, and start with a different type of man, one who had all those paternal traits that I wanted so much."

"So that's what Nick is to you? A father figure?"

"Not exactly. I'm just now understanding that maybe what I need in a husband is a man who can love me as a wife, cherish me and enjoy me, and be attracted to me and flirt with me . . . but also nurture and protect me with that fatherly security I never had. It changes everything, Mike. I wish I'd known it before, when I was choosing rogues and rats to go out with. I wish I'd known that I could have what I always wanted. But I didn't know. I thought I could find what I wanted by choosing unavailable men like Dad, and through my wiles and my looks, capture them into falling for me. But men like that never do fall that hard for a woman, and they're never more available than Dad ever was."

Mike frowned as he let her thoughts sink in. "I should have been that for you. I was your big brother. I was supposed to take care of you."

"But you were as neglected as I was. How could you know any better? We were two kids bringing ourselves up. You did the best you could with what you knew."

His eyes misted over. "What if it doesn't work out with Nick, Issie? What if he never asks you to marry him?"

Her gaze drifted out that window again. "I'll be disappointed, but not broken. Because Nick will have given me something pretty important. He'll have shown me, just for a while, what God's father-love for me is all about. And I know God can take it from there."

● ● ●

The next afternoon, a huge portion of the town turned out for the drill that would help the emergency personnel of the town prepare for another disaster. They staged a hurricane with tornadoes, and mock casualties lay all over the school grounds.

Attired in his turnout gear and his mask and tanks, Nick helped with the triage operation that the paramedics were involved in. They ran from actor to actor assessing invisible wounds.

He saw Issie across the bodies, watched her pretending to administer care to a victim.

Nick found it hard to concentrate. He'd been trying to ask her to marry him for the last week, but every time he got close to her, his heart raced and his palms sweated, and he found himself gazing into her eyes and forgetting any rational thoughts he'd ever had.

He knew he should just come out with it, tell her he loved her and wanted to spend the rest of his life with her, but some part of him feared that she would say no. He didn't want it to end just yet. He'd been carrying the ring every day in his pocket, and he had it on him now, but he didn't know when he would get the chance to ask her.

He looked around for where he was needed and saw that the firemen were almost finished with their work. The paramedics had the wounded under control. They were nearing the end of the day, and he knew the drill had been successful.

He went back to the fire truck and took off his mask and cap, hung his tanks on the back of the seat, opened his turnout coat. Issie came around the truck, hurrying to put her crash cart away in her own rescue unit.

She winked at him as she passed. "Kind of a fun day, huh?"

"Yeah, fun." He reached down and grabbed her arm, pulled her back. Her eyes brightened into that flirtatious look he loved, as she looked expectantly up at him.

He leaned back against the fire truck. "You know, it's not so easy being around you, keeping my thoughts to myself."

She smiled. "I know the feeling."

He leaned down and kissed her. The fact that she didn't recoil, that she always let him come close, continually surprised him. "So what are you going to do after this?" he whispered.

She slid her arms under his turnout coat and around his waist, and threw her head back to look up at him. "I don't know. I thought I might rent a movie, invite a nice man over to watch it with me. A preacher type, maybe. You know anybody like that?"

He shook his head. "I wasn't talking about today."

"Oh?" she asked.

"I meant what are you doing for the rest of your life?"

Her eyes grew serious as she gazed up at him, unable to answer.

"That's my stupid way of asking you if you thought maybe you'd like to spend it with me."

For a moment the shock on her face was hard to read. He wasn't sure if she was thinking of a nice way to let him down easy, or if she was so stunned that she couldn't think of a way to say yes.

Then she burst into tears. He let her go, suddenly ashamed and full of remorse. It was too soon to ask her, he thought. How could he have been so stupid?

But then she threw her arms around him again, raised up on her toes, and kissed him with all the heart and enthusiasm that he had hoped for. Pulling back slightly from his lips, she whispered, "The thought of being your wife is just one more example of grace in action," she whispered. "That in my wildest dreams, you would pick somebody like me."

"I could never pick anybody else," he whispered. "Then you'll say yes?"

"Yes!" she cried. "Yes! Yes! Yes!"

She threw her arms around him again and he lifted her up and spun her around. Others started to come around to see where all this noisy joy originated.

None of them had to ask what had happened. Everyone knew. Some things were just meant to be.

Afterword

Last night as I was trying to relax and fall asleep, I began reflecting on the 23rd Psalm and all the riches layered in that passage. And I came to the phrase I've repeated and read many times before.

He restores my soul.

Always before, I dwelled on the verse before it, about his leading me beside the quiet waters. That is, after all, a wonderful thought in such a stressful, noisy world. And I've pondered the verse after it, about the Lord guiding me in paths of righteousness. That's particularly important to someone like me, who has no sense of direction.

But this is the first time I've lingered on his restoring my soul.

And I realized that he does, in such a merciful way. He has restored my soul when I've beaten it and bruised it through my careless actions and terrible choices. He has restored my soul when I've allowed it to run empty, and he's restored it when I've filled it up with things it wasn't made to hold. He has restored my soul when others have crushed it. He has restored it when there was no hope for restoration.

And I wondered what my life would look like now, if I had never allowed that restoration. What if I had pushed God away when he reached down for me like a daddy reaching for his toddler? What if I had not reached up to him, allowing him to lift me? What if I had not laid my head on his shoulder?

Where would I be if I'd had to take the punishment I deserved for the sins *I* committed, and if I'd had to walk through life without that perfect, unconditional love? What if I'd had to face a future eternity with only hopelessness and fear?

Thank God for Jesus Christ, who loved me so much that he took that punishment for me, cleaned my slate, restored my soul . . .

I can't wait to see him face-to-face.

God bless all of you!

Terri Blackstock

Last Light

A Restoration Novel

Terri Blackstock,
#1 Bestselling Suspense Author

Today, the world as you know it will end. No need to turn off the lights.

Your car suddenly stalls and won't restart. You can't call for help because your cell phone is dead.

Everyone around you is having the same problem ... and it's just the tip of the iceberg. Your city is in a blackout. Communication is cut off. Hospital equipment won't operate. And airplanes are falling from the sky.

Is it a terrorist attack ... or something far worse?

In the face of a crisis that sweeps an entire high-tech planet back to the age before electricity, your family faces a choice. Will you hoard your possessions to survive — or trust God to provide as you offer your resources and your hearts to others?

Yesterday's world is gone. Now all you've got is your family and community. You stand or fall together. Like never before, you must rely on each other.

But one of you is a killer.

Number one bestselling suspense author Terri Blackstock weaves a masterful what-if novel in which global catastrophe reveals the darkness in human hearts—and lights the way to restoration for a self-centered world. *Last Light* is the first book in this exciting series.

Softcover: 0-310-25767-0
Audio CD, Unabridged: 0-310-26880-X

Pick up a copy today at your favorite bookstore!

Night Light

A Restoration Novel

Terri Blackstock, #1 Bestselling Suspense Author

In the face of a crisis that sweeps an entire high-tech planet back to the age before electricity, the Brannings face a choice. Will they hoard their possessions to survive — or trust God to provide as they offer their resources to others?

Number one bestselling suspense author Terri Blackstock weaves a masterful what-if series in which global catastrophe reveals the darkness in human hearts — and lights the way to restoration for a selfcentered world.

An era unlike any in modern civilization is descending, one without lights, electronics, running water, or automobiles. As a global blackout lengthens into months, the neighbors of Oak Hollow grapple with a chilling realization: the power may never return.

Survival has become a lifestyle. When two young thieves break into the Brannings' home and clean out the food in their pantry, Jeff Branning tracks them to a filthy apartment and discovers a family of children living alone, stealing to stay alive. Where is their mother? The search for answers uncovers a trail of desperation and murder … and for the Brannings, a powerful new purpose that can transform their entire community — and above all, themselves.

Softcover: 0-310-25768-9
Audio CD, Unabridged: 0-310-26921-0

Pick up a copy today at your favorite bookstore!

ZONDERVAN®
.com

True Light

A Restoration Novel

Terri Blackstock, #1 Bestselling Suspense Author

The darkness deepens in a world without power.

But, daring to defend a young outcast, one family strikes a light.

In the face of a crisis that sweeps an entire high-tech planet back to the age before electricity, the Brannings face a choice. Will they hoard their possessions to survive—or trust God to provide as they offer their resources to others?

Number one bestselling suspense author Terri Blackstock weaves a masterful what-if series in which global catastrophe reveals the darkness in human hearts—and lights the way to restoration for a self-centered world.

Now eight months into a global blackout, the residents of Oak Hollow are coping with the deep winter nights. But the struggle to survive can bring out the worst in a person—or a community.

A teenager has been shot and the suspect sits in jail. As the son of a convicted murderer, Mark Green already has one strike against him. Now he faces the wrath of all Oak Hollow—except for one person. Deni Branning has known Mark since high school and is convinced he is no killer.

When Mark finds himself at large with a host of other prisoners released upon the unsuspecting community, Deni and her family attempt to help him find the person who really pulled the trigger. But clearing Mark's reputation is only part of his battle. Protecting the neighbors who ostracized him is just as difficult.

And forgiving them may be the hardest part of all.

Softcover: 0-310-25769-7
Unabridged Audio CD: 0-310-26922-9
Audio Download, Unabridged: 0-310-26948-2

ebook:
Palm™ Reader: 0-310-27484-2
Adobe® Reader: 0-310-27474-5
Microsoft Reader®: 0-310-27477-X
Mobipocket Reader™: 031027480x

Pick up a copy today at your favorite bookstore!

ZONDERVAN®
.com

Read an excerpt from

TRUE LIGHT

BOOK THREE OF THE RESTORATION SERIES

TERRI BLACKSTOCK

THE BUCK FELL WITH THE FIRST SHOT, AND ZACH EMORY couldn't help being impressed with himself. From his deer stand, it looked like an eight- or ten-pointer. If the weather stayed cold, he'd be able to make it last for several weeks' worth of meals.

He climbed down from his deer stand and pulled up the collar of his jacket. It was so cold his ears were numb, and his fingers had begun to ache. But it was worth it. Even in the pre-outage days, Zach had spent many mornings sitting in a deer stand freezing to death, just for sport. Now it was a matter of survival.

He jogged toward the animal that lay dead twenty yards away. His brother Gary would be crazy with envy. They had a competition going, and Gary was two up on him. Zach hoped Gary had heard the gunshot and would come to help him move the deer. It would take both of them to lift it into their rickshaw.

He bent over the buck. Ten points. And a perfect shot right through the heart. His dad would finally be proud, and if he was lucky, his mother would drag herself out of bed to get a look.

He heard footsteps behind him and turned to see a man emerging from the trees, walking toward him. Zach squinted, trying to place him. He'd seen him before, but he couldn't remember where.

"Did I score or what?" he asked as the man came closer. "He's a ten-pointer. Got him in one shot, right through the ticker!"

The man didn't look like he'd come to celebrate. He stopped about thirty feet away ... and raised his rifle.

Was he going to shoot? Zach's hands came up, as if that would stop him.

The gun fired—its impact propelling Zach backward, bouncing him onto the dirt.

two

THE BUILDING SMELLED OF MOTOR OIL AND GREASE — A SCENT
Deni Branning associated with progress. A symphony of
roaring engines brought a smile to her face as she rolled
her bike inside. Oh, for the days of noise pollution and
hurry — of bumper-to-bumper traffic, honking horns, blaring radios, and twenty-four-hour TV.

All over the large warehouse, mechanics and engineers
with black-stained fingers worked at converting engines. The
building had been purchased by the feds a few months ago,
when they instituted the draft. Instead of drafting soldiers,
the government had conscripted all of those with experience
as mechanics. Later, they'd added others to the conscription
list: electricians, scientists, and engineers. Many of them
were allowed to live at home and work in the local conversion plants, but others had been sent across the country to
serve where they were needed.

Pushing down the kickstand on her bike, she reached
into her bag for her notepad and looked around for someone in charge. She saw Ned Emory, from her neighborhood,
standing nearby with a clipboard, instructing a group of
mechanics with a disassembled engine laid out in front of
them. She headed toward him.

"Excuse me," she yelled over the noise. "Mr. Emory?"

He turned. "Yeah?"

She could see that he didn't recognize her, even though
his son Zach had been close friends with her brother for
years. "Deni Branning. Jeff's sister?"

Recognition dawned in his eyes. She reached out to shake hands with him, but he showed her his greasy hands. "Better not shake. What brings you here?"

"I'm writing an article about your work here. Do you have time for an interview?"

As if he hadn't heard her, he turned back to the men, barked out some orders that she couldn't hear, and started walking away. Glancing back over his shoulder, he said, "I heard the newspaper is back up and running. They hired you, did they?"

She caught up to him and tried to match his steps. "That's right. the *Crockett Times*. They liked what I'd been doing on the message boards around town. This'll be the cover story for next week's issue."

He didn't seem impressed, so she pulled out her big guns. "You guys are like rock stars. Everybody wants to know what you're up to."

Pride pulled at the corners of his mouth, and she knew she'd struck a chord. "Sure, I can give you a few minutes. What do you want to know?"

He started up a staircase, and she blew out her frustration as she followed him. "Is there someplace we can sit down?"

"I don't have time to sit down." He reached the top of the stairs and headed across the concrete floor to an area where a dozen mopeds sat in various stages of completion. "Hey, Stark! I need at least four of these done by the end of the day. Get Bennett over here to help you."

Deni's gaze swept over the bikes. "Wow. How can I get one of those?"

"You can't. They're not for the private sector." He was walking again, but she hung back, unable to tear herself away from the coveted mopeds. She stepped toward one and touched the seat.

He turned back and gave her an impatient look. "Do you want to do the interview or not?"

She shook off her longing and forced herself to focus. "Of course."

He led her past a table filled with generators, and again, her longing kicked in. "Do those work?"

"They do after we harden them against the Pulses."

Her heart quickened. If they were making hardened generators here, it wouldn't be long until they actually had electricity. Could there really be lightbulbs at the end of the tunnel?

"When will those be available for the public?" she asked, catching up to him again.

"Our illustrious supernova will burn out before we can finish supplying the hospitals. They're priority number one for the generators right now. Without robotics, assembly lines—electricity, for that matter—we have to do everything by hand, one at a time. And even if we could produce enough for the public, there's one missing ingredient."

"Gasoline," she said.

"You got it." He reached a series of offices with glass walls, overlooking the work on the floor below them. "We can't get enough gas without operating tanker trucks, and once we get it here, we don't have electricity to work the pumps."

She was well aware of the chain of problems. "But aren't you guys all about creating work-arounds?"

"Right now we're just trying to help critical services operate. Like I said, the star will likely burn out before we get caught up with that. Then we'll shift our objectives from sustaining to rebuilding." He headed into one of the offices, dropped his clipboard on his desk, and motioned for her to take a seat.

As Deni sat down, something outside the glass caught Ned's eye, and Deni turned to follow his gaze. Someone was running up the stairs.

Ned frowned as his son Gary came running toward his door. "Dad, Zach's been shot!"

"*What?*"

Deni caught her breath and got to her feet.

"We were hunting at the Jenkins's place. I heard some gunshots and ... when I found him ..."

"Is he dead?" Ned blurted out.

"I don't think so. I got help and somebody went to get an ambulance. They're taking him to University Hospital."

Ned grabbed his son's shoulders. "What condition was he in when they took him?"

Gary trembled as he raked his hands through his hair. "There was blood all over his shirt ... front and back."

Deni's heart stopped. Her brother's best friend ...

Ned raced out of the office and hurried down the stairs, Gary on his heels. Deni followed them as far as the top of the stairs, then waited there as they hurried through the building. All the engines went quiet, and everyone stared as Ned ran to a beat-up Buick. "The keys!" he shouted. "Where are the keys?"

Someone tossed them to him, and he got in and started the engine. Gary jumped in beside him. Two guys pulled up the garage door and the Buick rumbled out.

Deni muttered a prayer for Zach as they drove off—and then a thought struck her. Jeff, Deni's brother, sometimes hunted with Zach. Could they have been together? What if he'd been hurt too?

She had to get to the scene of the shooting. She ran downstairs, grabbed her bike, and pedaled out behind them.

three

"ZACH? ZACH, CAN YOU HEAR ME?"

Zach tried to open his eyes, but they were glued shut. Something was shaking and bumping him — and with each jolt, pain exploded through him.

"Zach, we're getting you to the hospital, okay, buddy? Stay with me."

Was he in an ambulance? How long had it been since he'd been in a running car? Weeks? Months? Years? His brain couldn't find the answer.

He tried to breathe, but something was crushing his chest. Drowning ... choking ... gurgling.

Something sliced through his throat. "We're gonna help you breathe, buddy. Hang on, we're almost there."

He couldn't breathe. Gagging. Smothering. Gasping.

The ambulance jerked to a stop, people all around him yelling, probing, pushing.

As they rolled him into the building, Zach knew he was dying.

More great books from
Terri Blackstock

Sun Coast Chronicles

Softcover 0-310-20015-6

Softcover 0-310-20016-4

Softcover 0-310-20708-8

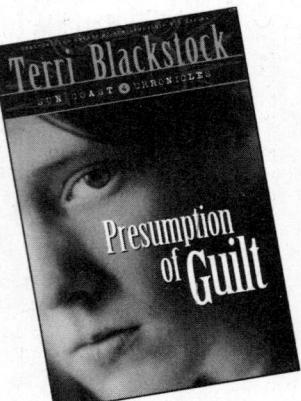

Softcover 0-310-20018-0

Pick up a copy today at your favorite bookstore!

Cape Refuge Series

This bestselling series follows the lives of the people of the small seaside community of Cape Refuge, as two sisters struggle to continue the ministry their parents began—helping the troubled souls who come to Hanover House for solace.

Cape Refuge
Softcover: 0-310-23592-

Southern Storm
Softcover: 0-310-23593-6

River's Edge
Softcover: 0-310-23594-4

Breaker's Reef
Softcover: 0-310-23595-2

Pick up a copy today at your favorite bookstore!

About the Author

*T*erri Blackstock is an award-winning novelist who has written for several major publishers including HarperCollins, Dell, Harlequin, and Silhouette. Published under two pseudonyms, her books have sold over 5 million copies worldwide.

With her success in secular publishing at its peak, Blackstock had what she calls "a spiritual awakening." A Christian since the age of fourteen, she realized she had not been using her gift as God intended. It was at that point that she recommitted her life to Christ, gave up her secular career, and made the decision to write only books that would point her readers to him.

"I wanted to be able to tell the truth in my stories," she said, "and not just be politically correct. It doesn't matter how many readers I have if I can't tell them what I know about the roots of their problems and the solutions that have literally saved my own life."

Her books are about flawed Christians in crisis and God's provisions for their mistakes and wrong choices. She claims to be extremely qualified to write such books, since she's had years of personal experience.

A native of nowhere, since she was raised in the Air Force, Blackstock makes Mississippi her home. She and her husband are the parents of three children—a blended family which she considers one more of God's provisions.

Three ways to keep up on your favorite Zondervan books and authors

Sign up for our *Fiction E-Newsletter*. Every month you'll receive sample excerpts from our books, sneak peeks at upcoming books, and chances to win free books autographed by the author.

You can also sign up for our *Breakfast Club*. Every morning in your email, you'll receive a five-minute snippet from a fiction or nonfiction book. A new book will be featured each week, and by the end of the week you will have sampled two to three chapters of the book.

Zondervan *Author Tracker* is the best way to be notified whenever your favorite Zondervan authors write new books, go on tour, or want to tell you about what's happening in their lives.

Visit *www.zondervan.com* and sign up today!

ZONDERVAN®

ZONDERVAN.com/
AUTHORTRACKER
follow your favorite authors

We want to hear from you. Please send your comments about this book to us in care of zreview@zondervan.com. Thank you.